SCHOOL'S OUT

A NOVEL

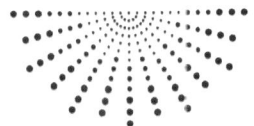

BRUCE ROGERS

WAYZGOOSE PRESS

Edited by Maggie Sokolik

Cover design by D.J. Rogers at Bookbranders

ACKNOWLEDGMENTS

Thanks to the late Donald Barthelme, whose advice helped shape this novel when it was still a short story. Thanks to Diane McWhorter for early encouragement and help. Sincere thanks to Dorothy Zemach, publisher, and Maggie Sokolik, senior fiction editor at Wayzgoose Press. My thanks also to beta readers Barbara Sihombing, Eliza Mimsford, and Jim Price.

"Goals incapable of attainment have driven many a man to despair, but despair is easier to get to than that—one need merely look out of the window, for example."
— Donald Barthelme

"School's out, school's out,
Teacher let her monkeys out.
One went east, one went west,
And one went up the teacher's dress."

— Children's song

INCLUDING THE CIRCUS

Laurel had no real use for the Five Sorrowful Mysteries, but through a fluke of the airwaves, all she could get to come in clearly on her radio was a broadcast of the Family Rosary Hour out of Iowa somewhere, and she needed something to distract her. She felt giddy after a day's driving.

"The Second Sorrowful Mystery: The Flagellation of Christ. Christ is taken like a common criminal, bound to a pillar, and..."

Laurel turned off the county highway at Matt's Store and took the gravel road that led past School's Out. There, almost right around the corner, a flock of guinea fowl were shuffling around in the middle of the road. The birds probably felt pretty safe; there was never much traffic there. All but one moved to the side of the road or fluttered up into the trees. One stood its ground.

Laurel slammed her foot down on the brake. It felt like she was stepping into a bucket of oatmeal. The speckled bird loomed up in the twilight. It seemed to grow as she got closer, becoming man-sized and more. And it didn't seem as if she were bearing down on it; the bird seemed to be advancing on her. She swerved, but that didn't help. At the last second, the bird launched itself, evidently planning to soar right over the truck, but it misjudged the speed of the truck or its own take-off velocity. It hit her grill and then, with a dreadful thump, she ran over it. Her truck ended up halfway in the roadside ditch, and her engine died. The surviving fowl let out a horrifying squealing and squawking. The males' call was a metallic clicking sound: "Chi! Chi! Chi! Chi!" The hens sounded like they were saying, fittingly enough, "Come back! Come back!"

"Save us from the fires of Hell, lead all souls to Heaven, especially those in greatest need..."

Matt's Store was closed, and Laurel didn't feel like explaining how she had squashed one of the guinea fowl. She would have to walk the rest of the way, to leave her truck where it was and ask Matt to work on it tomorrow. She couldn't make the trip home without brakes. The bird was under her truck. It was a male—its crest was larger than a hen's. This flock of guinea fowl was more or less Matt's now, but their ancestors had once belonged to her and Ross. Laurel put the mashed bird in her backpack and started walking uphill, toward School's Out.

Ross had just put his son to bed when the phone rang.

"Hi Ross. You remembered I was going to call tonight, right?" He'd remembered. Laurel had sent him a postcard telling him when to expect her call. But she was supposed to call several hours earlier—right after seven, when the rates went down. "Have you had a drink or two?" Laurel was convinced that their conversations went more smoothly when they were lubricated with alcohol. "I finished off most of a bottle of Mateus during dinner," she said.

He'd known all along that Laurel wouldn't call when she said she would; she never did. If he'd started drinking when she was supposed to call, he might be recklessly drunk by now. When that happened, he tended to get maudlin and say things he didn't especially want her to hear.

"Sorry I'm so late calling. I had a problem." She told him about the guinea fowl incident.

"I don't know why you gave Matt those guineas anyway," Ross said.

"I didn't exactly give them to him—they sort of migrated down there. But I wasn't sorry to see them go," Laurel said.

"Why not? They eat ticks. They eat a lot of ticks." At one time, Colorado tick fever had been a problem at School's Out. "And they're better watch dogs than dogs."

"They're loud, they're obnoxious, and they were always picking on the chickens. I hate bullies."

"Were you drinking before you ran over that poor bird?"

"No, that thing with the guinea fowl was earlier. I was coming back from a fair down in Denver, and I was tired." Laurel designed and made electronic jewelry and sold it at arts and crafts fairs. "It was because of the brakes. You know, I'm so sick of things screwing up on that truck. Last month it was the clutch, now the brakes. If I ever meet a dashing mechanic, I'm going to get him to fall in love and travel with me everywhere.

"In fact, at this point, I'd settle for a boring mechanic with crooked teeth and a bad complexion, as long as he could keep the Grape on the road." The U.S. Grape was a 1958 Dodge postal truck that had been painted purple a long time ago. "It's a good thing the brakes went out where they did, so I could walk home. A good thing for me, I mean—not for that guinea fowl."

He could picture Laurel walking the road between Matt's and School's Out. She'd walk up Harmony Hill, past the abandoned school bus in the woods, past the cottonwood with the word TREE painted on its trunk, past Mushroom Rock. She'd be looking up at the sky, her arms folded across her chest. The hem of her long, striped Mexican coat would be flapping around her knees. She'd be wearing one of her own necklaces, which would be glittering in the twilight. Occasionally, she'd flip her dark hair out of her face; she did that a lot. She'd be irate, but not so irate that she couldn't enjoy the walk.

Ross sat down in an ancient easy chair and swiveled it around so that he could look outside. His living room windows looked out on an alley. Directly across the alley, a light in a fourth-floor apartment came on.

"By the way," Ross said. "I was at a movie at the Orson Wells last week over in Cambridge, *The King of Hearts*, and I..."

"Oh, I love that movie! What is it that the boss lunatic tells the soldier? You should be a beautiful woman until you're thirty, a general until you're sixty, and the rest of your life, you should be the Pope. I guess next year I have to become a general."

"I've seen it three or four times. It's been playing at the Wells for years now. Anyway, a woman in the row behind me was wearing a piece of your jewelry. One of your sparkly mushrooms."

"You sure? I haven't made mushrooms for ages."

"I'm sure. A guy sitting near her asked her to turn it off. Said it was distracting."

"Were you at the movie by yourself, or did you have a date?"

"I was with someone, but she thought the movie was stupid, so I decided not to go out with her again."

"Good call."

Across the alleyway, a woman appeared in the lit-up room and answered the phone. She sat down on a window seat to talk. Ross wondered who was calling her. It would create an interesting geometry if she were talking to an ex-husband. *Although Laurel's not exactly an ex; not exactly.*

Ross stood up from his chair so he could see better. The woman in the window didn't appear to have any clothes on.

"So put Jeremy on, will you?"

"Huh? Oh. No. No, I'm not going to do that." Ross was finding it difficult to talk as if nothing were happening across the alley. "I had a hard enough time getting him to bed as is."

"That's because he wanted to talk to me."

"That may be, but he has school tomorrow, and it's late here. I'm not going to wake him up."

"You can be so tight-assed sometimes. I'm already missing him like crazy. Summers go by so fast."

"Not for me," Ross said. Jeremy spent his summers with Laurel out in western Colorado.

"Well, if you aren't going to let me talk to him now, I'll have to call back later in the week. And I'm calling collect."

The woman across the alley stood up and was walking around as far as the phone cord would allow. Once or twice she bent over, as if to pet a small dog or a cat. She was laughing. *That means she's probably not talking to her ex.* He wished the woman didn't have so many plants in her window.

Ross tried to remember the last time he'd seen anyone in that apartment. Last summer, there had been a guy living there who would sit out on his fire escape in his underwear, drinking beer and listening to the Red Sox on the radio. The odd thing about that guy was, every time Ross had seen him, he had a different head of hair: a blond shag, a flattop, an Afro, a fifties' greaser do, a pompadour, a mohawk. At first, Ross wondered if there were a bunch of beer-and-baseball fans living there, but once he spotted him with no hair at all, and he decided the man must collect toupees.

A definite improvement on the toupee collector.

"One reason I called was, I wanted to tell you, we're having another reunion this Thanksgiving. You didn't come last year, so this year you should, you definitely should. You and Jeremy both. We're inviting anyone who ever lived at School's Out."

"That must be fifty or sixty people."

"Cap and Poppy and I sat down the other night and came up with almost a hundred names. And I know we must have missed some. Course, we'll never be able to get in touch with all of them. Some of them are probably dead."

"I don't know," Ross said. "I'd like to come. I wanted to last year, but... but the restaurant is liable to be at a pretty critical stage right around then. I'm sure Dean would just love it if I picked up and went to Colorado for a week."

"Who cares what Dean thinks? What do *you* want to do?"

"You're always getting down on Dean. You barely know him."

"I know him well enough to know he's another one like you. Someone who can't make up his mind about anything. He's another person who talks about doing things instead of actually doing anything. Not a good partner for someone like you, Ross."

"That doesn't sound at all like Dean to me. And what about the restaurant? That's something Dean and I are doing, isn't it?"

"You haven't opened it yet. You said it was going to be open way back in..."

"I know, I know, but we *are* going to get it up and running. It's just that everything takes longer and costs more than you think it's going to."

"Besides, you ask me, you're doing that restaurant just to prove to me that you *can* do something. That's what I think. In a way, that makes it partly my restaurant."

Ross wondered what Dean would say if he knew that Laurel considered herself a part owner.

"So, is it fun for you?" Laurel asked him.

"Is what fun?"

"Working on your restaurant. Is it fun?"

He had to think about that. The concept of *fun* was a knotty one. "It's absorbing," he told her. "Absorbing is about the best I can hope for these days." The woman he'd been watching had hung up the phone and walked into another room. She was definitely not wearing any clothes.

"I just hope you don't lose interest."

"What? Why would I lose interest?"

"That's a pattern with you. Remember that time you were going to write a book about tending bar in Mexico? You were all hyped up about that, then one day you could care less."

"What do I know about writing? This is different. This is something I care about."

"Well, we'll see, I guess. So, are you coming out for Thanksgiving or not?"

"Umm, unlikely, I have to say. Right about then..."

"Don't bother explaining," Laurel said.

Across the alley, a pale arm reached back into the living room, and the lights went off. Ross sighed a long, deep, husky sigh. A sigh that belonged in the Sigh Hall of Fame.

Laurel asked him what the matter was.

"Nothing's the matter. People are always asking me what the matter is. I just come across like something's the matter."

"That's true, but I can tell when something's really bothering you."

"Damn it, Laurel, nothing's the matter."

"Don't get all pissy with me. I wish you would have had a couple of drinks. Listen, if you won't come out here, then right after the reunion, maybe I'll come to Boston. Maybe I could be there for your grand opening. Would that make you happy?"

"I'll have to think about that some."

"That's soooo Ross-ish of you, my God. Do you want me there or not?"

"I don't know. I guess it would be all right, but..."

"You don't want me to come."

"I didn't say that."

"Yes, you did. You just didn't use those words."

"I was thinking about the last time you were here."

"'Damn everything but the circus,'" Dean said. "You know who said that? It was e. e. cummings, that's who."

The big cats were performing in the center ring. One of the lions snarled and was slow to get up on his seat until the lion tamer nudged him with a chair.

"Why are lions scared of chairs?" Jeremy asked.

"Excellent question," Dean said. "See, the lion tries to focus on all four legs of the chair at the same time, so his focus is divided—you know, like if you tried to do your homework and listen to music, talk on the phone and watch TV, all at the same time."

"My dad won't let us have a TV."

"Yeah, well, your dad's a bit of a Luddite, but you get what I mean. So the lion gets confused and doesn't know what to do next, so he just does what the lion tamer wants him to do."

"You're making that up," Amy said.

"He's probably not," Ross said. "Dean is a font of useless knowledge."

"I think the lion's just afraid the lion tamer will jab him in the eye with a chair leg. And that's just plain mean," Amy said. "Or maybe the lions have been condi-

tioned. They know that every time they don't pay attention to the chair, they get hit by that whip."

Halfway through the trapeze act, Laurel said to Ross, "I want to take Jeremy back with me when I leave tomorrow. It would just be a few weeks early. Why can't I?"

"Because he can't miss two whole weeks of school, that's why," Ross said. "Let's not talk about it now, okay? Let's talk about it after the circus."

"Okay, but I'm going to take him."

"Not until school's out."

"Yeah, that's where I'm taking him. Back to School's Out." Laurel found what she'd said pretty funny. When she'd quit laughing, she popped a second Quaalude.

Amy came back from the bathroom. "It's so gray and depressing out there, out on the concourses. Everything in here is all glittery and circusy, but out there, it's like it used to be during hockey games, and it smells like antique hot dogs. That's another thing I don't like about the circus—you feel cheated, somehow, when you leave, even if it's just to go to the bathroom."

Dean asked her when she'd ever been to a hockey game. Even back then, Dean was suspicious of things Amy had done without him.

"Daddy used to take Claire and me to Bruins games all the time when we were little." Claire was Amy's twin sister.

"Figures Dorky Dan would like something as brutal as hockey. And drag his kids to watch it."

"Well, I hated hockey, and Daddy wanted us to get autographs from the players. He'd take pictures of us when we did, so I've got all these photos of Claire and me and guys with no teeth. And it wasn't just hockey, he took us to see the Celtics, and wrestling, and boxing, too. He was always dragging us here. I have nightmares about being lost in Boston Garden and wandering around forever."

Dean gave Amy's arm a squeeze. For once, she was siding with him against her father. "You'd be like the monkey," Dean said.

"What monkey?"

"Years ago, three monkeys escaped in Boston Garden when the circus was in town. They put out peanuts and bananas and trapped two of them, but they never got the third one. Supposedly it's still here, wandering around late at night. Night watchmen claim they've seen it and heard it screeching. It's like the phantom of the opera, only it's a monkey."

"I wouldn't mind sheeing a phantom monkey," Laurel said. "But right now, my mouse is so dry, I need a Coke, and I bet Jeremy wantsh one, too. Where'sh zat Coke man?" Laurel was starting to seriously slur her words, thanks to the Quaaludes.

"I don't think he'll be back this way soon," Dean said. "He looked like a rational young man. I think it bothered him philosophically to see you lying in the aisle instead of sitting in your seat."

"I fell. Ish not a girlsh's fault when she fallsh, ish it?"

"And when you elbowed him in the throat when he was trying to help you up…"

"I din't try to elbow him. It was an ashident. Anyone can have an ashident. I said, 'Eshcoosh me' to him, din't I?"

"Jeremy," Ross said, "look at that bear riding a bicycle. Not something you see every day."

"I think he's gone to sleep, Ross," Amy said.

"Asleep? How can anyone fall asleep at a circus?"

"Maybe he's upset about his turtle."

Ross looked into the cardboard box again, the kind of box Chinese restaurants use for takeout. He gave the turtle a little poke. "Maybe it's only sleeping. It's hard to tell with turtles, don't you think?"

"It looks pretty dead to me," Amy said.

"Damn. I tried to pick the liveliest one."

"At least he didn't have time to get attached to it," Dean said.

Laurel stood up and waved. "Up 'ere, Coke man."

"That's the balloon man, Laurel," Ross told her.

Amy said, "I saw the balloon man at work when I went to the bathroom. He sticks those fancy balloons of his right up in kids' faces and says 'Don't you wanna take home a souvenir of the circus, kid?' So either the kids wind up crying because they can't have one, or the parents wind up buying some stupid, expensive balloon that won't last more than…'

"That's just good marketing," Dean said. "Balloon men have to make a living like anyone else."

"I don't like it, that's all. And I don't like the way they treat their animals—I read an article about how they train the elephants, and it's just awful. They use this horrible thing called a bullhook to poke them with. And I don't like the way they only sell the crappiest trash to eat. I guess I don't like the circus very much."

"Donsh you even like the clownsh, Amy?" Laurel asked. "They're my favorish."

"How many clowns do you think Picasso painted during his Rose Period?" Dean asked, "He painted a buttload of clowns. In fact, if you count the harlequins, he painted over…"

"Clowns are creepy," Amy said.

"There he ish," Laurel shouted. "Thersh's that old Coke man." It was, in fact, the same young man that Laurel had elbowed in the throat, only he had traded his soft drinks for snow cones. "Over 'ere, Coke man!" Laurel reached across Dean *and was able to grab the snow-cone man by an apron string. The snow-cone seller kept climbing the stairs as if nothing untoward were happening, but Ross could see the panic in his eyes. His apron came undone, his neck was wrenched to one side. He spilled red and blue ice on the concrete steps. Gamely, though, he plunged on, his legs pumping like a fullback's, and managed to tear free.*

"Come back, Coke man."

"Maybe we should go," Ross said.

"Come on, Jeremy, you sleepyhead, time to go," Amy said. "Upsy-daisy."

"Anyone know where that phrase 'upsy-daisy' comes from?" Dean asked. "It's kind of interesting. It..."

"No, and right now, I don't want to," Ross said. "Let's go."

"All right, fine, lesh go," Laurel said. "I'm getting up now, and when I've finished getting up, we'll leave." It took her a long time. Then she tottered, tried to correct herself, and as if in slow motion, sprawled across Dean's lap. "Am I up yet?"

"Damn everything," Dean said, "including the circus."

"Okay, that was horrible," Laurel admitted. "Really, really horrible. But it was all because of the 'ludes. I'd never taken one before and I haven't taken any since. I was stressing about leaving Jer. Someone told me they make you mellow and peaceful, and when the first one didn't, I took another one, but they made me stupid and sloppy instead. And they gave me this creepy feeling, like spiders were crawling around on the inside of my skin."

Ross looked across the alley again. The lights were still off. "Where are you calling from, anyway?" he asked Laurel. "Matt's Store?" Matt had the phone that was closest to School's Out.

"Not after smooshing that guinea fowl. Besides, Matt's been closed for hours."

"That taco place?"

"These days that taco place is a McDonald's. But it's closed now too. Guess again."

"The Lucky Café? The Grandview Hotel? The Snake Pit Bar? That phone booth by the Mushroom Museum?"

"No, no, no, and no way. That booth's been gone for years. The Mushroom Museum's been gone for years. When it closed, Cap wanted to steal that giant red-and-white, polka-dot plaster mushroom they had by the front door and bring it out to School's Out, but someone got to it first."

"I give up. Where are you?"

"That's you, always giving up. Come on, guess."

"For God's sake, Laurel, just tell me."

The correct answer: Ross's parents' house.

Ross wasn't sure how to take this news. The idea of Laurel allied with his parents was a bit disturbing.

He remembered the first time, years before, when he brought Laurel to his parents' house late one night. He had her sleep in his family's fallout shelter. He didn't think, at the time, that his parents were ready to meet Laurel.

"I was supposed to have dinner here," Laurel said, "but there was that business with the bird, and then I couldn't drive the Grape in because of the brakes. So, finally, your brother came out to School's Out in his truck to see what was going on. He brought me into town. We had a late dinner. But at least there was Mateus."

"I bet Dad was pissed. He hates when people are late."

"He wasn't too upset. Although he ate dinner before I got here. Do you want to talk to your mom? I think she's out on the balcony having a cigarette. Or Marshall? You know he has a girlfriend now, right? A girlfriend named Nikki."

"I did know that, but no, I don't want to talk to anyone else, not right now. I'm having a hard enough time with this conversation as is."

"See, Ross, I told you something was wrong. Why won't you admit it?"

"There's nothing wrong. How many times do I have to tell you that?"

"There is. There's bound to be."

There probably is, Ross thought. *I just wish I knew what it was.*

DOS GRINGOS

Ross walked around the block to Marlborough Street. He hesitated in front of the building that he reckoned was directly behind his, thinking that he wouldn't go in. The next thing he knew, he'd left the sidewalk and was standing in the foyer, examining the names on the mailboxes. There were twelve apartments in the building, same as in his.

The woman he'd seen the night before had been in a fourth-floor apartment facing the rear. *That would make it... let's see, number 10, 11, maybe 12.... if they're numbered logically.*

Not that he could count on that. Not in Boston.

A MRS. BUDWIG lived in Apartment 10. P. FAIRBAIRN and J. PECK lived in 11. *Maybe she's one of those two. Maybe she's the toupee collector's roommate.*

In Apartment 12, there lived a THEA DE WITT. That name was printed in pencil on a ragged strip of paper. Under her name was another name, but it had been crossed out.

Ross plucked a flyer out of one of the mailboxes and wrote the names on the back. The front of the flyer read:

HELP FOR THE PERPLEXED
SISTER JUDITH, SPIRITUAL READER AND PSYCHIC ADVISOR
DO NOT FAIL TO VISIT THIS GIFTED WOMAN
ALL QUESTIONS ANSWERED SATISFACTORILY

Ross wished Sister Judith were here. He had a question for her.

~

"There's the big guy now," Dean said when Ross came in. "I brought doughnuts, and I got you a coffee. Hey, guess what, the urinals are here. Finally." Dean was sitting at what had been the counter when this was Spiro's Super Sub Shop and what would eventually become the bar. Dean's coffee cup was covered with a legal pad to keep the plaster dust out. He had his Pentax with him.

"Yeah? How do they look?" Ross asked Dean. He took a Boston kreme and a honey cruller out of the box.

"Couple of real beauties. The plumbers are putting them in right now, so we don't have to keep running next door to the Bean's." Chris Bean owned Copenhagen Cream, the ice cream parlor next door, and was their landlord. "Anything the matter, Ross? You're looking a bit distracted this morning."

"Hmm? No, nothing. Well, Laurel called last night."

"Again? Well, that explains it. You always look gloomy after you talk to her. And nobody does gloomy better than you. Oh, another thing. The Bean came by earlier and said his customers have been complaining about the noise."

"It does sound like a bowling alley in here," Ross said. "Hey Lizard, you hear that? We're getting complaints about you." Lizard—real name Anthony Lizaro—was their carpenter and contractor. He was removing a wall. Lizard always said he liked tearing things down more than he liked building things.

"What's that?" Lizard shouted.

"You're being too damn noisy," Dean told him. "You're upsetting the rumdums eating ice cream next door."

"Tell me how to do this quietly." He started whistling.

"Use a rubber crowbar," Dean said. "Hey, you sure that's not a load-bearing wall?"

"Pretty sure," Lizard said. "We'll find out soon enough, I guess."

Lizard disappeared and came back with a coffee. He snagged one of the doughnuts.

"Eww, you dunk powdered donuts?" Dean asked. "That's disgusting. The way the powdered sugar just sits on top of..."

"Ross has powdered sugar floating in his coffee, too. Why are you picking on my coffee?"

"That's not powdered sugar," Dean said. "That's construction dust."

"Anything's better dunked in coffee. I even dunk bananas in coffee," Lizard said.

"That should be illegal. I think it is in some states," Ross said. "Hey Dean, what's with the camera?"

"Documentation. Remember back when Spiro first pulled out, I took all those pictures?"

"Yep," Lizard said, "back when you guys were still in the finger-fucking stage with this place. You were so excited, you even took pictures of me."

"I wanted to take some today because I don't think it's ever going to look worse than it does right now."

"You kidding? Oh, it's gonna look worse, a lot worse," Lizard said. "Wait'll you see what the bathrooms look like when the plumbers get done. Plumbers are all like messy little kids. And hey, what were you thinking with those urinals? *Black* urinals?"

This was the first time Ross had heard what color the urinals were. "They were cheaper than your urinals that come in standard colors," Dean explained.

"Do you know what those are going to look like after a couple of months of being pissed in? They're going to turn a hideous shade of gray. I could have gotten you some white ones that don't look used at all. In fact, if you're interested, I can get you some for home use. And even have them installed. I know a plumber who owes me a favor."

"Why would we want home urinals?" Ross asked him.

"I don't understand why every bathroom doesn't come equipped with one. Ours has practically saved my relationship with m'lady. I never have to worry about whether I've left the toilet seat up. Let me tell you, m'lady's not pleased, not pleased at all when I do, and she doesn't mind letting me know."

Dean said, "I've never understood that. I think women should be happy we put the toilet seat up *before* we piss. If they have to put it down themselves afterwards—how hard is that?"

"M'lady says—it's a matter of chivalry."

Ross shrugged. "It's just me and Jeremy at my place, so... no complaints."

Dean said, "Haven't you ever noticed that, when it comes to urinals, guys don't aim real well? There's always a puddle of piddle. That's why I don't eat at Japanese restaurants. They expect you to take your shoes off. So then you drink sake or Sapporo, you have to go to the bathroom, and you have to put your forehead up against the wall and your feet way back. You have to stand at almost a forty-five-degree angle while you..."

"Not a problem with these babies. They've got this long lower lip. You practically have to straddle it. So... no spillage. No dribblage."

Dean said, "Now, if you could get me a bidet..."

"A bidet! I wish! No, but you know what I *can* get you? I can get you one of those bathroom heat lamps. You know, the ones you see in motels? You can't believe how sweet it is to have one of those suckers in your bathroom on a cold morning. M'lady's quite pleased with ours. Although they do make you look like you've got terminal sunburn."

"Where on earth did you get one of those?"

"Oh, I don't have just one, I have dozens. I helped tear down that old motel, what was it called? Umm, the Skyway Motel, I think, out on Route 1A. And I got a sparkie to install one of them in my bathroom for free. He owed me a favor."

"Lots of people seem to owe you favors," Dean said. "Isn't your coffee break about over?"

Lizard returned to demolishing the wall. Dean said, "I got a call from Rafael last night."

"Yeah, he called me, too. I had Jeremy tell him I wasn't home. He calls all the time, wanting to know when we're going to be open."

"Well, he's got these industrial-strength peppers he ordered from Mexico, bushels of them, and he's tripping over them at home. He wants to store them here and get paid back for them."

"He can put them in the basement, but I think we should tell him he's going to have to wait on the reimbursement. He went ahead on this pepper business without so much as a by-your-leave from anyone."

"That's what I told him. And of course, he got pissed. That was nothing, though. His mother got on and ripped me a new one. She said it shouldn't take normal people anywhere near this long to open a restaurant. She said she and Rafael opened Estrella Maya in three weeks."

"Yeah, and they closed a month or two after that."

"Then she said that we should put her and Rafael on the payroll right now. At least, I think that's what she said. Mama's Spanish is pretty colloquial, and she really fires it out when she's worked up."

"I wonder if it was a mistake, promising Mama a job here."

"Well, you're the one who said we had to have Rafael in the kitchen, and he said they'd only come as a team. Besides, when the kitchen door swings open, and customers see *her* back there, they're going to think, 'Authentic. Damned authentic.'"

"You won't actually be able to see into the kitchen from the dining room, but I know what you mean," Ross said. "I'm going next door to the Bean's to make a few phone calls."

"Oh, that reminds me. They're going to install the pay phone on Friday. We have to decide where we want it. God knows when we'll get a phone down in our office. God knows when we'll actually have an office."

~

Ross asked the woman scooping ice cream at Copenhagen Cream if he could borrow a phone book. His question seemed to startle her. It was as if she'd never heard of phone books, but then she found it. For some reason, it was kept in the freezer, sitting on top of a huge drum of rocky road. A few minutes with the cold phone book, and he had a number for a P. Fairbairn and J. Beck and for an Evelyn Budwig at the address on Marlborough.

"Hello, this is Peter and Joel's answering machine," said a crotchety voice. "I don't think they're here right now, but I guess I could check if you really want me to." Ross heard footsteps walking away from the phone. "Oh Peter, Joel, yoo-hoo? Are you around? Peter? Joel?" Then footsteps seemed to approach the phone. "No, just as I figured—they're not in right now. If you want to leave a message, I guess I could take one for you. Wait till you hear me beep. And for pity's sake, keep it clean!" *Beeeeeep*....

Ross didn't want to leave a message for Peter or Joel. He hung up and dialed the number for Mrs. Budwig. "Hello, Mrs. Budwig?"

"Yes, this is she. This is Evelyn Budwig," the woman said. She spoke with a fluttery elegance.

"Who's calling, please?"

Mrs. Budwig sounded far too much like a little old lady to be anything else. He couldn't picture someone with that voice answering the phone in the nude. Now he had to think of a way to get off the line. He felt too guilty for bothering her to just hang up. "Umm, Ms. Budwig, sorry to disturb you, but I'm offering magazine subscriptions: wrestling magazines, gun magazines, drag-racing magazines, that sort of thing. I don't suppose you'd be interested in something like that, would you?"

While he was talking, Ross looked over at the woman behind the ice cream counter. A badge on her pocket said ROBIN. On her breast pocket. He remembered, when he was about thirteen, reading the phrase "the waitress's breast pocket" in a novel and getting a raging erection.

Chris Bean was fond of fifties' music and had a tape that played doo-wop on an endless loop. When Robin wasn't scooping, she was dancing around behind the counter as if she were at a sock hop. He watched as she leaned over to get a customer a scoop of caramel carob chip.

"No. No, I wouldn't be, I'm afraid," Mrs. Budwig said. It was hard to hear her with the Platters playing loudly in the background.

"Well, that's too bad. I'm sorry I bothered you. I..."

"The reason I wouldn't be is that I'm blind. More than ninety percent blind, anyway."

"Oh, that's terrible."

Ross heard her laugh. A lovely laugh. "No, it's not so terrible. I'm used to it. But you can see why I don't need any magazines, although the drag-racing magazine sounds interesting. But only if you can send me a new pair of eyes."

"Umm, well, I'll let you go, then, Ms. Budwig."

"Do you have to? I haven't gotten a phone call in weeks. In months, maybe."

"Well... I have a lot more calls to make."

"I understand. But... I hope you don't mind me saying this, young man, but... I wonder if there's some other field, something other than phone sales, that interests you. I mean, I hate to say this, but... you're not very good at it."

A pair of cops came into Copenhagen Cream. One was a pretty Chinese cop, and one was a friendly-looking old cop with hair growing out of his ears. Ross waited for them to get their sundaes before he made his third call. He didn't like the idea of making shady calls while there were cops around, even inoffensive-looking cops like these.

There was no listing in the phone book for a Thea de Witt, but Directory Assistance had a number for her and was willing to give it to him. He was pretty sure, at this point, that she was the party he was interested in. He put in another dime and called her number, but no one answered.

Ross ordered a butter brickle and watched as Robin bent down and scooped it out.

"You want jimmies on that?" she asked him.

"Okay, have a seat," Dean said. "I want to try these names out on you." He picked up the legal pad. "Zapata's Mustache. What do you think?"

"I don't know. A lot of people will have no idea who Zapata was. And it kind of reminds me of that place I used to work, Yer Fadder's Mustache."

Yer Fadder's Mustache was the first place in Boston where Ross had tended bar. The waitstaff—even the women—had to put on fake mustaches, and they all had to wear suspenders, bow ties, bowler hats, and garters on their sleeves. There was a nickelodeon in the bar, and the waiters were always trying to get customers to sing along with old songs.

"I remember hearing about it. Never went there," Dean said.

"No? Too hokey for you?"

"It wasn't that. It's just that no one ever wanted to go there with me, and I never wanted to go alone."

"That's too bad. Just think, if you'd been a regular at the bar there, we might be a year further along."

"I don't know if I would have trusted someone in a fake mustache."

"I was the only person who didn't have to wear one because I have a real beard. Let's hear some more names."

"El Sótano."

"The cellar. Except we're on the first floor."

"Point taken," Dean said, and crossed out the name.

"Wait a minute, that's my pen."

"So?"

"So it's all bent. It looks like Uri Geller got to it."

"I've been biting it. I've been trying to cut back on my smoking, and I have to do something oral. It's not like it's a Montblanc." It was, in fact, a lowly Paper Mate. "All right, another one—Tortilla Flats."

An electrician called from downstairs, "Are the lights in the kitchen off?"

"No, they're on," Ross shouted down to him. "What else you got?"

"What's wrong with Tortilla Flats? Pretty damned clever, I think. Okay, what do you think of La Cochara Grasienta?"

"*Grasienta*? Oh, greasy... I get it. The Greasy Spoon. Interesting. But I'm not sure people will know we're being ironic."

"And too many syllables. Won't roll off the tongue," Dean said. "No, I think I like Tortilla Flats best. Even if you don't get the reference to Steinbeck, it's a good name. If you do get it... everybody likes lovable drunks."

A chunk of the wall Lizard had been working on came crashing down. "There you go. You could drive a tank through that," he said.

"A go-cart, anyway," Dean said.

Satisfied with his progress, Lizard made his way over to the counter, stepping through the rubble. Lizard had a huge, fierce-looking mustache, fully twice the size of Dean's. He could have been a waiter at Yer Fadder's Mustache. He could have been Zapata. "You've got powdered sugar in your mustache, Lizard," Ross told him.

"You've got ice cream in your beard. I'll give you a good name for this place—call it Hecho en Boston."

"I didn't know you knew any Spanish, Lizard," Ross said.

"There are a lot of things about me you guys don't know."

Dean said, "We don't want to call attention to the fact that people are having dinner in Boston—we want them to feel like they've been magically transported to Old Mexico."

"You don't like that one, how about this... call it Dos Gringos."

The electrician's voice came from the basement again. "How 'bout them lights? They off now?"

"Nope, still on."

"Sparkies are such lunatics. They must have a rule that you have to be crazy to get into the Electricians Guild. I was working a job out in Quincy and I heard one electrician say to his assistant, 'Grab one of them two wires. Okay, you feel anything? No? Well, don't grab the other one then, or you'll get a nasty shock.'"

"Quiet," Dean said. "Don't alienate another one of the subcontractors. The heating and air-conditioning guy won't come back here unless you're gone. And what are you doing, anyway? You can't be on a coffee break, you've already had two of those."

"*Correcto.*"

"And it's too early for lunch."

"*Correcto también.*"

"So you must be fucking around, fucking around on our time."

"You're hurting my feelings, Dean."

"Oh my God, now he has hurt feelings. What are you going to do, take your tools and go home?"

"I wouldn't do that. I love this gig. It's indoor work, you pay me off the books, and you have no idea when I do something wrong, so long as I keep whistling."

When Lizard had gone off to demolish another wall, Ross said, "I kind of like it."

"Like what?"

"Dos Gringos. It's apt."

"Come on. It may be apt, but it sucks."

"Still, I like it." Ross picked up Dean's camera and pretended to take a picture of him. "Do you have all your lenses in your camera bag? Do you have that big mother zoom lens?"

"Yeah, but I don't know why I brought it. Not like I need a long-distance lens to photograph urinals. Why do you ask?"

"I was wondering if I could borrow it."

"Now the lights are off," Dean hollered down to the electrician. "Yeah, sure, I'm not really planning to go on safari anytime soon. What do you need it for?"

"Off? They can't be off *now*!" The electrician came rushing up the stairs. "They *are* off! Oh my God, what have I done?"

"It's just amazing, how many things can go wrong," Dean said.

3

NEW ENGLAND BELL

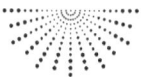

"Open one more button," Dean told Ross. "That's good, now fluff up your chest hair."

"I've been here before, I think. What was this place before it was New England Bell?"

"Dante's. Appropriate name. There's a certain resemblance between hell and Kenmore Square."

"Oh yeah. When Laurel was in town, she wanted to hear some punk music, so we came here. We saw The Scabies before they made it big, and Roadkill, and a band called Slime Mold, I think... or maybe it was Pond Scum—oh, and The Garage Band."

"What garage band?"

"No, that was their name—The Garage Band. Place looked a lot different then. The walls were black, and there weren't any hanging plants. I wonder if it took them as long to remodel as it's taking us."

"I don't know. I know they had to put in a lot of telephone equipment. Okay, what I think we should do tonight is try to look sad. That's easy for you, that's your fallback demeanor, but I have to work at it."

"What do you mean, sad?"

"Sad. You know, gloomy... morose... glum. But with just a trace, just a twinkle of enigmatic humor lurking behind the sadness. Get it?"

"I'm not sure. And why is it easy for me?"

"You know why. You always look like this big old galoot whose horse just died. Me, I always look chipper."

"Who told you that you look chipper? And why are we trying to look sad?"

"To stand out against all these vacuous smiles. And because melancholy men are mysterious, and mysterious is interesting."

They found a table. There was a big sign on the table that said Extension 23, and there was an old-fashioned candlestick phone. Dean lifted the receiver to his ear and dialed O. He spoke into the top of the phone and ordered a beer for Ross and a scotch with a twist for himself.

"What do you think of those two that just came in?"

"They look like a couple of keypunch operators."

"So what's wrong with that?" Dean asked. "After a long, tedious day punching keys, I bet they..."

"I don't have anything against keypunch operators. I have no idea what they even do. I'm just afraid you'll try to stick me with the one in the pink jeans."

"Hmm, I was hoping to. Okay, forget them. What about the ones over at Extension 36?"

"Better, but... one of them looks awfully angry about something."

"Well, maybe she's just pretending to look angry to seem interesting. I think I'll give ol' Extension 36 a ring."

"All right, go ahead, just don't ask them to dance."

"What's the matter with dancing?"

"I didn't mind so much when the point of dancing was just to throw yourself around and jump up and down now and then. But I've been watching, and the people here, they all seem to know what they're doing."

"Yeah, I've seen you dance. You dance like you've got bumblebees in your underwear."

"Besides, I hate strobe lights. Those things can give you seizures."

"Only if you're prone to seizures. But okay, we'll tell them you had polio as a kid or something, so no dancing. Hey, nobody's answering."

"Maybe their phone's out of order. Call a repairman."

"Better idea—let's just walk over and say hello."

~

"My friend and I were wondering if maybe we could buy you drinks."

"We already have drinks," one of them said. This was the woman they thought looked angry. From up close, she looked positively rabid.

"Want to dance, then?"

"Dean, I told you..." Ross was fighting down an impulse to hit Dean in the face.

"I don't," answered the angry woman. "Do you?" she asked her friend. The other woman had feathered hair, as if she'd just come from a salon. This, and a tendency to tilt her head to the side, made her look a little like a sparrow.

"No," the sparrow said, "I guess I don't either."

"Well, in that case, maybe we could all move to a bigger table and just talk."

"We're already talking," the first woman said, "to each other."

"I suppose, then," Dean said, "a couple of blow jobs would be out of the question, huh?"

"Did someone drop you on your head when you were a little kid, Dean? Is that why you act the way you do?"

"So I overestimated their senses of humor. I wish I had my camera with me. I would have loved to have caught those expressions."

"I thought that one was going to bite you or try to poke out your eye. Or at least call the manager."

"Who comes into a place like this for a quiet little chat? They were misrepresenting themselves by being here."

"I think I'm misrepresenting myself, too. I liked this place better when it was the Inferno, and I didn't like that place at all."

"Not the Inferno, Dante's. Let's have one more drink," Dean said. He was reaching for the phone when it suddenly rang.

"Probably a wrong number," Ross said.

Dean picked it up and listened for a minute. Then he covered the mouthpiece. "It's someone wanting to know why we look so unhappy," he told Ross. "See, I told you a little Weltschmerz would go a long way." He spoke for a few minutes more and then said, "She wants to know if we'll buy her a Long Island iced tea."

"Where is she?"

"Extension 11."

Ross looked around and saw her. She waved. "That's a god-awful drink but... tell her yes."

The woman came and sat between them. Her name was Gail, they found out. Dean ordered her drink of choice.

"Did you just come in? We didn't see you earlier."

"I was in the game room with my roommate Darla."

"Oh, that's where those ungodly sounds are coming from. You have a roommate here?"

"I did, but she left with the guy she was playing Space Pirates with." Gail sighed. "Are either of you guys a third?"

"A third what?" Ross asked.

"You know, a third. If I meet one more guy with a III behind his name..." She left the threat dangling. "So, what are your job titles?"

"Our what?"

"Your job titles. What do you do? Isn't that what I'm supposed to ask you?"

"We don't know either. We're kind of new to this," Ross said.

"Well, I think it is." She laughed. Her laughter seemed discharged at nothing in particular. "Now, you take that guy Darla left with. He came up to me back in the game room, and he said, 'Hi, I'm Barnet Kingston the Third, and I own Kingston's Records and Tapes. How do you like me so far?'

"And I said, 'Not so much, Barnet, so far.' And he said, 'That's okay, I'm the kind of guy who grows on you. Who are you, and what's your job title?' He was a retread, a real retread. I can't believe three generations got stuck with that dorky name. Barnet! Bar-fucking-net Kingston. And so then I asked him if he was married, because he had a white circle on his ring finger where you'd wear a wedding band. You know what he said? This is precious. He said, 'To a certain extent.' Unbelievable, just unbelievable. But Darla went off with him. They're all retreads, thirds are." She laughed again, her laugh a little more high pitched.

Ross realized this woman was not entirely sober. It didn't take many Long Island iced teas to get a person drunk.

"Well, if that's what we're supposed to do, I guess we'd better get on with it," Dean said. "We don't want to violate custom. You first. What's your job title?"

"Ticket taker," Gail said, "at the Mini Cine."

"How do you like ticket taking?"

"Usually it's pretty much okay. Sometimes there are things... things that just annoy you. Like last night, this couple came in, and they had a diaper bag. A diaper bag but no baby! I'm sure it was full of popcorn. Too damn cheap to buy from us."

"Ma and Pa Kettle go to the movies," Dean said. "Well, I used to be a consultant for a window-installation agency. I designed window displays for clothing stores."

"Oh, my roommate Darla works in a clothing store."

"Well, then, maybe you've heard from her that there are some appalling things that happen in clothing stores..."

"They may not seem all that appalling to you," Ross said to Gail. "Dean appalls easily."

"Some appalling things," Dean insisted. "Things more dramatic than people bringing their own popcorn. I could give you an example—what went on with the Duchess of the Denim Den."

Gail gave him a puzzled look.

"I guess I'd better explain. You may have noticed, there are two distinct schools of mannequin design. One school goes in more and more for abstraction. They churn out those featureless, metallic, android mutants you see in some stores. A lot of them don't have faces, or even heads. Now, the other school makes mannequins that look human. Not like those mannequins you used to see, the ones with about as much expression as a lump of dough. These mannequins—you'd swear they were human."

"Those are the dummies I like best," Gail said. "Ones that look real."

"Don't call them dummies," Ross warned her. "That term upsets Dean. Appalls him."

"In the biz, we never use that term, *dummies*. We call them mannequins. Mannequins. Well, the Duchess, she was the most realistic of any of them. State of the art. Now, they say mannequins are named after the model who posed for them, and the rumor was, the Duchess really was an aristocrat from some defunct little country somewhere. I don't know, but whoever she was, she must have been one hell of a good-looking woman. Her hair felt"—Dean rubbed a strand of Gail's hair through his fingers— "felt every bit as real as yours. Her skin"—he briefly touched Gail's cheek—"was as soft as yours. She even had nipples"—Gail quickly scooted her chair out of Dean's range—"as I'm sure you do too. Anyway, I convinced Lance--Lance was the manager of the Denim Den—I got him to order a Duchess. But I never got to put so much as a halter top on her. Lance had her uncrated, took one look, and locked her in a dressing room they weren't using. He'd spend all his breaks and lunch hours with the Duchess. Now, I didn't exactly blame him. Working at a clothing store is incredibly boring, and..."

"I don't know about that. Darla likes it, and she gets her clothes forty percent off," Gail said. "She can even buy clothes for me."

"Trust me—I've put in plenty of time in clothing stores. Selling clothes is so boring, it withers the soul," Dean said. "Next time you go into a clothing store, take a look at the people working there. They all have these glassy-eyed expressions. They look like brook trout. So I don't blame

Lance for taking advantage of any diversion that came along. And like I said, the Duchess was a looker. And she was probably a better conversationalist than half the people who worked at the Denim Den. But he shouldn't have monopolized her."

Gail wanted to know what, exactly, the manager did with a dummy.

"With a mannequin, you mean. There's no point in going into details. The thing is, he was squandering a resource. The Duchess was so spectacular, she may have helped turn things around for the Den. If people had seen *her* in the window, smartly dressed, of course, they would have come flocking in. As it was, that store went under a few months later."

"You know what?" Gail finished her cocktail quickly. "I'm beginning to think you guys are a couple of retreads."

"Don't get discouraged, Ross," Dean said when Gail had gone. "I don't think we're missing much. Her nose whistled when she breathed, did you notice? Can you imagine sleeping with her? She must sound like a little steam calliope." Dean pulled Ross's pen out of his pocket and made a note on a cocktail napkin. "I've got to remember that line, 'How do you like me so far?'"

Dean was about to dial O to order more drinks. "Don't order one for me," Ross said. "I'm leaving."

"Leaving?" Dean chomped on Ross's pen. "Why are you leaving? They have a late happy hour."

"Because, I told you, I don't like it here. If I actually got together with someone in a place like this, I'd feel sort of shallow. But since I haven't, I feel even worse. I'm not even successful at being shallow. I'm not even a good retread. Whatever that is."

"Don't go. Sit back down. Amy's gone somewhere, and if I get home before she does, she'll think I spent the whole evening pouting at home."

"What do you mean, she's gone? Like on a date?"

"Tell you the truth, Ross, I don't know where she's been going lately. She won't tell me. She says I never tell her where I go, so why should she?"

"But you think she's seeing someone?"

"Maybe. Probably, even."

"That might be for the best. You're always saying she doesn't have much experience in the real world. What is it you always say she is?"

"Pathologically unsophisticated?"

"Right. Well, I never thought that was true but... at least now she's getting new input."

"I don't know how you can say that. You know she's never gone in for this sort of thing, and now, maybe she'll sleep with someone and it will seem terrific to her, not because it's any better, because I guarantee you it won't be, but because it's different, and she'll be dazzled. Dazzled. She's a rookie at this, Ross. She doesn't even know when she's supposed to feel guilty."

"She's just bored. I'd be bored if I did what Amy did all day."

"I think it's more serious than boredom. Want to hear what she told me? She said that, since every cell in a person's body is replaced by new ones over a seven-year period, why then, less than half of me is the person she fell in love with four years ago."

"Well, that could explain the seven-year-itch theory," Ross said. "She was serious when she said that?"

"Semi-serious, anyway. You know where she's getting this drivel, don't you? She's getting it from that guy Chewy."

"Chewy? That's someone she's seeing?"

"No, you know Chewy. Amy went to grade school with him. Remember, he gave that Halloween party we went to down in the North End?"

"Oh yeah. He came as a butterfly or something. Bald guy, right?"

"He shaves his head, I think."

"Isn't he supposed to be gay?"

"I don't know what he is. He never talks. Not to me, anyway. Amy's taking some kind of karate lessons from him. I don't get why she wants to be his good buddy, but, whatever. Hey, instead of going home, let's go somewhere else. We could go down to the Combat Zone. The Naked i or the Teddy Bear Club, maybe. You can always get strippers to smile at you."

"But they smile at everyone. That takes all the fun out of it."

"Come on."

"No, I need to go pick up Jeremy at his friend Mojave's house. He spends more time over there than he does at home these days. They play these endless war games."

"What, like Gettysburg? We used to stay up all night playing that in my dorm. I was good at it, too. If General Lee had used my battle plan, the South would have won the war. But those games are pretty complicated for a kid Jeremy's age, aren't they?"

"Yeah, he says Mojave always beats him. Anyway, I'm going to get Jer and then I have some things I want to do at home. You go to the Combat Zone by yourself."

"Maybe I will."

"On second thought, maybe you shouldn't. You might get beat up if you do. I remember you talking about that time when you first got to town and..."

"I'll be fine. I've learned how to handle myself up here at night. You never want to make eye contact with anyone. It was different down in Virginia. You could look at anyone whenever you liked. Up here, you can't make eye contact with people after dark, or else they think you want to screw around with them."

Dean came out of Dunkin' Donuts on Boylston Street trying to get his umbrella open. There were three kids huddled together just outside the door, wet hair hanging in their faces. They were speaking softly together in a language Dean couldn't identify. He looked at them and listened, trying to place the language. Then one of them said to him, "Ay, you, what you looking us for?"

"Oh, no, I wasn't. I was just..."

"Give us you hwalled."

"Give you what?"

That particular kid didn't say anything else. Maybe he was upset because Dean hadn't understood him. Another kid pulled out a knife. "We have knife," this one said. "Give us wallet."

Knife against umbrella; Dean tried to calculate the odds. The umbrella had the longer range, but the knife was sharper. But what exactly had the kid meant by "We have knife?" Did he mean that we, collectively, have one knife among us, or that each of us have one knife apiece? That would make a difference.

Another one of the kids reached into his coat pocket. Dean heard the snick of a switchblade opening.

Dean shifted his umbrella to his left hand and drew out his wallet. "I'm afraid I find myself basically impecunious at the moment."

They gave him a puzzled look. "Give us wallet."

"There's nothing in it, see?" He held it upside down and shook it to emphasize its emptiness. "See, nothing. I had two dollars, but I spent most of it on doughnuts."

Dean thought that, at this point, maybe he could simply walk off. The holdup had been pretty informal up to this point. He put his wallet away and opened his umbrella.

Those who had knives out brandished them. "All right," Dean said. "Here, take my thirty-seven cents and my doughnuts. That's the best I can do."

They seemed pretty unhappy at this arrangement and consulted among themselves in their unknown language. In the end, they accepted, but without grace. They took his umbrella, too, while they were at it. They didn't want soggy donuts.

Dean said, "Nowadays I don't have any trouble. I just never look at anyone."

"Be careful, anyway. You still might get mugged. Or walk into a parked car."

"I don't think I'm going to go if you don't. If I went into a strip joint by myself, I'd be liable to take it seriously. I guess I'll just sit here and have another drink."

"See you tomorrow, then. Don't drink too much. We have to finish sanding the floor in the bar tomorrow."

"I'm sick of sanding. I don't know why we're paying all those people, and we have to do our own sanding. Maybe I should have stuck with mannequins. Mannequins were boring, but at least I knew what the hell I was doing."

4

CAUSALITY

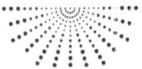

AFTER PUTTING JEREMY TO BED, ROSS SAT FACING THE WINDOW WITH THE phone in his lap. For a long time, he just stared across the alley. Then he dialed all but the last digit of the number Directory Assistance had given him for Thea de Witt. *Why am I doing this?* he wondered. *This is ridiculous.* He was about to put the phone back in its cradle, but somehow, as if acting on its own, his finger completed the call.

A light came on and a woman came into the room. There was a flash of pale, lithe limbs and flowing hair. The woman—Thea de Witt, he assumed —picked up the phone.

Cause and effect.

He'd fitted his camera with the lens he'd borrowed from Dean. It was the size of a howitzer. He saw her mouth the word "Hello," then actually heard the word through the phone. He could dimly hear music in the background—Fleetwood Mac, maybe.

She was in the nude again.

Using Dean's gigantic lens, she seemed to be about two feet away. "Hello there," he said. "I'd like to order a pizza. A medium pizza with— let's see, it says I get two free toppings, so mushrooms and pepperoni. Oh, and I want black olives. I guess I'll have to pay extra for those, huh?"

"I'm having a hard time understanding you."

This was because, as a precaution, he was covering the mouthpiece of his phone with a handkerchief. *Must sound like I'm talking through a milkshake.*

"Now as I understand it," he said, "you guarantee *hot* pizza. I don't even have to pay for it if it arrives cold, it says here in your ad. Last week, I ordered kung pao chicken from the Double Happiness House, and by the time they delivered, it was stone cold. And they still expected me to pay for cold Chinese slop. Can you believe it? I hope I don't have to go through *that* again. Not all of us have microwaves, you know."

She was standing in the window. He fiddled with the lens and a mole just above her left breast came into sharp focus. However, the most interesting parts of that breast were screened by the plantlets of a spider plant. The bottom of the window frame cut her off below the waist. He trained the lens on her face. Her eyes were blue, deep blue, a startling, icy blue.

"I still can't hear you very well, but I'm sure you have a wrong number." Thea de Witt had a slight, unplaceable accent. British, but not quite British. It was so slight that Ross wondered if it was an affectation.

He kept returning to those eyes.

"You mean this isn't Hot to Trot?"

"This isn't what?" She sat down sideways on the window seat.

"This isn't Hot to Trot Pizza? You're not the pizza lady?"

"No, I'm not a pizza lady. I'm going back to bed. If I were you, though, I'd gargle with salt water." She sounded kind; she sounded, somehow, like someone used to dealing with the misguided.

She didn't go right back to bed. She lay back on the window seat for a few moments, her legs crossed at the knees. One foot was bouncing up and down, probably in time to the music. He'd been wrong—she wasn't completely nude. She was wearing socks.

Jeremy came into the living room as if on a solemn errand. He had their cat, Swizzle, draped around his neck, wearing her more than carrying her. His face was creased from his pillow. "Pizza?" he asked.

Ross hurriedly pulled the curtains closed. "Sorry, Jer, no pizza tonight."

Jeremy yawned operatically and tossed his dark hair out of his eyes.

Exactly how Laurel would toss the hair out of her face.

"Why do you have a camera?"

"Uh, no reason, I was cleaning the lens. You should go back to bed. It's late."

Jeremy went into their tiny kitchen.

"I'm going to have Cap'n Crunch, then. Do we have any cat-beer?"

That was what Jeremy called milk.

"I bought a half gallon a day or two ago. It's gone already. You drink a lot of milk."

Jeremy opened the refrigerator. "There's some half & half."

"Half & half is for coffee," Ross said, "and there's only a little." He closed the refrigerator door. He tried to give Jeremy a frosty look, but when it came to his son, his looks were never all that frosty.

"Come on, give it."

"Let's talk about it."

Jeremy huffed and said, "S'it!" He had problems pronouncing his sh's sometimes.

"All right, all right already," Ross said. He got the carton of half & half out for Jeremy. "You can be pretty hard to live with sometimes, you know that?"

5

WHOPPERS

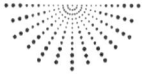

"Yo, Ross, I'm just gonna have a seat in this booth. You go order for both of us, okay? I want one of their... their big burgers," Dean said. "And fries."

"Why should I do that? I don't like standing in line either."

"If I don't get us a place to sit, there might not be any left."

"There are plenty of empty tables."

"Listen, there are some words I have trouble saying, okay, and that happens to be one of them."

"Okay, fine, but you have to tell me why when I get back."

When Ross returned with their lunch, Dean whispered urgently to him, "See those two guys in the booth next to us?" Ross looked around. There was a white guy and a black guy, both with ample sideburns. "Well, get this: the white guy told the other guy that he was at a disco last night, and he met this redhead. This *smokin'* redhead, is how he put it."

"Let me guess—you think he was talking about Amy?"

"Why not? She was out again last night. And listen to this: The black guy asked the other guy if he banged her, and he said, no, 'cause she had someone waiting for her at home,' and he did, too, so they didn't have anywhere to go."

"I wouldn't worry too much. Probably tons of redheaded women roistering around last night. Besides, Amy isn't exactly a redhead. I'd say her hair is more auburn."

"I'd say mahogany... maybe russet... but those are all shades of red."

Dean snatched up a couple of fries. "The fries are better at McDonald's," he said. "The ones here are too skinny."

The two men in the next booth laughed uproariously about something. Ross asked Dean why he couldn't say that word.

"You remember me telling you about that motorcycle accident I had down in Virginia, right?"

"I've seen those scars on your knee."

"The way it happened was... my buddy Eugene and I, we were out riding—we both had Yamaha Bearcats back then—and we were riding on a little country road outside of town, moving along pretty good, and... those helmets can get hot, so I opened the face shield. And a June bug drilled me right between the eyes. It was like being shot with a custard-filled bullet. It hit me so hard I lost control and I laid my bike down, and my bike and I went sliding along the blacktop for about fifty feet.

"I not only blew out my knee, half my body was covered with third-degree road rash, and I had a concussion even though I'd been wearing a helmet. When we got to the hospital, I overheard the ambulance driver tell the ER nurse, they found me squirming around on the pavement, screaming like a scalded chicken. And you know, when you have a concussion, they wake you up every couple of hours and ask you questions, like who's president, and I'd say things like, President Pat Paulsen or President Norman Thomas, just to mess with them. So, when the nurses would wake me up, they'd always come to my room in teams of two or three, and they'd all be giggling, and they'd lift up my sheet. I finally figured out why. I'd been wearing this pair of underwear that an old girlfriend gave me. The underwear said—it said, Home of the... Home of... of that really big hamburger."

"That's why moms always tell you to change your underwear before you go out."

"My undies were clean—they were just embarrassing. I mean, not that it was false advertising or anything, but..."

The two men in the next booth stood up and shook hands elaborately. Both were wearing silk shirts and beltless pants and lots of aftershave. Enough aftershave to make eyes water.

"Tell you something else: Amy's talking about getting a permanent."

"So? What's wrong with that? Everyone's getting perms. She'd look good with one."

"It's not that there's anything wrong with perms, per se, it's just that they're so banal. So banal it's pathetic. First it was that blue hat, then the giant orange sunglasses, then the jacket with epaulets, then those knee-high boots, now a perm."

"Anything's banal, if you want to look at it that way. You're being pretty banal right now."

I know, but banality's like shit. You don't mind your own so much. So, last night, she didn't come back until almost two. Johnny Carson was already off. God, I hate Johnny Carson."

"You're kidding. Nobody hates Johnny Carson."

"I do. And then, even when she did come home, she didn't come to bed. She paced around the living room for... for I don't know how long. Do you know you can tell if a woman's been unfaithful by the sound of her boots on a wood floor? There's a special cadence for infidelity. And those boots she was pacing in, they cost more than a hundred dollars... a hundred dollars, for boots, are you freaking kidding me? And who do you imagine paid for them? My Frye boots cost me maybe thirty bucks, tops. What are you grinning at, Ross? That's sick, sick and evil to smirk like that when I'm feeling miserable."

"I'm sorry, but... but I was thinking of two things. One, if Amy was at the party with that guy who was sitting over there, she wasn't unfaithful, because you heard him say they didn't have any place to go. Two, I was thinking about that time around a year ago when you were almost ready to leave Amy for Sarah... Sarah... what was her name, again?"

Ross knew full well what Sarah's name was; he had slept with her himself, but he and Sarah had mutually agreed that it was best to never mention that to Dean.

"Sarah Jefferson? It wasn't so much that I planned to leave Amy, it was that I almost got caught and didn't have much choice."

"I love you. I love you. I love you, Dean. I love you, love you so much, love you, love you." Sarah kept frenetically saying things like that. He knew she didn't mean it. Before the first time they went to bed together, she told him that she'd be talking that way. To Sarah, it was as much a part of sex as breathing hard.

In the later stages of lovemaking, she paused her litany of "love you's" briefly, and Dean became aware of a wet chomping noise coming from under the bed. When they'd finished, Sarah rolled over, pulling the sheet off him, and had a look. "What have you gotten into now, Yo-Yo? Oh-oh. Bad Yo-Yo! Oh, she's a very bad, bad girl, Yo-Yo is."

"What did that bad Yo-Yo do?" Dean asked.

"She ate your shoes. One of them, anyway." Sarah handed him his left shoe. It was shredded and sodden and nasty, like a mutilated fish. Dean felt like grabbing that bad Yo-Yo and grinding her fool face into the carpet.

"Hey, isn't that one of those weird shoes, what do they call them? They're supposed to make you feel like you're walking in sand, right? You like 'em?"

Dean didn't, actually. "They were a gift."

"I'll buy you another pair of shoes," Sarah said, and kissed him on the forehead. "If it makes you feel any better, Yo-Yo chewed up a pair of my strappy sandals and one of my running shoes."

Dean couldn't imagine why that should make him feel any better. "I'd just like to know how I'm supposed to go home half-shod," he said.

And Sarah said to him, "Don't. Stay here. Stay as long as you like."

Dean tried to think of how he could tell Amy about his missing Earth Shoe. She'd given him those shoes for his birthday. He could tell her he'd been mugged by a one-legged bandit. Or that his foot had gotten stuck in trolley tracks, and it was give up a shoe or give up a leg. Or he could forget about telling her anything, and he could spend the night with Sarah. He could spend the rest of his life with her. Sarah had blond hair that went halfway down her butt, she had striking green eyes, and she moved like a dancer. In fact, she'd studied ballet in Denmark. She'd lived in Paris. She spoke four languages and she had a masters in comp lit. She read stories to children at a bookstore, and she was an actor. She was reasonably good in bed, although all that "love you" business was distracting.

On the debit side, her breath smelled like a combination of industrial glue and spoiled fish. Dean had encountered people who had issues with their breath, people whose breath smelled like Vienna sausages or like Fritos or like falafel. Those people had come by their breath problems naturally—that is, without having eaten Vienna sausages or Fritos or falafel—but this smell, this glue plus fishy smell, was in another class altogether. It was noisome. It was vile.

"Ouch, you're kneeling on my hair!" That was always a danger with people who had hip-length hair. "What are you doing?"

"I'm putting on my clothes, and then I'm going to put on my shoes—my shoe—and then I'm going to try to find an all-night shoe store."

∾

"I just couldn't face a lifetime of glue-flavored, tuna-fish kisses," Dean said.

I know. Me neither. And there was something Dean didn't know, because he could never spend the night. There was the snoring. The awful snoring.

When Sarah snored, it sounded like a buzz-saw going through corrugated metal.

"You're lucky Amy never found out," Ross told him.

"You're right about that. But I've been clean since then."

"Clean? Weren't we trying to pick up women at New England Bell last week? Without success, yes, but still..."

"I mean until Amy got crazy and started going out every night and doing God knows what. Hey, want to go to the Crow Bar with me tonight?"

"I went there once with Lizard. That place is a dump. Depressing."

"Wait, what? You're going places with Lizard? Without me? Well, it may be depressing, but I heard that after the shift changes at eleven, lots of nurses from Mass General show up. Nurses are always up for a good time. Because they're around death so much."

"I'm going to stay home tonight. I haven't spent much time with Jeremy lately."

An old man had moved into the booth next to theirs. He was carrying on a dialogue with God. He left gaps in his conversation where God could insert comments or questions if He wanted.

"You still telephoning your neighbor?"

"I have, once or twice," Ross admitted.

Ross had called and, trying to copy Amy's South Boston accent, he pretended to be from the Nielson Company and asked her what she was watching on TV. She replied that, while she'd once had a TV, it no longer worked. At first it would work for a while when she banged on it, she told him, but then it stopped working altogether. Another time he'd called and tried to imitate Dean's Virginia drawl, pretending he was a drunk who needed a taxi. She'd kindly looked up the number for Metro Taxi and gave it to him. Once he'd used his friend Wade's British accent, or his best approximation of it, and asked her if she needed a Diners Club card. She said she'd never be able to qualify for one. Since then he'd mostly been silent, looking through Dean's lens and listening to her say, "Hello? Hello? Who is this?" He'd run out of accents he could plausibly imitate.

"Be careful, though. My friend Eugene, the guy I was riding with when I wrecked my bike, he inherited an Amoco station from his dad. He installed one-way mirrors between the men's room and the ladies'. Every time a remotely attractive female came in, Eugene would trot off to the men's room and catch the show next door. So, one day a motorcycle cop pulled in and headed for the washroom. There was a permanent OUT OF ORDER sign on the men's room, but the cop didn't pay any attention.

While he was in there, some little sweetheart came in and took a leak next door. Eugene got busted. It was an ugly situation."

Oh my God, I'm Eugene. Ross thought. *I'm worse than Eugene.*

"We'd better go," Ross said to Dean. "We've got a lot to do this afternoon."

The man in the next booth was asking God for clarification. "You still want me to be your spy down here, right?"

Dean said, "I don't want to go back there right now. Lizard's going to be using the table saw all afternoon. I hate the noise that thing makes. It's like a giant dental drill. Or a billion mosquitos. Besides, I'm meeting Amy for lunch."

"Lunch? What the hell was this? Didn't we just have lunch?"

"I had *this* lunch because I was hungry. Lunch with Amy is going to be a serious affair. You can see we have a lot to talk over, can't you? And we're going to Quetzalcoatl's, so I can report on the competition."

"Now that's a bad name. Who can pronounce Quetzalcoatl's? How long is this luncheon of yours going to take? We're supposed to be at the ABCC at two-thirty to talk about our liquor license."

"Yeah, but do you need me there for that? I don't want to restrict myself too much. If lunch goes well, maybe we'll end up back at our apartment together. But I could come by your place tonight. Are you planning to give your neighbor another little call?"

"Probably not. I haven't done that for a while. Besides, it's a kind of a... a private thing."

"Hmm. So what kind of film are you shooting?"

"I'm not taking pictures. I'm just using your lens to look through."

"No pictures? Ross, you should always get documentation. Of everything. Tell you what: You take the pictures, and you can use my darkroom to develop them. I'll even help."

6

RED BRIEFS

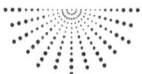

Usually, Thea de Witt answered her phone promptly, even if she'd been sleeping. Tonight, though, the phone rang eight or nine times and Ross was about to give up. Then a curly-haired, unhappy man in red undershorts came into the living room. "Hallo!" The man shouted angrily into the phone. Ross was about to hang up when the man shouted something else. "*Klootzak!*" Ross wondered who, or what, a *klootzak* was. It didn't sound complimentary.

The man put on a pair of round, steel-rimmed glasses—real John Lennon glasses—and bent forward with his hands on the window seat. He was staring across the alley. Ross dropped Swizzle the cat out of his lap and ducked below the windowsill, sitting in something crunchy, crunchy like the bones of a tiny bird.

> Section 259, 14c, of the Massachusetts General Laws: Whosoever telephones another person, or causes a person to be telephoned to, repeatedly, for the sole purpose of harassing, annoying, or soliciting such person shall be punished by a fine of not more than $500, or by imprisonment for not more than three months, or both.

"What are you in for, pal?"
"Oh, you know, harassing, annoying, soliciting—the works."
The phone rang, startling him. He expected it to be the police. *"This is Sergeant Fred Schmidt of the Shady Phone Call Squad. We know what you been*

up to, buddy. You wanna put that phone down and come outta there with your hands up?"

"Collect call for anyone from a Laurel Jarboe. Will you accept charges?"

"Goddamn it."

"Beg your pardon, sir?" The operator had a Midwestern twang. Ross wondered if he could imitate it.

"Uh, yes, operator, sure, why not? I'll take the call."

"Were you swearing at me or at the operator, Ross?"

"I was swearing at the radiator. I burned my elbow on it when I answered the phone."

"How did you manage that?"

"I was sitting on the floor next to the radiator when the phone rang."

"Oh. Well, I'm sure you had a good reason to be doing that. Why are you whispering?"

Whatever it was that Ross had sat in, it was pulverized now. He sniffed the powder. *Cap'n Crunch? Sugar Pops? Fruit Loops?"*

"Am I whispering? I didn't realize it. I guess I didn't want to wake up Jeremy." Irrationally enough, Ross had thought that the man across the alley might hear him. He risked an exploratory glance over the windowsill. The man had lit a cigarette and was still lurking in the living room. Without the lens, it was like looking at him on a tiny TV screen. He had an outsized head made larger by all his hair, and his red briefs were narrow, really narrow, not much wider than a rubber band.

"He's asleep already? Couldn't you just... oh my Lord, you should see what I just saw!"

Laurel had just seen two women walk by the window of her motel room. They were identical twins, wearing identical polka-dot maternity smocks. They both seemed to be in the exact same stage of pregnancy.

Laurel told Ross about the spectacle. "I wonder how they arranged *that*. It couldn't have been a coincidence."

"You know, I hardly ever see pregnant women around here."

"That's because cities are dying. That's what your father would say, anyway."

"Boston doesn't feel like it's dying."

"I know, but you know what your dad would say: The band on the *Titanic* went right on playing..."

"Even after it hit the iceberg. Yeah, I know. So Laurel, why are you calling?"

"I told you I was going to. I wanted to talk to Jer. And I wanted to tell you about a dream I had. You want to hear about it?"

Ross sighed. "I suppose," Ross said. He didn't want to stir until the man across the alley had gone away. Because Ross was so tall, scrunching down below his windowsill was not very comfortable. Inches away from him, the radiator was clanging and hissing and gurgling.

"Well, I was in this city I'd never been in before. I had some important reason for being there; I was on some sort of mission, but I don't know what it was. The whole city was quiet, no people around at all. I tried knocking on a few doors. No one answered, but I could hear shuffling sounds inside. I was having these weird feelings..."

"What kind of feelings?"

"Hard to say, exactly. I mean, feelings of longing, or loneliness, maybe, but mixed with a bit of curiosity... I can't describe them, exactly. There are emotions you have in dreams that you don't have anywhere else. And sometimes in dreams you can have two completely contradictory emotions at the same time. It's like colors—I see colors in my dreams that I've never seen in real life. So anyway, one place I walked by, it looked somehow familiar, so I just went in. And I realized something. The furniture in there was *alive*." Laurel was munching something on the other end of the line— potato chips, from the sound of it. "The only thing that was alive in this whole city was the furniture. And I realized something else. The furniture in this particular house wasn't a bunch of strangers. I mean, there were people I knew there, only they looked like furniture. Cap was there; he looked like a king-sized bed. Poppy was a kitchen table. Jeremy was a little ottoman stool."

"What about me? Was I there?"

"Uh-huh, you were there. You were a hot-water heater."

"A hot-water heater! That's not even furniture."

"I can't help it. That's what I dreamed."

"You and your dreams."

"That's what you always used to say when I'd tell you my dreams. 'Oh, Laurel, you and your dreams.' That is, when you said anything at all. Sometimes you'd just roll your eyes. Don't deny it, you did. And when I'd ask you about your dreams, you wouldn't tell me anything."

"That's because I almost never remember my dreams."

Ross heard Laurel start in on another handful of potato chips. Or perhaps it was ice. Laurel had a habit of crunching ice after she'd finished a drink, something Ross always found irritating.

"The other thing I wanted to tell you... when I told Cap you weren't coming to School's Out for the reunion, he said, 'You tell Ross he'd better get his ass out here, and no damn excuses.'"

Ross could picture Cap saying that, his big red beard bobbing up and down. "I'd love to see Cap, and everyone. And tell him, the only reason I can't is..."

"... is that you don't want to, or else you would. Okay, this is Jeremy's turn to stay with you over Christmas, and I just can't wait till next summer, so I'm going to have to take you up on your offer. I'll come there."

Ross didn't remember inviting her to visit, but he didn't say anything.

She said, "I know you'll be busy with the restaurant and all, but maybe I can help. And I want to get some shops back there to carry my jewelry. The more I can do that, the less I have to go to these fucking crafts fairs."

The man in the red briefs was gone now, though the lights were still on. It suddenly occurred to Ross that there had been no real reason to crouch on the floor. He could have just closed the curtains and walked away from the window.

"And I want to do a lot of things with Jeremy, too. I'll take him to the zoo..."

"There isn't a zoo in Boston. Well, there's one in Franklin Park, but it's not a very good zoo."

"Stop being so goddamn overwhelmingly enthusiastic," she said. "You're sweeping me off my feet. All right, you don't have a decent zoo, then I'll take Jeremy to the aquarium. You have one of those, don't you?"

Ross thought Laurel was sounding seriously upset with him, but then she unexpectedly giggled. "Here come those pregnant twins again, coming back to their room. They aren't just a little pregnant, either; looks like those kids are going to drop out of the hopper any minute now. I don't think I ever looked so pregnant."

Ross got off the floor and sat back down in the armchair. He thought of Laurel, rushing through the marketplace in Mexico in the rain just before Jeremy was born. "You looked pretty damn pregnant," Ross said, remembering.

7

VETERANS DAY

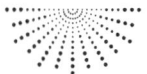

TWO BASS DRUMMERS FROM THE MARBLEHEAD MARCHING MARINERS WALKED past the laundromat. Behind them came a majorette with a white rifle over her shoulder. There were squads of soldiers from Fort Devens wandering aimlessly along Newbury Street. Three women dressed like nurses from the Great War came by, one of them eating a giant pretzel with mustard on it. She'd gotten mustard on the front yoke of her apron.

Jeremy found this flotsam from the Veterans Day parade disquieting. He was trying to convince Amy and Dean, and especially Ross, that this laundry was ill-timed. "We could be out on Valerie's fire escape right now, watching the parade." Valerie lived across the hall from Ross and Jeremy in an apartment on the more expensive side of the building, the side that overlooked Commonwealth Avenue. "The parade's going right by our house."

"Take a little responsibility, huh, Jeremy," Ross said. "Neither of us have any clean shirts, and all our socks are crispy."

"The red light went off," Jeremy said. "You can put the clothes in the dryer now. If you hurry..."

"*We* can put the clothes in the dryer. Get the basket."

Dean and Amy's laundry was done, too. "Hey, Ross, want to make a bet on whose dryer finishes first?" Dean asked.

"What kind of bet is that? They're both the same kind of machine."

"I know, but this one looks like a real thoroughbred of a Maytag to me. Come on, where's your sporting blood?"

"All right, you're on. What are the stakes?"

"Man with the losing machine has to fold all the clothes. I hate folding clothes."

"Okay, it's a bet, but if I lose, I'm not folding any underwear. I don't do underwear."

"Who folds underwear anyway?"

"I do," Amy said.

"What's that poster mean?" Jeremy wanted to know. The poster had an undertaker rubbing his palms together. DON'T DYE HERE! it said. "What if you couldn't help it? What if you had a heart attack or something?"

"It's a play on words," Dean said. "An ironic warning."

"You mean it's supposed to be funny?" Jeremy asked skeptically.

"Yes, mildly."

"What I think is funny," said Amy, "is watching Dean trying to decide if he should put that sweater in the dryer."

"Well, as Nietzsche put it, 'Live dangerously. Build your cities on the rims of volcanoes.'" He tossed the sweater in. "You ready, Ross?" Dean plopped a quarter into the slot and jerked the knob. "Go baby. Run your heart out." He patted the machine's flank. "Let me have some of that wine, Amy."

"I thought you didn't like it." Dean had given Amy money to go out for wine earlier, and she'd come back with Japanese plum wine.

"I don't, it's cloying, but it's all there is. Pour me some, will you?"

"Why can't you pour your own wine?" Amy asked. "Tell me, Ross, why is it that men think it's cute to be helpless?"

"Who says they do?"

"They must. Some men must, anyway. Can you think of any other reason they act so incompetent? You take Dean as an example. He..."

"Why take me as an example?"

"Because I know your case best, honey bun. Now Dean, when he used to decorate windows, he had the most impeccable dummies..."

"Mannequins! You call them mannequins, not dummies. How many times have I told you that?"

"Okay, *mannequins*. But when he takes a shower or he's getting in bed, he just throws his clothes on the floor."

"At least I know where everything is. It's on the floor," Dean said.

Amy said, "And when he does the dishes, I have to do half of them over. When he irons—which isn't very often—clothes look worse than before he ironed them. He doesn't even pick up his own toenail clippings. The only reason I can think of that he's so helpless and rotten at doing simple things is that he thinks it's sexy or something. Or he figures that if he does a terrible job, then I'll do it for him."

"It's just that there are some things a person can do and some things he can't," Dean said. "I accept that. Sure, I'm not great at domestic things. And I'll never learn how to do macramé, or vector analysis, or basic home wiring, or square dancing..."

"You're just lazy, Dean. You could learn how to do any of those things. Except maybe macramé. I can't see you ever being good at macramé."

"Lazy? She thinks I'm lazy? Ross, you're my witness—you heard her say that. This is the lady who takes three days to go to one job interview: one day to psych herself up, one day to actually do it, and one day to rest up from the experience."

"Doesn't mean I'm lazy."

"Well, at least I've always held down a job."

"Oh, you're not lazy when it comes to making a living. You're just lazy when it comes to living. A lot of that is your mother's fault. Jeremy's lucky, in a way. Laurel isn't around all the time to spoil him silly."

Jeremy, who hadn't been paying close attention, asked, "Why am I lucky?"

"You're lucky Amy's not your mother," Dean said. "Would you please give me some of that Chateau Robitussin?"

Ross decided to change the subject drastically. "I wonder how a restaurant in a laundromat would do? Suppose you put in tables and a bar, hired a strolling violinist..."

"I can see it," Dean said. "You'd want some of the old laundromat ambience to seep through. Keep the bulletin board and the change machine and the rack for lost socks and that sign on the rack—I love that sign." The sign read CAN'T FIND YOUR MATE? CHECK THE BARS.

Ross said, "You know what else I was thinking? Since we'd need oversize water heaters anyway, we could put in a couple of hot tubs."

"Now you're talking. Forget the washers and dryers; we'll just have hot tubs."

"Think it's too late to switch concepts?"

"Yeah, by a few months but... if the Mexican restaurant goes over big, we'll open a hot tub café. Maybe a laundromat bistro, too."

"You still haven't gotten the first one open," Amy reminded them.

Someone opened the door and let in a few bars of distant martial music. A woman with a white sack over her back came in. Her head was swathed in a long scarf and she was wearing a trench coat of some nameless shade between gray and beige. Her coat was stained and the cuffs and hem were frayed. There was a nondescript dog with her, some sort of a terrier. The dog had a severe underbite; its lower teeth stuck out over its upper lip like a miniature boar's.

As the woman was unwinding her scarf, Ross realized it was Thea de Witt. He hadn't called her since the man in red underwear answered the phone. Ross grabbed a tattered copy of *Redbook Magazine* and opened it in front of his face. The article that he opened it to turned out to be "Dr. Spock Warns Against Nudity at Home."

The woman was having trouble with the dollar-bill changer. "You have to put the bill in face up," the attendant told her.

"But it *is* face up."

"Then just shove old George in, and out comes your change. But it doesn't like dog-eared corners."

She tried it again, and it came back again. She stared forlornly at her unchanged bill. "I hate to bother you, but do any of you have change for a dollar?"

Ross put down the magazine. *She's not going to recognize me, no way. How could she?*

Dean said, "Your problem is, you need change for a five. That's not old George, that's old Abe."

"Oh, you're right. They all look so much alike."

"I think I have four ones and four quarters," Amy said. "And here, you can use some of our detergent. Those little packages you get for a quarter from the vending machine are a rip-off."

Thea loaded her clothes into the washer. She came back and took off her coat and sat down in the row of colorful plastic chairs facing them. She was wearing a vest that looked like it was made from carpet remnants.

She's a bit older than I thought she was. And her eyes are even bluer—they're an unbelievable blue. Like chips of sapphire. Sapphires in a laundromat.

"Are you British?" Dean asked her. "If not, you sound a little pretentious."

"That's a pretty pretentious way to put it," Amy said to Dean.

"No, I'm not British, I'm Dutch. But in the Netherlands, they teach you to speak English the way they speak it in England. And I worked in London for a couple of years."

"Well, I figured you weren't from around here when you couldn't tell a single from a fiver," Dean said.

"They're all the same size and they're all the same color," she said. "You have such ugly money."

"Form follows function," Dean said.

She rummaged in her purse and found a yellow fifty-guilder note with a sunflower on it. "See? Pretty, isn't it?" she said to Jeremy.

"Pretty," Jeremy agreed. "Can I have it?"

"I'm afraid not. This is about all the money I have. I was going to change it at the bank. I didn't realize all the banks would be closed today."

"By the way, your dog took a leak over by the Pepsi machine," Jeremy said.

"*Vervloekt!*" Thea shouted. "*Komt u hier, hond. Voort! Voort!*"

"What did you just say?" Jeremy asked her.

"I was calling my dog. His name is Vervloekt. That means... well, it means something like 'Damn it' in Dutch."

"Your dog doesn't speak English?"

"He doesn't speak anything," Thea told him.

"No, I mean..."

"I know what you mean. At home, I speak to him in Dutch. I don't know if he understands English or not."

"Damn It is a funny name for a dog."

"I didn't name him that, a friend did. What's your name?"

"Jeremy. Jeremy Jarboe. But I like to be called Jer."

"Some people might think that's a funny name."

"Nuh-uh, it's not."

"I didn't say *I* thought it was funny, I just said some people might."

"Do you know what my best friend's name is?"

Thea said that, no, she had no idea.

"It's Mojave. That's funnier, isn't it? And there's a girl in my class named Wildrose, and one named S'adow."

"You mean Shadow."

"That's what I said."

"Well, my name is Thea. Do you think that's a silly name?"

So that's how you pronounce it, Ross thought.

"Would you like some plum wine?" Dean asked her.

"No thanks, I don't drink much. Not during the day."

"How about an orange, then?" Ross asked her. He tossed one over to her.

"That's my orange. You said."

"If you come over here, I'll give you half," Thea said. "Here, you throw the peel away. I hope the man didn't see Vervloekt do that on the floor. I'll go clean it up as soon as we finish the orange."

"He can't see anything. He's blind."

"Jer, shh, he'll hear you," Ross whispered.

"So? He knows he's blind, doesn't he?"

"My neighbor in my apartment building is almost blind," Thea said.

"One time I was coming out of Grolier Bookshop and I saw this blind woman," Dean said. "She had a Seeing Eye dog, but it wasn't a retriever or a shepherd, it was this little mutt, half dachshund and half something else. She was picking her way through traffic on Plympton Street like a broken-field runner. And I was so busy watching her, I stepped off the curb and fell on my face."

"Dear me," said Amy.

"Jeremy, why don't you offer your mother a piece of our orange?" Thea said.

"That's not my mother. I'm lucky she isn't."

"Why is that?" Thea asked.

"I don't know. That's what Dean said. My real mom lives in School's Out. That's in Colorado."

"I see."

Thea got some paper towels from the restroom and wiped up the puddle her dog had made. She chastised her dog for making a mess.

Dean asked Thea if he could take a picture of her dog.

"Of Vervloekt? Why?"

"Dean takes pictures of anything that moves," Amy said. "And some things that don't."

"Well, if you want to. He's not in a very good mood because I scolded him."

Dean got down on hands and knees to snap the dog's picture. Vervloekt growled peevishly to confirm that he was in a foul mood. "He has quite a malocclusion," Dean said.

Amy asked what that was.

"It's overbite. Or underbite," Dean said. "I can never keep those straight. Like stalactites and stalagmites."

"Underbite," Thea said. "That looks like a good camera. Are you a professional?"

"He's only an amateur," Amy said, "but a committed one."

"I was just wondering," Thea said, "I'm a model. Sort of."

"Our dryer's stopped," Jeremy said. "We win."

"Look again. Mine's stopped, too. It nosed yours out, I'm afraid," Dean said.

"How do we know that?" Ross asked.

"I knew you'd say something like that. Since you weren't paying attention, I took a picture. It'll show my machine clearly at rest while yours is in its last tumble."

Ross asked Thea, "What kind of modeling do you do?"

It took Thea a long time to answer. She brushed an orange pip from her vest. "Figure modeling. For art classes. Places like Boston College. Tufts. The School of Art and Design."

Ross wondered if he could sign up for one of those classes. Maybe just audit it, since he couldn't draw.

"I went to Tufts for a while," Amy said. "But I didn't take any art classes."

"I took one class there, too," Dean said. "Women's studies. I was the only guy in the class. In fact, that's where I met her," Dean said, nudging Amy. "Hey, Ross, clothes get wrinkled if you leave them in the dryer too long. I don't want to have to iron them."

"He won't, anyway," Amy said. "He'll try to get me to. Or wear them wrinkled."

"You don't expect me to do anything until I've seen that photo, do you?" Ross asked.

"What do you think this is, a Polaroid? Come on, Ross, don't you trust me?"

"Can you tell me," Thea asked, "what the parade is for?"

Dean explained, "It's for Veterans Day. Veterans Day used to be Armistice Day. It was to celebrate the end of the First World War. That was a terrible war, an awful war, a war for no good reason—thousands of soldiers would die just to capture a few hundred yards of mud and muck. So, in 1918, after four years of this bullshit slaughter, early on the morning of November 11, they agreed to stop all the killing, but it didn't go into effect until eleven minutes after eleven o'clock. A couple of hundred guys died just so the war could end at a catchy time—on the eleventh of the eleventh month at eleven-eleven in the morning. Anyway, we don't celebrate Armistice Day anymore. Now we celebrate Veterans Day, and it's the last Monday of October, not the eleventh of November. I just think that's wrong, really wrong. Veterans can have a day, fine, I don't begrudge them that, but they shouldn't have stolen Armistice Day."

"Are you a veteran?" Thea asked him.

"No, but my father was missing in action in Korea."

Then Thea asked, "Are you going to be here much longer?"

"As long as it takes to fold all these clothes," Ross said.

"Could I ask you a favor? My washers are nearly finished. Would you put my clothes in a dryer for me? I'd like to watch the rest of the parade."

"Take me," Jeremy suggested. "I want to watch the rest of the parade too."

"I will," Thea said, "if your father says it's all right."

"I'll help you fold, Ross, even if you did lose." Amy stood up and pushed her giant orange sunglasses on top of her head. "You know, I think one of the hardest things about living alone must be folding sheets by yourself—especially fitted sheets."

"Why would you worry about something like that?" Dean asked belligerently. He took a sip of plum wine.

"I'd tell you, Deanikins, but you said you don't want to talk about it."

"You're right. I don't. It's absurd to discuss things that aren't going to happen. Here, Ross, let me have a look at that sweater. Didn't turn out too bad—only shrank a little, and that sweater was always big on me."

Ross left Dean with the sweater and walked to the front of the laundromat and looked out the window.

Dean said, "You know, Ross, something just occurred to me... she said her name was Thea. Isn't that the name of your...?"

"Yes," Ross said hurriedly, "it is."

"What are you guys talking about?" Amy asked, "You know her from someplace, Ross?"

"Not really."

He could still see Thea and Jeremy out on Newbury Street. Thea was talking to a group of soldiers. Jeremy looked impatient. He looked like he was about to cross his arms and start tapping his feet.

8

ETHNOCENTRISM

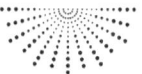

Ross put Thea's birthday present down on the window seat next to her phone. There didn't seem to be anywhere else to put it. It looked faintly pitiful sitting there, like some equipment a clown had left behind. The present itself was small and dome-shaped, but the wrapped package looked like a sausage. There was as much scotch tape as wrapping paper. If anyone asked, Ross was prepared to blame the present-wrapping job on Jeremy.

He watched Thea give his son such a vigorous hug that Jeremy was embarrassed. She had invited Jeremy to come to her party on the day of the parade and told him to bring along anyone that he liked. All the other guests seemed to be Dutch.

Ross and Dean and Jeremy sat down on the window seat. "I can't understand what anyone's saying," Jeremy told him. "All the words sound like *moose* or *cream cheese*."

"Not much I can do about that, Jer."

"I'm ready to leave," Dean said.

"We just got here," Amy said.

"You said we could leave whenever I wanted to," Dean said.

"Oh, sure, let's go home and argue some more. Forget it. I'm sick of arguing. Go home and argue by yourself."

"I don't want to argue," Dean said. "I just don't like parties where I don't know anyone."

"You don't like parties where people don't make a fuss over you."

"The Cheetos are stale," Jeremy said.

"Cheetos," Dean said, "chips and California dip. I expected something a little more Dutch. Smoked eels. Salted herrings. Bitterballen."

"Dutch apple pie," Amy suggested.

"That's not even Dutch," Dean said. "It's from Pennsylvania. The Pennsylvania Dutch actually..."

"Yes, Dean, I know. It was a joke, okay? Think I'll mingle a little."

A man with unruly hair and round wire-rims came in. He had a birthday present meticulously wrapped in gold foil and fitted with a gold bow. He turned it over to Thea and then put his arm around her. He whispered something to her and she shook her head, which seemed to make him angry, but he didn't take his arm away, and he didn't stop smiling. Ross went into the kitchen for a beer.

Two women were in the kitchen. One of them was trying to open a bottle of wine and had broken the cork.

"This is a job for a bartender," he said.

One of the women smiled at him, but the one holding the bottle said, "We don't need any help." Her accent was much thicker than Thea's.

"Okay, then." Ross grabbed a beer from the refrigerator and went back to the window seat.

"Why doesn't she have any furniture?" Jeremy asked him.

"Her décor *is* pretty minimalist," Dean said.

"She does have *some* furniture." Ross had seen a card table and two folding chairs in the kitchen and a mattress on the floor in her bedroom.

Thea was still talking to the man in the wire-rim glasses. He whispered something else to her and this time she nodded. This nodding seemed to make him even madder. Thea's gaze was ranging around the room during the exchange. It stopped when it lit on Ross, moved on, then returned and locked in.

"She has plenty of plants, though," Jeremy said. Ross and Jeremy were sitting directly below the spider plant that had obstructed his view. He considered emptying his beer into the hanging pot like indoor Agent Orange, but then he remembered it didn't matter; he wasn't calling her anymore. He'd even returned the lens to Dean.

"Her plants look a lot better than ours do," Jeremy said.

"Maybe she remembers to water them once in a while."

Thea was definitely looking him over. She smiled covertly. Ross was the first to break eye contact. He took a book from an orange crate. It turned out to be a book called *Important Idioms in English*.

When he looked up, the red-underwear guy had taken Thea by the elbow and sternly led her into the bedroom. He heard him shouting at her. He couldn't understand what he was saying, but he kept hearing the words *teef* and *kut*. And *slet* and *hoer*, which he could puzzle out. Some of the other guests were looking uneasy.

A few minutes later, he stormed out of the bedroom. Ross expected him to charge out the front door, perhaps screaming in anguish, but instead he went up to Amy and started chatting her up.

Thea came out shortly after, looking pale as milk. She moved a coleus plant and sat on the window seat between Jeremy and Ross. "I didn't know there were so many Dutch people in Boston," Ross said, in lieu of anything better to say.

"Practically all of them will be here tonight,"

More and more people kept arriving.

Jeremy had knocked over Dean's wineglass, or maybe Dean had. There was a puddle of red wine shaped like South America on the windowsill.

Ross said, "That guy you were talking to..."

"His name is Wim." She pronounced his name *Vim*. "He's an old friend of mine. Kind of. I guess you could say we're all old friends here." She turned to Jeremy. "Jer, do you want a piece of cake?"

"Don't you have to blow out the candles?"

"We don't usually use candles in Holland. We just eat the cake."

"Maybe. Do you have any cat-beer?"

"I have Narraganset." She asked Ross, "But you don't let Jeremy drink beer, do you?"

"You bought 'gansett?" Dean asked her. "What's wrong with Grolsch? Or Oranjeboom? Or even Heineken? Where's your ethnocentrism?"

"Oranjeboom—that's made in my hometown. But those cost too much here. And I can't tell the difference. I don't like beer very much."

"Don't like beer? Are you *sure* you're from Holland?"

Ross explained that cat-beer was what Jeremy called milk.

"Oh. No, there isn't any milk. I'm sorry, Jer, I should have gotten some."

The pool of wine was expanding. Brazil was creeping across the Atlantic.

"Well, the cake is in the kitchen if you want some." Thea stood up to greet three new guests. They exchanged kisses on the cheek with Thea. They all said something to her. It sounded to Ross a little like gefilte fish, but probably wasn't.

"I'm going to get another beer," Ross said.

"Get me another glass of wine while you're going that way, would you?" Dean asked. "Mine spilled."

"Get me some cake," Jeremy said.

There had been a turnover in the personnel in the kitchen. There were half a dozen people in there now. One was an overweight guy whose toupee was askew. He was speaking animatedly to a woman who was leaning heavily against the refrigerator. Ross thought of the toupee aficionado he used to see over here and wondered what it was about this apartment that attracted self-conscious bald guys.

Vervloekt was in the kitchen as well, dancing nervously on the linoleum.

The man grabbed Ross's arm. "Tell her it's truth," he demanded.

"What do you mean? Tell her what's the truth?"

"That at American parties, people amuse themselves with cooking oil. On their bodies."

"Wesson Oil, you mean. Yes, that's true, at some parties. Well, sort of true."

"Vesson Oil, yes. See? Truth." He tapped his drunken friend on the forehead. She was looking woozy.

"Not so much now as they used to, though. I don't think," Ross said. "It's a custom that's dying out."

"Dying?" The man sadly shook his head. Some of the grandeur had gone out of his idea of America. "What about pudding—Jell-O, I mean—in the bathtub?"

"I don't know much about that. Excuse me," Ross said to the woman, "I need to get into the refrigerator." The woman tried to move out of his way, but she didn't do well. She slid slowly down the refrigerator door. He was reminded of Laurel's slow-motion topple across Dean's lap at the circus. Ross and the man helped her up. She was limp. Dead weight. Once they got her sitting down on one of the two folding chairs in Thea's kitchen, Ross grabbed a can of beer from the refrigerator and took a couple of spares. He poured Dean a glass of wine and cut Jeremy a piece of cake.

When the talk in the kitchen turned to edible panties, Ross gathered his things and made for the bathroom.

A woman in the bathroom snarled, *"Doe de deur dicht! Er is iemand in hier!"* She kicked the door shut.

"Beg your pardon." In the fraction of a second that the door had been open, before her foot hit the door, Ross had peeked in, more out of habit than out of any genuine urge to see anything. He wasn't surprised to see that the woman inside was the woman who had been struggling with the cork in the kitchen.

Although he'd just had the door kicked in his face, Ross somehow kept control of the wine, beer, and cake. He reeled back into the hallway so that when the woman in the bathroom came out, she wouldn't connect him with the intrusion. Thea's bedroom was smoky and dark and teeming, a dangerous place for a man with his hands full. In the living room, people were dancing, and the menace was even clearer. He slumped down in the hallway, hoping to look like a harmless drunk.

The woman took her time. When she finally came out, she wasn't taken in by his pose. She glared at him.

Once inside, Ross unrolled a tremendous amount of toilet paper to wipe up the wine spill on the window seat. Just then Thea came in. Ross realized that the lock on the bathroom door was inoperable. Her hand still on the doorknob, she stared at him. It was a continuation of the stare she'd begun in the living room. Her eyes seemed even bluer in here, with the white tiles and the fluorescent lighting.

He expected her to say something, perhaps about the ungainly pyramid of beer cans, wineglass, and cake plate sitting behind the toilet or the wad of toilet paper in his hand. Instead, she came up to him and, on tiptoe, gave him a kiss. It was a brief kiss, and not a particularly passionate one, the equivalent, among kisses, of a reassuring nod.

"Pull a Steve Brody," Dean said to Ross when he rejoined Dean and Jeremy on the window seat.

"Do a what?"

"That's an important idiom in English. It says so right here in this book. 'To pull a Steve Brody: To jump from a high place.' What took you so long?

I felt pretty exposed sitting here. Everyone is talking to someone else, and I couldn't think of anything interesting enough to break in on them with. I hate parties."

"You could have talked to Jeremy,"

"You didn't bring me a fork," Jeremy said. "I want a fork."

"People ate before there were forks. Use your fingers."

"Actually, the fork first came along in the fourth century," Dean said. "One of my favorite poems is about forks. 'This strange thing must have crept / Right out of hell. / It resembles a bird's foot / Worn around a cannibal's neck.'"

"Here," Ross handed Dean the wad of toilet paper.

"What am I supposed to do with this?"

"Clean up that wine spill behind you."

"Oh. Thea already came by and did that. You know what, though? You got cake crumbs in my wine."

"Look," Ross said wearily, "I want both of you to stop your bitching."

Thea came back into the living room. Ross's present had somehow rolled off the window seat and onto the floor. She saved it from getting danced on.

"What did you end up getting her?" Dean asked Ross.

"I got her that paperweight."

"Ha! The one with the scorpion in it? What did you really get her?"

"That's what I really got her," Ross said. "You're the one who suggested it." They had been walking down Newbury Street and had seen the paperweight in the window of an antique shop. "You said that because she was a Scorpio, that..."

"All I said was, it's cheaper than diamond earrings."

"No, I distinctly remember you saying it was perfect."

"Ross, I thought you of all people would know when I wasn't being serious. I hope she doesn't open it in front of all these people."

"You know, you're a son of a bitch, Dean," Ross said. "I should have given her one of Laurel's necklaces. I still have a few. I don't have any electric scorpions, but I have a nice electric unicorn or an electric dolphin I could have given her."

Thea was now in the center of a group of people, all of whom seemed to know her better than Ross did. They were discussing a painting on the wall above a pile of cushions that served as her couch. The painting featured a pastel-pink-and-mint-green room, a child's bedroom with a small bed and a wardrobe in it. There was a young child in the bed. Ross thought the child looked like Thea might have looked when she was about six. A huge black rhinoceros with glowing red eyes was crashing through one of the walls of the child's bedroom.

"Tell me, Dean, what do you think of Thea?"

"Hubba, hubba."

"Hubba, hubba?"

"Another important idiom," Dean said. "'An expression of approval, often said of women.'"

"Come on, tell me what you think."

"Well, you've seen more of her than I have, ol' buddy. But she's very graceful. And you're right, her eyes are amazingly blue."

"Aren't they? When I was in high school, there was this resort, sort of a dude ranch that opened outside of town. They had a swimming pool, and one summer I got a job as a lifeguard there. The pool was made of blue tiles, and on a sunny day, the water was this sparkling cobalt blue. That's what her eyes remind me of."

"Her nose is a little funny. Makes her look a little like a duck, somehow."

Ross considered that. "Maybe. A pretty duck. I don't mind a slightly funny nose. I think that nose looks good on her. But I don't mean the way she looks."

"I don't know. Seems smart. Nice. Nice in a sort of distant, noncommittal way. She's a bit like you that way."

"You're right about that, I think. We're both kind of... I don't know, private. But I feel drawn to her."

"You just feel guilty because you were the peeper, and she was the peepee. No, wait, that doesn't sound right. You were the Peeping Tom, and she was the person who got peeped at."

"Maybe that's part of it. But there's more to it than that. I think that, if we ever got to know each other..."

"She could use a fashion upgrade, though. She should come to me for wardrobe tips. If there was an Academy Award for best-dressed mannequins, I'd have a couple of Oscars on my mantelpiece."

"I'm sure you would, Dean."

"I was serious about my work, I mean really serious. I read every book ever written on the subject. In fact, the first book on window displays was *A Guide to Window-Dressing*, which came out in the 1880s. There are only two copies of that book still around, one in Oxford and one in, of all places, Buffalo. So who do you think drove his motorcycle all the way to Buffalo and spent a day in the rare book room of the Buffalo and Erie County Public Library? And I'll tell you something, those librarians never let me out of their sight. I guess not many people who arrive at the library on a motorcycle want to browse their rare book collection."

"Have you read every book there is about opening a restaurant?"

"No. I started to, but it was depressing to see how much we were doing wrong. Damn, look at Amy," Dean said. Amy and Wim were dancing together to *Layla*. Amy was an uninhibited dancer. She would link her hands behind her head and pull her long auburn hair through her fingers, over her head and out to its full length. "She says dancing is therapy, better than meditation. She doesn't look too meditative, though, does she? She's dancing like a dervish. A dervish on drugs."

"She always dances like that," Ross told him. "Even with you."

"What do you mean, *even* with me? Of course she dances like that with me."

When the song slowed down and the piano kicked in, Wim took Amy's hand in his, put his arm around her waist, and waltzed her around the living room. He twirled her and dipped her a couple of times.

One of Thea's friends had asked Jeremy to dance. Ross had to admit that Jeremy could dance better than he could. He could dance better than his partner, who was maybe twenty years older than him. *Where did he learn how to do that? From Mojave's mother?*

The song ended, and Jeremy came back to the window seat. Amy and Wim went and stood in the doorway to the kitchen. They looked sweaty. Wim got them both a glass of wine. "Now check her out," Dean said, "Look how she's standing. Look how she's flicking her tongue out, and how she's leaning forward so she won't miss a word." Amy did look remarkably attentive, as if someone was going to give her a pop quiz on what Wim was telling her.

Dean said, "That guy, Wim, looks like a real smug bastard."

"Thea told me he's an artist. He did these paintings."

"I noticed he has paint splatters on his glasses," Dean said. "That's bad. Amy likes art. And I'll bet he has cocaine. Artists would tend to, wouldn't they?"

"Possibly," Ross said, "Several people here seem to be coked up and giggling."

"I want a Coke," Jeremy said.

"I didn't see any in the fridge. You'll have to ask Thea," Ross told him.

"There, he did it again. Did you see that sneer? I've never seen anyone who could muster so much contempt into one sneer."

"Tell you something else," Ross said. "He wears red underwear."

Dean looked at Wim with even stronger dislike, though he had a couple of pairs of red jockeys at home himself.

Thea detached herself from her circle and again squeezed onto the window seat. She was drinking white wine. The last time he'd seen her, she'd been drinking diet Coke.

"To throw a wingding. Do you know what that means, Thea?" Dean asked her. "No? You should. It's from your important idioms book."

"Oh, that book. My father gave it to me before I left home. It's old. I've never really looked at it. My father came to the States for a few months in the thirties, and maybe he got it then. He stayed in Boston. That's one reason I came here myself. Do any of you need anything?"

"I need something to wash this cake down with," Jeremy said. "Can I have a tonic?"

"Tonic?"

"A tonic. A soda. Coke, or Mountain Dew, or Orange Crus'."

"Oh, Jeremy, sorry, all the Cokes are gone. I think I may have drunk the last one myself."

"Figures," Jeremy mumbled. His mouth was full of cake, and his fingers were coated with frosting.

"Would you like to meet some of the people here?" Thea asked them.

"Not me," Dean said, "I have to go to the bathroom. Ross, save my place."

"The bathroom door doesn't lock," Thea warned him. "It seems to, but it doesn't. How about you, Ross? Can I introduce you to some of my friends?"

"I already met some," Ross said.

"You've been sitting over here all night."

"Not quite all night. I've gotten up a few times. How do you say happy birthday in Dutch?"

"*Gelukkige verjaardag*," Thea told him.

"When those three people over there came in, they said something to you that sounded like…"

"*Gefeliciteerd*. It means congratulations. We use it for birthdays, too."

Gefeliciteerd. Ross concentrated on memorizing that word. He opened another can of Narraganset. "Jeremy was admiring your plants. They're doing well. Especially this spider plant."

"They *are* doing well. I'm proud of them. We say in Dutch, '*Ik heb een groene duim*.' 'I have a green thumb.'"

"We say that in English, too. But I don't have one. I have a black thumb." Ross's apartment was like a hospice for plants. They went there to die.

"My plants are really the only nice things in my apartment."

"There are the paintings," Ross said.

"Yes, the paintings. Wim left them here when he moved in with his cousin Hendrik—that's Hendrik dancing with those three women—because there's no room to hang them there. But he'll probably give them to someone else now."

"You and Wim—you're not getting along?" Ross asked, although he knew they weren't.

"Not really. You know, I think the reason my plants do so well is because I get such good sun for most of the day. And I don't have any curtains."

"Why not?" Jeremy wanted to know.

"I just don't. At our home in Amsterdam, we didn't have any either."

"Did you have furniture?"

"Yes, Jeremy," she said, and put her arm around him. "We had beautiful old furniture. We just didn't have curtains. A lot of people who live in Amsterdam... "

"Hamster dam?"

"Amsterdam. It's the biggest city in my country. A lot of people who live there don't have curtains. There used to be curtains, before the war, but during the war, the German police—the Green Police, they called them—came around and told everyone they had to nail black curtains over their windows."

"Why?" Jeremy wanted to know.

"Because they thought the city was going to be bombed, and that the pilots could see the lights if the windows weren't covered. The day after the Germans left, people ripped them down, and they never put up any curtains at all after that. We moved to Amsterdam when I was about your age, and my mom didn't put up curtains either. I remember her saying, when I was young, 'Don't sit around in the kitchen, Theatje. Go read in the front room. The sunlight in there is the color of yellow roses.' It's funny that she would say that, now that I think of it. That's not the way she usually talked. Anyway, e ven these days, a lot of people in Amsterdam don't have curtains."

"That's where we live," Jeremy told Thea before Ross could stop him. He pointed at the dark windows straight across the alley. "We have curtains."

"I didn't realize you lived so close."

≈

A line had formed in front of the bathroom. Dean was next but one when Amy found him. "Someone burned a hole in my hat with a cigarette," she said unhappily. "You should have kept an eye on it. It was on the floor over by you."

"I had more important things to do than guard your fedora. I was talking to Ross."

"That's one of your problems, babycakes, you shouldn't have been talking to Ross. Both of you should have been talking to someone you've never met before. That's what parties are for. Doing that doesn't come natural for me either, but I force myself."

"You forced yourself pretty hard tonight, I noticed. I saw the way that guy Wim kept waving his arms around. What were you two talking about for so long? Action painting? Modern dance? Tai chi? Guerilla warfare?"

"No, actually, we were talking about baseball. Wim likes baseball because it's so graceful. He said, this summer, he went to a lot of baseball games—he calls them baseball matches—at Fenway Park. It's one of the only things he likes about America."

"Baseball? What do you know about baseball?"

"I know quite a bit. Daddy used to take Claire and me to Fenway for Red Sox games all the time. We have a book full of autographs of Sox players somewhere. We even have Ted Williams' autograph. He signed it, 'To a couple of cute gingersnaps, the Thumper.' Listen, Dean, I'm going to take off."

"Okay, fine. Just let me get into the bathroom, and..."

Now Dean was next in line.

"No, what I mean is, I'm going to go out for something to eat. After we talked about baseball, we started talking about food, and Wim found out I'd never tried Indonesian food, so he's going to take me to this place called the Barong Grill over in Cambridge."

"I like Indonesian food," Dean said, though he'd never had any. "Am I invited?"

"Tell you what, Dean, if it's any good, maybe you and I can go there sometime." She reached over and pulled his shirt collar out of his jacket and smoothed it over his lapels. "There, that's better. Don't look at me that way, Dean lovie. 'Never say no to anything,' right?"

The bathroom was free. The woman in line behind Dean was urging him to either go in or get out of the way.

"What did you say?" Dean asked Amy.

"I said, 'Never say no to anything.' Nietzsche said that, didn't he? You told me he did." She rubbed Dean's stomach with one hand and the back of his neck with the other.

"Are you going to do cocaine before this little Indonesian feast of yours?"

"Not that I know of. What gave you that idea?"

"Never mind. Just take your hands off me."

"Don't be such a bozo, Dean."

"Just take your hands off. I hate condescending women."

"I hate condescending women," Dean said, this time to Ross. "I feel like pulling a Steve Brody."

"Steady, Dean."

Amy and Wim had their coats on. Thea got up to whisper something to Wim on his way out. Whatever she said to him made him look surly and scornful again.

Thea's apartment was so small that the party didn't quite fit in it. Some of it had oozed through the front door and onto the landing. Part of it was trailing down the stairs. Amy, Wim's hand on her arm, left the party proper and plunged into its fringes. In a moment, she was back.

"I knew it," Dean said. "She's feeling guilty. She's come back to apologize."

Amy hadn't come back to talk to Dean, though. She had something to tell Thea. "There's a woman outside who wants to talk to you. An older woman. I think she might be blind."

"Oh, no," Thea said. "Mrs. Budwig. I'd better go see what she wants."

Thea didn't have to get up. Mrs. Budwig made her way in. The party drew itself up and parted and made a path from the door to the window seat.

"How much longer is this little party of yours going to last, Thea?" Mrs. Budwig asked. "I haven't complained all evening. You know I never complain, even when you play your music late at night. But now, I can't hear my news, and you know how I depend on that, and since I can't actually *see* the television..."

"I understand, Mrs. Budwig. It'll be over pretty soon. And I'll try to get people to quiet down."

"I'm ready," Jeremy said to Ross.

Ross asked him what he was ready for.

"Ready to go home."

9

SALUTE TO THE SUN

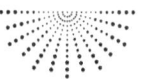

"WHAT DO YOU THINK THEY'RE DOING RIGHT NOW?" DEAN ASKED ROSS. "I'LL bet Wim's saying, 'This is delicious, wanna try a bite of mine?' And Amy's saying, 'You're right, that *is* yummy. Here, try some of mine now.' And he'll take her hand to steady the fork. And under the table, he'll start rubbing his knee against..."

"Dean," Ross said, "don't think about it if it upsets you."

"I can't not think about it. It's like when you get something in your eye, or when you've got a loose tooth." Then Dean said, "This has been about the worst wingding I've ever been to."

"You must be having a pretty bad time then. I'm sure you've been to some pretty awful wingdings."

"Well, true, but I have to go way back to top this. There was a Halloween party I went to in junior high. That was worse, you'd have to say. It was supposed to be a costume party, only no one came in costume, no one but me. Oh, this one girl had a sailor's cap and an eye patch, that was supposed to make her a pirate. One guy wore a fright wig and a mortarboard hat and sunglasses. He was supposed to be... I don't know what he was supposed to be. Me, I came as a tropical bird. My mother had spent weeks sewing my bird suit. It was elaborate; well, elaborate doesn't begin to describe it. It had these tail feathers that were like three feet long and aqua blue, and a yellow comb, and a big orange beak. And all I had on underneath was my underwear, so I couldn't..."

"Hey, Dean, are you ready to go?"

"More than ready. Been ready since we got here. Let's boogie."

"No, what I mean is, I want you to take Jeremy. Take him back to your place. I want to stay a little longer."

"All right," Dean said, after considering this for a minute. "All right, I'll do that for you, but you'd better come by for him before Amy gets back. You don't want your child to overhear the sort of things that are going to be said." Dean predicted scenes of rage and despair.

"I'll try," Ross said.

Dean and Jeremy and a clump of people from the kitchen left. Soon, the only guests left were Ross and Hendrik, Wim's beefy cousin. Hendrik had large hands and a square face. Square except for a deep cleft in his chin. It was the deepest cleft Ross had ever seen. It looked like a baby's butt.

According to Thea, Hendrik had been a dockworker in Rotterdam before he came to Boston with Wim. He'd become a Maoist while working on the docks.

Either Hendrik's English wasn't very good, or else he didn't enjoy talking to Ross. Conversation collapsed. They drank beer in silence. Near silence; Hendrik incessantly made little grunting noises. He occasionally lit a spicy-smelling cigarette. His cigarettes crackled and sparked every time he inhaled. Just when Ross was sure Hendrik was about to leave, he took off his heavy work boots. Not only were his hands big, so were his feet.

When Hendrik went to the bathroom, Thea said, "Hendrik can be quite nice when he's sober. He wouldn't hurt a... do you say a fly or a flea?"

"Fly. Or wait, no, flea. Or, I don't know, maybe either one. But Hendrik's a long way from sober. He's been drinking two for every one of mine, and I'm fairly far from sober myself."

"He'll pass out soon. He does that a lot. I hope he doesn't lose his temper first. One time at a party, someone ripped the medicine chest right off the bathroom wall. We didn't know for sure that it was Hendrik, but..."

"I think he's staying here to protect you from me," Ross said.

It took another hour of steady drinking and smelly cigarette smoking before Hendrik became unconscious. Thea whispered, "Let's go in the other room. We don't want him waking up."

Ross had never seen her bedroom before tonight. There weren't any windows. Her bike was propped up against the closet door, taking up almost a quarter of the space. There was a mattress and a sea chest.

"It's after midnight," Thea said.

"Considerably after," Ross agreed. Thea had a digital clock on a cardboard box that served as her nightstand. He watched it change from 2:12 to 2:13. The glow from Thea's clock reminded Ross a little of Laurel's jewelry.

"Today is my actual year day," she said. "Birthday, I mean. I had the party last night because I like to be alone on my birthday."

Then why am I still here?

She left him in the bedroom for a few minutes. When she came back, she had changed into a purple leotard and black tights. The tights were wearing a little thin around the knees. She put an album on her record player. For some reason, he'd been expecting Fleetwood Mac—it was hard to avoid Fleetwood Mac that fall—but it was classical. Lots of French horns. Ravel, maybe. Maybe Debussy. It had been a long time since Ross had taken a music appreciation class. Thea turned the music down as soon as it came on. She didn't want to wake up Hendrik or disturb Mrs. Budwig. It was the kind of portable three-speed record player Ross's mother had once bought for him and his brother Marshall with five books of S&H Green Stamps. Ross remembered sitting at the kitchen table with Marshall, licking the trading stamps and pasting them into books. He could still taste the glue.

Thea got a mat out of the closet and unrolled it next to her bed. "You don't mind if I do some yoga, do you? I've wanted to start exercising again for months. I thought, since it's my birthday..."

Ross couldn't imagine anyone not under considerable duress exercising at 2:17 in the morning, but it seemed boorish to say so. He sat on the mattress to watch. She stood quietly for a moment, her hands folded in prayer position, taking deep breaths, and then she began to move. It was a complex exercise. It involved, at different times, touching the floor with the palms of her hands, bending backwards, kneeling, crouching, and deliberately breathing at different speeds. She wound up standing with her legs apart and her arms forming a circle over her head. Then she suddenly lurched forward onto the mat.

Ross was afraid she'd had a seizure. Vervloekt, who had just come into the room, was equally startled. He turned around and went back to the cushions he'd been sharing with Hendrik.

"No, I'm all right. That one is called Salute to the Sun. It's actually a salute to the Hindu sun god—I forget his name." She rolled on her back, and her arms and legs shot up in the air. "This one is called Starfish Enfolding Itself."

"I was on my high school basketball team for a few years. We had to do calisthenics at the beginning of practice, but none of them had such... such fancy names."

"I took a class at the Free University called Living in Our Bodies. We did meditation, and breathing exercises, and yoga. These are yoga poses, but not exactly the traditional ones; the teacher kind of changed them around. Do you want to do some with me?"

"Umm, no, I think I've had too much beer." That, and he was awkward.

Ross glanced at the leotard where it narrowed into a strip and plunged between her legs. He remembered her leotard from the laundromat. It had been a damp purple wad that he'd tossed into the dryer. He also recalled a pair of skimpy red jockey shorts that had been in her wash.

She lay on the mat for a while after the starfish had finished enfolding itself. She was breathing deeply. "The other day at the parade, Jeremy told me a little about your wife."

Ross decided that he needed to have a little talk with Jeremy about the kinds of things he should and shouldn't discuss with his women friends. "What did he tell you about her?"

"He said she might be coming here for a visit."

"Well," he said, "she might. I don't know. We're not actually married anymore. What I mean is, we're still legally married, I guess, but we don't see much of each other. I've only seen her a couple of times in the past four years or so. Of course, Jeremy spends all of his summers with her, out in Colorado. And every other Christmas."

"You're both from Colorado?"

"Umm, not exactly. It's kind of complicated. Laurel was born in Michigan and grew up in California. I was born here in Boston, but I grew up in Colorado."

"Why did you move to... is it Denver? That's in Colorado, yes?"

"Umm, yeah, but we lived way out in the western part of the state, a long way from Denver. My father... my father had some weird ideas. He decided, about twenty years ago, that things looked pretty bleak, and that there would be a war. A nuclear holocaust."

"I don't think that's so weird. He's probably right. There probably will be a war."

"I don't know. Maybe. Anyway, he decided that if our family was going to survive, we were going to have to move. He figured that Boston would be one of the first places to disappear in a mushroom cloud, so he traveled around trying to figure out the safest place to wait out the war. He decided on a small town on the Western Slope of Colorado. It would be protected by the mountains, and there were old mines where you'd be safe from fallout."

"Does he still think there will be a war?"

"Probably. I've heard him say that, the more time goes by, the worse it'll be. But he thinks that, even without a war, civilization will collapse."

"I think maybe it's already started to," Thea said. "And your wife? She thought there would be a war too?"

"No. No, Laurel was just traveling through. She'd been in Mexico learning how to make jewelry, and she came back when she ran out of money. She had some friends who lived at a place outside of the town where I lived—School's Out, this place was called."

They kept turning up in town all summer. Three or four of them would appear on a street corner, looking around like anthropologists from another planet. New ones would arrive in gaudy Volkswagen vans, or they would hitchhike into town or come on a bus. They'd ask for directions to School's Out, which were given grudgingly if at all. Once, on a Saturday afternoon, they all descended on the town en masse. They piled out of an old school bus and a couple of vans, and armed with push brooms, they swept up half a dozen blocks of Main Street before inquiries could be made. They were the subject of an editorial in the Daily Searchlight: *"We can all get along." Some people in town hoped so. A few others disagreed, and they threw bricks through the windows of the* Daily Searchlight *office.*

"School's Out used to be the Rocky Mountain Methodist Youth Camp," Ross told Thea. "When that folded, a speculator bought the land. I think he was planning to build a plush hunting lodge or something. No one knew for sure because he had a heart attack and died. He didn't have any family except a nephew—Cap is his name—who inherited the land. Cap moved into the chaplain's cabin with his girlfriend Poppy. After a while, they took out ads in some underground newspapers around the country."

SCHOOL'S OUT!
FREE LIVES! FREE MUSIC!
HARD WORK! JUBILATION!
SCHOOL'S OUT! WHERE IT DOESN'T FUCKING MATTER!

Ross was driving home from Winifred's house one night. Winifred had been his girlfriend the last two years of high school. She was one of the few people in town who'd talk to him after he'd let everyone down by quitting the basketball team. Ross seldom wrote to Winifred while he was away at college, though she often wrote to him, but he'd seen her during Christmas breaks and now, home for the summer again, he'd looked her up. He and Winifred had been watching The Smothers Brothers *and making out in her living room tonight when her mother had come in and caught them and started yelling at Ross. She had a gravelly voice from smoking too many cigarettes. She called him a big baby for quitting the team and she drunkenly told him to get the hell out.*

As Ross drove past the Safeway, a grocery cart came rolling out of the parking lot. He almost crashed his father's Jeep into it. When he got out to move the cart, a man with a big red lumberjack beard came running out from behind the building. He was carrying a burlap sack and he was smiling. Three others appeared, each with a sack of their own.

"Sorry about the shopping cart." The man smiled some more. "I'm Cap." The others were Stash, Marjorie Microdot, and Aspen. Aspen had a baby in a sling across her chest. The baby smiled at Ross, too.

"What were you up to in the parking lot, Cap?"

Cap pulled some romaine lettuce out of his bag. "Take a look at that, man. Nothing wrong with this lettuce, is there?" The lettuce was badly wilted. "And they were just going to throw it away. There's all kind of stuff in the dumpsters still worth eating."

Ross considered this. "Why don't you come with me, Cap?" He led them to his house.

Ross unlocked the fallout shelter and filled their sacks with tuna fish and Spam and dried apricots and powdered milk and powdered eggs and sardines and biscuit mix and instant mashed potatoes, all from his father's stockpile. He offered them canned peaches, but Cap said they had peach trees at School's Out.

"You sure your dad won't miss this stuff?"

"I doubt it." At least not for a few months. His father had just finished his quarterly inventory a couple of weeks before.

Cap and his friends were grateful. They invited Ross to dinner at School's Out.

"I had trouble finding the place at first. There's a little country store, Matt's

Store, where you turn off the county highway. Then you climb up an unpaved road for a couple of miles. I thought I was lost but then I realized I was going the right way."

Ross saw a cottonwood with the word TREE spray-painted on it. There was an old school bus parked by the creek. He came around a curve and saw a couple of women, bare to the waist, picking peaches. He slowed down as he drove past the peach orchard. Then he saw the mailbox: SCHOOL'S OUT—MAILMAN, EVERYBODY LIVES HERE!

Thea was doing another exercise, this one called Pigeon Pose. Something about this exercise made her tights bag at the knees, and it made her joints pop.

~

Ross was sitting on the stone steps of The Earth Cult Lodge. Before, it had been the camp chapel. He was drinking wine with Cap and Cap's girlfriend Poppy. He'd brought three bottles of cheap red wine as a dinner gift, but only a few people at School's Out seemed to drink wine. Poppy had a butter churn between her knees; every now and then, she'd turn the crank.

A woman came out of the lodge, drying her hands on her jeans. There were bits of mirrors on her bright blue blouse and tiny bells in her hair and rings on almost all her fingers. She sparkled and jingled. "I hate doing dishes," she said. "But no one else around here seems to think dishes have to be done." She said to Ross, "I'm Mountain Laurel." That's what she was called back then. "And I'd like a little more wine."

He handed her the bottle. "Did you like dinner?" she asked him.

"Wasn't bad," he said.

"I thought it sucked," Laurel said.

Poppy commented: "I hate brown rice."

"The vegetarians are taking over," Cap said sadly.

Laurel said, "I have a couple of Snickers in my backpack, if anyone wants one."

Someone crossed the creek and came out of the woods and into the clearing in front of the lodge. The way he was dressed would have made a pimp blush. He was wearing gaudy striped pants, a flowery shirt, a fringed leather vest, fringed leather boots, and a purple hat with a long white feather in it. He pulled down his baggy pants, squatted behind some bushes, and went about his business.

Apparently, a number of people had used this meadow as a toilet in the past, because there was a sign nailed to a tree warning against it:

YOU CAN ONLY SHIT IN YOUR OWN NEST FOR SO LONG.
AFTER THAT, YOU'RE NESTING IN YOUR OWN SHIT.

Cap shouted at him, "Hey, bro, what the fuck, go use the outhouse!"
He replied by giving Cap the finger.
"Who's that?" Ross asked.
"That's Sweet Mystery," Poppy said. "He's Laurel's boyfriend."
"He's NOT my boyfriend," Laurel claimed. "He picked me up hitching, and he
wasn't going anywhere in particular, so I got him to bring me here. I'm sorry I
did."
"He's kind of an asshole," Cap said.
"He's a little strange," Poppy said, "but that's okay. There are a lot of strange
people here."
"Are you missing a bottle of wine?" Laurel asked Ross.
Ross checked his pack. The third bottle wasn't there.
"Sweet Mystery ripped you off," Laurel said. "I thought I saw him take it."
Sweet Mystery finished his chore, doffed his hat, bowed in their direction, and
disappeared back into the woods.
"How's the butter coming?" Cap asked Poppy.
"You churn for a while. My arms are tired."

"Laurel and Poppy had gone to school together at a little college in Ohio.
She needed to take two years of a foreign language. She tried French, she
tried Russian, German... she just didn't have a knack for languages. So... so
she made a deal with the college: If she took an intense Spanish course and
then passed a test... she could graduate. So Laurel went down to Mexico
but the town she went to was this big silversmithing town, and she got
interested in making jewelry, and she dropped her Spanish class and
became a jewelry maker's apprentice. She never did graduate."

Ross's girlfriend Winifred had broken the clasp on her mother's amethyst necklace
that she wasn't supposed to wear. Winifred's mother drank too much, and could be
pretty nasty to Winifred when she was drunk. A broken clasp would have been
enough to touch off a burst of fury. Ross took Winifred out to School's Out and
asked Laurel to fix it. After repairs were made, they went down to the creek.
Almost everyone in School's Out went down to the creek in the late afternoon to

wash clothes, to wade in the icy water, and to get high. In the days before School's Out, it had been called Coyote Creek. For a little while it was known as Ho Chi Minh Creek, then it became Karma Creek, but now it was known as Dream Catcher Creek. There were dozens of dream catchers hanging from the trees in the woods on the other side of the creek.

Everyone by the creek was naked except for Winifred, who sat on the bank fully clothed and unhappy. At one point, she unbuttoned the top button of her blouse. Then she hurriedly buttoned it again. Guillermo played his guitar and Stash played an autoharp and Andromeda danced.

Cap was talking to a man who had arrived the night before. He said he was from National Geographic, *and that he was doing a story on communities like School's Out. He'd been to New Atlantis in Oregon, and Urge City and the Funny Farm in California, and Erewhon in Utah. He was going to Far and Away in New Mexico next. No one knew if he was actually from* National Geographic, *but he did have a tape recorder and an expensive camera.*

Cap and the reporter were talking about the firebombing of the night before. Someone had lobbed an amateur Molotov cocktail at the stand down on the county road where they sold fruit and jam and honey. They'd missed, and Matt had to put out a brush fire so his store didn't burn down. "It's not that big a deal," Cap said. "Hardly anyone stops there, anyway. And if they do, a lot of the time they don't pay." The stand operated on an honor system. And they gave Matt half the proceeds because he let them set up right by his store.

Ross waded out into the creek. He got in up to his thighs before he felt too cold to go any farther. The creek was basically snow melt from the San Juan Mountains.

"Why are you taking pictures?" Poppy asked the man from National Geographic. *"You can't run pictures like that in your magazine."*

"I don't know about that," Cap said, "I remember seeing plenty of boobs in National Geographic. *Anytime a* National Geographic *photographer showed up to take pictures of some exotic tribe, out came the boobies. It was basically* Playboy *for twelve-year-olds."*

"We're an exotic tribe now?" Laurel asked.

"These are just background photos," the man said. "They won't run in the magazine, I promise."

"So they're for your private collection?" Poppy asked.

Sweet Mystery appeared out of nowhere and sat down next to Winifred. He had a hunting bow, a quiver full of steel-tipped arrows, and a knife in his rainbow-colored belt. The belt was all he was wearing. He said to Winifred: "We can't let them get away with this firebombing shit. For sure they'll be back. Do you want to stand a watch with me tonight?" Winifred turned her head away from him. She looked as if he'd offered to poke her in the eye with one of those arrows.

"What about you?" he asked Ross. "You're always coming and going. Are you here or not?"

Ross told him that, although he was here in some senses of the word, in other senses he was not, and besides, he wasn't very good with a bow.

"What are you going to do if you see someone suspicious?" the reporter asked Sweet Mystery. "Are you going to shoot him with an arrow?"

Sweet Mystery told the reporter that it was none of his fucking business what he was going to do. He went on to tell everyone in the vicinity of the creek that the reporter was not from National Geographic *at all. Funny, Sweet Mystery said, how the stand was bombed the same evening that this so-called reporter showed up. Sweet Mystery accused him of being from the FBI or the CIA. According to Sweet Mystery, that's why he kept taking pictures and making tapes.*

Guillermo and Stash struck dramatic chords on their instruments.

Sweet Mystery walked out to the middle of a log that spanned Dream Catcher Creek and asked if anyone at all had the balls to come stand guard with him. Marjorie Microdot said she would, but Marjorie had eaten some 'shrooms and was wandering around asking people if they thought trees could dream. Aspen offered, but she'd have to bring her baby, and the baby might give away their position. The reporter volunteered too. Sweet Mystery declined their offers and went off to stand his lonely watch.

"God, he's obnoxious," Cap said. "We ought to throw his ass out of here."

"We can't throw him out just because he's obnoxious," Poppy said. "This is the place where it doesn't fucking matter, remember?"

"I'm afraid he's going to rip me off," Laurel said.

"Rip you off for what?"

"My hash. He asked me for a taste the other night, and I think he followed me to see where I was hiding it."

When Laurel came back from Mexico, she was planning to smuggle a few keys of marijuana across the border, but Heriberto, who had been teaching her silver-smithing, said that was a bad idea. Marijuana was too bulky, too dangerous. He'd fashioned a homemade hashish press. Mexican hash was not as well-known as, say, Moroccan hash, but according to Laurel, it was every bit as good.

"I've sold some already," Laurel said. "When I sell the rest of it, I'm gone. I'm heading back to Mexico."

~

"What's that one called?" Ross asked her. Thea had worked through the

Plumb Line, the Rain Storm, and the Turtle Dance. Now she was sitting on the mat bending her leg so that her foot was in her face. Ross was amazed at how effortlessly and fluidly she moved her body.

"This isn't a pose," Thea said. "I've got a splinter in my toe. Well, did he steal it?"

Ross was sleeping that night in Marjorie Microdot's yurt. Ross had told Marjorie, when he was helping her put up her yurt, that he didn't think she'd be very comfortable in a tent in Colorado in the winter. She told him that if yurts were warm enough for Mongolians, a yurt would be warm enough for her. Besides, Marjorie told him, she was into roundness. Just after her yurt was finished, Marjorie disappeared. No sign of her anywhere. There was a rumor going around School's Out that she had been kidnapped by a yeti and bundled off to a cave on Uncompahgre Peak. In her absence, Ross commandeered her yurt for the nights he spent at School's Out.

Mountain Laurel reached into the yurt and shook Ross awake. He crawled out and stood there shivering. "He did it," Laurel said, "He actually did it. My hash is gone, and so is my truck."

"Your truck? I thought..."

"He was selling it to me. Whenever I sold some of my hash, I'd give him some money. So it's half my truck. More than half."

"Oh," Ross said. He glanced up; there was an amazing swarm of stars up there. He saw a meteor fall. "What are you going to do?"

"Go after him. If you let me borrow your Jeep. Or take me."

"Go after him? He could have gone anywhere."

"He's not going to get far. I siphoned off all but a few drops of gas."

They found the truck on the side of the road to School's Out near the tree with the word TREE painted on it. Ross approached the Grape with caution, not wanting to get an arrow though his spleen. Sweet Mystery wasn't there, though. Neither was the hash. "He must have taken it with him," Ross said.

Laurel wanted to look around a little. Wedged between a fence post and a rock, she found the cigar box with her bricks of hash in it. She squealed with girlish delight.

"Put it in the Jeep and let's get out of here," Ross said. But Laurel was pouring a can of gas into the truck. She threw Sweet Mystery's sleeping bag and his bow and his other belongings on the side of the road.

"You're not going back to School's Out, are you? He'll come looking for you there."

"I don't have anywhere else to go for now. Soon as I get rid of the rest of this hash, I'm off to Mexico."

"I know this guy, he was the corridor advisor in my dorm in Boulder. He was always selling weed to everyone who lived on our floor. He'd probably be interested in your hash."

"It's good stuff," she said. *"I'd give him a decent price."*

"Let's stay in town tonight, and drive to Boulder tomorrow. We have to take your truck though—this Jeep is my dad's."

Laurel followed him to his family's house. They hid the U.S. Grape behind the hill the house stood on. Then they went into the kitchen and made coffee. Ross had to keep telling her to keep her voice down. He definitely didn't want his father coming down.

And what if Sweet Mystery came looking for them?

Laurel said, *"I thought School's Out was a weird place to live, but this place—weird ain't the word, boy, weird ain't the word."*

"Shh," Ross said. He was used to people saying things like that about this house. *"What will you do down in Mexico?"*

"Go back to being Heriberto's apprentice. I still have a lot to learn about jewelry."

"How about I go with you? For a little while. If you want me to."

"Seriously? You'd want to come with me? What about Winifred?"

"She'll understand," Ross said, though he knew she wouldn't. Not in a million years.

"Well, sure, if you want to. I think I'd like that."

Ross didn't think it would be a good idea for her to spend the night in the house. Mountain Laurel would be a little hard to explain to his parents. He got a flashlight and led her along the base of the hill.

An old wooden sign said TUTTLE HILL MINE. They went through some bushes and past piles of mine tailings and around some barbed wire and into a mine shaft dug into the hillside.

The mine shaft gave Laurel the jitters. *"I don't know if I want to spend the night down there. All night I'll be thinking it'll cave in on me."*

"Don't worry about that. It's been shored up with steel I-beams and concrete shielded with tungsten." They went down about twenty feet and came to a metal blast door, nearly thick as the door of a bank vault. Ross entered a code and it swung open. There was another door, and Ross used a key to open it. Then they were in a large knotty-pine room. It looked like the living room in a mobile home.

"Where are we?"

"It's a fallout shelter," Ross said. *"My father had it built. You'll be safe here."*

"I should be okay here no matter what happens," Laurel said. "Even the apocalypse."

Ross lit a Coleman lantern and showed her around. There was a galley and a small bathroom with a chemical toilet. Behind two curtains there were two bedrooms, each with a bunk bed. Past the living room, there was an immensely long storeroom. In the storeroom, there were shelves of supplies stretching far back into the mine, farther than the light of the lamp carried. There was a Geiger counter and four gas masks on a nearby shelf. On another shelf there was a shotgun, a semi-automatic rifle, four handguns, and enough ammunition to fight a small war. There were canned and dried foods, a year's supply at least, packets of seeds and canning jars. There were first-aid supplies and a cache of emergency drugs. Laurel took a few Dexedrine tablets and a couple of Dilaudin and slipped them into the pocket of her jeans. There were hundreds of jerry cans of water, gasoline, and kerosene. She saw a set of the Encyclopedia Americana, a book on edible mushrooms from the Mushroom Museum, and a leather-bound set of books called The World's Greatest Literature. There was roll after roll of toilet paper, fishing gear, boxes of Kotex, a shortwave radio and spare parts for it. There were board games: Scrabble, his father's favorite; Monopoly, Clue, and Risk. Risk, the game of world conquest.

"Did you come down here much, when you were a kid?"

"We had drills. Once a month or so, my father would set off this alarm system we had in our house, usually in the middle of the night, and we'd have to scurry down here as fast as we could. My father would be standing by the entrance back there with a stopwatch. He never told us it was just a drill. During the Cuban missile thing, we had drills almost every night. One day, it was a Saturday, we were down here and we heard planes flying overhead. I remember my mom saying, 'I hope to God those are ours.'"

Laurel decided she was hungry and took a can of fruit cocktail off the shelf, but they couldn't find a can opener. "Imagine how frustrating it would be if you had to come down here and there wasn't a can opener. You'd have to bite the cans open."

"My dad probably could," Ross said.

They looked for an opener by the stark light of the Coleman lantern. Shadows danced and the lantern hissed. They came across a shoebox full of Topps baseball cards. "Those must have been my brother Marshall's," Ross said. "I never collected baseball cards."

Laurel looked through the cards. "Moose Skowron, New York Yankees. Don Drysdale, Los Angeles Dodgers. Harmon Killebrew, Washington Senators. Wouldn't it be strange to be down here and come across these cards and realize that there wasn't a New York or a Los Angeles or a Washington anymore?"

Though they were more than ten years old, the cards still smelled faintly of bubblegum.

Thea had finally finished her workout. Finally. "Do you want another beer?"

"I don't think there are any more. Hendrik drank the last one."

"I think there might be some scotch in the kitchen. Wim likes scotch. But you might have to drink it without ice."

Ross said he'd drink it without a glass if he had to.

"You might have to." She tiptoed out of the bedroom and returned with a bottle of wine for herself and a half-full bottle of scotch: MacDougal Scotch. Thea sat down on the mattress next to him. Her nose was sweaty. They both drank from their bottles. "You must have been in love with Laurel, then, if you went all the way to Mexico with her."

"I don't know," Ross said. "If I was, I didn't realize it at the time. There was something appealing in the idea of just taking off to Mexico, though, for no reason."

Laurel had gone to Midnight Mass with Heriberto and his family. Ross had been invited, but he didn't like going to church here. He didn't like looking at the blood-stained, brown-skinned Christ squirming in agony on His cross above the altar. He went to the Zócalo with Laurel and Heriberto's family but he didn't go into the cathedral with them. He sat outside a cantina and ordered a Noche Buena *beer. He'd brought a book with him. He was wearing a raspberry-colored guayabera with yellow pockets, an early Christmas present from Laurel. Before long a woman from Montreal named Lili said she liked his shirt and asked if she could share his table. She'd been sitting with other Canadians, but they didn't care for her views on independence for Quebec. He bought her a paloma. Lili was in Mexico to learn Spanish, although she was struggling. Ross had no French, and Lili's English was weak, so they tried to communicate in Spanish. Under the table, Ross felt a warm pressure against his leg.*

Ross asked her how old she was.

"Yo tengo veinte anos."

He told her that the word she wanted was años, *not* anos, *and he explained to her what she'd said.*

"Oh no! Estoy muy embarazada!"

"Don't worry about it," Ross told her, and explained to her next what embarazada meant.

Ross felt sorry for this girl, who not only had twenty assholes but was pregnant to boot.

The pressure beneath the table gently increased, and quivered. An erotic quiver? Lili asked if he wanted to come back to her room to talk some more. He thanked her for the offer but told her he had other plans. There was a party at Heriberto's house after Midnight Mass.

Lili shrugged and finished her drink. "Maybe I'll see you around town."

"Buenas noches," he said to her. A waitress walking by thought he was trying to order another Noche Buena beer. Lili went to sit down with someone else. The pressure on his leg was still there. Ross looked under the table, and the dog that had been leaning against his leg looked up at him with soulful brown eyes. It then scratched behind its ears.

Mass let out, and a crowd pushed out of the church and into the Zócalo. Church bells were ringing, shrill whistles were being blown, and dazzling fireworks lit up the sky. He didn't see Laurel or Heriberto and his family in the mass of churchgoers. The waitress brought him the beer she thought he'd ordered and he drank it, and then he paid the bill and started walking up the hill toward Heriberto's house. There were parties going on everywhere. On one corner, some boys were lighting firecrackers and burning old tires, creating an acrid stench. A woman carrying a gigantic cake crossed his path. There was a group of pretty teenage girls walking the other way. One smiled and said, in English, "Merry Christmas."

"Feliz Navidad," Ross said to them. They giggled.

Ross walked by a small park where there was a basketball court. Some boys, dressed in their best clothes, were playing basketball. There were about ten of them on each team, and there seemed to be three teams. Whenever the players lost control of the ball they were dribbling, they'd kick the ball around the court as if they were playing soccer. It reminded Ross of the way he'd played basketball in high school.

A few blocks farther on, a party was spilling into the street. An old man with a bottle of mezcal offered Ross a drink.

Ross came to the house where Heriberto lived with his mother and uncle and assorted other relatives. A little girl in a party dress let him into the courtyard. She was one of Heriberto's nieces or cousins. He had a lot of those. "¿Papá Noel?" The girl seemed to be seriously asking if he was Santa Claus. It was possibly the beard that fooled her. Ross had a beard, though otherwise he looked nothing like Papá Noel.

"No," Ross said, "I'm not."

Either the child didn't understand or didn't believe him. She went into the house announcing that *Papá Noel was here.*

"What you want to drink, Ross?" Heriberto asked him. Heriberto was dressed like a charro, a Mexican cowboy. He was wearing a black hat and a black shirt studded with silver gewgaws. Ross wondered, not for the first time, if Laurel was sleeping with him. Sometimes they went away together in the U.S. Grape for a couple of days—on business. Still, it was hard not to like Heriberto.

"Brandy," Ross said.

"What kind of brandy you like?"

"Presidente?" That was the only kind of Mexican brandy Ross knew by name.

"Not very good," Heriberto said. "You like Courvoisier?"

Ross said Courvoisier would be fine, too.

Ross brought him a snifter with a generous amount of cognac in it. "You must be sad, not to be in your home for Christmas."

"A little," Ross admitted.

"I been to your country before. To Chicago. Very clean. Very cold. There was extremely a bunch of snow." It sounded to Ross more like a description of Switzerland than of Chicago. "I say myself, I am going to live someday there. But no, I never will. I stay here. Business."

Then Laurel appeared and tried to get Ross to dance with her but he declined, so she grabbed Heriberto, and the two of them went off to dance. Ross sat on a wooden bench in the courtyard by himself and watched. Heriberto was an excellent dancer. Of course he was.

Outside the courtyard, out on the street, cars and trucks passed by. About half seemed to lack mufflers. They sounded like tanks rumbling by on their way to some battlefront. There was still the sporadic noise of firecrackers popping off.

Heriberto's uncle was on a ladder hanging a piñata from the branch of a tree in the courtyard. Laurel came from the dancing and sat next to Ross on the bench. She bumped her hip against his. "Hello, Señor Jarboe," Laurel said. "That shirt looks nice on you. Did you get something to eat? The food's incredible."

"I'm not all that hungry."

"Want to see what I made today?" She lifted a silver squash blossom from between her breasts. "Heriberto helped, but mostly I did it. And look at these earrings." Laurel flipped her hair out of the way so Ross could see. "Do you know what stone that is? No? It's ojo del tigre. Don't you just love that? Eye of the tiger."

"Uh-huh. Look at that piñata."

"I saw it earlier. Great, isn't it? I hope I get a whack at it."

"It's shaped like a pony. Almost all piñatas are shaped like animals."

"So what?"

"So... I just don't think people down here have much respect for animals. That's why they wallop the shit out of piñatas. It's symbolic."

"Oh, poo. It's just different down here, is all. You're always down on them."

"I'm not down on them. I just don't like the way they relate to animals."

"What's the matter with you, Ross? You seem so unhappy lately."

Ross wasn't sure himself what the matter was. Nothing was wrong, exactly. It was just that nothing had made much sense since he'd been in Mexico. He didn't think it was Mexico, though; he thought it was probably himself. Things just seemed to happen here, without any significance or meaning. Maybe things would make sense in retrospect. Maybe they would make sense as memories.

"Next month there's going to be a fiesta. Heriberto was telling me about it. The kids all dress like roosters, and they have cockfights in the streets."

"Que terrífico."

"Maybe we should move into town," Laurel said. She rubbed her nose and flipped her hair. They were living at the time at Dama Elena's campground, a few miles outside of town. It was cheap. "And you could get a job. Heriberto's uncle needs a bartender at his restaurant. We could use the money."

"Yeah, maybe," Ross said. "Or maybe I should just go back home. Go back to school. I could be back in time for the second semester."

Laurel rubbed her nose again and stretched out her legs. "Ross," she said, "I think I might be pregnant."

A stray orange-and-white cat squeezed through the bars of the gate and wandered into the courtyard. It reminded him of his mother's orange tabby, Dundee. It walked past Ross and on its way rubbed against his leg. My legs are certainly attractive to animals tonight, Ross thought. "Feliz Navidad, gato," Ross said to the cat. He expected Heriberto's sister to look at him like he was crazed, but she just smiled. "Watch," he said to Laurel. "She's going to tell the cat to vamoose and give it a kick to show she's serious."

"Shh, she'll hear you," Laurel told him.

Heriberto's sister reached down and patted the cat on its head. "Feliz Navidad," she told the cat.

"Okay, I was wrong," Ross said. "Christ, pregnant. Embarazada. Are you sure?"

"No, I told you, I just think so. I'm not sure. I'll know soon"

"Oh."

"But I have a feeling I am."

❧

Thea drank some wine. Ross took a swig of scotch from the bottle. Ross had never heard of MacDougal Scotch, but he wasn't much of a scotch drinker. There was a picture of a guy in a kilt on the label. It tasted faintly of machine oil.

"We talked about going to Mexico, Wim and I," Thea said. She was lying down on her mattress now, with her head against Ross's leg. Her long hair fanned out over his knees. "We were going to buy a van and drive down there, and then drive all the way to South America."

Ross could see the mole over her left breast, the mole he'd seen through Dean's lens. It was like meeting an old friend in an unexpected place. *Why, hi there, Mr. Mole!* "I don't know if you can. There's a stretch of the Pan-American Highway through Panama that hasn't been finished. I read about that in *National Geographic*. It's really wild jungle."

"It doesn't matter. We won't be doing that now. Besides, neither one of us can drive," Thea said. "How long did you stay in Mexico after that?"

"Well, I started working as a bartender at Heriberto's uncle's restaurant. We left a few weeks before Jeremy was supposed to be born. We stopped at a town near the border. We were in Mexico for over a year and somehow never got around to buying souvenirs."

∿

Ross was about to let Laurel out of the truck and go find a parking place, but a car pulled out of a spot right across the street from the market. Someone yelled at him that he couldn't park there, but Ross ignored him. There was a light rain, somewhere between a mist and a drizzle. "Chipi chipi," Ross called it. Of all the phrases he'd learned since he'd been in Mexico, that was by far his favorite.

Laurel must have sensed that there was some urgency because she started running from stall to stall. She bought a serape for her mother and Ross wrapped it around her. She bought a pair of huaraches for Poppy. She found an onyx burro for her sister and an onyx owl for her aunt. Ross was wearing a sky-blue sombrero trimmed in silver which was meant for Cap. She was carrying a set of mounted bull's horns to give to her father. The tip of one of the horns caught on the canvas of one of the stalls and that threw her to her knees, and then she rolled over on her back. She landed near an Indian woman who was squatting on the sidewalk, selling nail files. The woman had her files arranged in front of her as if they were exotic fruit. She let out a shriek when Laurel rolled across them. Her blouse hiked up when she fell; rain glistened on her bare, swollen belly. "Ross, it's starting."

Ross grabbed the nearest passer-by, a man with a friendly face and a sinister mustache. He asked the man where he could find a hospital, a clinic, a doctor's office, anything. Ross's Spanish was never that fluent, but it was made weird and ungrammatical by the stress of the situation. "No comprende ni jota, señor," *the passerby said.*

Ross shook his head and was about to try again but at this point, the only Spanish that occurred to him was chipi chipi. *He abandoned language altogether. He pointed to Laurel, lying amid the nail files on the sidewalk. He rocked an imaginary baby.* "Ah, sí, sí, sí! Ahora entiendo!" *the man said.*

The man hadn't understood, though. He directed them to an abortionist's office. Fortunately, the abortionist had been a first-rate gynecologist at a government clinic in Veracruz before he'd taken up the more lucrative abortionist's trade. And even more fortunately, there weren't any complications.

"That *was* fortunate," Thea said. "Sometimes there are."

Ross kissed the crown of Thea's head. He suddenly remembered times when he was a kid, going out to his Uncle Earl and Aunt Sophie's summer house in the Berkshires and seeing thousands of fireflies flashing in the twilight. He and his brother would capture some of them in mayo jars. For some reason, he associated the smell of Thea's hair with the smell of lightning bugs. He imagined her head ringed in a glorious lightning-bug halo. Or perhaps she just used some unusual Dutch shampoo. "After a couple of days, we drove to Colorado and moved back to School's Out."

"What about... what did you call him? Sweet something?"

"Sweet Mystery. He was gone. He'd been busted a couple of times in town, and the county sheriff told him that if he ever came back, he'd never get out of jail.

"There'd been a lot of changes. We hardly knew anyone there except Poppy and Cap. A few months later, Cap married us... he'd bought a certificate through the mail that said he was a minister of the Universal Church of Latter Day Druids or something. Cap and I—mostly Cap—fixed up the old crafts cabin for Laurel and me. Laurel made her jewelry, and I helped her run her business, and Cap and I worked a few days a week at a couple of restaurants in town. That's how we lived for a few years.

"But then... sometimes Laurel seemed perfectly happy, but other times I'd catch her crying out in the woods. She was smoking a lot of hash. Sometimes she'd leave School's Out by herself. Once she was gone for a week or more, and when she got back, she acted like nothing had happened. I asked her not to do that again, not to take off without letting me know where she was going. But a few days later I woke up and she was gone again, and I realized, I couldn't do this anymore. I borrowed some money from my brother, and he drove Jeremy and me to Denver, and we flew to Boston."

"Why did you come here? Why Boston?"

"Well, I kind of bounced back. This is where I lived as a kid. I have a slightly crazy aunt who lives not too far from here. I was thinking about going back to college and finishing my degree, but I never did. I got a job tending bar at a place called Yer Fadder's Mustache. My Aunt Sophie, she would watch Jeremy while I was at work. She's been generous, really generous to me, but she's a bit odd. She gets all dolled up..."

"What's that mean, dolled up?"

"She wears her best clothes. She gets all dolled up to watch Mike Douglas and Merv Griffin. Those are television shows. Daytime televisions shows."

"I know. I used to watch those, too, sometimes."

"You have a television?"

"I found one in the alley. It was old. It didn't work very well. The picture would go off, and I would hit the TV and it would come back on for a while, but then it stopped working at all."

"Oh yeah, I remember you telling me that."

Thea looked at him oddly.

"Well, anyhow, I guess my aunt must like me. She inherited a lot of money from my Uncle Earl, and she's giving me the money to get the restaurant started. Maybe she's doing that to get back at my father. She thinks he's a lunatic for moving us to the middle of nowhere—to the back of beyond, is how she always puts it. We stayed with her for about a year, and then Dean and Amy let us stay with them until we got a place of our own—the one across the alley from you."

"What restaurant are you talking about?"

"Didn't I tell you? Dean and I are opening a restaurant. A Mexican restaurant."

"You are? No, I don't think you told me that," Thea said. She drank more wine. "Where is Laurel now?"

"She still lives at School's Out. Cap and Poppy are still there, too, but I think they're the only ones left. She's still making jewelry, only now it's electronic jewelry with LEDs. Little twinkly lights. She travels around and sells her jewelry."

"I'd love to have that kind of job. I'd like to be creative. And to travel."

"You *are* traveling. You're a long way from home."

"It doesn't feel like it. I haven't been out of Boston since I arrived here, and that was almost a year ago."

"Why did *you* come to Boston?"

"For some reason, Wim thought people in America would appreciate his art more than Europeans. He thought he'd become a rich, famous painter, and I came with him because... well, I'd lost my job, and I was tired of working in hospitals, anyway. It was depressing and stressful, and sometimes it was disgusting and the doctors all thought they were gods and... I was ready to go somewhere else and do something different. Kind of like you going to Mexico, I guess. Wim wanted to go to New York or Los Angeles, but my father told us we should go to Boston. He was here years ago, before he was married, and I guess there was something—or someone—that made him love this city. So... that's why we're here. But I didn't think we'd just stay in Boston. I thought we'd travel around and see the country."

"You should go somewhere, then."

"I don't have any money. Besides, I'm afraid to travel by myself."

"What are you afraid of?"

"Of everything," she told him.

"I'm afraid sometimes, too."

"You? You don't seem like the sort of person who would be."

Why not? Ross wondered. *Because I exude confidence? Because I look fearless?* Those didn't seem likely answers. *Because I'm tall?*

One of the candles that Thea had lit was dribbling wax on the lid of her old footlocker. He didn't want to say anything about the candle, though, because once she got up, she might start doing yoga again. Instead, he asked her about the painting over her bed. "I guess Wim did that painting of you?"

In the painting, Thea was sitting in an open window. She was backlit by orange light. She was nude except that she was wearing a nun's veil and wimple. It was a flattering portrait except for the hands. Her hands looked like twisted rodent paws. "Do you like it?" she asked him.

Ross didn't want to appear too appreciative of anything that Wim had done. "I don't know... do you?"

"I don't know either. I guess it's a kind of a... a joke. You know, umm, that prostitutes in Amsterdam sit in windows that way?"

"I've heard that," Ross said. He thought it ironic that this was the way he was most used to seeing her—framed in a window. But without the nun's headgear. "Why did he make your hands look that way?"

"Wim could never paint hands. Anything else, yes, but not hands."

After this, Thea was quiet so long that Ross suspected she'd gone to sleep. It was late. Finally she said, "Do you remember, at the laundromat, I told you I was a model?"

"I remember that, yes."

"Well, I do model sometimes. For art classes, I mean. I don't like it very much, though."

"You model uh, nude I guess? Does that bother you?"

She took a while to answer. "I love being nude when I'm alone. Usually, as soon as I get home, I take off my clothes. And around other people... being nude, it doesn't bother me too much. Once Wim and I went to Greece, and we lived for a few weeks in these caves on a beach in Crete. We didn't wear clothes that whole time. And there were twenty or thirty other people living there, too, people from all over the world, and none of us wore clothes. But it's different when you're the only one in the room naked, and everyone is looking at you. One time, I went into a classroom and took off my robe, and it turned out I was in the wrong room—it was an engineering class. That was embarrassing. Very embarrassing. Anyway, I don't mind the quick sketches, but I hate the thirty-minute poses. My entire body starts to itch. And it's not like I get asked to work every day. They don't want the same model all the time. I was running out of money, so I asked Wim if he knew of any way I could get work without a green card, and he gave my phone number to Mr. Q.

"Mr. Q is a lawyer. He had some clients who were involved in... in pornography. I guess that's how he got interested. He bought a Super 8 camera and a lot of equipment, and he and his wife started making their own films on weekends.

"Once Wim had an exhibition of his paintings at a little gallery in Cambridge. Mr. Q bought one of his paintings, and he asked Wim if he knew any models. So... a few months ago, I got this call from Mr. Q. He wanted to know if I would have lunch with him."

Mr. Q studied the wine list for a long time. He seemed to be trying to memorize it.

Thea was feeling a little self-conscious about what she was wearing: jeans, a tan T-shirt, and a secondhand vest she'd bought at Morgan Memorial, the only place she could afford to shop for clothes. She hadn't thought Mr. Q would take her to such a nice restaurant. He was wearing a three-piece, dark gray suit with chalk stripes, a teal silk tie, and a radiantly white button-down shirt.

"You may not believe this," Mr. Q said to her, "but I was having lunch in a restaurant a few weeks ago, and they had a wine list at least twice as long and

twice as good as this one. And that restaurant was in Omaha. Omaha, of all places!"

"Omaha? Where is Omaha?"

"You know," Mr. Q said pleasantly, "I'm always surprised at how Americans... well, not all Americans, but many of them... know more about Europe than Europeans know about the United States. You'd think, with all the "made in the USA" films and TV shows... Anyway, Omaha is in Nebraska, and Nebraska is a long way from the East Coast and a long way from the West Coast. It used to mean something to live in Boston. Or San Francisco. I've always maintained that those are the only two American cities worth living in... but places out in the hinterlands... like Omaha, Kansas City, Denver... they're catching up." Mr. Q smiled. He had incredibly white, even teeth.

Would he ask her to take her clothes off before he offered her the job? It seemed reasonable that he would. What if she had a horrible scar or a birthmark or something?

"Of course, America doesn't have the restaurants that Europe does. Mrs. Q and I had some lovely meals in your country. I still remember fondly the rijsttafel we had in that wonderful Indonesian restaurant on Hoofstraat. Do you remember the name of that place?" He almost seemed to be testing her, to see if she was really from Amsterdam.

"The Samo Sebo?"

"Yes, I think that's right. Lord, what a meal that was. If we'd tried to eat everything they brought, we'd still be sitting there. And there was this Surinamese place where we had lunch a few times. We had those fried plantains they serve with peanut sauce... I can't remember what they're called, but... "

"Bakabana. *They're called* bakabana."

Thea said, "We talked about restaurants, and about paintings, and about films. We had lobster thermidor for lunch and a bottle of pouilly fuisse. And over coffee he told me that, so far, most of his models had been college girls. But some of his clients were looking for... for somewhat older women. Then he asked me if I'd be interested. I never thought I'd do something like that but—I nodded and said yes.

"He came by the next Saturday and picked me up. There was another woman in the car, Margreet, a friend of Wim's and Hendrik's. I'd met her once at a party back in Amsterdam, but I didn't know her very well.

"Mr. Q lives out in the suburbs—I don't really know where. His wife had coffee waiting for us in the kitchen. We sat around drinking coffee, waiting for the Star to show up."

"You both speak English extremely well," Mrs. Q said.

"Didn't I tell you?" Mr. Q said. He nodded proudly, as if he had taught them the language himself. "Of course, everyone in the Netherlands is fluent in at least two or three languages."

They were sitting at a table in the Q's kitchen, filling out forms that affirmed that they were over eighteen, that they were there of their own free will, that they weren't drunk or on drugs.

"This is Koffie Dutch you're drinking," Mrs. Q said. "'It's just an instant mix, but I wanted you to feel at home."

When Mr. and Mrs. Q weren't looking, Thea made a face at her coffee. Margreet smiled at her for the first time. They hadn't talked much in the car.

"Of course, I know it's not as good as the coffee you get in Holland," Mrs. Q said.

"No, of course it's not," Mr. Q said. "You Dutch still have connections in Java and Sumatra. They send the best beans to you and the stuff they send us, they sweep off the warehouse floors."

Mrs. Q was staring relentlessly at Thea. "I know I just met you this morning, Thea, but I feel like I already know you. Maybe because I've been living with you for a couple of weeks." Thea gave her a puzzled look. "You don't know what I mean, do you, dear? Come with me."

Mrs. Q led her into the living room. There were a dozen or more paintings hanging there. Over the sofa was one of Wim's portraits of Thea. In the painting, she was sitting on a swing inside an immense birdcage. She was wearing a jester's hat and collar but nothing else. Outside the birdcage, there was a man-sized canary playing a violin for her. The bird was wearing round glasses and had a crown of curly yellow feathers on its head. She surmised that the canary was meant to be Wim.

She remembered posing for Wim's sketches for that painting on a swing in the Vondelpark. She hadn't been nude then, but Wim had insisted that she wear that ridiculous hat and collar. The children sharing her swing set found that amusing.

It made her uneasy to see herself here, in the Q's house, in the nude. Maybe that was why Mr. Q hadn't asked to see her naked before he hired her. In a way, he already had. In the painting, her eyes were shining, but her hands grasping the chains of the swing inside the cage were gnarled; her knuckles looked swollen, her

nails misshapen. Wim said that she kept moving her hands, and that's why he had
trouble. Thea knew he was just lousy at painting hands.

There was a mechanical ruckus outside the house. It sounded like a small plane
was landing in the Qs' front yard. "That will be Ricky," she said.

"Who?" Thea asked.

"Why, Ricky! Ricky is... Ricky is our Star," she said reverently. "You know...
the talent. The male talent."

Thea had never heard a person called a talent before.

Ricky arrived on his rider mower. Besides acting in most of Mr. Q's films, he
also mowed lawns around the neighborhood. Saturday was his busy day. He cut a
swatch across the Qs' lawn and parked by the front porch. Now he was ringing
the doorbell.

"Mr. Q said it was just a routine film. It was going to be called *Dutch Treats*.
He said he'd done dozens like that one. I don't know. I've never seen any
pornography." Thea's voice had become flat, as if she were reading into a
tape recorder rather than speaking to an actual person. "In the first scene—
the first scene in the movie, not the first scene that we shot—Margreet and
I are playing tennis. In the next scene, we're having drinks outside, and
I'm supposed to act like I've pulled a muscle in my back during the match.
She asks if I want a back rub, and then I take off my blouse and she starts
rubbing my back. One thing leads to another. We go inside to her
bedroom. Then the Star comes home and catches us. He's supposed to be
Margreet's boyfriend. He's shocked, he's angry. He says he's going to give
us a rough time. But we get him to come to bed with us instead.

"We actually shot the last scene first—the one of all of us together. We
shot it in the Qs' basement. The unfinished part of the basement was full of
lots of antique stoves and a few... what are they called? Junk boxes?"

"Jukeboxes?"

"Yes, jukeboxes and old stoves. I don't know why. One room in the
basement had been finished. It was full of lighting equipment and sound
equipment and cameras on tripods. There was a bed covered with a dark
red bedspread and a leopard-skin rug on the floor. Mrs. Q worked the
video cameras. Mr. Q said she had a better eye than he did, and was better
at giving directions. Mr. Q took still shots."

Once or twice, Thea almost fell off the bed. Once Margreet actually did, almost knocking over a tripod. It was only a twin bed, and it was pretty crowded for three people. The Star moved around a lot. He was as limber as a nightcrawler. "Margreet, Thea, try to look like you're having fun," Mrs. Q said a couple of times. "You're supposed to be enjoying this."

Mr. Q was on his knees practically doing contortions to get the camera angles that he wanted. He called them "undercarriage" shots. Thea wondered why anyone would want to see photos taken from those vantage points. They were the most unflattering angles for viewing human beings she could think of.

"Come on, stroke him, really stroke him," Mrs. Q said at one point. "You're not at a petting zoo."

After some stroking, they thrashed around some more and tried different positions. Mrs. Q explained what was to happen next. "This is the one scene you have to get right. It's the most important scene in the movie. That's why they call it the payload shot," she told the actors.

"I believe it's called the money shot, darling," Mr. Q said.

"If you say so," Mrs. Q said dubiously.

For this scene, Mrs. Q had Thea and Margreet kneel on the leopard skin rug in front of the Star. They were each to take him in their mouths for a moment, and then pass him to the other. Thea tried to make her mouth as unexciting as possible so that his climax wouldn't be her responsibility.

"Cut!" Mrs. Q said, after a few moments. "You need to be more sensual. Less mechanical. Let me show you." For a moment, Thea thought Mrs. Q was going to demonstrate on the Star, or on Mr. Q, but instead, she sucked on Thea's and then on Margreet's fingers. She made loud slurping sounds as if she were eating noodles, and she employed a lot of tongue. "Like that," Mrs. Q said.

They went back to work. The Star was scarcely breathing hard. She had a feeling she and Margreet could pass him back and forth all day and nothing would happen. He looked bored. Thea's jaw was starting to ache. "When you get close, tap them on the shoulders," Mrs. Q told Ricky.

Finally, the Star tapped. He'd been silent during the whole process, but now he suddenly sounded like a sick walrus. Margreet frantically handed him over to Thea, but Thea dodged. Some of the payload landed on Margreet's knee, and one drop, somehow, got in Thea's eyelashes, but most of it plopped on the leopard skin rug. "Oh dear," said Mrs. Q. "That wasn't what was supposed to happen, exactly."

Thea apologized. Mrs. Q said, "Don't worry. It's not real leopard skin. And worse things have happened to it." She handed them both a baby wipe.

Thea tried to imagine what those things could possibly be.

"We can shoot that scene over again later," Mr. Q said.

"Or we could fake it with some fancy film editing and some Jergens Lotion," Mrs. Q said.

"No need," Mr. Q said. He told Margreet and Thea, "Our young Ricky can recharge quickly, trust me. That's why he's the Star."

"Yes, that's one reason," Mrs. Q said. "And because of his umm... dimensions."

After that scene, the Star got to take a recuperative break. Margreet and Thea put on the little white tennis outfits Mr. Q had bought them. Thea's didn't fit well: Too big. They went upstairs and out to the backyard. They were shooting the scene that took place after their tennis match. The two of them were sitting at an outdoor patio table having cocktails, although they were actually drinking iced tea. Mrs. Q told Thea to put her hand on the small of her back and wince. Margreet, on cue, offered her a massage. Thea nodded and took off her white top.

Mrs. Q spread a picnic blanket on the grass in her backyard and Thea lay down on it. "We ran out of massage oil, so we'll have to use olive oil. Don't worry, though—it's good for your skin. I use it instead of moisturizer sometimes." Margreet poured the oil on Thea's back and began massaging her. It felt pretty good, although it made her smell like a salad. The day was warm and sunny. Thea almost drifted off to sleep. Then she heard Mrs. Q say, "Okay, you two, enough rubbing. Let's go back downstairs and get down to business."

Thea said to Ross, "It was hard for me, but it was even harder for Margreet. She was raised Dutch Reformed, and she's from Nunspeet. That's in... we call it De Bijbelgordel. The Bible Belt."

"I didn't know you had a Bible Belt, too."

"We do. It's very traditional and religious. Margreet probably thought she'd go straight to hell for acting in the Qs' film. She must have needed money even more than I did."

Thea had her eyes closed, but the klieg lights were so bright that a red-orange glare soaked through her eyelids. The lights made the room unbearably warm; she was sweating and so was Margreet. She opened her eyes and saw Margreet's breasts floating in front of her face. They were larger than they had looked when Margreet had her clothes on. There were some faint, wiggly stretch marks on the underside. "For heaven's sakes, do something, Thea!" Mrs. Q said. Thea did a few things. A drop of Margreet's sweat fell on Thea's shoulder. Despite the heat, Thea shivered.

Margreet had opened her eyes too. For a moment, they looked at each other. Thea had seldom seen eyes so sad.

"Now, Margreet, I want you to go down on Thea, please."

Margreet looked over at Mrs. Q. "What?"

Mrs. Q explained the idiom.

Thea lay back and waited. She heard the cameras start to whir, but nothing was happening. When she looked up, Margreet was putting her clothes back on.

Mrs. Q gave Margreet a robe, and Mr. Q took her into the furnace room to talk. Thea couldn't hear what was being said, exactly, but his tone was fatherly and technical. She imagined him talking that way to a jury, asking them to acquit.

Ricky put his feet up on the bed. The soles of his feet were grass-stained. He was drinking a can of 7up and reading a comic book. Thea was wickedly thirsty, but she didn't feel like asking Mrs. Q for a drink. Thea dug her purse out from the pile of clothes in the corner. Three people's clothes made for quite a pile. She got a mint out of her purse. It helped a little with the thirst. Could she ask for a robe, too?

Mr. Q led Margreet back into the bedroom. She was looking shell-shocked. Mrs. Q reapplied Margreet's makeup and brushed her hair and took her robe. "Okay. Let's get back to where we were."

Thea tried to disassociate herself from what was going on down there, to detach her mind from her body. She stared at the ceiling. There was a dark stain on the ceiling, as if someone had spilled a cup of coffee up there. It reminded her of an inkblot in a Rorschach test. Staring at the ceiling helped for a while, but then her body started to betray her. She became aware of what Margreet was doing, and doing pretty well, and begrudgingly, she had an awkward orgasm.

This was Ricky the Star's cue to come stomping in, shaking his fists and looking murderous.

"Cut!" Mr. Q said. "That big jar of Vaseline was in the background for that whole scene."

"I don't mind that," Mrs. Q said. "I think it's a nice touch. Some authenticity."

"I think it's tacky," Mr. Q said. "I think we should do a retake."

Margreet bolted out of the room again.

"I think she threw up," Thea said.

Ross wished she hadn't mentioned someone getting sick. He was feeling more than a little queasy himself. Mixing beer and spirits had that effect on him. "What were your reactions to all this?" Ross asked her.

"I tried not to have any."

Mr. Q shook his head and smiled resignedly when Margreet left the set a second time. "There are positive aspects to working with amateurs, but there are definitely some drawbacks."

"Maybe we should shoot the tennis sequence next," Mrs. Q suggested.

Thea wondered if now was the time to mention that she didn't know how to play tennis.

Mr. Q looked at his watch. "We'll never get a court. Not at this time on a Saturday."

"Well, then, maybe we should break for lunch. You could go out and get us all a bucket of chicken," Mrs. Q suggested.

"I guess I could do that. All right, that's what we'll do. Crispy or spicy?"

"Spicy," Thea said.

"Crispy," the Star said. It was possibly the first thing he'd said all day.

Thea heard giggling and looked at the basement window. It was covered with plastic, but she could see children out there. "Umm, Mr. Q," Thea said, and pointed.

"Xong! Non Dai! Thuy! You get out of here! Beat it!" The kids took off as fast as Margreet had. "They really tee me off!"

"They're our neighbor Frank's kids," Mrs. Q explained.

"Our neighbors' adopted kids," Mr. Q said. "They know we do this on Saturdays. My theory is that Frank's trained them to come over here to take photos through the window. That's why I put the plastic up."

Ross moved his leg a little. It was getting numb, but he didn't want her to take her head away. There were a lot more questions he would like to ask and details he would like clarified. He decided, though, that she had said as much as she cared to. He only asked her this: "Would you do it again?"

"I wouldn't have done it at all, but I really needed the money," she told him. For the first time, her voice was clouded with emotion. "The money was good. Wim told me Mr. Q pays better than most people who make these films, even though he's only an amateur, really. But... the money I made, it's gone now. Nearly all of it."

Ross felt a sudden pang of nausea, together with a surge of sympathy and guilt. He felt sorry for her, being pressured into making that absurd porno film. Then he remembered how he'd spied on her. He was as bad as Wim and the Qs.

"But no, I don't think I would. It took... it took a lot away from me. I've been thinking lately that I might go home, back to my own country. There's not much here for me anymore."

Ross sensed that Thea was about to say something more, but the phone rang.

"Would you answer it? There's someone who keeps calling me in the middle of the night." She moved her head off his leg.

Ross didn't think it would be that person who sometimes called, and he didn't want to get up. He could keep his nausea in check as long as he didn't move, but if he stood up, it might be all over.

But Ross did as she asked. He tiptoed past Hendrik and Vervloekt. The dog woke up but Hendrik didn't. "Quiet," Ross whispered, although the dog hadn't made a sound. Hendrik's snoring was as loud as Sarah Jefferson's.

Ross answered the phone. A man, sounding annoyed, asked to speak to Thea. He had a heavy accent. The connection wasn't very good. It sounded as if someone were frying bacon in the background. Ross told him he'd get Thea. He heard the man take a deep breath and say, "Aduh."

He waited in her bedroom while she spoke on the phone. She spoke so softly that he wasn't sure if she was speaking Dutch or English. When she finally came back to the bedroom, Ross had his coat on.

"You're leaving?"

"Well, I told Dean that I'd come by for Jeremy before Amy got home."

"Do you want to hear something funny? Wim thought Amy was *your* girlfriend. When he saw you talking to me, he wanted to get back at you, and so he decided to ask her to have dinner with him. Right before they left, I told him that she was with Dean, not you."

"Who was calling just now? It wasn't Wim, was it?"

"No, that was my father. My father is one of those people who forgets about time zones. He called to wish me happy birthday."

"He hasn't had a lot of international experience?"

"I wouldn't say that. Like I said, he was here before, in Boston. And in the 1940s, he was an engineer on a railroad in the East Indies—in Indonesia. Indonesia was a Dutch colony back then. He was captured by the Japanese and spent three years in a prison camp in Singapore. I'd say that's pretty international."

"Uh, yeah, I'd say so. When I said I'd get you, he said, I think he said, 'Aduh.'" What's that mean in Dutch?"

"It's not Dutch, it's a word he picked up in Indonesia, but he uses it a lot. It means something like... alas... or ouch... or oh, shit."

"Did he ask who I was?"

"I told him you were a new friend." Thea sounded tired, as if new friends were exhausting. "He offered to wire me money so I could come home, even though he doesn't have much, only his railroad pension. He's lonely."

"He's lonely? Are he and your mother..."

"My mother passed away about a year ago. Exactly a year ago—on my birthday. Not long after that, my father moved from Amsterdam back to a small city called Breda where he and my mother lived when they were first married. That's where I was born. But by the time he got back there, there weren't many people around who remembered him. You're really going home?"

"I think I'd better. To tell you the truth, I think I might get sick. That beer and scotch got to me." Ross imagined the MacDougal Scotch and the Narragansett beer roiling and frothing inside of him, as if in a blender. "And it's been a long night." He felt like the sun should be up by now, but it was still utterly dark.

"You could be sick here if you want. I don't mind."

"Thanks, but I'd feel better about it at home." Ross was a noisy vomiter. He made loud, monkeylike noises that might wake up Hendrik. "Will you be all right? With Hendrik here, I mean?"

She assured him that she would be.

"Well, there's something I'd like to talk to you about. Could we get together tomorrow?"

"I don't know. I'll have to see. You'd better go now, if you're feeling sick."

"Okay, well, good night. Oh, and by the way..." Ross tried to remember the Dutch phrase but he couldn't.

"Yes?"

He kissed her. It was a brief and chaste kiss, a cousin of the kiss she'd given him in the bathroom. He kissed her the way someone might kiss a sleeping child. "Happy birthday," he said to her.

THE CLASSIFIEDS

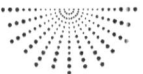

MAUD GONNE, DEAN AND AMY'S IRISH SETTER, WAS BARKING AT ROSS WHEN he got off the elevator. Maud always barked, no matter who got off the elevator or how well she knew them. The barking hurt his head. Amy, wearing an emerald silk robe, her hair up in a yellow towel, was standing in the doorway. "You should have asked who it was before you buzzed me in. Who knows, I might have been the Boston Strangler."

"They caught him years ago, and he's dead now. And the intercom is broken. It's always broken. Besides, I was hoping I'd get some company," Amy said. "You don't look so good, Ross."

"Don't feel so good either. I wish I had some menudo."

"Menudo?"

"Menudo... it's soup, Mexican soup... tripe and cows' hooves soup. It's the world's best cure for hangovers."

"Oh my Lord, seriously? If I were hungover, just thinking about menudo would make me barf," Amy said.

"Do you have any aspirin?" Ross asked her.

"I have Tylenol. How many do you want?"

"All of them," Ross said.

Amy tossed him the bottle. It had a childproof cap. Ross found it frustratingly difficult to get it open and was about to start using his teeth when Amy took it away from him and shook a couple of tablets into the palm of his hand.

"I'll make some coffee. Remember when we used to have coffee together every morning?"

Ross remembered. When he lived with Dean and Amy, he worked nights, tending bar first at Yer Fadder's Mustache and then at Maxwell's. Amy wasn't working at all. Mornings, he and Amy would sit by the window drinking coffee and talking. Sometimes they'd smoke a joint. A wedge of warm, buttery sunlight would move across the table. Motes of dust would swim in the light. Time flowed by like syrup on those mornings.

The sunlight was back again today, illuminating the classified ads from the *Boston Globe*. "Looking for an apartment?"

"No, not yet. First I need a job."

Amy tossed a handful of shiny black coffee beans into the coffee mill.

"What's that smell?" There was a sour, wet, heavy smell coming from the kitchen.

"French roast."

"Not that. Something stinks."

She shrugged and cranked the coffee mill. "Hey, Ross, tell me this: why doesn't the *Globe* put its want ads in alphabetical order?"

"No idea. Must be like area codes."

"Area codes?"

"Those aren't in any order either."

Amy got the coffee brewing and sat down at the table. "Here's one I circled. It says 'I'm looking for a tiger to fill a slot on my executive sales force. Must be the self-starter, go-getter type.' You think I'm a tiger, Ross? A tigress, rather?"

"Umm, in some ways, maybe. I don't know about the go-getter part, though."

"I *could* be a go-getter, I think, if I wanted to, and if someone gave me a chance to go get something. A lot of the jobs in here, I could do if they'd let me. Like this: 'The City of Tucson, Arizona is looking for a director for the newly completed Tucson Arts Center. Must be able to work with community and arts groups.' I could definitely do that, don't you think? But then it goes on and says, 'Must have MBA and at least two years' experience in arts administration and grantsmanship.' I don't have any experience in anything, really."

"I wonder why Tucson is advertising in a Boston newspaper. It's like admitting they don't have any local talent."

"Here's one for a word processor. What do they do?"

"No idea," Ross said. He imagined people tossing dictionaries into a giant Waring blender.

"The problem is, a lot of the things I'm good at don't look impressive on a résumé. Like the other night, I found a mouse in the pantry. I got a salad bowl and I was quick enough to trap him under it, and then I slid a piece of cardboard under the bowl, and I took him back in the alley and let him go, and the mouse wasn't hurt at all."

"You're right, though. Not many opportunities for mouse catchers. How are you with roaches? I pay Jeremy a dime for every roach he kills. He might cut you in, and you could take them alive. In fact, they'd probably all surrender to you. It would be like the Germans trying to surrender to the Americans instead of to the Russians."

"I hate roaches," Amy said, and shuddered. "Did you have a good time after the party last night?"

"It was interesting. We talked a lot."

"Thea's a Scorpio. Scorpios are very sensual."

"I know she's a Scorpio. But... I drank too much, and I started feeling sick to my stomach and I had to go home. I was supposed to come by here to get Jeremy last night, but I felt too bad to."

"Oh, you wild men with weak stomachs. You know she's older than you, don't you? She's in her thirties."

"Dean is thirty-two. I was thirty in September."

"And I will be, too, in two years. I can hardly believe that sometimes. Dean says there should be a decade between your twenties and thirties. I think that's one of his better ideas."

"He also thinks there should be a month between October and November. That's a good one, too. Especially this year, with all we have to do."

"But anyway, Thea is in her *late* thirties."

"She told me she's thirty-six. That's not really *late* thirties."

"You know she was in medical school for a couple of years? She dropped out because she wanted to spend more time with Wim."

"That's what Wim told you, is it?"

"Yes, that's what he told me. Doesn't he have a sad smile? I'm a sucker for a sad smile."

"I wasn't that impressed."

"Oh, don't get me wrong. I think he's an asshole, but I like the way he looks. He has terrific laugh lines. I don't know how he got them, though. He doesn't laugh much."

"It seemed to me that you two were getting along just fine last night."

"We were, at the party. But then we got on the subway to go to this restaurant on Dana Street over in Cambridge and he didn't say a thing. Then we couldn't find the restaurant, and it started to rain, and then we did find it but it was closed. So you know what he did? He just walked off and left me standing there in the rain. He didn't get me a cab or even walk me back to the subway in Central Square. Asshole."

"So you didn't have a very good time last night?"

"It got better. I got home before Dean did. Dean was so glad to see me that after Jeremy went to sleep, he gave me a back rub with chocolate-mint flavored massage oil. And this morning he brought me coffee in bed."

"He was pretty upset when you left with Wim."

"I know, but you know how Dean loves drama. At least, he used to."

"He was sure you were going to spend the night with Wim."

"Wim doesn't even have a place to go. He used to live with Thea, but they were having problems, and now he's crashing in some tiny rented room with his cousin. And Dean thinks I want to sleep with everyone I meet just because he does. Well, maybe, after I move out, I'll be a little more like Dean is."

"You're really going to move out?"

"You bet I am. I don't know why you're surprised. I've been saying for months that's what I'm going to do once I find a job. You know what worries me, though, a little? What if, after I find a place, I get fired or something and can't make the rent? I've been fired from jobs before. Then I wouldn't have any place to go."

"Dean would take you back."

"No, once I leave, I'm gone. And I couldn't go back to my parents' house. Did I ever tell you that, right after we got out of high school, my sister Claire and I got an apartment on Hemenway Street? We sold the *Free News* for a while. You know, you sell those papers for a quarter but you only get to keep a nickel. You have to sell a lot of papers to make eighty dollars. That's what our rent was, back then. So... what else we did... this is terrible, but we bought a gas can and we'd stand by a car and ask people passing by for just enough gas money get us back home to Connecticut."

"Why Connecticut?"

"I don't know. I guess we figured it would take three or four gallons of gas to get to Connecticut, so maybe people would give us a dollar. We still couldn't make our second month's rent. Daddy had to come down and move us back home. It was awful."

∾

Amy's father Dan carried a lava lamp and a teapot downstairs and fitted them in the trunk. Those were, thank God, the last things to bring out. He was glad he didn't have to go back into that building. For one thing, the stairway smelled like pee. He got in his car to wait for Amy and Claire. They were upstairs saying goodbye to their neighbor, Sam. Sam had once given them mescaline and then suggested that they all three get undressed and daub one another with body paints. All Amy and Claire could do was to sit on the floor and giggle and cry.

Their father was getting tired of waiting. He wanted them away from that pee-smelly building, away from Sam, away from this neighborhood NOW. He beeped his horn, but they still didn't come out. He rolled down the window, put his fingers in his mouth, and whistled. That always worked. His whistle was loud as any air-raid siren.

"He actually whistled for us, like we were dogs. He used to do that when we were kids out playing, when it was dinner time. It embarrassed us then, too. No, I couldn't go back there. I guess I could stay with Chewy, but Hector—that's his boyfriend—he pays most of Chewy's rent, and he wouldn't want me hanging around."

"If it ever came to that, you could stay with me."

"You'd give me sanctuary, Ross?"

"Yeah, sure. You and Dean took us in, after all."

When Ross arrived at Dean and Amy's, he had a large suitcase, a duffel bag, a briefcase, and his son. His son had two small suitcases and a backpack. A redheaded woman met them at the elevator. There was a barking dog with a coat exactly the same shade of red as the woman's hair. She'd left her apartment door open; she was watching TV and burning incense, which struck Ross as an odd combination of activities. She was watching a fishing show with the sound turned off.

"You must be Amy."

"I'm Amy. Did you say your name was Russ?"

"Ross. And this is Jeremy. Isn't Dean here?"

Dean had come to Maxwell's last night and sat at Ross's bar. He often came to Maxwell's after work. Ross had told him that he was tired of staying out in Boxborough with his Aunt Sophie. It was a long commute from Boxborough to Boston. Dean had offered the spare room in this apartment as a place for Ross and

Jeremy to stay temporarily. Of course, Dean had already had a few drinks when he'd made the offer. Ross hoped he would remember it today.

"No, he called and said he'd be late. He's still working on a window at some jeans store."

"My arms are falling off," Jeremy said.

"You can put those things down anywhere," Amy told Jeremy. Ross looked around the living room. There were a number of black-and-white photos of a woman taken from behind. The woman wasn't wearing pants in any of the photos. Jeremy was looking at one that featured dolls drinking tea from tiny white teacups. They were using the woman's behind as their tea table. Ross wondered if the woman in the photos was Amy.

"How are things in Virginia?" Amy asked Ross.

"Virginia? Okay, I suppose."

"You're not from Virginia? I thought you must be friends of Dean's from down there. You look like you just got to town."

"No. No, we've been in town for a while."

"You're going somewhere then?"

Ross and Jeremy exchanged glances that said, "This lady's a little slow on the uptake, isn't she?"

Jeremy was the first to hint at the nature of their visit. "Which room am I going to live in?"

~

"I liked it when you and Jer lived here. Everything was more fun."

"Dean was probably sorry he asked me. He had to give up his darkroom."

"I wonder if I'm going to hate living alone."

"As long as you have plenty of friends, I think you'll be fine."

"That's the problem. I don't have all that many friends. In fact, besides you and Chewy, I hardly have any. I wish Claire would come back home." Amy's twin Claire was in the Peace Corps in Ghana and still had another six months to go. "I thought about joining the Peace Corps myself, but I don't know if they'd send me to Ghana, and even if they did, she'd be about to come home by the time I got there. Or maybe I could become a nun. Nuns never have to worry about a job or a place to live or being lonely."

"When Laurel and I split up, I thought about going to Vietnam."

"You?"

"Why not me?"

"I think that's hilarious! For one thing, you're kind of... clumsy. Yes, you are, don't deny it. You probably would've shot yourself or blown yourself up with a grenade or something. You're just not the Green Beret type. I thought you were against the war."

"Of course I was against it. I didn't say I was going to join the Army. I wanted to go as a journalist or a photographer or something like that. It just seemed... it seemed like I was missing the biggest show I'd ever be likely to see."

"You talk about it like it was some kind of a movie. You might have been killed. A lot of people were. A kid I knew in grade school was."

"I know. That's why I decided not to go. Well, that, and the fact that I don't know anything about journalism or photography. Now it's too late."

"I guess it would have been okay if you had some sort of assurance that you wouldn't get hurt. I mean, like you were in your own car at a safari park instead of walking through a jungle full of wild animals."

"You miss the point."

"I didn't know there was a point," Amy said. "All that energy, all that money that went into that stupid war. What if they'd used it for something constructive and decent, like building new cities?"

"They probably would have turned out like Disneyland."

Amy said that she had to go dry her hair.

"First tell me what's causing that stink. It's like something crawled behind your refrigerator and died."

"It's just garbage," Amy said. "Do you know, I've taken out the garbage ever since I moved in here. I wouldn't mind if Dean would acknowledge it, if he'd say, 'Ame, you're doing fine work with that garbage.' But no. So I wanted to see how long it would sit there before he took responsibility."

It had obviously taken quite a while.

Amy went into the spare bedroom to use the blow-dryer. That was the room Ross and Jeremy had lived in for almost a year. Dean used it now as a darkroom and to store boxes of books and mannequin parts from his window-dressing days. There were limbs and heads and torsos scattered around. It looked like there had been a bloodless massacre in there.

Ross used the phone on the wall in the kitchen to call Thea. He had her number memorized by now. No answer.

"One other question—what's in the box?" The box Ross was asking about had been shipped to Dean by the Mad Mountain Outdoor Equipment Company.

"Oh, that. I was wondering that, too, so I opened it. It's a rubber raft."

"A rubber raft? I see. Dean's taking up white-water sports now?"

"It's a prop for another one of his damn photos," Amy said. "He's planning to bring it along when we go to Vermont."

For the past three years, Dean had been working on a series of photos he called "Amy's Derrière." Over the stove in the kitchen hung a photo of Amy walking down a railroad track at night with no pants on. There was the headlight of an oncoming train shooting past her. Over the desk in the living room, there was a photo of her posed on a branch of a bare tree. She was wearing a tropical bird suit. She was bent over so that the tail feathers stuck up in the air. The bottom of the bird suit had been cut away so her butt was clearly visible. In the photo hanging in the hallway, Amy was lying face down in autumn leaves. Hanging from invisible threads, seemingly flying over her ass, were two model biplanes looking as though they were about to engage in a dogfight. Over the fireplace, there was a photo of Amy sitting on a tombstone, taken from the rear. The tombstone said O'DELL. Amy's last name. "The ass," Amy said. "Always the ass. Dean's so obsessive."

"Where is Dean, by the way?"

"Don't know. I asked him to come and talk to me while I took a shower. I looked out once and he was sitting on the toilet seat, drinking coffee and grinning. Then I mentioned that I was going out tonight, and the next time I looked out, he was gone. Did you come to see me or Dean?"

"Actually, I came to pick up Jeremy."

"Oh, he got up early. Ate some Cheerios and watched cartoons for a while. Then he said he was going to meet his friend... Albuquerque?"

"Mojave." Mojave and Jeremy went to school together at Innisfree; Ross's Aunt Sophie didn't want Jeremy going to public school, so she was paying his tuition. Mojave was a couple years ahead of him. "So who are you going out with tonight?"

"Oh. With my friend Chewy's father. His name is Gus."

"Chewy fixed you up with his dad?"

"No, I met him kinda by accident. His father is a subway operator for the T, and he happened to be on the train I was on, going to work. I mean, he was going to work. He recognized me, and he got in touch and asked me to have drinks with him."

"He must be a lot older than... "

"Somewhat older, yes. Ross, I've got to take Maud out. Want to go for a walkie-walk, Maudie?" Hearing that, Maud seemed to lose her mind. She started barking and running in circles. Her tail lay waste the bric-a-brac on the coffee table.

Amy said, "Want to hear something incredible? The other day I bought some peacock feathers down at Quincy Market. I was putting them in a vase in the living room, and when I turned around, Maud had them at point. Her DNA kicked in, and she was a hunting dog again. Isn't that wild?"

Ross agreed that it was, although he wasn't sure that Irish setters had ever hunted peacocks.

"You always look so bored when anyone starts talking about dogs," Amy said.

"I think what it is, is that I always look bored and you only notice it when you talk about dogs."

"Well, I have to take Maud for a walk now that I've said the word *walk*." More frantic barking from Maud. "Do you want to come with me or wait here for Dean?"

"I'll come with you. I'm going to try to find Jeremy and then go home and take a couple more Tylenol and get a little more sleep. I still don't feel great." Ross pulled the black plastic garbage bag out of the trash container, although the smell sent his stomach into a tailspin.

"You shouldn't do that," Amy said.

"I can't stand the thought of anyone living with this."

Maud hesitated before getting on the tiny cage of an elevator. Amy had to shove her on from behind. "She hates this elevator, "Amy said. "So do I. I'm afraid the cable will break, it's so old."

"At least you have an elevator. Try living in a fourth-floor walk-up. Half the time, I get to the bottom, and I realize I left something I need back in the apartment."

The garbage filled the elevator with a grand stench.

Dean was coming into the lobby when they arrived there. He was wearing a motorcycle helmet and a leather jacket and was pushing a bicycle. "Ross. What are you doing here?"

"I called him as soon as you left," Amy said. "We inflated your raft and we were bouncing up and down on it."

Dean blinked at her.

"Actually, I came by to get Jeremy," Ross said.

"Oh. I was expecting you to do that last night. He already left. What's in the bag?"

"Our garbage," Amy said, "Why don't you take it from him?"

Dean did. "It reeks. It smells like a zombie fart. I don't even remember where it goes." Shaking her head, Amy pointed to the garbage room under the stairs.

"Where did you go this morning?" Amy asked Dean. "You disappeared."

"I went out for a ride on my bike. And no, it's not the same as it was with Cinnamon Girl, not the same at all." Cinnamon Girl was a red Bridgestone motorcycle that Dean had sold to raise capital for the restaurant.

"It's better for you. You get some exercise, and you can work out your hostilities on a bicycle. That motorcycle was just an ego pump."

"I don't have hostilities. Hey, Ross, Amy tell you she has a date with a bus driver tonight?"

"A train operator," she corrected.

"Excuse me. A subway jockey. Did she tell you his name was Gus? Can you believe it? Gus!"

Amy walked to the right of a parking meter, Maud to the left.

"So, Ross, what are *we* going to do tonight? Let's go out and pick up some women."

"I was thinking about asking Thea out for dinner," Ross said, "since it's her birthday."

"Oh. How did that go last night?"

"Well, tell you the truth, I..."

"Dean, I've told you again and again, don't do that." Dean had been walking along with his hand Amy's back pocket. She moved his hand away.

"You're always telling me how important touch is, how you don't get enough touch."

"I like to be touched, not groped. Especially not in public."

"I like the motion. It's a very complex motion." Dean tried to put his hand back more or less where it had been before. She bent a finger back and pushed his hand away again.

"Do that again, Cupcakes, you're going to be very sorry. That's such an invasion of my space."

"Invasion of space. Hostilities. Ego pump. You never used to talk like that. Where are you picking up that gibberish?" Dean asked her.

"Oh, fuck," Amy said. She handed Dean the leash. "You finish walking the dog. I can see you still have some hostilities to work out."

"Ame, I'm sorry. I..."

"Take her for a good long walk," she told him. "Bye, Ross. Hope you feel better." As she walked off, she gave them the peace sign.

They both stood and watched her trim ass as she walked away. Dean was right about it being a complex motion. As soon as she turned the corner, Dean lit a cigarette.

"Thought you were trying to quit."

"Yeah," Dean said, "I am, but it's hard at a time like this. Besides, these cigarettes are ultralights. It's hardly like smoking at all. When I came back from the party last night, you know what she was listening to? That Stevie Nicks song, the one she listens to over and over."

"'Landslide?'"

"Yeah, that one."

"Nice song. I heard she wrote that song in Colorado. While she was in her bathtub, I heard."

"Nice enough song, I suppose, but it's subversive. What did she tell you?"

"Stevie Nicks?

"No, not Stevie Nicks—Amy. Did she tell you she's been sleeping with this Gus guy?"

"No, she's not, but she did let him touch her breast. Just once, though, and only for a few seconds."

"She *what*?"

"I'm kidding, Dean. This is the first time she's gone out with him."

"Oh well, it's not like I give a shit. I don't give a shit at all."

"You don't?"

"No, I don't." Dean stared for a moment at his burning cigarette, as if not sure how it came to be in his hand. "Actually, I'd like to nail her shoes to the floor. You see what she's trying to do, don't you? She's trying to piss me off so much that I leave. That way she won't have to deal with feeling guilty. And she'll get to keep the apartment. Not that she can afford it."

They came to the Public Garden. "I'm going over to Beacon Hill to see if Jeremy is at Mojave's place. You know what, though? I think, deep down, you're enjoying all this."

"You're crazy, Ross, I've been..."

"Come on, admit it. You sort of like it."

"I admit, it was pretty boring when things were just going along the way they always did, but..."

"See?"

"But that doesn't mean I like it. Doesn't mean I like it one damn bit."

YELLOW ROSES

THEA WOKE UP FROM A DREAM OF BEING PARALYZED. SHE SAT UP QUICKLY TO assure herself that she actually was able to move. Out in the living room, her phone was ringing. Sometimes it seemed as if her phone was always ringing. She decided not to pay any attention to it. Vervloekt was half sitting on her chest and staring at her. His overbite gave the impression that he was smiling.

She couldn't remember many of the particulars of her dream, only that she was lying in the grass on a sunny day while people walked by. She was able to open her eyes, but the rest of her body felt like machinery that had rusted shut. At first, this wasn't all that unpleasant or disturbing. Mobility seemed more like a luxury than a necessity, and it was restful, lying there in the sunshine. But then she realized that she had to pee. She had to pee bad, so bad she might wet herself. And she was thirsty; she was dehydrated, and she couldn't get herself a drink of water. She surely was going to die of thirst. She couldn't even open her mouth to call for help. The passersby must have thought she was just relaxing there in the grass, in the sunshine, not realizing she was dying. She felt a pressure on her chest, as if someone was kneeling on her. She couldn't breathe. Her panic mounted until finally it woke her up.

After Ross left last night, she couldn't get to sleep even though she'd drunk a lot of wine, far more than she usually did. She finally took one of the sleeping pills that her father had given her. He hadn't been able to sleep well in the days after her mother died. He'd given her a few pills before she left Amsterdam in case she had trouble sleeping too. Wine and barbiturates might explain her dream. Or maybe it was because she'd fallen asleep so suddenly once she'd popped the pill that she hadn't taken off her leotard and tights. Wearing anything but socks to bed always made her feel constricted. Or maybe it was because Vervloekt had been lying on her.

Fully awake now, Thea looked down at her body. It still didn't feel quite right. If her body were a sweater, she'd have it on inside out. She flexed her arm and wiggled her toes. Her muscles hurt. At first, she thought this was the aftermath of her dream. Then she remembered the yoga she'd done the night before.

She took a deep breath, got out of bed, and went to the bathroom. Her need to pee hadn't been a dream. Then she took off the clothes she'd slept in and looked at herself in the bathroom mirror. The sight of her own body startled her, but then it always startled her. Nothing amiss. She'd picked up another kilo, perhaps, in the last month or so. Until last night, she hadn't been exercising. And she shouldn't have bought that birthday cake. She'd been overweight as a child; she never wanted to be again. She turned around and looked at herself over her shoulder. Thin arms, thin legs, but *huisvrouw* hips; hips to sling a jug of milk or a basket of fish on. She shook her head and got in the shower.

As she was getting dressed, she noticed that someone at the party last night had put out a cigarette in her jewelry box. All the jewelry she owned had been her mother's: a wedding ring, a pair of diamond earrings, a pearl necklace, some Balinese baubles her father had brought back from Indonesia. The candle she'd lit the night before had guttered and spilled wax on her footlocker. Her father had given her that footlocker when she'd moved to London. Besides her mattress, the card table in the kitchen, and a pile of pillows, it was the closest thing she had to furniture.

She found a note from Hendrik taped to the refrigerator. In Dutch, it said THANKS FOR THE SPACE ON YOUR FLOOR. I HOPE I DIDN'T CAUSE ANY TROUBLE LAST NIGHT. I HONESTLY DON'T REMEMBER. Lifting her hair, she bent over the kitchen sink and drank straight from the tap. Every cup and every glass in the place was polluted from the party last night. The part of her dream about being thirsty hadn't been a dream either.

She fed Vervloekt and made coffee in her secondhand percolator. The living room was filling up with sunlight. *"Get out of the kitchen, Theatje. Go read in the front parlor. The sunlight in there is the color of yellow roses."* She poured her coffee into an empty sugar bowl and took it into the living room. *Yellow roses. Gele roos.*

Her living room looked especially empty in the morning light. She thought of the sturdy mahogany furniture in her parents' house. She remembered her mother lovingly polishing it.

Some birthday presents were lying on the window seat next to the coleus. She unwrapped the ragged cylinder that Ross and Jeremy had brought. They'd used Christmas wrapping paper. Inside was a paper-weight with a tiny scorpion sealed in it. *What am I supposed to do with that?*

She tore the shiny gold wrapping off Wim's present. He'd given her a framed photograph. It was one of the stills that Mr. Q had taken. She and Margreet were kneeling on the leopard skin rug. The Star was standing in front of them. He was wearing a baseball cap but nothing else. Margreet's face was mostly hidden, but Thea was glancing at the camera. So much makeup ringed her eyes that she looked like a panda. Her lips looked like they had been colored with a garish red crayon, and the fake eyelashes Mrs. Q had fitted her out with looked like spider legs. Her skin was shiny from the olive oil. HAPPY 36th, Wim had written in one corner.

Thirty-six. That seemed impossible. Her last birthday felt like it was about a month ago. On the day before her thirty-fifth birthday, she and her father were sitting by her mother's bedside in the Antonie van Leeuwen-hoek hospital in Amsterdam. Her father had called her in London and asked her to come home. The doctors had told him her mother had a matter of days left, but the days turned into a week and then into two. Thea was missing day after day of work. When she called her supervisor in the hospital where she worked in London, he told her that if she wasn't back by the start of next week, she shouldn't bother coming back at all.

For two weeks, the woman lying in the hospital bed had been nearly unrecognizable. She barely spoke. But that morning she woke up, and she was Thea's mother again. She sat up in bed and put on lipstick. She asked Thea to brush her hair for her. She insisted that she was going to be fine and encouraged Thea to go back to London. When her doctor came in, he said the same thing. He said her mother should be released from the hospital in a day or so. Thea made plans to leave the next day.

Thea was on the ferry to Harwich when her mother died. On her birth-day. She found out when she called the hospital from a pay phone in the ferry port. She bought a ticket and took the next ferry back to Hook of Holland. By the time the funeral was over, she had no job and no plans. That's when Wim said, "Let's go to America."

Without thinking about it, she took the photo Wim had given her out of its frame and began to rip it to shreds.

Feeling a little groggy, Thea sat where Ross had been sitting last night. She leaned her head against the window. The pane was warm against her forehead and she could smell warm dust. Whoever had painted the window frame had been inept; there was paint on the glass and finger-prints in the paint. There was a blister of dried green paint on the white wooden window seat. She pushed at it and worried it and it popped open, and unbelievably, there was a droplet of liquid paint inside, even though it had been dripped there years ago, or maybe decades ago.

Thea picked up a tiny piece of the photo Wim had given her. Tiny pieces were all that were left. The scrap she picked up was a triangular piece with a nipple on it. At first, she thought it was Margreet's; then she realized it was her own.

A pigeon landed and walked along the ledge outside her window. It strutted past like a man with his hands in his pockets. The colors on its neck were the iridescent colors of an oil slick. She tapped on the pane and the bird fluttered off.

Across the alley was Ross's apartment. That's what Jeremy had told her. The curtains were closed.

Why did I tell him all that last night? She'd tried to tell him the story as evenly as she could, so he wouldn't be influenced by her tone. She wanted to see if he would be surprised or excited or disgusted. He didn't seem to be anything. She might as well have been telling him about a job at a dry-cleaning plant. But even though he was indifferent, there was something about him that made her want to go on. There was something soft and comfortable about him, like an old slipper. *I wonder why he wanted to talk to me today? Maybe he won't when he's sober.*

She was hungry. There was a chunk of birthday cake left but that had no appeal. In her refrigerator, there was half a jar of mustard, an almost empty bottle of white wine, a jar with a couple of olives in it, a withered lemon, and a carton of black cherry yogurt. She poured more coffee into the sugar bowl and grabbed the yogurt.

The phone was squatting smugly on the window seat, daring her to pick it up. *I could call KLM and be on a plane tonight. But what about Vervloekt? Could I take him on a plane?* She didn't know. Instead of calling the airline, she got her purse and found the number that Jeremy had written down for her on the day of the parade.

∾

"Hello, Jeremy. Do you know who this is?"

"No."

"It's Thea. How are you this morning?"

"Okay."

"Could I speak to Ross?"

"No."

Jeremy didn't sound like he was in much of a mood to chat. "Why not?"

"He's not here. I don't know where he is."

"I guess he must be feeling better. He wasn't feeling very well last night."

"From drinking? He doesn't get sick from that. He has a trick. He sleeps with one foot on the floor, and that keeps him from puking."

"It does?"

"Uh-huh. They teach you that in the Army."

"I didn't know that Ross was ever in the Army."

"He wasn't. He just knows the trick."

"You're there by yourself?"

"No. My friend Mojave's here. And Maxine."

"Maxine?"

"Mojave's dog."

"Well, tell Ross..."

"Wait a minute," Jeremy said. She heard barking in the background. "Someone's coming up the stairs. Might be him."

It was. He stopped in the bathroom to grab a couple more Tylenol before coming to the phone. "How are you feeling?" she asked.

"A little better," he said. "Still a bit shaky."

She felt shaky, too, even though she hadn't drunk as much as Ross. Or Hendrik. But her dream still haunted her. "Jeremy told me about your trick from the Army—to keep from getting sick."

"Oh. Yeah. Planting a foot on the floor. I think it's from the Navy, though. They call it dropping anchor. That works sometimes. It keeps the room from spinning around so much. But it didn't work so well last night. I called you earlier. What are you doing now?"

"Eating yogurt."

"I was going to see if you wanted to go out for dinner this evening. A birthday dinner."

"I don't know. I don't know if I can," she said, although she didn't have any plans. *Then why did I say that?*

"Oh. Well, I was thinking of going down to the Esplanade this afternoon and just sitting in the sun. Down by the Hatch Shell. We won't have weather like this for much longer. Could you meet me there? Around two?"

"Maybe." When Ross didn't say anything to her *maybe,* she said, "I always say maybe because I never know for sure what I'm going to do. I don't know; I shouldn't have called you. I'm in a funny mood today."

"No, I'm glad you called. I do want to talk to you about something."

"I know, you said that last night. I'll try to come, then."

Ross could see Thea through a gap in his curtains. She was cradling the phone between her head and her shoulder. That left both of her hands free to deal with her yogurt.

UMM...

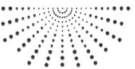

TWO WOMEN, JOGGING IN OPPOSITE DIRECTIONS, PASSED EACH OTHER IN FRONT of Ross's bench on the Esplanade. They smiled at each other but not at him. One was wearing peach-colored jogging shorts. There was a hole in the seat of her shorts which had been repaired with a patch meant for a bicycle tire. The patch was starting to peel off, but wouldn't come unstuck in time to do Ross any good.

It was a difficult business, getting the attention of jogging women. Their eyes glaze over, they think only of their own bodies. Stationary women were enough of a challenge. Now suppose he'd jumped up and tried to match speeds with the one in the peach shorts—what could he possibly have said to slow her down? Could he even have caught up with her? Unlikely—Ross was a famously slow runner. And the thought of running with a hangover made his head pulse with pain. Not that it mattered. It didn't matter because he was here to meet someone. Well, maybe.

Ross sat back and opened a letter from his mother he'd grabbed from his mailbox on the way out of the building.

Dear Ross dear,

Well, here's the front-page story: Your brother and Nikki getting married. I think the wedding will be in February. I say "I think" because Marshall has scarcely spoken to me for the last few days. I suppose I wasn't enthusiastic enough when he told me his news. I like Nikki, don't get me wrong. She's a good-natured person, but a little hard to get to know. She's quiet. And this whole thing came up so suddenly. She works at the Grandview Hotel. Hmm. She came out here to ski and she just stayed.

Marshall's first wife, Annabelle, had also been a maid at the Grandview Hotel. Ross's mother seemed to be implying that Marshall had an unhealthy fixation on Grandview maids.

Marshall and his first wife moved to New York after they were married. Marshall was studying to be an architect.

∾

When Marshall went to class in Brooklyn, Annabelle went to a department store. She tried on a long black leather coat slit up the back from ankles to hips. The puffy white down parka she'd brought from Colorado didn't seem appropriate in New York City. She thought it made her look like the Michelin Man. After that, she had lunch in the tea room on the fifth floor. She decided to put the coat on her Christmas list. On her way out of the store, she stopped and looked at some soft gray leather gloves in a basket marked SALE. They'd look good with the coat she had her eye on. She reached into the basket and felt a sharp prick of pain between her thumb and her index finger. Walking past Women's Shoes, she suddenly felt dizzy and couldn't catch her breath. She sat down in the shoe department and propped her feet up.

The clerk in Women's Shoes, a young man in a red-and-black sweater vest, had been due for a break for over an hour. He was staging a personal slowdown until he was relieved, so he took his time about waiting on Annabelle. By the time he went over to her, she was almost unconscious. He called his manager.

The manager arrived in time to see Annabelle stand up and try to walk away. She stumbled over a shoe-fitting stool and sprawled on the carpet. Her lips were spotted with saliva and her legs twitched. Her breathing was labored. "Drunk, I bet," the manager said, "or on drugs." But she sent for the store nurse and an ambulance anyway.

Annabelle whispered to the clerk, "My bones are melting. My mouth is cold."

The clerk didn't think she was drunk or high. "Look," he said to the manager. There were two red puncture marks at the base of her thumb, and her hand had swollen to an alarming size. It looked as though someone had inflated a rubber glove. "I'm going up to Sporting goods to get a snakebite kit."

The manager told him not to be ridiculous: How could there be a snake in a department store in Manhattan? Besides, they could be sued. And where the hell was that nurse? Where the hell was that ambulance?

Ross heard a sound from under the bench where he was sitting. He looked down and saw a listless man lying in the grass under the bench. It surprised him that he hadn't seen him before. He didn't seem to mind Ross sitting over him. Maybe it made him feel secure.

Marshall hasn't been able to find a very good job either. He's doing roofing for a construction company. He says he likes it but I think it must be depressing for him, and now that winter is almost here, there won't be much work. He was hanging out with Laurel and Cap and Poppy for a while, but now he's spending most of his time with Nikki. And he plays Scrabble with your father. I'm glad your dad has someone to play with. I stopped because I never won. Never. Not one game.

They spent most of the day at the hospital. Annabelle was being treated with antivenom and steroids. At 2 a.m., they finally persuaded Marshall to go home. When they got him there, he went straight to his studio and put his head on his drafting table. He wouldn't talk, he wouldn't get in bed. Ross and his father sat down at the kitchen table.

Ross's father looked uncomfortable. He was thinking, perhaps, that it would be just his luck that World War III would break out when he was at ground zero at the juiciest target in North America. A submarine lying off the Atlantic Coast could lob missiles into New York City before the first siren sounded.

"They have fallout shelters here, too, you know. There's one right down the street. I saw one of those black-and-yellow signs with the triangles," Ross said. "It was in a church basement."

His father snorted. "Don't be ludicrous. A church basement is a good place to play bingo, not to survive a thermonuclear attack."

Ross began to dig crumbs out of the crack in Marshall and Annabelle's kitchen table. He used a Maxwell's matchbook cover. It was something to do.

"Stop it," his father said.

Ross drummed his fingers on the Formica.

"Stop that, too."

Ross stopped. He could see that his father was close to sailing off into one of his rages. He'd been afraid of those all his life. "I'm going to fix something to drink."

"This isn't the time to be getting drunk."

Ross had been thinking of coffee, although getting drunk didn't seem a bad option either, come to think of it. Ross had worked late at Maxwell's the night before and had come down to New York from Boston on an early morning train and gone straight to the hospital. He was in that threshold state between exhaustion and nausea. His head kept nodding like a bobble-head doll's.

"Make some hot chocolate. I'll take it up to Marshall. Then we'll get him into bed."

Hot chocolate seemed grossly inadequate, but Ross poured milk into a saucepan and turned on the gas. "I still can't believe it," Ross said. "Bitten by a snake in New York City. Imagine."

His father didn't have any trouble believing it. Nothing that happened in a place like New York City would surprise him.

That afternoon, Ross and his father had gone to the department store where the attack had taken place. The manager was baffled. "Of course, strange things happen in a big department store." As an example, she told them about a putrid smell that came from Home Furnishings once. They'd searched everywhere and, after a day or two, they found portions of two dead cats sewn up in a brand-new sofa. No one had been able to explain that one either.

Now, in this particular case, according to a consulting herpetologist, the snake that bit Annabelle was an eyelash viper. The gloves in the basket were from Belgium. Eyelash vipers were indigenous to Central America, not Belgium. If it had happened in Gourmet Foods, where there were baskets of tropical fruits, it might have been a little more understandable. But Gourmet Foods was on the third floor, and no one could picture an eyelash viper on an escalator coming down to Ladies' Accessories. More likely, this was the work of a crackpot who raised snakes in his basement and left them in places where they would bite the unwary. The store was, of course, prepared to provide Annabelle and Marshall with a sum to cover her medical care and for damages. The manager said she hoped no one would find it necessary to talk to the newspapers.

Ross found a bottle of Tia Maria in the cupboard and slipped some into Marshall's hot chocolate when his father wasn't looking. "This is for you, Hotshot," Ross said to himself. His father took the liqueur-laced cocoa up to Marshall's studio. He rapped imperiously on the railing. Marshall still had his head down.

Ross's father rapped again. "It is I," he said.

It is I, my ass, Ross thought.

~

Ross watched a natty black man come along the Esplanade with a metal detector. White hair rose from his head like steam. His machine started to squeal. He dug in the ground with a screwdriver and unearthed a bottle cap. He threw it into the river. His expression never changed. He seemed inured to disappointment.

> Laurel has been coming over for dinner sometimes. She said she's been talking to you. I didn't ask her what you've been talking about, but I think it's encouraging that you two are still in touch.
>
> I know Marshall would love for you to come for the wedding. And we'd love to see you and Jeremy. I can't believe how long it's been since I've seen my grandson. Not since August. By the way, is your restaurant open yet?

The man under the bench made another sound, and not a happy one. Maybe security wasn't as important to him as the sensation of warm sunlight coming through the slats.

> Your father just came into the room and I asked him if there was anything he wanted to say. He said to tell you to use a dictionary the next time you write. He was kidding, of course, but you did spell a lot as if it were one word, and you wrote it's when you meant its.

"What's the password?"

Ross looked up. Thea was sitting next to him. He hadn't seen her coming.

"Password?"

"Yes, the password. I'm going to pay you for your secrets and then a submarine"—she pointed toward the River Charles—"is going to pick me up and take me away. But first you have to give me the password."

In her trench coat, Thea did look a little like a foreign agent. The hint of an accent helped.

Ross looked out on the Charles. He didn't see a periscope. All he could see was an eight-person shell, with eight women rowers providing the propulsion. He could faintly hear the coxswain barking directions to the rowers. "Number six, you're early!" It seemed to Ross, though, that the oars moved in perfect unison.

"I don't know the password, I'm afraid."

"Well... is that a secret document you're looking at?"

"This? Not exactly. It's a letter from my mother."

"What's your mother say?"

"She wrote to tell me that my brother's getting married. For the second time." Ross told Thea about Marshall's first wife.

"Did she die from the snakebite?"

"No, she recovered, but she still had problems. She dreamed about snakes all the time and would wake up screaming because she thought they were crawling all over her. And she didn't trust anything or anybody. Including Marshall."

"I can almost understand that. Sometimes I don't trust anything or anybody either."

"Well, Annabelle went into different kinds of therapy. One was group therapy for people with phobias, and she fell in love with one of the other people in the group. He was afraid of earthquakes, I think. Or spiders. Or maybe both. They moved in together."

"Your poor brother."

"I guess that's why my mother isn't more enthusiastic about Marshall getting married to another maid at the Grandview Hotel. After all the trouble he had with the first one."

"Did you know there's someone under our bench?"

Ross looked down. Vervloekt was there, too, lying near the man down there.

"Uh-huh, he's an FBI man. He's been taping everything you've said."

"What was it you wanted to talk to me about?"

"Oh. Well. You remember last night when I told you about the restaurant?"

"We talked about a lot of things last night. I kind of remember you mentioning a restaurant."

"Dean and I are opening a Mexican restaurant in a month or so. And I was wondering... since you need a job... if you might want to work there. When we get it open."

"What would I do?"

"You could be a waitress, or a hostess, or something."

"I've never worked in a restaurant before."

"We've never opened one before. It's nothing you couldn't learn. What do you think?"

"Umm..."

"What's that mean?"

"It means 'Umm...'"

The man under their bench began to shout in a hoarse voice. "Yink, erggh, fuck."

Vervloekt came out from under the bench, alarmed. The man's spotted fingers curled around a slat between Ross and Thea. Thea jumped up. "*Komen*, Vervloekt," she said.

Ross picked up his letter and came, too. "I should go find Jeremy, anyway."

"Did you see his arms? They were all covered with scabs. From falling down when he's drunk, I guess."

"I guess." On his way home from Thea's last night, he'd tripped on an uneven slab of sidewalk. His palms were scraped and his right knee was sore. "Will you think it over, about the job?"

"I'll think about it. But I'll probably go back home before long." She sounded sorry, sorry that there wasn't a submarine out there, standing off the Esplanade, waiting to whisk her and her dog away. "Thanks for asking me, though."

They walked off. He put his arm around her. She didn't seem to mind that. After a moment, he took his arm away. She didn't seem to mind that either.

ON THE ARTHUR FIEDLER FOOTBRIDGE

JEREMY DROPPED A HIGH-GRADE DOG TURD FROM THE ARTHUR FIEDLER Footbridge onto the traffic on Storrow Drive below them. It was an oddly shaped dog turd, rather like a pork chop. Possibly it was two or even three dog turds fused together. A standard poodle had left it behind. Jeremy meant for it to paste the windshield of a westbound Plymouth Volare, but he released it too late, and the car passed under the bridge unsullied.

"You have to lead them," Mojave told him. "You don't wait until they're almost under you. Those cars are going *fast*."

"It stuck to the bag," Jeremy explained.

Jeremy was still unclear as to why, exactly, they were bombarding cars with dog poop. Mojave told him he got the idea from his cousin, who said he did it to express his utter contempt for humanity. Mojave's cousin had a number of ways to express his contempt for humans. He'd go to grocery stores, for example, and put jars of pickled pigs' knuckles in people's shopping carts when they weren't looking.

Jeremy suggested dropping eggs instead, and Mojave was amenable, but when they went to Flagg's Market to buy a dozen eggs each, the clerk had looked them over and said, "You boys are up to no good." He wouldn't sell eggs to them, but he did let them buy a package of brown paper lunch sacks and some rubber gloves.

They still had four rounds of dog shit in those bags. They'd gathered it from the Esplanade, where there was plenty to choose from. Mohave favored those turds firm enough to remain intact during the descent but soft enough to splatter on impact.

"Here, my turn." Mojave loosed his load too soon, and it fell harmlessly in front of a taxi. "He slowed down," said Mohave. "He saw it coming, and he slowed down."

Flies were crawling on the paper bags. Jeremy approached them quietly and slapped his hands together above one of the bags, hoping to squash a fly or two as they were taking off.

"You can't kill flies that way. Flies are too fast. And too smart. Flies are so smart they can read your mind. They can tell when you're coming to get 'em."

"It's easier to kill roaches," Jeremy admitted.

"Roaches are *stupid*," Mojave said. "Anyone can kill roaches."

"I smooshed a hundred and seventeen of them in October, and my dad gave me a dime each."

Mojave did some multiplication. "That's pretty good. Would he give me a dime for each one I kill? We have lots of roaches, too."

"No, just at our apartment."

"I could kill them in my apartment, and bring them over, and you could say you killed them and we could split the money."

"I don't know. I don't think so." Jeremy didn't want to jeopardize his income by padding body counts.

"Here comes a cop car. Wait'll I say NOW!" Mojave said. "NOW!" This time Mojave's calculations were impeccable. A cluster of Scottish terrier droppings peppered the police car's windshield like grapeshot. A solid Weimaraner turd plopped onto the roof of the black and white. "Did you see? Mine landed on his windshield. That cop didn't know *what* was happening."

Jeremy looked back. He was afraid the cop would take the Copley Square exit and come back for them.

"I had the little ones that landed on the windshield," Jeremy claimed.

"Nuh-uh, 'fraid not," Mojave said.

"'Fraid so."

"'Fraid not. Hey, Maxine, cool it!" Maxine, Mojave's Doberman, was tied to a light fixture on the bridge. She had a woman who had been riding her bike over to the Esplanade cowering against the other side of the bridge. "She won't hurt you, lady. She just barks a lot. Is that a Raleigh Sprite? Those are cool bikes."

The woman nodded and hurried past. Her bike wasn't any kind of

Raleigh, but she would have agreed to anything to cross the bridge with her flesh still attached to her bones.

Mojave took Maxine's muzzle in his hands and gave her a kiss.

"Yuck," Jeremy said.

"Dogs' mouths are cleaner than people's," Mojave said, "Everybody knows that. Want to have a sleepover tonight?"

"Your bed's too little."

"Come on. We can play Normandy Landing or Waterloo."

Jeremy said he would consider it, although he'd already decided to ask his father if he could, not because of the war games, which he always lost. Jeremy actually preferred video games like Space Pirates to board games, but Mojave said those were for dorks. He would consider a sleepover, though, because of Mojave's mother. Jeremy had a serious crush on Mojave's mom.

"Here comes your dad," Mojave said. "Who's that with him? Does he have a girlfriend now?"

"That's Thea. We went to her party. She's a doctor, sort of."

"She is not. Look at her."

Jeremy had to admit that Thea didn't look much like a doctor. What kind of a doctor would wear a coat like that? "She is too. Ask her."

Maxine, straining at her leash, snarled at Ross and Thea. Vervloekt snarled back. He had a nasal growl, as if he had adenoid problems. Thea picked him up and walked behind Ross. Clearly, she didn't trust Dobermans.

"Maxine!" Ross shouted, "What's your problem!"

Maxine sat back on her haunches and wagged the stub of her tail, as if that snarling business had been some kind of a joke.

"That woman on the bike told us to watch out," Ross said.

"Maxine scared her," Jeremy said.

"I can understand why," Thea said.

"Are you really a doctor?" Mojave asked her.

"No," she said, "I'm not."

"I told you," Mojave said. "She was kidding you."

"I went to medical school for a while. I worked in a hospital."

In that case, Mojave had some questions he'd been saving up to ask someone with a medical background:

- Why do you say "Bless you" when someone sneezes, but not when they fart?

- Why do you have stuff in your eyes when you wake up in the morning?
- Why do some people walk funny?
- Why do you pee sometimes when you laugh real hard, but not when you cry?
- Why do you get hangnails on your hands but not on your feet?
- When people who have blue eyes look at things, do they kinda look blue?

Thea couldn't answer any of his questions except the one about blue eyes. "You'd better ask someone who's *really* a doctor."

Ross put his arm around his son. "What have you and your colleague been up to?"

"Watching cars."

"Sounds fun. We got a letter from Grandma. Uncle Marshall's getting married in February. She wants us to come out for the wedding."

"Us? You mean me too?" Jeremy asked

"We'll see. You'll be in school then."

"I want to go to Colorado," Jeremy said.

"Me, too," Mojave said.

"Me, too," Thea said.

Ross turned and looked at Thea. "You do?"

"Sure. I'd like to go anywhere," she said. "What do you have in the bag, Jeremy? Your lunch?"

"Dog s'it."

Mojave corrected him. "Dog *shit*. My mom makes me pick it up. She doesn't like Maxine just to leave it on the sidewalk."

"Be sure to wash your hands," Thea and Ross said simultaneously.

14

POSSUMS

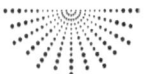

"Were you starting to wonder if I was ever coming back?" Amy asked. She'd just returned to their table after almost a quarter hour in the powder room.

"No, Red," Gus said. She looked at him. Had he actually called her Red? "I knew you'd be back. You left your purse here."

"Let's have another drink," Amy suggested.

Their waitress, a rangy woman in a gray silk blouse, was leaning against a counter over by the coffeemaker. Her arms were crossed, her eyes unfocused. Gus waved in her direction, fiddled with his tie, waved some more, and called, "Miss, oh, miss." No response.

"I think you're supposed to use this phone to order more drinks," Amy said.

"That's dumb. She's standing right there."

Finally, Amy marched up and tapped her on the shoulder. The waitress told her that they should use the phone on their table.

"Out of order," Amy told her.

When Amy got back to the table, Gus asked if she wanted to eat there. "We could get some appetizers here in the bar, or go into the restaurant and..."

"Go ahead and order something, if you like. There's hardly anything on the menu I can eat except some lame salads."

"You don't eat meat?"

"Never red meat. Or chicken. Fish sometimes."

"My wife—my ex-wife, that is—she's vegetarian, too. And so is Chewy, of course. Chewy *never* liked meat. He used to spit out his strained peas and ham when he was a baby."

"And people always gave them a hard time, I bet."

"Well, it was hard on my wife, especially back when. In those days, she was probably one of the only vegetarians in South Boston. But she was strict. She even sent off for shoes and belts from some company out in California. They claimed all their leather goods came from cows that died a natural death."

Amy looked under the table at her leather clogs. She'd bought them at Jordan Marsh, not from a humane company in California.

"She used to say, all she got was the cabbage, not the corned beef. But she never wanted to live anywhere else. 'South Boston is part of my karma,' she'd always say." Gus pronounced the word *comma*. "I guess it's part of mine, too," he said. "And yours."

"We could sing a few bars of 'Southie Is My Hometown,'" Amy suggested.

For a horrible moment, Amy thought he was going to accept, but then the waitress darted over to their table. Once she'd been stirred, that woman could move. She snatched up Amy's empty wineglass with a back-handed flick of the wrist and popped a full glass of red wine in front of her. She acted like she was scoring a goal in a game she'd invented to make the hours go faster. Then she lunged across the table to give Gus his beer. *And give him a nice look down your gray silk blouse.*

If Gus enjoyed his look, he didn't let on. He opened a pouch on his belt and paid the waitress. Gus had a money belt with secret zippers, as if he were planning to travel to some dicey part of the world. He practically had to take his pants off to pay the bill.

Gus clinked his beer mug against her wineglass and smiled at her. He'd been smiling, too, on the train that stalled between Kendall Square and Central Square.

It was hot on the stalled Red Line train, hot and crowded as a henhouse. There was no sign of the camaraderie and good humor that supposedly crop up when strangers are trapped together. Everyone kept getting on Amy's nerves. The man

in front of her had on an enormous backpack, and he kept taking little steps back-
wards. His pack drove her into the pole she had been leaning against. A baby was
crying toward the rear of the car. A nearby four-year-old kept asking his mother
endless questions: "Do babies come out of their mommies' tummies wearing
clothes?" His mother ignored him. The woman hanging on the strap beside Amy
was continually adjusting her underwear, and nearly everyone on the car seemed
to be breathing too loud. It was like being on a train full of wheezing asthmatics.

The only person on board who was smiling was a barrel-chested, guppy-faced
man who was seated nearby. He was wearing the uniform of an MBTA driver.
She assumed he was on his way home after driving a train all day, or maybe he
was on his way to start his shift. Amy wondered if train drivers got to ride the
subway free on their way to and from work like deadheading pilots. His uniform
made him look a little like a pilot, in fact, except he had a T insignia on his
sleeve. He had offered his seat to her when she'd boarded the train at State Street.
Now she wished she'd accepted. There was something mildly familiar about him.
Had he been the assistant volleyball coach at her high school? One of Dean's
window-dressing colleagues? The ice cream man in her old neighborhood? One
of the Santas she'd worked with when she was a helper elf? She couldn't
place him.

After a great deal of time had passed, Amy began to wonder if they would ever
get off this train, or if they did, if anything would be the same when they surfaced.
They might arrive at the end of the Red Line to find that Cambridge had vanished,
and that in its place a dark forest had sprung up. After a few days of hunger and
panic, someone would take a deer. They'd chop down trees and build rude cabins
in the clearing. There might be a struggle to see which woman would live in which
man's hut. She thought she would make a desirable mate in this apocalyptic place;
more so, she thought, than the woman fiddling with her bra or the mom who
refused to answer her son's questions. Maybe the man in the MBTA uniform and
the backpacker would come to blows over her. Maybe the backpacker was younger
and more skilled in woodcraft, but there was something about the off-duty driver
that might make him formidable.

Amy wished they'd move on, either to the forest or to Harvard Square.

The man kept smiling, smiling at her. All these people on the train and he was
smiling at her. *She took his smile to mean, "We subway men, we know all that is*
worth knowing about waiting."

"What are you making?" Gus asked her.

Amy was carefully folding a dollar bill. "A swan. It's called origami when you fold paper like this. It's *very* Japanese. Can I ask you something, Gus? Do you subway drivers make good money?"

"Oh, more than you might think."

"How about school bus drivers? I keep seeing ads in the paper for school bus drivers, and I was thinking about applying."

"They get union scale, too, and they don't even have to join the union. But you don't want to get involved with that busing thing."

"No? Why don't I?"

"You just don't," Gus said. "They throw rocks at school buses, some places."

"Places like South Boston."

A middle-aged woman walked by on her way out. The woman had spikey hair and was wearing a stainless steel choker. She smiled at Amy and waved goodbye. "That's Sister Agnes. That's who I was talking to for so long in the ladies' room."

"Sister? You mean like a nun? Here?" Gus seemed to find the idea of a nun in a bar in Kenmore Square farfetched.

"She's not a nun anymore. She's Agnes McGarrity now. She was my sixth-grade teacher at Saint Mike's. Turns out, Sister Agnes likes punk music, and she thought this place was a punk bar—it used to be, I guess. I would never have recognized her. I didn't even know what color her hair was, and I remember her being about seven feet tall even though I'm taller than she is now. She recognized me right away, though."

"That's because you haven't changed much. I recognized you too, on the train."

"I don't know how. We moved from South Boston when I was eleven. I was skinny, and I had buck teeth, and..."

"You look the same, though. Same hair. Same freckles. Same expressions. I remember how you and Claire and Chewy used to play together back when you were in grade school." Gus was Chewy's father, and Chewy was Amy's oldest friend. That's why Gus had looked vaguely familiar to her on the stalled train. She hadn't seen him, though, for nearly twenty years.

"You not only recognized me, you tracked me down. Did you ask Chewy how to get in touch with me?"

"No, Chewy doesn't know I called you. But it wasn't hard. I remembered your name. And you were in the phone book."

"How did you know it was me on the train and not my twin sister?"

"I could just tell," Gus said. "And Claire wasn't in the phone book."

"That's because she's in Ghana. Anyway, Sister Agnes was my favorite teacher. She used to write books for Catholic girls, and some of the students in her classes became characters in her books. She put me and Claire in one of her books. In the book, my name was Angela, and my twin sister was named Claudia, and we had beautiful voices, but we used them to sing in seedy bars."

"But you didn't really do that? You..."

"No, *we* didn't, of course we didn't. She made that part up. Come to think of it, I've never heard of a bar where they have young schoolgirls singing, but I guess back then, Sister had a hard time doing research. All the same, I knew Angela was me and Claudia was Claire. They both had red hair in her book, and they said things that I remembered us saying in class.

"Sister Agnes put herself in those books, too. Her name was Sister Lucy, and she went around solving people's problems. In the book about Angela, Sister Lucy stormed into the bar and told Angela and Claudia that she wanted them to sing in the girls' choir. And they said they couldn't, they needed the money to support their family because their father was a drunken lout."

"I remember your father. Dan. He wasn't a drunk."

"You're not keeping up, Gus. This was just in the book, not in real life. Anyway, Sister Lucy found him a job as a janitor at the school, and both the girls joined the church choir and Angela became the soloist." In the book, it was Claudia who had become the soloist, but Amy didn't think that was fair because she was a better singer than Claire.

"Poor Sister. In real life, her students never got in much trouble, so she never got to act like Sister Lucy. There, it's finished." The dollar bill she'd been folding did look a little like a swan. "I'll leave it as part of the tip."

"That book, I'd like to read it. Where can I get it?"

"I have no idea. I don't even have a copy anymore. It's been out of print for years, I imagine."

"I'll look in used book stores," Gus said. "I didn't like nuns very much." Gus, like Amy and Claire and his son Chewy, had gone to Saint Michael the Archangel's grade school in South Boston. "There was this one nun, Sister Generosa, who used to grab me by the ear because my penmanship wasn't very good. My capital G's looked like capital S's, she said. She used to call me Sus. Here," he said. "I'm going to leave a dollar for the waitress." He extracted the bill from his belt. "I'm going to keep the swan for myself. You're good with your hands. My ex-wife was good with her hands, too."

Now we know Gus's type: Irish-American vegetarians. Irish-American vege-tarians with small motor skills.

The old-fashioned phone at their table rang. Amy picked it up quickly. *It's going to be Dean. He followed me.*

"Hi. What do you think of me so far?" someone asked. It wasn't Dean.

"Well, I don't know," Amy said.

"You look a lot like my next girlfriend," the voice said.

"Who is this?" She looked around the bar to see who else was talking on their phones. It turned out a lot of people were.

"I'll meet you out on the dance floor. Then you'll see."

"I don't think so."

"Suit yourself. I just thought you might want to get away from that old fart."

Amy hung up.

"Who was that?" Gus asked her.

"Wrong number."

"Why don't we forget about getting another drink and get out of here. Unless you want to dance."

"No, I don't feel much like dancing tonight."

Gus looked relieved. "Let's go, then. I'll take you to see something interesting."

"What?"

"It's a surprise."

"I don't really like surprises all that much."

"This is one surprise I think you'll like." Gus stood up and looked around. "Crazy place, don't you think? Everybody phoning people they don't even know. What kind of people do that?"

"Crazy people, I guess." It occurred to her that Gus had practically done that when he called her.

"They should do well, then. Plenty of crazy people around. You run into all of them, sooner or later, on the subway," Gus said, and smiled his underground smile.

"There," Gus said, "my ex-wife designed that."

"Your wife designed the Boston Aquarium?"

"Not the aquarium. The seal tank."

"Oh. Are there seals in it?"

"During the day. They used to leave them out at night, but one of them

—Smokey was his name—just disappeared one night. I always wondered what happened to Smokey. Did someone grab him and take him home and keep him in a kiddy pool? And another one, Pierre, got sick and died. When they cut him open, they found ten dollars' worth of change inside of him."

"Ten dollars?"

"Ten dollars. Well, it probably wasn't exact change, but..."

Amy said, "In the San Diego Zoo, someone once threw marshmallows that were soaked with LSD to one of the polar bears."

"That's terrible. Were you there?"

"No," she admitted, "I've never been to San Diego. It *is* terrible but... you can't help wonder what polar bears hallucinate when they're tripping."

"I was at that zoo a couple of times when I was in the Navy. I wonder which one of the polar bears it happened to."

Looking at the seal-less tank, Amy shivered. Her feet were cold in her open-toed clogs. She could smell the harbor, only a few hundred yards off. It smelled like a cellar closet.

"It was nice when they were out at night," Gus said. "There weren't any tourists crowding around. When we'd first get down here, we'd just smell them, and the fish they ate, and hear them swimming around and around in the tank. And we'd hear them barking. You know seals sound a lot like dogs, the way they bark? And then we'd get closer and watch them swim. Seals, they're shaped like torpedoes. My wife used to say, whoever designed seals knew a thing or two about hydrodynamics."

I wouldn't mind being a seal. Not a seal in an aquarium. A freewheeling seal, out in the harbor.

"The kids used to love coming down here—Chewy, before he got too old, and Babette, and Brigid—well, she was too young to enjoy it, but I'm sure she would have. We'd stop at a fish market and buy some fresh fish and feed them. I suppose we shouldn't have, but hey, it's not like we threw spare change into their tank."

The harbor's probably too polluted to be fun for seals, though.

"Brigid died. I don't know if Chewy ever told you about that. It was that crib-death thing. One minute they're asleep, the next minute they're gone, bingo, just like that. What's the matter?"

Amy had been jumping up and down to stay warm. "Nothing. Just a little chilly. I guess it was more fun when the seals were out, huh?" Gus took a step closer to her. He seemed huge and dense and inert.

"You don't much like it, do you, Red?"

"My name's Amy."

"Amy, Red, what's the difference? You don't much like it."

"I like it fine." *What does he want from me?*

"But not the way *I* like it."

"Maybe not, but I think it's a fine seal tank. I can't imagine a better one." *I wish I could say something funny, something to make him lighten up. But what's funny about a seal tank? Especially one with no seals. What's funny about a dead daughter?*

"We'll go." His expression lacked all point or edge. "There's something else I want to show you, anyway."

"I don't know, Gus. I'm starting to get pretty tired. Besides, you make me nervous, the way you drive."

"It's just that I forget, sometimes, that I'm driving a car, not a train."

Dean would be happy if I got home early. But I don't know if I should be trying to make him happy right now. I ought to be seeing how much bad news he can take. Still, if I got home early, he might give me a massage. With one of those edible oils. Almond coconut. Or mint chocolate. Yum.

Gus said, "I won't forget, though, now that you've reminded me."

"There's something funny in the shrubbery," Amy said.

"You're not afraid, are you? There's nothing to be afraid of. I come here all the time."

"Yeah, but at night?"

"All the time."

Something rustled in the dead leaves again. "There *is* something over there. A cat."

"What, you're afraid of cats? No, it's not a cat, it's a possum."

She could see now that he was right. It *was* a possum. The possum was the color of tiles in a public restroom. It had a long snout and a mouth full of vicious-looking teeth. She'd never heard of people being chewed up or mauled by possums but still... those teeth.

"Possums like graveyards. Darned if I know why, but they do. I've seen my share of possums around here," Gus said. "Don't worry, though, they won't hurt you."

"Are they possums or opossums?" Amy asked him.

"I don't know. What's the difference?"

"Opossums are Irish," Amy said.

"Irish? But... oh, I see. I get it."

They were going to see the monument that marked where Brigid, Gus's daughter, lay buried. "It's not like these," he said contemptuously. "Not like these statues of Jesus and of sad angels with clasped hands and..."

"Angels with glass pants?"

"Not glass pants, clasped hands." Gus held his hands together to show her what he meant. "It's pretty unique—at least, *I* think it is. My ex-wife drew the plans for it, and I had it built. The graveyard people didn't want it here, but I said I'd take them to court. They don't much like innovation, graveyard people, but they like lawsuits even less."

A possum pair crossed the path in front of them. One seemed misshapen, but then she realized it was carrying half a dozen possum babies on its back. The possum mom turned and hissed at them. "Is it much farther?" she asked plaintively.

"Just over this hill. Come on." He tried to take her hand to hurry her along, but she wouldn't let him. She was walking slowly and gingerly, as if crossing a minefield.

A trio of turnip-colored possums crawled out from behind a statue of the Virgin Mary. *Enough!* She turned back the way they'd come. Gus was in such a rush that he didn't notice.

The clouds opened, and the graveyard was drenched in moonlight. It looked as though the moon would be full in a night or two.

The cemetery, Amy reasoned, was laid out in a way that gave the impression that it was larger than it actually was. The footpaths wound around like intestines, separated from themselves only by a few plots, a few trees, and lots of shrubbery. *So I think I can take a shortcut back to the parking lot by going through this hedge and going down into this little valley, and, oh my fucking God, where did all these fucking possums come from?*

There were an implausible number of possums milling about in the moonlight in this spooky little hollow. Possums were crawling over the raised surfaces of new graves and into the sunken surfaces of old ones. Possums scurried between the trees and scrambled amid the marble monuments. *I can't believe it, I can't believe all these fucking possums.*

She skirted Possum Hollow and regained a path on the other side when she heard something or someone moving in the leaf litter off to the right and a little behind her. She thought about what she'd do if someone jumped her and grabbed her from behind. She'd kick back at the attacker's kneecap, then bring down the heel of her clog, scraping down his shin, then come down with everything on the arch of his foot, crushing those little bones around the instep. Just the way Chewy had taught her. *And if one of my arms is free, I'll jab over my shoulder and poke him in the eye with a stiff thumb.*

The bushes moved again and yet another possum appeared. It was a mangy, one-eyed grandfather possum. "You old bastard," she yelled, and she stamped her foot. "Your buddies are all back that way!" She pointed with her thumb toward the possum jamboree.

She thought it interesting that the popular notion of how possums act when they are alarmed corresponded so neatly to the way this possum was behaving. This one was sprawled out in the fallen leaves as if it had been run over by an eighteen-wheeler. Its mouth was open and its lips were foamy. *Rabies?* Its eyes were glazed and it was producing a powerful, evil odor.

Who did I imagine might jump me? Gus? He wouldn't do that. Poor old Gus. Now Dean might. Dean might think it was hilarious to jump out and startle me while I was walking through a graveyard. No, actually, I doubt it. He wouldn't do that. I love you Dean. You hear that, sugar bear? Do you? I need my freedom, and you make me crazy, but I love you just the same.

She followed the meandering path and came out of the cemetery, but not at the place where they'd gone in. She crossed the street and walked on. From every living room she passed came the shifting blue-gray light of televisions.

There were signs on many of the lawns that said, NEIGHBORHOOD WATCH: WE'RE STOPPING CRIME! From what she could tell, the neighbors weren't watching anything but the eleven o'clock news. ROYCE STREET. FLINT STREET. LINSLADE COURT. BERKSHIRE AVENUE. *Who gets to give streets their names, anyway?*

And where the hell am I? Quincy? Braintree? Weymouth? All she knew was that they had driven one hell of a long way on I-93 from the waterfront where the aquarium stood. *Why didn't I pay any attention to where we were going?*

Ahead about five or six blocks, there was an island of light, a Sinclair station. *They'll have a phone, and a place to pee, and maybe even a coffee machine. It'll be warm.*

When she was still three blocks away, the lights at the station went off. When she arrived, there was still a skinny kid in there behind a counter using an adding machine. There was a throng of inflatable plastic dinosaurs sitting on the counter. *Jeremy would like one of those*, she thought. Amy rapped on the glass but he kid wouldn't open the door, and the phone was inside the station. The kid was looking at her as if he'd been held up by any number of shivering redheads in the past month.

Fucking kid, it's cold out here, and I don't know what to do. This is some first date.

Maybe he would at least call her a taxi. She dumped the contents of her purse out on the hood of a tow truck. She came up with sixty-five cents. That wouldn't buy her a taxi ride. Her last dollar had been folded into a swan. Then she thought about writing a note asking the kid to call Dean. Except what could Dean do? How could he get to her? *Right now, I wish he hadn't sold Cinnamon Girl. It might be a cold night for a ride on a motorcycle, but it would be better than being stranded out here in the boonies.*

She walked back toward the cemetery, thinking, *Now what?* The kid from the gas station drove past slowly, and then did a U-turn and came back for a second peep. She was alarmed, not for herself, but for the kid if he tried anything. She was ready. "Beat it, twerp!" She felt better after shouting at him.

I doubt if Dean would give me a massage, anyway. He's not going to be happy with me.

The kid was driving past again. "Go on, scumbag, get the fuck out of here. You don't know who the hell you're messing with!"

But it wasn't the kid this time, it was Gus. His rubbery, round face was pressed against the driver-side window and was looking at her as if wondering who she could possibly be. "Hello there, Gus," she said. "How 'bout a lift?"

When she'd climbed in, Gus told her about his visit to Brigid's grave. "The moon came out from behind the clouds while I was on the way there. And I played the video..."

"Video?"

"Uh-huh. Didn't I tell you? There's a video player built right into her tombstone. The screen is covered by a solar panel and when you lift up the panel, the video plays. It's a five-minute movie about Bridey from the moment she was born, right up until... you know. I wish you could have watched it with me. Where did you go off to?"

"I had some trouble with the possums."

"Oh. I was worried about you. I heard someone shouting once. Was that you?"

He looks like he's still worried about me.

"I'm sorry I punked out on you, Gus," Amy said, although she was glad she hadn't had to watch a five-minute film about a dead baby. "Your pants are wet. Did you slip in the grass?"

"After I watched the film, I was running around, trying to find you. I tripped over a tree root."

"Well, now what? Any more surprises?"

"I'm hungry. We could go down to Chinatown and get something to eat. They have some dishes you could eat—sweet-and-sour shrimp, things like that."

"I have to go to the bathroom someplace first," Amy said. "Why do you suppose Chinese restaurants are open so late?"

"Well, for one thing, they sell beer after all the other bars close. They call it cold tea. They put it in teapots, and you have to drink it out of little teacups."

"I thought maybe it was because they still go by China time. It's the middle of the day in China, right?"

"Yeah, China's on the other side of the Date Line," Gus said. "I crossed that a lot of times when I was in the Navy."

"What does it feel like?"

Gus said it didn't feel like much of anything. "Same for the Equator. But, you know, when you're in the Navy, and you cross the Equator the first time... they call you pollywogs. And the sailors who've crossed it before—they're called shellbacks—they make the pollywogs duckwalk around the ship, and they pour disgusting stuff all over you, and smack you with paddles. But only the first time. After that, you're a shellback, too."

"Sounds like a fraternity," Amy said. "Do you know of any Chinese restaurants that have pinball machines?"

"Uh, I don't think so. I don't think I've ever seen a pinball machine in a Chinese restaurant."

"Hmm. Me neither, come to think of it. I just really enjoy playing pinball."

"Let's forget about Chinese. I know this place called Jimmy's in South Boston. They have a whole room full of pinball machines in back. And some pretty good fish sandwiches. How long have you been playing pinball?"

"Just a few months. Your son's been teaching me."

"Well, I taught Chewy, a long time ago."

"You must be good, then."

"Pretty good, but he's gotten better than me. What about you? I'll bet if Chewy's been giving you lessons, you must be hot, huh?"

There was, for the moment, pact between them.

THE TURK

IF YOU SAY CHECK, YOU MUST MEAN YOUR OIL.
IF YOU SAY CHARGE, YOU MUST MEAN YOUR BATTERY.

THAT'S WHAT THE SIGN IN THE GAS STATION SAID.

Ross had gone in to get keys to the restrooms. He came out with only one. Someone had driven off with the other years ago. He gave the surviving key to Amy. It was attached by a chain to a horseshoe so that no one would drive off with this one. "The ladies' room is co-ed these days," he told her.

Dean muttered, "Oh ye of little bladders." This was the second time they'd made a bathroom stop. They'd also stopped once so that Maud could pee. And once so that Amy could buy maple syrup.

"It's nasty in there," Amy came out saying. "Really nasty. And the light doesn't work."

Ross took a deep breath and plunged in. The darkness was absolute. He aimed by dead reckoning and was cheered by the sound of liquid against liquid. Two thirds of the way through, he ran out of air. He tried breathing through his mouth, but the smell was so thick, so noisome that he could taste it. Then the door wouldn't open. Maybe the other key hadn't been stolen at all. Maybe a traveler had fainted from the fumes and was entombed next door along with the key to the inaccessible men's room.

Ross threw his weight against the door and burst out into the light. "Your right, it is bad in there," he said to Amy. "Worse than your kitchen."

"My kitchen isn't always that bad," Amy said. "At least you didn't have to sit down."

Thea said that she'd wait and go later. Dean groaned, anticipating another stop.

They got back in the truck, Lizard's truck, and Dean started the engine. "Look at those gas pumps," Dean said. The pumps in front of the station were cylinders with glass globes on top. The globes looked like a 1950s concept of space helmets. "Vermonters sure love anachronisms."

"Not all of them do, I bet," Amy said.

"Why do you have to contradict everything I say?"

"I don't. But you're always telling *me* not to speak in generalities. You're always saying, 'All generalities are false.'"

"Including that one. Ross, did you ask in there how to get to the Round Barn?"

"They were pretty vague," Ross said. "In fact, they seemed almost hostile. We'll have to go by those directions you got over the phone."

"Those were pretty vague, too," Dean said.

Ross wrote down the price of gas in a little notebook for expenses. "Their pumps may be old-fashioned, but their prices are smack up to date."

There had been a sign for the Round Barn Restaurant out on the highway, but it looked as if someone had written graffiti on it and then taken a chainsaw to it. They almost missed the turnoff. The gravel road led them through a patch of woods and a pasture and then past a distant pond.

"I thought you said we'd see some beautiful foliage," Amy said.

Dean said, "We would have if we'd made it up here when we were supposed to, back in October. But..."

"Yes, I know—things are just creeping along at the restaurant. What else is new?"

They came to a parking lot between an old farmhouse and a substantial round barn made of gray stone. There were plastic blisters on top of the barn where skylights had been let in the roof. "I thought it was going to be hokier," Ross said. "That's one hell of a barn."

"That shows you how important names are. You thought it would be hokey because of the name. It made you think of Red Barn, which is a pretty cheesy restaurant chain. Although their Barney Burger isn't bad."

"Why is it round?" Amy asked.

"The Barney Burger?"

"The barn."

"Oh. Because round barns stood up better to storms. And they cost less to build. And because people thought the devil could hide in corners, so..."

"Oh, come on!"

"It's true. Look it up next time you're in the BPL," Dean said.

A sign on the front door said SORRY, WE'RE CLOSED, but the door wasn't locked. They stood in the foyer by an oaken host stand that looked like a pulpit in a church. There was a leather-bound reservation book there. "They must have closed back in September," Dean said, looking at the last entries.

They entered the dining area. Six columns of dusty light, pouring in from the skylights, seemed to be holding up the roof of the barn. The smell of the interior was complex. The top note was woodsmoke. The heart notes were the smell of cooking mixed with the smell of furniture polish and gasoline. The bass note was the smell of cow manure.

There were tables scattered around the main level, some of them in the wedge-shaped livestock pens up against the round walls. There were tables up on platforms and tables down in pits. There were tables on three ascending balconies. "There's someone up there," Thea said. She pointed at an arm that was dangling off the highest balcony. It was as big around as a telephone pole.

Dean led them back to the kitchen.

"Shouldn't we talk to someone first?" Thea asked.

"We're just going to take a quick look at the merchandise," Dean said, "God, but it's a big mother." He was talking about the cookline. He got a measuring tape and a legal pad out of his briefcase. There was a sketch of their own kitchen on the pad. "Look, Ross, if we put the dishwasher here, and the counter over there—good thing Lizard hasn't gotten around to putting that in yet—then I think we can shoehorn this cookline in right here, don't you? Looks like it's in cherry condition, too." He looked at the dishwasher. "Why don't we put the Hobart through its paces and see what this mother can do?" He tried to turn the dishwasher on.

Ross noticed that Thea was not with them anymore.

"What's this thing?" Amy asked, holding up an attachment for a big commercial mixer.

Dean glanced up. He was trying to figure out why the dishwasher wasn't starting up. "It's a marital aid," he said. "Can't you tell? Hey, Ross, see if this thing is plugged in."

"Yeah, it is. Where'd Thea go?"

"She left, I guess," Amy said. "She was getting nervous, being back here. I am, too. Maybe she went back to the truck."

"Or maybe she's looking for a bathroom," Dean said. "Hey, Ross, see if you can find a light switch, will you?"

~

The truck was empty except for Maud. There was now a car in the parking lot, though, a station wagon that had THE ROUND BARN logo painted on the door. Ross knocked on the door of the farmhouse several times. When he got tired of knocking, he sat in the sun on a front-porch swing for a while, then he went around back, where there was a greenhouse. He heard voices coming from back there. And music. Abba, singing about money.

"How far were you dilated then?" he heard Thea ask.

"I was only at around two centimeters. Not far enough. I was standing by the fridge when my water broke. I asked one of the kids to get me some ice chips, and he slipped in my water and almost broke his neck. After my water broke, I stopped. For no reason at all, I just stopped. And then, after I'd been in labor all night and most of the next morning, the midwife gave me castor oil mixed in orange juice. That's a folk-medicine thing, that castor oil can speed your delivery. She was a sweetheart, my midwife was, but she wasn't all that bright. All the castor oil did was give me the runs. Really bad. After that, the kids decided I needed to go to a hospital whether I wanted to or not." The woman Thea was talking to had a sweet, tinkling voice. It was like listening to wind chimes reciting poetry, even though she was talking about diarrhea.

Ross heard Thea say, "Sometimes castor oil can help, if you're ready— but if you're not... it can actually hurt your baby. Going to the hospital was probably a good idea at that point."

"Well, at the time, I didn't think so. I'd been so sure of delivering at home that I had a hard time letting go of the idea. I had everything just the way I wanted. I had good music—I'd decided the first music Joe ever heard should be Sibelius. I had good people around, all the kids, and there was a fire in the fireplace, and candles. I wanted Joe to think that the world was a pretty swell place to be born into. And I was dreading what would happen if I went into some small-town hospital. Caesarian city. And I was right, that was exactly what happened. The doctor made me feel like I'd be killing my baby and maybe myself if I tried to have a vaginal birth."

Thea said, "I understand. A lot of doctors don't know how to talk to people very well. In fact, I think a lot of them don't even *like* people. When I was in medical school, we'd make rounds with the doctors sometimes. There was one old doctor who would talk about patients as if they weren't there. We'd all be crowded into this poor patient's room, and he'd say things like, 'Now this is an interesting case. Unfortunately, he won't be around much longer, but...'"

"Oh, dear God! Well, when the kids took me to the hospital, the doctor... he wasn't that old but he had old ideas. In his way, he was a real dinosaur. I still think... oh, hello there..." she said to Ross, who had gotten tired of eavesdropping and had come into the greenhouse. Both Thea and Irene were on their knees on the hard dirt floor of the greenhouse, their backs arched, their hands on their heels, their breasts pointed at the sky. "Are you the one I talked to on the phone?"

"That was my partner, Dean."

"Oh well, he sounded like a nice person, as I'm sure you are too. I'm Irene. Your friend here has been teaching me some yoga poses. I'm in ruins after having Joe, but I never could get interested in exercises like sit-ups and so on. Thea just taught me how to do the Salute to the Sun, and... what did you say this one was called?"

"The Camel Pose," Thea said. "It's supposed to open your heart chakra. That's what my yoga teacher said."

"Yes, of course. The Camel Pose." She asked Ross, "Do you want some sun tea?"

Irene was a small woman. Her hair was pulled back into a French braid that fell halfway down her back. It was entirely gray, the color of the stones of her barn, but her face was like a child's face.

Ross sat on a wooden bench. "We were just in the barn, in the kitchen. We couldn't get the dishwasher to work."

"That's because Yankee Electric cut off our power a few days ago. Are you going to buy it? I hope so."

"Probably. We'll probably buy quite a few things. Your prices are... well, they're pretty reasonable."

"Are they? You know, I can't even remember what we paid for most of that stuff. I suppose we should have looked for used things, like you're doing, but we bought everything new. Everything but the host stand—that we got from a church down in Stockbridge. My husband would know what all those things are worth, but he never comes near this place, not anymore. My husband doesn't like anything that doesn't make it. He thinks failure is contagious, I guess, so he stays in New York."

Irene got Maud water and Amy and Dean sun tea when they showed up at the greenhouse. "You can just about taste the sunshine in it." She poured the weak-looking tea into tall, thin glasses. "And it didn't take any power. Yankee Energy uses nuclear, you know."

"I noticed your power was out," Dean said. "We couldn't see if everything works, like the dishwasher or the ice machine or..."

"Oh, everything works. Believe me."

There was something about Irene that made one want to believe.

"I didn't see those water glasses and bar glasses we talked about on the phone," Dean said.

"A nice man who's opening a Chinese restaurant in Brattleboro, a Mr. Chang, he came up yesterday and bought some things. Do you need silverware? Flatware?"

Dean told her they were buying their plates from Mexico and inheriting their cutlery from Spiro's Super Sub Shop.

"Mr. Chang may have bought the silverware anyway. How about a microwave oven?"

"You don't want one of those," Amy said. "Microwaves aren't good for you. They mess with your blood cells."

"They do? I didn't know that," Irene said. "I'll have the kids throw it in the pond then."

"Don't do that," Dean said, "We'll give you thirty-five dollars, considering it's unsafe."

"But now I don't want to sell it. How about candles? I have boxes and boxes."

"You can't have real candles in restaurants in Boston. Because of a fire years ago," Ross said.

"The Coconut Grove fire," Dean said.

"No candles?" Irene said. "How sad for Boston. I guess that's okay, though. We need candles around here in the evening."

They discussed the cookline and the dishwasher, stockpots and sauté pans, meat cleavers, barstools, a deep fryer, a coffeemaker, a cash register, the vacuum cleaner, a couple of lowboy refrigerators, the host stand, and the huge supply of swizzle sticks that Irene had on hand. Dean made an offer for the whole package. Ross thought he was being facetious, but Irene said, "That sounds fair to me. Make the check out to Irene Pearlmutter. That's P-e-a-r-l-mutter, not P-e-r-l-mutter."

Dean looked surprised but whipped out the checkbook. Ross wrote down the figure in his notebook.

Then Dean asked Irene if he could make use of the pond on her property.

"How do you mean, make use of? You don't mean swim in it, do you? There are leeches in there. Besides, the water's icy."

"No, no, I'm just going to take a few photos."

"Oh, sure, take all the pictures you like. Too bad you missed the Canadian geese. They stopped by the pond last month. Geese are very photogenic, don't you think?"

"That wasn't much money for all that stuff," Ross said. He wouldn't have said anything if Dean had still been there, but Dean and Amy were on their way down to the pond.

"Do you have much?" Irene asked him.

"No, not really."

"Then it's all right. I didn't even count on getting that much. It's a good feeling, isn't it, starting something new? A beginning is always better than an ending. Although endings... endings have their own sweet charm."

Thea was examining the plants in the greenhouse. They didn't look healthy. "There's nothing you can do for those, dear," Irene said. "It's too cold in here for them at night. You can see your breath. Hey, do you want some plants? Everybody has plants in their restaurants these days."

Thea was looking at him. Her look said that she wanted him to buy the plants, to rescue them. "I'll have to ask Dean how much we can spend on plants. Dean doesn't like plants much, so we weren't planning..."

"No, I want you to just take them. Before they all die."

"We could take a few, I guess. I have a feeling that there won't be a whole lot of room in the truck."

"You can have some of these herbs, too—you'll need fresh cilantro if you're going to be cooking Mexican food, I think."

"I suppose so. I'm not a big fan of cilantro—tastes like dish soap to me. Like metal shavings soaked in dish soap. Can I ask you something, Irene? Why did you close? Not enough business?"

"Oh, we did all right—at first. We were only open about eight months a year because the barn costs so much to heat, but we did okay. There's some summer stock close by, and people would come by after the plays. And in the fall, lots of leaf-peepers would drop in for dinner. We were getting by.

But the locals, they didn't like us, and they did things, different things, to make it hard on us."

Joe, the baby, woke up and started to cry, and Thea lifted him out of his bassinet. The bassinet was dangling from a macramé plant hanger. Joe pawed at the buttons on Thea's blouse. "He wants to nurse you," Irene said. "A boob's a boob to Joe."

"I'd better give him to you, then."

"You can try it. Before I got pregnant, I tried it out with a friend's baby, just to see what it's like. It's quite pleasant, actually."

Thea smiled. "He wouldn't get what he wants."

"I think it's being close to someone that he likes as much as anything. Go ahead, Joe won't starve. You can see what a little fatso he is."

"Oh, thanks, but that's all right," Thea said, handing Irene her child.

Ross had been hoping...

Amy said: "If hair didn't turn gray because you were getting older, if it was a color you were born with, like blonde or red, then Irene would have beautiful hair, don't you think?"

"I don't like gray hair," Dean said.

"Too bad, 'cause you're getting a few."

"Shut up, I am not."

"What are these for?" she asked him. They were walking over a grate of metal pipes set in the road where the road went through a fence.

"It's a cattle guard. When this was a working farm, it kept the cows from wandering off—and you didn't have to get out of your truck to open and close a gate."

"*This* kept in cattle? I don't believe it."

"Nonetheless, it's true. Look—it works for dogs, too."

"Come on, Maud sweetie." But Maud didn't want to. Amy had to go back and carry her over the pipes.

"There, you see? Believe me now? It's sort of like a ha-ha."

"A ha-ha?"

"That's right, a ha-ha. That's what they used to use on estates in England. For a while, it was fashionable to have the parks on those estates come right up to the stately mansions. But they didn't want sheep wandering into the drawing room, naturally, so they built ha-ha's. They could have built walls, but those would have blocked the view. Ha-ha's were basically just trenches with stone walls down inside them. They called them ha-ha's, see, because the dukes or other honchos that owned estates would have guests come out for weekend soirees, and these guests would be strolling around the grounds, admiring the topiary or something, and sometimes they'd fall into the ditches. And of course, the duke would say, 'Ha-...' Goddamn it, why did you hit me?"

"Oh, Dean, I'm sorry. I only meant to give you a little tap on the nose. It was my ring; my ring did it. Poor thing—your lip's bleeding. Here, I'll kiss it."

Dean was staring at the blood on his fingers, flabbergasted. "Your ring! You sure you weren't wearing brass knuckles?"

Don't laugh, Amy told herself. *Whatever you do, don't laugh.*

"You got my blood on your collar," he said to her, after she'd kissed him.

"That's okay. I love you Dean, you little pumpkin." She gave him a tissue from her purse. "Here, I'll carry the raft. I can't believe my ring did so much damage. I really am sorry. It's just that sometimes your little stories, sometimes they seem so, I don't know, so inappropriate. I mean, ha-ha's? You know, I used to think that if there was anything I ever wanted to know, I could just ask you."

"You don't think that anymore, I take it." Dean was trying to staunch the flow of blood from his lip.

"No. For one thing, I realized you don't know everything. Just things that amuse you. For another thing, you won't always be around to ask."

"I'm not going anywhere."

"I am, though."

"I don't want to talk about that," said Dean.

"Fine, me neither. Let's just enjoy the walk. Isn't the foliage beautiful?"

"There hardly is any foliage. The trees are almost bare."

"I'm kidding, Dean."

"So you figure you'll buy a set of *Encyclopedia Britannica* and strike out on your own?"

"Just this minute you said you didn't want to talk about it."

"I only want to know what you've got in mind. I deserve that much, don't I?"

"I've told you lots of times what I have in mind. You don't pay attention."

"That's because I don't accept it. Listen," he said. They turned off the road and took the path that led to the pond. "I've got a plan. An amazing, marvelous plan. Let's get married, and then..."

"Married? Are you crazy? Come *on*, Dean. I can't believe that's you saying this. Married! 'Marriage is an institution—to be married is to be institutionalized.' Whenever I used to even mention getting married, that's what you'd always say."

"Just listen, don't interrupt, I'm explaining the plan. Okay, now, say we get married. Right after the honeymoon..."

"Where would we go on our honeymoon?"

"How should I know? Would you just listen?"

"Okay, but I'm not going anywhere corny, like Disneyland. Maybe Paris. Or Bali. Bali sounds like a good place for a honeymoon. Or no, wait... Japan! We could stay at a ryokan up in the mountains. That would be soooo Japanesey."

"We can go to the far-flung Islets of Langerhans for all I care. Okay, so after we get back from our honeymoon, we go our separate ways. Then, at the end of a certain period, a year, say, we get back together for the rest of our lives."

"Why do we have to get married to do that? Why can't we just do it?"

"Getting married makes it a formal contract, a commitment. It ups the stakes."

Amy thought about it for a few minutes. She and Dean got along well enough, usually. He tolerated her idiosyncrasies and she tolerated his, although she had to tolerate a lot more than he did. "I've got to hand it to you, Dean, that's an interesting plan. I almost feel like saying, 'Okay, great, let's get married.' It would be fun, and we could have a big party. But I'm not going to."

"We could throw a *monster* party. We could have it at the restaurant, and..."

"I'm not going to because that limitation would still be there. A year seems like a long time..."

"Make it two then."

"But that's still a limitation. We'd only temporarily be split up, and that's not what I want. I want to be unconditionally on my own and then, if we do get back together in a year or two, fine. But we can't force it."

"That's what you think, huh?"

"That's what I think. But there's no reason why it has to be antagonistic. Our separating, I mean. We can be respectful to each other, and open with each other, and..."

"As long as we're being open with each other, tell me what happened Saturday night."

"What happened Saturday night is none of your business, gumdrops."

"That doesn't sound very respectful. You could have called and told me you were going to be late. You didn't get home until almost three in the morning."

"I didn't want to. It would have interrupted the flow of the evening."

"So how did the evening flow? Did your subway driver show you a good time?"

"You won't let that go, will you? You're worrying it like Maud with a bone. All right, I'll tell you what happened. We played pinball."

"Yeah, I'm sure you did. You know, it was Saturday night—Sunday morning really—when you had that screaming nightmare."

"Was it?" *God, what if I'm sleeping next to someone I don't know that well and I have one of those nightmares? That could scare the hell out someone.* She had one of those every month or two.

"Maybe it was because you felt guilty."

"Maybe it was because I feel trapped. Why should I feel guilty? I'm not doing anything wrong."

"Then why are you having nightmares?"

"You think, just because you feel guilty all the time, everyone else does. Listen, Dean, I want you to smile."

"To what?"

"To smile. You know what smiling is, right?"

"My lip hurts too much to smile."

"Come on, you can manage a smile. It's a sunny day, you just bought all that restaurant stuff at Filene Basement prices, and I've said I'm going to pose for you again. So smile, won't you?"

Dean's smile was brief and ghastly. The blood on his lips didn't help.

"There's something wrong with you, Dean, something seriously wrong with you if that's the best smile you can manage."

"Come on, let's run," Thea said. Thea took his hand and they ran through a field of gray boulders. The boulders looked like stunned sheep. Ross eventually stopped running because he got a stitch in his side. Also, he felt a little ridiculous.

"God, it feels good to be out of the city," Thea said. She was breathing hard from the run. "Do you know this is the first time I've been out of Boston since I got here? Look at those mountains!"

"They're not that big compared to the ones in Colorado."

"They're huge compared to the ones in Holland—since there aren't any mountains in Holland. You know, this is my favorite time of day. Everything looks so soft when the light's like this. It's like everything is melting."

"Photographers call it the golden hour. Dean likes to shoot at this time of day." Ross kissed Thea on the back of her neck. "You taste salty."

"That's from running. And from the yoga."

"You're a salty dog."

"I didn't know Amy was going to bring her dog," Thea said. "or I would have brought Vervloekt. He'd love it here."

"You still haven't told me," Ross said. "Are you going to take the job?"

"I don't know yet. My father always told me, never make promises unless you're sure you can keep them. I wish we'd seen the Canadian geese."

"It's actually Canada."

"What is Canada?"

"Their real name is Canada geese, not Canadian geese. You know, I remember my father telling me that, back in the 1950s, radar operators saw a huge flock of Canada geese on their screens, and they thought they were Russian missiles. The Air Force went on Red Alert and everything. Geese almost touched off World War III."

"I don't care. I still wish we'd seen them."

They came down to the pond. "Watch your step," Ross said to Thea. "The geese may be gone, but they've left plenty of mementos behind."

The raft was lying on the bank like an orange plastic puddle. Dean was swearing. "Goddamn them."

"Goddamn who?" Ross asked him. "The geese?"

"Goddamn the Mad Mountain Outdoor Equipment Company, and fuck anyone who ever worked there, and super fuck anyone who was friends with someone who worked there. This raft won't inflate."

"We could hold it under water," Ross said, "and find out where the leaks are."

"You can see the holes," Thea said. "Here, and here, and..."

"Maudie was kind of playing with it the other day," Amy said. "I didn't think she'd hurt it, though."

"That dog should be shot at dawn," Dean said.

"Dean! Don't you dare say that! She can understand you."

Maud looked up at Dean. She didn't appear alarmed.

"What happened to your lip, Dean?" Thea asked him.

"I belted him one in the mouth," Amy said, "because I knew he was going to say something mean to Maud."

There was a dull, booming roar, as if a flight of heavy bombers were coming in at treetop level. "What's that?" Amy asked.

"Bikes," Dean said. "Big ones."

"Sounds like they went right up to the restaurant," Amy said.

"Nah, they're out on the highway."

"You wouldn't think Vermont would have motorcycle gangs," Amy said. "It seems so civilized. And so tidy."

"There's a little boat over there," Thea said, and pointed. "Can you use that?"

"It's full of water. It'll sink," Amy said.

"That's just rainwater. Ross, give me a hand, huh?"

Together they wrestled the old rowboat over on its side and dumped the water. Ross got his pant leg

soaked with scummy water. They hauled it to the bank, and Dean almost lost a shoe to the mud. They pushed it into the pond.

"Well, this isn't what I had in mind, but at least it floats. I like the form better, anyway. Go ahead and take your clothes off and get in the boat."

"Can't I leave my clothes on for this one? It's pretty cold."

"Don't be ridiculous. Come on, before we lose the light."

"Not unless you take off your clothes too."

"Me? What good would that do? I have to concentrate on taking the photo."

"I think it would help you relate to your subject. You feel what I feel."

"That's just silly. Besides, women have an extra layer of fat under their skin that keeps them warmer than men."

"I think that's a myth, Dean," Thea said.

"Made up by a man, no doubt," Amy said. "Come on, sweetcakes, let's get undressed." Amy unzipped her jeans.

"Ross, would you mind turning the other way?"

"For God's sake, Dean, your apartment is plastered with pictures of Amy."

"Yeah, well, that's finished product. This is raw material."

"Look, I've got goose bumps," Amy said.

"What are goose bumps?" Thea asked. "Oh, I see. *Kippenvel*."

"Wow," Ross said, "Those are some wicked kipperfelt," Ross said.

"*Kippenvel*," Thea corrected him.

"I wonder if they're Canada goose bumps."

"Ross, now come on, turn around," Dean said.

"She *said* to look."

Amy hung her pants from a pine branch and pulled her sweater over her head. "Dean, if you don't drop trou, I'm not going any further."

"Thea, would you turn around, too?" Dean threw most of his clothes off. "Here are your wings." He handed Amy a pair of wings made of blue gauze on a silver frame. There were little silvery stars glittering in the gauze.

"Where did you get the wings?" Thea asked.

"My friend Chewy made them," Amy said. "Chewy is good with his hands. He gets that from his mother. The wings were part of his Halloween costume last year. You should have seen what Dean wore to that party. He couldn't think of anything else, so he tore the stuffing out of an old sofa and pasted it all over his body, and he went as mildew."

"I used the wrong kind of glue, though," Dean said. "I had little bits of cotton batting stuck in my chest hair for weeks."

Amy asked how she was supposed to get aboard the rowboat. The bank was steep and muddy.

"Jump," Dean suggested.

She looked at Dean as if he were speaking a language she didn't know.

"Go on, jump, you can make it." Sighing, Amy closed her eyes and jumped into the boat. It skimmed toward the center of the pond, taking on an inch of water. "Use that little paddle that came with the raft."

"I think I left it ashore. No, here it is. What do I do with it?"

"Paddle."

"The seat's all slimy. It feels horrible."

Dean knelt down on one knee. "Don't worry about that. I can't see your butt, so I need you to sit up on the back of the boat, not on the seat. Careful, don't fall in. Okay, now look over to the left. That's good. That's very good. Look at the tops of trees over there. Semi-smile. Lean forward a little. Perfect."

"This is the last time, Dean, the very last."

"You don't know what you're saying. Okay, this is it. 'The moment of decision,' as Cartier-Bresson puts it. Can you straighten up the boat a little?"

"Paddle to the right. That'll turn you to your left," someone said.

"Who said that?" Dean wanted to know. He didn't look up from his camera.

"Uh, Dean, we have company," Ross said.

Dean took his picture. "Company? Company? What kind of company?" Through his lens, Dean saw a foreshortened arm reach in front of him, and the camera was snatched away from his eye.

"Do you mind if I take a look?"

"Who are you?"

"I'm the Turk." The Turk was an anguished-looking individual wearing earrings made from dimes. He had a set of spectacular tattoos, long, stringy hair with a bald patch on top, and a beard that was braided on one side. He was large but not overweight. "Hey, that's gonna be an all-right picture. You didn't center her in the shot, did you? You know about the rule of thirds, right?"

"Of course I know about the rule of thirds," Dean said. He remembered someone talking about that in a photography class he'd taken at the Free University, but he didn't remember exactly what it was. He considered himself more of an intuitive photographer than one who followed rules, including the rule of thirds.

"I wish I had my camera with me," the Turk said. "That's gonna be a fine photo. Maybe you should take a couple more, just to make sure you got it. That's what they always tell you, isn't it? The more you shoot, the better your chances of getting a great photo."

Dean stood up. "Amy, cover yourself."

Amy didn't have much to cover herself with. Her wings were nearly transparent. "Hi," she said to the Turk. "Where'd you come from?"

"Irene sent me down to invite you to dinner. They're making it now." He asked Dean, "You want to get out on the boat, and I'll take a photo of you both?"

"No, no, that's all right." Dean seemed to suddenly realize he wasn't wearing anything but his boxers.

"Can Thea and I turn around now?" asked Ross.

Amy zigzagged back to shore while Dean hurried into his clothes. She tried to clamber up the bank, but the mud was like jellied consommé and her feet slipped. She grabbed a root, but the root snapped off and she found herself sitting in six inches of water. "Oh, *fuck* that's cold!" Dean helped her up the bank before the Turk could and stood in front of her while she put her panties on. "Oh my God, there's a leech on my leg!"

"Let me see," said the Turk. "There are lots of leeches in this pond." He took her ankle and examined the inside of her calf. An amber triangle of sopping pubic hair was showing through her panties. Her skin was covered with wicked goose bumps, and her wings flapped feebly.

Dean snatched Amy's ankle away from the Turk and almost spilled her back into the muck. "Thea, what do you know about leeches?"

"Umm, I must have dropped out of medical school before we got to leeches."

"Don't you put lighter fluid on them?" Ross asked. "That's what we used to do with ticks."

"How about gasoline? I could syphon some from the bike," the Turk offered.

Then Thea said, "I think I'd just grab it and pull it off."

"Right. That's what Rose did for Charlie in *The African Queen*," Dean said. "Well, here goes."

"Hey, wait," Amy said. "It's not a leech after all. It's just a blob of mud."

16

COOL BREEZE CHARLIE

"Look at that sky," Thea said. The sun was setting flamboyantly, and the clouds in the west had turned purple and gold. The light seemed to have congealed.

"Purple and gold," Dean said. "Those were my high school colors. Go Bulldogs."

Ross was looking at Thea's hair. The light of the setting sun was playing there, highlighting gold strands in her light-brown hair. Her hair seemed as fine as corn silk.

"Are you cold?" the Turk asked Amy. Amy was still shivering from her dunk in the pond. She nodded. "Let's go in the barn, then."

"We still have to load the truck," Ross said.

The Turk told them that the truck had already been loaded.

Dean looked at line of motorcycles in the parking lot. "I used to have a bike myself," he said, "not that long ago."

"It was red," Amy said. "He named it Cinnamon Girl."

"He still has the leather jacket," Ross said.

"Let's go inside," the Turk said.

Inside the barn, candles had been lit. The silo in the center of the barn had been modified into a fireplace, and a fire had been laid there. Men with orange-lit faces were putting chunks of meat on a grate over the fire. Other men were sitting at tables drinking beer or wine. There was a lot of smoke and more shadow than light.

There was a round of introductions. They met Rudy, Lucky Jack, Erik the Red, the Good Time Bomber, Roach, the Wild Yak, Duffy, Popeye, Tank, Pinko, Dirty Ernie, Wino, and the Iceman. Then they met Molly, Measle, Raisin, Denim, Rita, Rain, and Emma. The Turk also alluded to Big George, who was lying way up on the third balcony. They'd seen his meaty arm hanging down when they'd come into the barn before. He was still sleeping. Or passed out. Or dead.

The Turk led them to a table on the first balcony, overlooking the fireplace. "Customers used to ask for this. It's the primo table," the Turk said.

"What's for dinner?" Amy asked.

"Whatever was left in the freezer when the power went out a couple of days ago," the Turk said. "We can find you a nice filet. Won't be long, all that meat's gonna get raunchy."

The Good Time Bomber—or maybe it was the Wild Yak—brought them steaks. Amy took a plate when it was offered to her. It seemed easier than explaining.

"Why'd you take that steak?" Dean asked her. "You're not going to eat it, are you?"

"Be quiet, Dean," Amy said. "You know I'm not."

The Turk had overheard. "You don't like filets?"

Amy told him about her vegetarianism. She ate fish sometimes, she told him, but rarely, and never red meat.

"I bet we can find something for you," he said, "Come with me to the kitchen."

Irene and Molly were in the kitchen. Irene had been changing Joe's diaper by lantern light. "There you go, boyo. All dry again."

"Not for long," Molly said.

The Turk shone a flashlight down into the freezer. Soggy white packages were floating in the water. "I thought I saw a package of asparagus in here. I guess not." He went to a cupboard and got down a #10 size can of baby peas. "You like peas?"

"I'd turn green if I ate that many peas. Don't worry about me. I'm not that hungry, anyway," she said, although she was.

"Hey, I know something you might like." He got a cheesecake from the top of a cupboard. "I have to keep this hidden, or some scroungy mother will come along and scarf it all up in one sitting. Where are the knives and forks?" he asked Irene.

"I think I sold them."

"Well, here." He tore off a chunk and handed it to Amy. "I heard that, in Europe, people eat their desserts before they have dinner."

"Mmm, s'rich," Amy said, her mouth full of cheesecake.

"The Turk made it," Irene said. "He was a chef. Most of the kids worked here."

"I got the recipe from a box of cream cheese. It's supposed to be served with a cherry sauce, but that's all gone," the Turk said. "Tell me, those photos you were taking today, were they some kind of advertisement? For your restaurant?"

"It's not my restaurant. It's Dean and Ross's. And no, it wasn't an advertisement, exactly."

"It was like art, then?"

"You could call it art," Amy said.

"The Turk's an artist too," Irene said. Molly snickered. "He is," Irene insisted.

"I'm not really an artist." He managed to get a deprecating shrug into his voice. "I do a little photography now and then. But mostly I do tattoos."

"Tattoos?"

"Yeah, back when I lived in Tulsa, I had a shop there. Well, actually, it was just the back of Sherry Lynn's beauty parlor—Sherry Lynn was my ol' lady back then. See, tattoos, they're like bikes, in a way. You get tired of the way other people screw up a job, so after a while, you figure out how to do the work yourself. Look at this dragon here." He rolled up his sleeve. "I got that at a swap meet. That's where you get the world's worst tattoos, at swap meets. I touched this up later myself, but you can still see what a wimpy dragon it was."

It looked to Amy like a kid's drawing of a dragon. Jeremy could have drawn a better dragon. "Your first customers must have been pretty brave," Amy said.

"My first customer was Chopper—Chopper was Sherry Lynn's cocker spaniel. I did a skull and crossbones on his tummy. After that, I did a few prospects..."

"Prospects?"

"Prospects are like pledges in a fraternity. Or a sorority," Molly said.

"Molly went to Dartmouth," Irene said.

"Oh yeah, I went there for like two weeks," Molly said. "Some college girl I was."

"I could do one for you," the Turk told Amy. "I've got my needles. Just a little feminine kind of tattoo. Like a rose. Or, I know, a butterfly. I could do a good blue morphine."

"Morpho," Amy said. She thought of the parrot that Laurel had tattooed on the side of her left breast. Amy had never actually seen it, but Ross had told her about it, and it intrigued her. "A friend of mine has a tropical bird tattoo."

"I could do that. Piece of pie."

"Piece of cake," Molly corrected him.

"Shut up, Molly," the Turk told her.

Amy didn't want to copy Laurel, though. Maybe a ladybug. Or a turtle. Amy liked turtles.

"The Turk gave me a tattoo," Irene said. "He's very good."

"I'll have to think about it," Amy said.

"You can't think about something like that," Irene said. "You just have to do it. Go with the flow."

"Aren't your needles electric?" Molly asked. "How're you going to work them with no electricity?"

"Shit, I forgot about that. Well, we could go somewhere where they have electricity. A bar. Or a motel."

"Some other time, maybe," Amy said.

"Well, okay, but I don't know how much longer I'll be around," the Turk said. "I'm going up to Alaska to work on that pipeline thing."

"I think they finished that," Amy said. Molly snickered again.

"Well, if they have, I'll do something else. Work on a fishing boat, maybe. They always need people on fishing boats, I hear. I just know that, soon, it's gonna be time to go. The good Lord, He got me out of Tulsa just in time. It was like He shook me awake one morning and said, get out of town now, Turk, before the shit hits the fan. When the good Lord tells you it's time to move on, you'd be crazy not to listen, wouldn't you?"

Molly asked, "Did the good Lord give you those hot credit cards?"

"Shut up, Molly," the Turk said. He said to Amy, "Hey, you want to go for a little putt? We could go up to the Gap. You can see the lights of New York from there."

"He means the state, not the city," Molly said.

"You *should* go," Irene said. "There's nothing like a night ride."

"I'd like to, but Dean and Ross might want to leave soon."

"It doesn't take long to get to the Gap," Irene said. "Don't worry, I'll tell them where you went. Molly, go get Amy a dome and some leathers."

"I will if I don't have to do dishes again tonight," Molly said.

"Just do what Irene said," the Turk told her. "Move."

~

"What do we do," Dean asked, "if these guys get so bored they turn violent?"

Ross looked around. No one in the barn looked especially violent at the moment. They looked as placid as milkmen. "I think we're safe for the time being."

"I don't think they'd do anything with Irene here," Thea said.

"See, these guys can be peaceful one moment and turn into savages the next. They're nihilists, and don't forget it. Not that I have anything against nihilism, *per se*, but it has its seamy side. Have you noticed anything strange about these guys?"

"Umm, aside from the fact that everything about them is strange?"

"Well, there's one thing in particular. Almost none of them is wearing colors from the same club. I've seen a Visigoth and an Outcast and two Gypsy Marauders. The guy in the Knucklehead T-shirt is a Tarantula. There are a couple of Renegades and a few Devil's Dukes and a Head-hunter. It's like a bikers' all-star team."

"How do you know so much about this stuff?" Ross asked Dean.

"Back when I had a bike, I subscribed to *Iron Horseman*. I guess I never let my subscription lapse."

The front door of the barn opened, slowly at first, and then banging wide. No one seemed to be there. A voice from outside called in, "You thought it was the wind, but it's Cool Breeze Charlie." With a roar, someone drove a motorcycle through the doorway and parked it near the fireplace.

"Pretty impressive entry," Ross whispered.

No one else in the barn seemed impressed. They all looked bored. Maybe that was how Charlie always came in. "How you riffraff doing this evening?" Charlie asked. Irene came out of the kitchen, nursing Joe. "Hey, rug rat." Charlie acted as though he was going to pry Joe from her nipple. Instead he kissed Irene on the top of her head. "Who them?" he asked, jerking his thumb toward the first balcony.

"They're from Boston. They came up to buy some things for their restaurant. I'll introduce you."

Irene and Charlie climbed up to the first balcony. Charlie put out his hand for Dean to shake but instead he whacked Dean on the bicep. "Got you," he said.

"So you did," Dean said, rubbing his shoulder. "Got me good."

"Looks like someone already got you today. Somebody punch you in the kisser?"

Charlie was wearing a cut—a denim jacket with the sleeves chopped off. His cut was covered with patches and buttons. One big button proclaimed HELMET LAWS SUCK.

"Everyone ought to wear a helmet," Dean said. "I had an accident on my bike once, and I got a concussion even though I *was* wearing a helmet. Imagine if I hadn't been. My head would have popped open like a ripe cantaloupe."

"Best way to avoid that… don't have accidents."

Irene told them that Amy had gone for a ride with the Turk.

"She *what*?"

"She went for a little ride. Don't worry, they'll be back soon. And the Turk is an excellent driver."

"How long do you think they'll be gone?" Ross asked Irene. "We were planning to leave soon."

Cool Breeze Charlie answered for her. "Depends."

"Depends on what?" Dean asked.

"Depends on if she's a good hump."

Amy walked across the parking lot carrying a helmet and a bottle of wine and wearing a leather jacket far too big for her. The Turk walked beside her, his engineer boots crunching in the gravel. The starlight was thick as heavy cream. "God," Amy said, "look at them all. You never see the stars like this in Boston."

"You'll see more than this if you ever go to Oklahoma. When I was a kid, I lived on a farm, and I was kind of scared of them."

"You were afraid of stars?"

"Well, like when I'd finished my chores and was walking from the barn to the house at night, I'd look up and there would be all these stars, and sometimes, I'd run back to the house."

"But why? Stars are so far away."

"I know. That's why I'd run. See, the light from those stars is really moving out—something like thirty-eight thousand miles an hour, but it takes years, hundreds of years, for it to get to Oklahoma. And there were so many stars, but they were so far away, that..."

"I think I see what you mean." She shivered and slung her leg over the motorcycle. It was a familiar move. She'd ridden with Dean many times, though not on a bike so big. Not nearly this big.

"The bitch seat is nice and comfy. Irene says it's like a Barcalounger." Turk got on the bike in front of Amy.

When Amy didn't say anything, the Turk said, "Sorry, I didn't mean that you..."

"It's all right. Sometimes Dean called it a bitch seat too." She put her hands on the Turk's sides and her feet on the pegs.

The Turk eased the bike off its side stand and slammed down on the starter pedal with all his weight. Through his leather vest, she could feel the barging urgency in the muscles of his back. BAROOOOM! The sound was like a sudden roar of greasy thunder. The bike shuddered between her legs. The Turk eased out the clutch and opened the throttle. The back wheel spit up gravel. They were on their way.

The bike moved forward about ten inches, and then the engine died. The silence was dramatic after the roar of the Harley.

The Turk kicked the starter pedal again and then another time. *He's carrying a lot of tension in his back,* Amy thought. *He needs to take deeper breaths.*

"Come on, honey," he said to his motorcycle. He tried again. BAROO..." The motorcycle started but died instantly. Amy smelled gasoline.

"I don't know much about motorcycles," she said, "but maybe your battery's dead, or..." She remembered a problem Dean had once had with his bike. "Or maybe it's your solenoid." She had no idea what a solenoid was, or what it was meant to do. She thought it sounded like something from a science fiction story.

The Turk suddenly dismounted and walked in front of the bike. He seized the handlebars and stared into the headlight. "Now *look*. You *are* going to start. Got it? I've had about enough of this shit from you, you hear me? Start, you whore!"

Amy decided to get off the bike, too. The Turk was starting to sound a little hysterical. She took off the helmet and shook out her hair.

Someone was coming through the gravel toward them. "Turk," Irene said, "get a grip."

"Again," he said to her. "She won't start again. There's nothing wrong with her either. I've gone over her again and again, taken her apart and put her back together, and there's nothing wrong with her. She just won't fucking start when I need her to. Just like that time when..."

"Look," Irene said, "there's no sense getting mad at a piece of machinery."

"A piece of machinery? You think she's a piece of machinery? I thought you understood. I thought..."

"That's what it is, Turk, a machine. Now, why don't you take the station wagon? You and Amy can go up to the Gap and still see the lights." For some reason, this suggestion infuriated him and drove him to despair. He knelt down in front of his motorcycle. Amy thought she heard him sobbing.

He's taking this a little hard, thought Amy.

"I'm going to go," Amy announced. Neither of them seemed to notice her walking away. When she turned around and looked back, Irene was kneeling in the gravel by the Turk, holding his hands in hers. It appeared as if she were teaching him how to pray.

Dean was leaning back in his chair with his mouth open, looking as if he were about to have some painful dental work done. His lower lip was cracked and swollen.

"I guess you're pretty pissed, huh?" Ross asked him. "Have some more wine."

Thea patted Dean's hand and poured the wine for him. "Maybe you should put some ice on your lip."

"I just want to get out of here. Right now," Dean said. "I feel like we've been here for weeks."

"How would Amy get home?" Thea asked him.

"She can stay here. She can be the Turk's ol' lady."

"I think he already has one," Ross said. "Irene has a little tattoo on the inside of her arm of a guy in a turban."

"You mean, you think it's 'Pass the Vaseline, Irene?' And 'Let's get down to work, Turk?'"

"Wouldn't surprise me."

"Except Turks don't actually wear turbans. Well, never mind, I'm going to go the bathroom and slit my wrists," Dean said. "Anybody wants me, I'll be back there bleeding to death."

"Shh," Ross said.

Cool Breeze Charlie was coming up the staircase.

He was earnest-looking and he had apple cheeks. His blond hair was wild and tangled from riding without a helmet. He looked like a Hitler Youth with a bad haircut. "No more meat," he said sadly.

"You can have Amy's steak if you want it," Thea said. "She won't eat it."

He picked it up and took a big bite from her cold steak. "Thought you'd never ask," Amy's steak was quite rare, and a trickle of blood dribbled down his chin.

The giant who was lying on the third level gave out a loud groan and rolled over. The balcony creaked as if it were about to give away. "Is there something the matter with him?" Thea asked.

"Something the matter with Big George? Well, tell you the truth, we don't exactly know. He's been that way pretty much since the Battle of the Rockaway Market."

"The what?"

"Well, see, George went into the Rockaway just as it was closing to pick up a few things we needed out here at the Barn, and the guys that worked there, I guess they didn't like the way he looked or the way he smelled, or who the hell knows what they didn't like about him, so they told him they were closed, would he please go away? Well, George didn't pay any attention, he just went in and started grabbing the stuff we asked him to get, and all of a sudden, a bunch of the clerks jumped him in the frozen foods section."

Ross had to hand it to the fearless clerks of the Rockaway Market; Big George made the Turk look puny. He weighed about as much as everyone else in the barn put together. He was around ten feet tall and looked bulletproof. The "Big" in Big George's name was pathetically inadequate. He should have been known as Enormous George. Or Colossal George. Gigantic George. Mega-George.

"Georgie went berserk and was throwing those assholes all over the aisle. But then he went down—they'd just mopped the floors, and he slipped—and they started wasting him with their mop handles and whacking him with broomsticks and dropping humongous cans on his head."

"He may have concussed," Thea said. "Anything can happen with head injuries."

"Maybe so. He came back here, and he went up to the top balcony, and he hasn't stirred much since then. He sure hasn't been much fun lately.

Why don't you take a look at him? Irene said you were some kind of a doctor."

"I'm not a doctor. I was just in medical school for a little while."

"Yeah, but hell, you know more than these shitbags around here. Tell you what, you look at him and you say he oughta go to a hospital, we'll take him there tonight."

Thea looked up at the balcony where Big George lay.

"Thea," Ross said, "you don't have to."

"I'll take a look," she said. "I don't know what good it will do, but I'll look."

George was drooling a little. Thea didn't know if drool was a good sign or an ominous one. That was another thing they hadn't covered before she left medical school. There was a scar that started on the bridge of his nose, crossed his forehead, and disappeared beneath his leather cap. It didn't look like a recent wound, though. There was no sign of bruising. There was a strong smell of whisky. It seemed more likely that George had passed out drunk than that he was suffering from a concussion, although it must have taken a case of booze to render someone the size of Big George unconscious.

She had the feeling that everyone in the barn had stopped talking and was staring up at her and George. She lifted his eyelid to see if his pupil was dilated. It seemed to be, but it was hard to judge how big George's pupils normally were. She struggled to lift George's huge hand to take his pulse. There was a jingle of chains, and then George suddenly reached up, grabbed her wrist, put one massive arm around her waist, and pulled her on top of him.

Ross jumped out of his chair, but Dean put his arm out, holding him back. Up on the third balcony, Thea was putting up a forlorn struggle. It was like watching newsreels showing children trying to stop tanks by throwing rocks at them. George gave Thea a kiss, forcing a tongue as big as a calf's liver into her mouth, and then broke off the kiss with a loud, wet smack. With a laugh, he let her go. She was up and running. She flashed past their table with a look of pure apprehension on her face and kept right on going. She slipped on the last step and took a pratfall on the stone floor of the barn. "*Schijt!*" Everyone—nearly everyone—in the barn laughed and clapped. She picked herself up and fled out the front door.

"Look at that!" Charlie said. "She fixed old Georgie boy right up."

Amy knocked on the window of the truck. Thea let her in. "Hello Maudie. Hello Thea. Scooch over." Maud was resting her chin in Thea's lap. Thea scooched. Maud had to scooch as well.

The plastic seat was warm from where Thea had been sitting. "You know, you always open the truck door with your left hand. Are you left handed? I am."

"No. That's just how they teach us to do it in Holland. If you open the door with the hand farthest away from the door, it makes you look over your shoulder. That way, you see anyone coming on a bicycle, and they don't run into your door when you open it."

"That's a good idea. I'm going to start doing that, too," Amy said. "I was out in the parking lot and I saw you run by. What's the matter?"

Amy didn't think Thea was going to answer. *The first time I saw her, I thought she needed a friend. A woman friend. I don't know if it's me, though. It might be. I could sure use one myself.*

Thea told her what had happened up on the third balcony.

"Did he hurt you?"

Thea looked at her wrist. There were large crescent-shaped welts where George had grabbed her thin wrist. And she knew she'd have a spectacular bruise over her tailbone from her fall. "No, not really. I just felt ridiculous. Especially when I fell. I felt stupid and clumsy and fat."

"Fat? You're not fat. Not even close to fat."

"Yes, I am. I might not look fat now, but I am. My mother was fat, and my father is fat, and I was a fat child. When you're fat as a kid, you're always fat. Sometimes when I wake up in the morning, I look in the mirror and I expect to see myself with fat little legs, and arms like little sausages, and..."

"Don't," Amy said. "Don't talk about yourself that way. You're not fat anymore, not at all, not by a longshot, and that's what counts. When I was a kid, I was skinny. Really skinny."

"You're not skinny now. I could tell, down by the pond today. You looked like a butterfly in your wings."

Amy giggled. "A butterfly? I think I was supposed to be a fairy."

"You missed it," Charlie said. "The Doc fixed Big George." Irene and the

Turk had come back into the barn and were sitting at a table with Molly. Irene was setting up the pieces on a chessboard.

Dean and Ross had come down from their table on the balcony and were on their way out of the barn. "It was a joke," the Turk told them. "They're always playing jokes on each other."

"Charlie put itching powder in Rita's and Rain's sleeping bags the other night," Molly said.

"No more jokes," Irene said. "They're our guests."

"I guess we'd better get going," Ross said.

"You don't have to," Charlie said. "Crash here tonight and drive back tomorrow."

"We borrowed the truck from our contractor. He needs it first thing in the morning." *Although I'm sure Lizard would love having an excuse to come into work late tomorrow.*

"I was gonna get you guys stoned," Charlie said, "Well, what the hell, I'll lay this on you." He took out a large lump of hashish and cut it in half. "It's good shit, really good shit. All the way from Nepal. Don't smoke this shit all at once; it'll really fuck you up."

"You tell Amy I meant it," the Turk said to Dean. "If she still wants it, tell her to come up and get it. Before I split for Alaska. No charge."

Out in the truck, Thea told Dean, "No, I'm not hurt."

"I guess you had to do it, right? I mean, aren't even med students bound by the Hippocratic Oath?"

"Shut up, Dean," Amy told him.

"Don't tell me to shut up. By the way, the so-called Turk had a little message for you, Amy. You can come up and get *it* anytime you want."

Ignoring this, Amy said to Ross, "We have a little problem, though."

"I lost one of my contact lenses," Thea said. "It must have popped out when he grabbed me."

"I'll go back and look for it," Ross said.

"Will you take this jacket? And this helmet? And this wine?" Amy asked.

"Leave the wine," Dean said.

"You don't want to go back in there, do you?" Thea said.

"I don't mind," Ross said. He did, though.

Ross, down on his hands and knees, was waiting for Big George to reach out and collar him. Would he be kissed too?

No one paid much attention to him when he'd come back into the barn. He grabbed a couple of candles from downstairs tables and brought them up to the third balcony. He mentally divided the territory around George into a grid and was conscientiously searching each square. *There, what's that glittering over in D-5?* That, it turned out, was a piece of a broken glass. *And hadn't George been lying on his back when Thea was up here?* George was lying on his stomach now. *If the lens popped out on his chest, then, Christ almighty, it'll be under him now. And sorry, Thea, but that's where it's going to stay.*

Someone tapped on his shoulder. Ross almost jumped on top of George, he was so startled.

"What are you doing up here?"

It was Iceman who wanted to know. Iceman was short and scrawny compared to the other bikers. He had a thin face and a sharp nose. He looked more like a rodent than anyone Ross had ever met in person. The resemblance was made more distinct by the sharpness of Iceman's teeth. Ross wondered if Iceman stayed up nights, filing his teeth to a point. *But that would be too grotesque even for someone like Iceman—wouldn't it?* Say, then, that Iceman simply had a set of abnormally pointy teeth that increased his resemblance to a malevolent rat.

Ross stood up, brushing grit off his palms. "I was looking for a contact lens."

"Well, you'd better not. You don't want to wake George up again. And anyway, Charlie wants to talk to you."

Cool Breeze Charlie was drinking a Côte Rôtie wine. He spilled a little on Ross's shoe when he poured more. "Hey hey Ross. You know, me and Iceman here, we were just talking about human nature. We were just commenting about the fact that there are different kinds of people." Ross waited for Charlie to go on. There wasn't much that he could reply to that. "Now, one kind of person, he'll get himself on top, no matter what. He always comes out ahead. This kind of person says, 'I'm one lucky son of a bitch,' but that's not it, not it at all. It's just that everybody else is too polite, or too chickenshit, or too stoned to disagree, or to stand up for themselves. Or maybe they just don't like hassles.

"Our Irene, now, she's one of those people who hate hassles. Hates 'em!

Like, she let the assholes around here run her out of business. Me, I would have been tempted to stomp some ass. When in doubt, stomp ass, right?"

Ross nodded, not sure what he was agreeing with.

"Now, Iceman and me, we were just talking about what a great deal you guys got on that stuff you bought today," Charlie said.

Ross glanced over at Iceman. His fangs were glittering in the candlelight.

"Yeah, we did. That's why we drove all the way up here. But Irene went along with the price. In fact, she even..."

Charlie interrupted him by belching. He dragged the belch out to two syllables, with the accent on the second syllable. Bur-RUUP. "That's just like Irene. Ain't that just like Irene, Iceman?" The rodent nodded. "She's one kind lady. I mean, where would we be, where would any of us be, without our Irene?"

Ross said, in his most reasonable tone of voice: "Well, gentlemen, how much more do you think she wants?"

Charlie said, "It's not what she wants; it's what you think she deserves. For being the kind of lady she is."

"I'll have to go out to the truck to get the checkbook."

"Hey, now, I think you've just come up with a plan!" Charlie said earnestly. Charlie could come across as earnest as any encyclopedia sales-man. Iceman smiled, showing his dagger-sharp teeth. Charlie offered Ross his hand, removing it at the last second and punching Ross in the upper arm.

Irene and the Turk were playing chess by the light of an oil lamp at a table near the door. Molly was watching. Irene said to Ross: "Charlie asked you for more money, didn't he?"

"We did agree on a price."

"I know we did," Irene said. "But the kids, they're always worried about me being taken. I keep telling them not to worry. I tell them, I've been used by some real experts, and not just anybody is going to take advantage of me now."

The Turk said, "You sure you want to move your knight there? You're going to lose it if you do."

"See?" she said. "Everybody thinks they're looking out for me. Go ahead and take it. I'll have you in checkmate in two moves if you do."

Ross looked down at the board. As near as he could tell, she was bluffing.

"Tell you what," Irene said to Ross, "I'll tear up your second check."

"Then what's the point of writing it?"

"Well, just so Charlie doesn't get irritated."

"That Charlie's an asshole," Molly said. "He shot a hole in Denim's waterbed."

"Just shut up, Molly," the Turk said.

Ross could well imagine Charlie in a firefight with the furniture.

"Or we could just leave," Ross said.

"Yes," Irene said, "but go quickly."

"I couldn't find your contact," he told Thea. She'd moved into the back seat. She opened the door for Ross with her left hand.

"Ross, I'm so sorry; I had it all the time. It was bothering me because of all the smoke in the air and I took it out without thinking about it."

"Oh. Well, good. Dean, let's get out of here. Now."

It seemed to Ross that the tires made an awful lot of noise in the gravel as Dean pulled out. The headlights tracked across the long row of bikes and the bare trees at the end of the parking lot.

Thea said, "Thanks for going back in, Ross."

"No problem. Are you sure you're not hurt?"

"No, I'm okay. Just embarrassed. I've never been so embarrassed."

They turned off the unpaved road and onto the highway.

"Never?" Dean said. "Never? You must have led a life remarkably free of embarrassment if this breaks your record."

"Dean, I'm sure Thea doesn't want to talk about embarrassing moments right now," Amy said.

"Are you kidding? Everybody loves to talk about embarrassments, embarrassments from their past. It gives them a chance to relive the awfulness without any real threat. It's like eating a Twinkie. It's shameful, but at the same time, it affords a certain pleasure."

"I don't eat Twinkies," Amy said, "but go ahead."

"Go ahead and what?"

"Go ahead and tell us something embarrassing."

"Not unless everyone does."

"Not me," Ross said. Ross was looking out at the side mirror of the truck. Were those the headlights of a car tailgating them, or were those two motorcyclists riding abreast? Charlie and Iceman?

"Come on," Dean said. "It'll be more fun than playing Botticelli."

Thea wasn't interested either. She'd had enough embarrassment for one night.

"Well, okay, I'll play with you," Amy said. "But you go first."

"Let's play rock, paper, scissors to decide who goes first. Ready? One, two, three..."

Amy slapped her palm down flat on her thigh with a clapping noise. Paper. At the same time, Dean dropped his arm and formed a circle with his index finger and thumb, as if making the okay sign. "I win," Dean said.

"What the hell is that?" Amy asked. "That's not a rock, or a..."

"It's a lens. A lens burns paper when the sun shines through it."

"That's nuts. What makes you think you can just add a..."

"The more variables a game has, the more fun it is. Okay, I'll give you a break. We'll do two out of three."

This time Amy did a lens. Dean thumped his fist down on the seat between them. "Rock smashes lens. I win, and that's two out of three."

"You cheated," Amy said. "No one's ever heard of rock, paper, scissors, lens. Have you ever heard of that?" she asked the back seat.

"No. In Holland we play *steen, papier, schaar*. Only those three. Dutch people are very good at it, though. We seldom lose when we play people from other countries."

Ross wondered why that would be. And he reminded himself not to play that game with Thea.

"Okay, okay, I'll be magnanimous and go first, even though I won. Let's get the rules down. It has to be something you've never told anyone before."

"Okay. And it has to be embarrassing," Amy said.

"Absolutely humiliating," Dean said.

"Go ahead, then."

After that, Dean was quiet.

"Change your mind?" Amy asked him.

"No, no, I was deciding what would be the *most* embarrassing incident. It's hard to choose just one. Okay, I've decided. Pass me the wine, Amy."

"No, you're driving."

"I'll just take a swig. All right, this happened when I was thirteen or so. That's when all disgraceful things happen. It has to do with hormones."

Ross tried to picture Dean as an adolescent. All he could come up with was an image of Dean exactly as he was today, only proportionally smaller. In Ross's imagination, teenage Dean had the same mustache he had now, only it was miniscule.

"Now, this particular time, I'd gone over to my girlfriend's house after school. Penny was her name, Penny Blackwell. She was a perky little thing. A majorette like you, Amy. She..."

"I was a cheerleader, not a majorette. Claire was the baton twirler in the family." In fact, both Amy and her sister had started off as baton twirlers, but once Amy flung her baton high into the air and it landed on a middle linebacker's head. If he hadn't been wearing his helmet, he might have been seriously hurt. The coach took her baton away from her for good after that.

"Well, anyway, Penny's parents were having a barbecue. We went up to her room before dinner. Our pretext was, we were going up there to listen to music, maybe some Herman's Hermits, I forget, but our real intention was to make out. I was hoping for a little boob-through-the-bra. I'd gotten boob-through-the-blouse once, but that was about the extent of it. I even saw the possibility of getting a little bare boob, but you know me—ever the optimist.

"But before I could do anything else, I had an urgent matter to take care of. I had to take a dump, and I had to take one bad."

"This is going to be crude, isn't it?" Amy asked him.

"Of course. How could it be embarrassing and not be crude? Let me get on with my story. Pass the wine back first, will you?"

"No more for you."

Dean sighed. "Well, I knew this was going to be one hellacious crap. It'd been brewing and building up since fourth period English class. I'd had cramps. And frankly, I was nervous. Just taking a piss at someone else's house gave me the jim-jams. You left the water running in the sink, you aimed above the waterline to minimize splashing noises, and you flushed early and got out quick. Even then, when you came out of the bathroom, you felt like everyone was staring at you. Were there wet spots? Did you zip up all the way? Taking a shit, though, that was a different sort of undertaking altogether. Up until then, I'd always made my excuses and gone home to poop in peace."

"Dean, this is getting gross, really, really gross."

"No, wait, it gets worse," Dean said. "Anyway, I excused myself and went into the bathroom. It was the kind of bathroom that had charcoal-gray-and-pink tiles instead of black-and-white ones. There was pink shag carpeting on the toilet seat, and on the back of the toilet and a pink shag bathmat, pink-and-gray-striped towels, and a rose-colored shower curtain.

There were boxes full of glistening bath-oil lozenges and tissues in a deco-rator box and soap in the shape of a microphone for singing in the shower. There were two cans of room deodorant—Spicy Mist and Spring Breeze, take your pick—and there was a pink Princess telephone and a copy of *Jokes for the John*.

"So in I went, and after a few painful moments, I'd dropped the biggest turd anyone has ever seen. It was lying in the toilet bowl like a beached battleship. That baby was huge. It should have been featured in *Ripley's Believe It or Not*. No wonder I'd been in pain. If Big George took a dump, it..."

"Dean, this isn't embarrassing, it's disgusting. And puerile. Please stop. And turn on the heater."

"What, four warm bodies in here, and you want heat?"

"I've been cold since I fell in the pond, and that was your fault, so let's have some heat."

"All right, all right. Then I reached behind me to flush. Nothing happened. Must not have hit the old handle hard enough. Tried again. Nada. The water in the toilet bowl didn't even ripple. I tried so many times, the handle almost came off in my hand. I lifted the shag carpet cover off the back of the toilet and looked inside. I remembered my mom jiggling something when our toilet wouldn't flush, so I jiggled anything jigglable, but that didn't help at all."

Ross imagined young Dean sitting on the pot, pants around his ankles, tiny mustache quivering with despair.

"As you can imagine, I was about to completely freak out. But I got a hold of myself and considered my options. One: I could leave it where it lay. Maybe, under ordinary circumstances, but I did *not* want to be associ-ated with this abomination. Second: I could open the frosted glass window and heave it out with all my might. But that window looked out on the backyard, and Penny's parents were out there drinking gin bucks and grilling steaks. What would Penny's father do if he got hit in the chest by something the size of a zeppelin? It might have broken a couple of ribs. Third option: I could put it in that cute filigreed silver waste basket. There were quite a few tissues in there, mostly covered with lipstick smears, that I might have been able to use to hide it. But even if I'd emptied both cans of air freshener on top of it, it would have betrayed itself.

"By this time... I'm squeezing the story... I'd been sitting there quite a while, sweating. I heard Penny's father calling, from the backyard, 'You kids want your steaks well done, or what? Heh-heh-heh.' That's how he laughed: Heh-heh-heh.

"So what I did was, I put the turd and the TP in her mother's pink shower cap, wadded the whole thing up, and stepped on it. Then I stuffed it into my pants. It was a tight fit. It was like trying to shoplift a loaf of bread and a pound of hamburger and the Sunday *New York Times*. Of course, I knew her old lady would eventually miss the shower cap, but I figured she might not connect me with the heist. What kind of a thirteen-year-old has a shower-cap fetish? As a precaution, I doused my pants with about half a bottle of her old man's Jade East.

"Then I used the Princess phone to call my friend Eugene. I told Eugene to call me at Penny's house in about five minutes and tell whoever answered that there was an emergency and that I had to come home right away.

"Penny grabbed me when I came out of the bathroom and said, 'For God's sakes, Dean, let's get out there! What are they going to think?'

"It was an awkward cookout. I grabbed my plate and pulled a lawn chair over to the far corner of the yard. Penny's mom had tomatoes growing over there. I thought, *you tomatoes are going to get the fertilizing of your life. You're going to be as big as volleyballs with all the night soil you're going to get.*

"But I never got a chance to ditch my load. Penny was keeping me under tight surveillance because I was acting unbalanced. I was sitting so far away from everyone else that they had to shout. 'You want some A.1. Sauce for your steak, son?' her father hollered.

"No thanks, Mr. Blackwell, putting sauce on a steak like this would be criminal," I shouted back to him, although the steak was practically cremated.

"Then the family dog started limping toward me. The Blackwells had this vintage Chihuahua named—creatively enough—Pup-0. Pup-0 must have been older than Penny. He was coming toward me, I have no doubt, to sniff me out. I had a feeling, for some reason, that if Pup-O ever got to me, he'd start sniffing my crotch like mad, and the jig would be up.

"I kept wondering why the hell Eugene hadn't called yet. And Pup-O was creeping closer and closer. I thought, I'll try telepathy. *Okay, Pup-O buddy, just hold it where you are. One step closer and I'll come back tonight with Gravy Train laced with ground glass and strychnine.* No effect. *You don't know who you're fucking with, Pup-O. You come any closer and I'll come back and douse you with kerosene and put a match to you.* I broadcast a mental image of Pup-O looking as if he were Joan of Arc. That didn't do any good either. Fucking Pup-O had no latent telepathic powers. He just came shuffling along, making this repulsive wheezing sound that he made instead of barking."

"Dean, I think that's absolutely awful, that you would think about killing a poor little dog," Amy said.

"So do I," Thea said. Ross was surprised she'd said anything; he thought she'd been asleep. Maybe she had woken up just in time to hear about Pup-O.

"You don't know how scuzzy Pup-O was. He was more like a furry cockroach than a dog. But I was just projecting threatening thoughts. I wasn't planning to do him any harm. I was so busy worrying about Pup-O that I barely saw Penny's mom walking out of the house and coming up to me. I was afraid she'd already missed the shower cap, but all of a sudden, she burst into tears.

"Eugene had called and told her my mother had fallen down a flight of stairs at work and broken her back. Mrs. Blackwell offered to give me a ride to the hospital, but I said I'd take my bike. Even though I hadn't actually brought my bike there."

There was a flat, dead silence. It was so quiet, it felt like it might start snowing inside the truck. Then Ross said, "That's pretty embarrassing. Is any of that true?"

"Most of it," Dean said. "Almost all of it."

"So how do you feel?" Amy asked him. "Was it therapeutic?"

"Yes and no." Dean was bouncing up and down behind the steering wheel. "I feel terrific. But I also feel embarrassed all over again. Now it's your turn."

"Oh, I don't have anything nearly that embarrassing to tell," Amy said. "Not even remotely close."

"No? How about that time when..."

"No! It has to be something no one knows about, remember?"

"Well, come on. Air out that dirty linen. Let's go. The more painful, the better."

"All right, then. When I was a kid, I used to keep fuzzies in my pocket."

Thea whispered a question to Ross. "I don't know," he told Thea. "Amy, what *are* fuzzies?"

"Fuzzies were like little balls of wool. I'd get them by playing with the hem of my cardigan sweaters. Then I'd save them. When I got nervous, I'd roll them between my fingers like woolly nervous beads. Well, once, during Sister Philomena's religion class, I was standing by my desk reciting from the Baltimore Catechism, and I couldn't remember but six of the seven Sacraments. And there I was, rubbing my fuzzies a mile a minute. Then I dropped a couple of fuzzies right in front of Sister Philomena."

"And she asked you about them?"

"Oh no. No, I'm sure she thought they were just balls of lint if she noticed them at all. But I *thought* she must know about fuzzies. I thought she knew about everything. And I figured that anything that felt as good as fuzzies had to be a mortal sin."

"I still don't see where the embarrassment comes in."

"I don't think you understand about fuzzies. I have these moments from the past, these moments when memories appear in absolute crystal clarity, and one of those moments is when my fuzzies hit the floor. I couldn't have been more embarrassed if I was suddenly standing there naked. And Sister Philomena... she was not the nicest of nuns. She'd whacked me over the head a couple of times with a missal. I thought for sure... "

"She did what with a missile?"

"Not like a guided missile. A missal. A prayer book."

"Okay, but nothing happened. She didn't do anything. She didn't know you had a lint fetish. No one did. So I don't know why..."

"Listen, I was humiliated. And anyway, no one knew about the smooshed kaka in your pants. Technically, it wasn't embarrassing, it was just potentially embarrassing. It would only have been embarrassing if Pup-o had sniffed you out."

"Jeez, here you have us expecting something mortifying, and what do you give us—fuzzies! You give us fuzzies! No, that's unacceptable. Take another turn."

"Nope."

"You agreed. Now come on."

"Dean," Ross said, "that was a stop sign you just went through."

Ross heard the brakes on the truck squeal. In the right-side mirror, he saw the headlights of another car behind them. He saw that car fishtail and estimated that it was going to be a near miss.

The car hit them from behind. Not very hard, but a solid bump.

Thea made a sound that was half shriek, half sigh. Maud started to bark.

"Is everyone okay?" Everyone was, apparently. Dean got out. The driver of the other car was looking over the front bumper of her Saab with a flashlight. It was hard to tell if there was any damage to the truck since there was already a plethora of dings. "Doesn't look like there was any real damage," he said to her. "We were lucky."

"Lucky!" the other driver said, turning on him. She had a round pink face, frizzy hair, and extraordinarily short lashes. "Why did you stop in the middle of an intersection? If you're going to run stop signs, you don't get second thoughts."

"Look, what I did doesn't matter. If you rear-end someone, it's your fault, no matter what."

"That doesn't apply," the woman said with a sniff, "if you're behind an idiot."

"Why didn't *you* stop at the stop sign?"

"Because I was following you," She started to get back into her Saab.

"Then you're the idiot," he said. To underscore his point, he kicked her door shut, leaving a scuff mark on the white finish.

"Dean! Get back in here!" Amy shouted from the truck.

Dean got back in the cab. "Can you believe that? What a bitch. I should have known when..." He looked up and saw the other driver out his window, her nearly lashless eyes scowling at him. She aimed a kick at his door, went back to her car, and drove around them.

Dean got out and looked at the dent left by the woman's boot. "Well, at least it's not my truck," Dean said. "And I doubt if Lizard will care too much." Lizard's truck lacked a paint job; its finish consisted of primer and rust. Dean got out and opened the back of the truck. "Oh, this is just wonderful; we've got maple syrup all over the coffee machine. Amy, I want you to put that woman on the List."

"Yes, Dean."

Back on the road again, Ross thought about the highway in front of them, and the dreary drive down the Mass Pike. He thought about unloading the truck at the restaurant, and cleaning up the maple syrup, and then returning the truck to Lizard. He thought about getting a taxi, picking up Jeremy at Mojave's, taking Thea home. He thought about climbing those steps, all those steps, carrying Jeremy because he'd be asleep, putting him to bed, and then collapsing into his own bed. He skimmed back and forth over his immediate future so many times that actually doing anything seemed redundant.

"Did you hear me, Amy? I want her name on the List."

"All right, Dean,' she said, pretending to write something. "I didn't catch her name, though. Can I just write 'kinky-haired lady in the white

Saab?'" *Pretty soon,* Amy thought, *he'll have to keep his own damn List.* But she decided not to mention that now. Dean was already in a bad enough mood.

"The List got a *lot* longer today," Dean said crossly. "Big George, and the Turk, of course, and that demon rat-bastard Charlie, and..."

"Yes, Dean," Amy said, "Turn up the heat a little more, please."

17

HARD CHAIRS

THE LIST THAT AMY KEPT FOR DEAN WAS MODELED ROUGHLY AFTER A LIST kept by Richard Dadd. Richard Dadd was an artist, a water colorist who lived in England when Victoria was queen. He took a trip to the Ottoman Empire and painted charming, exquisitely detailed watercolors of the Blue Mosque and Hagia Sophie and other sights. He then journeyed on to Egypt with friends he'd met along the way. On a voyage down the Nile, he suffered a severe sunstroke and had to return to London. While still in a care ward in the Southwark Wing of Guy's Hospital, he began to halluci-nate fairies. And it was there he began keeping a list, a list of people who deserved to die. Richard's father's name was the first to make this list. His father came to see him in the hospital. He asked a few polite questions, made a few sympathetic noises, and left after ten minutes. His father was unaware that he was being possessed by a demon. Richard only knew this for certain because the Egyptian god Osiris had told him so.

A nurse handled him clumsily while giving him a sponge bath. He wrote her name down. After being released from the hospital, the list grew much faster. He took down the names of shop girls, cabmen, other artists. He added, in one day, a dumpling-shaped waitress in the tea shop at the Aerated Bread Company, a dandy with nasty comb tracks through his hair, a deaf man who sold newspapers, two members of Parliament, and a drunken, foul-mouthed subaltern of the Royal Welsh Fusiliers. The list was starting to get unwieldy. Richard considered writing down only the names of those who deserved to live, to save on paper and ink. Instead, he decided to act. He would strike the first name off the list and work his way down.

Richard accosted his father in front of his club in the Pall Mall, slung him over his shoulder fireman-fashion, and trotted off toward St. James Park. "Where are we going, Richard?" his father asked amiably. So far, this impromptu piggyback ride seemed a kind of a joke.

"You're going to your reward, Pater," Richard said. "You are going to your death."

"Is that what you suppose I deserve? Who helped get you into the Academy? Who paid your passage to the Ottoman Empire? Who paid your hospital bills?"

"You deserve it more than anyone. You head the list. And while I know you don't realize it, there is a demon living inside of you."

"Isn't that something one would know?"

"Apparently not," Richard said.

By the time they reached St. James Park, they had an escort of small children scampering along behind them. They were surrounded by clouds of fairies, which Richard knew weren't real although they certainly seemed to be. There were also enormous white pelicans, some sitting on park benches, which Richard assumed were also hallucinations, though they weren't. The elder Mr. Dadd said, "Put me down under this tree, Richard, and we'll sit here and thrash this out." Richard didn't even break stride. "Very well, put me down here by the banks of the duck pond."

Richard instead put his father down *in* the pond and held him underwater. His drowning seemed to take forever, so Richard hurried the process with a straight razor which he'd stropped on leather the night before.

On his way to Guy's Hospital to deal with the second person on his list, the clumsy nurse, he was arrested. Found to be criminally insane, he spent the rest of his life in Bedlam. His doctors urged him to keep painting, as a kind of therapy, and he painted his most noteworthy pieces there, including many featuring fairies.

Like Richard Dadd, Dean would have begun his List with the name of his father, only he didn't know his father's name. Dean's mother would never tell anyone who had gotten her pregnant, and his grandparents had packed her off to a home for unwed mothers. Dean told people that his father had been MIA in the Korean War. That sounded tragic, but better than what had actually happened. The number one slot on his List remained an anonymous blank.

∾

"Who told you you'd be making big bucks driving a school bus?"

"Gus," Amy said. "Gus told me that beginning school bus drivers make the same as beginning drivers on the MBTA." Amy was getting ready to go to an interview. She was in her panties, ironing a blouse. Stevie Nicks was singing "Landslide."

"I think it's time Gus went on the List, then. I've heard enough about him," Dean said. He was also thinking about adding Stevie Nicks to the List.

"Poor Gus. What are you doing home, anyway? I thought you and Ross were painting this week."

"We can't start painting until Lizard finishes up with the carpentry, and who knows how long that will take. Otherwise we'll end up with sawdust in the paint. I told Ross my hemorrhoids were flaring up and that I was going to shoot home for a little Prep H."

"I hate the smell of that stuff."

"It's the shark's liver oil they put in it."

"You mean they kill sharks just so..."

"I don't know why you're always bad-mouthing my 'rhoids. Those babies helped keep me from being drafted. Anyway, they're fine. That was just an excuse to come home."

"Well, I'm sure there are other things you could be helping Ross with."

"I just wanted to talk to you. To spend some time with you."

"You haven't wanted to *just* talk to me for years."

"I was thinking we could talk in bed. I brought a bottle of Liebfrau-milch—too sweet for me, but I know you like it—and a nice bottle of white Bordeaux—and we can take our wine to bed with us."

"Can't do it, Dean. I told you last night I have an interview today. Excuse me, I've got to get into the bathroom."

"I not only have wine, I got pears and cheese. Your two favorite kinds of cheeses: camembert and taleggio. We can have a picnic in bed."

She hesitated just for a few seconds. "You and Ross and Lizard can have a nice little snack."

Dean tried the bathroom door. "Hey, how come you've got the door locked?"

"You're not going to like what's going on in here, babes."

"What are you talking about? Would you please open that door?" He heard the lock click open. "My God, Ame, what are you doing??"

Amy was shaving under her arms. For the first time in years. "I told you, I have an interview."

"And you're going to it nude to the waist?"

"I think I'll feel more... more streamlined, you know? More professional. Besides, everyone shaves there these days. I go out in something sleeveless and people look at me weird. I would have started shaving years ago, but I knew you'd kick up a fuss."

"Not everyone shaves. And why are you using my razor?"

"It's sharper than mine."

"Don't you think it's unnatural? You know, hair is what makes you a mammal. It's what separates us from..."

"What, you think I'm going to turn into a lizard if I shave my pits? I've paid my dues, Dean. I'm not the little hippy girl who moved in with you four years ago. I don't know why you're so fixated on my underarms, anyway. I've always shaved my legs, and you never complained about that."

"You know, this French writer Huysmans wrote about women's underarms. He called them 'spice boxes.' He said..."

"More like sweat boxes in my case. God, I almost shaved off a mole. I forgot it was there."

"Well, it's no big deal. Shave anywhere you want, I don't care," Dean said, though he cared bitterly. "Actually, I've been thinking about shaving off Melvin."

"You're the only man I know whose mustache has a name."

"My college roommate liked the idea that my mustache had a name so much that he gave his a name too. He called it Mr. Tickles."

Amy splashed water under her arms and dried herself. "Maybe you *should* shave it. It's starting to look a little seedy."

Dean sounded hurt. "I've had this 'stache since 1969."

"So don't shave it. Do what you want with it, it's your Melvin." She sprayed on deodorant. "Yow, that stings!"

"You know you're destroying the ozone layer, every time you spray," Dean said darkly.

"Like you don't use Right Guard. Excuse me again," she said. She went into their bedroom.

Dean looked in the bathroom mirror. Melvin *was* looking a little unkempt. *Though not as scruffy as Ross's beard.*

He looked at the photo of Amy over the toilet. Amy was seated on the back of a large sheep. She wasn't wearing any pants, of course. Amy and the sheep were juxtaposed on a photo of a tornado ripping through a trailer park. It looked as though bare-ass Amy was riding her sheep right into that twister.

He followed Amy. "Why is it, Dean, that no matter what room I'm in, there you are, leaning against the doorjamb?"

"A bra," he said accusingly. "She's actually going to wear a bra. I can't believe what I'm seeing."

"It's called a no-bra."

"A no-bra is still a bra."

"I've worn this a number of times—you've just never noticed," Amy said, "I was thinking about wearing this hat." She put it on and set it at a rakish angle. "Too much, do you think?"

Dean snorted and mumbled. She did look pretty jaunty, though, standing there in a hat and her underwear. It was a pastel-blue fedora, like the one Robert Redford wore in *The Sting*.

"Well, *I* think it's too much," Amy said. "Besides, there's a cigarette burn in it. Thanks to you." She doffed the hat and tried to twirl it on the tip of her finger, but it spun away.

"Dean," she said, "I'm really nervous about this, do you know that? I haven't had a successful interview since I got my Christmas elf job."

He came up behind her and folded his arms around her waist. "Two kinds of cheeses. Pears. Oh, and dates and tamari almonds. German wine for you, French wine for me." His hand slid downward. "It would be a lot more fun than this interview, I promise."

"God, I ask him for a little reassurance, and he thinks I want an orgasm." Amy twirled away from him. "I have to finish getting dressed."

They were waiting for the elevator. "How do I look? Do I look employable?" Amy was wearing a Cossack blouse and whipcord trousers tucked into her high boots.

"Where's your horse?"

"You know, Dean, you've become quite conservative." The elevator creaked its way up to their floor, and she pushed aside the heavy iron door. Dean was whinnying like a horse. "You have. You really don't like change anymore. You used to say that the flux is in flux and even the pieces fall to pieces, and that's the way you like it, but you can't stand the fact that..."

They reached the lobby. "You want to know something? Those pants are too tight on you."

"You can't stand the fact that I'm changing right before your eyes, that I'm evolving, that I'm not just your Amy baby anymore. You can't stand that, can you?"

"And your makeup..."

"Dean, stop it. Just cut it out. Stop criticizing me. Daddy me instead." *Daddy me* was one of Amy's stock expressions. By it, she meant, "Give me comfort. And a hug." Paradoxically, her real daddy seldom, if ever, comforted her.

Dean daddied her half-heartedly, and then they went outside. It was drizzling and cold. "Wish me luck, cupcakes."

"Luck," Dean said. He sounded like he was being strangled. "I hope everything turns out the way you want it to."

"There's something sinister about the way you say that, but it'll have to do. Can you pick up some dry dog food at the market? Maud's almost completely out."

Dean's hemorrhoids gave an authoritative twinge just at that moment, as if to prove that the distress they caused was not entirely fictional.

He watched her walk off. He could smell her flowery perfume on the wet air. Amy rarely wore perfume. Her pants weren't really too tight; they fit her butt perfectly, and she had a nearly perfect butt. No, not nearly perfect... perfect. "I love you, Amy," he said, but she was too far off to hear.

Amy stood in the parking lot of a furniture store across the street from the bus barn, watching a school bus come home. It had taken a ride on the subway and on two buses to get to this remote corner of Mattapan. The left turn into the barn seemed impossibly sharp. The doorway looked way too small, and it was set at an odd angle. Traffic was backing up behind the bus. There was a steady stream of cars coming the other way.

The bus driver turned on the flashing lights and the stop signs on either side of the bus flared out to halt traffic. That, Amy assumed, was something a driver should do only when kids were getting on or off, not when one wanted to make a left turn. The driver whipped his bus across the other lane, and when it was clear he wasn't going to make the turn in one try, he slammed into reverse, adjusted the angle of entry, and scooted smartly into the barn. *Could I do that? I have trouble parking Daddy's Pinto.*

She thought about rescheduling her interview, or canceling it entirely. She wondered if Dean realized how tempted she'd been to spend the afternoon with him, eating soft cheeses and drinking wine in bed. She could practically see the image of the nun on the blue bottle of Liebfraumilch and taste the tangy cheeses. But she hadn't had much luck finding a job so far. She'd interviewed for a job delivering flowers and for a job at a gourmet food shop, but she hadn't gotten any callbacks. She'd applied to be the assistant manager of a bookstore, which struck her as an almost ideal job, but when she went to be interviewed, she discovered that the bookstore was a dodgy adult bookstore on the fringes of the Combat Zone, so she turned around and went home.

But I can do this. If I can get an A on my Wollstonecraft paper in my Women's Studies class, I can learn to drive a school bus. Professor Franconi said she almost never gave A's.

Of course, Dean did help me write that paper.

I even got a better grade than Dean did in that class. I told him Grace Slick wouldn't be a good subject for a final paper. I doubt if Professor Franconi had ever even heard of Grace Slick.

The bus barn was a huge concrete cavern. Once it must have been an indoor parking garage. After that, it clearly had been a used car dealership. A few cheerful plastic pennants were still hanging on the somber gray walls. SIT ON HARD CHAIRS, SAVE HARD CASH, they said.

The driver who had pulled in so adroitly was sweeping out his bus. She boarded the bus and said hi. The muffler was making pinging noises as the hot metal cooled. The driver was sweeping a few Cheetos, an empty pack of Vantages, a bloody Band-Aid, a comb with almost no teeth, and an empty condom packet down the aisle of the bus. He wore a gray cap with a black visor. If there had been a red star above the bill, he would have looked like a Soviet Army officer.

"Hibe," he said. He sounded like he had a juicy head cold.

"I'm lost. Can you tell me where to find Carol?"

"In duh disbatcher's oppice." He sniffled. Amy badly wanted to tell him to go blow his nose.

"That's what I figured. But where's the dispatcher's office?"

"Dust keep walking up duh ramps." The driver was trying to sweep up a cough drop, but it was stuck to the matting on the floor.

"I watched you come into the bus barn. You drive very well," she told him. "Is it hard?"

The driver upended the broom and used the handle to deftly pry the cough drop off the floor. Then he sneezed. "No," he said, "dribing... dad's not duh hard pard."

"That's a wicked bad cold you have there," Amy said. "Are you taking vitamin C or anything?"

"I always hab a code, because..." He broke off in midsentence to stare at her chest. The Cossack shirt was made of flimsy linen. "Because of dem damn kids. Dey gib me codes by sneezing and coughing on me."

Amy was glad she was wearing a bra. Even a no-bra.

Carol was on the phone when Amy came into the dispatcher's glassed-in office. She covered the mouthpiece with her palm. "Sit down, hon. With you in a sec." Amy removed a Styrofoam cup half full of cold coffee from the wooden chair and sat down. When the used car company had pulled out, they'd left their hard chairs behind. *Dean would be in agony sitting here, what with his hemorrhoids.*

Had she overdone it with the White Shoulders? The scent of her perfume seemed to fill the small office.

"I don't think you're getting me," Carol said into the phone. She spoke slowly and precisely. "It isn't a question of you getting a refund, it's a question of you reimbursing us for the damage to two seats and the cost of recharging a fire extinguisher."

Amy's hair was wet but she didn't dare shake it; she might splatter rainwater all over those papers lying on Carol's desk. She spotted a box of Callard and Bowser butterscotch in Carol's inbox.

Carol said into the phone, "Let me ask you: If you were a bus driver, and someone tried to set fire to your bus, would *you* keep going?" She looked up at Amy, rolled her eyes, and smiled, including her in the joke. "The way I see it, if someone had given those kids a little more supervision..."

Oh my God, did I really just do that? Did she see me? Amy, without thinking, had helped herself to a piece of Carol's candy. *How could I have done that? Will she not hire me now?*

Carol, in the meantime, had finished talking on the phone. "Charters!" she said. She made the word sound obscene. "I hate 'em sometimes. You'd think a bunch of blind kids..."

Amy's mouth was too full of butterscotch for her to say anything, but she made her eyes round with surprise.

"That's right, blind kids. Blind firebugs. So, you're the gal that called me about a job, right?"

"Uhm-hmm," Amy said, nodding her head and trying to chew the candy unobtrusively. She was afraid she might lose a filling. It was like chewing on a chunk of sugary rawhide.

"And you used to drive a tour bus out in California?"

"Um-umm." Amy shook her head. She wanted to tell Carol that she'd never even been to California, and that she had never driven anything bigger than a Pinto, but she couldn't on account of the butterscotch.

"Must have been someone else. But that's all right. Sometimes it's better if people have no experience than if they have the wrong kind of experience. You have a driver's license, don't you? Okay, that's a start. Now this is what you have to do before you can drive for us."

First, she had to take a written exam to get a Class II license. Carol gave her a fat booklet to study before she took the test. Then she had to get a physical, and after that she had to take a road test to get a school bus permit. The whole process would take some time. "Have you got all that?"

The candy was beginning to soften. Amy forced the gob of butterscotch down her throat. *God, don't let it lodge anywhere. That's all I need, to choke to death here in the disbatcher's oppice.* "Do I need to get a hat like the one that driver who just pulled in has?"

"Who, Paulie? No, Paulie has really long hair, which is against company policy. So he wads it up and sticks it under that stupid cap of his and we pretend we don't notice. The license will cost you a few bucks. So will the physical. We can advance you the money if..."

"I think I can swing it." *I can borrow it from Dean. No, not a good idea. I'll borrow it from Daddy.*

The phone on Carol's desk rang. Amy got ready to leave, but she couldn't find her sunglasses. They weren't in her purse or in any of her pockets.

Carol covered the phone with her hand. "What are you looking for?"

When Amy told her, Carol said, "You don't mean that pair of big orange sunglasses sitting on top of your head, do you?"

Oh Lord, that's what I did with them. "Oh no, not those. That's my *main* pair. The ones I'm looking for are my spare sunglasses. I must have left them at home or something."

Carol looked her over for a few seconds longer, and then went back to her call. *She doesn't believe me. She thinks I'm a dingbat. She may be right. And she's wondering why I need sunglasses on such a dreary-ass day.*

As Amy was walking out the office door, Carol said, "Those butterscotches are good, aren't they? You should try their toffees sometime too."

∿

Paulie, the bus driver with the head cold, was getting into his car, parked just outside the bus barn. He'd taken off his Red Army hat, and his hair came well past his shoulders. "Hey," she called to him. "Guess what? I got the job."

"Eberbody duds," Paulie said in his raspy voice.

"Pardon?"

"Nudding."

"This friend of mine, he works for the MBTA, he was telling me there are different kinds of buses. Which is the easiest kind to drive?"

"I never dought of it dad way."

"Well, what kind do you drive? Yours seemed to handle really well."

"Well, dey almost all hab duh same engines, but dey hab different bodies. Today I was dribing a Bluebird—stubid name 'cause dey're all yellow—but usually I dribe a Ward or a Crown or..."

"A Bluebird!" Amy said. "That's what I want to drive. I can't imagine myself driving anything but a Bluebird."

PEOPLING

NEW MEXICAN RESTAURANT NOW PEOPLING. *MUY INTERESANTE* PLACE TO WORK. BARTENDER, SERVERS, KITCHEN STIFF, HOST-ESSES, BUS PEOPLE ALL NEEDED. EXPERIENCE A PLUS. CALL DEAN OR ROSS, 555-7447.

BUZZ TIBBETS, JR.

DEAN: So you're Buzz, is that right? (*Dean suddenly snaps Buzz's picture with his Pentax, then makes a notation on his legal pad. Buzz blinks from the flash.*) Don't let that worry you—we're taking pictures of everyone we interview today.
BUZZ: (*rubbing eyes*) Yes, sir, I'm Buzz. But only temporarily. I'm planning on changing my name as soon as I can.
DEAN: Changing it? To what? (*Gets ready to make another notation.*)
BUZZ: I don't exactly know yet. I got one of those little name books from the supermarket...
DEAN: *What to Name Baby*?
BUZZ: Yeah, like that, and I've been going through it and marking ones I like. But I don't have to make up my mind too quick. It costs more than you'd think to change your name. Officially, I mean.
ROSS: What's wrong with the name Buzz?
BUZZ: Well, nothing. It's an okay name, I guess. But my dad was a Buzz too, and people back home called him Big Buzz and me Little Buzz, and I

didn't much like the sound of that, and in high school, some people started calling me Buzzsaw and Buzzard, so...

ROSS: (*Looking at Buzz's application*) So why did you leave Texas, Buzz?

BUZZ: I'm not exactly from Texas. I'm from Texarkana, but from the part that's in Arkansas, not the part that's in Texas.

ROSS: All right, why did you leave Arkansas?

BUZZ: Not all that much to do there.

DEAN: There was this movie, a late, late movie I saw a couple of weeks ago about some kind of monster like Bigfoot from down around Texarkana.

BUZZ: Yes, sir, that would be that Boggy Creek movie. One night, we were camping, and we thought we saw the Boggy Creek monster coming toward us, but it was just my dad, Big Buzz, coming back from the jakes.

ROSS: So, how do you like Boston?

BUZZ: I haven't seen all that much of it, this time around. People seem super nice, but I've been too busy trying to find work to poke around much.

ROSS: You've been here before?

BUZZ: Way back, when I was a little kid, my dad Big Buzz brought me and my brothers here 'cause he thought we should learn about history. I don't remember much except the Liberty Bell.

DEAN: That's in Philadelphia.

BUZZ: (*yawning*) You sure? Maybe that's where we went, then. No wonder nothing looks familiar.

ROSS: You say on your application you've worked in a bar before.

BUZZ: (*finishes yawn*) Right, great little place back in Texarkana, place called The Joint. It was right on State Line Avenue on the Texas side, but if you crossed the street, you were in Arkansas.

ROSS: And you tended bar there?

BUZZ: No, what mostly I did was check people's ID's. But I hung around with the bartenders enough so that I learned how to make all kinds of drinks. Tell you what, you name a drink, I'll tell you what's in it.

DEAN: I'm sure you can. Now...

BUZZ: Come on, try me.

ROSS: All right, what's in a Manhattan?

BUZZ: Uh oh... I don't know that one. No one much ordered Manhattans at The Joint. Ask me about a Pink Pull Your Panties Down, though.

DEAN: That's an easy one. Now, what we...

BUZZ: Hawaiian Punch, beer, lemonade, and Everclear. One-ninety proof Everclear. Packs a wallop.

DEAN: Sounds about right. Now, what we're going to do is give you a hypothetical situation and find out how you'd react, okay? Say it's a busy Saturday night and the servers' drink orders are getting backed up, and this character bellies up to the bar and says, "Make me a margarita and make it snappy." What do you do?

BUZZ: Let me think about that for a minute. (*thinks*) Well, I suppose what I'd do is, tell him real polite, have a seat, and I'll be with you quick as can be.

DEAN: Suppose he still insisted?

BUZZ: I'd tell him, "Keep your pants on, buddy, can't you see I'm goin' just as fast as I can?"

DEAN: Suppose he started getting nasty about it? Making a scene?

BUZZ: Then I guess I'd get him his drink out of turn, just so he'd quit his squawking.

DEAN: And if he said, "I wanted this margarita without salt," what would you do then?

BUZZ:

DEAN: Buzz?

BUZZ: Huh? Sorry, what'd you say?

DEAN: I said, what if he wanted one without salt?

BUZZ: I guess I'd tell him to go scrape the salt off and get away from me quick before I open a can of whoop ass. (*yawns again*)

ROSS: Is there anything the matter, Buzz?

BUZZ: Nothing particular's the matter. It's just that I don't have an alarm clock and so I had to stay up all night so as to be sure I could get here on time.

ROSS: Let me ask you, Buzz—if we couldn't use you as a bartender, would you consider doing something else? Not sure we want anyone opening cans of whoop ass in the bar. How about washing dishes or busing tables?

BUZZ: I was thinking I'd like to tend bar but... what the hey, I'd consider anything right about now.

ROSS: Do you have any questions for us?

BUZZ:

DEAN: Come in, Buzz. This is the mother ship calling.

BUZZ: Huh? Oh, sorry, guess I spaced out again, huh?

ROSS: I asked you if you had any questions for us.

BUZZ: No, but... well, you guys say it'll be a couple of weeks before you open? I was just wondering if there might be something I could do around here in the meantime.

ROSS: Most of the things we pay people to do around here at this stage—
you have to be union.
BUZZ: Yeah, I heard that about Boston, but still, when I was coming in
here, I saw some things that
needed doing. It's kind of a mess up there. And you could pay me whatever you think is fair. You wouldn't have to pay me like I was in a union.
DEAN: I suppose, when we're painting and so forth...
BUZZ: I'm handy at painting. I'm good with a roller, and I'm good with a
brush, and I don't get paint anywhere but where it's supposed to go. And
I'm not a bad carpenter either. My uncle Ray's one of the best carpenters in
Texarkana, and he taught me a few things.
DEAN: We already have a carpenter... sort of. We could think it over, I
guess. There might be some things... (Looks at application) You didn't put
down a phone number where we could get in touch with you.
BUZZ: I don't actually have a phone yet.
DEAN: Put down your address, then.
BUZZ: I don't have an actual address yet either. I'm sort of temporarily
living out of my car.
DEAN: Well, put down your license number.
BUZZ: What I'll do is, tomorrow morning, I'll drop by and see if there's
anything that needs doing, and if there is, I'll do it.
ROSS: Check with us before you actually start doing anything.
BUZZ: Oh, sure, I wouldn't want to do anything you didn't want done.

ROSS: Well, it looks as though we've hired someone whether we intended
to or not.
DEAN: But not as a bartender.
ROSS: Definitely not. But there might be things he can do.
DEAN: God, that haircut; like it was done with a combine. And that
accent.
ROSS: Your accent was pretty thick when I first met you. It still is when
you're upset.
DEAN: Are you kidding me? I have a warm hint of the Virginia Piedmont.
You're comparing that with
Buzz's Texas twang?
ROSS: He's from the Arkansas part, not the Texas part. Anyway, I don't
think we want him in the front of the house. But he seemed enthusiastic
enough.

DEAN: Oh, he's plenty enthusiastic. At least when he's awake. Normally, I'm a little suspicious of enthusiasm, but I have a feeling Buzz might work out for us. He probably knows more about carpentry than Lizard does.
ROSS: Don't let Lizard hear you say that.
DEAN: No, I bet he does. He's like those kids you see hanging around gas stations, drinking Cokes. They always know more about cars than the guys that actually work there.

~

PATSY KALCEVIC

DEAN: (*looking over Patsy's application*) It says here you're a student? (*Patsy nods*) And a philosophy major? (*more nodding*) So how are you this morning, ontologically speaking?
PATSY: What?
DEAN: Just a little joke. What branch of philosophy are you interested in? Phenomenology?
Epistemology? Or are you one of those Logical-Positivist creeps?
PATSY: I just started back to school in September. Boston State. I had to write something where it said "Intended Major" I haven't gotten to any of that stuff yet.
DEAN: I was a philosophy major myself. Well—double major, philosophy slash English lit. Okay, well, what else—do you have any kids?
PATSY: No. But I don't see what difference that makes.
DEAN: (*soothingly*) It doesn't make any difference. We just want to get to know you better.
ROSS: I don't think we're supposed to ask about kids, Dean.
PATSY: I think the only important thing to know about me is that I'm a quick learner and a terrific waitress. I've waited tables for almost fifteen years. I've done it all, from fast food to fine dining.
ROSS: I see that. On your application, it says that you're currently the manager of a bakery.
PATSY: Yeah, it's called the Muffin Man.
DEAN: Is that the one on Drury Lane?
PATSY: God, if you knew how many times...
DEAN: Sorry. So why do you want to go from being a manager to being a waitress?
PATSY: Because I'm sick of doing everyone's job for them. If a dishwasher doesn't show—and one doesn't about once a week—then I wash

dishes. If a waitress doesn't show, I wait tables. And I have to do all that plus my own work—all the ordering, bookkeeping, scheduling, training, all that. I've been putting in fifty or more hours a week, and I'm taking nine credit hours. No, I've got to find something else before finals, or I'll die. I'll die.

DEAN: Do you know anything about Mexican food?

PATSY: Not that much, except that I love nachos. But I didn't know a cranapple muffin from a jelly doughnut when I started at the Muffin Man. I'm a quick learner.

DEAN: I think we have what we need, Patsy. We'll be in touch, one way or another.

PATSY: I live with my mom. If I'm not at home, leave a message with her. I'm not there very much.

ROSS: Great, now I'm going to have that damn muffin song going through my head all day long. Jeremy used to listen to it constantly. So, what did you think? She seemed awfully defensive, didn't you think?

DEAN: Yeah, she's bitter about something. But anyone who majors in philosophy...

(*Patsy comes back into the office*)

PATSY: Sorry to bother you, I just wanted to know if there's any chance at all you might hire me.

DEAN: Well, we just started interviewing.

PATSY: I always try to be one of the first persons interviewed. But they always say, "We have lots of people to talk to still." Unless I don't get there early. Then they say, "Sorry, we hired someone right off the bat this morning."

ROSS: We just want to have the best waitstaff we possibly can.

PATSY: Look, I know, I understand that. But I had to cut two classes to come to this interview. It takes a lot of time, looking for a job, and that's one thing I don't have much of. If I didn't have to keep skipping classes, maybe I'd know about that phenomenology stuff you were talking about —although so far, we just keep hearing about Plato.

ROSS: I'm sorry you had to miss classes. We really will let you know as soon...

PATSY: (*shaking head*) If someone decides not to hire you, you never hear a word. You call and you just get the runaround. Look, I'm sorry I keep going on like this. If someone came into the Muffin Man and acted the way

I've been acting, I wouldn't give her a job either. So I wouldn't blame you if...

DEAN: All right, then. We were going to surprise you, but we'll tell you now. You've got the job.

PATSY: I do?

ROSS: You know, Amy told me the same thing about interviews. That it doesn't matter if you interview first or last.

DEAN: Well, she's not interviewing anymore. She's taking that job pushing school buses.

ROSS: Is she really?

DEAN: Yeah, but I predict she won't last more than a week. Can you see Amy waking up at five every morning? Amy has a hard time getting up at the crack of noon.

ROSS: I don't know, she's been showing a lot of determination lately. Tell me, why did you hire Patsy right off the bat like that? She's not exactly... sparkling.

DEAN: Yeah, she's about as charming as a gargoyle. That might come from being a philosophy major.

ROSS: You know, on her application, it said she worked was Durgin Park. They encourage their waitresses to be crabby. They're famous for that.

DEAN: I don't think Patsy would need a lot of encouragement to be cranky.

ROSS: So I still don't quite get why you hired her.

DEAN: I think we should consider making her head waitress. Someone around here has to know what they're doing.

~

KEITH HARTSAW

KEITH: I'll be damned, Ross, you've just about pulled it off. I mean, just about everyone who's ever worked in a restaurant says they're going to open a place of their own someday. But you walked out and damn it, you're doing it.

ROSS: (*to Dean*) You remember Keith? We used to work together at Maxwell's. (*turning to Keith*) You know, Rafael is going to be working here too.

KEITH: Is he? That's great. He's a hell of a good chef. He was kind of wasted, cooking at Maxwell's. How much imagination does it take to grill a steak or boil a lobster? But I thought I heard he was opening his own place.

ROSS: He did, he and his mom—they opened Estrella Maya. Out in Brighton. It went belly up after just a few months.

DEAN: It's a risky business we've gotten into.

ROSS: So how's everyone back at Maxie's? How's uh, Kandi doing?

DEAN: Kandi? I remember her. She was the hostess, right? Classy looking lady.

KEITH: Kandi left just a week or so ago. I guess her husband's tired of her working nights. But I told her I was going to interview here, and she told me to ask you if you were still going out with that woman from the bookstore... what was her name? Sarah something? Or Susan...?

ROSS: (interrupting him) And Michael? How's Michael?

KEITH: Michael's been gone for a while. You know he makes pottery, right? Well, he had some pieces in a show at a gallery in Newton and he sold quite a few of them. The next day he walks into Maxwell's and his name's not on the schedule. James only wants people who are completely dependent on their job at Maxie's to work there.

ROSS: God, James is such a control freak. And Wade? He still around?

KEITH: He went back to London a couple of months ago, back when James was thinking of turning the place into a Wild West bar. Wade said waiting tables was unpleasant enough; he said he had no fucking intention of doing it in a sodding ten-gallon hat.

ROSS: (shaking head) I can just hear Wade saying that.

KEITH: I guess I'm about the last of the old crew left. Except for James, that is.

ROSS: Maggie? Don't tell me she's gone.

KEITH: Maggie left when... did you ever hear anything about the Punk? No? Well, James hired the Punk as a dishwasher. He was this cute little blond number with a nasty temper. James fell madly in love with him and pretty soon, he was promoted to waiter, even though other people had to serve his drinks for him because he wasn't old enough. James was having dinner with some of his artsy-fartsy friends, and he had the Punk wait on them to show him off. The Punk got behind on his other tables and told Maggie to pick up a couple of them. She told him she had plenty of her own tables going—it was a busy night. So the Punk said that if she didn't take those tables off his hands, he was going to cut out her liver with a steak knife. She said "Okay, if you feel that way about it, fine," Then she took off her apron and walked out the back door for good.

ROSS: (*to Dean*) Maggie's this great waitress with a photographic memory. James didn't approve of people writing down orders unless it was a really big table; he thought it looked tacky. But Maggie could take orders from a table of ten and not write anything down and still not screw up.
(*to Keith*) So, is the Punk still there?

KEITH: No, that's the best part. He stayed around a few more weeks, getting together as much cash as he could, then he used James' Bank-Americard to book a flight to L.A., and he vanished. Damn near broke James' heart. So Ross, what do you think? I'd love to go in to Maxwell's this afternoon and tell James I'm quitting.

ROSS: Well, I'd wait on that, but I think we'll be able to use you.
(*a pause*)

KEITH: You know, Ross, when you left Maxie's, I wanted to walk out right behind you.

ROSS: I appreciate that, Keith, but it wouldn't have done any good.

KEITH: It would have made me feel better. We all knew it was crap, that bit about you dipping into the till.

ROSS: James just wanted to get rid of me. I knew too much.

KEITH: I was glad you didn't take that polygraph test.

ROSS: I could have. But it was beneath my dignity.

KEITH: Some of us—Michael, Wade, Maggie, couple of others—we talked about walking out together that next Saturday night. As a protest. That would have shaken James up.

ROSS: For one night. He'd have replaced you by Sunday.

KEITH: You know what surprised me? You never stopped by, just to see how things were going.

ROSS: I said when I left that I wasn't coming back.

KEITH: Yeah, I know, everyone says that, but just about everybody who ever worked there shows up eventually. You see them sitting at the bar like they just happened to be in the neighborhood and had some time to kill. They sit there and say, "God, this place has changed!" Course, it never seems to change to me. But it's funny, much as people hate working there, it seems to get in the blood. Michael's there all the time, Wade calls from London sometimes to see what's going on, and Maggie started dropping by once the Punk was gone—Maggie's in law school now, by the way.

ROSS: Is she? I was hoping I could get her to work here. Well, tell you the truth, I've thought about coming by but... I can't stand the thought of seeing James.

KEITH: I can hardly stand seeing him myself. Tell you something else: We haven't had a decent bartender since you left. Guy working there now, he has to look up gin and tonic in Old Mister Boston...

ROSS: Wow. All those people I used to work with, they're all gone. All but Keith. And James.

DEAN: What did you expect? It's been over six months. You know what turn-over is like in restaurants.

ROSS: I don't know. Whenever I picture Maxwell's, it's exactly the way it was the night I left. It's a good thing I never went back. I'd be one of those sad people sitting at the bar saying "God, this place has changed!"

DEAN: You never told me about the polygraph test or any of that.

ROSS: It pisses me off too much to talk about. You know, it's funny. When I started at Maxwell's, James was just another waiter there. Not a bad guy. Then he got to be maître d, and then manager, and he got to be progressively more and more a bastard.

DEAN: Sounds like he deserved to be ripped off.

ROSS: Maybe so, but I didn't. What, you think I'd rip you off if I thought you deserved it?

DEAN: (*sincerely*) Of course not, Ross. You know I trust you explicitly.

ROSS: You shouldn't do that, but... I'd never rip you off. Because I don't want to end up on the List.

DEAN: It turned out to be a good thing that you got fired. It was a week or so after that we definitely decided to turn Spiro's Super Sub Shop into ¿Por Que No? If that's the name we're actually going with. I'm not in love with it.

ROSS: Me either, but It's the only one we could halfway agree on. So, what do you think of Keith?

DEAN: You know him a lot better than I do. I just remember he worked at Maxwell's. What do you think?

ROSS: I don't know if he's all that good a waiter. I remember Maggie saying he was always out in the weeds. He didn't have the kind of memory that she did, and he gave the kitchen the wrong orders sometimes. He ordered the wrong drinks from me too. But... if he can write down his orders at the table—I don't think that's tacky—maybe he'll do fine. Anyway, I'd like to help him get out of that place.

DEAN: I think that what you like is the idea of him going in and saying, "James, I quit. I'm going to work at Ross's new restaurant."

MEREDITH FISCUS

DEAN: Relax, Meredith. We're probably as nervous as you are.

MEREDITH: I'm not nervous at all.

ROSS: Seems you travel around quite a bit. (*reading from application*) Chez Fondue, Aspen. King Henry VIII's, San Francisco. Bianca's in Santa Barbara. Le Poirier in Montreal. Tito's in Santa Fe. And this one, I like this one: Mom's Apple Pie, Kabul, Afghanistan.

MEREDITH: It's pronounced *KAH-bull*—kinda like cobble stone. Not kah-*BOOL*.

DEAN: So what was that like?

MEREDITH: Interesting place to work. All these homesick Americans passing through Kabul on their way to getting holy in India would stop in. You could get burgers and fries and regular coffee. And apple pie, natu-rally. But I couldn't make any money there. Backpackers aren't big tippers. (*Enter Lizard*)

LIZARD: Who wants coffee? (*sees Meredith*) Hey, hello. Didn't see you come in.

DEAN: This is Lizard. He's the carpenter.

LIZARD: You hear the way he says that? It's like, "This is Lizard. He's shit wrapped in skin." This guy has no respect for people who do physical labor, people who get their hands dirty.

DEAN: Are you kidding me? I used to be a hod carrier.

LIZARD: You were a hod carrier? That's damn hard work. I wouldn't have thought you'd had it in you, Dean. (To Meredith) Want to get coffee with me?

MEREDITH: I'm afraid I have to finish this interview.

LIZARD: All right then, I'll bring you one back. You take your coffee regu-lar? And who's paying?

DEAN: We've already given you all our money.

LIZARD: I'll start a tab then. (*to Meredith*) Don't go away.

DEAN: (*to Ross*) If someone would just plug in the coffee machine, he wouldn't have to make three coffee runs a morning.

ROSS: Lizard likes going out. Besides, the coffee machine's not working right.

DEAN: It's not? Damn, that's because it got drenched in maple syrup. Well, I don't guess we can't go back to Irene for a refund, but we should get one of the electricians...

MEREDITH: Uh, I have another interview at eleven thirty.

DEAN: Oh, sorry. Let's see, we were talking about places you've worked. What about King Henry's? What was that like?

MEREDITH: Oh, you know, it was one of those medieval places where everyone eats with their hands, and there was a jester, and the customers called the waitresses wenches and the waiters knaves, and...

DEAN: Did the diners throw their bones over their shoulders to the hounds?

MEREDITH: They threw the bones, but we couldn't have dogs because of the health department.

ROSS: The customers called you wench? That didn't bother you?

MEREDITH: No, why should it? It was all theater. In fact, a lot of the wait-rons there were actors. And the tips were good.

DEAN: (to Ross) Could be we're on the wrong tack here. Maybe we need a historical context. Caligula's Kitchen—you like the sound of that? Maybe Bonaparte's Bistro?

ROSS: Any questions for us, Meredith?

MEREDITH: Is this going to be a good money house?

DEAN: We hope so. It'll take time to build up a regular clientele, of course, but we hope no one starves in the meantime.

MEREDITH: Are you doing anything to help the servers out? When people are tipping, they have to decide for themselves how much to leave. And people aren't used to making up their own prices for things. I mean, a lot of people still think 10 percent is an okay tip.

ROSS: Yeah, true, tipping is pretty arbitrary. But we're not going to tack on a service charge, if that's what you mean.

MEREDITH: I mean just a reminder. Like, this one place I worked, Bian-ca's, they had a little notice at the bottom of the menu that said: WE SUGGEST A GRATUITY OF 15%.

ROSS: What we've thought about doing is to have the waiters and wait-resses pool their tips and give a cut to the kitchen staff and the other people who don't get tips. That way everyone has a stake in what goes on out on the floor.

MEREDITH: I worked at a place in Santa Fe where they did that. What happened was, a few people did all the work, and everyone got a share. It was like socialism.

DEAN: It's just something we've considered. We haven't made any final decisions yet.

ROSS: Meredith, let me ask you—you relocate quite a bit. Suppose we offer you a job here—how do we know you won't be moving to Morocco or Maui or someplace in a month or two?

MEREDITH: You'll just have to trust me, I guess. I'm planning to be around for a while, though. I just signed a year's lease on an apartment in the South End, and I just bought new skis so I can go skiing up in Vermont on my days off. A friend of mine has a condo up in Snowbury.

ROSS: Well, see, my point is, Dean and I want to hire people who are definitely going to stick around a while. That's the only way we can do some of the things we want to do. We eventually want to get health insurance and things like that for our employees. You don't usually get that sort of thing in restaurant work.

MEREDITH: No, you don't, but really, I wonder if that matters much to anyone. The only kind of restaurants where people stick around are places where they have a wine steward and the waiters wear tuxes.

ROSS: If they were treated okay, people might stick around longer.

MEREDITH: I don't know. Maybe. But most of the people I've worked with have been people who were waiting for something better to come along. None of them planned to be doing restaurant work more than a few years.

DEAN: She has a point, Ross. We're dealing with a very mobile class of people.

ROSS: She does have point, but I think...

DEAN: We can't exactly ask people we hire to sign a binding contract, can we?

ROSS: (*closing eyes in frustration*) No, Dean, I guess we can't.

DEAN: We'll just have to see how it goes. If Meredith says she's going to be around, I think we can trust her.

MEREDITH: Does this mean I've got the job?

DEAN: Well, that's encouraging. We're going to have at least a couple people here with some real restaurant experience.

ROSS: Yeah. I guess.

DEAN: You're pissed off, aren't you? Don't bother denying it. I can tell when you are.

ROSS: I guess I just wasn't as sure about her as you seemed to be. And you were acting so gaga...

DEAN: I wasn't exactly gaga... I just wanted to nail her down. Maybe at that next interview she was going to...

ROSS: Right. There are probably people who do nothing but follow her around all day, tripping over themselves, trying to offer her jobs.

DEAN: She does have all that experience.

ROSS: Says she does. Are we going to call Kabul—I mean *KAH-bull*—and get a reference from Mom? Maybe she never worked there. Or maybe when the backpackers didn't tip enough, she got rude and Mom gave her the sack.

DEAN: Okay, sure, she comes off as a tad greedy, but that can be a positive attribute in a waitress. And you have to admit, she's a real healthy looking lady.

ROSS: You like 'em flashy. But we aren't going to hire people just because they look pretty.

DEAN: No, of course not, but if we were, she'd be overqualified.

ROSS: Tell you what, Dean, I think we're making up our minds too fast. We've seen four people and more or less hired all of them. Didn't we say we were going to wait and talk it over before we hired anyone?

DEAN: Okay, from now on, we discuss.

ROSS: You know, it's just that we've talked about this place for so long. We...

DEAN: That's right. And everyone, I mean everyone, thought it was just talk. I kind of thought so myself.

ROSS: But we pretty much decided what kind of a place we wanted. We shouldn't chuck all that just because it doesn't jibe with what someone who comes in looking for a job wants. Even if she is real healthy looking.

DEAN: No, we shouldn't. Absolutely not. Of course, we do have to be a little expedient. Just because we figured something out when we were sitting in a bar a year ago doesn't mean it's going to work in the trenches.

ROSS: We haven't tried *anything* yet. We have no idea what'll work and what won't. And by the way, you were never really a hod carrier, were you?

DEAN: Yeah, I was a hoddie. For a little while. I only lasted till lunchtime.

ROSS: Why's that?

DEAN: It was a hot day. And hods are heavy. Really, really heavy.

~

HOWARD DILBECK AND FRIEND

HOWARD: You guys are younger than I thought you'd be.

DEAN: (*making a check mark on Howard's application*) That's one point in your favor.

HOWARD: And I thought you'd probably be Mexican.

DEAN: No. No, we're not. Now, it says on your application that you've done a little cooking and a little waiting, too. That's good. We're going to have a small staff, so versatility is appreciated.

HOWARD: Oh, I can be versatile all right. Can I ask you guys something? Are you going to be open for lunch?

HOWARD'S FRIEND: Howard, I don't think you...

DEAN: We thought we would be, yes. Why do you ask?

HOWARD: Because I can't work lunches on Monday, Wednesday, and Friday. I'm in class then.

ROSS: Well, we'll be closed on Mondays, but we can talk about scheduling later.

HOWARD: But see, with me, scheduling is a major concern. Now, there would be a conflict on Thursday, too, because of student council meetings. I wouldn't have to go every week but sometimes I would because I'm the representative for the Telecom Department, and I have a certain responsibility.

ROSS: So really, you could only work lunches on Tuesday, right?

HOWARD: And weekends, usually. Now Wednesday evenings, I do a work-study project with these kids from Columbia Point, teaching them how to run a radio station. Really, I don't teach them anything, I just turn them loose. I wouldn't even have to be there except that the administration is afraid they might break something or say something dirty over the air. But they're great. They're real. They're really real. They know everything about music, and the patter they come up with... amazing... you'd be amazed. You should listen some Wednesday evening.

ROSS: So let's see... Wednesday dinner shift is out. That leaves...

HOWARD: And Friday night, but just temporarily. There's a film series... classic films... hey, we're showing *Citizen Kane* next Friday if you...

DEAN: Seen it. Howard, it looks like it's going to be tough, trying to mesh your schedule with our needs.

ROSS: And we don't want to hire too many part-time people.

HOWARD: Well, I can appreciate that. (*to friend*) See? I told you this would happen.

HOWARD'S FRIEND: You don't have to do all that other shit. You could just go to classes and work here.

(*to Dean*) Could he do that?

HOWARD: I've told you and I've told you, going to college is more than just taking classes. It's the whole... the whole educational *gestalt* of...
DEAN: (*To Howard's friend*) What about you? Are you looking for a job?
HOWARD'S FRIEND: (*disgusted*) *I've* already got a job.
ROSS: Why would someone bring a date to a job interview?
DEAN: I don't think she was a date, exactly—more like a chaperone.

ROBIN LINDERSMITH

ROSS: I wonder why you look so familiar?
ROBIN: Maybe because I uh... work next door? At Copenhagen Cream?
DEAN: Are you asking us or telling us?
ROBIN: Huh? (kneads purse in lap) Uh, telling you, I guess. I only work there part-time.
ROSS: Oh yeah. I think I've seen you over there.
DEAN: Does the Bean know you're here? We don't want him thinking we're trying to lure his help away. Got to keep up good relations with the landlord.
HOWARD: Oh, he knows. Chris is the one who suggested I come over here.
DEAN: He suggested it, huh.
ROBIN: Uh-huh. He thought I could make more money working here.
DEAN: Well, Robin, working at an ice cream parlor isn't exactly the kind of experience...
ROBIN: That's not all I've done. I was the hostess at a place called the Beef and Booze out on Route 128, and I was a cocktail waitress at this bar in West Newton, the Blue Moose. It's closed now. But I've got a letter from the... the uh...
ROSS: The manager?
ROBIN: Yes, the manager. I'll show it to you. (*Begins looking in her purse*) (*Enter Lizard*)
LIZARD: Coffee break time. Hey, what'd you do with that other chick? We were just starting to hit it off.
ROSS: She's been gone a long time.
DEAN: So have you. This coffee's cold.
LIZARD: Well, I met up with this old buddy of mine. We used to be on the golf team together back in high school.
ROSS: I didn't know you played golf, Lizard.

LIZARD: Like I'm always telling you guys, there are a lot of things you don't know about me. (*To Robin*) You want a coffee, kid? We've got an extra here.

ROBIN: Coffee?

LIZARD: You know, that stuff people drink during coffee breaks. Here you go, drink up. Hey, you've got carpenter pants on.

ROBIN: I what?

LIZARD: It's people like you make those pants so expensive that carpenters can't afford them anymore.

DEAN: Are you kidding? There's nothing carpenters shouldn't be able to afford.

ROBIN: I didn't know they were carpenter pants. I just thought they were cute.

LIZARD: That loop on your thigh—why did you think that was there? It's to put your hammer in.

DEAN: I've never once seen a carpenter with a hammer in that loop.

LIZARD: That's because, every time you move, the hammer falls out and lands on your foot.

(*Lizard exits, shaking head*)

ROBIN: I don't think I want this coffee. I don't like coffee.

DEAN: That's all right. Just set it down. (*Robyn starts to put the coffee cup in a basket full of Rafael's chilies.*) No, on the desk. There, that's fine. Now, Robin, imagine yourself in this situation. One of your reservations has requested a table by the window. Then another party comes in and asks for that table. You say, someone reserved it for seven o'clock. They point out that it's quarter after seven. What do you do?

ROBIN: *I* don't know.

DEAN: You don't know? You don't want to make a guess or anything?

ROBIN: I'd rather be a cocktail waitress than a hostess. They make more money.

LIZARD: (*from upstairs*) You wanna move that over just a pussy hair?

ROSS: Sorry. That's just our carpenter talking to his assistant. Could you close the office door behind you, please?

ROBIN: Me?

ROSS: Never mind, I'll get it. (*Ross walks around the desk and closes the door but stands for a moment near Robin.*)

ROBIN: I just can't find that letter. (*Empties purse on the desk; a penny rolls around on the desktop in a concentric circle*)

DEAN: Well, it's easy to lose things. There are a lot more places where things aren't than places where they are.

ROSS: (*assuming seat*) Just relax.
ROBIN: I'm trying. Maybe if I take a deep breath?
ROSS: Sure, try that.
(*Robin closes eyes, takes a couple of very deep breaths*)
ROSS: Robin?
(*Robin opens eyes and exhales; she appears to be seeing them for the first time.*)
ROSS: Is there anything you'd like to ask us?
ROBIN: Ooh, that made me a little dizzy. Anything to ask you? Uh, can you tell me if this is a safe neighborhood at night? We're only open during the day next door. And I had a friend—my brother's friend, really—he was walking along one night not far from here, near Back Bay Station,
just walking down the street, minding his own business, and he got all sliced up. These two guys came along. And they had potatoes...
DEAN: Potatoes? They were slicing potatoes?
ROBIN: No, they had potatoes on a string. And there were razor blades stuck in the potatoes. They were swinging them around, and they hit my brother's friend with their razor potatoes, one on his left arm and one on his right. And even though he was wearing a leather jacket, the razors cut right through it and he had to go to the hospital.
DEAN: Interesting. Irish gangs used to use razor potatoes back in the twenties. I guess they're making a comeback. But I don't think this neighborhood is so bad that you'll be attacked with potatoes at the hostess stand.
ROBIN: Like I said, I'd rather be a cocktail waitress. Or any kind of waitress.
ROBIN: We'll keep that in mind. And we'll get back to you. At least we know where to find you.
(*Robin shovels things back into her purse*)
DEAN: That's Ross's pen you're taking, Robin.
ROBIN: Is it? Are you sure?
DEAN: I can tell. It's got my tooth marks in it.
ROBIN: Oh. Well, here, I'll give it back to you.

DEAN: You were the gaga one this time—I saw you casing her boobs.
ROSS: God, was I? I didn't even realize it. Think she noticed?
DEAN: Any earthling would. Especially when you got up for an aerial view. Some women have built-in detection devices, like those fighter

planes that can tell if they're being scanned by radar. But... with Robin, I think you're safe. I don't think she noticed much of anything.

ROSS: I could tell, you thought she was an airhead.

DEAN: I wouldn't go so far as to say that, but every time she opened her mouth, Ferris wheels dropped out.

ROSS: That's because she was nervous. I think she'd make an okay hostess. Or waitress.

DEAN: You do, huh. I think we should wait to decide. You're right, we still have a lot of people to talk to. Hey, what's up with all these restaurants that have meat and alcohol in their names? The Beef and Booze. The Burger and Beer. Maybe we should change the name of this place to the Sirloin and Sangria. Or the Veal and Vodka. (*Goes upstairs and looks around. Ross joins him.*) Who are all those people milling around up here? Why are there always people here who don't belong?

ROSS: Well, that's Lizard and the assistant Lizard, you don't mean them. There's a sparkie and a plumber, they all belong.

DEAN: Who's the little guy?

ROSS: The guy who wants to sell us matchbooks with our logo on them?

DEAN: No, I met him. I told him to come back when we had a logo.

ROSS: The beer distributer? The insurance guy? The guy bringing the jukebox?

DEAN: Don't think so.

ROSS: A reporter from *Boston Magazine*? A spy from Casa Rubio?

DEAN: Nope, nope. I'm thinking he might be from the Building Inspector's office.

ROSS: Could be. He might have come by to see if we really widened the doorways.

DEAN: Or maybe he came by for a bribe.

ROSS: That's possible, too. Why don't we ask him?

DEAN: Or I could call up some friends and have his legs broken.

ROSS: You have friends that break people's legs?

DEAN: Well no, not really. We need to cultivate friends like that, though, going into business in this town.

WALKER BRODY

ROSS: We thought maybe the Building Inspector sent you.

WALKER: No, Mr.... what did you say your name was, exactly?

ROSS: Ross.

WALKER: Mr. Ross. No, he didn't. I came on my own.

ROSS: Not Mr. Ross, just plain Ross. And this is just plain Dean. So, it says on your application that you used to be a jockey?

DEAN: Where did you ride?

WALKER: Got my start at Douglas Park down in Louisville. That place is long gone now. I raced at Hialeah and Aqueduct and Churchill Downs and up here at Suffolk Downs and lots of little places you probably never heard of.

DEAN: Churchill Downs, huh. Ever ride in the Derby?

WALKER: No, I never got to, but I rode Roman Coins in the Preakness in '63.

ROSS: How'd you do?

WALKER: Not in the money. But not last either.

ROSS: So you retired and...

WALKER: Well, I had a bad fall riding at Centennial out in Denver. Broke my femur in two places and wrecked my knee and messed up my back pretty bad. If I'd been a horse, they would have shot me. I was laid up for months.

ROSS: And after that, you started tending bar?

WALKER: Well, I wasn't just a bartender at the Julep Cup. I owned part of it too.

DEAN: Okay, so there seems to be a... a gaping hole in your résumé. From '69 to '74.

WALKER: That's right. I was in LaGrange then.

DEAN: LaGrange?

WALKER: Oh, right, I forget people up here don't know what that is. It's a prison down in Kentucky. (A pause) Now I know you're gonna want to know what I was doing there in the joint. Well, I'll be honest with you, Mr. Dean, Mr. Ross—I almost killed a man. (Another pause) It was a terrible, terrible thing. This man, I knew him from my racing days, he'd been a trainer. Then he came to work for me at the Julep Cup. He played the electric guitar. Played it real good. He could even play it with his teeth. One night, we got in a fight—over a woman, of course—and I hit him way too hard with a bottle of Maker's Mark. Gave him a concussion.

DEAN: Concussions, those are nasty things. Had one myself. Is that how you, uh, lost your eye? In the fight?

WALKER: No, uh, that happened right after I got out of Lagrange. We were celebrating, my ma and my brother and my lady friend and me. We'd drunk a few bottles of champagne and I was opening one more. I twisted off the wire hood and then I tried to get the cork out but it was struck in there good. Finally it sailed out and hit me...

ROSS: You're should always point the bottle away from...

WALKER: I know that, but I was feeling kinda loopy, right out of the joint like that, and at least half in the bag, and that cork popped me right in the eye. Nothing the doctors could do. Not seen a thing out of that eye since that day.

DEAN: Well, one good thing... I don't think we'll be selling a lot of champagne here. I'm glad you didn't try to bullshit us... about your time in, uh, Lagrange.

WALKER: You know, I could have. I could have told you that I worked some place but it burned down. You probably wouldn't have checked. You probably have better things to do. But I thought it would be better just to be up front with you. Because I might have forgotten what I told you originally, don't you see? Then where would I be?

ROSS: What are you thinking?

DEAN: I was just thinking, it's a good thing the plumbers mounted one of those urinals lower than the other one. I mean, if we hire him.

ROSS: I think they have to. I think it's a law or something. No, really, what did you think of Walker?

DEAN: I think that, if we go for the business-type customers at lunch...

ROSS: So you want to dress Walker up like one of those jockey lawn ornaments and tell him to do some fancy cocktail shaking and...

DEAN: That's not it at all, I just think he would make a really steady bartender for the lunch shift.

ROSS: Steady? I guess. He did almost kill someone.

DEAN: Guy probably provoked it, playing guitar with his toes.

ROSS: Not toes, teeth.

DEAN: Right, teeth. I just think we should shoot for a quiet, masculine ambience at lunch.

ROSS: Masculine? There are more women working around here than men.

DEAN: Yeah, but the secretaries bring yogurt for lunch and eat at their desks, and the women execs—they'll feel like they've arrived.

ROSS: I don't know that I trust your logic. So, you think we should hire him? You have to watch it with experienced bartenders. They know all the tricks. They can short ring you; a customer comes in and orders a two-fifty top-shelf tequila, and they ring it up as a dollar-fifty well drink. If they're closing, they can void out cash receipts and pocket the money. Or they can just give away booze to friends, or give free drinks to regular customers so they get better tips. There are lots of ways they can rob you.

DEAN: You think Walker would do any of that?

ROSS: Umm, no, I don't think so. I just think he knows how to. I mean, I never did any of that either, except give a few drinks to friends. Like you. But I knew how to.

CECILY DE PAUL

ROSS: You've never worked in a restaurant before, Cecily?

CECILY: Never have. But I'm a good cook. I have five nieces and nephews and a lot of friends who like to drop by at dinner time, so it's almost like a restaurant around my house. All my friends tell me I should open a place. I'm sure it takes a lot of money, though.

DEAN: It does. More than you can imagine.

ROSS: So what are your specialties?

DEAN: Oh—well, cookies of course. I guess you guys know...

ROSS: Know what?

(*Cecily takes a couple of packages out of her purse*)

ROSS: Wait—Aunt Cecily's Cookies. You're Aunt Cecily? You kidding? Those are amazing cookies! I get them all the time, but my kid usually eats all of them before I can even get one.

DEAN: Aunt Cecily—hell yeah, look, that's your picture on the package. This is like interviewing a celebrity. You must be making bundles. You could open your own cookie café.

CECILY: Well—these are my cookies—my recipes—my life's blood. But I sold out to California Brands a few years back.

DEAN: Big mistake?

CECILY: Oh, I don't know. Sometimes I think I should have waited. But making cookies is easy compared to marketing them and distributing them.

ROSS: Of course, we won't have cookies on the menu.

CECILY: I'm good at other things, too. Desserts for sure. Soups. Seafood. Steaks. Anything.

DEAN: Do you know anything about Mexican food?

CECILY: Umm, no, not too much. But... *yo hablo español. Un poco.*

DEAN: *Muy bien.* That's a plus. Our chef Rafael doesn't speak great

English and his mother—she'll be working here, too—she doesn't speak any English at all.

CECILY: Well, my ex was from Venezuela, so...

DEAN: Cecily, let me pose a hypothetical situation to you. Suppose a waiter brings you an order for carne asada—

CECILY: Now, what's that, exactly? I know it means "roasted meat," but...

ROSS: It's basically just marinated skirt steak.

DEAN: Okay, so, say this waiter asks for it medium-well, and you cook it that way, and then he says, "Sorry, I meant medium rare." What would you do?

CECILY: Well, you can't uncook steak. So I guess I'd talk to that waiter.

DEAN: What would you say?

CECILY: I'd say, "You'd better get your shit together, hon!" I'd cook him a medium-rare steak and I'd set that other steak aside in case some rube comes in later and orders burnt meat.

DEAN: I like a woman who kicks butt and spits on the floor.

ROSS: Wait, she did what?

DEAN: I don't mean she really spit on the floor. I just mean she's not going to take any crap from the waitrons. But there's more to her than that. Didn't you get the idea that she was basically... wholesome? I mean wholesome like baking soda or...

ROSS: Baking soda is wholesome?

DEAN: I think of it that way. I liked her a lot.

ROSS: How could anyone not like her? She's the cookie lady.

-?-

-?-: Don't take my picture!

DEAN: We've been taking everyone's picture. We're just...

-?-: (filled with a burly dread) Not mine! Don't!

ROSS: Don't take his picture if he doesn't want you to, Dean. Now, you didn't put your name on the application. Or your social security number, or...

-?-: I don't have one. It's not safe to.

ROSS: One what? A social security number or a name?

-?-: You're not going to have a microwave oven here, are you?

DEAN: Not right away. We almost bought one. It's probably at the bottom of a pond now.

-?-: Good. That's where they belong, all of them. They put out rays, you know. Make you sterile.

ROSS: So, about dishwashing, we know it can be a pretty unpleasant job, but we see it as a very important one. I know all about it. I used to be a pearl diver myself.

DEAN: Little Richard was one too. And Malcolm X.

-?-: Don't call it pearl diving! There aren't any pearls. I've never seen a pearl, I've never...

ROSS: Right, sorry. Anyway, we know it's about the crappiest work in the house, and it usually pays the least.

-?-: That's just the way it is. If it was fun, I'd have to pay you to do it.

ROSS: You may have a point, but here, we're planning to pay our dish-washers decent wages, and they'll get a certain percentage of the tips that the servers get.

-?-: I don't want any tips. If I were a waiter, I'd give people back their tips and tell them not to do that again, ever.

ROSS: In fact, we're considering having everyone on the staff work as a dishwasher for one night—just to see what the job is like.

-? -: And are you going to have everyone on the staff work as managers for one night? To see what that's like?

ROSS: No, but that's not...

-?-: It's exactly the same. You don't want amateurs poking around in your manager business and messing things up. Well, neither do I. So, will there be many things that have to be washed by hand?

ROSS: Not too many things, I don't think—just stuff that won't fit through the dishwashing machine. Big pots and so forth. And chef's knives. Rafael would get very upset if you put his knives through the dishwasher. Or his cast iron skillets.

-?-: If it was up to me, I'd do everything by hand. That's the only way you can be really, really 100 percent sure things are completely clean. You'll need to get me some sand for the pots and pans.

DEAN: Sand? Like on beaches?

-?-: Of course like on beaches, what did you think? I need fine white sand, not that ugly gray stuff you get around here. Pure silica sand. White sand. Or pink sand from Bermuda—that's good sand, primo sand. And you rub and you scour them and... and wait a minute. Wait just a damn minute. Do you have any fluorescent lights around here?

ROSS: In the kitchen. Why?

-?-: In the *kitchen*! Where do you think I'm going to be washing dishes, in the cloakroom? In the men's room? Do you have any idea what fluorescent lights do to you?

ROSS: Uh, no.

DEAN: (*in a loud aside*) Ross, I'm beginning to think...

-?-: They put out your eyes, is all. They burn out your retinas. They... they put out rays...

DEAN: I should hope they put out rays.

-?-: (*fervently*) Will you get rid of them?

DEAN: We just spent a lot of money having them put in.

-?-: Money! Oh, well, I can see it won't do any good talking to you about it, since it's a matter of *money!* (-?- *stands up*) Well, fine. You get yourself some other sucker, someone who doesn't mind washing dishes with the help of a Seeing Eye dog. (*rushes out*)

DEAN: Do you suppose Seeing Eye dogs can actually help wash dishes?

AMY O'DELL

DEAN: All right, let's take a look at your application here. Your last job, it says, was as a Santa's helper at Jordan Marsh, and that was two Christmases ago.

AMY: No. No, my last job was giving away sample packs of fake cigarettes last summer. Those cigarettes made of cabbage and green tea.

DEAN: Oh, yes, I see, you put that down. Those cigarettes were hideous, by the way. Nasty smell, nasty taste. Okay, before that, we have to go back quite a few years to your job at FotoHut. Suppose you tell us why you left that job.

AMY: You already know why.

DEAN: Just tell us, please.

AMY: All right, I will. There was a big sign on the drive-thru that said CLEARANCE: 8 FEET. Well, one night, someone stole that sign. Or maybe the wind blew it away, I don't know. But... it wasn't there, and I didn't notice that it was gone when I opened. So a truck with a camper came through, and...

DEAN: (*gleefully*) And it sheered the canopy of the FotoHut right off, didn't it?

AMY: If you knew what happened, why did you ask?

DEAN: No need to get defensive. Let's continue. Now, it doesn't appear as if you have any actual restaurant experience. Am I correct in assuming that?

AMY: You know you are. But your ad didn't say you had to. It said EXPE-RIENCE A PLUS.

DEAN: True enough, but we've been getting people in here today with years and years of experience, haven't we, Ross? We even had a woman in here who started her own cookie company.

AMY: Yeah, but don't you think that someone who was responsible— don't look at me that way, Dean— someone who was responsible and had plenty of common sense, that he or she could pick it up? I don't have any experience driving a bus, but the bus company is willing to take a chance on me. Restaurant work—I don't think it's as complicated as you make it out to be. Besides, Ross offered Thea a job, and she's never worked in a restaurant either. She didn't even have to come for an interview.

DEAN: No, but she worked at a hospital in London. She knows what it's like to hustle. However, that's beside the point. Okay, let's do a little hypo-thetical. (*Looks at legal pad.*) Pretend you've just finished up with a table and given them the check, and they pay with a twenty and a ten. You take it to Ross in the bar, he rings it up, and you bring your customers their change. One of them tells you they gave you two twenties. How do you respond?

AMY: I know it wasn't two twenties?

DEAN: Yes.

AMY: And Ross is sure too?

DEAN: Yes.

AMY: I'd tell them to kiss off then.

DEAN: Wrong. Absolutely wrong.

AMY: What do you mean, wrong? What should I have done, according to you?

DEAN: What you should do in a case like that is take the customer's name and address and tell him that if, when the bartender cashes out at the end of the shift, he comes up ten over, you'll see to it that a check for ten dollars will be mailed to him, pronto. You never, under any circumstances, tell a customer to "kiss off."

AMY: I didn't mean I'd actually say it in those words. Ross, what would you have done?

ROSS: I guess I...

DEAN: (*Overlapping him*) Don't try to pull poor Ross into this.

AMY: It's just that it's the oldest, lamest trick in the world. Even my boss at FotoHut warned me about that.

DEAN: Maybe. Or maybe it was an honest mistake. But even if it wasn't, you always treat paying customers with respect. Even if they're bunco artists.

AMY: No matter what I said, it would have been "Wrong, absolutely wrong." You just don't want me working here because if I'm around, you won't be able to act like a big shot, and you won't be able to come on to all the waitresses. Or you think you won't be able to. Why should I care what you do once we've split up?

DEAN: Bullshit. Just because you're not qualified to...

AMY: Ross, am I qualified or not?

ROSS: Well, I'd have to say...

DEAN: (*overlapping him again*) You're always doing this. We're having a personal discussion and you have to enlist a referee. You did that the whole time Ross lived with us.

AMY: You seem to forget, gumdrops, this isn't a personal discussion. It's a job interview, and Ross has half the say in deciding.

DEAN: Didn't he just say that he didn't want to get involved?

AMY: Dean, Dean, Dean, sometimes you make me laugh. And sometimes you make me feel so tired. Anyway, it doesn't matter. I just filled out an application and came to the interview to see what you'd do. You did exactly what I thought you'd do. You're predictable, honeybun, so predictable. Ross, did you hear about my new job?

ROSS: A little. Are you going to be able to get up that early? I know you like to sleep in.

AMY: I hope so. I'll have to practice first. Last week, Daddy told me I can use the Pinto while I'm working there.

DEAN: Great. A goose-turd green Pinto with a Nixon bumper sticker. Some ride.

AMY: I'm not one of those people who cares what kind of car they drive. And I've been trying to scrape that bumper sticker off, but it's really stuck on there. I can only peel off one tiny scrap at a time.

ROSS: Maybe you can find a "Don't blame me, I'm from Massachusetts" bumper sticker somewhere to cover it up with.

AMY: Oh, Daddy would love that! Anyway, getting that car was a biggie, because the bus barn's way out in Mattapan. Daddy's being super supportive, for a change. He wants me to be independent.

DEAN: He's not being "supportive." He's being hateful toward me. Dorky Dan's always resented me.

AMY: Not always he hasn't. And Ross, I finally passed the written test for a Class II license, after failing it two times. They ask you these absurd questions, like about the pressure in air brakes—our school buses don't even have air brakes. At least, I don't think they do. And I passed the physical too, although that doctor that the bus company sent me to was sort of a lech, I thought.

DEAN: He was? What did he do?

AMY: I'm sure you'd love to hear the details.

ROSS: So—you looking forward to it?

AMY: I don't know. It's... it's a little scary. One of the drivers, Paulie, he's been driving since the whole busing thing got started. He told me that, the first few weeks he was driving in South Boston, he got stoned a couple of times.

ROSS: Really? That doesn't sound like such a good idea—to get stoned when...

AMY: Ross, I mean with real stones!

DEAN: You ask me, the most dangerous thing will be driving around in that Pinto. A car taps your rear end and it's going to erupt into a fireball.

AMY: I'll just have to be careful then. I'll have to avoid running stop signs and then stopping suddenly when there's a car right behind me. Oh, by the way, Ross, did you know that KITCHEN STAFF was misspelled in your ad? it said KITCHEN STIFF.

ROSS: We know. Dean said it wasn't his fault though.

AMY: Don't you know that about Dean yet? He has to be right even when he's wrong

~

ROSS: Tell me, Dean, why are you so bent on self-destructing?

DEAN: What? What are you talking about?

ROSS: For months, I hear about how you want Amy to stay with you and how painful it all is. Then she comes in and asks you to do something for her, and you...

DEAN: Christ, Ross, don't you see what's going on here? She's sly. She's trying to maneuver herself into a position where it seems like logic is on her side. Obviously, it's working with you. Listen, there are a million good reasons why she shouldn't work here. She wants to destroy everything we've done by...

ROSS: You know what? I think, deep down, you're afraid of her.

DEAN: Afraid? I'm not afraid. I just know how treacherous she can be.

ROSS: Treacherous? Amy?

DEAN: Believe me, she can be. You've just never seen that side of her. Besides, I *do* want to act like a big shot, and I *am* planning to come on to the waitresses. Well, some of them, anyway.

ROSS: Tell me another thing: Why does Amy's dad dislike you so much?

DEAN: I don't know. Lots of reasons, I guess. Partly on political grounds. We were in Dorky Dan's car at Arby's—me and Amy and her sister Claire and Dorky Dan—and the news came on the radio that Nixon was finally going to resign, and I started cheering and whooping it up in the back seat. Dorky Dan got out of the driver's seat and pulled the back door open—I swear, until the last second, I thought he was just fooling around—and the son of a bitch yanked me out of the car. I got horsey sauce and jamocha shake all over my second-best shirt, and I had to take a taxi home. No wonder Amy turned out the way she did, with a father like that.

ADRIANA RUIZ-CRUZADO

DEAN: So you're waitressing now?

ADRIANA: Yes, I am, at another Mexican restaurant. Quetzalcoatl's, it's called.

DEAN: Quetzalcoatl's. They're going to be our main competition, I think. Quetzalcoatl's and Casa Rubio.

ROSS: Why do you want to leave Quetzalcoatl's? Aren't you happy there?

ADRIANA: I was at first...then I started having problems every time I went into the kitchen—the kitchen staff... this is sort of embarrassing...

DEAN: You can tell us. We're very discrete.

ADRIANA: Well, the kitchen staff... sometimes they... they harass me.

DEAN: Harass you how? You mean they... say things... or they...

ADRIANA: At first, yes, they just said things and made noises... like kissy noises...

DEAN: This was everyone... all the kitchen staff?

ADRIANA: Most of them a little. Some of them a lot. Especially Paco the sous chef and Bob the dishwasher. And it got worse... nearly every time I walked by, they patted me... pinched me... grabbed me...

DEAN: Where did they grab you?

ADRIANA: Mostly in the kitchen.

DEAN: No, I mean...

ROSS: Dean, we don't need to know that.

ADRIANA: It's mostly when they're drinking... but they're almost always drinking.

ROSS: You talked to your manager about this?

ADRIANA: Yes... I went to his office and told him what was going on in the kitchen. And he... he kept asking questions. What did they say? What did you do? How did you feel when they patted you? Can you show me where they pinched you?

ROSS: You need to get out of there. I guarantee you we won't let that sort of stuff go on around here.

ADRIANA: I worked with Rafael at Estella Maya before it closed—he wouldn't have tolerated it either. In fact, he's the one who suggested I look for a job here.

ROSS: Oh, you know Rafael? Oh yeah, I see he's a reference on your application. He and his mother will both be working here.

ADRIANA: Oh. Mama will be here? Well, I still want the job.

DEAN: Are you from Mexico?

ADRIANA: I was born in the DR—but I've lived here since I was nine. That won't make too much difference. Most Americans—they don't know much about other countries. The other night one of my customers asked me where I was from, and I told her, the Dominican Republic, and she said, "I'd love to visit your country someday. I've always wanted to see South America."

DEAN: That doesn't surprise me. It would be nice to have another person who could talk to Rafael and Mama.

ADRIANA: When I wait tables, I can do a Mexican accent.

DEAN: I don't think that will be necessary. So, one more question—are they worried about us over at Quetzalcoatl's?

ADRIANA: No, I don't think so.

DEAN: Feeling pretty sure of themselves, are they?

ADRIANA: I don't think they know about you.

ROBIN SHUTE

DEAN: You're the second Robin to come in here today.

ROBIN: (*laughing*) I certainly hope that won't keep you from hiring me.

DEAN: (*seriously*) It might. That could get pretty confusing.

ROSS: We can assign them numbers.

DEAN: What made you decide to become a waitress when you've been a teacher for so long?

ROBIN II: I was afraid you'd ask that. I just didn't feel safe teaching anymore.

ROSS: You mean because of the busing problem, or...

ROBIN II: No, that wasn't it. It's just that these crazy things... these nasty things have been happening to me lately, and...

DEAN: We'd like to hear about that.

ROBIN II: I was afraid you would. (*Sighs*) I was teaching at Bunker Hill High. One day I came back to my classroom during the lunch period to do some grading. There's a storeroom behind the classroom where I usually teach. They keep football jerseys and trophies and things like that in there. I found one of my juniors—Vince is his name—climbing through the transom. I asked him what he thought he was doing, and he said, "You can see what I'm doing." So I reported him to the principal and he got suspended. Because he was suspended, he got kicked off the hockey team. I guess hockey meant a lot to Vince—he was kind of a star at Bunker Hill, and he was hoping to get a scholarship to play in college and maybe play in the NHL someday. It was right after that, these weird things started happening.

DEAN: What sort of weird things?

ROBIN: Little stuff, at first. Pizzas would show up when I hadn't ordered them. Then a couple of Jehovah's Witnesses came over to talk to me. They'd gotten a postcard saying I wanted more information. Someone sent off for stamp collections and coin collections in my name. Someone collected subscription cards from magazines and filled in my address. Oh, except for some horrible sex magazines—those he filled in my name but wrote in my neighbors' addresses. Book of the Month Club, Columbia Record Club—I was signed up for those too. When I finally got all that straightened out, he went to the post office and filled out a change of address card—my new address was in Guam. Then it started to get more malicious. One day my car was towed right out of my parking spot. When I finally tracked it down, this garage was just about to put a new transmission in it. I drove home, and there was about ten tons of crushed gravel in my parking place. And then I started getting calls from people who'd seen my number in men's rooms stalls all over Boston. Someone had written, NAUGHTY GIRL NEEDS SPANKING BAD, CALL ROBIN AT... and then he wrote my number.

DEAN: And you're sure this guy Vince was behind all this?

ROBIN II: Yes. I mean, I don't have any proof, but there's no one else who would do things like that. I moved to a new apartment. I got an unlisted phone number. Now what I need is a new job. And when I saw your ad in the paper, I...

DEAN: What did you think of the ad?

ROBIN II: Did you know that you misspelled kitchen *staff*. It says kitchen *stiff*.

DEAN: Yes, we know. That was the *Globe's* fault. I mean, what did you think of it from a stylistic point of of view?

ROBIN II: I don't know. I don't really like using nouns as verbs.

ROSS: You mean "peopling?" "To people" is a real verb.

ROBIN II: I suppose. It just reminds me a little of words I don't like... parenting, and gifting, and decisioning, and stonewalling... oh, and you know what was confusing? I didn't know what you meant when you said "New Mexican restaurant." I mean, it was hard to tell if this was a Mexican restaurant that was just opening, or if it was a Santa Fe-style restaurant.

ROSS: Tell me... were you an English teacher?

ROBIN II: English and drama.

ROSS: You sound a lot like my father.

ROBIN II: He's an English teacher?

ROSS: He used to be. Now he's a principal. He also publishes a little magazine called *The Lonely Grammarian*.

ROBIN II: I think I've seen that.

ROSS: I doubt it. It has a circulation of about two hundred. It's not even a real magazine—my dad cranks it out on a mimeograph machine at his high school.

ROBIN II: No, I really think I have. Was there an article in there a couple of months ago about how we're giving up the subjunctive without much of a fight?

ROSS: I don't know. Could have been.

ROBIN II: And an editorial about how there ought to be an Academy of the English Language like there is for French?

ROSS: He's been writing about that for years now. I think he wants to be head commissioner of the Academy. I'll be damned.

DEAN: Robin, suppose we don't have a position as a waitress available just now, would you consider being a hostess?

ROBIN II: What does being a hostess entail?

DEAN: Mostly wearing a long skirt and saying *hola* to people and showing them where to sit.

ROBIN II: That sounds pretty easy. Yeah, I'd consider that. I'd consider anything at this point. Listen, about my application....

ROSS: Yes?

ROBIN II: Don't give that telephone number to anyone. No matter what anyone says to you, don't give it out.

ROSS: God, I'm exhausted. And we have to do this all day tomorrow.

(*Dean gets up and goes into the bathroom adjoining the office*)

DEAN: Yeah, and you know who our first interview is tomorrow? Sarah Jefferson.

ROSS: You mean, THE Sarah Jefferson? The one whose dog...

DEAN: Yes, the one whose dog ate my shoe. Christ, are we ever going to get hot water around here?

ROSS: She's not the story lady at the bookstore anymore?

DEAN: (*slightly suspiciously*) How did you know she worked at a bookstore?

ROSS: I used to take Jeremy to that bookstore... to hear the stories.

DEAN: Well, I don't guess there's much money in storytelling.

ROSS: By the way, I don't think I can make it tomorrow at nine. I have to go by Jeremy's school tomorrow.

DEAN: She's going to expect me to hire her because we have a history. But... I don't know.

ROSS: Well, since you and Amy are calling it quits...

DEAN: That's just temporary... most likely. And besides... there were issues with Sarah Jefferson—not just the shoe. I don't think I want to go back down that road. Damn. I just got lather on my tie.

ROSS: You're shaving? And wearing a tie? What's up?

DEAN: I'm having dinner with my... well, for want of a better word, backers.

ROSS: Oh yeah, those mysterious backers of yours.

DEAN: Nothing particularly mysterious about them.

ROSS: Is it true that they're tree surgeons?

DEAN: Did Amy tell you that? They own a tree-trimming company, and a lot of other things too. They're new in town, but they're already involved in a lot of operations. Real California sharpies. Marauders in three-piece suits. And... as it happens... they're very big into Mexican food.

ROSS: So where are you going to dinner? Quetzalcoatl's?

DEAN: No, to Rafael's house. He and Mama are making dinner for us.

ROSS: You're kidding. Why wasn't I invited?

DEAN: I was going to invite you, but you told me you and Thea were going out for dinner tonight.

ROSS: She canceled. Again.

DEAN: Things are going a bit slow on the Thea front, I take it. Are we still saving a spot for her on the waitstaff?

ROSS: I don't know. She won't commit. So, don't you think I should meet these guys?

DEAN: You will, eventually. You've already got your pile together, thanks to auntie.

ROSS: I thought you did, too.

DEAN: I thought so myself, but... this is costing big bucks, more than I ever figured it would. (*Comes out of bathroom*) There, what do you think?

ROSS: You look like something out of *GQ*. Where'd you get the suit?

DEAN: I bought it at Bruno's back when clothing stores gave me a discount because I did their windows. I wasn't talking about the suit, though. What do you think of the new me?

ROSS: I don't know. Something's different. You're not wearing your glasses?

DEAN: Ross, I've never worn glasses. Laurel was right when she said you're not very observant. Open those baby blues.

ROSS: My eyes are gray.

DEAN: Look again. Melvin is gone.

ROSS: Melvin? Oh yeah, Melvin. (looking) You shaved off your mustache! I knew you were missing something.

DEAN: Yeah, only now I'm not sure I like the effect. I guess it's bound to look a little strange to me, since I'm seeing my upper lip for the first time in about eight years.

ROSS: Dean, these backers of yours—where did they come from?

DEAN: I told you, California.

ROSS: No, I mean, where did you meet them?

DEAN: In a class. A Free U class.

ROSS: I didn't know you were taking any classes. What sort of class?

DEAN: Well, don't tell Amy—she thinks it's a management techniques class. It's a massage class.

ROSS: Seriously? You don't strike me as a massage sort of guy.

DEAN: Massage is good for you. It relaxes you. I know I don't show it, but I actually operate under a lot of stress.

ROSS: No, you show it.

DEAN: And I thought there would be mostly women in the class, but it's mostly guys. Guys hoping to massage women, I guess.

ROSS: Including your West Coast tree surgeons.

DEAN: They'd been to Esalen, a few years back, and they're into massage.

ROSS: You know, Dean, tell you the truth—I kind of liked Melvin. I don't know why you shaved him off.

DEAN: (*Goes back and looks in the mirror; his expression turns horror-stricken*) It does look awful, doesn't it. Awful! My upper lip looks naked. Pink and naked. God, why did I do it? Why? I wonder how long it'll take to grow back.

ROSS: People used to say that smoking pot makes your hair grow faster. Your mustache too, I guess.

DEAN: I think that was meant figuratively. Couldn't hurt to try, though, I suppose.

19

THE SECOND ANNUAL SCHOOL'S OUT
REUNION & THANKSGIVING PIG OUT

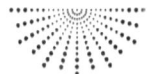

THERE WERE TWO BMWS PARKED IN FRONT OF CAP AND POPPY'S CABIN, ONE black and one silver. ILLINOIS, both the plates said, LAND OF LINCOLN. Laurel had left the U.S. Grape there yesterday; the black one was blocking her in.

"Wait here, Ollie," she told her dog. Ollie whimpered but lay down with a sound like a sack of bones being dropped on the porch. Heavy brass wind chimes bonged together. The porch swing swayed in the wind.

Cap and Poppy's living room was strewn with open suitcases and clothes and shoes and sleeping guests. Two guests were on the foldout couch. Three more were in sleeping bags on air mattresses: two under Cap's harpsichord, and one in the middle of the floor. The cabin smelled wonderfully of roasting turkey. Poppy was back in the kitchen, playing Happy Birthday on her new violin. "Hi, Pops, what doin'?"

"Practicing."

"Whose birthday is it?"

"No one's, as far as I know, but it's either Happy Birthday or Three Blind Mice, and somehow Happy Birthday seems more festive. I told Cap I wasn't ready to play in front of company. I haven't picked up a violin since I was ten. But when Cap saw that Guillermo had brought his guitar, he said, 'Hey, now you and Guillermo can jam.' I hope Guillermo knows Happy Birthday. Or Three Blind Mice."

"I can't believe Guillermo and Arthur are here."

"They got in late last night," Poppy said.

"Who's the Chinese woman under the harpsichord with Arthur? Was she ever here?"

"She's Korean, actually. That's Arthur's new squeeze, Tam Moon. Pretty name, don't you think? She's an actress. Arthur says she's up for a part in a movie about Vietnamese boat people, even though she's not from Vietnam. Arthur's taken a leave of absence from his job, he told me, to help her with her pronunciation. He said it's okay with the producer if she has a bit of an accent, but she still has too much of one."

"Who are the two on the sofa?" Laurel asked.

"That's Eliza and..."

"Eliza? Eliza who used to smoke a corncob pipe?"

"That was Eliza back then. But I don't think she's into corncob pipes anymore. She's all glitter and flash now. She runs a modeling agency in Chicago."

"And that's her boyfriend?"

"Not exactly, no. That's Jay. You remember Jay, don't you?"

"Jay. Let's see. Did he used to live in that old school bus with Johnny AWOL?"

"No, you're thinking of Stash, I think. Jay lived in a couple of cabins, and then he moved into that geodesic dome with Cascade. Back then, people called him Blue Jay. You don't remember?"

"He was Cascade's old man?"

"Well, sometimes. He sort of got around, I think."

"When was he here?"

"Oh God, way back. Maybe the second year we were here, but I'm not sure."

"That might have been when Ross and I were in Mexico. Must have been; otherwise, I'm pretty sure I'd remember him. I like the way he looks."

"You do? God, Laurel, we never agree on men."

"Only on Cap. I've always thought Cap was a cutie."

"Want him? He's yours. I'll even throw in the pigs."

"Where's this Bluebird live now?"

"Blue Jay, not Bluebird. Only now it's just Jay. Chicago. He's a lawyer or something. Or maybe an accountant."

"And that's where he and Eliza met? That's so cool, a couple of School's Out alums running into each other in..."

"They didn't meet in Chicago. They met on the couch last night. They were at it all night long. I wanted to throw a bucket of water on them about three a.m."

"Is that black BMW out there Jay's?"

"I think so. Eliza's is the silver one, I think. Why? Is there supposed to be something special about BMWs?"

"I don't know," Laurel said. "I was just wondering because he's blocking me in. Hey Poppy, where's Cap? I have to ask him something."

"He's probably down priming the pigs."

"We going to have pig tricks again this year?"

"Pig tricks and Happy Birthday. That's the best the Entertainment Committee could come up with."

"Better than last year. Last year, it was just pig tricks."

"We're expecting a bigger turnout this year. Maybe another ten or twelve people here by dinnertime. What was it you wanted to ask Cap?"

"Ollie got skunked night before last. I wanted to ask Cap if there's anything I can do about it before everyone gets here."

"I'm sure he'll know what to do. Even if he doesn't, he'll be happy to make something up."

"It's been terrible," Laurel said. "I can't let Ollie in the house, he smells so awful. Last night he sat in front of my bedroom window and barked all night. He's usually not a big barker. I mean, if he spots an animal near my cabin, he barks, but only once or twice. Doesn't matter if it's a mountain lion or a chipmunk, it's the same bark, so I never know if I should be alarmed."

"Last night, he sat on our porch and barked some too."

"Oh no, Poppy, I'm sorry."

"It's okay. I was awake anyway, with those two on the couch going at it like minks in heat."

~

"Hi, Cap," Laurel said. "What doin'?"

"Cleaning Dotty's tail."

"Why are you doing that, Cap?" Laurel knew what she was getting into by asking, but she never tired of Cap's phony pig lore.

"You have to keep a pig's tail clean, Laurel, you should know that. Because if a pig's tail is weighed down by mud, it pulls the skin on the pig's rump, and that pulls the skin on the pig's back, which pulls on the skin on the pig's shoulders, and all of that stretches the skin on the pig's forehead, and then that pulls on those little piggy eyelids. Before long it pulls them right open, and soon they're open all day and all night. And of course, the pig can't sleep with her eyes open all the time, who could? So, pretty soon, the poor pig dies of exhaustion."

"What are you *really* doing?"

"Putting disinfectant on Dotty's tail. Lola took a little nip out of it. Damn pigs; they'll eat anything, even each other. Won't you, ladies?" Cap was an innocent-looking man with kindly eyes, a nose too big for his face, and a huge, cinnamon-colored beard. "Shake," he told the pigs. One by one, they offered Laurel a hoof.

Laurel told Cap her problem.

"Tomato juice," Cap said. "That's the only substance known to man that can de-skunk a dog. Pour it all over him, rub it in good, then dunk him in the creek."

"How am I going to get him in the creek? Ollie hates water. Especially cold water."

Cap shook his head. "The only Lab in the world that hates water."

"I saw some of our guests are already here," Laurel said.

"More coming, too. Wendy and Ben are coming up from Denver. Stash said he's going to try to make it. Buffalo's going to be here. Aspen might be coming and bringing her baby, only he's not a baby anymore. A few folks are flying into Grand Junction and renting a car and coming down here this afternoon. We might have twenty people or more."

"If they need a place to stay, a couple of them can crash in my cabin."

"The one thing we got around here is plenty of room," Cap said.

"Yeah, but some of those cabins aren't in great shape, and they're full of spiders," Laurel said. "You know, I wish everyone, even people who were here for only one day, could be at the reunion."

"Except Sweet Mystery."

"Right. Definitely not him. By the way, sorry if Ollie kept you up last night. I wouldn't let him in, 'cause he smelled so awful."

"Go change your underwear, Ollie," Cap said to the dog in a stern voice. Ollie was sitting on the other side of the fence, eyeing the pigs, and looking ashamed of the way he smelled. He smelled even worse than the pigs.

"I guess Ollie thought you guys would be an easier touch. That you might let him inside."

Cap just said, "He's a dog. Dogs bark."

Laurel thought about that. "Uh-huh. That's right. Dogs do bark. You gonna get the girls to do tricks after dinner?"

"Thought I might. I dunno, Lola's been acting real ornery lately. She might not be feeling cooperative. We should have a little dress rehearsal, huh?" Cap waded through a gumbo of mud and pig poop and went into a shed. He came back with a box of Zagnuts. The pigs wagged their corkscrew tails.

"Where'd you get all the candy bars, Cap?"

"Matt gave 'em to me. Zagnuts aren't big sellers around here, I guess. He said he'd had these on the shelf for years." He unwrapped a couple of Zagnuts. "Look at that," he said, handing one of the wrappers to Laurel. "Five cents. They're twice that now."

"Well, I can see why they weren't popular. Who wants candy bars with no chocolate?"

"Pigs do," Cap said.

Cap held up one of the Zagnuts. "Want one, ladies?" The pigs obviously did. "You have to stand." With a bit of a boost from Cap, they stood up, balancing on their rear ends and their hind trotters, and they batted their pink eyelashes at him, snorting with anticipation. "If you want a Zagnut, you'll dance for us. Come on, dance." Obediently, the two pigs moved in circles—clumsy porcine pirouettes. "Curtsy now," Cap told them. They curtsied as well as pigs possibly could curtsy. "Here you go. Damn it, Dotty, greedy little bitch. You almost took the tip of my finger off."

"Maybe you'd better not give them any more," Laurel said. "If they're not hungry, they won't want to dance when everyone gets here."

"They're always hungry when it comes to stale Zagnuts. C'mon, Lola, you swine, get your foot off me!"

"Cap," Laurel said, "do you think we'll ever be coming to a reunion at School's Out?"

"If we ever leave, Laurel, there won't be any reunions. They're won't be any School's Out."

"God, how did *we* end up with that responsibility?"

"Tomato juice! That sounds like one of Cap's instant fantasies," Poppy said. "I bet he just made it up on the spot." Still, she checked the cupboard.

"If you don't have any, I could go down to Matt's Store. Except I don't guess he's open today," Laurel said.

"There's a can of V8 juice. Think that would do?"

"I don't see why not. It's mostly tomato juice."

Poppy opened the oven and peeked inside the blue-flecked pans.

"Two turkeys? Two giant turkeys?" Laurel asked.

"Three. I cooked one last night. And Ben is bringing a ham he smoked himself. People packed it away last year. We ran out of food, remember?" Poppy threw more wood into the wood-fired stove and basted the turkeys.

"They're doing fine, I already made the pies—I made them with peaches we canned last summer—and I've got Happy Birthday down pretty well. Think I'll come along with you."

"I'll bring some of the milk punch I made for the reunion."

"That's something I really like about you, Laurel. You make a celebration out of everything."

The people who once lived at School's Out had peppered the area with proper nouns. Nothing went nameless. There were more place names per acre around School's Out than anywhere else on the Western Slope. New names were superimposed on old ones; names shifted and evolved. Some features picked up four or five names over the course of time. Sometimes one name competed with another. Many names wouldn't last till the next weekend; others endured.

Poppy, Laurel, and Ollie walked on the Jimi Hendrix Highway—which was a gravel road—down Harmony Hill. They left the road near Mushroom Rock and crossed Ghost Dance Meadow. The Earth Cult Lodge, which had once been the chapel for the Rocky Mountain Methodist Youth Camp, and had been the hub of School's Out, once stood in this meadow, but there had been a fire. Two freestanding chimneys were all that were left. People driving on the little road that led past School's Out sometimes stopped and took pictures of the chimneys, thinking they were the sad aftermath of some pioneer disaster.

The two women and the dog sat down on the banks of what had been Dream Catcher Creek. Now it was just called the creek. The dream catchers that had hung from the trees along the creek were long gone. The forest on the other side of the creek had been known as, at different times, Lothlórien, Sherwood Forest, and the Hundred Acre Woods. Now it was just called the woods.

"All right, Ollie, time to take your clothes off." Laurel untied the red bandana Ollie wore around his neck and undid his collar. Then she poured V8 juice all over him and massaged it into his fur. Ollie turned from gold to orange. "Hold still, Ollie. God, but you stink, stink, stink!" Ollie shook himself and sprayed them with a fine mist of vegetable cocktail. "Stop shaking!" She asked Poppy "Any ideas about how we get him into the creek?"

"Will he chase a stick if you throw one in?"

"Hah, you kidding? Ollie sits back and laughs when you throw sticks. He's not into sticks at all."

"I guess we'll have to give him a shove."

They shoved. Ollie wound up paw-deep in the icy water. "Look at you," Laurel said to her dog. Ollie looked up at her dubiously. His long lashes and sad eyes reminded her a little of Ross. "That's his Bambi look," she told Poppy. "It's meant to make me feel guilty."

"I can see shoving isn't going to get it," Poppy said.

"C'mere, Ollie." Ollie climbed out of the creek, looking grateful. Laurel picked him up and carried him upstream, where a log spanned the creek. She eased him into about three feet of water. He took a few strokes toward the bank and then began splashing. He looked like a sinking steamboat. Poppy said that, in her opinion at least, the dog was drowning.

"He's fine. Come on, buddy, quit faking it."

Ollie swam a couple more strokes and scrambled up the bank. "Watch out, "Laurel said. "He's going to shake."

Ollie shook vigorously and showered them with cold creek water.

"Poor thing, he's freezing. I should have brought another towel."

"Freezing? I can't believe it's this warm in late November. It's positively balmy. Remember what it was like for the first reunion? Eight inches of snow."

"Come sit in the sun, Ollie. You'll be fine in a few minutes." Laurel took off her serape and draped it over the miserable, shivering Ollie. "You want some milk punch?" she asked Poppy.

"Of course I do. Did that help? Does he smell any better?"

Laurel sniffed her dog. "He smells like vegetables gone bad."

"I told you Cap was bullshitting about this."

"No, seriously, rotting vegetables is a big improvement. Maybe when he dries, it'll be even better." Laurel picked up the empty can and shielded it from Poppy. "Okay, Pops, bet you can't tell me what eight vegetables are in V8."

"Let's see. Tomatoes, obviously."

"Tomato concentrate, actually. That's one."

"And celery, right? And carrots. I remember seeing a carrot on the label. And... how many have I got so far?"

"Three, I think."

"Only three, huh. Spinach? Onions?"

"Okay on the spinach, no to onions."

"Potatoes? Asparagus? Broccoli?

"Nope, nope, nope."

"Lettuce?"

"Right. Three more to go."

"Cauliflower? Radishes? Eggplant? Cabbage? Lima beans"

"No to all those. Not even close."

"I can't think of any more vegetables... oh, parsnips? Kohlrabi? Kale? Squash? Cantaloupes?"

"Don't be silly. Cantaloupes aren't vegetables."

"I know, but neither are tomatoes, they say. And there aren't any more vegetables. I give up."

"You missed beets, watercress, and parsley."

"What? Okay, I can accept beets. Maybe even watercress, though that's a stretch. But parsley? That's no more a vegetable than a cantaloupe is. It's an herb."

"You're just a sore loser, Pops."

"I'm going to write a letter. They should have to call it V7."

They drank more milk punch. "So, Laurel, did you ever get in touch with Ross? About coming to the reunion?"

"Ross?" Laurel tried to look puzzled. "Now who, exactly, is this Ross?"

"You remember Ross," Poppy said. "You went to Mexico with him. You married him; he lived in your cabin for a few years. Jeremy's father, remember?"

"Oh, that Ross. No, it doesn't look like he's going to make it. Not this year. All the pressure of opening a restaurant, you know. And it's just as well."

"Are you saying that because you believe it? Or because you couldn't handle it if he came out."

"What's there to handle? 'Can I handle it?' that's not the question. The question is, 'Why should I give a shit.' You know, Cap said something pretty profound this morning."

"Cap loves being profound," Poppy said, "especially in the morning."

"This time he wasn't even trying. I was apologizing to him about Ollie's barking all night, and he just shrugged and said, 'Dogs bark.'"

"Wow, that is profound, even for Cap."

"No, I really think it is. It's like Cap accepts that things do what they're meant to do. Dogs bark. Trees grow. Fires burn. Ross rosses. I just wish I could accept his rossing as well as Cap accepts Ollie's barking."

"Dogs bark," Poppy said, "and guests screw on the couch."

"Right," Laurel said.

"Cap accepted that pretty well. He pretended to sleep through it, but I just know he was listening. Tell me, how does a person go about rossing?"

"It's more a state of mind than a course of action. A rosser at the top of his form will put off doing anything for years, put off making any kind of decision, and then he'll throw himself into some project and ignore everything else going on around him. Although who knows how long he'll stick with it. Oh, and a real rosser... a real rosser is emotionally constipated. Nothing fazes a rosser. A real rosser just... slides through life. No, I take that back; he doesn't slide through life. He just sits there and lets life slide by him."

"But you still love him anyway, don't you? That's why you haven't taken up with anyone else."

Laurel shrugged and petted her wet dog. "Not like I've had a lot of offers."

"Tell me something else. If Ross rosses, do I poppy?"

"Of course."

"How do I know if I'm poppying right?"

"Oh, you poppy beautifully," Laurel said. She put her arm around Poppy and gave her a squeeze.

Poppy said, "You really think so? Because I think I might have to poppy somewhere else. Away from School's Out."

Laurel shivered. It seemed like, every time she turned around, part of her life fell apart. "Where would you go?"

"I don't know. Back home first, I guess. Some place where the winters don't last six months. Somewhere where you don't have to drive twenty miles to a town where there's never a good movie or a good place to eat."

"There are a few places these days, in Olde Towne, that..."

"Yeah, I guess, but I probably couldn't afford to eat at those places. Anyway, I'm just sick of being a mountain mama, and taking up the violin isn't going to change that. I'm a city girl—yeah, I know, Tallahassee isn't much of a city, but still... look, I've spent almost ten years of my life up in the mountains. It may not be the middle of nowhere, but you can see it from here. I know, you have, too, but you went to Mexico, you went to Boston, you go places to sell your jewelry, you get around. I never go anywhere. And this may be okay for Cap, he's from a small town, and besides, he's easily amused. You give Cap a piece of bubble gum, he's happy for the rest of the day."

"Poppy, that's not fair. About Cap. He's..."

"I know, I know, I'm being bitchy. But seriously, do you know anyone who can sit on a porch swing and look through a kaleidoscope for as long as Cap can?"

Laurel thought about that. No, she decided, she definitely didn't.

"So just let me be bitchy, okay?"

"Okay, Pops. What does Cap say? Is he willing to go with you?"

"I haven't told him what I've been thinking. Or rather, I kinda told him, but I pretended I wasn't being serious."

"What did he say?"

"Nothing. He thought I was kidding. But... if I go... I mean, if Cap wants to come with me, fine. But once I make up my mind... I'll go with him or without him."

Laurel tried to imagine what life would be like if she and Ollie were the only ones left at School's Out.

"I don't think Cap would leave the pigs behind, though, and it's hard for me to imagine Dotty and Lola in Tallahassee."

"I think we should have a little more milk punch," Laurel said.

"What's the matter, Laurel?"

"Nothing. I'm just thinking that I miss Jeremy. I miss the hell out of Jeremy. And I even miss Ross. And now I've found out that I might be missing you... I don't like missing people."

"Drink up," Poppy said.

"You know what I think," Laurel said. "I think..." Laurel never got to say what she thought. A deer came out of the scrub oak down the creek from them and took a few mincing steps into the clearing. Something long and green was dangling from its mouth. Ollie saw the deer and was up and after it. The deer bounded across Ghost Dance Meadow.

The first shot hit a rock and flew off with a piercing whine. It sounded so much like a ricochet in a cowboy movie that it didn't seem real to Laurel. She'd seen the truck up on Hendrix Highway but assumed it was more guests arriving for the reunion or tourists wanting a chimney photo. When she looked again, the truck had stopped and there were two gun barrels poking out of the windows. There was a sudden PAP-PAP-PAP and the deer went down. Ollie had been following a few yards behind the deer; his momentum carried him right over the deer and he landed hard. He stood up and then stumbled. Laurel started to scream and to run toward her dog, but Poppy knocked her legs out from under her and rolled her down to the creek. There was another rapid burst of firing, almost like automatic weapon fire. Laurel and Poppy dug their toes into their shoes and clenched every muscle in their bodies. They were covered with milk punch. Ollie and the deer weren't moving. The firing stopped.

Laurel ripped off her blouse, popping the buttons, and waved it like a semaphore flag. Screaming, she charged the truck. Poppy came behind her. One more shot zinged past. Laurel scooped up her dog and they ran across Ghost Dance Meadow as fast as they could.

~

"Holy fucking shit," said one of the hunters. Vern was his name.

The two hunters had not been seriously hunting when they saw the deer break across the field. They'd been driving down the road eating donuts. Vern had been eating donuts and drinking a Coors, a combination that the other hunter found repulsive. They were more or less lost. "Holy fucking shit," Vern said again. "Am I crazy, or were they topless?"

"One of them was," said the other hunter. Both of the hunters were dressed in camouflage jumpsuits.

"You shouldn't of fired off that last shot. We could of gotten a better look."

"Didn't want them to get the license number. Besides, I did get me a good look, right through here." He patted the scope on his rifle. "She had a sparkly necklace, and she had a little birdie painted on one side of her titty."

"You just meant to scare 'em, right?"

"What do you think I meant to do?" Vern wasn't sure, but then the other hunter said, "If I'd meant to do more than that, I would've done it, and no fucking around."

"That *was* a dog, wasn't it?"

"Didn't see no dogs. All I saw was a deer." The other hunter unsheathed a huge hunting knife.

"I don't know what I saw either, it happened so fast. What if they call the cops on us?" The license number bit had never occurred to Vern, but then, he didn't have the training his friend had. The other hunter had gone to the police academy, back in Dayton. However, he'd flunked out halfway through and had never actually become a cop.

"It's Thanksgiving. No cop's gonna want to come all the way out here for something like this on Thanksgiving. And if they do get around to comin' out here, we'll be gone." He headed across the field. He was going to field dress the deer they had shot.

Vern opened another can of beer on the way across the field. They didn't have Coors, back in Ohio. Colorado Kool Aid, they called it there. His friends had made him promise to bring back a whole case. "Tell you one thing, they sure hightailed it outta here." Vern liked the way that sounded so much that he said it again. "Yes, sir, they sure hightailed it outta here. I don't ever want to hear someone say that hippies can't run."

Just before Laurel and Poppy stumbled up to the pigpen, Cap had been holding two Zagnuts up in the air. All the guests who were there so far for the reunion were watching. The pigs had been dancing, in their fashion. These were not the serious postprandial pig tricks Cap had in store. He was saving the heavy-duty tricks—Pigs Play Soccer, Pigs Kind of Jump Rope, Pigs Do Their Multiplication Tables, Pigs Stand on Their Heads with Some Assistance, Pigs Climb Stepladders, and their finale, the Incredible Piggy Swan Dive—for after dinner, when the audience would be in a more receptive mood. The pigs weren't going to wear themselves out in the meantime. They weren't about to do any more than whet the guests' appetite for pig tricks. Pigs know how to work an audience.

Cap hurdled over the fence around the pigpen and looked at Ollie's wound. Blood was trickling from the dog's mouth and there was a dark string of blood hanging from his nose. There was a black, bubbling hole in the fur of Ollie's chest. Laurel's white blouse was buttonless and stained. The pink stains were V8 juice; the darker ones were from Ollie.

"Where did this happen?" Cap wanted to know.

Poppy told him. "And they tried to shoot us, too, I think. At least, they fired in our direction."

Cap went toward his cabin, trailing pig shit.

"Did you get the license number of the van?" This was Jay, the lawyer. He was wondering if this was the same dog that had barked outside the cabin for hours last night. Had he been armed, he might have shot that dog himself.

Poppy and Laurel shook their heads. It hadn't occurred to them to get a license number. "It was an out-of-state plate, though," Poppy said.

"Isn't that illegal?" Guillermo asked Jay. "You can't hunt from a truck like that, can you?"

"Beats me," Jay said. He didn't know much about Colorado's fish and wildlife regs.

"Well, it's definitely illegal to shoot at people."

"Under ordinary circumstances, anyway," Jay said.

"Roller, the dog not dead," said Tam Moon, the Korean woman. "He bleating."

"It's *Laurel*, not Roller," Arthur said, correcting her out of habit. "He's br*eath*ing."

Ollie let out a soft, strangled bark.

"Shouldn't we try to do something for him?" Eliza asked.

"He shiveling. Lap him on a branket," Tam Moon said.

"Shivering," said Arthur. "*Wrap* him in a blanket."

Poppy was going to get a blanket when she ran into Cap. He was loading his guns. It was a slow process. The only weapons Cap owned were antique guns made from kits that Poppy had given him three Christmases ago. One was a flint-action muzzle-loader and the other was a Confederate cavalry pistol. Cap looked like a guerrilla who'd been hiding in the mountains for years, waiting for word that the revolution had finally broken out.

At another time, Poppy might have fallen off the porch laughing. As it was, she gently disarmed him. "You can't just go shoot them, Cap. Besides, they're long gone by now."

"The motherfuckers," Cap said. There were tears in his eyes. The wind chimes rang like cathedral bells. "Poor Ollie. Poor, poor Ollie."

Laurel, her dog in her arms, was walking toward her truck. Jay caught up with her. "We can take my car. It'll be faster." He tried to pry the dog from her, but she wouldn't let go. One of her breasts was fully exposed now; he could see the wet-purple wings of the parrot. There was an elegance and a desolation in the tableau: tit, tattoo, and dying dog. And the violent reek of skunk and brandy and blood. Laurel whipped her hair out of her face.

"Please," she squeaked. She didn't mean, "Please, let's do take your BMW" or "Please don't touch the dog" or "Please don't stare at my breast." She meant, "Please don't let this be happening."

Jay opened the passenger door of his BMW.

Lola and Dotty were still sitting up back in the pigpen. Their snouts were twitching; they grunted with impatience. They were still waiting for those Zagnuts.

There was no sign of the hunters; just the picnic blanket, the V8 can glinting in the sun, and a heap of deer innards. Already there were buzzards circling. They drove quickly past the tree marked TREE and

through the flock of guinea fowl. Just before they got to the county highway, Jay heard the bubbling, wretched breathing come to a stop. He pulled
over and took a look at Ollie. "The dog's dead, I'm afraid. I'm sorry."
Laurel nodded; she seemed almost relieved. She let Jay take the dog and
the blanket out of her lap and put him in the back seat. She got out of the
car and she let him hold her for a minute.

After the hug, Laurel went mutely up to the door of Matt's Store and
stared at the CLOSED sign. She looked at it for a long time, as if it were
written in an unknown alphabet. Then she went around to the house
behind the store where Matt lived. Jay followed.

Matt and his wife and his daughter, who was home from college for the
long weekend, were just finishing their Thanksgiving dinner. Instead of
turkey, they were having roast guinea fowl. They seemed undismayed by
Laurel's appearance or her smell. She asked Matt if he could let her into
the store so that she could use the pay phone in the back room. Matt told
her she could use their personal phone. They offered Jay coffee and
pumpkin pie.

Jay had left Chicago Tuesday morning and spent a day and a half
driving across the Midwest and through the mountains. Last night he'd
been with... Elisa? Electra? Eliza? Whatever her name was, she'd been a
bear in bed. On a foldout sofa, actually. Almost all night. *If I started to put
my head down now, I'd be asleep before it hit the table*, Jay thought, *and I
wouldn't wake up for days.*

Jay assumed that Laurel would call the county sheriff. Back when Jay
had lived at School's Out, relations with the sheriff's department hadn't
been cordial, not cordial at all. But Cap had told him that lately, he'd been
getting high with a couple of the sheriff's deputies, so things must have
improved.

But no, Laurel was calling long distance. At first, Jay thought, it
sounded as though Laurel was talking to a child. Her words were blurred
by crying. She made another call, and her tone changed. She was now
talking to someone she had once cared about, but was no longer sure of.
At first her words were infused with sorrow, then with annoyance. Then
she seemed to be talking about him; he heard her refer to him as "Blue
Jay." No one had called him that in a long time. Was she trying to make
someone jealous? And did that mean she would want to sleep with him?
He foresaw the possibility of another long night without sleep. His joints
ached. And now, for some reason, she seemed to be talking about a tree
that ate babies.

Jay tried to tune out her conversation. He sipped his coffee and tried to follow what Matt was saying instead. Matt was telling him that when he, Matt, had owned a ranch, he would tie blaze orange ribbons around the livestock during deer-hunting season to prevent an incident like the one that had happened this afternoon. Jay tried to envision Matt's ranch. In his mind, there were farm animals strolling around the barnyard, all wearing orange neckties.

20

GODZILLA VS. KING KONG

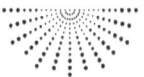

GUS WASN'T A RESOURCEFUL COOK. EVEN WITH FOOTBALL BLASTING FROM THE TV, Amy could hear him groaning in the kitchen. She got up from the game of Clue she'd been playing with Chewy and Babette and went to see what the problem was. The game had been fixed anyway.

"Where's that wrapper the turkey came in," Amy asked Gus.

Gus fished it out of the trash and rinsed turkey blood off of it. Amy read the label. "Well, here's your problem. It seems you should have defrosted the bird a day or so ago and started cooking it about ten a.m." Their Thanksgiving dinner was supposed to be at three. It was now nearly one. "We'll just turn the oven up a little," Amy said.

"It's still pretty frozen," Gus said unhappily.

Amy put her hand on the turkey breast. It felt like a chunk of cold marble. "Guess you should have given that wrapper a read yesterday, huh."

"My ex... she left right after Christmas last year, so this is the first time I've ever cooked a turkey," Gus said. "Can you start cooking a turkey when it's still mostly frozen?"

"I honestly don't know. Isn't there some sort of a hotline you can call?" Amy had never cooked a turkey either. She and Dean had gone to her parents' house until things became too tense between Dean and her father. After that, Ross made Thanksgiving dinner for her and Dean and Jeremy. She didn't eat turkey anyway. "You could start on the dressing."

"The recipe I looked at said you need giblets for the dressing, and the giblets are frozen inside the turkey."

"What I'd do is, I think, is put that old Butterball in the oven and crank up the heat and go ahead and make the dressing. When it thaws out a little, pull those giblets out and stuff the dressing in then. I can take the giblets home to my dog. If there aren't any giblets in the dressing, I'll eat some. But giblets—ick!"

"The dressing will still have turkey juice in it. You and Chewy..."

"I'm not a fanatic. I can live with a little turkey juice."

"Chewy can't. Maybe we should go to a restaurant. I have to go to work later anyway."

"Stop worrying. Everything's basically okay. And going out for a Thanksgiving Special at some restaurant is pathetic. Here, I'll take the cranberries out of the can." She used Gus's electric can opener, patted the side of the can, and the ribbed, crimson cylinder slid onto a platter with a sucking sound. It quivered for a few seconds. For some reason, she imagined that it was giggling. "You know, when I was a little kid, I didn't realize cranberries really were berries. I thought they grew like this, in cylinders. I pictured these trees with can-shaped fruit hanging from them."

"My wife used to make cranberry relish with fresh cranberries and orange juice and a little horseradish, I think. But she took all her recipes with her. And I figured I had enough to do, what with the turkey and dressing and all."

"Well, I'd better get back to playing Clue."

"Sure, go ahead. You're the guest. Go play Clue." Amy had a feeling that Gus would love it if she volunteered to finish making dinner so that he could watch his football game. "Hey, Red," he whispered, "you don't think Chewy knows anything, do you?" Gus didn't want his son to know he was seeing Amy. Not yet, anyway.

"No, I'm sure he has no idea," she told Gus. She wasn't ready to tell Chewy either. "Chewy thinks he invited me. In fact, he did."

"Dinner's going to be a little late," Amy told Chewy and Babette.

"You did it." Babette pointed at Amy. Babette was Chewy's little sister, the one who had given him the nickname Chewy, her baby version of Charlie.

"I didn't do anything. Your dad just didn't defrost the turkey soon enough."

"No, you *did* it," Babette insisted. "You were Miss Scarlet, and Miss Scarlet killed Mr. Boddy. In the billiards room. With a lead pipe. I win!"

∾

Mr. Boddy was lining up a double bank shot and didn't look up when Miss Scarlet entered the room. She took off her shoes and left them by the door. She glided up to the billiards table in stocking feet, quiet as thistledown.

"Why, little Miss Scarlet. You startled me. Still, I'm pleased to see you." He didn't look startled. Or pleased. "Been mucking about in the secret passages, I see. No doubt with your charming Colonel Mustard. Your dress is a bit dusty."

She smiled thinly.

"You know," Mister Boddy said, appraising her. "I've always thought that women with red hair should never wear red. That blood-red dress clashes rather unpleasantly with your mahogany hair. I have to admit, the red fishnet stockings are a nice touch. And the long red gloves. I assume you're wearing blood-red underwear? But your shoes, where are they? Oh, I see, over by the door. Those red stiletto-heeled numbers. Not bad. Not at all bad. Did you know, the first known instance of a woman wearing stiletto heels only dates back to the 1920s? There's a photo of a singer at the Folies Bergère wearing them while sitting on a piano—Mistinguett, her name was. At one point, her legs were insured for five hundred thousand francs. Someone once asked her to explain why she was so popular with men. Do you know what she said? No? Well, I'll tell you. Her answer was, 'It's a kind of magnetism. I say 'Come closer,' and I draw them to me.' I find that interesting because you have the exact same effect on men. You're magnetic as well, you draw them in without even trying. And Mistinguett often wore red—like you. When she died, Jean Cocteau said..."

"I don't care what he said. I'm not interested in Jean Cocteau, or Miss Tingly, or whatever her name was, or her legs. And I'm especially not interested in your fashion opinions."

"You almost pull that outfit off, Miss Scarlet, but not quite. Not quite." He was wearing a charcoal-colored smoking jacket and a plum-colored ascot. There was a smudge of blue pool-cue chalk on the side of his nose. That irritated her. "I stand by my opinion," he said. "Redheads should not be wearing red."

"That may go for your dummies, but not for me."

"Not dummies, damn it." he shouted. "They're called mannequins! Mannequins!" His face turned nearly as red as her outfit. She thought for a moment that he was going to swing on her with his cue stick. She was ready. But then, he composed himself. "Tell me, Miss Scarlet, what have you got there behind your back? What are you hiding? Something for me?"

"Oh, nothing much." She shifted the length of pipe from her right hand to her left; she was left-handed. There was a satisfying heft to it. "Just a little surprise."

~

"What happened?" Gus called from the kitchen. The cheering from the TV had become even more frenzied.

"I won," Babette shrieked "Miss Scarlet did it with a lead pipe in the billiards room. I'm the best detective."

Some detective. You looked at the cards.

"I think someone got a touchdown," Amy called to Gus.

"Who? Which team got a touchdown?"

"I don't know," Amy said. "Who's playing?" Although she'd been a cheerleader, Amy never paid much attention to football specifics.

In the kitchen, Gus groaned.

"Who wants to play again?" Babette asked. Amy didn't, and she couldn't imagine Chewy wanting to. Chewy was speaking as little as possible today. He was hoping to leave language behind, to eliminate needless speech from his life. While they were playing Clue, he wouldn't even make accusations out loud; he'd just point and grunt and use pantomime, which couldn't have been much fun. She did, however, enjoy his pantomime of "with a noose;" his tongue lolled out and his eyes rolled up into his head. "Come on, let's start," Babette said. She put the three cards in the secret envelope, taking a good look at them this time too. "Only I don't want to be Mrs. Peacock. I want to be Miss Scarlet this time."

I'm always Miss Scarlet, Amy thought. When I was a kid, if I couldn't be Miss Scarlet, I wouldn't play. No way I'm that dowdy Mrs. White or Mrs. Peacock.

The doorbell rang. "I'll get it," Amy said. *That'll be Hector.*

Babette said, "You can't get it. You don't live here. I'll get it."

~

When Chewy called Amy on Tuesday, he told her he didn't want Hector there for Thanksgiving dinner with them.

"Then don't invite him," Amy said.

"Not easy. Wants meet family. See house." Even when Chewy broke down and spoke, he used words sparingly, as if writing a telegram.

"Tell him no," Amy suggested.

"Can't," Chewy said. "Binary personality. Tell him no, hears NO! NO! NO! NO!"

Hector Bird, Chewy's lover, was a call-in radio talk show host. He was known for his hatefulness on the air. His trademark technique was to trap callers into degrading themselves and then make his escape by suddenly hanging up on them.

"Well, it might not be too bad," Amy said. "Hector's usually okay when he's not on the air. And your father isn't the sort to pick fights."

"Not what he does. No fights. Let's you come at him. And come and come. Wears you out."

"Oh dear," Amy said. "I didn't realize that. This could be bad then. Like Godzilla versus King Kong."

"Who?" Chewy didn't know, or pretended he didn't know, who Godzilla was. King Kong either.

"So," Gus said. "Chewy tells me you're his teacher."

Without hesitation, Hector leapt into the lie. "Chewy's absolutely right. I'm for sure his teacher."

"How does that work?" Gus wanted to know. "I mean, you become a regular dentist, and then, if you're good at it, they ask you to teach?"

"Quite the contrary. Your really good dentists make far too much money to want to teach. Even mediocre dentists make more money than us teachers. No, what you get at the academy is the bottom of the dentistry barrel."

"Oh, come on, Dr. Bird. I don't believe you," Gus said. "I've broken people in on my job—I drive for the T, in case Chewy didn't tell you—and I know it's a lot harder to teach someone how to do something than it is to just go ahead and do it yourself. What, exactly, do you teach?"

"Drilling."

"Drilling. Well, I guess that's important. Dentists have to know how to drill."

"It's crucial."

"Say, you want a drink, Dr. Bird?" Gus asked, as if coming up with some novel idea for home entertaining.

"I think I'll have two," Hector said. "That way you don't have to get up and get me another."

"Just one will do for me," Amy said.

"Okay. And Chewy doesn't drink," Gus said.

"I know. Which is surprising. As a general rule, we dentists drink hard and live fast and die young."

Gus came back with drinks on a tray. Hector balanced one on each knee.

"Chewy not only doesn't drink, he doesn't eat meat either," Gus said to Hector. "Neither does his friend Amy here."

Hector said, "They could eat turkey if they wanted to. Turkeys aren't all that different from vegetables. In fact, some vegetables—asparagus, for example—have higher IQs than your average turkey."

Gus ran his fingers through his dark, curly hair. "Speaking of turkeys, I guess I'd better go check on the one in the oven."

Amy thought, if Hector was Godzilla, he was definitely ahead of King Kong on points.

~

"Can't stand," Chewy said. "Walk."

"You said we could play Clue," Babette said. "Do you want to play Clue, Dr. Bird?"

"No more games," Chewy said. "Walk."

"Oh, puh-LEEEZE," Hector said. "Why do we want to walk?"

He says that a lot on the air, Amy thought. *Oh, puh-LEEZE! You can't get the full effect of it, though, listening to him on the radio. You can't see how disgusted he looks and how he rolls his eyes way back in his head. Like Chewy did when he was pretending to be lynched.*

"I'm watching the game," Hector said, "and I haven't finished my drinks. Besides, it still hurts to walk." A year ago, during a show about busing in Boston, a man in a ski mask had stormed into the studio. He had fired a gun into the glass booth at WQBX where Hector was talking into a microphone. The bullet had hit Hector in the thigh instead of smashing into his heart; possibly the refraction caused by the glass had spoiled the gunman's aim. His producer kept a handgun behind the control booth. She got the drop on the intruder and had him lie on the floor until the police and the EMTs arrived.

Hector still walked with a limp.

"I wouldn't mind going for a walk," Amy said. "I haven't seen the old neighborhood for a long time."

"Okay, then," Babette said. "I'll go too."

"Stay," Chewy told his sister, as if talking to a pet.

That's what you get for cheating, Mrs. Peacock.

~

Next door to Gus's house, in the tiny front yard, there was an upended bathtub embedded in the ground. Inside the porcelain grotto was a plaster statue of the Virgin Mary. It was not by any means the only one of those in South Boston. *Our Lady of the Bathtub... or Madonna on the Half Shell, that's what people call them.* There was a garland of white plastic flowers circling the inside of the tub, where the bathtub ring would have been. The flowers had once been blue, but sunlight and time had bleached them.

"What the hell's taking him so long?" Hector asked. They were both waiting for Chewy to come out.

"I guess he's talking to Gus," Amy said. *Or rather, Gus is doing all the talking.*

Hector had his hands stuffed into the pockets of his pea coat and his watch cap pulled down. *Gus was the one who had been in the Navy, but Hector looks more like a sailor. I just wonder why he's so uncomfortable around me. Dean's like that, too, around Chewy. Neither one of them can understand why Chewy and I are friends.*

"Look," Amy said. A white van was driving by. WHO NEEDS NIGGERS? It said on one panel. BUSING SUCKS it said on another. Amy shook her head sadly. "I'm going to be driving a school bus soon," she told Hector.

"You believe in living dangerously, don't you? People in this town are totally irrational when it comes to busing. They're even willing to shoot people who don't agree with them. There's some major craziness going on here."

"Gus thinks I'm crazy too," Amy said. "Tell you the truth, I'm a little scared myself." *More than a little.*

"Well, don't get yourself shot. It hurts like hell."

Chewy came out of the house frowning. Wrinkles creased his shaved head.

"Come on," Hector told Chewy, "You wanted to walk, let's walk." They walked up D Street toward West Broadway, past solid blocks of clapboard triple-deckers: Irish battleships, people called them. Amy's family had once lived on the third floor—the top deck—of one of these battleships, before moving out to Lexington. "You might have told me I was supposed to play your teacher. I could have gotten together some better lines."

Chewy didn't answer. Amy told Hector that Chewy was being particularly quiet today. "In one of his cosmic phases, is he? He's the Cosmic Kid, this one." Hector's tone was as dismissive as ever, but Amy could tell from the way Hector looked at Chewy that nothing Chewy could say or do would really upset him.

She remembered Chewy telling her that about once a week, Hector would come over to his apartment in the North End in the late afternoon after Chewy got home from classes. Chewy would take a nap and Hector would watch. Nothing else, just watch. He'd drink rye—he kept a bottle at Chewy's place—and sit there as it became dark, and watch Chewy sleep. Eventually, he would have to leave for the studio for his evening call-in show. When Chewy woke up, he'd find his week's spending money under the pillow, as if the Tooth Fairy had left it there.

In fact, that's what Chewy called Hector, because Hector was helping pay his way through dental school. He called him the Tooth Fairy.

They were walking down the sidewalk where Mike the Crazy Kid used to ride his tricycle. Even after Mike grew far too large to comfortably fit on a trike, he would ride back and forth, back and forth along this stretch of sidewalk every day for hours at a time, making a pitiful sound deep in his throat. *Gluck, gluck, gluck,* it had sounded like to Amy when she walked by.

"So, I hear you're going out with Chewy's dad," Hector said to Amy.

Chewy does know, then. And he told Hector.

"We've only gone out once," Amy said.

"He probably has shoes older than you."

This remark seemed unfair, since Hector must be at least as old as Gus, and Chewy was the same age as she was. "In that case, he should go shoe shopping," she said.

But then Hector said, "No, I approve. He seems like a nice enough old fart. And us old farts should stick together."

Maybe Godzilla and King Kong can form an alliance... monsters against Tokyo.

"That bowling alley over there... my sister Claire and I used to bowl there every Saturday. We were on a team and we had our own shoes and our own balls. I loved bowling. Hey, maybe some time, we could all go bowling."

"What you people up here call bowling, that's not real bowling. Those wimpy little candlepins fly around like matchsticks. And those dinky balls you use..."

"I don't know," Amy said, "My dad told me candlepin bowling was harder than tenpin bowling. Or duckpin bowling. He's done all three."

"Hey Chewy, did you listen to the show Tuesday night?" Hector asked.

Chewy shook his head. He listened to Hector nearly every night, but always denied it.

"There was this caller who might have interested you. She's a regular—calls once a week or so. What we call a Killer down at the station. She is bor-RIIING. Every time my producer hears her voice, she goes like this..." Hector sliced his throat with a forefinger. "So Tuesday, this Killer gets on and she says, 'Hector? You there, Hector?'" Hector imitated the falsetto quiver of an old woman. "'Are you there, Hector?'"

~

"You'll want to turn down your radio, caller. Way down." There was a sharp screech of feedback. Hector was sure his producer had already told her to do that.

"Then I won't be able to hear you."

"You can hear me through the phone."

"Oh, okay, Hector, is that better? Do you know it took me almost thirty times to get through to you tonight? And I have arthritis in my knuckles—well, not just in my knuckles, all over—so it isn't easy for me to dial the phone. My sister lives downstairs from me. She's the one you were talking to Sunday night, about Jesus, remember?"

"Sure, I remember. She's another Killer."

"What's that, Hector?"

"I said, go ahead, dearie."

"Well, she gets through easier than I do because she's got one of those push-button type phones. But you think she'd let her own sister use it?"

"You can't expect to compete with the pros with shoddy equipment."

"Well, anyway, I was wondering if you saw the Herald-American *this morning."*

"Nope. I'm a Cronkite junkie. Never read newspapers. If that's all you were wondering..."

"Well, no, I was wondering what you thought of an article in there. Wait a second, I'll go find it." It took her quite a bit more than a second. Too much dead air. *"Okay, here it is. Since you didn't see it, I'll read it to you. Let me grab my glasses."* More dead air. *"Okay. 'Grannies learn karate.' That's the title. Then it goes, 'If you're a purse snatcher, and you're working the North End, and you spot a little old lady, you might get the biggest surprise of your entire life. Because...'"*

"Why don't you just give me the gist of it? Put it in a nutshell, huh?"

"Well, it's about grannies who are learning how to karate."

"Imagine my surprise," Hector said.

"I think, personally, it's a good idea. You know, my purse was snatched right

in a subway station on the Orange Line a couple of weeks ago, and my fingers were almost broken—they still hurt. Although maybe that's the arthritis. Anyway, I was just wondering what you thought."

"Well, I'll give you my opinion, caller, if you really want it. Let me ask you, dearie, do you think criminals are dumb? Do you think your average purse snatcher or mugger doesn't read the paper or listen to the radio? Sure they do. I bet we have some in the audience tonight."

She sucked in her breath. "Tonight? Do you really think so, Hector?"

"Sure, it's possible. More than possible—almost certain. So don't think that criminals aren't aware that everyone's taking up martial arts. And since they don't want to be at a disadvantage, they take up karate, too. Or they might decide that, to maintain their advantage, they should start carrying weapons: brass knuckles, baseball bats, broken bottles, socks full of sand or full of quarters, potatoes studded with double-edged razor blades that you swing on a string. There are lots of ways these thugs can maim you or even kill you if you get them scared enough. Of course, that's saying nothing of guns. Give one of these criminals a gun and he'll have a hole blown through you before you can let out your first pitiful little "Haiii!"

"I just thought if I could learn to karate a little, then..."

"Oh, puh-LEEEZE," Hector said. "I just explained why that won't help. Now, you might say, you could arm yourself with the same kind of weapons that are in the criminals' arsenal. You could carry a knife or a broken bottle or a razor-studded potato in your purse—be careful, though, when you go to get a stick of Juicy Fruit. You could even get a gun and find some fool to teach you how to shoot, turn you into a regular little sharpshooter. Then what happens? The arms race heats up, that's what. Street criminals start packing heavy weapons. Never mind that stuff's illegal, what the hell, these guys don't care, they're not exactly law-abiding citizens. They graduate to assault rifles and fully automatic weapons and street-sweepers and..."

They were walking past St. Mike's—St. Michael the Archangel parochial school. She and Chewy had both gone there; so had Gus. In fact, almost everyone that Amy knew had gone there, all but a couple of non-Catholic friends. In those days, it seemed to Amy that there were only two religions in the world: Catholic and Public.

Amy saw paper turkeys in the windows of some of the classrooms. *We cut out those turkeys, too and colored them with crayons.* Amy had colored each of her turkey's feathers a different color, so that it looked more like a peacock than a turkey, but then, she'd never seen a real turkey, not one that was alive, anyway. She still hadn't.

Then they were at the place where Leo Donovan had been the crossing guard. He'd been in the seventh grade when Amy was in the sixth, just before her father had moved their family to the suburbs. She could picture Leo in his white canvas Sam Browne belt with a silver-and-red sergeant's badge pinned to it. Since only eight graders could be lieutenants or the captain of the cross-ing-guard force, he was only a sergeant, yet he somehow seemed to outrank and outshine the eighth-grade officers. He had the plum crossing to patrol, the one right in front of the school. When traffic was flowing, he held his arms up protectively. No one, not even a first grader, could get past Leo. Everyone had to wait for him to give the all clear. Schoolgirls in checkered waistcoats and white blouses and blue skirts would giggle. When all was safe, he'd walk out into the middle of the street holding his portable stop sign and he'd wave the students across. All the sixth-grade girls—in fact, nearly all the girls at St. Mike's—had a crush on Leo. Amy did too, but she never spoke to him, on or off duty, because he'd been unimaginably out of reach. He went about the business of being a crossing guard with a grim sense of purpose. When it rained, he wore a bright yellow slicker and a yellow rain hat. Amy liked him best in his vinyl yellow rain gear. He looked like a captain standing on the deck of his ship in a squall, wearing his foul-weather togs.

Leo was the only person Amy had known who had actually died in Vietnam. He'd been piloting a Huey gunship when it was blown out of the sky.

"... recoilless rifles and grenade launchers and wire-guided missiles. Then where are you? You think things are bad now, wait and see what a nightmare it will be. The whole city will be a free-fire zone."

"Well, but..."

"And I've got more news for you, dear caller. When you get old, your bones get brittle. I hate to be blunt about it, but that's the way it is. At your age, you take up martial arts, you're begging for compound factures. Besides being brittle, old bones take a long time to heal. Say you're thrown down hard on the mat and you break your hip. You're laid up for months. How do you get to the grocery store? How do you go to church or visit your sister? You can't even get up to dial the phone, or go to the bathroom on your own, for crying out loud. You get bedsores, and they fester. No, caller, you take my advice and leave karate to the

Japanese. To young Japanese. To young Japanese males. Now good night to you!"
Blang!

That blang! sound was supposed to be the sound of Hector triumphantly
flinging the phone against its cradle, but it was actually produced when he nodded
to his producer and she pushed a button. In his first few months at WQBX, he'd
broken a couple of phones. Besides, the recorded blang! sounded more dramatic
than an actual hang up.

∿

"That's completely absurd," Amy said, "and vile."

"I get paid for being absurd and vile, honey."

"Do you believe what you told that poor lady? Do you believe one word of it?"

"Doesn't matter if I do or don't," he said. "I get paid for saying 'down' when someone says 'up.'"

"Did you tell anyone over the air that it was your boyfriend who was teaching karate to those grannies in the North End?"

"Sor-REEE, no, I did not. They pay me to be absurd, not to be honest. You know, when I relocated here from Cincinnati, everyone kept telling me what a tolerant city Boston is. Bullshit, bullshit, bullshit. When I did a show on being gay in Boston, people started calling the station and making threats. They threatened me, they threatened my producer and the station manager, they even threatened our receptionist. Someone claimed he was going to plant a bomb under the transmitter tower. I was lucky I didn't get shot again. No, radio is a dangerous enough business as is. You don't need to go looking for trouble."

"I think we're plenty tolerant here in Boston—most of us, anyway. Maybe it's just that there are a bunch of intolerant weirdo fanatics in your radio audience, people who have nothing better to do than listen to talk radio."

"You told Chewy you listen to it sometimes," Hector said.

They came to St. Michael the Archangel church. It was an enormous red-brick building. Amy thought it looked smug and pleased with itself, somehow. "We had to go to Mass at St. Mike's every morning before school. And of course, we had to go on Sundays too."

"They made you go every day? That amounts to theocracy."

"Every day but Saturday."

Without warning, Chewy bolted up the steps and into the vestibule.

"What the hell is he up to now?" Hector asked her. "I can't believe they don't lock the damn doors."

Amy shrugged. Maybe he hadn't cared for Hector's story. "I'm going in too. Do you want to come with me or wait out here?"

Hector considered this. Then he said, "I've never been in a Catholic church before."

"Never?"

"Well, places like Notre Dame and Duomo di Milano, but not your basic Catholic church."

They went in. Everything looked exactly the same as it had when Amy had been in the sixth grade. It even smelled the same. After nearly a hundred years, the smell of burning incense had become engrained in the wood of the pews. "I feel funny, not wearing a hat. When I was a kid, and one of us girls would forget our hat, the nuns would bobby-pin a Kleenex on top of her head."

Hector was peering into the holy water font. "Here, this is what you do with that." She dipped her finger into the water and made the sign of the cross. When Hector tried, he splashed water on his pants and crossed himself backwards.

"It burns! It burns!" Hector cried. "Just kidding," he said, when Amy looked at him oddly.

Chewy was the only other person in the church. He was kneeling in the pew closest to the altar. They walked to the front of the church. "Like this," Amy said, showing Hector how to genuflect.

"No way I can do that. My leg's too stiff." Hector sat next to Chewy and Amy knelt beside him on the hard wooden kneeler. "What's with you, boy? Looking to rejoin the fold?"

Chewy didn't answer.

"Why are you kneeling?" Hector asked Amy.

"It's what Catholics do," Amy said. "When I was a kid, one time my friends and I were on the beach on the Cape. Some boys said, bet you girls go to a Catholic school. We asked them how they knew. 'The knees. The knees give you away. You Catholic girls always have callouses on your knees.'"

Hector was looking at the huge statue of Christ crucified over the altar. "I think it's so tacky," Hector said, "hanging Him up there like that. Look how white His skin is. Did anyone in the Middle East have skin that color? Not only that, he's scarcely bleeding at all. You take a man out and crucify him, he'd be bleeding like a stuck pig." It was true; the statue over the altar had white skin, white as marshmallow topping, and there were only little dabs of blood, as if from paper cuts.

"You know, my friend Ross—he lived in Mexico for a while—he said that a lot of the crucifixes you see down there, they're really gory. Lots of blood."

"What's with the candle?" Hector asked. "Is it supposed to be lit, or did someone forget to blow it out?"

"That's the sacristy lamp. It's always burning. It's meant to tell you that God's really here. They call it the Silent Presence."

"The Silent Presence. That sounds kind of sinister. Kind of creepy, actually."

Amy was watching the candle burning in its red glass cylinder. "There's something so intriguing about candles," Amy said. "They're almost hypnotic. When I used to trip, I could watch candles for hours and hours."

Hector snorted. He didn't approve of drugs. "No wonder. You turn your brain to mush, it doesn't take much to amuse you."

Chewy stood up. All of a sudden, he seemed congested with things to say. Amy figured he'd talk about candlelight and psychedelics and religion. Instead he said, "Let's steal it."

"Steal what?"

"The lamp." He climbed over the top of the pew and vaulted the communion rail. "Help me."

"He's crazy," Hector said. "He's finally flipped. Where are *you* going?"

"To help him."

"You've both gone totally nuts. I'm going to call the cops."

Amy had never been on the far side of the communion rail, never been in the sacristy itself. In her day, women weren't generally welcome up there, unless they were getting married or putting fresh flowers on the altar. She looked up at the marshmallow Jesus to see if He was taking any notice. He didn't appear to be. She fought down an urge to genuflect again and took hold of the ornate bronze base of the lamp. It was much heavier than she thought it would be. Chewy blew out the flame. "I hate the way blown-out candles smell," she told him.

They hustled the lamp down the left aisle, past the stained-glass windows and over patches of colored light on the marble floor. About two thirds of the way to the vestibule, they heard the front door open. "Oh my God," Amy said. She realized in that second how much trouble they'd be in if they were caught, and how embarrassing it would be. Amy remembered when a couple of her classmates had stolen an angel from the school crèche. Her parents had been horrified; it was a sacrilege, they said. Stealing a sacristy lamp was so much worse than taking a statue from a nativity scene. Her parents would disown her. There'd be no more Pinto.

Chewy drew her over to a confessional booth. They hastily hid the lamp where, usually, the priest would sit. Amy and Chewy both ducked into the side of the booth where the penitent would kneel. It was a tight fit for the both of them. They heard Hector talking to someone and then heard the front door open again.

~

Amy and Chewy were standing by the bushes in front of the church. Amy remembered hearing rumors that young couples used to have sex behind those bushes on Saturday afternoons, when the priests were hearing confessions. After consummation, they would dash into the church. If they'd done it anywhere else, they might have been hit by a car before they could confess their mortal sin, and they would have gone straight to hell. This way, they didn't have to risk crossing any streets when not in a state of grace.

"Where have you been?" she asked Hector. "We were cold." *I was cold anyway. I don't know if Chewy gets cold.*

"I've been talking to young Father Cardoza," Hector said. "He's the new pastor here. I lied; I told him my wife and I were thinking about converting, but we were having trouble with that whole birth control thing. He took me to his office in the rectory and we had yerba mate, because he's from Argentina. Well, he's from Paraguay, but he went to seminary in Argentina. He told me he has some problems with the contraception bit, too. He's quite nice, and kind of cute for a pastor."

"The priest who was pastor here when I was a kid, Father Ryan, he wasn't at all cute," Amy said. "He was cranky and creepy and old. He used to smack me on the butt sometimes, even if I hadn't done anything wrong."

"Just a quick little swat? Or more?" Hector asked her. He was wondering if he had a theme for an upcoming show.

"They were kind of slow-motion smacks and... sometimes they ended with kind of a fondle."

"Were you the only one who got spanked like that, or did he spank other girls too?"

"Other girls, too. I don't know how many. We didn't talk about it much. Boys, too, I think."

Chewy nodded.

"Well, if I hadn't done something when Father Cardoza walked in, you know where you'd be? You'd be spending your Thanksgiving in the South Bay Jail."

"How are we going to get the lamp home?" Amy asked.

"You mean you've still got it?"

"It's in the bushes."

"Good Lord, haven't you two gone far enough with this? The only reason I intercepted the priest was so you'd have a chance to put it back."

Chewy came out of the bushes carrying the lamp. He was just going to march home with it. "Wait, Chewy. Put it back for now," Amy said. "I'll go get my car." It was nice to have a car to go get.

Gus was standing at his front door. He was looking forlorn. "You took a long walk," he said. "Where's Chewy? Where's Dr. Bird?"

"They're uh, with the stuff."

"Stuff? What stuff?"

"Umm, just stuff we bought at a yard sale."

"Thanksgiving seems a strange day to have a yard sale."

"It's great stuff. It was a very intense yard sale. What's the matter, Gus?"

"Nothing. Nothing's the matter."

"Come on, tell Amy."

"Nothing went the way I wanted it to today. The turkey's still not done, not nearly. And I don't know if it will be any good when it is done. I doubt it."

"It seems to me," Amy said, "that the most important thing is, we all got to be together on Thanksgiving."

"But we weren't all together, except for a few minutes."

"Well," Amy said, "true. That's true. We'll all have to get together some other time, then. Maybe for Christmas. Or just some weekend. We can all go bowling. So what else is bothering you? Did your team lose the game?"

"No," he said heavily, "they won, but after the game, I watched the news, and there was a big fire downtown today, in a building with a cafeteria on the first floor."

"Uh-huh."

"And there were these old people there, having their Thanksgiving dinners. Lonely old people, I guess, or they wouldn't be at a cafeteria for Thanksgiving. But it turned out, they all got out okay."

"Well, that's good, isn't it?"

"Yes, but after everyone got out, the building collapsed, and there was still a fireman inside. They said on the news he was missing, but then they showed a video of the building right after it collapsed, and there were flames shooting up all over. Nobody could have lived through that."

"That's awful, Gus, but..."

"And I was thinking... I don't know. I kept thinking about that fireman's family, how they're holding up Thanksgiving dinner, waiting for him to get home. Only he won't be. He won't be coming home."

"Gus, don't think about that kind of thing. There's no sense making yourself miserable." But by now, he'd gotten *her* thinking about that fireman too, and his family, and how they would be looking at the clock, waiting for their fireman to happily burst through the door, home for dinner after fighting a fire. They'd be waiting and waiting. She started feeling seriously unhappy herself. She felt like putting the sacristy lamp back where it belonged and living a righteous life thereafter.

"I've got to go to work," Gus said. "Why don't you stay, though, and have dinner when the turkey's finally cooked? If it ever is."

"Okay, I might. I can have some cranberries and maybe some dressing."

"And, well, it'll be a long time, but if you're still here by the time I get back, maybe we could go someplace."

"I don't know. Where would we go?" *Not back to the graveyard.*

"We could go by that building where the fire was. You know, just drive past."

"Gus, that's pretty morbid. And... and you just can't feel responsible for..."

"I don't feel responsible. Heck, I know it wasn't my fault, I had nothing to do with it. I just feel like... I feel like we'd be honoring him if we just... just visited that place. What do you think, Red?"

"Honoring him? I don't know," Amy said, "Maybe."

21

BARBED WIRE

Mr. and Mrs. Q's neighbor Frank knew all about the women who'd appeared in their films. He'd watched all of those movies, many times over. Frank had been looking forward to Thanksgiving at the Qs' for a while now.

"Which one is that one?" Wim asked Frank. He was asking about the woman in the long purple dress sitting on the stairs.

"That'd be Pamela," Frank told him. "Isn't she something? I don't know how Mr. Q finds 'em. Pamela was in *The British Pound* and *English Muffins*. Those are some fine little films. And she *is* British. She wouldn't have to be, I don't suppose, but she is. Mr. Q's a real stickler, you know, a real perfectionist." Frank drained his drink.

"And the one over there?" This time he was asking about the tall blonde woman in the black sweater, black velour bell bottoms, and glittery silver pumps who was helping herself to one of Mr. Q's crab puffs.

"Ramona, from *Rubber Maid*. Nice little film if you care for that sort of thing. She had a supporting role in *Sleazy Rider*, too. And that woman she's talking to"—he meant the one in the fawn-colored jumpsuit—"her name is Svetlana. She was in *The Russians Are Cumming*."

"And who's that talking to Mr. Q?" Mr. Q was sitting on the ledge in front of his fireplace with a woman on either side of him.

"Her name is Thera, or something like that. She's in *Dutch Treats*. Not a bad movie, but not one of his best. I understand she's really Dutch."

"No, the one on the other side of him." The svelte woman sitting next to Mr. Q had a cascade of flowing black hair; she was wearing a dark red sweater and a short black leather skirt. "Who is she?"

"Funny you should ask," Frank said. "Be damned if I know. Been trying to place her all afternoon."

After a while, Mr. Q came by with a plate of artichoke hearts and a bowl of yellow stuff with black specks in it. "That's some shirt you're wearing," Frank said to him. "Looks like you're going to a prom."

Mr. Q ignored Frank's comment on his ruffled shirt. "Have an artichoke heart," he said to Frank.

"Who's that you were talking to?" Frank asked Mr. Q. "Is that Chloe from *Brand Spanking New*?"

"Nope. Chloe was much more petite than this girl. And much more vulnerable looking."

"Regina from *Bottoms Up*? Misty from *Going Down South*? Amber from *What the Doctor Did*?"

"No, those were all very early efforts. I'd have no idea how to get in touch with Regina or Misty. Amber is suing me right now, but there's no way she's going to win."

"There was something to be said for those early flicks," Frank said. "That was before you bought good lights, so they had that grainy look, and it was before Mrs. Q took that videography class, so the camera work was all jumpy, but I like those early films a lot. They're gritty. They're authentic. Anyway, who is that girl? What was she in?"

"That's Velveteen, and she hasn't been in anything yet. I'm saving her for a special project I have in mind. Here, dip the artichoke in this." He meant in the yellow stuff. "Isn't that delicious?"

"Not bad. What is it?"

"You won't believe it when I tell you. It's mayonnaise. Plain old mayonnaise. That just shows you how different something that's made at home, made with respect for the ingredients, how different that can be from some mass-produced crap."

"What are those black thingies?"

"Coarse ground pepper." He asked Wim if he wanted an artichoke heart. He made it sound like he hoped Wim didn't.

"No, I don't want some," Wim said. "I burned my tongue on those crap pup things..."

"Crab puffs. And I suppose you'll hold a grudge against my food all day long?"

Wim shrugged and whipped a clove cigarette out of his shirt pocket.

"I don't want you smoking inside the house. You know that. Dinner in half an hour."

"That gives me time for another drink or two," Frank said. "What's for dinner, gourmet stuff?"

"No, not gourmet stuff, whatever that is," Mr. Q said, "Just plain good food." He went off to offer artichoke hearts to other guests. Wim lit up.

"Doesn't he have the most incredible voice?" Frank asked Wim. "Did you ever hear anyone who sounded like that? No wonder he does voice-overs for some of his films." Mr. Q's voice was large and round and honeyed. "He talks the way Burl Ives sings. I'll bet that's why he makes such a good lawyer. Who can argue with Burl Ives?"

"I don't know," Wim said. He had no idea who Burl Ives was. Some sort of rock star?

∽

Wim sat next to Thea, where Mr. Q had been sitting before. "You smell like a campfire," Thea told him.

Wim's cousin Hendrik had been evicted from his rented room and was sleeping on the floor at a neo-Marxist commune, but the neo-Marxists wouldn't let Wim stay there because he didn't give a damn about politics. So Wim had been living in Wampatuck State Park outside of Boston. "And what's wrong with smelling like campfires? The smell of smoke is a good, honest smell. What were you talking about to Mr. Q?"

"He asked me if I wanted to be in another one of his films."

"I thought he might. And what did you tell him?"

"I told him that I have another job, working in a Mexican restaurant."

This was disappointing news for Wim, who had received a finder's fee for lining up Thea and Margreet for *Dutch Treats*. He'd been hoping that he might get paid if Thea made another movie.

"And what did he say then?"

"He said he hoped they would make their own tortillas." Thea got up and left him alone with Velveteen. Wim turned to her and introduced himself.

"Your name's *Vim*?" Velveteen smiled. "That sounds like a breakfast cereal or something."

"No, it's spelled with double chew."

"You mean a double u." She traced the letter in the air.

"Yes, that's what I said. And your name, what is it?

"I'm Velveteen."

"Yes, but your real name?"

"Velveteen," she insisted. "My mother named me after the velveteen rabbit."

Wim smiled, to show he wasn't being taken in by this rabbit nonsense.

"I'm serious. It's from a story for kids, a really, really sad story called *The Velveteen Rabbit*. My mom loved that book, so she named me Velveteen. Look, I'll prove it." She got a red leather wallet out of her purse and showed him her driver's license.

"Okay, I believe." Wim flipped through her wallet and came across a picture of an old man standing in front of an ersatz Christmas tree. "This is your father?"

"No, my boyfriend."

"*Boy*friend?"

"Yeah, my boyfriend. He has this big old house out on a lake. He used to let me use his credit card to buy clothes and stuff, and he took my kid fishing on the lake." She showed him another snapshot, one of a child holding a tiny fish up to the camera. "This guy," she said quietly. "I live for this guy."

"And you live in this big house with your boyfriend?"

"Not anymore. See, I have this other boyfriend, and I borrowed the old guy's Cadillac, and we went for a ride. We were sort of driving it together. He was steering and I was working the gas and the brake, but that didn't work too well. We totaled the Caddy."

"I think you have a lot of boyfriends."

"Not really. Just the two. Just one now. After the wreck, I was in the hospital for a couple of days, and when I got out, my old boyfriend was gone. His daughter came and took him with her back to California. She was afraid we might get married, and he might leave all his money to me."

"What about this other boyfriend of yours?"

"You're pretty curious about things, you know that? You always ask a girl so many questions?" Velveteen wanted to know. "I see him every day, almost. He's the assistant manager of the place where I work. But he's not much of a boyfriend. And I think there are other girls he likes better."

"And this you don't care about?"

"I don't much care about that, no. It's the other things. This job... I make a hundred fifty, two-hundred bucks a night in tips most nights, and he keeps almost all of it. I don't know what he does with it. What do you do with that kind of money?"

Wim could imagine a lot of things that could be done with that kind of money. Being Velveteen's boyfriend appeared to have solid advantages.

"So one time, I needed a little extra money for the kid. Not much, just some. I held out on him, and he found out, and he beat me up. Beat me up pretty bad. He's just this little guy, but he can play real rough."

"You should have called the police up," Wim said.

"I did. Or rather, my sister did. And the cops came and took him away. And then, the next night, his brothers—his brothers are even meaner than he is—they came and beat me up worse. They gave me a shiner, and they broke one of my fingers."

Velveteen had used makeup to cover her black eye, but looking closely, Wim could see the faint outline of a fading purple bruise.

"You need another kind of job, *ne*?"

Velveteen unrolled her turtleneck and covered half her face with it. She was cold, even by the fire. "I was taking a course in the mail: 'How to Get Your Real Estate License.' See, that's what the old man was into—real estate, and he'd done well, really well. I can read and write, and..."

Wim looked at her to see if she were joking. She took his look to be one of doubt. "Well, I can. Get me a book, I'll read it for you."

"No, I believe."

"But my other boyfriend found out what I was doing, and he tore up all my real estate books and papers and burned them. He likes me to work where he does, I guess so he can keep an eye on me." She pointed to the painting of Thea over the easy chair. "Mr. Q told me you painted that. It's really good. It looks just like that girl who was sitting over here, except for her hands. I like art. I've never known any real artists. Maybe you could paint me sometime."

"I could do that. We could go on a date, and I could do a few sketches."

"A date?" she snickered through her cranberry-colored sweater. She was imagining a malt shop and a movie. "No one's asked me out on a date in a long time. Do you mean a money date, or..."

"We can go tonight. Right after dinner," Wim said.

"Tonight? Where would we go? Do you have a car?"

Wim shook his head. He didn't even know how to drive.

"What about your place?" she suggested.

"This is my place now," Wim said. "I live in the basement."

"You do?" Velveteen's eyes, just above her upturned collar, showed surprise. "I don't think Mr. Q would like it if I spent the night with you in his basement. And we can't go to my apartment, because of my kid, and my sister lives there too. And my boyfriend might come around later."

Wim agreed; going to her place was a bad idea. He didn't want a run-in with her boyfriend, or with her boyfriend's vindictive brothers.

"I guess we could go to a hotel," Velveteen said. "You could do your sketches there."

A night of drawing Velveteen at a hotel suited Wim perfectly. A one-night stay might turn into a permanent place to live. Anything would be better than living in a tent. Or staying with the Qs. There might be room service. There might be a bar in the lobby.

"Do you have any money?" she asked him. "No, I guess not, not if you're living in someone's basement. I'll have to get some, then, before we can go."

⌁

Mrs. Q found Thea in the basement, sitting by the bed where much of *Dutch Treats* had been filmed. This was Wim's bed now. "*There* you are," Mrs. Q said. "Bad news. He isn't going to make it to the party."

"Who isn't?"

"Why, Ricky. You know, the Star."

Does she expect me to be disappointed?

"He said he had to rake leaves today." Mrs. Q sighed. "He's so dedicated to all his little jobs. I like that in him, but raking leaves on Thanksgiving?"

Mrs. Q's mention of the Star brought back more memories of that afternoon in this room. She looked down at the leopard-skin rug, but there was more than one stain there. She wasn't sure which one she and Margreet had helped produce. She remembered that infinitely sad look in her eyes. *Did they invite Margreet to the party today?* The Qs had not been very pleased with Margreet's performance. But it had been in the contract they'd signed before making *Dutch Treats*. They had to agree to come to the Qs' Thanksgiving dinner party.

"Your friend Wim doesn't take much pride in the way he makes a bed, does he?" Mrs. Q said. She tried to straighten the spread but that didn't help much. The problem was more fundamental. Mrs. Q tore off all the bedclothes and came back with clean sheets. "I don't mind telling you, Thea, that your friend Wim is somewhat... well, *trying* to have as a houseguest. Quite trying."

"I can imagine," Thea automatically began working the right side of the bed, helping Mrs. Q. First they put on the fitted bottom sheet—bright banana yellow, with big blue flowers.

Mrs. Q said, "When I heard Wim was living in a tent, I almost cried, it sounded so pitiful. Wim has so much talent, and who can paint in a tent?

And it was starting to get cold about then. One day I said to Mr. Q, let's get in the car and drive to the park and bring Wim back here." Now Mrs. Q unfurled the fresh top sheet. It snapped like a sail in the wind, then settled onto the bed. "But staying here hasn't seemed to have helped him as an artist. I haven't seen him paint anything. He was supposed to do me, you know. That was part of the agreement. He was going to do a portrait of me in exchange for room and board. I was looking forward to posing for him. But no, not even a sketch so far. He doesn't do anything but watch TV. His cousin Hendrik comes out here, and the two of them sit around and monopolize the couch and eat smelly cheeses and smoke those nasty clove cigarettes."

"*Kreteks*," Thea said.

"What's that?"

"That's what those clove cigarettes are called, *kreteks*. They're from Indonesia." Thea's father smoked them too.

"Wherever they're from, they stink. Well, they don't smell too bad when someone's actually smoking them, but afterwards? And even though we've asked him and asked him not to smoke in the house, he doesn't pay any attention. It gets just awful in the den. We had to air it out before the party. And when those cloves burn, they pop and send out sparks. There are all these tiny burn holes in our couch. Say, you do good hospital corners, Thea."

They laid the red comforter on the bed. "I could have told you that Wim is a hard person to help," Thea said. "I was in med school when we first met. Wim and Hendrik were sleeping in the Vondelpark. I let them move into my apartment there for a while. Then he stayed with me when I was working in London." She shook her head. "And no, he's not an easy person to live with."

"Well, I wish you had told us that, dear. The other day he was talking about going back to Holland. He said you'd be going back with him."

"That's not true. We're not friends like that anymore."

"Then he said he and Hendrik might go to South Africa. Hendrik and Wim have an uncle who lives there, Wim told me. But I don't know where he thinks he's going to get money for these trips. Between you and me and the walls, I don't think he can afford carfare into Boston. He's borrowed money from Mr. Q, and I'm pretty sure he's taken money from my purse. And I'll bet those cigarettes of his aren't cheap, if they come all the way from Indonesia."

Thea finished stuffing Wim's pillow into the pillowcase and fluffed it up. She wondered if that was the same pillow that Mrs. Q had at one point put under her ass.

Thea was sorry when they'd finished making the bed. Making the bed had been something comprehensible and concrete. It was something that needed to be done. She felt like ripping it up and starting over again.

"Thea," Mrs. Q said, coming closer and taking her hand. "There's something I want to show you. I bet you've never seen anything like it before."

Thea wondered distantly if she was being propositioned.

"I can't just tell you about it. It's something I have to show you."

Mrs. Q led her by the hand through the unfinished portion of the basement, which was packed with stoves, old wood-fired stoves, dozens of old stoves. Here and there were four or five jukeboxes, looking gaudy in comparison with the dark metal stoves. Thea banged her shin hard against the cast-iron leg of one of the stoves.

They went through a doorway and into an attached garage. It was a two-car garage, but there were no cars. There were twenty or more glass cases full of hundreds of strands of barbed wire, each with a plastic label. "This," Mrs. Q said proudly, "is our barbed-wire collection."

Thea looked in the case nearest the door. One rusty strand had particularly long and nasty-looking barbs.

GERMAN SPIRAL TRENCH WIRE, c. 1916
FOUND 3/9/72
NEAR THE POLYGON WOOD, FLANDERS

"You'd think it wouldn't be hard to find barbed wire around World War I battlefields. They say there was over a million miles of the stuff strung in front of the trenches. That's enough to go around the world forty times over. But it's been nearly sixty years since the war ended, so it's not like there are still clumps of it lying around. And you have to be careful; when we were tromping through the woods, we met this Aussie guy whose grandfather died in the battle there, and he told us there were still some unexploded artillery shells buried in the ground. He said someone had stepped on one a few months before and it exploded."

"But... why? Why do you collect barbed wire?"

This took Mrs. Q aback. She was ready for questions about the configuration of barbs or the thickness of strands. She could explain the purpose of individual specimens. She was at a loss, though, when it came to answering Thea's question. "I don't know. We like to collect things. Mr. Q collects art, of course. We collected antique stoves and old jukeboxes, but both of those are so big, you can only collect so many. And jukeboxes are getting to be very expensive. We tried collecting antique beer cans, and matchbooks from famous restaurants, and we thought about merry-go-round horses for a while, but for some reason, we like barbed wire better. I guess we got interested when we were traveling out west and we stopped at a barbed wire museum in Kansas. We stopped there just by chance—but it was a revelation. What a collection! And since then... well, I guess you'd say we became obsessed with barbed wire. It's given us a chance to travel to some interesting places, and... and it's just given us purpose. You need purpose, don't you think?"

Thea realized she was crying. She didn't know when she'd started, or why.

H. M. ROSE'S KINK-LINE BARB, 1877
FOUND 7/16/69
NEAR GILLETTE, WYOMING

"You'd be surprised, the people who collect barbed wire," Mrs. Q said. "We went to a traders convention in Salt Lake City a couple of years ago, and there was a dentist and a professor from Berkeley and the CEO of a lawn-care company and... oh, and there were these two nuns there who had the most complete collection of moonshine wire anyone had ever seen. Moonshine wire—that's wire that's made without a patent—these nuns had strands of moonshine wire that the experts at the convention had never seen before, or even heard of, if you can believe that."

BRINKENHOFF FLAT RIBBON, 1883 or 1884
PURCHASED 10/07/75
SALT LAKE CITY, UTAH

Thea rubbed her shin. She'd really banged it; it had started bleeding. Her crying had become more pronounced now. She realized she wasn't going to be able to keep it from Mrs. Q.

～

Wim was coming out of the upstairs bathroom; Mr. Q was waiting to get in. "Hey, man," Wim said to him.

"You know, it's funny. Once I got into a discussion with a German fellow. He told me the thing that annoyed him the most about Americans was the way they always say, 'Hey, man' when they want to talk to each other. The reason I say that's funny, is that I don't think I've heard one American say 'Hey, man' to another in the last five years at least. The only people who ever say that nowadays are foreigners who think they're mocking Americans."

"Klootzak!" Wim said under his breath. Mr. Q was becoming progressively less friendly and increasingly annoying. Wim felt like grabbing him by his lacy shirtfront and hurling him down the stairs. The stairs were carpeted with such thick, spongy shag carpeting that it probably wouldn't do him any harm. *Not yet, though.* He didn't want to go back to living in a tent. "Listen," Wim said, "When you take Velveteen home, you can take me, too. We're going to a hotel."

"I told Thea I would give her a ride. Won't that be a little awkward?" Mr. Q said and sneered.

But Wim had a sneer that could wither lesser sneers. "You let me worry about the awkward," Wim said.

Mr. Q pressed on past Wim into the bathroom. The he spun around and accused Wim, "You were using the guest towels."

"And aren't I a guest?"

"No, you live here," Mr. Q said. His tone of voice indicated, *but not for long.*

～

Mr. Q's neighbor Frank was drunk. Dangerously drunk. "Let's all go in and get a massage."

Mr. Q's Lincoln was parked in the lot behind the Lucky Star Spa in Lynnfield where Velveteen worked. Mr. Q and Wim were in the front seat, Thea and Frank in the back. Frank had come along because he was drunk and thought it might be fun. What else was there to do on a Thanksgiving night? His wife and their adopted kids were spending Thanksgiving with her family in Indiana.

"Do you imagine, do you actually imagine, Frank, that I would want a massage at a place like that?" Mr. Q asked him. "Or that Thea would?"

"Why not? *Ev*-ry-one wants a massage. *Ev*-ry-body *needs* a mas-*sage*," Frank claimed. He was trying to sound like a carnival barker.

"We don't have time anyway, Frank." Mr. Q said to him.

"I don't have to work tomorrow. You don't have to work tomorrow.

Nobody has to work the day after Thanksgiving. So let's stay out late tonight."

"I have to be somewhere tonight," Thea said. "I promised. I should have been there an hour ago."

Up in the front seat, Wim made a rude noise.

"You can't say that you've been to America until you've had a good massage," Frank said. He slipped back into carnival-barking mode again. "A real pro-*fes*-sion-al mas-*sage*. Guar-an-*teed* to be to-tal-ly sat-is-fy-ing for men and women, boys and girls, dogs and cats."

"Shut up, Frank," Mr. Q said.

Frank had only had one massage in his life, and that one had been less than totally satisfying, quite a bit short of satisfying. He'd been a traveling man a few years back, and one morning when he was driving through east Tennessee, he heard over his CB radio that there was a massage parlor being run out of a truck stop on Route 11E. The trucker who'd sent this message said it was only for the desperate. Nevertheless, Frank made a long detour, found the diner, and went in.

Frank had to wait for the lunch rush to end, as the two masseuses doubled as wait-resses. To kill time, he ordered a meat loaf sandwich and mashed potatoes. Twice he went to the bathroom and drank from a half pint of Jack Daniels Black. He had three cups of coffee after lunch, waiting for the waitresses to get free. They were taking their time. The lunch rush was over, but they were talking to some truckers and to a couple of men who looked like farmers. The women had a baby in a bassinette sitting on the counter, and they were cooing to her. Frank made one more trip to the bathroom, killed the rest of the Black Jack, and went up to one of the waitresses. She was counting her tips. "What about me?"

"What about you? You want to pay your check?"

"No, remember, I ordered the blue plate special." The blue plate special was the highest priced item on the truck stop's "other" menu, the Rub-a-Dub menu. It was described as "a delightfully sensual, four-paw body rub."

The waitress looked at Frank, then at the other waitress, who nodded, and then she looked at her watch. "All right, but we're going to have to hurry it up. We have to start setting up for dinner pretty soon."

Frank followed them into the kitchen, and he paid his money to the cook, who gave him a sly wink. According to the Rub-a-Dub menu, a blue-plate special should run him forty dollars. Frank gave the cook a fifty-dollar bill and waited for his change. The cook said, "Tip." Frank followed the waitresses out the kitchen door and into a trailer parked behind the diner. It was messy inside, with laundry everywhere. One of them had to move the ironing board so that the other could set up the massage table.

"You gotta take a shower first," one of them said. Frank looked into their shower stall; the plastic tiles were cracked and stained, the floor was moldy, and the stall smelled like rotten eggs. He told them that he had just taken one before he came to the diner. They let it go at that.

Frank took off his clothes and lay down on the massage table; the waitresses took off their uniforms. They left their slips and the rest of their underwear on. According to the Rub-a-Dub menu, a blue-plate special was to be served up entirely in the nude, but Frank figured they'd work their way into nudity.

One of the women started rubbing his shoulders, and the other one rubbed the back of his legs. They were pretty half-hearted in their rubbing, but Frank managed to get a little excited, anyway. He started moving his hips rhythmically. "What's he doing?" one waitress asked the other.

"He's humping the table," the second waitress said. "You're humping the table, aren't you?"

"You do that at home?" the first one asked him. "You get up on your kitchen table and hump that?"

"What would your wife say if she came into the kitchen and saw you humping the table? What would your kids say?" Frank didn't have any kids then, but he and his wife were in the process of adopting three orphaned children from Vietnam.

The baby started crying in another part of the trailer. "I'll take care of her," the second waitress said. "You finish up here." Half of Frank's blue-plate special went off to tend to the baby. After a few more minutes of rubbing, the other half called out, "You'd better get back here. Come back and see what he's done now. And bring some paper towels."

~

"Come on, let's go inside," Frank said. "Anything's better than waiting in the car." Frank was willing to give massage another chance.

"We won't be waiting much longer," Mr. Q said.

Velveteen had said that she was just going in to pick up her paycheck. That had been over an hour ago.

"We'll all get blue plate specials," Frank said. "I'll pay for everyone."

"You're drunk, Frank."

"Listen to him. He says I'm drunk, so I must be. Who can argue with Burl Ives?" Wim had thrown his sketch pad and a box of charcoal pencils into the back seat between Frank and Thea. Frank had moved them to the other side of the seat so that he could sit closer to Thea. He put his hand on her knee, not because she'd been in one of Mr. Q's movies, or because her boyfriend was fooling around with a massage-parlor girl, but because he was drunk and would have done the same with any knee. "Hey Burl, give us a song, how about it?"

Mr. Q ignored him. "Wim, if you're going to light up one of those putrid cigarettes, you have to go outside the car."

Wim said it was cold out there.

"Please smoke outside," Thea said.

Wim snarled and opened the car door. "I'll go to see why she takes so long."

A dapper man behind the desk inside the massage parlor was cleaning his nails when Wim came in. He was wearing a plaid vest. "Half hour or full hour?" he asked Wim.

"No, I don't want a massage. I want to talk to Velveteen."

"She's busy."

"I need to talk to her."

"We don't want any trouble here. You remember that, huh?"

When Velveteen opened the door, Wim got a glimpse of a heavy-set man coated with oil, lying on a massage table. The flocked wallpaper in there was a deep red. The light was pink, from two red light bulbs in wall sconces. The oily man looked like a plump, rosy baby on a changing table. "I'm sorry," Velveteen said. "I figured it would be totally dead around here when we came by to get my check. It's Thanksgiving night—who the hell wants a massage when you're all full of turkey? But it was super busy and I got recruited. What the hell, I figured, I need the cash."

"Everybody is waiting out in the car."

"Well, I said I was sorry. I won't be much longer, but if you want, you can just take off and go without me."

"We'll wait."

"Really? In that case, would you go down to the front desk and ask my boyfriend..."

"Boyfriend? That's your boyfriend?"

"I told you, he's the assistant manager here. Go down and ask him for a jelly bean, okay?"

"A chili bean?"

"A jelly bean. Or a black beauty. You know, a pep pill. I work a hell of a lot better, and I'll get done faster if I'm speeding. Tell him it's for Velveteen. He'll give it to you."

"Hey, man," Wim said.

"What did you say?" the assistant manager was still looking critically at his fingernails. They were tiny but exquisite. "What do you want now? You want a rub after all?"

"I want a pep pill. A black beauty or a chili bean for Velveteen."

"What does she think this is, a fucking pharmacy?"

"She said you would give her one. It helps her work."

"You can go tell her to fuck off."

Wim grabbed the man by the vest and yanked him up. He had only meant to haul the assistant manager to his feet. Instead, he had him dangling in the air. The man was practically a midget. No, he *was* a midget. If his brothers were the same size as he was, one would have had to climb on the other's shoulders in order to punch Velveteen out. They must have looked like a circus team gone berserk. "Sorry," Wim muttered, letting go of the assistant manager and letting him drop back on his stool.

It was then he noticed the nail file. It had gone right through his denim jacket and was embedded in the fleshy part of his forearm. He hadn't even felt it go in. It was sticking there now.

Wim slammed the door behind him as he got back in the car. "Well?" Mr. Q asked him.

Wim gave him an exaggerated, frustrated shrug.

"Come on, Burl, sing it for us. 'Go tell Aunt Rosie. Go tell Aunt Rosie...'"

"If you don't shape up, I'm going to throw you out of this car, Frank, so help me," Mr. Q said.

"And I'll help him," Wim said. Wim and Mr. Q exchanged glances. It made them uneasy, being allies.

"I'm serious, Frank," Mr. Q said.

But in fact, they were bluffing, and it's hard to bluff a drunk. "Go tell Aunt Rosie,'" Frank sang, "'the old gray goose is dead.'"

"Shut up, Frank," Mr. Q said. "And it's not Aunt Rosie, it's Aunt Rhody."

"You sure? I always thought it was Rosie. But I guess you should know, Burl," Frank said. "Go tell Aunt Rhody...'"

"I have to go, Wim," Thea said. "I'm really late. When is she coming?"

"I don't know."

"Go back in and find out," Mr. Q said.

"I can't."

Mr. Q saw the blood from Wim's nail-file wound. "Criminy, Wim, you're bleeding. You're dripping blood all over the upholstery."

"Let me see," Thea said.

Wim jerked his arm away from her. "Leave me alone."

Frank sang, "She died in the mill pond, while standing on her head."

Velveteen and the assistant manager appeared in the back doorway of the massage parlor. The assistant manager was glaring at the people in the car. Thea saw Velveteen reach down and brush something out of the little man's hair. At first, that seemed to annoy him, but then he smiled up at her. With that, Thea knew that Velveteen wasn't going anywhere with Wim tonight.

"We're getting out of here. I don't like the looks of this. I don't like the looks of this at all," Mr. Q said.

Wim said something, but Thea couldn't make out what. She reached up and patted him on the shoulder. His life seemed to be going seriously wrong, and she felt somehow involved in the defeat with him.

Frank said, "How about 'A Little Bitty Tear Let Me Down'? That's a great one, Burl. Sing that one, huh?"

Mr. Q started up the Lincoln. Velveteen waved goodbye. She had a fast, semicircular wave that made her look like a gas-station attendant cleaning a windshield.

Thea felt Frank's hand on her knee again. She removed it. He put his hand back, a little higher on her thigh.

22

CITY OF DREADFUL NIGHT

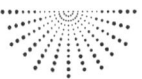

"You know what I think the problem is?" Dean asked Ross.

"Not enough paint?" Dean and Ross were painting the kitchen of their restaurant.

"No, not enough forests."

"Forests? I didn't know you cared much about forests. I wouldn't have thought so."

"I like forests fine, but... I'm not talking about my personal problems," Dean said, "not right now. I'm talking about the problem in general. The unhappiness problem. Back when people lived in forests, they were happy, because they knew what was expected of them. Men went out and killed animals with spears and stuff and brought them home, and that gave them status. Plenty of status. Women didn't much like stabbing bears and boars and so forth, and weren't all that good at it, because stabbing stuff takes quite a bit of upper-body strength. But you can bet that women appreciated the stabbers, because they liked eating as much as anyone."

"And there weren't any problems back then?"

"Oh, there were plenty of problems, I'm sure. Like, sometimes the stuff that the men planned to eat wound up eating them instead. That sort of thing happened routinely, I'd guess. But that's pretty uncomplicated, compared to what we have today."

Ross looked carefully at Dean, trying to gauge his seriousness. With Dean's penchant for the dramatic, it was often difficult to tell.

"And then, there's the fire-control factor."

"Be careful, Dean. You're getting paint on the deep fryer."

"I *am* being careful. This is just cheap paint—it's too watery."

"And you're getting it all over Buzz's bed."

"Oh, like that matters."

They were allowing Buzz to camp in the kitchen until the restaurant opened. He had a stained and tattered Boy Scout sleeping bag spread over a cot. There were Burger King wrappers, crushed Styrofoam cups, empty matchbooks, a beer can, half a bear claw, dirty socks, a dead spider, and unidentifiable detritus on the cot. His bed couldn't have looked messier if a dog had had puppies in it.

"I was talking about the fire-control factor," Dean said. "Say these guys, these hunters, bag a buffalo and drag it home, and that night, the whole clan has a big party to celebrate, and they build a bonfire to cook buffalo steaks. They drink a little too much prehistoric beer, and they're whooping it up, singing, dancing, not paying attention to the fire, and it starts to spread. Panic! But, all of a sudden, a dozen or so of the hunters turn into volunteer firemen. They form a perimeter around the fire, whip out their wangers, and bingo, you've got fire control."

"That's a good way to smell up a campground," Ross said.

"It's a good way to take charge. When you live in a forest, fire control is crucial. Women don't have the right equipment. Their stream is too diffuse. Their aim's too inaccurate. Their range is too short."

"And they might get burned."

"Yikes! Imagine how painful that would be."

Ross poured more paint into the tray. "You know what, Dean, I think your theory sucks."

Dean blinked at him. "Maybe. Maybe so. But explain to me why..."

"For one thing, you know what they call these people you're talking about, right? They call them hunter-gatherers. Who do you think did the gathering bit? Women went out and found... they found nuts and berries and seeds and herbs and all kinds of shit like that. And they fetched the water. Don't you think there might have been a few gourds full of water around to throw on the fire instead of pissing it out?"

"Yeah, okay, forget fire control, but bringing down a wooly mammoth with spears—those gatherers must have found the hunters pretty impressive when they did something like that."

"Was that as impressive as having babies? Can you imagine how weird that must have been, seeing a woman's belly swell up, and her boobs get all heavy, and then all of a sudden, a tiny human pops out? It must have seemed like magic. Like some powerful juju."

"Well, then, explain to me why today, women are so happy, comparatively, and men are so miserable. It has to do with a fall from power,
believe me," Dean said.

"I still don't agree with your premise. I don't see that women are all
that happy. Lots of women aren't, particularly. And not all men are
unhappy. I'm not, for instance." Ross looked over what they had already
painted. The paint *was* too thin, and the old blue paint job was showing
through the new white paint. The blue-white color of the kitchen walls
reminded Ross of the color of Laurel's breast milk. She used to store it in
baby bottles in the fridge. Sometimes, when they were out of half & half,
Ross would squirt a little into his coffee.

"You just *think* you're happy. You sure don't look it. You always look
morose."

"I didn't say I was happy. I said I wasn't *un*happy. Big difference."

"And the reason you're not unhappy is, you're using the roller and I'm
stuck with the brush."

"You want to roll for a while?"

"No, you go ahead. You know what you remind me of, Ross? You
remind me of those films they used to show in Driver's Ed class."

*Black-and-white footage—overhead shot of a '57 Bel Air convertible. Background
music involving dark and ominous chord progressions. Camera pans down.
Medium close-up of four young people barreling down a two-lane. Passengers
laughing, singing, hugging. Gleeful shrieks and tinny rock and roll, barely audible
over the soundtrack and the growl of the eight-banger engine. They appear to be
driving directly into the looming clouds of a thunderstorm.*

*Close up of a teen driver with a thin mustache. He takes a drink from a bottle,
passes it to the woman in the seat next to him. Her long hair is streaming in the
wind. She takes a nip and passes the bottle to the back seat. The tall passenger back
there takes a slug, too, and then gives it to the woman sitting beside him. Sitting
between them is a large, friendly dog. They offer the dog a drink.*

*Background music turns even more portentous. It begins to rain. Tires squeal
as the Chevy barely negotiates a turn. Tension mounts.*

*Sudden silence. Screen goes black. The sound of screaming brakes, the crash of
impact, the cascading sound of breaking glass, the sickening thud of bodies hitting
the wet blacktop. Then: actual Highway Patrol footage spliced in. Jagged scrap
metal wrapped around a bridge abutment. Somber, tight-lipped highway
patrolmen moving around amid the wreckage, covering bodies lying on the road*

with tarps. One smaller bundle presumably represents the friendly dog. Significant close-up of a cherry-top spinning around.

Belligerent, basso-profundo announcer: "This could be you..."

"Why do I remind you of that? You think I'm heading for a crack-up?"

"Not necessarily. All I'm saying is, reality has thin walls and unexpected disaster is always punching its fist through them, and you don't act like you're aware of that particular facet of reality."

Ross thought of Wim's painting in Thea's living room, of the rhino crashing into the child's bedroom.

"Not that I blame you," Dean said, "I wasn't either, really. I had no idea what sort of nastiness life had in store for me." Dean dropped his voice several octaves: "This could be you..."

"I've had my share of problems. Besides, you're going through a bad breakup, which is tough, for sure, but it's not like you've been in a terrible crash or you're being carted off to a concentration camp," Ross said. "You know, we're going to have to give these walls two coats."

"We're not going to have enough paint to give them *one* coat today," Dean said. "Remember, the only people who are going to see these walls are going to be working here. No need to impress them."

Out in the bar, the phone was ringing.

"I've got wet paint on my hands," Dean said. "Can you get it?"

"I've got paint on my hands too. Tell Buzz to get it."

Buzz had been painting the name of the restaurant and the logo on the front window.

"I sent Buzz out to get lunch. Who the hell even has this number?"

"Jeremy does. I guess I'll get it."

Laurel told Ross what had happened to Ollie. Ross told her he was sorry, really sorry, and that it was a horrible, hideous thing that had happened to her dog.

"You don't give a damn. I can tell from your voice."

"You can't tell anything. I have a naturally flat delivery."

"*I* can tell."

"I didn't even know you had a dog, Laurel."

"Jeremy must have told you about Ollie. Jeremy loved that dog. When I told him what happened, he freaked out. He..."

"You talked to Jeremy?"

"Yeah, I called your home number and nobody was there, so I called the number he gave me for his friend... Sahara?"

"Mojave."

"Yes, Mojave, and Jeremy was there, and so I told him what had happened, and he was really bummed when he found out."

"Jeremy may have told me about Ollie and I forgot about it. But still, I can sympathize."

"Oh great, you can sympathize," Laurel said. "Don't get all emotional on me. *I* could have been shot—I almost was—and you'd say, 'Aw, Jeez, that's too bad, poor Laurel. I can really sympathize.'"

Ross could picture Laurel at the other end of the line. Her anger would be making her blush. Laurel had an uneven, splotchy way of blushing when she was pissed off or when she was about to have an orgasm. "I do care, Laurel. Like I said, I..."

"Said, said. What are you going to *do*?"

"What do you want me to do?"

"Come out here and be with me."

"I would, Laurel, but I just can't now. I mean, we're painting the kitchen today, even though it's Thanksgiving. That should tell you..."

"Bullshit. To hell with your painting. Go to Logan and get on a plane. I'll drive to Grand Junction and pick you up. There are a lot of people here this weekend for the reunion. You'd have a good time. Blue Jay is here. Blue Jay's helped me a lot since this happened. Do you remember him?"

Ross didn't remember anyone named Blue Jay. "I'd like to, but I can't. I'd never get a flight out on Thanksgiving without a reservation, and..."

"That's bullshit and you know it. No one travels on Thanksgiving afternoon; I'm sure you could get a flight. You know what you're doing now?" she asked him. "You're rossing."

"I'm what?"

"Rossing. Same as not doing anything. Being inertial. Unemotional and inertial."

"Oh, rossing. I thought for a minute you said rolfing."

"Come on, Ross, talk to me. Stop acting so Deanish for a minute and really talk to me."

"Talk about what?" Ross had a hard time being empathetic on demand.

"Tell me what you're feeling, what you think about me. You never said, even when we were together. 'Laurel, you look so beautiful today,' or 'Laurel, how can you say such stupid things.' You almost never said anything to me, except occasionally, 'I don't care,' or 'Whatever you want, that's okay with me.'"

"That's a major exaggeration. I said plenty of things to you," Ross said, "but all right, I'll tell you what I'm thinking right now. I'm thinking, I'm glad Laurel still calls me when she's feeling down. I hope she always does."

"Really?"

"Really."

"Do you remember those long letters you wrote me when we first split up—when you left for Boston? There was so much sadness in those letters, it scared me. That's about the only time you've ever let your feelings hang out, at least to me. And now you don't write me at all."

"That's because you told me I was wallowing in the past."

"Well, you were, but I guess that's okay, sometimes. We're all wallowing like Cap's pigs out here this weekend."

"I've been trying to be a little more blasé about the past."

"You may have gotten too blasé." Then she said, "Tell me."

"Tell you what?"

"You know."

"Oh. Yeah. It's gonna be all right, babe."

This was part of a tradition of theirs. They would tell each other "It's gonna be all right, babe" even when the odds were stacked against it. When they were in Mexico and the fan belt on the U.S. Grape snapped on a Sunday night fifteen miles from the closest town, Ross was kicking the truck when Laurel told him, "It's gonna be all right, babe." When Laurel went all the way to Kansas City to a crafts fair and sold only three pieces of jewelry, Ross told her, "Don't worry, it's gonna be all right, Babe."

"Tell me again."

And he did.

"I hope so," she said. "I can't wrap my head around the fact that my sweet dog is lying dead in the back seat of Blue Jay's car."

"It'll take time to..."

"And I can't believe that you're not having Thanksgiving with Jeremy."

"He's perfectly happy having dinner with Mojave and his mom."

"I worry about him. I had a dream the other night. I was walking through the woods, and I saw a leg hanging out of a hole in a tree, a baby's leg, and it had sort of turned purple. And the tree was sucking the leg in, like someone slurping spaghetti. The leg kept kicking, but it was being pulled in. And I grabbed hold of the leg and yanked and yanked and finally got the baby out of the tree, but it was too late. The baby was already dead."

"And you think the baby was Jer?"

"I think it must have been."

"You've always had morbid dreams, Laurel."

"A lot of my dreams happen in forests. I wonder what that means."

"Dean thinks that's the biggest problem today, not enough forests."

"There are plenty of forests out here," Laurel said. "I'm going to go. Blue Jay is driving me home. He's been... he's been a help. A big help."

"You mentioned that. You're still going to the dinner back at School's Out, aren't you? You've been looking forward to that for a long time."

"Ross, I'm covered in blood, my blouse doesn't have any buttons on it, and my dog is dead," Laurel said bleakly. "I just want to go home and go to bed and pull the covers over my head."

Did she mean, go to bed with Blue Jay? Laurel lightly sprinkled her sheets with oil of pennyroyal before going to bed. An aromatic nest for a blue jay.

"I'm sorry I can't come out there now," Ross said, "Jer and I will be there in February for my brother's wedding."

"Don't worry about it. I never thought you'd really come."

Dean wasn't painting anymore. He was smoking a cigarette and looking at an old copy of the *Boston Free News,* one of the newspapers they'd used to cover the kitchen floor. Buzz came back with a white paper sack. "You know," Dean said to Buzz, "women who put personal ads in newspapers sure can be picky. This one says, 'Looking for a guy who is sincere, warm, mature, and in touch with his own spirituality. No heavy drinkers and no smokers. Vegetarian preferred.' Okay, here's another one: 'Petite, deserted wife, 42, looking for a nonsmoking male of her own age, preferably a deserted husband or boyfriend.' And here's another: '27 yo SF likes waterfalls, playing Clue, going to Roller Derbies, walking across covered bridges, and lying in the grass looking for shooting stars. Want to join me? Nonsmoker only.'"

"Boston women sure don't like smokers."

"If you smoke, you might as well plan on being celibate forever. You take out an ad that says you're a smoker... you'd get more responses if your ad said, 'Trappist monk with herpes looking for a meaningless fling.'"

"I don't even get why you're even reading those things," Buzz said. "You have that foxy girlfriend. Grampy Tibbets used to say, whenever he'd see a pretty girl, 'She's cuter 'n a speckled pup under a red wheelbarrow.' That's what I thought, first time I saw your girlfriend. She's your typical speckled pup under your typical red wheelbarrow."

Dean grunted. "Grampy Tibbets had a way with words, no doubt about it, but... Amy's not really my girlfriend anymore. More like a roommate. A roommate who doesn't pay rent. And I doubt she'll even be my roomie much longer."

"So... no more Amy and Dean?"

"No more Dean and Amy, you mean."

"What's the difference?"

"I don't know. No one ever says Amy and Dean; it's always Dean and Amy. Amy and Dean sounds like Cher and Sonny. Or Garfunkel and Simon. Or Bullfinkle and Rocky. Just plain doesn't sound right. Not that it matters much anymore."

"It was Bullwinkle, not Bullfinkle."

"Yeah, you're right. I'm surprised you even remember that show."

"It was one of Big Buzz's favorites. He made me and my brothers watch it with him every Saturday morning. He said we could learn a lot about history from that dog with the time machine."

"Sherman."

"No, Sherman was the boy. The dog was Mr. Peabody. So what would you say, if you were writing one of those personals?"

Dean gave it some thought. "Let's see. How about, 'Looking for a philosopher and/or poet with a huge sexual appetite who enjoys country music. Nondrinkers and nonsmokers need not apply. Carnivores welcome.'"

"You like country music? If I'd known that, I would have..."

"I hate country music. I just want my next girlfriend to be a country-music lovin', cigarette smokin', carnivorous kinda gal."

"But what if she wanted to listen to Dolly Parton or Merle Haggard while..."

Ross came back to the kitchen. Dean said, "Let me guess, that was Laurel. You've got that Laurel-called expression. You know, as often as she calls you, she should get herself a WATS line. What did she want this time?"

"Some hunter shot her dog, and she wants me to come to Colorado."

"Oh my God, that's awful. If someone shot Maud..."

"I know. It is awful."

"Are you going to go?"

"With all we have to do here?"

"I'm glad you're so responsible, Ross. I'm glad one of us is. Is that all she wanted?"

"She told me about a dream she had, about a cannibal tree that was eating a baby. She thought the baby was Jeremy."

"That wouldn't really be a cannibal tree, then, would it? A cannibal tree would eat other trees."

"And she told me that I never talk about my feelings."

"Well," Dean said, "you don't, much."

"She used to always ask me, 'What are you feeling now?' I never knew what to say. I never seemed to be feeling much of anything, in particular. I guess I should have made stuff up."

"Face it, Ross, you're just shallow. You're shallower than a kiddie pool. People can barely get their feet wet in you. So Buzz, let's eat, huh?"

"Took me a while to find a place where I could get turkey sandwiches. But I couldn't find any batteries." They'd been listening to Buzz's transistor radio while they were painting, but the batteries had died. "I just found out Dean likes country music, so..."

"That's not what I said at all, but anyway, Happy Thanksgiving, guys," Dean said.

"Hey, I've had worse Thanksgivings," Buzz said. "Last year, all I had was a can of Campbell's turkey noodle soup. I didn't even have a bowl to eat it in, or a spoon, or a hot plate to warm it up on, or a real can-opener, just a church key. I sat it on a radiator for a while and then I slurped it out of the can like it was a beer. Hard to get the noodles out that way."

"Pitiful," Dean said. "Ross, eat."

Ross claimed he wasn't hungry.

"Ross has problems," Dean said to Buzz. "He just got a call from his ex. And he just found out he was shallow."

"You guys split my sandwich," Ross said. "I'll just eat the pickle. How's the front window coming, Buzz?"

"Finished," Buzz said, his mouth full of sandwich. Flecks of turkey breast rained down on the carpet of newspaper.

"Young Buzz does good work," Dean said.

"I'm glad I finished," Buzz said. "It was cold out there."

"Cold out where? In the dining room?"

"No, cold outside."

"Wait, you painted on the outside of the window?" Dean asked.

"Sure, what's wrong with that?"

"I don't know. Is that what people usually do? It seems like it would wear off pretty fast."

"I guess I could scrape it off and start again from the inside. I never made letters backwards, though. I had enough trouble with that upside-down question mark."

Dean said, "We'll probably be out of business by the time the paint wears off. But maybe you should scrape it off. I've decided I really don't like ¿Por Qué No?. I still don't know why you wouldn't go along with Tortilla Flats."

"Why wouldn't you go along with Dos Gringos?" Ross asked him. "Just because Lizard came up with it?"

"Just because it's a stupid name."

"Let's get back to painting. You can roll for a while, and Buzz and I will do the touch-ups."

"I could really get behind some pumpkin-pie ice cream," Buzz said. "Why don't I go next door and get us a quart?"

"Copenhagen Cream is closed today, and besides..."

"What I think we should do," Dean said, "is punt. I mean, we don't have enough paint to finish anyway, and we can't get any more today."

"Jesus, Dean, look around. Are we really going to open this place next weekend?"

"At first glance, I admit, it looks pretty bleak. But once we finish painting, get the newspapers off the floor, and get Buzz's cot out of here, it'll look a lot better. We've been putting in lots of hours, though, and no one else in the whole city is working today, so why should we?"

"I have this great idea," Buzz said, "for a national holiday that would last a whole year. To mellow the country out."

"Here's another idea—one day every month with no name and no number. That way no one could schedule anything for that day," Dean said.

"All right," Ross said hopelessly. "You want to punt, we'll punt." He sat down on the newspapers.

"You just sat in some paint," Buzz told him.

"I'm not surprised," Ross said.

Buzz had a suggestion: "Let's get stoned."

"You got anything to smoke?" Dean asked him.

"Not anymore," Buzz said sadly. "I brought a baggie of homegrown with me from Arkansas, but it's long gone. Wasn't very good, anyway."

"Guess we can't very well get stoned, then, can we?"

Ross sighed. "I might have some hash."

"Hash? Righteous!" Buzz said. "I didn't know you..."

"I don't, much, anymore. This is the stuff that guy up in Vermont laid on us. I'd forgotten about it until I put these jeans on this morning. I think it may have gone through the wash." Ross fished the chunk out of his pocket. It did look slightly pale and mildewed. "The guy that gave it to me, that Cool Breeze guy, Cool Breeze Charlie, he said it was from Nepal."

"Oh, good God, is that half a Nepalese temple ball? I thought those things were mythical. You know, they say Bruce Lee chewed a Nepalese temple ball before every one of his fight scenes," Buzz said.

"Charlie said be careful. He said this stuff could really fuck you up."

"I think I have a pipe somewhere," Buzz rooted through his Boy Scout knapsack.

"Were you a Boy Scout, Buzz?" Ross asked him.

Buzz gave them a crisp, three-fingered Boy Scout salute. "I sure was. Almost made Eagle. My dad, Big Buzz, was scoutmaster of good old Troop 210. Umm, maybe I don't have a pipe after all. But I can make one."

Buzz fashioned a crude pipe, cutting a hole in the cardboard tube from a roll of toilet paper and covering the hole with aluminum foil. He used Ross's chewed-up ballpoint pen to poke tiny holes in the foil. "This is what guys in Vietnam and guys in jail use to smoke hash. Down in Arkansas, we call it a steamroller."

"Were you in Vietnam, Buzz?"

"No, but my brother Skip was in jail."

"Your brother is named Skip? Your parents were into some pretty informal names."

"I have another brother named Chigger."

"Chigger? Seriously?"

"Not his real name. Not even my parents would name a kid after an ornery bug. But everyone's always called him Chigger. He likes it."

"Did you ever decide on a new name, Buzz?" Ross asked him.

"Not for sure, but I've narrowed it down some: Troy, Jason, Spencer, or Chad. I like Timothy, too, but it doesn't go well with my last name—Timothy Tibbets just doesn't sound good."

"Too alliterative," Dean said.

"Yeah, and I don't want to change my last name."

"Just don't change your name to Robin," Dean said. "We already have two of those."

"I won't. It sounds kind of girly."

"Okay, fire it up," Dean said. "We'll be *Le Club des Hashischins*." Dean rubbed his hands together. "I'll be Baudelaire, Ross can be Nerval, and Buzz, you're Dumas."

"Who's this Dumbass guy?" Buzz wanted to know.

"Not dumbass, Dumas. You know, *The Three Musketeers?* He wrote that."

"Oh yeah, saw that, good movie. Good candy bar too. So, we're the three musketeers?" He handed Ross the steamroller. "You have to cover the open end with your hand," he said. Dean got out his lighter.

Ross took one hit and started coughing. "That's enough for me."

Dean and Buzz passed the makeshift pipe back and forth. When it went out, Dean tried to relight it with his BIC, but the steamroller caught fire. "It's okay, it was pretty much gone, anyway."

"That's some good shit," Buzz said. "Anyone want a bite of a bear claw?"

Ross was feeling that one toke. He said, "I don't know, somehow getting high these days, it just feels kind of corny. It's not 1969 anymore." He suddenly had the munchies and was sorry he had passed on the turkey sandwich. He stood up and brought with him a few pages of the *Boston Globe* stuck with paint to the seat of his pants.

"Don't move," Dean told him. "I want to get a photo of you like that."

Ross ripped the newspapers from his seat before Dean could get to his camera. It was the business section of the *Globe*. He imagined a headline:

ROOKY RESTAURATEURS GET STONED,
BLOW BIG CHANCE

Mojave's mother rang them into her building. She and Mojave lived in a basement apartment on Beacon Hill.

"Listen," Ross said, "hear the music?"

"'Blue Moon of Kentucky'? Somebody's playing Bill Monroe?" Dean guessed.

"No, there's a tiny recording studio down here in what used to be the coal cellar. Mostly for bluegrass musicians." As if to prove that was true, a tired, pale man carrying four cups of coffee was buzzed in and came down the stairs behind them and the music stopped. A tired man holding a mandolin opened the door for him. They saw a woman with a stand-up bass behind him. The walls of the studio were lined with empty yellow egg cartons to soak up the sound. It was a cozy yellow cave in there.

"I hope you're not real stoned," Ross said to Dean. "Are you?"

"I'm seeing a pink fringe around almost everything," Dean said. "And my feet kind of feel like they're not actually touching the ground; I feel like my shoes are sort of cruising along an inch or two above the floor. Aside from that, I'm fine."

"Mojave's mother is real down on dope. Try to act normal."

Ross knocked, and the door opened as far as the police lock would let it. Then, in the space between the door and the frame, the muzzle of a black beast appeared, snarling and drooling. "Don't open that door!" Dean shouted. He'd turned a pallid shade of gray. It was too late, though. Jeremy had already disengaged the police lock.

"Calm down, Maxine, it's just me," Ross said. The growling subsided. Maxine backed off and curled up; she was ready to go to sleep.

Jeremy had his head tilted up; he had a wad of toilet paper stuck in one nostril and he had a bloody handkerchief in his hand that looked like a used tourniquet. "Did Cerberus here do that to you?" Dean asked him, pointing at Maxine.

"Uh-uh," Jeremy said, "I got another nosebleed. A bad one. And her name's Maxine, not Sarah Bus."

"Nosebleed. Epistaxis, huh," Dean said.

"I didn't hit him, Mr. Jarboe."

"Hush, Mojave, nobody said you did," Mojave's mother said.

"I just didn't want anybody to think I hit him."

"I believe you, Mojave," Ross said. "Is it still bleeding?"

"I don't know. Maybe a little."

Dean was intently examining the houseplants. He was paying far too much attention to the philodendrons, especially for someone who didn't particularly like potted plants.

"They were watching parades on TV," Mojave's mother said, "and then Jeremy got that call from his mom, about her dog. That's so horrible, that someone would shoot a dog. If someone shot Maxine, I'd hunt him down and blow him away." She said that with such somber determination that Ross had no doubt that she would do just that. Ross wondered what she would do if she saw a tree eating Mojave. Take a chainsaw to it, probably.

"His nosebleed started right after the phone call. Then they played some game—they love those games—but it still didn't stop. I cut out a little strip of cardboard and had him put it under his top lip, and I got him to put his pinky in a bowl of ice water. That's what my ma always used to say you should do about nosebleeds. I think it slowed down some then, but it was bleeding right through dinner."

"He got blood in his mashed potatoes," Mojave said.

"Didn't," Jeremy said.

"Did too."

"Hush, Mojave."

"He'll be all right," Ross said. "It's genetic." *Or was it?* "I used to get nosebleeds, too, when I was a kid."

"I used to get earaches," Dean said. "Wicked, horrible earaches. Acute otitis media." He clapped his hands theatrically over his ears.

"Did you have a good time, other than the nosebleed?"

"We played Normandy Beachhead," Jeremy said. "I lost."

Mojave explained how this had happened. "He was the Allies and I was the Germans. I hit him on Sword Beach with one of my infantry divisions. But that was just a diversion. What I really did was, I let him land on Omaha and climb up the bluffs and then I smashed his flanks with Panzer Group West. I wasn't afraid to use poison gas. And I had German pilots turn into kamikazes to take out his fleet."

"It's a good thing we had Eisenhower over there on D-Day and not you, Jeremy," Dean said. "Otherwise, we'd all be speaking German." Dean clicked his heels together and gave a straight-arm salute.

Ross glared at him. Dean was acting pretty damn stoned.

Ross thanked Mojave's mother for having Jeremy over for dinner. "Dean and I are pretty busy this week, so..."

"You're always busy," Jeremy said.

"... so I didn't have time to fix a big dinner at home like I usually do."

"Jeremy's no trouble. It was better than having Thanksgiving for just two. Here," she said, handing him a plate covered with aluminum foil. "Tell you the truth, I don't like turkey all that much."

There was someone at the door now. Maxine went into her attack-dog mode again. Dean turned ashen again. "Seriously, cool it, Maxine," Mojave told the dog.

It was one of the weary musicians from the studio next door. "I was just wondering," he said, "if we could borrow a spoon."

"A spoon? What for?" Mojave's mother's eyes narrowed with suspicion. Ross could tell that she was thinking, *"Drugs!"*

"What for?" the musician asked innocently. "Why, to stir our coffee with."

"I thought you were going to blow it," Ross said to Dean, "when you started in with that Heil Hitler bit."

"I was in control," Dean said.

"And the way you kept staring and poking at her philodendrons. I was afraid you were going to start talking to them."

"What do you mean? What are philotendrons?" Jeremy wanted to know.

"Her potted plants," Dean said. To Ross he said, "You'd have been focused on her philodendrons, too, if you'd been seeing them the way I was seeing them." Dean had seen Mojave's mother's plants limned in a shimmering pink glow. Who wouldn't look at something like that?

"I tell you, Ross, I was in control. Or at least, I was able to act like I was in control, which is all that matters. You know, I had no idea Mojave's mother was black."

"I think she's only half black, but yeah, he must have inherited most of his traits from his dad. Except for the curly-hair gene."

"Where's Mojave's father? Are they divorced?"

"He got killed," Jeremy said.

"He was a nice guy," Ross said. "He played the banjo, and he started up that little studio down in the basement there."

"Did drugs have anything to do with the way he died?" Dean asked, "Is that why..."

"He got killed in a car wreck," Jeremy said. "He was a race car driver." Jeremy was still walking along with his head held back. He seemed to be scanning the sky for kamikaze dive-bombers.

"Jer," Ross said to him, "I think your nosebleed has stopped. Why don't you try putting your head down? Otherwise, you might walk into a parking meter."

"I hate nosebleeds. I don't want any more."

"Anyway, Mojave sure has a gorgeous mother," Dean said.

This comment popped Jeremy's head right down. "Careful, Dean," Ross said quietly.

"Why, have you got a crush on her, Jeremy?"

"No!" Jeremy said, with emphasis.

"Jeremy, you little lover boy!"

"Stop teasing him, Dean," Ross said.

As they were crossing Berkeley Street, a car took the corner at break-neck speed. It came within a few feet of clipping Dean. "Go back to New York, you fuckers!"

"That wasn't a New York license plate," Ross pointed out. "It was from Oregon."

"Oh well... go back to Oregon."

"That wasn't nearly as satisfying, was it?" Ross asked him.

"You're walking too slow," Jeremy said. "I want to get home."

"You go ahead. We'll catch up with you."

"I was thinking you guys might want to come over to my place for a while," Dean said. "I don't really feel like being alone."

"Thea's coming by later."

"Finally getting her over for dinner, huh?"

"Not for dinner, actually. She's having dinner somewhere else. But she's coming over to my place after that. At least, she said she probably would."

"Even better. Coffee, cognac, the Brandenburg Concertos on the stereo... you may be heading for some premarital sex tonight, Ross. Although I suppose it's not premarital if you don't plan on getting married."

Ross shrugged. It was as if Dean had access to every detail of his plan for the evening. "I just asked her to come by and hang out."

"Hanging out? That's what you kids today are calling it? But, it's later this evening that she'll be coming by, right? Why don't you and Jeremy come over now?"

"I have to clean up some at my place," Ross said.

"No, you don't. Just take the vacuum out of the closet and leave it in the middle of the floor. That way, it looks like your intentions to clean were good, but you were too busy taking care of really important stuff to actually do anything."

"I really do need to spruce things up. We've been so busy, the apartment's pretty much in tattered ruins. Hey, Dean, don't be so hard on Jeremy. Especially about Mojave's mother. He's pretty sensitive about that, and Mojave gives him a hard enough time. Jeremy doesn't mind people having a little fun at his expense, but he hates to be humiliated."

"I'm pretty much that way myself," Dean said. "I hope he's not really upset at me."

~

Maud Gonne barked happily when Dean came home. She'd never spent so much time alone as she had in the last month or so, and she didn't like it.

Dean gave her a treat, then another one. He got down on the carpet and wrestled with her. Maud loved that.

This was the first Thanksgiving Dean had not spent with Amy since... since they first got together. She was at her parents' house. That's what she'd told him, anyway. He wondered. When she'd left this morning, she seemed to be trailing clouds of insincerity.

He looked around for clues. He thought he may have found one. There was a notepad on the table by the phone. He rubbed the point of a pencil sideways on the notepad to see if there was the impression of an incriminating phone number written on a page in the pad and then torn out. A phone number magically appeared. He called the number. No one answered, but there was a recording. Someone named Carol told him that, if he was interested in driving a school bus, he should call back Monday.

In their bedroom, he went through her top drawer. All that was in there was her blameless, neatly folded underwear. And, oddly enough, used bows from old Christmas presents and a recipe for meatless lasagna. He checked the medicine cabinet in the bathroom to find out if her diaphragm was accounted for. The round hot-pink case was there. He snapped it open to make sure the diaphragm was in its case and not in Amy. It was, but then he remembered her gynecologist had fitted her out with an IUD, so that proved nothing.

It was getting dark. It got dark early in late November in Boston. He went to the spare room, which was full of mannequin parts and darkroom equipment and boxes of books that his mother had mailed from Virginia. Almost every book Dean had ever owned was in those boxes. There were his Landmark Books, books about Bomba the Jungle Boy and Tom Swift and Sergeant Preston of the Yukon, and his high school algebra and Spanish books. It took a while, but he finally found what he was looking for, the textbook for his nineteenth century British poetry course. And he found the poem he was looking for: *The City of Dreadful Night*. It was long, but he read it all the way through. It was fully dark by the time he'd finished. As poetry goes, it was appallingly bad, but its dreary tone matched his mood precisely. And the hashish may have made the imagery more vivid.

No way I can stay here tonight. I need to walk. I need to walk through the City of Dreadful Night. Just like that guy in the poem.

Maud needed to go out. He thought about taking her with him as he prowled the city. But somehow, he couldn't picture a "spectral wanderer of the unholy night" with an Irish setter on a leash. He took Maud around the block, gave her another treat and a pat on the butt, and went out into the darkness. He heard her whimper as he left.

~

Ross finished vacuuming. He did the dishes. He took cleanser to the toilet bowl, which had been looking scummy. He folded the end of the toilet paper into a V shape, the way they did in hotels. Then he decided that looked silly, so he unfolded it. He fed Swizzle and gave her a saucer of warm cat-beer, and he changed her kitty litter, though, technically, it was Jer's turn. He dusted everything within the range of his feather duster, including the collection of masks he and Laurel had brought back from Mexico. He'd forgotten how grotesque a few of those were, especially the mask of the witch-woman with a devil popping out her forehead. Both the woman and the demon were grinning lasciviously. Maybe he should take that one off the wall. And maybe the wolf with the antelope horns and the goat's beard. It had shiny black marbles for eyes, which gave it a bored but wicked look.

Next, he changed his sheets. That gave him pause. His sheets weren't really in need of changing; he'd changed them only a few days before. Suppose Thea didn't show, or suppose she did but had no interest in getting between them. Sleeping alone on those freshly changed sheets might be pretty depressing. He almost took the clean sheets off and put the old ones back on, but that seemed even more pathetic.

In the shower, he scrubbed his hands and forearms until they hurt, trying to get those specks of white paint off. Of course, Thea must be used to a man with paint on his hands. While he was showering, the water turned too hot twice and icy cold once. Not too bad, for Ross's shower.

He tried to think of something else meaningful to do. He could put new shelf paper in the kitchen cabinets. The red-on-white-polka-dot shelf paper had been there since they'd moved in. Except he didn't have any new shelf paper. Or he could clean the oven. Or change the bag in the vacuum cleaner. Sort his socks. Give the cat a bath. Update his address book.

None of those had much appeal. What else? He could fill the salt shaker and pepper mill. *That* didn't seem too onerous. He went to the kitchen cabinet and got down the Morton's. He read what it said on the round blue box: WHEN IT RAINS, IT POURS. He'd been reading that for most of his life, but it finally dawned on him why it said that on a salt box. He topped off the salt shaker. There weren't any peppercorns, though, to refill his pepper mill. To make matters worse, the pepper mill itself was absolutely, thoroughly empty.

Well, that blows it, he thought. *There went any chance I may have had with Thea*. He pictured her racing down the stairs, shrieking, "No peppercorns! No peppercorns!"

He sat down in the chair near the window and tried to think of what he usually did when he was home and had nothing in particular to do. Nothing occurred to him; not one single thing.

Ross had taken off his watch when he was painting and left it at the restaurant. The clock on his stove hadn't been reset at the end of Daylight Saving Time, and it was inaccurate anyway. He dialed NERVOUS—637-8687. He listened to a short plug for a bank, and then the time lady told him it was 7:58 p.m. Eastern Standard Time. While Thea hadn't arrived early, she still wasn't late. No grounds for optimism, but none, as yet, for despair. He also found out that that it was thirty-four degrees Fahrenheit—1.11 degrees Celsius. While it wasn't freezing out, it was close to it.

He adjusted the clock on the kitchen stove and was on his way to synchronize the clock radio in his bedroom. On his way, he looked into Jeremy's tiny bedroom. Jeremy was sitting at his desk, drawing a picture of a dinosaur. Ross had found the desk and the bench that fit behind it at an antique barn in New Hampshire. He'd bought it because it was the same kind of desk he'd sat in when he was in elementary school. There was a round hole in the upper-right-hand corner of the desk for an inkwell, although by the time Ross was in school, pens that used bottled ink had pretty much disappeared. There were rumors, though, that earlier generations of boys would dip girls' hair in the inkwells. There were stains around the hole in Jeremy's desk. He imagined black ink dripping from some poor girl's pigtail.

Pretty soon, that desk is going to be too small for Jer; his legs don't fit where they're supposed to even now.

"What are you up to, Jeremy?"

"Homework," Jeremy said.

"I thought they didn't give homework at Innisfree."

"Now they do. The parents voted."

"They didn't ask me what my vote was."

"You didn't go to the meeting. I gave you the note."

"Oh. Well, how come you're doing it now? You don't have school until Monday."

"I don't know. I don't have anything else to do. I wish you'd let us get a TV."

"Right about now, I wouldn't mind watching a little TV myself. By the way, we're going to get some company later. Thea's coming over."

"She is?"

"I think she is, anyway. Why don't you clean up your room a little?"

Jeremy swiveled around in his seat. "Why?"

"So she doesn't think you're a crummy little slob, that's why." Ross sat down on the edge of the bed and rubbed his son's bony shoulders.

"Why should she care?" Jeremy asked.

"You got me there. No more nosebleed?"

Jeremy shook his head.

"I love you, Jeremy."

"I know," Jeremy said, in his tolerant voice. "You want to see my dinosaur?"

"Oh, it's a Brontosaurus." The dinosaur was standing near the foot of a waterfall, its long neck and head protruding from the mist. It was smiling —a slight, enigmatic smile.

"That's what they used to call it. I guess they called it that when you were in school. But really, the right name for it is Apatosaurus." That's how he'd labeled his drawing: APATOSAURUS.

Ross looked at Jeremy's drawing again. To him, that would always be a Brontosaurus.

"How's Cuthbert doing?"

"Fine. All he does is go round and round." Cuthbert, a gerbil, was Jeremy's class pet. Students took turns taking him home for weekends. Jeremy had him for the long Thanksgiving weekend.

"We should oil that wheel," Ross said. "It's so squeaky, you won't get much sleep."

Back in the living room, Ross sat down by the window and pushed open the curtains. There was a gob of peanut butter on one of the curtains. Across the alley, at Thea's, the lights were still off. Would she stop by her apartment to feed her dog or change clothes before she came here? He decided to just stand there and keep watch. After about a minute, he gave it up as too boring. *Too boring even for me.*

As soon as he sat down on the couch, the cat jumped up on his lap. He could try to call Laurel back. It must have been horrifying, seeing her dog shot down in front of her. He tried to imagine seeing someone shoot Swizzle. He stroked her soft fur. The problem was, he'd have to call Matt and ask Matt to drive two miles up to School's Out to let Laurel know that he was trying to call her, and it was Thanksgiving night. And anyway, Laurel might be busy entertaining Blue Jay, whoever the hell this Blue Jay was.

For just a moment, Ross remembered the smell of pennyroyal on Laurel's sheets, and the uneven blush spreading over her body as she approached her orgasm. Then his mind shied away from that image.

He tried to think instead of what other people were doing. What were the people who lived in the building next door doing? What were the people who lived in the next block up to? What if he had a cutaway view of every apartment in Back Bay: Was anyone putting cheese in a mouse-trap? Playing a zither? Were there two people making fudge and arguing about surrealism? Was someone making out a check to a funeral parlor? Was a wife trying to hypnotize a husband, or vice versa? Was a wife trying to hypnotize a husband, or vice versa? Had someone just finished typing the last line of an epic poem?

Probably not. Probably everyone was watching TV. By this time of year, there would be holiday specials on.

He wondered briefly if Thea would blush like Laurel when she approached a climax. He wondered if it was easy for her to orgasm. Did she make much noise? He wondered if he'd ever get to find out. The odds seemed against it at the moment.

His landlady had once told him that this house had been built about a hundred years ago for a wealthy Boston merchant named Ezra Cloud, who had vanished at sea. Did the Widow Cloud ever stand in this room, hoping for someone to come and keep her company? Doubtfully. These little rooms on the fourth floor had likely belonged to servants. Or maybe a crazy aunt was kept hidden away up here on the top floor. The widow would have done her pining in the first-floor parlor, where there was a big bay window looking out on Commonwealth Avenue, perfect for pining. Nowadays, that apartment was the most expensive one in Ross's building. Two women named Jade and Prudence and an old English sheepdog named October lived there now.

Thea had said, if she was going to be late or couldn't make it, she'd call. Ross put the phone in his lap. He imagined it ringing, and picking it up, and Thea saying, "Hello, Ross, I was held up for a little while, but I'll be right over. Why don't you turn down the sheets?" But stubbornly, the phone wouldn't ring. It just plain wouldn't ring. Because he wanted it to, it wouldn't. That was the problem. He stood up and turned his back on the phone, put his hands in his pockets, and walked away whistling.

"What are you doing," asked Jeremy. He was standing in the living room doorway, staring at Ross.

"Whistling. Just whistling."

"Why?"

"To keep in practice. I don't get that many chances to whistle. Isn't it about time for you to get ready for bed?"

"I can sleep in tomorrow," Jeremy said.

It was forty-seven minutes past nine now, according to the clock on his stove.

Ross remembered Thea telling him that she hated to say she'd be somewhere at a certain time. "I'm not good with promises," she'd said to him.

He got himself a beer out of the refrigerator. He realized that he didn't feel like drinking beer, but it was too late, he'd already popped it open. He sucked the foam off the top of the can. As he did so, the phone rang. Because he'd left the phone on his easy chair, the ring sounded sickly, but still, it was ringing. It was actually ringing.

"I'll get it," Jeremy said.

It was probably Mojave anyway. He called quite regularly. He probably wanted to gloat some more about smashing the invasion of France.

It wasn't Mojave, though. The call was for Ross. "Am I disturbing anything?" Dean asked.

"What do you mean, disturbing?"

"I thought you might be up to your ears in Dutch twat by now."

Ross took a deep breath. "No, she's a no-show. So far, anyway. But if that's what you thought, why... ?"

"Because Amy's still not home. I thought maybe she'd stopped by there or called or something."

"No. Why would she do that?"

"I don't know. No reason. Well, I'm going to call her parents, I guess. She said she was having dinner there."

"Maybe you should."

"You wouldn't want to call them for me, would you, and ask for her? If Dorky Dan answers and he recognizes my voice, he'll hang up on me."

"Disguise your voice."

"I'm not very good at that. People hear that little twinge of Virginia in my voice and they know it's me right away. Hey, since we're both womanless, why don't you come out with me for a while? We can have a drink or three. There are a few places open, even though it's a holiday."

Going out with Dean had a certain appeal. To hell with waiting. But Valerie, Ross's neighbor, who looked in on Jeremy when Ross was away, was in New Jersey for Thanksgiving weekend. Besides, Thea might show up any minute now. She wasn't *that* late. "I guess not."

"I'll just have to keep wandering the streets by myself then," Dean said.

"This is what Saint John of the Cross called 'the long dark night of the soul.'"

"Why don't you just go home?"

"No, I can't stand the idea of being there alone. I don't feel like doing anything, but I don't want to do nothing either."

"I know the feeling," Ross said. "So where are you calling from?"

"I'm at a bar on Mass Ave at the moment. They have really cheap beer. Too bad I don't like beer that much. I've been wandering from bar to bar and calling home every half hour or so to see if she's back yet. You know, there are some really sad-looking people out drinking on Thanksgiving night. Including me, I guess."

"You could go by the restaurant and hang out with Buzz. Do a little more painting."

"I've had enough of the restaurant for today," Dean said. "You know, that Nepalese hash was incredibly potent. I wonder if those guys doctored it with opium or something. I'm still feeling high. I'm starting to wonder if I'll ever come down."

"Well, Charlie warned me. But of course you'll come down. Eventually."

"I don't know. Once Jean-Paul Sartre took peyote, and he had hallucinations for years after that. He thought giant crabs were following him everywhere he went."

"Are you seeing giant crabs?"

"No... but I'm still seeing that pink aura around some things. There's one around my beer."

"As long as there aren't any big pink crabs following you around, I think you'll be fine. See you tomorrow."

Ross lay down on the couch after hanging up, staring at the ceiling. His landlady had painted it last year. She'd used that textured paint that looked like cottage cheese. He picked up a *Rolling Stone* he'd had since September. He forced himself to read about Elvis's demise. At the point in the article where the author said, "Heart attack, my ass," Ross dropped the magazine on the floor next to the sofa. He went back to staring at the ceiling.

The cat jumped up on his chest. He covered his face with a pillow.

Ross sat up suddenly; the cat tumbled to the floor. He'd heard something. It sounded like apples falling from a tree, one apple every second or so. *Footsteps?* But Thea couldn't be on the stairs. He'd have to buzz her in the front door first. He put the pillow over his face again and heard more apples. *Just blood pounding in my ears*, he decided. *Just my heart beating.*

Swizzle jumped up on the windowsill as if she were going to keep her eye out for Thea. *Let me know if you see anything.*

Once Amy had told him about alternative-nostril breathing exercises that she used to help her relax. That's what he needed to do: relax. Only he couldn't remember much of what she'd told him. He tried taking a deep breath out of his right nostril but couldn't figure out how not to breathe through his left nostril at the same time. Then he figured it out. *Oh yeah, use your finger.* After a few attempts, he started to feel a little dizzy. He thought of Robin I taking deep breaths during her interview. That didn't make her any less nervous.

Ross went to the window again and started petting the cat. Thea's apartment was still dark; it looked abandoned. He wished he'd gone to meet Dean.

Amy was struggling to untie Chewy's complicated knots. The trunk wouldn't close with the sacristy lamp in it, and they'd had to tie it in. The Pinto had the smallest trunk Amy had ever seen.

She sensed someone moving behind her, coming toward her. She pretended to go on with what she was doing, but she took the Screamer out of her purse and slipped it into her coat pocket. The Screamer would emit a tremendous, piercing shriek when its top was twisted. Once it had gone off by accident when she was taking the written test for her Class II license. She slipped the can of Mugger Mist out of her purse, flipped off the safety lock, and palmed it.

Someone said, "Here, let me..."

"Stop right where you are!" The light from the streetlamp glinted off the red-and-silver can of Mugger Mist. Her finger twitched on the button, ready to spray.

Dean was so surprised, he was thrown into sudden retreat. He tripped over the curb and sat down hard.

"Dean," she said, the nozzle of the can still aimed at his face, "why were you sneaking up on me? Where did you come from?"

"I was just over there by the bushes."

"Why were you lurking in the bushes?"

"*By* the bushes, not *in* the bushes. And I wasn't lurking. I was waiting for you to come home."

"Why weren't you waiting inside? I hate to feel like I'm being checked up on."

Dean, who always looked intense, contrived to make himself look more so. "Because I didn't feel like waiting inside. I felt like walking. I've been walking the streets all night. And thinking."

"Thinking? Good. You need to do some thinking. What were you thinking about?"

"I've been thinking about a certain line of poetry. I've been saying it to myself over and over." Dean spoke the line in such a somber tone that he was moved by it himself. "'The city is of Night. Perchance of Death, but certainly of Night.' Pretty fat line, isn't it."

"I don't get it."

"I think that line perfectly encapsulates all the despair of those lonely men, those infinitely lonely men—'the spectral wanderers of unholy Night'—who walk the dark streets of the city. You know, the poet who wrote that line, he was British. And a lot of British poets are afflicted with what's called the English disease. He .."

"What's this English disease?" Amy asked suspiciously. "Something to do with spanking?"

"No, nothing to do with spanking. The English disease is melancholia." He quoted another line from *The City of Dreadful Night*. "'My wine of life is poison mixed with gall.'"

"Christ on a crutch, you haven't been thinking, you've been brooding. Poison and gall, Jesus."

"I couldn't help brooding. I was worried about you."

Amy rolled her eyes.

"This is something new with you, isn't it, this eye-rolling bit every time I say something."

"I've always been an eye roller, even when I was a kid. You just started noticing it."

"Well, you've been doing it a lot lately. You know what Ross tells Jeremy when he rolls his eyes? He tells him he's going to sprain his eyes and that they're going to get stuck up inside his head. 'This could be you.'"

A light rain began to fall. Amy disarmed the Mugger Mist and slipped it into her coat pocket along with the Screamer. Dean got off the curb and brushed off his pants. He looked into the trunk of the Pinto. "What have you been doing, looting churches?"

She didn't like the sound of that. "I got it at a yard sale."

"Who was having the yard sale, the Archbishop of Boston?"

"You're starting in again. You know, Dean, you used to be funny. I thought you were one of the funniest people I'd ever met. I thought you were a real Chevy Chase. That was one of the reasons I was attracted to you. But you're not that funny anymore. You're just plain old sarcastic."

Dean helped her lift the lamp out of the trunk. "It's half mine and half Chewy's. I get it this month."

"You've been at Chewy's all day?"

"No, I... I was at my parent's house. I told you this morning that was where I was going to be. At my parents' house."

Dean blinked at her. "Well, you're here now. Let's go upstairs. We can have a little Thanksgiving party."

"What you mean is, we can screw. Isn't that what you mean?"

"Why is it that when you want to do it, which is never all that often, it's making love, but when I want to do it, it's screwing?"

Although he didn't remember falling asleep, Ross was sleeping on the couch when Thea buzzed. He let her in. "I was pretty sure you weren't coming," he said to her. He wondered if he sounded peevish. He hoped not. Peevish was not sexy.

Thea was panting from running up four flights of stairs to get to Ross's apartment. "I'm sorry," she said between pants. "I know I'm a little late."

Ross looked at the clock on his stove. *Almost three hours late.* "You said you'd give me a call if you were going to be late." *Definitely peevish. Cut it out.*

"I know. I wanted to, but I couldn't."

She was wearing the same battered coat that she'd been wearing when she'd come into the laundromat. It was dripping rainwater. He remembered a line from some old movie: "Let's get you out of that wet coat and into a dry martini." Only Ross didn't have any gin. Or vermouth, or olives. And he didn't think Thea would like martinis anyway.

"I was in someone else's car, and Wim... well, I just couldn't call. And, this is terrible, but I couldn't remember your last name, and I didn't have your number with me, so..."

"It's Jarboe," Jeremy said. Jeremy had been sleeping too. His sleepiness was still clinging to him like toast crumbs. He was wearing Star Wars pajamas, and his hair was sticking out in every direction.

Ross looked at Jeremy. In this light, his skin and his hair seemed a shade, just a shade darker than his, and a couple shades darker than Laurel's.

"Hello, Jeremy... Jer," Thea said. "You're up late."

"I'm hungry," he said.

"Have some turkey," Ross told him.

"I already had turkey today. I want Rice Krispies."

Ross got him Rice Krispies.

"I had a nosebleed at dinner," Jeremy announced. He obviously wanted to be the center of attention of this late-night gathering.

"You did?" Thea said. "Let me look."

"Epitaxi," Ross said. "That's what Dean called it."

"Epistaxis, I believe it is," Thea said.

"It's all right now," Jeremy said. "It stopped." But he let her look into his mouth and nose.

"I used to get nosebleeds too," Thea said,

"Guess we're all nosebleeders here, then," Ross said.

"Well, I can't tell much in this light. The next time it happens, pinch the top of your nose and use an ice pack."

"Mojave's mother told me to put my pinky in a bowl of ice water."

"Your... pinky?"

"His little finger," Ross said.

"Oh. I can't imagine how that would help."

"Do you know how to get splinters out of fingers? Without it hurting?"

"Do you have a splinter in your finger?"

"Not now. I did, but my dad got it out."

"Then you didn't need me."

"It hurt, though, when he did it." Jeremy turned his attention back to his cereal. From all the noise, it sounded to Ross like Jeremy had finished off the Rice Krispies and had started munching on the bowl. Both Jeremy and his mother were noisy chewers.

"Are you hungry too?" Ross asked Thea.

"A little."

"I could make you a turkey sandwich."

"Mr. Q had pheasant at his party, and I had some of that. I wasn't very hungry, but I tried it. It's a little like turkey, I guess. It was too rich for me."

So, Ross thought, *Mr. Q threw this dinner party. And Wim was among the guests. And pheasant was served. Quite the wingding.*

"Would you like some Rice Krispies then?"

"Yes," she said, "I think I would."

While Ross was getting her a bowl, a roach came out from behind the refrigerator and crawled across the kitchen wall behind Thea's head. He tried to ignore it.

Not Jeremy. When he caught sight of the roach, he hopped up and smashed it flat with the *Rolling Stone*. Some of the roach's remains were smeared across the photo of Elvis on the cover. Jeremy made a diagonal slash across four vertical hash marks on a chart that was held by ladybug magnets on the refrigerator door.

CONFIRMED KILLS, NOVEMBER, it said at the top of the tally chart. "That's a hundred and five so far this month," Jeremy said. "That means you owe me ten-fifty."

"I give him a dime per dead roach," Ross explained. "Don't just leave it hanging on the wall," he told Jeremy.

After the burial detail, Ross ushered Jeremy back to his bedroom. Thea was examining his wandering Jew when he came back into the living room. "Poor thing. It needs more light."

"It needs more water too," Ross said. "I always forget, and so does Jeremy, when it's his turn." *That's something I could have done—watered the plants. Now she thinks I'm a thoughtless plant owner.*

"It's pretty sick," she said, nodding. She hung the plant back up. "But then, everything's sick."

"You're not in a very good mood, are you?" She didn't answer him, but her eyes were wet, as if she had been crying, or was planning to start crying soon. He said, "I haven't been in a good mood myself, until you showed up. I hate holidays."

"I've decided," she said, "to take that job. If you still want me."

"Of course I do," Ross said, trying not to sound surprised. He'd told Dean a couple of days ago that he didn't think Thea would be working at the restaurant. He hoped Dean hadn't hired someone else. He knew that Sarah Jefferson had called Dean once or twice and asked him to reconsider her application. "What made you decide?"

"I just decided, that's all. It takes me a long time to make decisions."

"Same for me," Ross said, although he made decisions fairly quickly and then spent a lot of time questioning them. Ross realized that for the last few minutes, he'd been holding her hand. Her hand was full of crumpled dead leaves from his wandering Jew.

"Some of the masks on your walls are pretty frightening," she said. "But some of them are pretty funny. Especially that one with the devil coming out of her head."

"They're from Mexico. From Michoacán," Ross said, as if that explained everything worth knowing about the masks.

"It's nice for you," Thea said, "that you have a fireplace. I don't."

"Yes, it is nice," he said dreamily. Then he realized that she might expect him to build a cheerful fire. "I can't use it, though. The chimney catches fire."

"That's too bad."

"My neighbor Valerie has a working fireplace. She's gone for the weekend, but I have her spare key. We could go over there and build a fire and have coffee."

Thea nodded. "That would be nice," Thea said, her hand tightening on his.

"I'll get the coffee started," he said.

Instead of doing that, he kissed her cheek. Then he slipped his tongue into her ear. She seemed to like that. The inside of her ear tasted like green apples.

Amy felt better after a shower, much better. And she felt more benevolent toward Dean. She was even feeling a bit horny. She dabbed on White Shoulders perfume and put on the lacy red camisole and panties set that Dean had given her last Valentine's Day. She'd never worn it before. It still had the price tag on it. *Damn, he spent a lot of money on lingerie. I bet a pretty lingerie saleswoman talked him into it.* She went into their bedroom and bounded into bed with him.

Dean had been lying in their bed watching TV. "Wait," he yelped. Amy was kissing his neck and blowing in his ear. Dean was watching *Dawn Patrol*. It was one of his top five favorite movies.

"Wait? You want me to wait? I don't understand," Amy said. "I just don't. You're the one who wanted to have a little party, and now you want to watch some stupid World War II movie?" She reached down and turned off the TV at the foot of their bed and resumed kissing his neck.

"World War I," Dean said.

"World War I, World War II, World War III, what difference does it make?"

"See, it's about pilots in the First World War. Errol Flynn just ordered David Niven's kid brother to go out on patrol, and David Niven is pissed because his brother is just a rank recruit. They both know the Hun's going to blast him out of the sky. But Errol Flynn—he's the squadron commander —he thinks it wouldn't be fair to the other pilots if David Niven's little brother didn't fly, and you know how the Brits are about fair play, so... you interested yet?" Dean turned the TV back on with his big toe. There was a commercial on now.

"Some of you have said to me, 'Tommy, we just can't afford conventional housing, what with the way things are today. On the other hand, we're not sure we want to invest all our savings in a trailer.' Well, here's what I always tell people. 'If you're thinking of what trailers used to be like back in the forties and fifties, sure, I don't blame you. Those trailers were cramped and ugly and the trailer parks they were in, they were like Tobacco Road. Now, at New Morning Modular Housing, we don't sell trailers. No, we sell quality modular and mobile...'"

"Come on, Dean," Amy said, "turn it off. I've got to get up at five tomorrow."

Dean sang, "'Call me early, mother dear, for I'm to be Queen of the May.'"

"What?"

"It's a line from the movie. But originally from a poem by Tennyson. And why do you have to get up early? You don't start work until Monday."

"I'll never be able to get up at five on Monday if I don't practice."

"Why don't you get up at four, then, or three thirty? Like Roman soldiers—they'd drill all winter with really heavy swords so that when they actually went into combat, with regulation swords, it'd feel like they were wielding feathers."

"And some of you have come up to me and said, 'Tommy, if these new modular units are all they're cracked up to be, why don't you show us what they look like on the inside? So that's what we're...'"

"This," Dean said, "is a really homespun commercial. Watch how they're jiggling the camera around."

"... a look at that kitchen. Look how that design maximizes your work space. And look at these closets. Big, huh? And that wood-grain laminate paneling, how about that? Wouldn't this be a great place to hang your hat?"

"Wouldn't that be a great place to hang your*self*? I think we better get Tommy here on the List."

Amy got out of bed and went into the living room.

"All right, all right, I'm turning off the TV. There, it's off. You can come back to bed now." Amy didn't answer. He lay there a while longer, waiting for Judy Collins to come on in the living room. Generally, when Amy was upset, she'd dig out her old, scratchy Judy Collins albums. Sometimes Joni Mitchell, now and then Leonard Cohen or Jackson Browne, but usually Judy Collins. "Ame?" She still didn't answer. Maybe she was listening to Judy Collins with headphones on.

Dean turned the TV on with his toe again. There was the raucous buzz of biplanes. They sounded like lawnmowers. By this time, David Niven's brother was already dead. It had happened fast.

A few minutes later, she came back into the bedroom. The movie was practically over. Now Errol Flynn was doomed. His biplane had been riddled by machine-gun fire and was spiraling out of the sky, trailing a corkscrew of smoke. "'Oh, what a rotten war,'" Dean said. Another line from the movie. "What are you doing, Amy?"

What she was doing was getting out of her camisole and getting dressed: panties, jeans, socks, T-shirt. "Don't worry, I won't be disturbing you for long. You can watch all the television you want when I'm gone."

"You're going somewhere?" Amy had threatened to leave in the middle of the night several times before in the last few months. Once she'd gotten as far as putting her boots on. "Where are you going?"

"Home."

"Home? Really? Or are you lying about that again?"

She looked at him warily. "What do you mean, lying?"

"I tried to call you there this afternoon. I disguised my voice and asked for you. Your mother told me that you'd come by earlier and gotten the car and then went to have Thanksgiving dinner with Ross and Jeremy."

"You disguised your voice? She didn't know it was you?"

"She knew right away." Dean could see now that telling her about the phone call had been a tactical mistake. She was visibly turning from upset to furious.

"Thanks, Dean! Now you've gone and really fucked things up for me."

"You sure as hell weren't with Ross, because I was. And you weren't at Chewy's. I tried calling his apartment half a dozen times."

"I guess you think you're quite the little detective, don't you?"

"I'd just like to know where the hell you were all day."

"Chewy and I were at his father's house, if it's any of your fucking business, which it isn't."

"So why did you lie about that to your parents? Are you ashamed of Gus?"

"No, but... Daddy doesn't like Chewy. Not as much as he doesn't like you, but..."

"And why did you lie about it to me?"

She didn't answer that one. She grabbed her sweater off the dresser. Dean reached over to the nightstand where he kept his contraband cigarettes.

"Dean!" she said, her head popping out of her sweater. "Smoking!"

"I might as well tell you. I've been smoking all along, when you weren't around. I couldn't help it."

"I should have known. I guess I did know. I kept smelling the cigarette stink on you, but I didn't want to believe it." She sat down on the foot of the bed and pulled on her boots. "You made a commitment to quit and you broke it. You can't be honest with anyone, can you, even yourself?"

"You're calling *me* dishonest? You're the one who lied to people from one end of this town to another today."

She zipped up her boots. "Goodbye, Dean."

He put his hand on her shoulder, but she shot up from the bed and headed for the living room. Dean didn't like the way her boots sounded on the wood floor. "Aiii-meeee!" he called. He heard her get her coat from the closet. Whatever else happened tonight, a new record for closeness-to-leaving had been set. He heard the jingle of glass against metal as she struggled to pick up the sacristy lamp, and he heard the front door open.

Maud was awake now. She thought she was going for a midnight walk and was in a joyful frenzy. Her copper-colored tail was wagging furiously. "Aiii-meeee, goddamn it!"

He heard their front door slam. There was something dreadfully final about that slam. She wouldn't be back tonight. Or ever again, maybe.

Flight Sub Lieutenant Dean Burgess arrived at the aerodrome of the 59th Squadron only the day before his first flight. He'd come from the base depot in La Havre in an open Mitchel touring car along with four other replacement pilots. They'd talked their driver into stopping twice for wine at estaminets along the route. They'd all been singing "Pack up your troubles in your old kit bag and smile, smile, smile" at the top of their lungs as they arrived. Everyone, that is, but Flight Sub Lieutenant Burgess had been singing. When the Mitchel stopped outside the old farmhouse that served as headquarters for the 59th, the squadron's adjutant, Phipps, and his batman met them and ushered them inside.

The replacement pilots lined up at attention until Squadron Commander Scott told them to stand easy. "We're not much on formality around here," the captain said. "I want to welcome you to the slaughterhouse. Pleased to make your acquaintance, I'm the butcher. Tomorrow, A Flight has a new something nasty to attend to." They would be flying in support of yet another Big Push. As the Tommies went over the top, A Flight was to buzz the German trenches and then strafe all available targets behind the enemy's lines. They'd be carrying four Cooper bombs — the big ones, the thirty pounders — and they were to look for petrol stores and ammunition dumps. There would be heavy archie fire and it was all but certain they'd be intercepted by German fighters flown by seasoned pilots.

Captain Scott asked them all how many hours of flight training they had logged at Brooklands Training Station. One of the pilots, Sub Lieutenant Tibbets, had twenty-three hours in the air, and another one had nineteen. Sub Lieutenant Burgess had seventeen. The other two pilots had only thirteen apiece. "The three pilots with the most training will be in A Flight tomorrow." The other two pilots who would be flying were jubilant. The two who would be staying behind were despondent. So was Flight Sub Lieutenant Burgess. Adjutant Phipps added three names to the roster for A Flight on a blackboard.

The captain looked at them pityingly. Lieutenant Burgess had heard that the CO's younger brother had been assigned to the 59th and had not returned from his first mission. "Dismissed. Try to relax. Have a drink," the captain told them.

They crowded around the bar—actually a wooden door set on top of two barrels—and had a whiskey. Sub Lieutenant Burgess had another. And another. They heard the roar of B Flight returning, one plane at a time. Everyone in the bar counted out loud. Six planes landed. Seven had taken off. "Only one this time," someone said, sounding relieved.

The B-Flight pilots joined them at the makeshift bar. Their faces were grimy except where their goggles had been. The missing pilot, Lieutenant Jarboe, had pancaked down on top of a house in a French village behind German lines. They didn't know if he was a prisoner or another casualty, but either way, he wasn't coming back. The adjutant Phipps erased his name from the blackboard. Sub Lieutenant Burgess had another drink.

The veteran pilots began to sing, and after a few verses, the rookie pilots joined in on the chorus:

"So stand by your glasses steady
This world is a world of lies.
Here's a toast to the dead already
Hurrah for the next man to die!"

The next thing Sub Lieutenant Burgess knew, he was being awakened by Adjutant Phipps' batman. It was just getting light. Call me early, mother dear, for I am to be Queen of the May. *By the time he staggered downstairs, the other pilots were already on their way out to their machines. The adjutant said, "Have a nip o' tea and a couple headache powders on toast, then off you go." The adjutant's batman helped him into his flying jacket and handed him his leather helmet.*

Squadron Commander Scott was standing outside the farmhouse door. He was wearing his uniform trousers and a polka-dot pajama top. "You look terrible," the captain told him. "At Brooklands, they taught you the half loop and roll out, didn't they?"

The sub lieutenant nodded, although he couldn't, at this moment, remember anything they had taught him at Brooklands.

"Just keep watching your flight leader. And don't let Jerry get behind you." The captain shook his hand. "Goodbye, then."

Sub Lieutenant Burgess walked out to his Nieuport 28 and climbed into the bay. He had trained on a Sopwith Pup and wasn't familiar with the controls on this plane. The chief mechanic, Flight Sergeant Lizaro, asked him, "Has the officer got any maps or papers that might give information to the enemy?" Sub Lieutenant Burgess wanted to say, if it would get him out of this mission, that yes, he had a packet full of detailed battle plans for the upcoming British advance stuffed in his pants. "No? Best o' luck to you, then, sir."

He was third in line to take off. The first plane was airborne, barely clearing the trees. The second was bumping along the grassy runway. He set the fuel mixture to 100 percent to prime the carburetor, and then set the throttle to 10 percent.

Sergeant Lizaro took hold of the propeller. "Switch up, sir," he said.

"Switch up," the lieutenant said, activating the magnetos.

"Contact."

"Contact." Sergeant Lizaro turned the prop to the left. The engine fired. He pulled the chocks and the plane rolled forward. In the sky beyond those trees, a terrible menace was waiting for Lieutenant Burgess. The lyrics of the song he had heard last night kept running through his head.

"Here's a toast to the dead already
Hurrah for the next man to die."

Dean caught up with Amy in the hallway outside their apartment before the elevator came. "What a mess you are," she said. Dean was in his underwear. His hand with the burning cigarette twitched, dropping ashes on his bare foot. "Get back inside before someone sees you. Take Maud with you."

"I can't believe this is happening. I can't believe this is *you* doing this, Amy."

"You made your choice. Why don't you go see what else is on TV? You might be missing something good." She got on the elevator, and the elevator creaked and clattered as it took her away.

By the time Dean had gotten his clothes on and raced downstairs—Amy had left the elevator door open on the first floor—she'd put the lamp in the seat next to her and was driving off.

He stood in the space she'd pulled out of, wringing his hands. A half block away, her car stopped. He saw her backup lights come on and the Pinto came down Beacon Street in reverse. He put his hands in his pockets. Wringing them was too dreadfully dramatic, even at a time like this. Even for him.

"Here," she said, and tossed him a baggie. There were dark, wet, awful things in there. "Those are turkey giblets. Cook them up and give them to Maud. They'll be good for her."

"Amy," Dean said "wait a minute." He had a last-ditch, back-to-the-sea ploy he'd been saving. He didn't hold out much hope that it would work, but it was worth a try. "Mommy me."

"Mommy yourself," she said, and drove off with as much speed as the Pinto could muster. Dean closed his eyes and saw a biplane spiraling out of the sky.

∾

Ross was lighting Valerie's last two paper logs with one of her foot-long fireplace matches. He reminded himself to replace the logs before she got back from New Jersey, knowing that he would undoubtably forget, and that Valerie would be upset with him. He accepted that.

He brought a pot of coffee over to Valerie's, and half & half and sugar. He brought two snifters of Rémy Martin. He found Valerie's Brandenburg Concertos, because he didn't have any Bach himself, and he put the record on her turntable. He poked the fire. Then Thea went to the bathroom. Then he did. *Sometimes*, he thought, *it's such an effort, getting cozy.*

He'd set his snifter too close to the fire. When he went to take a sip of cognac, the rim of his glass burned the bridge of his nose and he spilled most of it. He had to turn on the overhead light so that he and Thea could try to clean the cognac out of Valerie's furry white hearth rug. *Nothing wrecks a mood like an overhead light.*

"I guess I'll go over and get some more cognac."

"Just relax. We can share mine. Does your nose hurt very much? There's a red mark."

"It's not too bad," Ross said, though it hurt quite a bit.

The cat had come over to Valerie's, too. She was sitting on the rug between them looking very nonchalant, as if waiting for a bus or something. "Is this where I catch the Dudley bus?" Ross could imagine the cat asking.

"He's a beautiful cat," Thea said, and began stroking her. "What's his name?"

"*Her* name, actually. I had a hard time coming up with a good name for her. The landlady doesn't allow pets, unless you pay extra, so I hide her whenever she comes over. For a while I was calling her Anne Frank." It occurred to Ross that Dutch people might not find references to Anne Frank amusing. "But then, one night, I was tending bar, and all of sudden, a name came to me. I decided to call her Swizzle."

"Swizzle?"

"Those little stirrers that you put in cocktails are called swizzle sticks. We got a bunch of them up in Vermont that day."

"Oh. Swizzle. I like the sound of that word."

Swizzle took the story of her naming as a cue to meow. It was such a perfectly pronounced, well-enunciated meow that she seemed to be parodying herself and cats in general. Ross joined in the petting. That made it possible for his fingertips to brush against Thea's in Swizzle's long white silky fur.

Ross said, "That's what Jeremy calls fourth gear."

"Fourth gear?"

"When the cat purrs like that, Jeremy says she's in fourth gear."

"*Purr.* I've been trying to think of that word. In Dutch, we say *snorren.*"

"*Snorren.* Like snore?"

"Yes. *Snorren* means purr and snore. It also means whiskers."

"How appropriate." Ross couldn't think of much else to say. He rubbed his nose where it had been burned. It hurt with a narrow, insidious pain. It had been a tough day for noses in the Jarboe family. Thea hit the cat's lick spot at the base of Swizzle's tail and she started licking, first her paws and then the empty air.

As soon as I take a last sip of that cognac, I'm going to kiss her, he thought. The interlude between social exchange and the onset of intimacy was an awkward time. On the recording, the ensemble paused and the harpsichordist launched into a passionate solo.

The cognac was gone, and abruptly, they were kissing. He wasn't sure if he had initiated it or if she had, but it didn't much matter. They kissed fiercely for a long time. At one point, Ross's leg flailed out and kicked the stereo stand, sending the needle skidding across the Fifth Concerto.

The cat downshifted and went off on some obscure cat mission.

With a little help from Thea, Ross had taken off her blouse and was working on her bra. Her bra looked as though it had been laundered too often. It was—to use one of his mother's favorite phrases—tattletale gray, and it had three snaps in back. A real prison-issue bra. He wondered if Thea bought her lingerie at the same place she got her raincoat.

Once he'd managed her bra, he started kissing her breasts. He undid her belt. To go much further, he'd need cooperation. Then she said, "Wait, Ross."

He tried to think what she'd say next:

- "I like it better with women."
- "I think I might have the clap."
- "I'm afraid you might have the clap."
- "I think it's a sin."
- "No matter what Wim does, I'm going to be true to him. That's just how I am."
- "I like you, but I don't like you *that* way."
- "I hate sex."
- "I want to do some yoga first."

Ross asked her gently what was wrong. He hoped he sounded gentle, anyway.

"I don't know," she whispered. He sat up. She stayed on her back. Her skin looked orange in the fading light of the paper logs. Her breasts were slick and shiny from having been kissed.

"What do you *think* might be wrong?"

"I don't know," she said again. "Maybe it's... I was in that basement at Mr. Q's today. Something drew me... dragged me... down to that basement. That horrible basement. You remember, I told you about..."

Ross said he remembered her telling him about that basement.

"I'm worried, I guess, that something happened to me that day. I don't think I've felt very good about myself since then."

Ross reassuringly touched her cheek and stroked her hair. *If I were to say, "It's okay, we can wait," would she think I was being sensitive? Or what if I said, "Come on, forget about that, let's get those pants off?" Would she think I was being decisive? Or a barbarian?*

He compromised by not saying anything.

"You know," she said, after lying there awhile, "that night, when you were at my party, I told you about Mr. Q and all that just to see how you would react. If you weren't too shocked, then I was going to make love to you."

"I wasn't shocked or anything. I was just... not feeling very well. From drinking too much, I mean."

"You don't have to explain," she told him. "It's probably a good thing that nothing happened. The reason I wanted to make love then was to see if I still liked it. To see if I was still normal. That's not a very good reason." She threw an arm around him. "I think I'd like to make love to you now, though, Ross."

"To see if you're normal?"

"No. Because I like you. A lot."

That was good enough for Ross. He reached for her jeans. She lifted her hips to let him take them off. That lovely little gesture was, to Ross, a green flag on race day. But then she said, "Wait."

He wanted to say, "Now what?" but he bit his tongue.

She laughed and touched his face. "Do you know that you've got white paint in your beard? There's even some in your chest hair."

"I thought I'd gotten it all out when I showered. Is that why you said, 'Wait?'"

"No, I just thought we should go back to your apartment. This floor isn't very comfortable, and I'm starting to get cold." She did have goose bumps, and the fire was almost out. He tried to remember the Dutch word for goose bumps, but he couldn't. Kipper something. "Do I need to put my clothes back on to go across the hall?"

Ross was afraid that, once she'd gotten her clothes back on, she might never take them off again. "Let's just make a dash for it."

∾

"TOO BAD. TOO BAD. OH! TOO, TOO BAD.
NOW WE SHALL HAVE TOO RETURN TO VIRGINIA."
(ROBERT E. LEE, AFTER THE BATTLE
OF GETTYSBURG)

Dean tore the sheet out of the Selectric and compared it to the original quote in Bartlett's. It was perfect, except for the typo. Even that was okay; it would confirm that he was distraught.

He folded the piece of typing paper so that he could stand it on their bedside table, then he turned off every light in the apartment except for a tensor lamp he used to read by in bed. It locked like a little lit-up billboard on the nightstand. He hoped that Amy would come back when it was dark, so she could get the full effect. It would be nice if he had a single, blood-red rose to put next to his note, but blood-red roses would be hard to come by at this hour on Thanksgiving night.

The tensor lamp didn't provide much light; it was too dark for efficient packing, but he didn't feel like turning the overhead lights on. He'd only packed a pint of Cutty Sark and a few pairs of jockeys when the entire unpleasant reality of a return to Virginia hit him. If he were to leave tonight, he'd have to hitchhike, but it was too late to hitchhike. About five years too late. He couldn't call a travel agency. He couldn't jump into a taxi and say, "Charlottesville, and step on it." Any chance he could get a flight out to Richmond first thing tomorrow? Doubtful. A Greyhound? A depressing way to travel.

He would have to sleep on a foldaway couch in his mother's living room when he got there. His mother lived in an apartment complex and right across the highway was a trailer park, and the people from the trailer park were always coming over and using the swimming pool, and the people in the apartment complex objected, and sometimes there were fist-fights. It would not be a cordial place for a man with a broken heart to recover.

What about the restaurant? What about Maud?

And, if he actually went back to Virginia, there'd be no Virginia left to go to. There would be no place to retreat to, no final refuge. *Appomattox, baby*. Dean gave up on packing. He put his note in the nightstand drawer. He turned off the tensor light.

He got the Cutty out of the suitcase, filled up a hip flask, and hit the streets again. *"The city is of Night. Perchance of Death, but certainly of Night / For never there can come the lucid morning's fragrant breath…"* His feet no longer felt like they were skimming over the sidewalk, but the pavement beneath his feet now felt like it was made of gelatin. He half expected to see giant crabs following him.

While Thea was in the bathroom, Ross gathered all the candles in the apartment and took them into his bedroom. Candlelight was his compromise between total darkness and light from the reading lamp on his nightstand. While Ross had no particular reason to believe that Thea preferred making love in total darkness, it was his experience that some women did, and he didn't want to take that chance.

Laurel always used to drape their bedside lamp with a red silk scarf.

That would bathe the room in a soft, rosy, exotic glow while they made love. Ross didn't own any appropriate scarves, however.

Thea called from the bathroom: "Could you get me something to put my contacts in?"

Brandy snifters would have been good, but he only had two, and he'd just poured a little more cognac into them. He brought her a shot glass.

"I need two," she said. "I have two contacts."

"Right. One per eye." He found a glass—an empty jam jar, actually—with pictures of the Flintstones on it. That would do.

The front-door buzzer rang. "I'm not going to answer it." He suspected it would be Dean.

"You have to," Thea said. "What if it's an emergency?"

I damn well don't have to, he thought, but he pressed the intercom button anyway.

"It's Amy," he told Thea. "She's on her way up."

"Does Amy come over so late very often?"

"No," said Ross firmly, not wanting her to get the wrong idea. "Never."

He could hear her climbing the steps. She seemed to be dragging something heavy behind her. Step, thump, step, thump. *Dean's body, maybe.*

"Dean's been looking for you," he told Amy when she came in. "He called me this evening, wanting to know if I'd seen you."

"He found me." Amy was white around the lips, and her eyes were grim, as if she were fresh from bloody combat.

Thea stepped out of the bathroom wrapped in a towel. "Oh, I didn't know you'd be here, Thea. I should have called or something. But I couldn't stay home, and Chewy was out, and..."

"It's all right," Thea assured her. She put her hand on Amy's arm. "Of course you can stay here tonight." She squinted at Amy's stolen sacristy lamp. Her vision wasn't very good without her contacts. "From a church?"

"Originally," Amy said. "I got it at a yard sale. I was afraid someone might steal it from my car. Ross, I'm going to need a place to stay until I can find my own apartment."

"Well..."

"So will you give me sanctuary?"

23

ALARUMS

THEA DROPPED THE TOWEL. THAT LEFT HER WITH JUST PANTIES AND WHITE socks on. And then just socks. Ross almost wished he'd told her to put her clothes back on so he could watch her get undressed with a bit more panache. This felt like she was getting ready for a shower. But then… there she was, in his bedroom, in the nude, so… could he complain?

I don't know about these candles, Ross thought. *They're not giving off enough light.*

"You're staring at me," Thea said.

Explaining or apologizing would have been complicated, so he put his arms around her instead. They stayed like that for a long time, a good six feet from his bed. It was as if they'd been spot-welded to the floor.

Ross thought, *Should I move her bedwards? Would that be rushing things?*

Or maybe she wants to make love standing up? To make love standing up, Thea would have to stand on the Boston phone book. And on the North, South, and West suburban directories.

Thea broke the impasse, backing up toward his bed with her fingers hooked in his belt. She sat down on the edge of his bed and tried to worry him out of his jeans. They got stuck around his ankles, as was the way with jeans.

Thea thought, *nothing looks quite so silly as a man with his pants partway down.* She managed to pry one of his feet out of his bunched-up jeans, but he wobbled and tumbled onto the bed. In a complex maneuver mostly involving his big toe, he worked his way out of his jeans altogether, but in the process, all of his loose change came out of his pocket and rolled across the floor. One quarter in particular seemed to roll on forever, finally coming to a noisy landing under the little table by the bedroom door.

Thea wondered: *Will he mind if I keep my socks on?* Thea's feet got cold easily. For some reason, it annoyed Wim when she went to bed in her socks.

He opened his eyes and looked at her pretty face in candlelight. As it turned out, her eyes were open, too. There were flecks of gold in her blue eyes—or was that a trick of the candlelight? He felt he was falling into a deep-blue mist when he looked into her eyes. She smiled and he smiled back. *This is the time you would say "I love you" if you were in love. Sometimes, even if you're not, you might say it at a juncture like this. Especially if you were Sarah Jefferson.*

They were kissing each other randomly now, all over. Ross's head wound up between her legs. She raised her hips off the mattress.

Thea was breathing with a sawing sound and was moving hard against his face. *"I thought you'd be up to your ears in Dutch twat by now,"* Dean had said. He was, practically. He reached up and cupped her right breast. He rotated her rose-colored nipple a quarter turn. She was caressing her other breast. With her free hand, Thea tugged on Ross's ear until it became almost painful. Only her shoulders and heels were still touching Ross's mattress.

Her hips bucked and her body trembled. She let go of her breast and his ear and clutched the bedspread with both hands. She made a sound between laughing and crying with a few yips and yelps and whimpers thrown in. *No way she's faking it. If she were, she'd make more plausible noises.*

He made it inside her for the tag end of her orgasm.

In a hoarse voice, she said, "I'm taking the pill. In case you wondered."

Ross was teetering on the edge of an orgasm when the cat bush-whacked his ass. Swizzle loved a moving target. His whole body went stiff, as if a crackling jolt of electricity had passed through him. The cat sank her claws deep into his butt.

Thea didn't see the cat, not at first. When he spasmed, she thought he was having an orgasm. Or a heart attack.

Cat may have done me a favor by attacking my ass. I think I can go a few more strokes, and that's it. No, got through those. Maybe one more. There, that wasn't so exciting, was it? Risk one more. That was close. A near thing. Countdown approaching zero. Slow it down. Think of awful things: dirty dishes, broken toys, stinky tennis shoes, piles of dead birds, people puking in the snow. No, that's no good, you're ruining it. Think about... think about that pubic hair caught in the back of your throat. Think about the cat scratches on your ass. Your sore nose. Think about Thea being with Wim all afternoon. What did they do? God, there's an awful thought for you.

That thought got him through another whole series of strokes.

Thea was watching one of the candle flames. It was out of focus because she didn't have her contacts in, but that didn't make it any less interesting. She saw a quivering orange aura, and a tapered yellow cone inside of that, and a blue kernel inside of that. She'd been watching it for quite a while, but just now realized how pure and lovely it was. She realized at the same moment that she might cum again.

Think of boring things: Tax forms, wiring diagrams, Moby Dick, Yoko Ono, Red Sox statistics. No, that's not working either. Feels too damn good. Closer than ever. All right, what's the square root of... Wait, I don't remember how to do square roots.

Before he could switch to long division, he felt his toes crimp and he came. He was even noisier than Thea had been. He kept going afterwards. Thea had squeezed her hand between their bodies and was flicking herself and then, amazingly, she came too. Again.

They lay together for quite a while without speaking or even moving. She trembled slightly a few times—aftershocks from her orgasms. Their breathing slowly settled down. Once she coughed and squeezed his cock. Finally, he slipped out with a plopping sound.

How to get that pube out of the back of my throat? What did Jeremy call things that were in your mouth but didn't belong there? Binkies, that was it. He took a straightforward approach, digging around the soft palate with his index finger. He gagged, a little. *Come out, you damn binky.* He gagged again but managed to hook the hair.

Pubic hair, he decided, was pretty exciting material when considered *en masse*, but alone and detached, a pubic hair was just another hair. It was only a binky.

Thea put her head on his chest and brushed her hair out of her face. Her hair was shimmery in the candlelight. Ross tried to think of something intelligent to say about what had happened, about what they'd just done. It was hard, though, to come up with an opening line that sounded right. Maybe he should introduce another topic altogether. The population explosion. African art. Child psychology. The bop style of jazz. Esperanto. Nuclear escalation. Vanishing species. Or he could pretend that the whole thing had never happened, that it was a mere coincidence that had landed them in bed together with all their clothes off, still breathing hard.

His head felt full of bubble gum. There was nothing he could say that wouldn't come out sounding absurd or trite, so he settled on, "That was nice."

The pillow had fallen off the bed during their lovemaking. He slipped his arm under her head. She raised her head and squinted at him. He took it as a disapproving squint. "*Nice* is pretty weak," he said. "What I meant is... that was fabulous."

That seemed to satisfy her. She nodded. "It was." He rolled over in the bed so that they were lying side by side. "It doesn't bother you, that you slept with a whore?"

"What! You're not a whore. You..."

"What is a whore? Someone who takes money for sex, right? I kept thinking about that today, at Mr. Q's party. I had sex. I took money. I'm a whore."

"No, don't say that. You just..."

"Ross, you're going to have to get used to something. Dutch people... we're very direct. When we have something to say, we say it. We don't... sugarcake it."

"Sugarcoat."

"Yes, we don't sugarcoat it. So I'm a whore," she said. "That was funny when the cat jumped on you. At first I didn't know what was going on. I thought something was the matter."

Ross could see the pattern his chest hair had made on her breasts. It looked as if she'd been sleeping face down in tall grass. "Yeah," he said, insincerely, "pretty funny."

Swizzle was lying next to Ross in the bed now. She was purring. *Snorren. I'd be purring, too, if I could,* Ross thought.

Thea rubbed her shin where she had banged it against the iron stove. It had stopped hurting while she was making love, but now it was throbbing again. Down in the alley, an electronic whoop kicked in. Thea asked him what was going on.

"It's a burglar alarm. In a car, probably."

"Someone is trying to steal a car?"

"Yeah, maybe. Maybe not, though. Those things don't work very well. They have a way of going off if someone just walks by."

"Should we call the police?"

"I don't think we have to. There are probably half a dozen people on either side of the alley dialing 911 right now."

She wrapped one of her legs around him and put her hand on his chest. There was still a faint set of bruises on her wrist where Big George had manhandled her. "When I'm home alone, I always hear noises coming from that alley. Sometimes I think I hear shots, or screams, or people fighting. I used to buy newspapers just to see if there were any stories about murders or rapes around here, but I never saw any. I remember reading about that woman down in New York who was being stabbed and all those people knew it was happening but didn't do anything. When I first read that, I thought that Americans were terrible people, but now I can see how it happened. I wasn't that they didn't want to help, it was just that they didn't know what was going on or didn't know what to do."

Ross said, "You know, I forget sometimes that we're all a bunch of foreigners to you."

"When I first came here," she said, "I couldn't believe it. I mean, there were Americans in Amsterdam and even more in London, but that wasn't the same. They were always self-conscious about being Americans. But here... coming into the city from the airport, I remember looking at all the cars and all the buildings and thinking they were all full of Americans. Americans just going about their business. And all of them different from me. Oh, not a lot different, but a little bit. They all walked a little differently and sat down differently, held their silverware differently, looked at people differently, thought differently. It was a little overwhelming. Do you know what I mean?"

"Not exactly."

"Well... have you ever been to Europe?"

He never had. He felt a little inadequate for that reason. He considered lying and saying that yes, he'd been lots of times, but she might press him for details, and he might end up saying something stupid about Europeans. "No. I've been to Mexico, though."

"That's right. You told me. Did you have any of those feelings?"

"I guess. Sort of. I remember thinking that there were an awful lot of Mexicans running around down there, and that they were all acting very Mexican. At first I liked that, then for a while it bothered me, and then... then, near the end of my time there, I went back to liking it. I liked it so much that I didn't want to come back. I wanted to be Mexican myself. Maybe that's one reason I wanted to open a Mexican restaurant."

She'd wrapped her legs around him. Semen was oozing out of her and dripping onto his thigh and from there onto the bedspread. They'd been in a rush and hadn't taken the time to get between the sheets, his fresh sheets, so it was going to leave splotches on his purple spread, splotches that shouted SOMEONE CAME HERE! SOMEONE CAME *BIG* HERE!

"That damn siren," Thea said.

"The guy who owns the car is probably down the Cape for Thanksgiving."

Thea was moving her hand around on his chest and stomach and thighs. So far it was more like friendly pats than anything else, but he found himself getting interested again. *But you can't trust that first hard-on afterwards; it can melt away without any warning. It's unreliable. Totally unreliable.*

Thea stopped petting him and asked, unexpectedly, "How many women have you slept with?"

Ross's worthless erection withered away. This was the first time a woman had ever asked him that. Most women, he'd been led to believe, referred to that sort of list contemptuously as notches on a gun, or on a belt, or on a bedpost. *If I were to say three or four, would she think I was an irredeemable novice? Or just loyal to my partners? If I told her twenty something, would she think I was worldly and experienced? Or a retread?"*

"I don't know, exactly," he said. "I suppose around ten."

"What do you mean you don't know? Everybody knows."

She was right. He knew, all right. Eleven. No, not anymore. Twelve, now, exactly twelve. A dozen. Like a dozen donuts. A dozen roses. A dozen eggs. A nice round number.

1) A prostitute. He'd gone to a whorehouse with his brother Marshall and their friend Skeets. She'd told them what her name was, but now he couldn't remember it. La something. Laverne? Latasha? Ladonna? It didn't much matter: For sure it wasn't her real name. She'd given him a bad cold. At least she hadn't given him something worse.

2) Winifred, his girlfriend in high school. She'd arranged for their first time to be the night of their junior prom. Imagine that. At a time when everyone in town was pissed off at Ross for quitting the basketball team, Winifred stayed with him and defended him. She stayed with him even though her mother, a drunken but loyal basketball fan, despised Ross. He still felt guilty for leaving Winifred without a word when he went to Mexico with Laurel.

3) Wanda, aka Big Red. It seemed like everyone had slept with Big Red at least once during the two years Ross was in college. He remembered seeing a graffito in a men's room at the stadium that said, "You meet the nicest people on a Wanda."

4) Dorcas, a slinky woman he'd met in a macro-economics class. He couldn't remember much about Dorcas except that she thought Friedman was cool and Keynes was not. She drove a red Camaro which she washed a lot while wearing a lime-green bikini. While they were having sex, she

would sometimes call him daddy and sometimes, paradoxically, she'd call him her naughty little boy. Sometimes she'd say "rhaar," but she didn't sound like she was growling. She sounded like she was reading the word "rhaar" from a script.

5) Marjorie Microdot, the first woman he'd slept with whom he'd actually slept with. That happened in the yurt she'd built at School's Out before she'd inexplicably vanished. After they'd had sex, and he was falling asleep, she told him that he had a long way to go before he found his center. "You need to be in touch with your body." Had a yeti really carried her off? Maybe she'd purposely gone with the yeti. Maybe the yeti was more in touch with its body than Ross was.

6) Laurel. Countless times. And he had a bruise to show for practically every time. Laurel was not gentle in bed. But the bruises were worth it. They were well worth it.

7) Lili, from Quebec. She was studying Spanish in Mexico. He'd met her on Christmas Eve and then he kept seeing her around town. When he became the bartender at El Pavo Real, Heriberto's uncle's restaurant, she started coming there for *hora feliz* and drinking Palomas, many of which Ross gave her for free. One weekend when Laurel went off with Heriberto on business, or on what she said was business, he slept with Lili.

8) Kandi, the hostess at Maxwell's. She was in her mid-forties, married with two kids, and had a regal air about her. She dressed elegantly and seemed haughty. She didn't need the money she made as a hostess; her husband was a senior engineer at a company that made punch clocks for employees. But she'd stayed at home for fifteen years taking care of kids and dealing with an unresponsive husband, and she was tired of that life, so she went to work in a restaurant. Ross was never more surprised than when, in the storage room in the basement of Maxwell's, Kandi came in, locked the door behind her, and slipped out of her long, royal-blue Laura Ashley dress with no prompting from him. They made love on a fifty-pound sack of all-purpose flour. Their affair went on for a couple of months. She wanted to make love more often—and more passionately—than any woman Ross had ever been with, before or since, but it was hard to find opportunities. Guilt gnawed at her the entire time they were intimate. She was terrified that her husband would find out, or that her kids would find out, or that the other people who worked at Maxwell's would find out. She kept saying they needed to end their affair and was constantly nagging him, telling him he should get it together and find someone else. Every time a female customer came into the bar, Kandi would urge him to consider this stranger as her successor, but at the time,

Ross was happy being with her and having a secret affair. One day, they walked together to Appleton's Booksellers on Charles Street to buy a book for one of her kid's birthday presents. Kandi saw a woman with long blond hair reading stories in the Storybook Corner and she urged him to take up with her. A few weeks later, he did. When Ross told Kandi, she was infuriated and felt bitterly betrayed.

9) Sarah Jefferson, the story lady at Appleton Booksellers. Soon after Kandi pointed her out, he started taking Jeremy to Story Hour. During pauses in her readings, he sometimes found her looking his way. They bonded over her reading of *Where the Wild Things Are*. He particularly liked the way she roared the terrible roars and gnashed the terrible teeth when impersonating the Wild Things during their wild rumpus. She was a dancer and a writer and also an actress. She had a role in a cheerless one-act play that Ross went to see. The characters in the play all dressed in black jeans and black turtlenecks and sat atop ladders for the duration of the play. She did look good, perched up there, her long blonde hair falling over her black sweater, but then, there was that problem with her toxic breath. And with her snoring. And with the fact that Dean was sneaking around with her at the same time

10) Stephanie, whom he'd met at a New Year Eve's party almost a year ago. They'd hit it off at the party and left together before midnight. They stopped and bought some cheap champagne and went to her apartment to watch the ball drop while in their underwear. Ross told her about the Mexican custom of eating twelve grapes at midnight for good luck, only she didn't have any fresh grapes, so they had to pop twelve raisins into each other's mouths. She was wearing a black bra and black panties; Ross told her that, in Mexico, wearing black underwear on New Year was considered bad luck. Mexican women wore red if they wanted love in the coming year, yellow if they wanted profit. She came back from her bedroom wearing festive red Christmas panties with Santa Claus on her butt and a Christmas tree on her crotch. "These are the only red panties I have," she told him. Ross was certain that they would be fabulous together in bed, only they weren't, they were so-so. So-so at best. The next morning, she said she would make an omelet with avocados and mushrooms if he took her dog, an Akita named Fuji, out for a walk. Ross walked Fuji and came back to her building. She'd never told him what her last name was, so he couldn't ask to be buzzed into her apartment. There were no first names listed next to the buzzers, only initials, and there were four initials S. He stood in the foyer a long time before a couple came out and he was able to sneak into the building behind them. He wasn't even sure which

apartment was hers, but luckily, Fuji knew. She was cooking breakfast wearing a bra-and-panties set the color of egg yolks. Red last night, yellow this morning—she had both bases covered: passion and prosperity. He asked her out again a couple of times after that, but she was always busy.

11) Valerie, his neighbor, but only that once. Because he didn't have a TV, he went to her apartment to watch *MASH* one Saturday evening, and he stayed over there and after *MASH* they watched *Mary Tyler Moore,* and after that, they were both bored, and so, what the hell?

12) And now, Thea. Thea, incredibly enough.

"How many men have you slept with?" He'd never asked a woman that question before either. Well, maybe Laurel.

"A few more than you. I only count the ones that I liked, though."

"That's an interesting way to count." *That would knock two or three off my list.*

"I don't think I'm very good at it."

She wants me to tell her that's not true.

"That's not true. I already told you... it was fantastic."

Or did I say fabulous?

"No, I just lay back and let you do things"

"That was mostly my fault. I get nervous when I'm not doing something, so I didn't give you much of a chance to do things. I'm sorry."

She kissed his stomach and then blew on it, making an uncouth sound. "Do you like that?"

"Umm. I used to do that to Jeremy when he was a baby. It made him laugh."

"I don't know what Americans like." she said. She started to experiment. "Do they like this?" She bit his chin and then licked his throat. "Or this?" She kissed his right nipple. "Or how about this? Do they like that?" she said, as she popped him into her mouth.

This is one American who likes that.

He tried to maneuver her so that they could do *that* to each other simultaneously, but she wouldn't budge, so he just lay back and relaxed. Her tongue felt indescribably soft and warm.

Thea was recalling the techniques Mrs. Q had demonstrated by sucking sensually on her fingers. And she was concentrating on the fact that this was Ross, and not the Star. And not Wim.

Ross was thinking about seeing her through Dean's lens, and how astonishingly desirable she seemed, even at a distance. Desirable, but utterly unreachable. He never dreamed she'd be naked in his bed giving him a blowjob. Then he stopped thinking. He let go.

Ross kept stroking her hair afterwards. Eventually his stroking became mechanical. Then it stopped. Thea decided he'd fallen asleep. Hanging on the back of his bedroom door, there was a chocolate-colored terry cloth robe and a silky silver one with red roses on it. *Whose robe is that?* She kissed Ross on the forehead, put on the silky robe, and then, on her way out of the bedroom, she banged her shin on the low table by the door. That was the second time she'd injured that shin today.

Ross said sleepily, "I do that all the time. I should put a blinking red light on that table."

~

Thea jumped when the bathroom door opened, but it was only the cat. The cat meowed with a definite interrogative note. "What are you doing in here?" the cat wanted to know. She felt more sticky fluid creeping down her inner thigh.

She tried to remember the cat's name. Sizzle? Skillet? Stickler? "You know what, Sizzle?" she said to the cat, "I think I'll take a shower."

Three minutes later, she was dripping water on the bathroom floor and squinting at the shower head as if it had been intentionally malicious to her. "It burned me," she told the cat.

Outside, the alarm rang on.

Coming out of the bathroom, she took a wrong turn and went into the living room. The curtains were pulled and it was completely dark. She ran into something that had no right being where it was and heard the clank of glass against metal. Suddenly, she was completely lost, lost in Ross's living room. She retreated a few steps and found the switch for the overhead light. She flipped it on, just for a second, just long enough to get her bearings. Out of the corner of her eye, she saw roaches quickly scurrying for cover. Maybe they thought she was Jeremy, coming to kill them.

It was Amy's sacristy lamp she had run into. Amy herself was lying on the couch on top of a sleeping bag, her hands clasped under her breasts.

"Oooh, that was like a flashbulb going off. I can still see orange balls of light floating in front of my eyes," Amy said.

Thea said, in an apologetic whisper, "Sorry! I forgot you were out here. Did I wake you up?"

"Not really. I haven't been able to get to sleep. I'm not used to sleeping on a couch, and it's kind of lumpy." The noises from the next room had been keeping her up as well. "I almost thought you were Laurel. I remember seeing her in a robe just like that one when she was here."

"I guess she left it here." *Maybe because she was planning to come back.*

"I almost fell asleep, but then that alarm went off. It's like it's coming from the inside of your head, you know?" Amy patted the couch. "Come sit down."

"It's getting a little weaker now," Thea said.

"Yeah, and it's starting to sound hoarse. Who were you talking to in the bathroom?"

"The cat. Do you always sleep like that, Amy?"

"No, I usually don't wear anything at all, but..."

"Neither do I. Except socks."

"But I thought Jeremy might get up in the middle of the night so I left my T-shirt on." Thea noted that she was concerned about Jeremy seeing her but didn't mention Ross.

"What I meant was, do you sleep on your back with your hands like that, usually?"

"Oh. I guess I do. Dean says all I need is a daisy in my hands, and I'll look like I'm dead."

"Dead people don't look like that. They just look dead."

"I don't know much about real dead people. It's funny, though, my friend Chewy said lying on your back like this centers you. He said it's the best position for astral projection. Do you believe in astral projection?"

"I don't know. I don't know anything about it."

"I don't either. A lot of the things Chewy talks about, I'm not sure I believe in. I believe in psychic experiences, though, because I had one." Amy waited for Thea to ask about her psychic experience. When she didn't, Amy went ahead and told her about it. "I woke up once in the middle of the night and heard someone out in the living room."

"God, I'd hate that. Ever since Wim... well, ever since I started living by myself, I've been afraid something like that might happen some night."

"At first I wasn't all that alarmed. I was in that state between being asleep and being awake where nothing seems exactly real, you know, so it somehow didn't bother me that much. And there was something about the way this person was moving around in the living room that made it sound like he or she belonged there. It almost sounded like someone was carefully rearranging the furniture."

≈

Amy heard someone walk from the living room to the kitchen, open the refrigera-

tor, and get something out. She thought, Oh, *it's just Dean. Then she reached over and found Dean in bed next to her.*

She heard this person, whoever it was, go into the bathroom. She heard someone bang down the toilet seat hard, almost angrily. Dean had no doubt left it up. Then she knew for certain from the next sound she heard that her intruder was a woman. I don't think a woman will hurt us. Maybe she's lost; maybe she's just in the wrong apartment. Maybe...

The bathroom door opened and she heard footpads coming toward their bedroom. It sounded as though the woman was wearing bedroom slippers. Suddenly it struck her that something was wrong, very wrong. What the hell is a strange woman in slippers doing here at three o'clock in the fucking morning?

She sat up. "Dean, wake up! There's a woman in the apartment with us!"

"What's she look like?"

"Dean, I'm serious! Listen!"

Dean sat up and listened. "I don't hear anything. You were dreaming." *He rolled over and went back to sleep.*

Amy didn't hear anything now either. She got up and looked down the hall-way. She went into the living room and looked around. No one.

She looked under the couch and moved the easy chairs to look behind them. Maud woke up and looked at her quizzically. If there had actually been a stranger here, Maud would have been barking her fool head off. Okay, I guess I did dream it, but it seemed sooooo real. *She got herself a drink of milk to help her get back to sleep, and she stopped by the bathroom to have a quick pee. As usual, Dean had forgotten to put the seat up. She was padding her way down the hallway, heading back to bed, when she stopped—she suddenly realized what had just happened.*

"I don't understand," Thea said. "What happened?"

"Don't you see? I heard myself. I heard future Amy. First, I heard myself in the living room, searching behind the chairs. That's why Maud didn't bark, because it was me. Then I heard future Amy getting something from the fridge, and then going to the bathroom. I'd been hearing things that happened a few minutes in the future.

"I told Dean what'd happened the next morning, and he said, 'It's a miracle. The world's most pointless miracle.' There's this woman, she says she's a psychic—her name is Sister Judith... "

"Yes, she's always leaving flyers in my mailbox."

"I called her to see what she thought about all this, but the woman who answered said Sister Judith was temporarily unavailable because she was in jail. So I called Chewy and told him about what happened, because he understands things like that, but he was in one of his silent phases. You call him up and he picks up the phone, but he doesn't say anything, not even hello. It's kind of spooky. And sometimes he calls me, too. He likes to listen even if he doesn't like to talk. The phone rings, and it seems like there's no one there, but I know it's Chewy, so I talk to him."

"I think this Chewy person calls me sometimes, too."

"He does? You know Chewy?"

"No, I don't know him, but someone has been calling me in the middle of the night and then saying ridiculous things or not saying anything at all."

"Oh. Well, I'm pretty sure it isn't Chewy. I don't think he quiet-calls anyone but me. And maybe his boyfriend Hector."

"It worries me, worries me a lot, that someone calls like that. Not so much lately, but for about a month, someone was calling once or twice a week."

"I wouldn't worry about it too much," Amy said. "You probably have a phone number that's close to someone else's. Once Dean and I had a phone number that was just one digit different from a radio station's. People would call at all hours and request songs. There was this one guy who would call almost every other day wanting to hear *In a Gada da Vida*."

"I don't know," Thea said. "It still worries me."

"You might have to get your number changed if it starts up again," Amy said. "We did. Did you and Ross have a nice Thanksgiving?"

"We weren't together for most of the day. I promised this man... this man I used to model for... that I'd come to his dinner party."

"Maybe I could be a model too. Do you think so? Tell you the truth, I'm a little nervous about driving a school bus. Those things are so huge, and Boston traffic is so crazy, and they haven't trained me very well. Being a model seems safer."

Thea didn't think Amy would like the kind of modeling that she had done for Mr. Q, but Amy didn't know about that. *At least, I hope she doesn't.*

"The only modeling I've done has been for Dean, and that's sort of amateur stuff, and it's photography, not drawing."

"You don't need any experience. I didn't have any."

"Do you have to take your clothes off?"

"Umm, yes, generally."

"I don't know. I'm a little shy, but... if it was art. I'm not ashamed of my body or anything."

"You don't have any reason to be," Thea told her.

"But it must feel kind of strange, a whole class looking at you, and you're the only one naked."

The phone rang.

"Would you get it?" Amy asked Thea. "If it's Dean, tell him I'm not here, okay?"

"Amy?" the voice at the other end said. Thea was glad there was *someone* there. The idea that her phantom phone calls might follow her around was terrifying.

"No, this is Thea."

Amy whispered, "Is it Dean?" Thea nodded.

"So you finally got there," Dean said. "Let me talk to Amy, please."

"She isn't here right now."

"I know she is. I walked by and saw her car parked on Comm Ave near Ross's building." Dean didn't sound accusatory when he said that. He sounded apologetic. "Let me talk to her. Please."

"I can't."

"Thea, what am I going to do?"

"I don't know what to tell you, Dean. I don't know anything about any of this."

"Really? You two haven't been talking? Well, listen, ask her again, will you? Try to persuade her. Tell her I only want to talk for a minute."

Thea covered the mouthpiece. "He says he only wants to talk for a minute."

Amy looked indecisive, then shook her head.

"She says she can't come to the phone right now."

"Well, it's all right," Dean said, a little too quickly for it to really be all right. "Just tell her..." His voice trailed off. Through an eerie cross-connection, she could hear faint voices on the line. She couldn't make out what they were saying, but one seemed to be trying to pick an argument with the other one; the other one seemed to be laughing.

"What do you want me to tell her, Dean?"

"Oh. Tell her that I vacuumed. I vacuumed. Even though I was tired from pacing the streets all night, and even though I'd been drinking, and even though I was still seeing a pink fringe around things, I vacuumed the whole apartment. Tell her that."

Thea promised that she would, though she had no idea what he meant by seeing a pink fringe.

"Tell her I didn't just leave the vacuum sitting out. I did a bang-up job. Wall to wall, every nook, every cranny." Thea could tell that Dean wanted to be forgiven for something by somebody. In a pinch, he'd even settle for being forgiven by her. But Thea didn't know how to go about it. "Oh, and tell her... tell her I love her."

When Thea had hung up, Amy said, "I wish you hadn't told him I couldn't come to the phone. I wish you'd told him I just didn't want to talk to him. What did he ask you to tell me?"

"He wanted you to know that he'd vacuumed."

"Oh. That figures. He always vacuums when he's feeling guilty. I bet he offered to give me a back rub, too, didn't he? That's another thing he does when he wants to make up."

Amy looked a little disappointed when Thea told her that he hadn't. "He did say he loved you."

The phone rang again. "That's probably my back rub now," Amy said. Thea picked up the phone before it could ring a second time.

"I forgot, there's something I need to talk to Ross about," Dean said.

"Ross is asleep."

"Really? Wore him out, huh. Well, get him up and ask him what he thinks of La Risa Final."

"Of what?"

"La Risa Final. It means The Last Laugh. See, neither of us like ¿Por Qué No? all that much as a name for the restaurant, so when I was out walking around tonight, I hit on La Risa Final. The Last Laugh. I think he'll like it. Tell him that, even though I was upset tonight, and even though I was drinking, a little bit, even though I was stoned all day long, that I had the best interests of the partnership in mind." Dean didn't mention that he had almost fled to Virginia earlier this evening.

"Can I tell him that in the morning?"

Dean considered that. "I guess. You want to write it down? The name of the restaurant, I mean."

"It's dark in here. I don't think I could,"

"Say it back to me, then, so I know you've got it."

She did.

Dean corrected her pronunciation. "You have to roll the r. R-r-r-r-r-isa."

"R-r-r-r-isa. You should go to sleep now, Dean. It's very late."

"'The City is of Night, but not of sleep / Sweet sleep is not for the weary brain.'"

"What's that?"

"Any messages for me?" he asked.

Thea didn't think *He always vacuums when he feels guilty* constituted a bona fide message. "No, not really. Go to bed."

"I have a hard time falling asleep when I sleep alone. You get so you expect someone to be there, and you keep waking up all night thinking, 'Something's wrong.'"

"I know," Thea said, "but you should try, anyway."

Thea told Amy that she was going back to bed now. She wasn't going to answer the phone again no matter what.

Just then another siren kicked in, a loud one. A police car, or an ambulance. And then, a block or so away, a dog began to bay in response to the siren.

"Okay, but what did he say this time?"

"He just gave me a message for Ross."

"About my staying here?" Amy wanted to know.

"No. About the restaurant."

"What was that you were saying? R-r-r-r something."

"It was Spanish. The Last Laugh."

"Oh. That sounds like Dean. Always worrying about who laughs last. Well, I guess I'll see you in the morning. I'm going to get up early and make breakfast for Ross and Jeremy. For you too, of course. Pancakes, maybe. I wonder if he has any whole wheat flour. Anyway, I want him to know I'm going to be a responsible guest while I'm here."

Thea opened the bedroom door. The doorknob felt sticky. It seemed even darker in there than it had in the living room. Ross must have gotten up and blown out the candles. The night seemed longer, deeper than a normal night. A night shouldn't have enough hours to be as late as it seemed. She heard a creaky, whirring sound, something spinning around and around. Did she not turn off the fan in the bathroom?

She took off her robe—Laurel's robe—and groped around for the bed. It wasn't where she expected it to be. Then she stumbled into it. Ross slept sprawled all over the bed. She touched his hand.

It wasn't Ross's hand. It was too little. Far too little. *Oh my God, what if Jeremy wakes up screaming. Ross will think I'm molesting his little boy.*

She backed away from the bed as quickly and covertly as possible grabbed the robe. Jeremy made a sound in his sleep, a grinding noise with his teeth.

The candles were still burning, and shadows were dancing around

Ross's bedroom. Ross slept with as much abandon as his son did, but he made room for her without waking up. The cat made room for her, too. "La Risa Final," she whispered in Ross's ear.

That made him smile in his sleep.

She got close to him so she could see his face by the light of the candles. The car alarm faded in and out. The ambulance siren, or perhaps it had been a police siren, was gone, and so were the dog's mournful howls. *I like the way he looks. I like the sound of his voice. I like the way he talks to Jeremy. I like the way he makes love. I like his gray eyes, his kind gray eyes. I wonder, though. I wonder if he has anything to do with me at all?*

24

THE WAY ORANGE JUICE GOES WITH
TOOTHPASTE

ROSS WOKE TO THE SOUND OF WATER RUNNING AND A WOMAN SINGING. THIS was Amy, taking a shower. Then her singing turned to a scream. He visualized her in there: lather in her hair, soapy water running down her body, eyes screwed up, cursing the showerhead. He went back to sleep.

When he woke up again, Amy was in the kitchen. "Morning." She was wearing her emerald-green bathrobe. She had gone back to her apartment on Saturday to collect some essentials when she knew Dean would be at the restaurant. Her robe was slightly ajar, showing a thin V of white, lightly freckled skin from neck to navel. She smelled minty.

"It's Dr. Bonner's peppermint soap," Amy said. "I don't use anything else. You want some O.J.?"

"No thanks. I just brushed my teeth. You know how orange juice and toothpaste are together."

"Have a bagel then. I stopped and got a few on my way back from the bus barn. I burned one. Your toaster was turned all the way up."

"Jeremy does that because he thinks his toast will get done faster. I can't believe you've already been out and come back."

"I feel like I've had a complete day, and it's not even ten o'clock." Amy sighed.

"I heard you screaming in the shower. What got you, the cold water or the hot?"

"Both, at different times."

"The cold's better than the hot."

"Not by much."

"You got spoiled, having a water heater right in your own apartment. What did Woody Allen say? Something like, whenever anyone on the Eastern Seaboard flushes a toilet, my water temperature changes. You know, you don't look like you're feeling so hot."

"I'm so tired, I feel nauseous. I felt better right after my shower, but now I'm back to flat-out horrible. It's all Dean's fault." Dean had been over the night before, trying to convince Amy to come home. He'd stayed and argued with her until well after midnight. "I kept hoping you'd come out and say something to him."

"What was I supposed to say? Dean's already pissed at me for letting you stay here. Listen, why don't you get some sleep now? You can use my bed. I'll be leaving right after I shower."

Amy shook her head. "I'd love to, but if I sleep now, I don't think I can get to bed early enough tonight. That's the kind of schedule I should shoot for. Tonight I'm going to bed right after Walter Cronkite."

"No TV, so no Uncle Walt. So how was your first morning on the job?"

Amy sat in the driver's seat of her bus at the street corner, her lights flashing. She felt profoundly depressed, although, so far, she'd performed faultlessly. She'd gotten up when it was still dark as midnight and driven the Pinto to Mattapan. She'd gassed up her bus and brought it here without any damage to her bus, other vehicles, pedestrians, or herself. Even her present difficulty could scarcely be considered her fault.

She'd spent Sunday in the Pinto driving the route she was supposed to take in the bus. Thea had come along as a navigator, reading directions from the itinerary Carol had given Amy. They'd driven the route three or four times. She was at the right street corner, she was sure of that; it was just that no one else was. Still, the lack of children did seem crucial. She was going to be late if she didn't leave soon, but arriving at the school with an empty bus would be pretty futile.

Maybe everyone was sick; a sudden outbreak of measles or chicken pox, maybe. Or maybe the kids loved their old bus driver so much, they were boycotting the new one. There was a little mom-and-pop grocery store on the opposite corner that seemed to be open. Would they have a phone? Who could she call? Carol, back at the bus barn? The school board? Dean?

A handsome black man with a dalmatian walked down the sidewalk beside her bus and smiled at her. It was one thing to get up early and take your dog for a walk, quite another to have to get up and drive a school bus. He didn't have to cope with missing children. Neither did his dog. She envied them.

Amy laid her head down on the huge steering wheel. She felt queasy and had to go to the bathroom. She considered abandoning the bus and walking home.

Someone was knocking on the glass of the school bus door. She pulled the lever, and with a hiss, the door opened. There was a young black man there. "Hi," she said. "Are you my first customer?"

"I'm Jerry," he said. "Didn't they tell you about me?"

She tried to remember. They'd told her a great many things, most of which she'd forgotten, but she was pretty sure no one had mentioned Jerry.

"I'm your monitor," Jerry said.

Amy felt a warm surge of relief. My monitor! I thought he looked way too old to be in junior high. *"Pleased to meet you," Amy said. "According to the stuff the bus company gave me, everyone was supposed to meet me right here. Where are all my passengers?"*

"At first, back in September, we used to wait here, but Steve, the old bus driver, he said that the turn up at the end of the next block was so tight, that it would be better to pick up the kids around the corner."

Oh, wonderful. If it was too tight for Steve, what's it going to be like for me?

"And it's a couple blocks shorter for them to walk. A lot of them live in the bricks."

"The bricks?"

"The bricks... the projects, the housing projects," Jerry said. "I'll go get the kids."

"No, uh, let's go around the block and then pick them up there, like Steve did."

"You'll still have to make that turn, now that you're pointed that way."

Yeah, but the kids won't be aboard to see me doing it. Don't want them to lose confidence so early on.

Jerry got on, Amy let out the clutch, and the bus lurched into the street. The driver of a panel truck behind them leaned heavily on his horn. She looked over at Jerry. He was smiling. But heaven knows what he's thinking. I wonder if he'd drive, if I asked him? I bet he knows more about driving and engines and things. He could drive, and I could be the monitor.

It was, as Jerry had warned, a turn not to be taken lightly, worse even than the turn into the bus barn. A narrow street made narrower by parked cars on the through street and the cross street, it angled off to the left at an oblique angle. She'd negotiated this turn in the Pinto several times yesterday, on her practice runs with Thea, without even thinking about it, but a school bus was about five times bigger than that little Ford. She took it in a series of small maneuvers, grinding the gears every time she went from reverse to low and back again. She knew she should be double clutching, but she'd forgotten how to do that, exactly. Her bus effectively blocked traffic going in every direction. In her rearview mirror, she could see the driver of the panel truck working his jaw muscles, his face going cherry red. Jerry offered to get out and direct her.

"No, we've almost got it." She was afraid to let Jerry out. She was afraid he'd run away. "One more time." And if I don't get it this time, too bad. I don't have enough strength left in my arms to turn the wheel all the way around again. *She ground the gears for the final assault, closed her eyes and shot it, not caring how close she came to the brown Dodge Dart parked on the street. She cleared it by inches.*

"This is my first day," she told Jerry.

He nodded agreeably. "First days are always difficult," he said.

"I didn't get in a whole lot of time behind the wheel before they sent me out." That would have been enough, but she went on to say, "I passed the driving test to get my license, but there were five new drivers on the bus taking the test at the same time. We only drove the bus about a hundred yards each, and after every test drive, the examiner would say, 'Not bad. Double clutch next time. Don 't forget to double clutch. Next driver.'" And when the women drivers got up from the driver's seat, he'd give each of them a pat on the butt.

That information would definitely have been enough, but she plunged on, determined not to keep anything from her monitor. "Until last week, I'd never driven anything but an automatic or anything bigger than a Pinto. You wouldn't think they'd trust a big, expensive bus, not to mention all these children, to someone with as little experience as I have, would you?"

Jerry smiled on, although by now she was convinced that his smile was pure bravado. "There are the kids," he said.

"I haven't completely gotten the hang of it, but I think I'll be able to do okay. At least I didn't wreck my bus or anything this morning."

"I'm glad to hear that," Ross said. He got himself coffee.

"I was hoping to drive a Bluebird, but I got a Crown Supercoach. I like the sound of Bluebird better, but Supercoach sounds okay too, don't you think? I just wish you were going to be my monitor, Ross."

"Why? You don't like your monitor?"

"No, Jerry is super nice. I'd just like to have a friend with me on the bus."

"No way I could get up that early every day. I still think you should get a couple of hours of sleep. What time do you have to drive this afternoon?"

"Not until two thirty. I think I'm going back to my place in a little while —to Dean's place, I mean—since he'll be at the restaurant. I need to get some more clothes and stuff, and I want to visit with Maud and just sit around. It's peaceful there, this time of day."

"Yes, it is," Ross said, remembering their languid mornings there. "Oh, you won't have to cook dinner for us this evening." Amy's vegetarian dishes hadn't been a big hit with Jeremy. He didn't much care for brown rice or tofu or raw veggies. Ross didn't much like them either; they reminded him of the meals he'd had in the early days of School's Out. "Thea and Jeremy and Dean and I are having dinner at the restaurant. It's kind of a dry run for the kitchen stiff."

Amy felt a pang of regret at not being included in this little soiree. But maybe it was for the best. Maybe. "You know, it's just so amazing that you and Thea met in the laundromat and now you're sort of going together. Of course, I guess people have to meet somewhere. Dean says all relationships are accidents of time and place."

"Dean may be right." Ross put half & half in his coffee and looked at her.

"What's the matter?"

"I was thinking about telling you something, but now I don't think I should."

"You must want to, or you wouldn't have mentioned it. Come on, tell Amy."

"You see, Thea and I didn't actually meet in the laundromat," Ross said. "No, that's not true. We met there, but I'd been... watching her."

"How do you mean, watching?"

Ross told her what he meant. He told her about seeing Thea that first night. About getting her name from her mailbox. He told her about borrowing a lens from Dean, about calling and asking for a pizza and about calling her several times after that. Sometimes he would talk to her. Mostly he wouldn't say anything; he'd just watch and wait for her to hang up. He told her about the time he called when Wim answered the phone.

"You don't look shocked," Ross said to Amy. She hadn't screeched in horror. She hadn't even pulled her robe closed.

"Most men are voyeurs," Amy said. "If you weren't always giving us lecherous looks, women would probably go around naked half the time."

"We men blew it."

"You blew it. I have to admit, I thought you were a little different. I'm kind of surprised you'd pull something so sneaky. There's something about you that makes a person want to trust you."

"It's the eyelashes. Laurel used to call them Bambi lashes. When I was a kid, I hated them. I'd trim them every week or so."

"No, it's more than just your lashes. Anyway... you're not still calling her, are you?"

"No, I haven't for a few weeks. Not since I met her in person. Now that I know her—I feel pretty horrible about all that. Really horrible. Besides, I gave Dean his zoom lens back."

"That's good, because you were scaring her."

"What do you mean? How do you know that?"

"Because, the other night, Thanksgiving night, she was here and we were talking, and the phone rang and she was afraid no one would be there. She said that used to happen at her apartment all the time. I could tell she was frightened. Anyway, you want some orange juice now?"

"Oh God, now I feel even worse." Ross got up and put his cup in the sink. "I've got to get to the restaurant. The fire department is doing a safety inspection this morning. We have a menu meeting with Rafael and Mama this afternoon. And we still haven't finished painting the kitchen. It needs a second coat."

"I don't think you'll ever get that place open."

"Don't say that. We're hoping to have a soft opening this coming weekend, and a real opening a few days after that. Anyway, I'm glad your school bus job is working out okay—I know you were nervous about it."

"Oh no, I think it'll be fine. Just fine."

Amy parked her bus in front of Crispus Attucks Junior High, her tires scraping the curb. Still no casualties. But there should have been a line of buses unloading in front of the school. Hers was the only one. She'd arrived either very early or very late. Probably very late.

A couple came walking along the sidewalk across the street from the school. They both wheeled around and gave Amy the finger. Redundantly, the man yelled, "Fuck you! Fuck you, bitch!" The woman snarled wordlessly. They were obviously no fans of busing. At least they didn't throw a rock at her bus.

"Those two, they walk by and do that at least once a week," Jerry told her.

She waited until everyone but Jerry had gotten off the bus. "I've got to go in for a minute. I've got to go to the bathroom really bad. I know we're running late..." They still had to pick up another load of students and take them to Bunker Hill High, "but I really have to go."

"No problem," Jerry said brightly. "No problem."

She wondered what made him such a pleasant person so early in the morning.

Amy caught up with one of her passengers, a kid wearing a red satin windbreaker that said YOUNG LIONS on back. "Where are you going?" he asked her. "You don't have to walk us to school too, you know."

"I got you here late," Amy said, "so I'm going to explain to your teachers that it was my fault." She had no intention of doing that; she only wanted to duck in and have a quick pee.

The kid snorted. He'd obviously had some practice snorting. "They don't give a shit."

"Tell me," Amy said, "why did you keep poking and pushing that kid across the aisle from you?" Amy had witnessed this in her rearview mirror. She was hoping Jerry would say something, but he never did. He never said a word to anyone, although there were times when things on the bus got a bit unruly. Kids were jumping from seat to seat. There were cigarettes being smoked, and near the back of the bus, a joint was being passed around. A couple was seriously making out.

"Because," the kid said, "he's fat and he's stupid and he keeps playin' with me."

"He's Vietnamese, though. They've already had such a hard time."

The historical irony didn't much matter to this kid. "He shouldn't be playin' with me."

"What do you mean, playing with, exactly?"

"Messin' around and sayin' shit to me."

"What are Young Lions? Is it like a club?" Or a street gang? Do street gangs have their own clothing lines these days?

The kid said, with exaggerated contempt, "It's a softball team."

That was good. She was afraid of gangbangers, but not of softball players.

Inside the front door, there was a sign that said, ALL VISITORS MUST CHECK IN AT THE OFFICE. Are school bus drivers considered visitors? She'd hoped there would be a bathroom right inside the door, but none was in sight. There was a surging mass of students in the corridor. It occurred to Amy that many of the boys looked like third graders, not junior high students. Many of the girls, on the other hand, looked like cocktail waitresses.

A bald man was standing at the intersection of two corridors in an island of empty hallway. The students passing by were giving him a wide berth. Amy guessed he was the assistant principal. He'd caught sight of Amy and was looking at her with disapproval. The man resembled the assistant principal at the junior *high she'd gone to in Lexington. Maybe it was the same man. Or maybe there was something about the job that molded the features of a person, making all assistant principals look alike.*

The bald man was bearing down on her. The crowd was parting like the Red Sea, letting him come through. "Help me out here, kid. Tell me where the girl's room is."

"You gonna start playin' with me too?" the Young Lion asked her. He disappeared into the flow of students like a fish being thrown back into a stream.

Ross was on his way out. "Amy, what I told you, it's a secret, okay."

"Sure, Ross, you can trust me. I'm sure you'll tell her when you think the time is right. Ross?"

"Yeah?"

"I have something to tell you, and it's a secret too. From Dean, I mean. It's about my job."

"What about it?"

"I hate it. I lied when I said it was fine. It's hard, really, really hard, driving a school bus, and I despise getting up that early, and I'm constantly afraid something awful is going to happen. I've been thinking about not going back this afternoon."

MARGARITA MADNESS

IN THE SERVERS STATION, JUST OUTSIDE THE KITCHEN,
Meredith struck a kitchen match on her zipper and lit a Virginia Slim. The servers station filled with sulfurous yellow smoke from her match. Everyone looked at her. Meredith loved the effect she achieved by lighting wooden matches on the fly of her Jordache jeans.

Patsy announced, "Meredith, I've got you working Section 2. Keith, you've got 3, and I'm taking 4. Thea, you're doing Section 1 and the Stag Table, and Robin II is going to follow you around. Robin, you just watch Thea and do what she does."

Robin II said: "I think we should call it the Community Table, not the Stag Table. Community Table just sounds... I don't know, more refined, I think."

"It's Dean and Ross's restaurant—they can call it whatever they want," Patsy said. "Does anyone know where Robin I is? She's got the bar."

No one knew.

"Maybe she's over at Copenhagen Cream," Keith said.

"What, she went for ice cream?"

"She's still working part-time over there."

Keith asked Meredith if it had been busy the night before. "I wasn't on last night, but it was wicked busy Thursday night," Meredith said. "So busy I didn't have time to pee. I cleared over eighty-five dollars, though."

"Wow, not too shabby for a weeknight. Hope I do that well tonight."

· · ·

OVER IN THE BAR,

Dean was putting a sign Buzz had made in the front window:

HAPPY HOUR 4-6

MARGARITA MADNESS!

TWOOFER MARGS $2.00!

"There," Dean said to Ross. "We can't just expect people to know we're having a special on bargain-basement margaritas." Ross had just hauled a case of Dos Equis up from the basement and was putting bottles in the lowboy refrigerator under the bar. "Hey, how do you think I look tonight?"

Ross glanced at him. "New haircut?"

"Not that new. I got it three, four days ago. You know, funny thing, my stylist kept rubbing up against me the whole time she was cutting my hair."

"How else was she supposed to get at your hair?"

"I don't know; seemed like the intimacy was a bit out of proportion, you know what I mean? But then later, I was paying for the haircut, and I asked her if she wanted to come by here for a drink sometime, and she got all huffy."

"Maybe she's schizoid," Ross said, "Or married. Or both. Who knows?"

"Anyway, what I was talking about was my tie. Since I'm hosting tonight, I thought I'd wear a tie, so I bought one at Bruno's. Even though I don't do their windows anymore, they still give me a discount, but even so, their prices are ludicrous. Seventeen bucks for a damn tie?"

"Pink is a good color for you."

"Coral. The guy at Bruno's said it was coral."

"Coral? I'd call that shade Pepto Bismol. It's kind of wide, though, and short, don't you think?"

"That's what's trendy, he said. He even suggested an ascot, a plum-colored ascot, but I think you have to be wearing a smoking jacket to pull off an ascot."

"You know you've got a big red stain on your shirt, right? Looks like you got shot in the gut."

"I had a salsa accident, and I've been too busy to do much laundry lately. But I bought a sweater to cover it up." He pulled a sweater out of a gold BRUNO'S bag. "You don't even want to know what this sucker cost."

"Gray, huh."

"Heather. Sales guy said heather and coral will look great together. Hey, I thought you were going to be wearing a tie when you were behind the bar? For the first few weeks, anyway."

Ross lifted his head up. Hiding behind his beard was a bowtie.

"You look like a Pez dispenser when you do that," Dean said. "Not much point in wearing a tie if no one can see it."

"This is the bowtie I had to wear when I worked at Yer Fadder's Mustache. I don't have a lot of other ties." In fact, he didn't have any. "Do you have chapped lips?"

"Chapped lips? Oh, you mean because of the ChapStick. I'm still trying to cut back on smoking. Anytime I want a cigarette, I just smear on the ChapStick."

"Now you're going to turn into a ChapStick junkie," Ross said. "Would you get me a bucket of ice?"

BACK IN THE SERVERS STATION,

Thea asked Robin I how she was tonight.

Robin I looked like she wasn't ready to answer such a difficult question. "Uh... okay? Okay, I guess."

Patsy upbraided Robin I, "You're late, you know. The cocktail waitress comes in at three forty-five to work happy hour."

"Sorry, Patsy. I was working next door until four."

"Why are you giving her a hard time?" Meredith asked Patsy. Between puffs, Meredith held her cigarette over her shoulder like a dueling pistol. "We haven't had one single customer in the bar so far."

"Ever hear of something called setup?" Patsy asked. "We'd all better get moving." She went to get the mop.

Meredith asked Keith, "Who told Patsy to release the flying monkeys? And since when is she telling people where to work and what to do?"

Keith said, "Since Dean and Ross made her chief server. Remember at the last staff meeting, Dean said..."

"I wasn't at that meeting," Meredith said. "I was skiing. But that explains why she's being such a bitch. And why is she going to clean the bathrooms?"

"She's doing Section 4. Section 4 cleans the restrooms. That's something else we talked about at the meeting—who does what during set-up. And since you're Section 3, you have to clean the lettuce."

"Cleaning the bathrooms should be Buzz's job. If you went out to eat, would you want someone waiting on you who'd been mucking around with toilets and mops?"

IN THE KITCHEN, BACK BY THE DISHWASHING MACHINE,

Thea said, "Eli, do you know if..."

"You can still call me Buzz for now. I can't decide between Eli, Jesse, Ian, or Spencer. Or maybe Cyrus."

"I like Cyrus," Robin II said. "Although I had a Jesse in my drama class —such a sweet kid. He was a good actor, too. I had him play Benjamin in *A Spoon River Anthology*."

"Benjamin, hmm. Benjamin Tibbets doesn't sound bad. Kind of a solid name. But nah, I'm leaning toward Ian or Spencer at the moment. It's a big decision, though, and I want to be sure it's a name I can live with. Don't want to have to change my name twice."

"Have you considered Toby? I had a student named Toby that I liked a lot. And I loved that movie *Toby Tyler* when I was a kid."

"*Toby Tyler*! Yeah, I liked that movie too, especially the monkey. But Toby's kind of a wimpy name, don't you think?"

Robin II thought about that. "I suppose. If Hitler had been named Toby instead of Adolf, there probably wouldn't have been a Second World War."

"Robin II is going to start waitressing soon. She's following me tonight," Thea told Buzz.

"I was wondering why you weren't wearing a long skirt, Robin," Buzz said.

"Buzz, we're setting tables and we're short of forks."

He poked through the silverware tray. "Only a few in here. I'll wash 'em by hand and keep my eyes open. And in case of a silverware emergency, I keep a secret stash hidden away."

Mama was standing in front of two huge pots of boiling water, almost hidden in the steam. Thea thought of a picture Jeremy had drawn and shown to her, of a dinosaur in the mist at the foot of a waterfall. Only the dinosaur had been smiling.

Mama fired a rapid burst of Spanish in Buzz's direction.

"What'd she say?" Buzz asked Cecily. Cecily was a line chef and Mama's *de facto* translator. She was also the only person on the kitchen stiff besides Buzz who wasn't related to Mama and Rafael.

"Couldn't quite catch it, hon," Cecily said. "Probably told you not to take any siestas tonight."

Thea whispered to Buzz that she was a little afraid of Mama. Mama was a dark, awesome presence in the kitchen.

"She likes you," Buzz said to her. "Cecily told me. Know what she calls you? Santa Thea."

"But why? I've never even talked to her. I've never done anything but give her my orders."

"I guess she just likes you."

Mama aimed more Spanish at Buzz.

"Okay, I got it this time," Cecily said. "She needs you to go downstairs and get a few things from the fridge."

DOWN IN THE WALK-IN REFRIGERATOR,

Meredith was eating guacamole from an enormous plastic vat. She was scooping it up with a spoon and really gobbling it down. The door of the walk-in opened and Buzz came in. "You scared me. I almost choked," she said. "I thought you were Ross the Boss. He yelled at me night before last for snarfing some shrimp."

"Ross yelled? I've never heard Ross yell at anyone."

"Well, he didn't exactly yell, but he told me to stop, and not in his normal tone of voice. He asked me if I wanted to keep working here."

"I don't think he meant it. I don't think Ross would fire anyone for snacking. He'd have to fire everyone. You ever notice, when you're in the kitchen, how everyone's mouth is always moving? And anytime a waiter has to return an order, you should see it, the kitchen stiff swarms around it like jackals going after a dead antelope."

"If he fires me, he fires me. I was looking for a job before I found this one. Damn," she said, "I got green goo on my jeans. I bet it's going to leave a stain."

"I like to dip pork cracklings in the guac," Buzz said. "I keep a bag of them next door in the office."

"That's right, you're still sleeping in the office."

"For now."

"Did you ever decide what you're changing your name to?"

"I'm thinking mostly of Ian or Jesse or Spencer, but I'm still not sure."

"Ian is a great name," Meredith said, "as long as you don't go to Bangkok."

"Why can't I go to Bangkok?"

"I was backpacking in Thailand, and I met this musician from Scotland named Ian, and we traveled around together for a while. Whenever he played a gig, he'd start off by saying, 'Good evening, I'm Ian,' and the Thai people in the audience would crack up. Finally, we found out that there's a slang word in Thai that sounds like Ian that means horny."

"Well, that fits me pretty well," Buzz said. The chill air in the walk-in was making Meredith's nipples press against the thin cotton fabric of her blouse. They looked like they could poke an eye out.

"I like the name Buzz, tell you the truth. I think *that* suits you."

"It's such a goober name," Buzz said. "It's not very Boston."

Buzz borrowed the spoon from Meredith and had some guacamole.

"I've never worked anywhere where you don't get a free shift meal," Meredith said.

"Mama doesn't like to cook any more than she absolutely has to. And she doesn't like the idea of people eating her cooking for free."

"We should at least have a chance to taste the specials. You shouldn't have to sell something you haven't tasted."

"At least we get a shift drink. Are you washing the lettuce tonight?"

Meredith said she was. She'd just learned that Section 2 had to wash lettuce.

"I hope you do a better job than Adriana did last night. A customer complained about dirty lettuce."

"It couldn't have been as bad as at Bianca's—Bianca's was this place I worked in Santa Barbara. One waiter served a salad that had a big green slug in it. He saw it just as he set it down in front of the customer, and he was too embarrassed to take it back. We were all hanging around the table, waiting to see what would happen. I thought I'd die when I saw it crawling along on the customer's fork."

"So what happened?"

"He ate it," Meredith said. "He probably thought it was an anchovy or an olive or something."

LEANING OUT OF THE PASS-THROUGH WINDOW,
Cecily said, "Spread the word: The soup tonight is cold sopa de lima and the special is pollo pibil." Pollo pibil had also been the special the night before. "Push the pollo."

"Who left this cigarette burning?" Patsy wanted to know. It was a long, skinny cigarette with white lipstick on the filter. Everyone knew it was Meredith's. "It's stinking the whole place up. We shouldn't allow smoking in the servers station."

"Thea, where are you working tonight?" Robin I asked.

Robin II answered for her. "Thea and I are working the South 40 together." The South 40 was Section I.

"The South 40," Robin I said, with a trace of nostalgia. "I worked the South 40 last weekend and I did really well. I was hoping to get a good section tonight. I never make all that much money working the bar. I still haven't paid my brother all my share of the December rent."

Thea thought about trading sections with Robin I and letting her train Robin II. Two people with the same name might cooperate nicely. And Robin I had more experience than Thea did. Thea had only been waiting tables for a few weeks herself. She'd started the first night the restaurant was open and no one had trained her. Her first table had been a party of three old ladies who were cussing and drinking and carrying on all during their meal, and she made every mistake a server can possibly make while waiting on them. They gave her the biggest tip she'd gotten so far. Even Meredith had been impressed.

SITTING ON A STOOL IN THE BAR,

Meredith looked like she was posing for a fashion photo. She always looked like she was posing for something. You could practically hear the shutters click around Meredith. "Can I have my shift drink now, Ross?" she asked him.

"That's not how it works," Ross said. "You know that. You work a shift, you get your drink then."

"Can't I have mine now? I'll be in a better mood waiting tables if I'm relaxed."

"That makes sense," Dean said, arriving with the ice. "Mood's all important when you're waiting tables. Guess what? Someone working lunch left the ice scoop in the machine, and now it's going to take Admiral Byrd to get it out of there. It's buried under about fifty pounds of ice cubes."

"We've got some real amateurs around here," Meredith said.

"Get Buzz to make a sign to put on the ice machine," Ross said.

"Buzz needs to go the store. We've run out of a lot of things Rafael says we have to have. We've got to work on our ordering techniques."

"Maybe we should put Patsy in charge of ordering," Ross said. "I need limes for the bar, too."

Ross gave Meredith her drink. "I didn't want my 'rita on the rocks, but... that's okay. Don't I get two, since it's happy hour?"

"No," Ross said. "Dean, there's a customer waiting at the host stand."

UP AT THE HOST STAND,

Dean said, "I thought you were going to be a real customer."

"Thanks a lot, Dean," Lizard said. "Why aren't I a real customer?"

"Well, for one thing, there's the way you're dressed."

"I came here straight from work. You think I work in evening clothes?" Lizard asked.

"You worked today? You never worked for us on Saturdays."

"You didn't pay me what I'm getting paid now. How come you're the host tonight? Did Robin II get canned?"

"She wants to be a waitress. She's training tonight. You going to the bar first, or you just want dinner?"

"I think I'll have din-din first. I didn't have time for lunch today."

"Din-din? What is this, Romper Room?"

"You can put me in Meredith's section." Lizard waved to Meredith, who was still at the bar.

"Let's see," Dean said, consulting the chart on the host stand. "No, Thea will be taking care of you tonight."

"Wait a minute," Lizard said. "There's no one else in the entire restaurant. Why can't I sit where I want?"

"Because," Dean said, "you're the first customer, and Thea's working Section 1. That's how it works."

"Robin II always put me in Meredith's section if I asked."

"I don't know why you're complaining. You're getting a free dinner."

"Free? *Free*?" When Lizard had finished up his carpentry work at the restaurant, Dean and Ross still owed him $3,600. Lizard had agreed to take the balance out in trade, and had been in for drinks and dinner nearly every night since the restaurant opened. "What do you mean, free?"

"Calm down," Dean said. "I was just kidding about the free part. Is it just you, or is your lady dining with you tonight?"

"M'lady and I have been, uh, well, lately, we haven't been seeing eye to eye, exactly. We're going through a rough patch."

"I know how that goes," Dean said.

"In fact, looks like we're going to go our separate ways."

"So that home urinal thing wasn't enough to keep her on the reservation, huh? You want to sit at the Stag Table?"

"Please," Lizard said. "I have *some* dignity."

AT TABLE 2,

Lizard said, "Someone is following you, Thea."

"She's supposed to be. She's training."

"I just wanted to make sure you knew." Lizard ordered a draft Carta Blanca and a tequila shot. "And ask Meredith to come by my table, will you?"

COMING INTO THE SERVERS STATION,

clutching her margarita, Meredith said, "I can't believe it. I just found out Lizard asked for me, actually asked for me, and Dean wouldn't seat him in my section. He tips really well, even though his meals are comped. I've never worked at a place where a call customer couldn't get the waitress he wanted."

"I always gave him to you when I was the hostess," Robin II said.

"I know you did. I'm going to have to have a little talk with Dean."

"You can still take him if you want," Thea said.

"Forget it. I don't want to be running from section to section all night." The South 40 was separated from the rest of the dining room by the bar.

"Hey Meredith," Patsy said, "Want to help us with these napkins?"

"I just got a table. Besides, it's not my job. Section 3 folds napkins."

"Buzz just got these back from the laundromat," Robin I said. "It's kind of fun, folding them now, 'cause they're still warm." She held one against her cheek.

IN THE BAR,

Dean said to Ross, "I can't believe the way Meredith was just sitting there with that spray of baby's breath in her hair, just sitting there looking the way she looks."

"How did you keep from throwing yourself at the foot of her barstool and professing your love?"

"It was a struggle. Did you check out those jeans she was wearing?"

"Yeah, I saw them. There was a big grease spot over one knee."

"That's not what I mean. What I mean is, you could read the date on a dime in her back pocket."

"I can't imagine how she could even fit a dime in that back pocket."

"Come on, don't tell me you don't find her amazingly beautiful," Dean said.

Ross thought about that. "I would say I find her annoyingly pretty."

"You should have seen her at lunch yesterday. This blouse she was wearing, it looked like a giant Kleenex with a Peter Pan collar. Whenever she got between you and the light from the window, she didn't have any secrets. Her boobs... they appeared to be standing at attention. They practically clicked their heels together and gave a snappy salute, and shouted, 'Yes, *sir*, sergeant major, *sir*!'"

Ross tried to envision that. It didn't seem like typical behavior for breasts.

ARRIVING AT THE BAR WITH ROBIN II IN TOW,

Thea ordered drinks for their tables in the South 40: another Carta Blanca and tequila shot for Lizard, two margaritas, a Bloody Maria, and a vodka and Coke.

"Vodka and Coke? That sounds just awful. No one drinks vodka and Coke."

"It was the guy at the Stag Table," Robin II said. "The one in the red pants."

"Saturday night brings out the amateur drinkers," Dean said. "Almost as bad as New Year's Eve."

"Vodka and Coke is a horrible combination," Ross said.

"There are worse," Dean said. "One night when I was about twelve, my mom was working the night shift and my friend Eugene came over. We found a fifth of bourbon in the cabinet over the stove and decided to have a drink or two, only we didn't know how to go about it. First we tried drinking it right out of the bottle. We were bewildered by how awful it tasted. We couldn't believe that something adults liked so much had such a hideous taste. Then Eugene remembered that his parents mixed their booze with soft drinks. The problem was, the only soft drink we had in the house that night was that red cream soda."

"Oh God, bourbon and Big Red? Hands down, that's the worst drink I've ever heard of," Ross said.

"I don't know. Adam Clayton Powell drank scotch and milk. Milk to soothe his ulcer, scotch to calm his nerves."

"Still not as bad as bourbon and Big Red. Did you and Eugene get sick?"

"Did we get sick? Of course we got sick. We were puking up our toenails before we were halfway through the bourbon. There was pink vomit everywhere: on the sofa, inside the refrigerator, under the coffee table, in the clothes hamper, in the kitty-litter pan, even on the ceiling fan."

My mom came home and found us passed out and she was about to rush us to the hospital. She thought we were throwing up blood. Ever since then, I haven't been able to drink bourbon or even smell it without feeling a little queasy. Same for Big Red."

Robin II said, "Dean, there's a couple waiting at the host stand."

Dean went off to seat them.

"I think Dean liked it better when you were the hostess," Ross said to Robin II.

"It's kind of boring, just showing people where to sit. And standing at that host stand... I always felt like I should be giving a sermon or something. It felt like a pulpit."

"It used to be."

BRINGING A COUPLE OF STAR MARKET SACKS TO THE BAR,

Dean said, "Buzz is back from the store. Here are the limes. Only half of them are yours. Rafael needs limes, too."

"What else did we run out of?"

"Toilet paper. And... damn, I told him to get single ply, but he didn't."

Ross said, "Single-ply TP is something that shouldn't even exist."

"But it's cheap. Mama also wanted him to get queso Oaxaca and crema, but the best Buzz could come up with was mozzarella and sour cream. She wanted him to get some pork, too, but he forgot."

"Mama's gonna be mad," Ross said. Everyone dreaded making Mama mad. "What's with this jar of pigs' knuckles?"

"Buzz said someone put it in his cart when he wasn't looking."

"Well, maybe Mama can figure out something to do with them. Why are you looking at those bags that way?"

Dean had been staring dejectedly at the brown paper grocery sacks Buzz had brought back from the market.

"Amy always brought groceries home in bags just like these," he said sadly.

"She still does," Ross said.

BY THE PINBALL MACHINE IN THE BAR,

two men were playing Captain Fantastic. The pinball machine had just arrived that morning. Robin I asked them if they wanted margaritas. "They're twofers," Robin I told them. "Two for the price of one."

"Yes, we know what twofers are. And the word twofer was misspelled on your sign."

"I'll tell one of the owners. I'm sure we can fix it."

One of the men ordered a couple margaritas. The other one said he didn't like tequila. "Do you have Irish whiskey?"

"I think we do. I'll be right back."

Robin returned to the pinball machine and said that they had several types of Irish whiskey.

"Okay, fine, I'll have an Irish with a splash of soda."

"What kind do you want?"

The man thought for a minute. "Do you have Black Bush?"

"None of your business," Robin I said, and indignantly danced away.

AT TABLE 4,

Thea and Robin II's two new customers were examining the menu. They were both sitting on the same side of the table. Dean had given them each a menu, but they were both looking at the same one. The man said, "Are you staring at me?"

Thea denied it, and Robin II shook her head; she hadn't been staring either.

"It's all right, it happens. You're trying to place me, aren't you? I'll give you a hint... IceTravaganza."

Thea didn't understand.

"It's an ice show," Robin II explained. "It's in town now. He skates in it, I guess."

The skater's date said, "Figure skaters have the most unique faces. I don't mean just handsome or beautiful, although a lot of them are, I mean unique. I don't know why that should be, but it is. Pity that, in an ice show, so many of them have to wear costumes so you can't even see their faces."

"You can't say 'most unique.' Something's either unique or it isn't," Robin II said. A few seconds later, she said, "I'm sorry, that was rude. I'm an English teacher. I mean, I was an English teacher and it... it just kind of slipped out."

IN THE KITCHEN,

Cecily was ladling soup into bowls on Patsy's tray. Dean had pushed two tables together and seated a party of ten in Patsy's section, a Free University group called Singles Dine Out. Cecily garnished the soups with a dollop of sour cream and a sprig of cilantro and hooked a sliced wedge of lime on the rim of the bowls. "You want to take these for now, and I'll have the rest ready when you get back?"

"No, I can take all of them. I used to lump a dozen cups of coffee when I worked at the Muffin Man."

Mama told Patsy, "*Ten cuidado.*"

"That means 'Be careful,'" Cecily told Patsy.

BARRELING THROUGH THE SWINGING KITCHEN DOOR,

Robin I knocked Patsy on her butt, drenching her in sopa de lima.

"I'll get the first-aid kit," Buzz said. "Someone go get Thea. Maybe she..."

"It's cold soup, Buzz," Cecily said.

"Forget the first-aid kit. Get the mop," Dean said. Dean had come in from the front of the house when he'd heard the hubbub in the kitchen.

"Ross told me, quick like a bunny, go get more ice from the kitchen." Robin picked cilantro from Patsy's hair. Her hands were shaking. "I'm so sorry, Patsy, I didn't see you coming."

"Why do you think we had that little window put in the kitchen door?" Dean asked her.

Robin I looked as though she was about to start crying.

"Patsy's going to be okay, Robin," Cecily said. "So take it easy, hon."

Meredith said, "I was working at this place called Chez Fondue in Aspen and a waitress tripped and splashed a super-hot cheese fondue all over another waitress. Hit her right in the numbers, as they say on Monday Night Football. It was horrible. We couldn't get the cheese off her skin. It was like she'd been napalmed She finally ran out and threw herself in the snow until the ambulance got there."

"¡*Qué doloroso!*" Rafael said. He'd been listening from the kitchen.

Patsy got to her feet. "You sure you're okay, hon?" Cecily asked.

"I'm fine, but I can't work like this." Patsy looked as though a bomb full of soup had exploded near her.

"I have some clothes downstairs. There might be something you could wear." Buzz's belongings were scattered all over the office, giving it the air of a Gypsy camp.

"I'll see," Patsy said, although Patsy and Buzz were nowhere near the same size.

"Yeah, go see if you can find something," Dean said. "Right now you look like a walking menu."

CUTTING THROUGH THE BAR ON HER WAY TO THE SOUTH 40,

Thea hurried past three young guys drinking two-for-one margaritas and looking over the selections on the jukebox. Every time she passed the jukebox, it reminded her of the Qs' basement. One of the young men stopped her. "Hey, you're an art model, aren't you?" he asked her. "I remember seeing you."

Thea nodded. Knowing this young man had seen her posing made her feel nude now. "You're an art student?"

"No, I'm an engineering student. You came into our class by mistake once, remember?"

AT THE STAG TABLE,

Thea asked the party in the polyester red pants how his pollo pibil was.

Her question caught him in mid-bite and she had to wait for him to finish chewing. "Not bad. Why, do you want some?"

"No, thanks," she said. "I don't like Mexican food very much."

He laughed into his napkin. When he finished laughing, he said, "So what part of Holland are you from?"

"How do you know I'm from Holland?"

"I'm good at placing accents," he said. "You're either from Holland or from Flanders."

"I was born in Breda. That's a town in the south near..."

"I know where it is. Never been there, but I know where it is, and I know some things that happened there. During the Eighty Years War, the Spanish captured the city. The city only surrendered because the Spanish promised not to plunder it, but I guess the Spanish had their fingers crossed. There was some serious mayhem in your hometown after the Spanish showed up."

Thea remembered hearing about that in school.

"And that's where the Treaty of Breda was signed. It let you Dutch keep your monopoly on nutmeg, but it gave New York to the British. Wouldn't it be interesting if the Brits got nutmeg and you got to keep your colonies? If New York—New Amsterdam, I guess it would be—still belonged to you? Would be a lot cleaner, I'm guessing, and a lot safer."

"I didn't live in Breda long. We moved to Amsterdam when I was pretty young. How do you know so much about Breda? Most people here have never heard of it."

The customer took another bite. "I'm interested in war, you see," he said. "The Punic War, the Crusades, the Napoleonic Wars, the Civil War, the Franco-Prussian War, any war up to but not including World War I. War wasn't so interesting after that, I don't think. Do you?"

Both Thea and Robin II shook their heads, though neither of them considered any war very interesting.

"Never been in one. I was in the service, but not in a war. I was in Army Intelligence, although a lot of people think that's an oxymoron. Guess I'll never be in one now. You think they'd let me back in the Army?" He nudged Robin II.

"No, probably not," she said to him. The man in the red pants was somewhere in his late sixties.

Dean seated another customer at the Stag Table, a tall woman with a long neck and a pageboy haircut. She had the carriage of a cadet, which Thea thought the party in red pants might appreciate. As soon as she sat down, she pulled a hardcover notebook with pictures of peacocks on it from her purse, and looking neither left nor right, began writing furiously.

Thea wondered if there was any chance that the two of them might leave together. Not much of one, probably, but some curious pairings had been formed at the Stag Table. The man in the red pants was lonely, she could tell, and the woman with the peacock notebook might like older men. He could tell her stories of wars he'd never been in, and she could take notes. They could drink vodka and Cokes.

Thea wondered why all restaurants didn't have stag tables. It seemed like a good idea.

"So tell me," said the man in the red pants, "how do you like us Americans so far?"

Thea thought about it. "I like you Americans better than I thought I would."

CROOKING A FINGER,

the skater's date signaled Robin II. "We'll have two more of those big blue margaritas of yours."

"Sure. But, you know, happy hour is over, so they're full price now. You could order a pitcher of them. It would be cheaper." The skater and his date had already had a pair of blue margaritas apiece.

"Yes, but we don't want a pitcher," the skater explained patiently. "Not before we have our dinners."

"Wait, Randy, let's look at this logically," his date said to him. "I'm in no mood to stop drinking margaritas, are you? We might as well save ourselves a little money."

"Why do you always side with waitresses against me?" the skater asked.

BACK IN THE BAR,

Ross was finally hanging up the phone. "Hey, Ross, come on, we're getting slammed out here," Dean said. Thea and Robin II, Meredith, and Robin I were all in line, waiting to place drink orders, and there were customers on most of the barstools.

"Just checking up on things at home."

"How's your roomie?"

"Jeremy? He's fine."

"You know I didn't mean Jeremy."

"Amy's fine too. Nice to have her around—she hangs out with Jeremy sometimes when I'm at work."*Except when she's with Gus.* "What do you need?" he asked Thea.

Meredith said, "I need a piña, a pisco sour, a bullshot, and a frozen strawberry daiquiri, and I need them on the fly."

"I think Thea was here first," Ross said.

Thea needed a pitcher of blue margaritas and two palomas.

"What's a paloma?" Robin II asked.

"Tequila, grapefruit juice, lime, and soda. It's on the drink menu because, when I was tending bar down in Mexico, hardly anyone ordered margaritas. Everyone drank palomas."

"Sounds tart," Robin II said.

Meredith asked Thea and Robin II how they did with the guy at the Stag Table that they'd been talking to.

"A little more than a dollar," Robin II told her. All of his tip had been in coins. He'd also left a button and some lint.

"A buck? That's it? Well, what can you expect from a guy in tacky red pants and a white belt."

"I don't know. In my country, that's not such a bad tip," Thea said.

"Yeah, but I bet in your country, they don't pay waitrons a shitty dollar twenty-seven an hour in wages."

Ross got Thea's drinks. He slipped a note he'd written on a cocktail napkin on her tray when she wasn't looking.

He started on Meredith's drinks. He threw ice into the blender. Ross told Dean, "I had this dream the other night that everyone kept asking me for cocktails I'd never heard of, like a Bull Moose and a Frisco Fizz and a Green Grog."

"I've never heard of those either," Dean said. "What's in a Bull Moose?"

"No idea. As far as I know, there's no such drink."

"Those are great names for drinks. Tonight you should try to dream what goes into them."

Ross poured rum, pineapple juice, and cream of coconut into the blender and hit the LIQUEFY button. He poured Meredith's piña into a glass, floated some dark rum on the foam, and garnished it with a spear of pineapple and a cherry. He washed out the blender so he could start on her frozen daiquiri. "Blender drinks are a pain in the ass. The only thing worse is a layered drink, like a pousse café. You have to be a real prick to order one of those on a busy night, but one night at Maxwell's, when it was really busy, some guy did. Seven layers: crème de menthe, crème de violette, chartreuse, grenadine, I don't even remember what else. It took me about five minutes to make—I screwed up once and had to start over. So finally I set it down in front of him and said 'tah-dah!' We had these silver straws you're supposed to use to drink one layer at a time, but he used it to stir his drink and he downed it all in one gulp."

"Definitely a prick," Dean said.

Meredith was waiting impatiently. If she were a waitress in a cartoon, steam would be coming out of her ears.

Ross thought, *I hope Thea notices that note on the napkin. What if she gives it to a customer?*

IN THE SERVERS STATION, DRUMMING HER FINGERS IN THE PASS-THROUGH WINDOW,

Meredith asked Cecily again when her orders were going to be up.

Cecily rolled her eyes and inclined her head in Mama's direction, saying, in effect, "Don't ask me, ask her."

"Everything's in slo-mo tonight," Meredith said tensely.

"What's it like in the bar?" Keith asked her.

"Backed up. And Ross is pulling this typical macho-bartender routine, making drinks as fast or as slow as he feels like. Why do bartenders always have to be such control freaks?"

"I don't think Ross pretends to be slow," Keith said. "I think he really is a little slow. But when things get hectic, he doesn't get rattled, and he doesn't make any mistakes. When I worked with him at Maxwell's, he..."

"He wasn't an owner then. Being an owner makes it worse. Owners want total control."

"I've worked for worse people, believe me. The manager at Maxwell's, anytime you'd relax for even a minute, he'd say 'If you can lean, you can clean.'"

"That must be line one on the first page of *The Restaurant Manager's Handbook*," Meredith said. "Hey Cecie, could you please ask Mama when those orders are gonna be up? That table has been waiting for like fifteen minutes."

"*Ya viene*," Mama said.

"She said they're coming."

"Tell her, so's Christmas."

"*Ya viene Navidad tambien*," Cecily told Mama.

Mama sounded like she'd backed onto the grill when she heard that. She brandished her bean masher at Meredith and Cecily both.

"You know, we should all pitch in and get Mama some valium for Christmas," Keith said.

PASSING BY TABLE 4,

Thea stopped long enough to ask the skater and his friend how their dinners were.

"Excellent," his date said. "Don't you think so, Randy?"

The skater nodded. He was looking more than a little drunk. So was his date. They'd worked their way through most of their pitcher of margaritas. Thea hoped he didn't have to skate tonight.

His date used her napkin to remove a dab of sour cream from the skater's nose and some guacamole from his mustache. "You know, one thing I like about Mexican food is that you can't eat it and stay dignified at the same time. No one can. Not even figure skaters."

TAKING A SEAT AT THE BAR,

Lizard ordered another Carta Blanca and another shot of tequila. A Mexican boilermaker, he called it. Ross brought him the tequila and a salt shaker and a slice of lime and poured him a beer. "Gracias, hombre." Lizard licked salt from the back of his hand and sucked the lime and shot the tequila. Then he banged his hands on the bar.

"I don't think you're doing that right. You're supposed to bite the lime after you drink the tequila."

"You can do it any order that you like, Ross: lime, salt, tequila... tequila, salt, lime... salt, lime, tequila, whatever. There's no wrong way to drink tequila. As long as you slap your hands on the bar afterwards."

"How was dinner tonight?"

"So-so."

"Just so-so? Not four star?"

"The rice was dry."

"I'll mention that to the kitchen stiff."

"The mole sauce wasn't bad. Spicy, but not crazy spicy. The chocolate taste was a tad overpowering, though. The chicken was cooked pretty well this time. Sometimes Mama overcooks the chicken, and it gets mealy."

"You should be a restaurant critic. How about the service?"

"Uh... so-so."

"Sounds like you had a pretty mediocre dinner."

"Well, I know you and Thea are an item now, and I don't want to get her in trouble, so..."

"No, just tell me what you think. I can talk to Thea if she isn't doing something right."

"It's not that she's doing anything *wrong*. She brought me my drinks, she brought my dinner, she kept my water glass full, she asked me if everything was okay, and when I was finished, she took my plate away. It's just that she didn't have any dazzle."

"No dazzle?"

"No dazzle," Lizard said. "No sense of theater. Not much in the way of pizzazz. People don't go out to eat just because they're hungry; they also go out because they want to be entertained. There was this song a few years back, a song about Gypsy Rose Lee, you remember? It was called 'Let Me Entertain You,' That should be your waiters' theme song. 'Let Me Entertain You,'" Lizard sang. "'Let me make you smile. Let me do a few tricks, I'm very versatile.'" Of course, what do I know? I'm just a carpenter."

"No, you may have a point there, "Ross said. "I just don't think Thea is the Gypsy Rose Lee type."

Keith came up to the service area of the bar. Ross didn't think Keith was the Gypsy Rose Lee type either. He ordered a bloody Maria with extra horseradish and a sangarita. "I think that's pronounced sangria," Lizard said.

Ross said, "No, a sangarita is a margarita blended with sangria. I thought I'd invented it but turns out... someone else invented it first."

Robin I danced by. She had a new table in the bar. Lizard said, "Now you look at Robin. Watch the way she dances from table to table. Now that's dazzle for you. That's theater."

"She always dances when there's music on." Steely Dan was playing on the jukebox. "Sometimes she sings too. For some reason, that annoys Dean."

"Dean gets easily annoyed," Lizard said.

"He does when it comes to Robin. It especially irritates him when she wears sandals."

Lizard tapped his beer mug.

"¿Una cerveza más?" Ross asked him.

"Sí, claro, mi amigo, y otro tequila, por favor. What's the deal with sandals?"

"Well, she has sort of hairy toes. For a woman, I mean. Dean calls her Frodo sometimes."

"You could get her little hairnets for her toes," Lizard suggested.

Keith said, "Or we could chip in and get her electrolysis for Christmas."

COMING UP TO TABLE 4,

Thea was about to ask the couple if they wanted dessert or coffee. The woman had disappeared, however, and the skater was slumped down in his seat, a goofy grin on his face. Thea didn't think his face was all that unique. She wondered if his date had gone to the bathroom or wandered out onto Isabella Street in a drunken daze. Then the table he was sitting at shuddered.

LEADING A COUPLE FROM THE BAR TO SECTION 1,

Dean was struck by a heavy-duty urge, an insatiable need for a cigarette. Maybe it was the woman who was walking behind him that brought it on. She had long blonde hair, hair that came down to her hips. She was much younger than the man she was with. She reminded Dean of Sarah Jefferson. A lot. A number of times he wished he'd hired Sarah when she'd applied for a job here. She'd been pretty displeased that he hadn't. Dean blamed it on Ross, even though Ross hadn't been at the interview. He told her that Ross didn't think much of her résumé.

Sarah had called Ross and asked him why he didn't want to hire her. Ross blamed it on Dean.

Dean reached into his pocket and got out his ChapStick and gave his lips a quick coating. When he was putting it back in his pocket, he missed and it slid down his leg. He caught it in mid-stride with his right foot and drop kicked it across the South 40.

UNDER TABLE 3,

Dean was searching for his missing ChapStick after seating the woman with the long golden hair and her older companion. He'd booted it over by the tables against the wall. He got down on his knees and looked under Table 3. There was a woman under Table 4. God knows what she would do if he startled her. He decided to forget about his ChapStick and to go have a cigarette. Except it wouldn't look good if he was smoking at the host stand. If he went somewhere else, though, he just knew five more parties would come in and want to be seated. Having customers stacked up in the entrance way wouldn't look good either.

RETURNING TO THE BAR,

Dean asked, "Did you catch a look at that blonde with all the hair?"

"It was a fall," Lizard said. "I can spot a fall a mile away."

"What do you know about falls? I'd love to ask her out to my van to do a little coke."

"She's with someone," Ross said.

"So? He doesn't look like much. And he must be twenty years older than her."

"Maybe he drove her here in a Jaguar," Lizard said, "or maybe he can lick his eyebrows."

"Besides, you don't have a van," Ross said.

"You can use my truck if you want," Lizard said.

"Your truck? You kidding me? Your truck looks like something a migrant worker would drive. And it smells like maple syrup. What does maple syrup make you think of? Waffles, not sex. No, what I need is a customized van with a kickass paint job and skylights and crushed velvet carpeting crawling up the walls and a futon on the floor and state-of-the-art sound and..."

"You not only don't have a van, you don't have any coke, do you?"

"No," Dean said regretfully. "No van, no coke."

"I have some downstairs," Buzz said. Buzz had come into the bar on his break. "You want some?"

"How can you afford coke on what we pay you?" Dean asked him.

"Robin I gives it to me. Someone keeps leaving it for her as a tip, and she doesn't do coke."

COMING INTO BAÑO DE DAMAS,

Thea realized she wasn't alone. Robin II had been following her pretty closely, almost like a remora. "You don't have to follow me in here, Robin. Just out on the floor."

OUTSIDE BAÑO DE DAMAS,

Dean finally found Robin II. He was sweating and wishing he wasn't wearing a sweater tonight, but he couldn't walk around in a shirt with a huge salsa stain. Dean felt a little like he had at the Halloween party when he couldn't take off his bird costume because underneath, there was only his underwear. "I'm going to give you a table of your own, one of Keith's. He's swamped, everybody's swamped, and even the bar is full. Robin I is out in the weeds. And I've been serving margaritas out on Isabella Street."

"I don't know if I'm ready. I'd rather follow Thea for a while longer."

"It's time for some experiential training," Dean said. "Go out there and shine."

IN THE SERVERS STATION,

Meredith was using the adding machine, making sure that her calculations were correct. Cecily stuck her head through the pass-through window. "Okay, everyone, eighty-six the poc chuc. Eight-six anything with pork in it."

"Eighty-six? What's that mean, Meredith?" Robin II asked.

"What? Oh shit, I just added eighty-six in as the tax."

"I'm sorry," Robin II said. "I just wanted to know..."

"It means there isn't any more of something," Cecily said. "The pork's all gone."

"It's all right," Meredith said. "It's just that I've been waiting on this five-top at Table 12. I think they must be tourists from Des Moines or Utah or someplace. When they first came in, Mommy wanted a sassy seat for baby, and all we had was a high chair. Then when they were looking at the menu, Papa pulled out this little flashlight to see the prices better. And then they wanted to know if there was a kiddy menu. Then they joined hands and said grace out loud. And all of them—including Mom and Dad

—wanted refills on their Cokes. I just know that when I bring Papa the tab, he's going to use a slide rule or a pocket calculator to check my math, so I want to get it right."

"I think we *should* have a menu for kids," Robin I said. "One that has pictures they can color while they're waiting for their little dinners."

"We don't want to encourage people to bring kids," Meredith said. "We don't want to be known as a family restaurant. Families don't tip."

"Guess what, Meredith," Robin II said, "I'm going to get my own table. One of Keith's. I can't believe Dean thinks I'm trained, but..."

Meredith looked up from her calculations. "I could handle one more, if you don't want it."

"No, I think I'm going to take it. I have to start somewhere. I just wish we could have a more systematic program for training new servers. Maybe I could write a manual. Once I really know what's going on here, I mean," Robin II said.

"I think that's a good idea," Robin I said. "I didn't know what eighty-six meant either, when I first started waitressing. I didn't know what it meant to be out in the woods, either."

"Out in the weeds, Robin, not out in the woods," Meredith said.

"Really? Well, anyway, people just expect you to know everything."

"Yeah, you should suggest that manual to Ross," Meredith told Robin II. "He'll say, good idea, and write it down on a cocktail napkin, and that's the last you'll ever hear about it."

Dean poked his head around the corner. "I just seated you at Table 19, Robin," Dean told Robin II.

Robin II rolled her head, shrugged her shoulders, shook out her arms, and threw a couple of punches at an imaginary speed bag. "That's my cue," she said. "I'm on."

"Go for it, kid," Meredith said. "It's showtime."

She stepped out of the station then ducked right back in. "Oh Christ, I know one of those people. She was a student teacher at my school."

"That's what I like about being a waitress," Robin I said. "You see all kinds of people you know. My brother and his girlfriend were here last week, and the other day my boss Chris from next door came in. Except the main reason he came in was to complain about how the smell of Mexican cooking keeps seeping into Copenhagen Cream, so Dean comped him lunch."

"I don't like it at all," Robin II said. "I want to wait on people I've never seen before and that I'll never see again."

· · ·

AT TABLE 6,

the man appeared to be trying to memorize the menu. Thea was getting a little impatient; she had other tables to tend to. The man asked her what she recommended. When Thea had told the man in red pants that she didn't like Mexican food, he'd laughed. She decided not to say that anymore. "The pollo pibil is very popular this evening."

"Hmm, pity you don't have cochita pibil, but I suppose it's hard to roast a suckling pig on a spit in your kitchen. All right, I'll have the pollo pibil and... and I'm going to live dangerously—I'm also going to have the tacos escamoles. And my companion Denise here, will have the... How's the pavo relleno negro?"

"I'm sure it's good," Thea said.

"Okay, she'll have that and the poc chuc."

They must be really hungry, Thea thought. The portions Mama and Rafael dished out seemed enormous to Thea. She couldn't imagine anyone eating more than one of them. "You both want two entrées?"

"Yes, that's right. The dinners come with the sopa de lima, right, and... you like guacamole, don't you dear?"

"I dote on guacamole," the young woman with the long hair said.

IN BAÑO DE CABALLEROS,

Dean was using one of the black urinals. He hated to admit it, but Lizard had been right. After just a few weeks of being peed on, the drain and the backsplash were starting to turn a ghastly gray. A mesh screen had been placed over the drain, and as usual, several wads of gum were ensnared in it. *What is it about peeing that makes men want to spit their gum out?* There was a soggy cigarette butt in this one too.

He looked up and started reading the graffiti. A small blackboard was mounted above the urinals to discourage people from writing on the wall. BE ALERT! AMERICA NEEDS MORE LERTS! was the first graffito to appear on the blackboard this week. Dean thought America already had its fair share of lerts. and maybe more. Somewhat more recent was MY MOTHER MADE ME A HOMOSEXUAL and beneath it, in what looked like another person's handwriting, WOULD SHE MAKE ONE FOR ME? One that Dean had not seen until tonight was more enigmatic—IN THE SUNSET OF EMPIRE, EVEN SMALL MEN CAST GIANT SHADOWS. He was washing his hands and mulling that one when a bald guy came in. Dean remembered seating him; he'd come in with another bald guy. They'd wanted to sit at the Stag Table, but it was full, so Dean had put them in Section 4. He had a roll of fat at the back of his neck thick as a burrito. He looked to Dean like a real lert. A first-class, red-hot lert.

The paper towel dispenser was empty. Dean told himself to remind Buzz of that. The bald guy said, without turning around, "Hey bub, you work here?"

Dean tried to remember the last time anyone had greeted him as bub; it had been a good long while. Possibly no one ever had. Dean felt like saying, "Yeah, you fucking lert, I work here. As a matter of fact, I'm one of the owners of this joint. What of it, bub?"

Instead he dried his hands on his pants and admitted that he did work there.

The lert turned around and was zipping up. "What's that waitress's name then?"

"Which one?" Dean figured he meant Meredith. Male customers often asked about her.

"I dunno, the one in overalls and the Texarkana College T-shirt."

Patsy. Patsy in Buzz's clothes. "Her name is Tomato," Dean told the lert, "but we all call her Toots."

"Tomato, eh. That's a funny name."

"Why do you think we call her Toots?"

IN THE SERVERS STATION,

Robin II asked Meredith, "So, what should I do first? I'm nervous."

Meredith said, "First, calm down."

Robin II had traded her table with the student teacher for one of Meredith's tables. Dean was seating them now.

"Then go introduce yourself. Just say, 'I'm Robin, and I...'"

"I don't do that anymore," Keith said. "Not since this one night at Maxwell's when I went up to a table and I said, 'Hi, I'm Keith, and I'll be taking care of you tonight,' and one of the customers said, 'We don't care what your name is. We don't want to be your friends. We just want you to bring us our food."

"So... should I introduce myself or not?"

"Play it by ear," Meredith said. "Just be friendly and keep checking with them to make sure everything's all right. Be *extra* friendly to the people at that table because they're Dean's backers and their wives. They own a piece of this place."

"Oh, great. Why'd you have to tell me that? Now I'm really nervous."

Thea came into the station and hung the dupe on the order wheel in the pass-through window. "Ordering," she called. "Cecily, one of my customers wants an escamoles taco. What are escamoles?"

"Ant eggs," Cecily said.

"Yuck," Robin II, Meredith, and Keith said.

"Yuck indeed," Cecily said.

Rafael said something to Cecily in Spanish. "He says they're actually ant larvae."

"Are they good?"

"I don't know," Cecily said. "I've never been brave enough to try them."

AT TABLE 11,

Robin II put a glass of water in front of each of the three backers and their wives. But there were four women, so one of them must not have been a wife. The backers looked like the Beach Boys would look if the Beach Boys were wearing bespoke Italian suits.

A few minutes later, she came back and asked, "Is everything all right here?"

They looked a little puzzled. One of the women said, "Yes. Our ice waters are just fine. Can we order some real drinks now, please?"

BEHIND THE BAR,

Ross was looking at an ID card. "I can't accept this, Keith. Go see if she has a driver's license or a passport or something."

"I already asked. She doesn't drive, she told me, and she's never been out of the country."

"See if she has a credit card, or a student ID, or..."

"I asked. This is all she has."

"I don't think I should take this."

"She doesn't have any cash, either," Keith said. "Maybe you should talk to her."

"I can't leave the bar right now. Go get Dean."

Dean came over to the bar, eventually. "You have to talk to someone Keith's waiting on. She wants to pay by check, and the only ID she has is a card from the Europa Health Spa."

"Oh, Lord," Dean said. "Why me? I was just going to sit down and have a drink with the backers."

"I'll talk to her, if you want," Lizard said.

"Never mind," Dean said, "I guess I can see what... well, wait a minute, maybe that's not a bad idea. Sure, you talk to her, and if you do a good job, the house will give you a free drink. Won't even come off what we owe you."

"Cecie!" Ross said, "Where you been? Haven't seen you all night." Ross was always happy to see Cecily.

Cecily licked pico de gallo off the back of her hand. She was wearing Army boots and an apron over a denim dress. "It's been real zooey back in the kitchen tonight," she said, in her sweet baby-girl voice.

"Well, it's finally slowing down a little."

"Maybe out here. Still *muy loco* back there. Right now we're almost out of plates. Have you seen Buzz?"

"He's probably down in the office with a dollar bill stuck in his nose," Dean said.

"He was here not long ago," Ross said. "Why don't you take a quick break? Sit down for a minute and have your shift drink. You look like you could use it."

"Give her a Southern Comfort on the rocks," Dean said.

"I was going to have a beer. I like that Bohemia beer."

"It's pronounced Bo-HAY-mia," Dean said. "It's Mexican."

"Oh, I thought it was Czech. But I don't care how it's pronounced, as long as it's nice and cold."

"We think you look like someone who'd drink Southern Comfort, don't we Ross?"

Ross had never thought anything of the sort, but he didn't say so. "Maybe it's because you look a little like Janis Joplin. That was her drink."

"Do I? Oooh, I like that notion. In that case, set me up with a Southern Comfort. And a Bo-HAAAAAY-mia back."

"How have things been going in the back of the house tonight, Cecie?" Dean asked her. "We're kind of out of touch with the kitchen stiff. If you're having any problems, we'd like to know about them."

"I think I'm going to like this," Cecily said. "It's like liquid candy." She lifted her glass again, and when she set it down, there was only ice left in the glass. "Course, I'm not hard to please." She grabbed her beer to take back to the kitchen. "Any problems? Well, I like working with Rafael. I like Rafael a lot—he's a real pro. He did get mad at Buzz for putting his cast-iron skillets in the dishwasher, but Buzz gave him a couple of lines to snort when Mama wasn't looking, so now they're friends again. Mama, she's been riding me pretty hard. Like, she started in on me because there was this plate going out, and she found a hair on it, and she said it was mine. It was black and thick and it had a split end. No way that was my hair."

Dean mimed a machine-gun attack on the kitchen through the wall of the bar. "Eat hot lead, Mama." He pulled an imaginary pin with his teeth and lobbed an imaginary grenade through the imaginary hole he'd cut in the wall with imaginary automatic-weapon fire.

"You don't like her either, huh," Cecily said.

BACK AT TABLE 6,

the man had a bit of pollo pibil impaled on the end of his fork. He was staring at it, and then he looked around suspiciously, as if he expected someone to snatch it away. Finally, he took a small bite and chewed it for a long time. It reminded Thea of the way Vervloekt chewed when she gave him a dab of peanut butter. "Is everything okay here?' Thea asked him and his companion. They'd each finished less than half of their two entrées.

Nodding, the man chewed on. Thea took that to mean, everything's just fine.

"Muy yummy," said Denise, his long-haired companion.

"I'm sorry we ran out of the poc chuc," Thea said. "It's been a busy night."

"That's okay," Denise said. "The shrimp were real tasty, too. But then, everything's good with lots of garlic and butter. If you put garlic and butter on a cement block, it would taste pretty good, don't you think? Tell me, you must make a lot of guacamole here, huh?"

Thea agreed. They made guacamole here by the long ton.

"What do they do with the avocado seeds afterwards?"

Thea didn't know. "Throw them away, I guess."

"Do you think you could get me one? I've been wanting to try my hand at growing an avocado plant."

The man finally finished chewing his chicken and pushed his plate away. "And waitress, would you please bring us the dessert menu? Oh, and would you kindly ask the manager to drop by our table when he or she has a moment?"

IN THE SERVERS STATION,

one of the women from the backers' table came in and refilled her own glass with ice water. According to Dean, she was one of the backer's sister-in-law. "It's okay," the woman told Robin II. "I used to be a waitress myself."

Robin was horrified. After the woman had gone back to her table, she said to Meredith, "I should have filled up her glass for her. She could see I wasn't busy when she came back here. I hope Dean didn't see. Or Patsy. I've got one measly table, and I can't even..."

"You worry too much. But yeah, you should try to anticipate what customers need and get to them first. Keep their water glasses full, empty the ashtrays, scoop the crumbs off the table, clear the dishes, see if they need doggy bags. That's what waitressing is all about." Meredith was smoking vigorously, trying to finish her cigarette before she went back out on the floor.

"That same woman got up earlier and was straightening the pictures in the dining room. You know, the ones of Dean's girlfriend."

"Well, you can't anticipate everything," Meredith said, and took another quick drag on her cigarette. "Some of those photos were pretty cockamamie. And Dean told me the woman in the photos isn't his girl-friend anymore. Are you still feeling nervous?"

"Not quite so much anymore. I remembered something I used to tell my kids who were acting in the senior play. I'd tell them, when you get stage fright, don't think of the people in the audience as flesh-and-blood people. Think of them as cabbages. Row after row of cabbages."

"So you've been thinking of your customers as a bunch of cabbages?"

"Well, no, not exactly. I guess I think of them more as... as a bunch of quasi-cabbages. As cabbages that have to get good service."

"Quasi-cabbages. That something they teach you in graduate school?"

"Well, kind of. I did hear about cabbages in my drama coaching methods class."

Patsy came into the station. "Look at this check," she said. "There's a note on it for me." HEY TOOTS, ARE YOU ON THE DESSERT MENU? WANT A DATE AFTER WORK?

"Toots? Kind of insulting, isn't it? And archaic?" Robin II asked.

"I don't know," Meredith said. "I wouldn't mind being called Toots. By the right person. Are you going to go out with him, Patsy?"

"I don't date customers. Or people I work with. In fact, I don't date much at all. Too busy."

"That's right," Robin II said. "You're getting your BA"

"In philosophy," Meredith said, and smiled.

"One of the things I like about waitressing is that you're almost always busy on Saturday nights. You don't have to sit home feeling sorry for yourself because you don't have anything to do." Patsy grabbed the coffeepot and left. She usually came and went with a military snappiness, but tonight, wearing Buzz's clothes, she wasn't dashing around quite so smartly. She'd rolled the pants legs of his overalls up so she wouldn't keep stepping on the cuffs, but they kept slipping down.

"I think that's sad," Meredith said. "Patsy *likes* spending her Saturday nights at work. I was about to say something smartass to her, but now I feel like crying, that's so sad."

Robin II didn't say anything. She felt pretty much the same way as Patsy did. When she'd been a teacher, she'd spent a lot of her Saturday nights at home alone, grading papers or writing lesson plans. Saturday nights at ¿Por Que No? were more exciting than that. Quite a bit more exciting.

IN SECTION 3,

Robin II, looking alarmed, waited for Meredith to finish taking an order from Table 27, the table where the student teacher had been seated. Robin was rattled, so rattled she didn't much care if she was spotted waitressing. And anyway, the student teacher didn't seem to recognize her.

"What's up?" Meredith asked her.

"Dean sat down with the cabbages," Robin II said. "I mean with the backers. And he ordered a Spanish coffee. Isn't that the one you have to make at the table?"

"Yeah, it's the one where you light the rum."

"I don't know how to do that! I'll light the table cloth on fire, or my hair. Would you do it for me? Please Mer?"

"Umm, I'm kind of busy, and it takes a while to do but... yeah, okay. It's kind of fun because everybody in the dining room turns around to watch," Meredith said.

"I was hoping you'd say that. I'll split my tip from that table with you."

"You know, this once, it's gonna be a freebie. But you tell Ross the Boss to ease off on Meredith a little. He's been on my case lately. Tell him what a nice, kind waitron Meredith is."

"I'll tell him. I'll get Thea to tell him, too. He listens to what she has to say more than he listens to me."

"Okay, and would you crank down the lights in the dining room a little? It's better to make Spanish coffee when the lights are low."

• • •

AT THE QUASI-CABBAGES' TABLE,

Dean was chatting with the ex-waitress, the sister-in-law of one of his backers. "Who took all the photos?"

"I did," Dean said modestly.

"Oh, did you?" she said, grinning. "Then tell me, why are they all..."

Just then Meredith arrived at their table to make Dean's Spanish coffee. First, she balanced a glass cup rimmed in vanilla sugar on the tip of her rhinestone shoe, then poured in a stream of 151 rum from a great height, not a drop going astray. Then she flipped the cup off her toe and snatched it out of the air. She put the cup in front of Dean, struck a kitchen match on her zipper, and with a flourish, set the rum ablaze. She sprinkled nutmeg and cinnamon into the fiery cup, creating dramatic sparks. She doused the blaze with Kahlúa, added coffee, a dollop of whipped cream, and chocolate shavings. Everyone at the table and most of the customers in the restaurant clapped. The woman sitting next to Dean gave Meredith a standing ovation.

"Excuse me, Dean," Thea said. She'd come up from behind during Meredith's coffee performance. "One of my customers wants to talk to a manager."

"Could you ask Ross?"

"I did. He told me to ask you." Actually, Thea wouldn't have minded if neither of them wanted to go to Table 6. She was afraid that guy was going to complain about something. About her.

"What about Lizard? Did you ask him?"

"Lizard? But he..."

"Never mind. I was just kidding about Lizard." Dean didn't want to go anywhere. He wanted to sit and enjoy his Spanish Coffee. He'd already had to get up three or four times to seat late customers. Besides, the sister-in-law was resting her knee against his now. Not enough pressure to be a signal of any kind, not yet, but the possibility was lurking there. On the other hand, he didn't want to appear wishy-washy in front of the backers. "I'll be right back," he told them, "just as soon as I've taken care of this little matter."

LEANING OVER THE BAR,

Lizard said to Ross, "See, that's what I'm talking about."

"What do you mean?"

"Meredith. The way she made that coffee for Dean. Didn't you hear the clapping? Meredith is practically made out of dazzle."

"I think she's kind of a showboat," Ross said.

"Nothing wrong with a little showboating," Lizard said.

IN THE SHADOWLESS KITCHEN, BACK BY THE GARBAGE PAILS,

Thea was washing coffee grounds and eggshells off two avocado pits that she'd found. She put them in a ramekin to take to the woman at Table 6. "I can run those through the dishwasher if you want," Buzz offered.

Meredith burst through the kitchen door. "Forks!" she shouted. "I need forks!"

Buzz reached behind the dishwasher. He had a secret cache of silverware back there. "I keep these stashed back there in case of an emergency."

AT TABLE 6,

The man said to Dean, "I just wanted to tell you how impressed we are with our visit to ¿Por Qué No?."

Dean was relieved. This was turning out better than he thought it might. This he could deal with. He smiled down at the couple benevolently.

"Denise... this is Denise... she wanted to try your poc chuc, but you were out. You see, last week, we had a citrus-marinated pork dish at that new Filipino restaurant, Café Ylang-Ylang, and Denise here was quite smitten with the flavors."

"You know how it is," Dean said. He shrugged, the way he thought a real maître d' in a swanky restaurant might shrug. "It's a Saturday night."

"I understand, I completely understand," the man said. "In fact, I'd prefer never eating out on a Saturday evening. Alas, I have to, most Saturdays. Well, I hope you prosper. You've got your own little niche carved out here. There's not much else between Taco Bell and Quetzalcoatl's in town."

Dean made a face like an offended gibbon at the mention of Quetzalcoatl's. The man smiled. "I know exactly what you're implying," the man said. "Quetzalcoatl's is excellent, definitely, if you like high-end Mexican cuisine, and certainly I do, but the ambience is a bit... a bit gaudy for my taste, a bit overblown. I admire the fact that you've kept things simple here. No need to match them bauble for bauble. Of course, there's also Casa Rubio. That place is an up-and-comer. Your closest competitor, I should think."

This guy was proving to be something of a lert, Dean decided.

"Denise's *camarones* were quite tasty, even if it wasn't her first choice. I think I detected a hint of Yucatan orange and perhaps a pinch of allspice and cumin along with the garlic in the butter sauce. Am I correct?"

Dean smiled enigmatically, to indicate that house secrets must be preserved. He had no idea what Mama and Rafael used when they cooked shrimp. They wouldn't tell anyone what they used to cook anything.

"I would do something about the rice, if I were you. It's a bit on the dry side. And one other thing I wanted you to clarify for me—was the pollo pibil actually cooked in a firepit?"

Again, Dean was on shaky ground, but he didn't think Mama had been digging holes and lighting fires in the kitchen. At least, he hadn't noticed any.

"I mean, by definition, it's not really *pibil* if it isn't cooked in an earthen pit, is it?"

By this point, Dean was ready to slap this customer around a little. He wanted to say, "Listen, you smug little lert, I can call it pollo pibil or any goddamn thing I want to call it, because it's my restaurant, see?" For good measure, he might give a savage yank on Denise's hair to see if she really was wearing a fall. She might be stunning, and she might look like Sarah Jefferson, but she was running with some bad company.

FINALLY, IN THE BAR, AT CLOSING TIME,

Buzz was trying to find out what everyone wanted on their pizza.

"Anything," Ross said, "anything but anchovies."

"I like the little fishies. Get one pie with anchovies aboard." Dean was in an expansive mood. He'd just seen his backers to the door. They'd given him a thumbs-up assessment of the restaurant. They'd been bedazzled by Meredith's fiery theatrics with the Spanish coffee. And the sister-in-law had given him her phone number.

Meredith was sitting at the bar with a big pile of money in front of her. This had been her best night here so far. She was putting some of her money into smaller piles. Robin I touched Meredith's hair. "Where'd you get your hair permed, Meredith? I've been thinking about getting a perm myself."

"This isn't a perm. My hair's just like this."

"Really? You're so lucky!"

"I used to think so. Now everyone has curls and more curls. I might even start straightening mine. Here, Buzz." She handed him one of the small piles of cash. "That's your share, and would you give this to the rest of the kitchen stiff? And... I don't have to tip you, do I, Dean?"

"Don't you always tip the host?"

"Sure, if it's Robin II or someone like that, but you're an owner. It's like at a hair salon. You tip a stylist who works there, but if the owner of the place cuts your hair, you don't."

"I've never tipped anyone who gave me a haircut. I didn't know I was supposed to."

"You'd better. If you don't, next time you go back, they'll butcher your hair."

"Oh. That might be why my stylist got so huffy the other day."

"Here's your free drink, Lizard." Ross set a tequila sour on the bar in front of him. "Thanks for helping out." Lizard was sitting at the bar next to Meredith, his stool as close to hers as feasible.

"Oh yeah, how did that thing with the ID card turn out?" Dean asked him.

"It wasn't so bad. I walked up to her and I said, '*Look*, lady!' It was kind of fun."

"And?"

"And then I took her check."

"You took her check? On a card from the Europa Health Spa?"

"It wasn't like she was trying to pay with beaver pelts. And what was I supposed to do after saying '*Look*, lady!' to her? If her check bounces, you can take it out of what you owe me. You know, Ross, I think this is the first time in my life I've ever had a drink on the house."

"You going to drink it or take it home and have it bronzed?" Dean asked him.

"Can I have my shift drink now?" Meredith asked Ross.

"You already had yours," Ross pointed out.

"Oh, make her another one," Dean said. "Meredith handled more tables tonight than anyone else.

Anyone except Robin I. I think it was a good idea, putting that sign in the window. The bar's never been so busy."

Ross said, "We have to get Buzz to change the sign, though, so it reads TWOFER *HOUSE* MARGS instead of just TWOFER MARGS. Some guy came in and ordered a couple of margaritas with Herradura tequila and with Grand Marnier instead of house triple sec."

"You're kidding," Dean said. "What did you do?"

"I mixed his drinks with José Cuervo and Hiram Walker behind the bar where he couldn't see me. He couldn't tell the difference."

Robin II said, "When Buzz changes the sign, you should ask him to spell twofers correctly."

Thea walked into the bar. Her last table had paid up. Dean said, "Thea, I hope I didn't blow it for you with that deuce at Table 6. That guy was kind of aggravating. They didn't stiff you, did they?"

"Stiff me?"

"Did he leave you a tip at all?"

"No, he didn't stiff me, he left me a good tip. And the woman who was with him left me another tip, folded up in her napkin. For the avocado seeds, I guess."

"Well, anyway, sorry. Ross, your girlfriend is sitting here without a drink in front of her."

"No, thanks. I don't really want one." Thea was trying to decide how she felt, being identified as Ross's girlfriend. She decided she didn't mind. In fact, she decided that she liked the way it sounded.

"Your free drink is part of your benefits package. In fact, right now it *is* your benefits package. Besides, around here, we don't trust people who don't drink, do we Ross?"

Thea wanted to be trusted. "I'll have a white wine. A small one."

Robin I said to Thea, "If you don't like the taste, get Ross to squirt a little ginger ale in the wine. And put some ice in it. That's what they call a wine spitter. Sometimes I have one of those for my shift drink."

"Wine spritzer," Ross said.

Dean took one of Meredith's cigarettes from her pack on the bar. He looked around for one of the matchbooks that had the ¿Por Qué No? logo on it, but Meredith said, "I got it." She lit his cigarette with one of her kitchen matches.

Patsy said to Dean, "You know that cigarette you're smoking is a Virginia Slim, right? They're chick cigarettes."

Dean said, "I've come a long way, baby."

"Dean," Ross said, "I'm disappointed in you. You went all evening without smoking, and..."

"The ChapStick just wasn't delivering the goods." Dean had slathered so much ChapStick on his lips that they seemed to be spackled. "I needed something to kill that cold, sick feeling in my gut."

"If you could have held out just a little longer, you could have killed it with pizza."

"Or coke," Buzz said. One of Robin I's customers had again tipped her with cocaine, this time in a Sucrets box, and she'd given it to Buzz. "Okay, I'm about to call Hot to Trot," Buzz said. "What's the consensus? Three large pizzas with the works?"

"Two of them with the works minus anchovies," Ross said. "Dean, you know your sweater is on inside out?"

"Is it? Oh God, you're right, it is! I thought it felt funny, but I figured that was just because it was new. I bet all the backers noticed. Why didn't someone tell me?"

"I didn't notice," Ross said, "until just now."

"I did," Robin I said, "but I thought you wanted it that way."

"Me, too," Lizard said, "I thought it was some new fashion."

Ross leaned over the bar when he gave Thea her wine. "Did you get my message?"

"Your message?"

The message I wrote on a napkin. Oh, no, I hope you didn't..."

"I'm kidding, Ross. I got your message."

"So what do you think?"

"Sure," Thea said, "I'll spend the night with you. I'd love to spend the night with you."

Dean went to reverse his sweater. On his way out of the bar, he told Buzz to make sure the pizza was delivered to the kitchen door. There were still a few customers lingering in the dining room. "It never looks good when the staff sends out for dinner."

TILL THE END OF THE INTERNAL COMBUSTION AGE

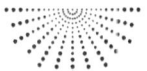

LAUREL WAS KNOCKING ON THE DOOR OF HER OWN CABIN. NOT KNOCKING, really, because her hands were full, but kicking. Finally, she heard someone coming, someone slow and unspeakably stiff. It sounded as if her oak dresser was on its way to answer the door. It made her think of a dream she'd had, about a city where the furniture was alive.

The door opened. Laurel was carrying two boxes of unsold jewelry and couldn't see around them into the cabin. She braced herself for Ollie's onslaught. When she went away for a weekend, Ollie would launch himself at her like a friendly torpedo when she came home. His tail would wag so fast that it would turn into a golden blur.

No onslaught. No torpedo. No blur. No Ollie. The pain came back.

Jay didn't greet her as brightly as Ollie would have. "You said you'd be back early this afternoon."

He was wearing light-blue silk pajamas and a black neck brace. Before Jay, she'd never been with a man who wore pajamas. Or a neck brace.

Laurel had been living alone for quite a while before Jay had come to stay, but she still remembered how important entrances are. A bad entrance could render an entire evening ruined beyond redemption. She made an effort to bury her own foul mood. She put the box down and kissed Jay on the nose. Jay sat down heavily in the chair by the wood stove. His posture was abnormally good because much of his body was in plaster casts. He'd had to slit the sleeve and the pant leg of his pajamas to accommodate the casts.

"I was having a little trouble with the truck," she told him.

"You should get a new truck."

"I'm not getting rid of that truck," she snapped. Jay was pushing his luck by criticizing the U.S. Grape. "I'm not getting rid of that truck until the end of the internal combustion age."

"That might not be so far off," Jay said, "the way gas prices keep going up. What went wrong this time?"

"Fuel pump, I think." She rubbed her forehead. She wasn't going to let him get her down. "It kept losing power on the way up to School's Out. It sounded like the engine had the hiccups. I'll get Matt to look at it tomorrow. How come you're watching Walt Disney?"

"I wasn't. I was watching football. Then I fell asleep."

"Big boys don't go to sleep until it's late."

"There wasn't anything to do, and the Demerol makes me sleepy."

"You could have come with me to the crafts fair."

He tapped on his leg. It sounded like he was tapping on sheet rock.

"I don't care, you still could have come."

"How much fun is Ogden, Utah anyway?"

"Last night, I went for a walk; you never saw as many Christmas lights as they have there. They take Christmas seriously in Ogden. They have this whole life-size Christmas village. With reindeer."

"Sounds exciting. But I'm in no shape to travel."

Actually, Laurel was glad Jay hadn't come with her. The heater in her hotel room didn't work well and he would have complained constantly about the cold. Last night, she'd wrapped herself in the bedspread and called Ross at his bar. He was too busy to talk to her. She could hear, in the background, the buzz of conversation and the clinking of glass. She heard a woman ask for two margaritas and she heard someone laugh. There was music—Steely Dan, maybe. It sounded like a much more exciting place to be on a Saturday night than a frigid hotel room in Ogden, Utah.

"Can I have one of your Demerol?" she asked Jay.

"I'm almost out. You don't need one."

"No, but I'd like one. You can always get more." She got up and took a pill from the bottle on the kitchen counter. She figured that, in a pinch, she could always outrun him.

"Don't do it," Jay said. "Just don't do it. You'll be sorry."

"You're just like a real blue jay—fuss, fuss, fuss." Once the pill had been safely swallowed, she came and sat on his lap.

"I hate you sometimes," Jay said, "and my fucking back itches."

"My poor little buckaroo," she said, scratching his back. "What did you do all day?"

"Nothing. Put your records in alphabetical order."

"Why do they have to be in alphabetical order?"

"When you want to hear a certain song, you don't want to page through every album in that orange crate. And you know, some of your albums, the dust covers are missing. You're just begging for scratches."

"I don't care. They're my albums."

"Oh, and I fixed the toaster." Jay was good at fixing things. He'd fixed the Mexican clock on the mantle that had never worked, and he'd fixed the electric water pump for the cabin. And then he decided to install an antenna on the roof of her cabin.

"It's still blurry," Laurel shouted out the window. Then she hurried back to the new television set. It was supposedly an early Christmas gift to her from Jay, but she knew he'd bought it because he liked to sit around in his silk pajamas and watch TV—especially football. It had a huge nineteen-inch screen and a built-in record player and radio. Jay had rearranged all her furniture to accommodate it in her living room.

"How about now?"

Back to the window: "A little clearer."

"Now?"

"Now it looks like it's snowing on the screen," she shouted up to him. "Snowing hard. A blizzard. Hang on, let me go check again. Still snowing. No, wait, now it's nice and clear."

Just then she heard a roar like an avalanche and she saw a dark shape plummet past the window in a shower of snow. Jay had slipped on the snowy roof and tumbled into the woodpile. He'd wrenched his neck and broken his right arm, a couple of ribs, and his right femur. Jay was handy but not surefooted.

"What else? Rearranging records and fixing a toaster couldn't have taken all day."

"Watched football. And now I don't even know if the Bears won. I fell asleep."

"They won—I heard it on the radio."

"Well, they oughta just give up and go home if they can't beat Tampa Bay—the Bucs haven't won a game ever. Not ever."

"You should have gone down and spent a little time with Cap. He's lonely."

"Cap bores me. All he talks about is Poppy and his pigs," Jay said. "You have to get off my lap. You're crushing me."

She stood up and pulled on his hand. "You have to get up, too, cowboy. You've been lazing round all day. Let's go for a walk."

"Right."

"Come on, there's only a little snow, and the moon is almost full. Everything's all silver and black. You can use your crutches."

"Right." Jay sneezed. "God, my ribs hurt when I sneeze."

"All right, fine. It's bedtime, I guess." Laurel wasn't sure she wanted to have sex right now, but at least they wouldn't have to talk.

"How was that? Did you like that okay?" Jay asked her.

"Uh-huh."

Laurel had gone from the bed to the kitchen, where she poured Stolichnaya over ice, and then to the chair by the front window.

"You don't sound very enthusiastic." Jay was never sure with Laurel. She certainly acted like she enjoyed it during the event itself. Sometimes she seemed to enjoy it a little too much, like someone doing a commercial for intercourse. But afterwards, she often acted like she regretted doing it at all. "You didn't hurt yourself, did you? You were hitting pretty hard against my cast."

The doctor had called the cast on Jay's leg a long-leg cast. If the break had been a bit higher on his thigh, he would have had to be fitted with a full-body cast.

"I have to do it hard," Laurel said. "Were you afraid I was going to crack the plaster?"

"I was afraid you were going to hurt yourself."

"I had a dream last night," Laurel said, "that I was having sex standing up."

"That was your dream? That's all there was to it? That doesn't come up to your standard for bizarre dreams."

"Well, there was more. In the dream, I was a Pepsi machine." Laurel got up to put a few more pieces of wood in the stove. She looked orange in the light of the fire. "You used all that wood I split on Thursday?"

"I was cold. I could get pneumonia easily in this condition."

"You don't have to explain." She closed the stove. "I just thought it was a lot of wood."

"I would have split some myself if I were able-bodied."

"You must be a lousy lawyer. You sound so insincere."

"I'm a brilliant lawyer. Come back to bed, why don't you?"

"I don't feel like it." There was nothing Laurel could do; there was no way now she could squelch the mood she'd been fighting for most of the weekend. She wished she could snuggle with Ollie. "I feel like sitting here. That's it."

"I thought it was only men who got depressed after sex. This is a hell of an atmosphere for an invalid. Cap's depressed, you're depressed, everyone's depressed. You haven't even put up a Christmas tree."

"Why do you care, you're Jewish. Besides, what's the point? Jeremy only comes out every other year for Christmas, and he was here last year."

"The crafts show you went to, how was it?"

"I was wondering if you were ever going to ask me about that," Laurel said. "It sucked. Most of the people who run these shows, they're basically crooks. They get rent from each booth and then they charge customers to get in. They promise you they'll have such-and-such a number of people there, and then there aren't half that many. And they give the best booths to people they know. In this case, they gave the best locations to Mormons and put me in a corner by the restrooms."

"Maybe that's what we should do. Put on crafts fairs."

"And they're supposed to screen the craftsmen. They couldn't have turned anyone down for this show. There were paintings of pink poodles on black velvet and Christmas trees made out of tomato cages and models of the LDS temple in Salt Lake City made out of popsicle sticks."

"So you didn't make a bundle—that's why you're mad?"

"Actually, I didn't do too bad. Compared to all that amateur crap, my stuff looked pretty good. It's a good thing, too; if I can't make money right before Christmas, then I can't make any money at all."

Laurel got up and poured herself more Stoli. "That's a hefty amount of vodka," Jay said.

"Utah has weird liquor laws. You have to fill out an application and join a private club before you can go into a bar. And you have to order food before you can order a drink. And then, for some weird reason, there's this partition made of frosted glass between you and the bartender so you can't see the drinks being made. They call it the Zion Curtain."

"So after one weekend of slightly curtailed drinking, you have to pour yourself a pint or so of Russian vodka?"

"You know, it's more fun drinking with a bunch of Mormons than it is with you." Laurel lapsed back into her preoccupation.

"So," Jay said, in his reasonable tone of voice, "just what *is* your problem?"

"Nothing. Nothing new. The Poached Egg Syndrome, that's all."

The Poached Egg Syndrome was Laurel's way of referring to her feelings of futility and ineptitude. She predicted her tombstone would read, SHE POACHED A MEAN EGG.

"I don't understand why you feel that way," Jay said. "You make your own jewelry, you run your own business, and you're good at it."

"You know this building, this cabin, back when this place was a summer camp, it was the arts and crafts cottage. There were Methodist campers here making jewelry twenty years ago. And it probably looked better than mine."

"I did crafts at summer camp. I made a birdhouse that fell apart when a bird first landed on it. I made this nifty bracelet out of... what do you call that plastic stuff? Blimp? Pimp? Gimp? I gave it to my mom and she never once wore it. That's not exactly the same as making electronic jewelry," Jay said. "I wish you'd come back to bed," Jay said. He meant it. He was beginning to find this depressed Laurel pretty interesting.

Laurel kept looking out the window. It was, as she had said, a landscape in silver and black. She could see the snowy road that wound past School's Out and she thought about driving home tonight and about seeing the flock of guinea fowl. It made her nervous to drive past the guineas, ever since she'd run over one of them. She always thought that they stared accusingly at her as she drove past. Then she thought about Ollie, and how he'd died at almost the same spot on the Hendrix Highway as she had run over that guinea fowl. Was there a karmic connection?

"I have to go to the bathroom," he told her. "I need you to help me out of bed."

"No, you don't, you can do it yourself," she said, but she gave him her hand. He pulled her down on top of her.

"Are you okay?" he asked her. She'd cracked her chin on his arm cast.

"You're an asshole," she said to him. She rubbed her chin.

"I think you're smoking too much grass," Jay said. "That's one of your problems. I threw your stash down the toilet."

"You did what?"

"You heard me, I think."

"Oh well, that was just Texas ditch weed. The good stuff was with me in the Grape."

"And you're drinking too much. Do you want to wake up in a dozen years after passing out on the floor in a puddle of vomit and realize this is the day Jeremy is graduating from college?"

"Fuck off. You don't know anything about what I want to do with the rest of my life, Jack." *Neither do I*, Laurel thought. "And I never get sick from drinking. I know a trick."

"I hate when you call me Jack," Jay said. "Another one of your problems, maybe your main problem, is this place. I think School's Out is depressing. I know it's depressing me. I mean, it was fine back in its heyday, but now, you're never going to get anywhere from here. Move to Denver. Move anywhere. Come back to Chicago with me."

"When *are* you planning to go back to Chicago? How long can you stay away from your lawyering?"

It took Jay a while to respond. "Right before I came out here, I had a problem, sort of a disagreement with one of the senior partners of my firm and then, when I called her to say I needed some time off... right after I fell off the roof, well... well, I guess I'm not welcome back to that particular position. But I'll end up at a better firm anyway."

Laurel said, "I don't even know if I am depressed, exactly. But if I am, it's because of the way you and I relate. When Ross lived here—I know you don't like to hear about Ross, but be a big boy—Ross and I were always thinking up these weird plans, and we were always getting ready to go places together. We had fun. We were like kids."

"You weren't *like* kids, you *were* kids."

"That's right, we were kids. We were clever. We were crazy. We'd scheme. We were always scheming." Laurel wondered if she was accurately remembering how she and Ross were together. "Of course, Ross wasn't that great at actually *doing* things. But he was a great schemer."

"Let's scheme, then," Jay said.

"What?"

"Scheming's something I'm good at too, only I know how to follow through. Let's scheme together, you and me."

WONDERLAND

DORKY DAN WAS STAKING OUT HIS DAUGHTER'S APARTMENT BUILDING. HE'D called his secretary and told her that he wouldn't be in until the afternoon, and he'd driven down to the North End. He saw his old Pinto and parked nearby. He noticed that she'd scratched off the NIXON, NOW MORE THAN EVER bumper sticker, or most of it.

He'd been sitting in the Café Firenze for over an hour now, keeping watch on Amy's front door, which was right across Hanover Street from the café. Whenever he ordered coffee, the waiter brought him tiny cups of espresso. It was the first time he'd ever tasted espresso. Too strong; he preferred his wife's coffee.

Dan couldn't explain what had drawn him to the North End this particular morning, except that he woke up with the suspicion that there was something wrong going on with Amy. Not that she was in danger, exactly—just that something was wrong. And Dan didn't believe that premonitions—especially premonitions about his twin daughters—should go unheeded. He sometimes had hunches that Amy's twin, Claire, faced dire troubles, but going to Ghana to check on her was beyond his abilities.

It didn't matter to Dan that he rarely had an accurate premonition.

At a little past ten, Chewy came out of the building across the street, books under one arm. Chewy was one of the twisted. Dan was convinced that there were forces abroad these days—he pictured them as tiny black tornados—that got hold of people and left them moral wrecks. He remembered Chewy as a child, before Dan had moved his family from South

Boston to Lexington. He remembered him as Charlie, before he got that ridiculous nickname, before he started shaving his head. He remembered Gus, his Dad. Chewy was a nice, polite, quiet kid back then, and Amy and Claire loved playing with him. But somehow, he'd become twisted.

With his third demitasse of espresso in front of him, Dan wondered if Amy had strayed too close to one of these little whirlwinds. Right out of high school, she and her sister moved into that hellhole of an apartment on Hemenway Street and were basically out on the streets begging. After they'd moved home, they started taking random classes at Tufts, although they seemed to spend more time at demonstrations than in the classroom. He'd seen a photo of them once, both of them giving the finger to a campus cop. Then Amy took some kind of women's lib class and there was one guy taking that class too, for some reason—well, Dan could guess why—and that guy was Dean. Dean was the shadiest whirlwind around. After years of living with that nightmare, she moved in with Dean's tall friend and his son. And now, here she was living in the North End in the same building as Chewy.

Dan had to go to the bathroom. He asked the kid behind the counter, the one who'd been making his espressos on that loud, hissing machine, to keep watch for him. When Dan came back to his table, the kid said that a redhead—a foxy redhead, he said—had come out of the building across the street and turned to the left. Dan paid for his coffees, left the kid a quarter, and rushed out of the café.

If she was on her way to meet Dean, he was taking back the Pinto, by God, and she could walk to Mattapan. A deal was a deal.

So far, though, no sign of Dean. Amy was going shop to shop, buying food. It wasn't hard to tail her. She was the only one in the neighborhood with hair the color of polished copper. When she turned down Prince Street, he followed her, still on the other side of the street.

Suddenly, she backtracked and went into a store she'd already passed. Dan had to quickly duck into a butcher shop on his side of the street. His reflexes seemed unusually good to him, but that might have been the effect of strong coffee.

The man behind the counter asked him what he wanted. Dan didn't really want anything. There were sausages of all sizes. There were plucked chickens and skinned rabbits that made his stomach churn. There was the smell of fresh blood.

He'd heard that the people who owned these little shops in the North End were connected with the Mafia. He found it hard to believe, though, that this scrawny old butcher was or ever had been a mobster.

When Amy came out of the shop carrying a baguette over her shoulder like a rifle, Dan noticed something. He wasn't the only one watching her. Nearly every man on the street turned and their eyes followed her. A taxi driver slowed down for a better view. Even the unlikely grandpa in the butcher shop gave her the eye.

∾

Thea got off the subway at Wonderland, the last stop on the Blue Line, and crossed a four-lane highway on a footbridge. For a long time, she'd wanted to be walking alone on a beach. When she lived in Amsterdam, she would take a train to Zandvoort and walk the beach there. Not in summer, when it was crowded, but on gray, blustery days like this.

A crowd of seagulls immediately began flying around her. There were a few other people on the beach, but there weren't any birds circling them. She wondered why the seagulls were finding her so fascinating. There was one gull in particular that kept hovering almost right in front of her. It had a bland face and insipid eyes.

A child was coming toward her. His face was the color of lard, and his cheeks were crisscrossed with blue veins. His expression reminded Thea of the seagull's. He was wearing a T-shirt that said I'M A LI'L DEVIL. He looked like he was about to say something to her, but an old woman called, "Storm! Storm, you come here!" Storm ran up the beach on stiff legs.

Ross had told her that there had once been a big amusement park at Wonderland. He said his Aunt Sophie and her rich husband Earl had met here, at one of the dance halls. Now there was just the dog-racing track.

The dogs must not be running now; the huge parking lot was nearly empty. There were still a few scattered remnants of the amusement park, though: a few places that offered carnival games: Pokerino, Skee-Ball, Fascination; the rusty remnants of a Ferris wheel behind a chain-link fence; a few food stands. Except for a small crowd at Kelley's Roast Beef, no one was all that interested in lunch on Revere Beach today.

The wind from the Atlantic kicked up the sand and blew foam from the surf. Someone had built a sandcastle, but the wind made it look like a castle that had been besieged and stormed years before. The sky was dark and cold and a little rainy; the air felt clammy. Thea turned up the collar of her raincoat.

She came to a gazebo on the beach, with concrete benches under it. THE OLDEST PUBLIC BEACH IN AMERICA, a sign said. It felt like the oldest beach in the world. A couple was sitting on one of the benches. The woman—a girl, really, not more than about fifteen—had her hand on the man's knee. A tattoo said, I'M IN LOVE WITH A CHILEAN BOY JUAN CARLOS. Thea wanted to sit down to empty the sand from her shoes, but the couple radiated the notion that they didn't want anyone to share their gazebo.

That's quite a commitment, to have someone's name tattooed on your arm. Especially at fifteen. Maybe it wasn't a permanent tattoo. Or maybe only the I'M IN LOVE WITH was permanent. At fifteen, the girl figured she'd be in love with *someone* the rest of her life and could fill in the blank as circumstances changed.

Not far from the gazebo, across the road, there was another subway stop, the Revere Beach stop. Whatever it was that she'd hoped might happen on her beach walk hadn't happened. She didn't have time to walk back the way that she'd come to give it another try. And she couldn't come back tomorrow. By tomorrow, she'd be hundreds of miles away from here.

She took one last look at the Atlantic. It stretched off to the east, gray and sullen and endless.

The rain was turning to sleet.

When she crossed the road, the gulls sounded sad to see her go. *But gulls always sound sad.*

∼

Amy answered the door with an ice pick in her hand. "Daddy!"

He asked her about the ice pick.

"I've been defrosting the freezer. There's so much ice, I couldn't even fit one ice cube tray in there. It's like chipping away at a glacier."

"You shouldn't be using an ice pick. You'll poke a hole into one of those tubes and let the gas out. That gas is dangerous. Why don't you use your blow-dryer?"

She gave him a hug, careful not to poke a hole in him. "How come you're here? Is Mom okay?"

"Your mother's fine. I was just in the neighborhood, that's all. On business. I thought you might want to have lunch. Maybe at an Italian place."

"This is Little Italy—all the restaurants down here are Italian places. I'd like to, Daddy, but I can't today. I'm having a friend over for lunch." She saw a shadow of suspicion cloud his face. "A girlfriend."

"Well... you know there are some cans of paint out here? You want me to bring them in?"

"That's okay, I'll get them later. My landlord said it was okay to paint as long as he didn't have to pay a painter. He's even giving me the paint." The current color of the walls was a nauseating green.

"Well... " He handed her a brown paper package. "I bought you a couple pork chops at the butcher shop down the street. For your dinner." He'd watched as the butcher cut them from a pork loin.

"Oh, Daddy, you know I don't..."

"That's right. I forgot. Here, I'll take them home to your mother then."

"I don't know how you could even stand to go in that shop, with all that blood and yuck."

"What's that voice?" her father asked. There was a strange combination of weird music and narration coming from the other room.

"Just a record."

"I can tell it's a record, but what..."

"It's a meditation record," she said, as if admitting that she was mentally ill. "I've had it for years."

Dan heard a voice from the stereo saying, "Imagine you are very small. Try to shrink yourself. You can do it, go ahead. It's difficult, but it's very simple. You are now as tiny as a grain of sand. No, you're smaller than that, you're small as the point of a needle, as a mote of dust, as..."

"How 'bout next week? Could we have lunch then?" Amy asked him. "I'll take *you* to lunch, how 'bout that?"

"Well, we'll see. How's that school bus thing going?"

"Oh, it's okay. I'm getting better at it. But I'm looking for another job."

"Good. I never liked the idea of you being involved in that busing stuff. So everything's all right? You're happy? Not having any problems?"

"No problems, Dad, honest." She gave him another hug.

"... small as an atom," the voice from the other room said. Whoever was speaking had a very calm voice. "You think you can't get smaller, perhaps, but you can. Now you are the size of a particle, a subatomic particle. Forces are whirling you around the nucleus. Whirl with them. You are now exactly the same size as God. Can you see him? He's there. You can if you try. It's difficult, but it's very simple."

On his way down the stairs, Dan encountered a pair of older women on the second floor. There was something about the way they looked at him that made him feel guilty, as if he were coming from a bordello. Not that he'd ever been to a bordello.

Walking back to his car, he felt somewhat relieved but still disquieted. Why hadn't she asked him in? Why didn't she want to have lunch with him until next week? Why was she listening to a record about gods the size of atoms?

He'd been bothered by the way everyone had looked at Amy when she'd come out of the bakery. It was more than her conspicuous hair color. She and Claire were identical twins, but for some reason, men didn't ogle Claire the way they did Amy. Amy emitted some sort of magnetism. Even though he was her father, he knew it was there, he was not immune, not entirely immune to it himself. He remembered one morning when, after a strange and sleepless night, there had been that incident by the clothes dryer.

Dan was driving home from Maine. He was doing 70, fifteen over the speed limit, and there was no traffic to contend with, but still, the trip felt endless. After more than three hours of driving, he was only on 495, skirting Portland.

He'd never felt this kind of lunatic urgency before. It might have been the smutty jokes he and his friends had told after dinner, except they always told racy jokes in the cabin at night. Maybe it was the Cokes and Jim Beam, but they always drank. It wasn't frustration from missing the buck; he'd missed plenty of deer in his day. He was a lousy shot. It almost felt as if someone had put Spanish fly or something in his drinks. But did Spanish fly work on men? In his fraternity days, he'd only heard of its supposed effect on women.

Whatever the reason, he couldn't sleep after he got into his mummy sleeping bag. All he could think of was being with a woman. The thought consumed him. Since he knew his wife's body best—actually, she had the only woman's body he knew at all—he concentrated on her. He began moving inside his sleeping bag. The down was soft and the slick silk felt good against him. The woman in the outdoor equipment store who'd sold him the bag said silk was soft and supple and breathable and was far better than a nylon or flannel lining. He had to agree. An image of that girl in the store flitted through his mind; she'd looked like she'd be soft and supple herself. Then his thoughts returned to his wife. The springs in the mattress were creaking. The man in the bunk beneath him was his accountant, and they were both Knights of Columbus. He didn't want his accountant and fellow Knight to wake up and hear him. He didn't want it that way anyway. What he wanted was his wife. He got out of his sleeping bag, climbed down the little ladder, dressed quickly, and grabbed his bag and his gun. Dan let his car roll down the hill in neutral so that no one in the cabin would wake up. He'd think of something to tell them later. He drove south in a white heat.

It was still dark when he crossed from Maine to New Hampshire, but twenty minutes later, as he was crossing the Whittier Bridge and coming into Massachusetts, the sky began to brighten.

His wife didn't wake up when he let himself into the house, or when he opened their bedroom door. She didn't wake up while he was undressing either, even though a couple of cartridges fell out of his vest and bounced noisily on the floor. His wife was a good sleeper. He lifted the bedclothes and looked at her. She was wearing a white cotton nightgown that came down to midcalf, but he could see the silhouette of her body through the nightie. He could feel the warmth radiating from the sheets. "Dan," she said, not opening her eyes, "I'm getting cold."

He took that as encouragement and got into bed, pulling her against him. "Dan?" She was more awake now, and slightly alarmed. "What are you doing home?"

"It's okay. I just wasn't having much fun up there and so I decided to come home. To be with you. I missed you."

"That's a first," she said, and rolled away. She added dismissively: "You smell like gun oil."

Never in any of his fantasies had his wife told him that he smelled like gun oil. He wasn't ready to give up, though. His new plan was to arouse her in her sleep so that she would be, when she woke up—what did his fraternity brothers used to say?—that she would wake up hot to trot. He had no idea if this would work, but the theory seemed sound. He started by stroking her back, gently rubbing her neck and shoulder blades and the small of her back. She didn't seem to mind. He thought he saw her smile in her sleep. He inched closer to her so that her hips were wedged up against him. His hand went down, way down to the hem of her nightgown. His fingers danced up her leg, her thigh, her tummy. When he reached the base of her breast, she said, "Knock it off, Dan, I'm trying to sleep."

So much for his hot-to-trot plan.

With that, he got out of bed and put his pants and shirt and hunting vest back on. He went downstairs. He tried sitting in the breakfast nook, but the bright yellow walls and the white table and chairs didn't match his mood. He went to the living room and sat in the La-Z-Boy his wife had given him for Father's Day two years ago. The living room wasn't a comfortable fit either. The chair's vibrations were merely annoying, and there wouldn't be anything on TV but kids' shows. He remembered watching Saturday morning cartoons with Amy and Claire when they were little. All three of them would be wearing their pajamas and they'd have a bowl of cereal while they watched. But he wasn't in the mood now to watch Speed Racer or H. R. Pufnstuff, or whatever was on these days.

He found himself, finally, in the basement, sitting in a pile of clothes between the washer and the dryer. He was cleaning his gun. It hadn't been fired since he'd *cleaned it last night sitting by the fireplace up in Maine. It was something to do, though.*

He vaguely considered driving down to the Combat Zone and trying to enlist a prostitute. But he knew little of the ways of prostitutes, being a family man. In college, he and his frat brothers would go to Chinatown after the bars closed at 2 a.m. to drink "cold tea"—after-hours beer served in teacups. To get to Chinatown, they would walk through the Combat Zone and leer at the prostitutes. There were plenty of them around. But at this hour, wouldn't they all be asleep, or surely in no mood for one last, desperate customer? He didn't know if there would be a morning shift coming on. Or if they took checks. He didn't have much cash, and his bank wasn't open.

A huge, glistening waterbug crawled out from under the water heater and skittered under the ping-pong table. He considered loading his rifle and opening fire on the creature. He'd heard that those bugs sometimes nip at people's toes. He'd be completely justified in blowing one away; it would be nothing short of self-defense. He looked at it through the scope on his rifle; it looked like something out of a science fiction movie. He might be a crummy shot, but he could hit that bug at a range of about six feet. What would a 30-30 slug do to a waterbug? But he'd wake up everyone in the house, and it would be hard to explain. The water-bug, as if telepathically sensing danger, disappeared abruptly into a drain under the ping-pong table.

He heard bare feet padding down the stairs, either Claire's or Amy's. It was Amy, most likely. They both liked to sleep in, but Amy was working at FotoHut and had to be there early. She bent over and put her head in the dryer, looking for her orange-and-blue FotoHut uniform. With a sigh of silk, her green robe fell open. He tried to force himself to look away, but he couldn't. Magnetism. "Cover yourself, Amy," he said thickly.

Amy bumped her head on the inside of the dryer and straightened up. She looked at him with terror. Her face was a livid white. She was too alarmed to speak.

Dan hadn't meant to take that tone with her. She certainly hadn't expected to run into anyone down here in the basement, especially since she thought he was in Maine. And she couldn't have known what kind of a night he'd had. Besides, she was afraid of guns, and here he was with a Winchester in his lap. "I'm sorry I startled you, Amy. Just close your robe. Please."

That came out sounding almost as bad, but at least she pulled her robe shut.

"Why don't we go upstairs and have ourselves some breakfast," he said, although he wasn't the least hungry. "Pancakes, maybe?" He hoped Amy knew how to make pancakes, because he didn't.

~

After her father left, Amy put another pan of hot water in the freezer compartment. She attacked the frost with her ice pick again. A satisfyingly large chunk of ice fell into the pan.

She couldn't believe that Mrs. D'Amato's sister would just move out and leave a freezer full of frost. For that matter, Mrs. D'Amato's sister hadn't swept the floor or cleaned the oven and she'd left a ring in the tub from her last bath.

Amy looked in on Gus. He was sitting cross-legged in her bedroom wearing her drawstring pants. They were the kind of pants that would fit anyone, even Gus. When he saw her, he started to smile but then thought better of it. *Gus must think it's not okay to meditate and smile at the same time.* The voice on the record said, "You are as big as a planet now, and you're growing bigger all the time. You are as big as a star, spinning through space." It had been a long time since Amy had listened to this record. She didn't remember the narrator sounding quite so simplistic. It sounded to Amy like he was lecturing preschoolers.

She got a blanket from a closet and laid it on the living room floor. She didn't have a dining room table yet, but this would be just as nice. It would be a picnic. She pushed a chair up to the kitchen counter and kneeled on the sink to get the silverware down. Her new apartment had a few quirky little drawbacks, including the placement of the silverware drawer.

"... the size of an entire galaxy. You are that cloud of stars and all the dark spaces between them. Forces whirl you through deep space. Whirl with them. Now you are as big as God. Can you see him? He's there, if you know where to look. It's difficult, but..."

Amy hoped Gus wasn't getting nauseous with all this talk about planets and stars and whirling. When they'd gone to the planetarium last weekend, he'd gotten sick listening to Pink Floyd and watching all those little lights revolving across the ceiling. Amy had been disappointed that they'd missed the end of the show, but she'd gone out and stood in the empty lobby while he was throwing up in the men's room. She'd looked at the photos that were hanging in the lobby, photos of the earth taken from the moon and of the moon taken from the earth. The man who had taken their tickets told her that sometimes people had strange reactions to the show. Once a woman had stripped off her clothes and started belting out "Dark Side of the Moon" along with Pink Floyd during the finale. "Of course," he said, "she was probably on drugs."

Amy looked at the clock. If Thea didn't get here soon, they wouldn't have time for lunch.

~

"I'm sorry I'm late," Thea said. "Sometimes it seems like I'm always late. Here, I brought you some flowers. I got them in the subway station."

"Lovely!" Amy said, though the daffodils looked a bit bedraggled. "Did you see my father on your way here?"

"I don't know what your father looks like," Thea said.

"Of course you don't. Well, he came by earlier. He said he was down in this part of town on business, but he works miles and miles from here and he never leaves the office. He was just checking up on me. What about Mrs. D'Amato? Did you see her? She's the old lady on the second floor."

"I saw two old women down there. They didn't look happy. They were staring at me."

"They always stare at me, too. Mrs. D'Amato's sister used to live here, in this apartment, but she couldn't make the rent, and she had to move in with Mrs. D'Amato. They blame me for that, for some reason. They remind me of that horrid woman that Dean has cooking for him."

"Mama. Yes, I can see why you'd say that."

"I'm going to make a loaf of banana bread and leave it in front of their door one morning with a nice note. That might help."

"I like your new apartment, Amy."

"I just love it. My friend Chewy lives right below me. I used to come over to visit and take self-defense lessons. When he told me this place was available, I shot down here as fast as I could."

"It's huge. It's about four times the size of mine." Amy's apartment was a place of odd angles and bare beams, of unexpected nooks and crannies, and of vast expanses of linoleum.

"I know. That's the thing about Back Bay—it's a great place to live, but it's ridiculously expensive and most of the apartments are miniscule. And there are roaches in almost every building."

"I know. Ross's building is infested with them. Mine isn't quite so bad, but I see them sometimes."

"One time, in our building—in Dean's building I mean—there was an electrical fire inside the walls on the first floor. They put it out right away, but it made a lot of smoke. So, every roach in the building came stampeding from downstairs up to our place on the fifth floor. Wave after wave of them. It was like those movies you see of terrified animals trying to escape a forest fire. It was awful! But this place, it doesn't have roaches—at least I haven't seen any—and it costs about half as much as the apartment where Dean and I lived, and it's much, much bigger. I could breed water buffalos up here. I know it looks empty, but... "

"My place looks empty too. I never got around to buying furniture," Thea said. "Well really, I couldn't afford to buy furniture."

"I like the way your apartment looks. Bare floors and pillows. It's kind of Japanesey. I love Japanese stuff. But I want furniture. I figure half the furniture in the apartment I lived in with Dean is mine."

Amy put the flowers in a glass and set the glass on the blanket.

"Do you have parakeets, Amy?"

"Parakeets? Oh, that's a record. It's called *Morning: The Sierra Nevadas*. It's mostly birds and creek sounds. There's this friend of mine, Gus—Gus is Chewy's dad—he's in the other room, trying to learn how to meditate. He's heard me talking about meditation and... and how it's been a big help when I've been going through stress, and so he asked me if I could help him get the hang of it, because he's been stressing out lately. He came over early this morning so that he wouldn't run into Chewy, because he thinks Chewy doesn't know about us, and he's been at it ever since. First we meditated together. I didn't want to get all metaphysical on him, but I gave him a few tips. Then I put on this old meditation record I have, but I think he went about as far as he could with that. So I put this nature record on and told him to relax. Anyway, I'm glad you could come by to see my place before you left."

"I'm glad I could come too," Thea said. "You know, I'm a little nervous about going."

"Are you? I always wanted to go to Colorado myself. I've never been west of Amherst. But you know, I used to tell people I was from Colorado. I thought it sounded way better than being from South Boston. I looked in an atlas and I picked out a hometown for myself. I was from Idaho Springs, Colorado. I liked the way that sounded. I was a cheerleader for the Idaho Springs High School football team. Our team was called the Mountaineers. Only, Ross told me his basketball team played the team from Idaho Springs once, and they're actually called the Gold Diggers, not the Mountaineers. That's a really stupid name, I think; it sounds like all they want to do is marry people for their money. My name was better."

Amy cut up an apple and a pear and arranged the slices on a plate with a wedge of taleggio cheese. She put out some bread and sliced some soppressata for Thea. She had panna cotta for dessert. "You can get food in the North End that you can't get anywhere else in town," she said.

"I've never been down here before," Thea said. "When I walked to your place from the subway stop, I felt like I was in Italy." Thea picked a slice of salami off the plate.

"I've never been to Italy, but I've heard other people say that too. Chewy and I are practically the only people down here who aren't Italian. Well, there are the tourists—I think every guide book ever written about Boston says come down here and see the Old North Church and have some pizza. But tourists don't count. Anyway, I think I'm going to like it here a lot. About the only drawback, my landlord doesn't allow dogs. Dean got Maud before I knew him, but she was still a puppy when I moved in. And he's always at the restaurant, so he's not spending nearly enough time with her or walking her enough. I think I ought to be able to have her half the time but... I'm sure Mrs. D'Amato would report me if I brought her here."

"If I weren't going to move in with Ross, I might move down here myself."

"Well, at least you won't have to move things very far," Amy said. "Just across the alley. I hope you like living there."

"I hope so, too. I've been there quite a bit since..."

"Since I moved out?"

"Well, yes, since you moved out. It wasn't that I minded your staying there. It's just that it's a small place for four people."

"At least you won't have to worry about getting anonymous phone calls in the dead of the night."

"In the what?"

"The dead of the night. The middle of the night."

"Oh. How do you know I won't?"

"Well, I don't but... you'll have a new phone number, won't you? Ross's number, I mean. Do you want a cup of tea with lunch? I was going to pick up a bottle of wine at Cirace's, but I have to drive in a little while and I have enough trouble handling my bus when I'm totally sober. I have Constant Comment, oolong, and Red Zinger. I did have chamomile and Mu #9, but I left them at Dean's even though he doesn't much like tea."

Thea left the choice to Amy. She asked where the bathroom was.

"It's off the bedroom, and like I said, Gus is in there. And the bathroom is tiny. You have to sit sort of sideways to pee, and the door doesn't close all the way when you do, but all he'll be able to see will be your knees."

That was all right with Thea. She didn't care who saw her knees.

"He wouldn't look anyway," Amy said. "I don't think." While the tea was steeping, she went back for one final assault on the freezer compartment.

The sound of birds and breezes and running water was louder in Amy's bedroom. Thea saw a pudgy man in purple pants sitting on a Japanese mat. His eyes were closed and his legs were folded beneath him. His hands were in his lap and his elbows were held closely against his body, as if he'd been tied up. He reminded Thea for some reason of a stuffed animal she'd had as a child, a big purple bear with brass buttons for eyes and a stitched-on smile. The bear nodded. Not at her, he just nodded. Thea realized he was asleep.

Sure enough, Mrs. D'Amato and her sister glowered at them as they were coming down the stairs. "That's just the way they *usually* look at me," Amy whispered to Thea. "Sometimes it's worse. You should have seen the look they gave me when I brought my sacristy lamp up the stairs."

They found Amy's Pinto tightly boxed in between two cars. It would take a crane to get Amy's car out of that space. "Sorry, I guess I won't be able to give you a ride home," Amy said. "We'll both have to take public transit. I'm probably going to be late."

"If we were in Amsterdam, we could take a white bicycle."

"You mean rent a bike?"

"No, these guys, they were called Provos, they used to leave white bicycles around the city, and you could take one and ride it wherever you wanted, and just leave it for the next person to take. I don't know if they do that anymore, though."

"That sounds like a good idea. Better than the subway."

"I'm used to taking the subway when I go someplace," Thea said. "but I hardly go anywhere except to the restaurant, and I walk or take my bike there."

"I'm not used to it, not anymore. What's the point of having a car if you can't use it?"

They started off toward Haymarket Square. "You won't recognize my place when you get back," Amy said. "I'll have all my stuff here, and I'm getting ready to paint, and I found out there are actually wood floors under the linoleum, so I'm planning to tear up the linoleum and rent a sander and..." Amy could tell that Thea wasn't very interested in her renovation plans. "What are you thinking about, Thea?"

"Amy," Thea said, "what did you mean about my not getting any more phone calls at night?"

Why on earth did I mention that, Amy thought. "I just meant that, because you're moving..."

"No, that's not what you meant. I have a feeling that I might know what you were talking about, but I'd like you to tell me."

I promised Ross. He's my friend. And he let me stay there all those weeks. For free.

But she told anyway. She told Thea everything she knew, in words as close to Ross's as possible. By the time she finished the account, they were on the platform, waiting for the train. "I'm surprised Ross hasn't told you anything yet. He's honest about himself, usually. He's probably planning to, right after you move in, I bet, or maybe on the trip. I know he feels bad that... you know. You know what guys are like. But he does feel really bad about it."

Thea didn't reply.

I'm sorry Ross, Amy thought. *I'm really, really sorry. I guess I'm not much good at keeping secrets after all.*

2 8

SO LONG LIKE A HOT DOG

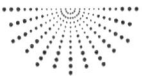

WIM'S COUSIN HENDRIK DROPPED THE DICE INTO THE LEATHER CUP AND SHOOK them hard. The cup disappeared in his hand. Hendrik's hands hadn't gotten any smaller since Ross had last seen them. "Thea tells to me that you're a *kapitalist*," Hendrik said.

Hendrik spilled the dice. Doubles again. "How do you mean, a capitalist?" Ross asked him.

Hendrik snatched up four more pieces from the backgammon board. Ross picked more of the label off the beer bottle he was holding. He'd only had a couple of sips, but Wim and Hendrik had insisted that he drink with them. "You own this place, ja?"

Ross tried to remember what Thea had told him about Hendrik's politics. He'd been a Maoist once, but Maoism had become too revisionist for him, so he'd joined some splinter group or another. Where would he look to for guidance now? Didn't Albania lean further to the left than China these days? *"This is Radio Albania, calling Boston. Radio Albania calling. Come in, Hendrik..."*

"Well, yeah, if that's what you mean, yeah, Dean and I are the owners."

"And you share profits with the workers?"

"So far," Ross said, "there haven't been any profits."

"Well, *heer kapitalische opperheer*, why don't you give another beer to us. If you can affording it."

Talk right, Ross thought at him. He found the way that Hendrik put on an exaggerated accent and peppered his speech with Dutch phrases annoying. Still, he got both Hendrik and Wim another cold Dos Equis.

"To each according to his need," Ross said.

Wim was wearing a Red Sox cap and he was sneering. He'd been doing a lot of sneering since he and Hendrik had come into the bar. *What the hell are they doing here, anyway?*

Hendrik drained his second beer in a matter of seconds. He sounded more like he was gargling beer than drinking it. A trickle of beer ran down the deep cleft in his chin. Wim drank his a little more deliberately.

Robin I skipped into the bar. She smelled of sandalwood. She gave her order to Ross: a tequila sunrise, an amaretto sour, a Harvey Wallbanger, and two frozen daiquiris. Ross got her drinks. It was better than standing there peeling the label off his beer. One of the drink orders Robin gave him was Thea's. Did she not want to see Wim? But she had been acting strangely since before Wim came in.

Robin I was looking at the backgammon board. "Who's winning?"

Dean was in the bar now, too. "Ross is getting his pants beat off," Dean told Robin.

"I know what, Ross. Pretend to sneeze and knock the board off the bar," Robin suggested.

"Now that's an old ploy for you," Dean said. "Voltaire talked about doing that."

"I don't know about Voltaire," Robin said. "I saw it on the *Andy Griffith Show*, a long time ago. Only it was with checkers."

"Probably Voltaire got it from Andy Griffith," Dean said. "Give me one of those Dos Equis, too, Ross. You know why it's called Dos Equis?"

"Because... that's how two X's are pronounced in Spanish," Ross said.

Robin said, "And there are two X's on the label. What a good name!"

"Yeah, but what do those two X's mean?" Dean asked. "What do you think of when you see two X's?"

"Pornography?" Robin wondered.

"No, Roman numerals. This German guy came over to Mexico and started a brewery right around 1900. XX is twenty—twentieth century."

"By century XXX, there will be Marxist governments in every capital of the world," Hendrik predicted.

"You mean XXI, I think," Dean said.

"Did you tell Thea I was here?" Wim asked Robin.

"I told her, but she's still pretty busy."

"I'll go find her. I'm busy myself," Wim said, though he wasn't.

Having finished peeling the Dos Equis label off his beer, Ross started tying knots in swizzle sticks. They still had thousands upon thousands of swizzle sticks that they had brought back from Vermont. Ross thought of Dorcas, a woman he'd known in college, who'd been able to tie swizzle sticks into a knot with her tongue.

Hendrik rolled again and picked his last man off the board. "*Jij verliest!*" Hendrik said. "You loose!"

"Lose, not loose," Ross said. Ross got the money he owed him from his tip jar.

Dean pointed out that Hendrik had won with a gammon. "That automatically doubles the bet," Dean said. Hendrik's gammon emptied the tip jar and Ross had to get out his wallet. *Thanks, Dean.*

Hendrik smiled and asked for—more or less demanded—another beer. He leaned way back on his stool to drink it faster. He lit one of his clove cigarettes. "Any snacks?"

Robin brought him chips and salsa. "Two thumps up," he told her.

When Wim came back, the two of them got ready to leave. Just before they walked out, Wim crooked his finger at Ross and leaned confidentially over the bar. The last thing Ross wanted was to have Wim whisper in his ear, but he didn't see any way to get out of it gracefully.

"I wonder if Wim does facial exercises so he can sneer better," Dean said, "or if he has a special sneer coach."

"Maybe he had surgery that allows his lips to curl more than a normal person's."

"What else is impressive," Dean said, "is how seamlessly he can transition from sneer to scowl to smirk. Hey, how come you kept giving Hendrik all that free beer?"

"He might have gotten violent if I'd cut him off. Hendrik doesn't believe in private property."

"Well, I don't either, in theory, but..."

"You could have written him up a bill if you were worried about it," Ross said. "That way he could have beat you up instead of me."

"We should start keeping a sawed-off shotgun behind the bar," Dean said, "to deal with drunken extremists. What did Wim tell you just before he left?"

Ross shook his head; he didn't want to talk about it. "What I'm wondering is, what did he and Thea talk about?"

"Tell me, and I'll ask her for you. I want to talk to her, anyway, before you guys leave town."

"Can't."

"Ross, you can tell me anything. I'm that kind of friend."

Anything except about Sarah Jefferson.

"He said, when... no, really, I shouldn't tell you."

"Come on, spit it out."

"He said, when Thea starts to cum, put your finger in her butt. That drives her absolutely wacky, he said."

"He told you that, huh? That's pretty hot stuff. Bet you can't wait to try that out, can you?"

Dean was sitting at a table in a corner of the bar, reworking the schedule for the next two weeks. He'd forgotten, when he'd made it up last week, that Thea and Ross were going to be gone. There were numerous additions, cross-outs, and footnotes. Up at the top of the sheet, he'd written, IF YOU DON'T LIKE THIS SCHEDULE, YOU CAN ALWAYS QUIT.

He saw Thea in the doorway to the dining room, trying to look the bar over without being seen herself. "Wim's gone, if that's what you were wondering."

She didn't look all that relieved, but she came into the bar. Dean asked her if she was busy right now.

"No, I have one more table, but they've finished dinner and they're sitting around drinking coffee and Rompope."

"Why don't you come sit with me for a while, then, and we can have a little talk," Dean said. "I have a present for you. A bon voyage gift." He handed her a gaudy tin box full of candy. The box had already been opened. "I saw these in the international foods section of Star Market, and I thought of you because they're made in Holland."

"Hopjes, they're called. They're from the Hague. I haven't had one of these for years." She unwrapped one and popped it into her mouth. "*Dank je*, Dean, that was nice of you. Do you want to try one?"

"No, thanks, I already did. Hope you don't mind."

"Of course I don't. Have another."

"That's all right. The aftertaste kind of reminded me of soap. So tell me, how did your tête-a-tête with Amy go? How is our little Amy?"

"It was nice," Thea said. "We had a picnic on the floor."

"Did she have anything to say about me?"

"Not really. Well, she said that you don't like tea very much, but she left you some anyway."

"That's it? That's all she said about me?"

"That's all I remember her saying."

"I see. Well, what I wanted were your overall impressions of the situation. Did you get the idea that she's serious about this? No, I mean, of course she's serious, but did you get the feeling that after a month or two of living alone, that maybe..."

Thea told Dean that she didn't think Amy could get much more serious about this. And that, while she didn't know for sure, she didn't think that a couple of months would have much of an effect on Amy's seriousness. "She said she's going to rent a sander and sand the wood floors. She wouldn't be sanding if she didn't plan on staying for a while, I don't think."

"You may be right," Dean said, "but I'm not completely convinced. See, Amy's never lived alone before. After a couple of months of coming home to an empty apartment... not even a dog there for company—well, we'll just have to wait and see, wait and see. Did she say anything about seeing anyone else?"

Thea thought about the stocky man sitting Buddha-fashion on the Japanese mat. *What was his name? Otto? Fred? Herman? No, wait... Gus. It was Gus.* "No, she didn't say anything about that."

"Maybe she wouldn't, though, because she knows you're my friend." Thea hadn't known until then that Dean considered her a friend. "I hate thinking about her with someone else. I hate it, but I can't stop myself. It's like I've got this movie, this X-rated movie starring Amy playing in my head all the time."

Thea wondered if Ross had told Dean about her own role in an X-rated movie.

She said to Dean: "Amy told me—not today, a few weeks ago—that she wasn't planning to get serious with any one person. She just wants to be on her own for a while." *Maybe I should have done the same. Did Ross come too soon after Wim? There wasn't more than a sliver of time between the two.*

"I hate the idea of her getting serious with one guy. I also hate the idea of a whole parade of men filing through her bedroom. I can't decide which I hate more. Anyway, I guess you're happy, now that Amy has moved out. That Ross, I'll tell you; one moves out, he's got another one waiting in the wings."

"But you don't... I mean, you don't think that Ross and Amy..."

"No, I don't think that," Dean said. "Back when I was in college, if you made the moves on a buddy's girlfriend, we called that snaking. I don't see Ross as a snake. But he encouraged her. Just by giving her a place to stay, he encouraged her."

"Well, it was convenient for him—he had someone to look after Jeremy most nights." Thea wondered why she was defending Ross. She had asked him, once, if he was attracted to Amy. He said he found her attractive, of course, but that he wasn't attracted. Sometimes, though, when she'd gone over there, she found them sitting around like an old married couple, maybe reading a newspaper and sharing things they found interesting or working a crossword puzzle together. There was an unspoken intimacy between them.

Besides, since this afternoon, she had a lot less reason to trust him. Still, she said, "I think Ross was just being her friend."

"He's supposed to be my friend too. My best friend. By the way, what did Wim want to see you about?"

"The people he's living with are throwing him out. He wanted to know if he could stay at my apartment while I was out of town."

"What did you say?"

"I told him I'd let him know. There are a few things I need to think about."

"Here comes friend Ross now."

Ross sat down with a sigh. "My feet hurt."

"You've got it easy, buddy, with those cushy rubber bar mats to stand on. Try working the host stand some night."

Ross looked at Thea. She didn't look very sympathetic. She seemed... wary. She was eyeing him with what felt like suspicion.

"Did you two decide to fly out to Spin-and-Marty Land?"

"We decided to compromise," Ross said. Ross wanted to fly both ways. Thea wanted to take a bus to see the land in between, even though Ross told her that the trip from Boston to Denver went through some of the most humdrum landscapes in North America.

Thea shrugged indifferently. Just this morning, she was acting enthusiastic about going.

Robin I pranced back into the bar and came to their table. "I need two cognacs," she told Ross.

"Why don't you get them yourself?" Ross said. "Get me one too, while you're at it."

"I've never been behind a bar before. I wouldn't know what to do."

"Hold the bottle upside down over the glass," Dean said.

In a few minutes, Robin returned to their table with three snifters on her tray. She gave one to Ross. "Don't you feel well, Ross?"

"His dogs are tired," Dean said.

"His dogs?"

"Ross has sore tootsies," Dean said. "Good lord, you've got enough cognac for three people in each of those glasses. That stuff is expensive."

"You didn't say how *long* to pour. Ross, if you need a foot rub, I'll give you one." Robin went off to deliver her drinks.

"The other day, Meredith called Robin I a space cadet. But I defended her," Dean said.

"You did?"

"I sure did. I said, 'Cadet, hell, she's commodore of a whole damn fleet of starships.' You know," Dean said, "maybe I should go to Colorado with you guys. I need a vacation, too."

"Who'd mind the shop?" Ross asked him.

"We'll let Patsy run it. And maybe we can open a new restaurant in Colorado."

"There are plenty of Mexican restaurants out there already."

"We'll open a New England restaurant. Clam chowder. Stuffed quahogs. Lobster rolls. Baked beans," Dean said. "Would you like to live in the mountains, Thea?"

"I don't know. I guess."

"How would you even know?" Ross said. "You said there aren't any mountains in Holland."

"I've been to Switzerland. I imagine the mountains there are a lot like the ones in Colorado."

"I suppose. I've never seen the Alps," Ross said.

Dean said, "I don't know either. I've seen the Alps but not the Rockies."

After she'd served the cognacs, Robin I came and sat down with them. "The man who ordered those drinks, I kept thinking I'd seen him before, or at least I recognized his voice. I finally figured it out. When the woman he was with got up to go to the restroom, he said, 'So long like a hot dog.'"

Dean said: "So?"

"So it's Uncle Billy!"

"You didn't recognize your Uncle Billy?"

"Not *my* Uncle Billy. *The* Uncle Billy. I guess none of you grew up in Boston."

"I lived here until I was seven," Ross said, "but I don't remember an Uncle Billy."

"Well, there used to be this TV show, back in the '50s, called *Uncle Billy's Magic Farm*."

"Oh, TV. My dad wouldn't let us have a TV."

"Uncle Billy would show Popeye cartoons and episodes of *The Little Rascals* and *Clutch Cargo* and things like that. Kids would come on the show on their birthdays. I was even on his show once, when I was six, I think. He had these two helpers, a cow and a chicken, Missy Moo and Pattycake. The cow was actually Uncle Billy's wife Jane, and sometimes he'd forget and call her Jane instead of Missy. What I remember best, though, is that, at the end of every show, he'd say a cute goodbye to the kids watching at home. He'd say, 'See you around like a doughnut,' or 'Catch you later, Tater,' or 'Ciao for now Brown Cow.' And 'So long like a hot dog,' that was my favorite."

"Uncle Billy must still enjoy the company of young friends," Dean said. "I'd be willing to bet that's not Missy Moo he's buying Courvoisier for."

"Oh, and 'Take care, Teddy Bear,' that was another good one. No, I don't think that's Jane, but I don't know for sure because on TV, she was always in a cow suit."

"That girl he's with tonight, she would have been in diapers in the 1950s."

"I just wish he and his teddy bear and those other people bivouacking in the dining room would get the hell out," Ross said. "I have a lot to do before we leave tomorrow."

"Relax, Ross, this is the best part of the evening, when everything is winding down."

"Poor Ross. You sure you don't want me to massage your feet?"

Ross still wasn't in the mood for a foot massage. "We could turn up the lights in the dining room a little. Or start vacuuming," he said.

"Or use a cattle prod," Dean suggested.

"When I worked at Maxwell's, we'd have someone scrape garbage cans across the concrete in the alley behind the restaurant. There was something about that sound that made campers want to leave. Get Buzz to take out the garbage."

"We have plastic garbage cans. Besides, I sent Buzz on an errand. Robin, I'll take that foot rub you were going to give Ross. Did I ever tell you I took a massage course last fall?"

"Did you? Fun!" Robin said. "Maybe sometime you can give me a back rub. My back hurts more than my feet when I work a split shift. Thea, what time are you bringing your doggie over tomorrow? I have to be here at work at eleven. I'm working a double again tomorrow."

"I'll talk to you about that later," Thea said.

"Buzz!" Dean said, "Did you come back by way of Texarkana?"

"I got lost. I swear, I never seen streets like you got around here. Some streets have the same name, but they're different streets. Some streets, you go along 'em for a while, and you're doing fine, and then they change names on you for no good reason. And about half the street signs are missing, and..."

"Yeah, it's a medieval maze out there. Did you get the paper?"

"Got it right here. They told me this was the first one off the press."

"Good. That way, we don't like the review, we still have time to steal every copy of the paper that we can find and drop off a satchel charge at the *Free News*. You'd better get back to the kitchen, Buzz, you've got quite a backlog of dishes. Mama's probably about to go into cardiac arrest."

"I wanna play a couple of games of Captain Fantastic first," Buzz said. "I've never played a pinball machine before that had more than two flippers. It's a whole new pinball universe. Besides, I live here, remember? I've got all night to do the dishes."

"You want to spend all your salary playing Captain Fantastic, that's fine, since we get a cut of the proceeds. Well, well, here it is." Dean opened the paper to the VICTUALS section and spread it out on the table.

Why Not, indeed?

L. Mitchell Ott

Reviewed: ¿Por Qué No?
95 Isabella Street
BankAmericard and Master Charge—no American Express
Reservations Accepted
Open 11-2:30 and 4-10, Tues-Fri
9:30-2:30 and 4-11 Sat and Sun
Closed Mondays

Dean said, "I hate when people put an initial in front of their names. Abraham Lincoln said people should part their names in the middle. I wonder what Mr. Ott's friends call him? L?"

"Maybe just plain old Mitch," Robin I said. She'd taken Dean's shoes off and was rubbing his feet.

I love good wine, as faithful readers of this column know by now. But as I have often said, while I love good wine, I like even mediocre wine. Being from San Antonio...

"That's not good," Ross said. "He's from Texas."

"What's wrong with being from Texas?" Buzz wanted to know. "I know plenty of good people from Texas. I'm almost from Texas myself."

"He'll think he's some kind of authority on Mexican food."

Being from San Antonio, I feel the same way about Mexican food. I love good Mexican food, but I can put up with even middling Mexican food. When I heard about a new Mexican place called ¿Por Qué No? (Spanish for "Why Not?") tucked away in Bay Village, Denise—my regular dining companion—and I went in enthusiastic search of it.

Waiting for a table to open up, we wandered into the bar. The bar at ¿Por Qué No? has the ambience of a beer blast. There's a loud pinball machine and an even louder jukebox, but it is a convivial place. Complimentary salsas and homemade tortilla chips are served, which makes sense from the management's point of view. Salty chips and *picante* salsa keep customers clamoring for more drinks. You have your choice of a standard tomato salsa, a mango and sweet corn salsa, or an incendiary salsa verde.

"If I were here tonight, he'd have to say the bar has the ambience of a mausoleum," Dean said.

Also available in the bar are some pretty exotic *antojitas* (literally, "small cravings"—best translated as "snacks" or "appetizers") from the Yucatan such as panuchos, codzitas, and my favorite, salbutes—a flash-fried Mayan taco. Just a taste of those brought back memories of a lovely afternoon at a beach bar on Playa Paraiso.

Denise wanted to try their nachos. She asked for them without jalapeños. Some weeks ago, at a restaurant I won't name, the server told her that the chef wouldn't prepare nachos without jalapeños because it would "ruin the integrity of the dish." There was none of that argle-bargle at ¿Por Qué No?. Denise got her nachos *sin jalapeños,* no questions asked.

I recommend the imported Mexican *cervezas*—most of them, anyway.

They serve Carta Blanca and Modelo (light and dark) on tap and Dos Equis, Bohemia, and Corona in bottles. I can't in good conscience recommend Corona, though—I've always found it rather skunky. Beer should come in brown glass bottles to protect it from the sun. The cocktail waitress said they also had Noche Buena, a seasonal beer available only around Christmas time, but then she came back and said they had sold out. Pity—that's one fine bock beer.

"He's right about Noche Buena," Ross said.
"And about Corona," Dean said.

I recommend the margaritas as well. They are served in giant snifters approximately the size of goldfish bowls and are half price during happy hour. Also available are blue margaritas made with Curaçao. They taste about the same as your standard margarita, but are the color of Windex.

The dining room has a pleasant and unfussy feel. At least the place is not packed with gaudy Mexican memorabilia. In fact, there are remarkably few concessions to a south-of-the-border atmosphere. The walls are white with only some framed black-and-white photographs here and there.

Typical Tex-Mex fare—burritos, enchiladas, tacos, flautas, posole—is readily available, but the menu also runs to some pretty exotic dishes from the Yucatan. Most of the kitchen staff, I was told, hails from that part of Mexico. The head chef and her sous chef once owned a restaurant in Merida, and they also operated the late, lamented Estrella Maya in Allston.

"Allston? I thought it was in Brighton," Ross said.
"Who can tell the difference?" Dean said.

Dinner was preceded by a cold, tangy sopa de lima, a Yucatecan twist on a classic Mexican tortilla soup. Roasted habeñero chilies add a smoky heat to this bright soup. Lovely! We also ordered guacamole. Not bad, but nothing spectacular. What is a little disappointing is that they don't make it tableside as they do at Quetzalcoatl's. That way, it's fresher, and it's a bit of a spectacle, watching it being made.

I ordered the *especialidad* of the day, the pollo pibil. This is chicken smothered in achiote paste and a goopy orange sauce, wrapped in a banana leaf, and cooked in an underground firepit. It was delicious and seasoned to perfection. My only complaint was that it was topped with sour cream rather than the richer *crema* it would have been topped with in Mexico. Feeling adventurous, I also ordered tacos made with escamoles. Escamoles—sometimes called Mexican caviar—are the larvae of ants that live under certain cacti in the Mexican desert. They were cooked with cilantro and chilies. This was my first time tasting escamoles. I found them buttery and citrusy and succulent.

My daughter Denise had the pavo relleno negro, an inky black turkey stew with a hard-cooked egg afloat in it. She also ordered the camarones yucatecos, jumbo shrimp served in a decadent sauce made with butter, garlic, spices, and a hint of Yucatan oranges. Mexican cuisine, like French dishes and Texas barbecue, is all about the sauces. And as my daughter pointed out, you could serve a chunk of cinderblock in that sauce and it would still be tasty.

"I know who this guy is," Dean said, "He was here a month or so ago, I think. Was kind of a pain. He was with that pretty woman who was wearing a fall. Wow, so that was his daughter."

Ross remembered his daughter. She looked like Sarah Jefferson.

"You remember that guy, Thea?" Dean asked, "You waited on him."

Thea nodded. She hoped he didn't have bad things to say about her in the rest of the review.

"I guess I could have asked her out to my van after all," Dean said. "since that was her dad and not her boyfriend."

"If you had a van," Ross said.

Our waitress was not, incidentally, a señorita with flashing eyes, but a young Englishwoman. She was attentive but not unctuous. She was a bit harried because it was, after all, a busy Saturday night. I'd prefer to never eat out on a Saturday night, but alas, duty called.

At least he called me young, Thea thought. *And attentive.*

By now, most of the waitstaff had gathered around the table. Adriana said, "Too bad I didn't wait on him. I have flashing eyes, don't you think?"

Robin I looked at her. "Oh, they definitely flash, Adriana," she said. "Thea, I thought you were English, too, when I first met you. You sort of sound like you are." Robin gave Dean's feet a pat and set them on the floor. "I should go check on my table," she said.

"Your table can wait a little while," Dean said. "Keep rubbing."

The entrées come with a serving of rice and refried beans, as per usual in most Mexican restaurants. The night we were there, the rice was dry and unpalatable, about the consistency of kitty litter. I've never understood why some restaurants are incapable of making good rice when it's so easy, and so important. Well-cooked rice can serve as the perfect blank canvas for almost any dish.

While all the entrées we ordered were tasty and the seasoning was spot on, I can't say much about the presentation. Now, I am aware that Mexican food isn't like Japanese food or classic French cuisine, where appearance is as essential as taste. And yes, there is more to fine food than a pretty plate. Still, the way a dish looks is important. My pollo pibil, for example, looked like an alien autopsy had been performed on a banana leaf.

"That does it," Dean said. "L. Mitchel Ott goes on the List."

Robin I wanted to know what list he was talking about.

"The Snuff List," Dean said. "The Richard Dadd Memorial Snuff List." Then he remembered that Amy was in charge of keeping the List up to date. He'd have to get it from her. "He's not interested in reviewing our restaurant. He just wants everyone to know that he can write prose shot full of fancy similes. Windex. Kitty litter. Alien autopsy. Bet you anything he has an MFA in creative writing."

Postres (desserts) can also be had at ¿Por Qué No?: coconut flan, sopapillas, pan tres leche, Rompope ice cream, mango soufflé. My daughter and I were, by the end of dinner, as stuffed as a couple of chili rellenos, so we ordered a light dessert and split it—a selection of fresh fruit (mango, cantaloupe, guava, and pineapple) sprinkled with *tajín* (a kind of chili powder) and a squeeze of fresh lime. *Tajín* magically transformed the taste of the fruit into flavors simultaneously savory and sweet. ¡*Delicioso!*

One more surprise: When the bill arrived, it was accompanied, not by a couple of trite chocolate mints, but by complimentary cookies. These were not your typical Mexican *galletas* but sturdy American Toll House cookies. Outrageously good Toll House cookies, I might add. Why cookies? Well, why not!

Cecily came into the bar. "Grab a chair, Cecie. You should see this too," Dean said. "He's going orgasmic about your cookies."

"I just came to tell you, there's this woman out in the dining room who's..."

"Come, sit with us," Dean said.

¿Por Qué No?, all in all, is not one of those restaurants that is falling all over itself trying to make it. You have to take it on its own terms. It is somewhat of a farfetched place, but everything holds together, *más o menos*. I wish them a hearty *Buena Suerte*.

Up next week: The Barong Grill
Indonesian food in Cambridge

"He definitely has a degree in creative writing," Dean said. "Not only that, but he must have taken an elective—Spanish for Smartasses," Dean said. "I don't know how he got such a plum job—I'd make a much better restaurant reviewer than him."

Ross said, "Well, I don't know that we want to have it blown up and put on an easel. And I don't know what's so farfetched about this place. But it could be worse. He's hard on restaurants. Did you see that review he did last week on The Matterhorn?"

"Yeah, he said their cheese fondue tasted the way dirty sweat socks smell. Still, I think he was unfair to us."

"I don't know. Sometimes the rice does taste like kitty litter. Want a Southern Comfort, Cecie?"

"Sure, hon," she said, "but I think you guys should know about this woman. She's taking all the pictures off the wall in the dining room."

"What woman? A customer?" Dean was thinking that someone might merely be straightening the photos again. Some of them needed straightening.

"I don't know. Just a woman. A woman with red hair. There's a bald guy too."

∽

Dean wanted to know what the hell was going on.

"Nothing much," Amy said. "Just taking these pictures off the wall and putting them in this box." Chewy was holding a big cardboard box.

"And then what?"

"Then," Amy said, "We're going to take the box and put it in the trailer."

"Why didn't you come and say something to me instead of sneaking around?"

"Sneaking? Do I look like I'm sneaking? I was going to say something to you, but you were so busy having that girl rub you that..."

"For God's sake," Dean said loudly, "those were my goddamn *feet* she was rubbing. You make it sound like..."

"Shh, Dean, don't get so excited. You'll disturb your customers."

"I don't care about the goddamn customers."

"Well, you should. Anyway, I don't care who rubs you, or where. I'm glad you're making new friends," Amy said, though in fact it had bothered her a little to see Dean's feet in another woman's lap.

Amy took another picture off the wall, the one hanging over Table 17. In that picture, Amy was lying down in a field full of flowers. It was broad daylight. Where Amy's hips should have been, there was a patch of night sky. Dean had wanted it to look as though you could see through the entire planet to the sky beyond by looking at Amy's butt. Instead, it looked more like she was wearing black panties. Black panties spangled with tiny white polka dots. It was not one of the more successful of the Amy's Derrière series.

"Those photos don't belong to you, Amy. I took them. With my camera. With my film. I developed them and matted them and framed them, and I hung them on the wall."

"I suppose that's all true," Amy said, "but it's my ass. I'll give you back the frames if you want. And you're about to light the wrong end of your cigarette. By the way, Chewy and I moved most of my stuff out of the apartment. We rented a U-Haul trailer and borrowed his friend's car. There are still a few things of mine there—we're going to get them now. Don't worry, though, we won't take anything that doesn't belongs to me."

The last customers, Uncle Billy and the woman who wasn't Missy Moo, had settled up and were hurrying out.

"See you around. See you around like a doughnut," Ross called, though not quite loud enough for Uncle Billy to hear him.

Ross was about to total up the night's receipts on the adding machine. He'd been waiting for Robin's and Thea's checks to come in. "At least now we know how to get customers to leave. We just stage a brawl in the dining room."

"I should go help Robin and Adriana clean up," Thea said.

"I've hardly had a chance to talk to you all night. Are you coming over later? Bringing the rest of your stuff?"

"There's not that much more to move. Mostly just Wim's paintings. I'm too tired to do that tonight."

Thea was supposed to move in with Ross after they returned from Colorado.

"Okay, well, I guess we'll be spending plenty of time together on the trip. We can talk then. Is everything okay?" Ross was used to people asking him questions like that. He didn't usually ask other people if things were all right.

"I was just wondering about someone who came in tonight. He was an older man, with white hair, and he was wearing a plaid jacket, and he sat at the bar. Do you remember him? He ordered three Screwdrivers and drank all three of them in about five minutes, and then he left without saying anything to anyone."

"What about him?"

"Oh, nothing. I was just wondering about him. He was sad looking, but he smiled at me."

"Tell you the truth, I don't remember the guy. It was pretty busy for a while there. When it gets busy, everything becomes sort of a blur. I don't even look at customers' faces."

"I should go help clean up."

"What did Wim have to say to you?"

"Nothing."

"Nothing?"

"Nothing important."

Thea left. Buzz, intently playing pinball, was the only other person left in the bar. His face was a ghostly electric white in the glow of the machine.

"It's going to be so nice to have a pet in the house again," Robin said to Thea. "Once my brother and I went to a music festival at a place in Connecticut called Powder Ridge, and we found this stray cat there, and I fed him hot dogs and made sure no one stepped on him. We took him home and I named him Powder. But he disappeared right after we got back to Boston. He came back, though, a few days later, and someone, for some reason, had put a collar on him made out of those pull tabs from beer cans. I could tell it annoyed him. I took it off and he acted really grateful for that, but then the next day he disappeared again and I never saw him after that. Poor Powder. I wonder whatever happened to him."

The story of Powder made Thea think of the man in the plaid jacket. They appeared for a little while, then they vanished.

"So you're going to bring your dog over what time tomorrow?"

"Our bus leaves around three, so..."

"I can't pronounce your doggie's name. Do you think it'll be okay if I just call him Damn It?"

"I think he'll know who you mean."

"And you'll bring his leash and his food bowl and everything?"

"Yes. But I have to tell you something Robin. I might not go. I might stay here. Then I wouldn't need you to..."

"Really? Well, I hope you go. You should. That would be so much fun, to go to Colorado. I've never been there, but I'd love to see the mountains. And I've been looking forward to having a dog around the house."

When Dean arrived back at his apartment building, there was a Ford Fairlane with a U-Haul behind it double parked in front. Chewy was loading boxes into the orange trailer. Chewy had borrowed the car from Hector. It was an enormous tan and white car that reminded Dean of a giant saddle oxford. "Didn't know you were going to help," Chewy said cheerfully.

At least he's talking. The last few time Dean had run into Chewy, he'd been under a scary vow of silence of some sort.

"Already took most furniture to Amy's," Chewy said.

Dean didn't respond. He was out of breath, having run most of the way from the restaurant. Chewy might think *he* was under a vow of silence.

"Maybe carry boxes. Some of them, heavy for Amy."

Dean nodded, thinking, *You sound like an idiot, talking that way. You're going on the List. Beyond question, you're headed for the List.*

Then he remembered that Chewy was already on the List—had been for a long time.

Upstairs, Amy said, "You're home early." She said this as if she'd been there waiting for him to come home from work while she was watching the late news. Instead she was packing to leave forever. Dean's favorite chair was gone. A lot of the living room furniture was gone. "Maybe you can help me clear up some mysteries. Is this *Return of Harmonica Slim* album yours or mine?"

Dean stopped panting long enough to say, "Mine."

"Thought so." She tossed the album on the larger stack. Amy came to the last album in the crate. *Learn Guitar with the Ventures.* He hadn't seen that album in years. His mother had given it to him one Christmas, thinking he might want to be in a band. She'd also given him a Silvertone electric guitar that she'd ordered from a Sears and Roebuck catalogue. Dean did want to be in a band, but no one he knew wanted to be in a band with him, not after they'd heard him play. No one but his friend Eugene. Eugene wanted to form a folk-rock duo, Dean and Gene, but Eugene was the only musician in town worse than Dean. "I guess that must be yours. I never knew you played guitar. Okay, and what's the story about this book, *Mining Techniques in Western Australia?* It looks like a library book. I'm sure it's not mine, but why..."

"It has the best recipes in the world for making homemade explosives. Never know when something like that might come in handy."

"It doesn't look like it was ever checked out."

"Of course it wasn't. You think I want everyone to know I have a book like that?"

"Well, I'll leave it on the shelf, and you can work out whether you should return it where it belongs. Then there's these copies of *The Bell Jar* and Anne Sexton's *Death Notebooks.*"

"Those are mine."

"I know they are, but you'll never read them. And I..."

"Ame," Dean said. "I want you to know, I love you. I love you and I want you to come back. Why don't you come back for a while, just long enough..."

"Too late, Dean. As usual, too late."

"I love you, though. What am I supposed to do about that?"

"Oh, Dean, Dean, that's just something you're saying. That's the problem. You've always just said things. What matters is what you do, not what you say."

"I've done plenty of things for you in my time."

"Name one," Amy challenged.

Dean disliked being asked for specific examples, preferring to argue the abstract principles at stake. While he was sure there were many instances of "doing things for Amy" to choose from, not one of them seemed supremely relevant at the moment. "I made soup for you when you had the flu."

"All you did was open a can. And it was soup made with chicken stock. I don't eat anything made from chickens."

"I helped you write that paper on Mary Wollstonecroft in our women's studies class. I even typed it for you."

"Yeah, and you laughed at my first draft. Besides, that was years ago, Dean, before we ever slept together. In fact, I think you helped me so I would sleep with you. And don't think that everyone didn't know why you were taking that class. Same reason you took Home Ec in high school. No, snookums, what matters isn't what you did five years ago, but what you do every day. Or rather, that's what used to matter. Nothing matters anymore."

She went into their bedroom. "You sure have been taking good care of this place. Have you changed the sheets since I left?" In fact, he hadn't even made the bed since she'd left. The top sheet was twisted up in the blankets and both the pillowcases had come off. "Looks like a drunk octopus's been sleeping here," Amy said.

She took the drawer from the nightstand and emptied it on the bed. There was a shower of ashes and cigarette butts onto the yellowed sheet. "I see you've been using the drawer as an ashtray. Nice." She picked up a sheet of folded paper and read, "Too bad. Too bad. Oh! Too, too bad. Now we shall have too return..."

He snatched the paper out of her hand and wadded it up. "All right, Dean, keep your secrets if you want." She paged through the December copy of *Penthouse* that had also been in the drawer. "God, how do they get those women to pose that way?"

"You mean in a Santa Claus hat?"

"I mean with their legs spread."

"For money. Lots of money. Here, this is yours. Take it. It might come in handy." He held out a vibrator that had been in the drawer.

"Oh, that," she said. "I won't have any need for *that* anymore."

Dean laughed. It was an utterly humorless laugh.

Amy walked over to the closet. She decided Dean needed some space. She hadn't liked the sound of that last laugh. She remembered that he'd wanted to name his restaurant La Risa Final. "Dean, I know you're feeling threatened. I know you've got a lot of anger in you right now. And that's okay, but it's no reason to act like a three-year-old."

She took an ankle-length, purple-and-white dress from the closet. *Granny gowns; that's what they used to call these dresses.* She tried to remember the last time she'd worn it, but she couldn't. *Still, you never know.* She tossed it in a box marked CAN'T BEAR TO PART WITH.

She was reaching for a blue sweater with a big gold letter L on it that she'd gotten for being a cheerleader. Just then Dean came up and pushed her. It wasn't much of a push, more of a small shove, but it caught her off-balance. With one hand she grabbed Dean and with another she grabbed the rod that the clothes were hanging on. She fell into the closet, pulling Dean with her. Then the rod gave way and all their clothes came down on top of them.

Not one of the self-defense moves that Chewy had taught her seemed appropriate for this situation. As far as she knew, nothing in karate, judo, tae kwondo, aikido, jujitsu, or any of the other martial arts addressed being buried under a boyfriend and their entire wardrobe. To make matters worse, Maud was barking furiously, trying to decide if they were in trouble or just playing, and if playing, could she play too? Amy groped around on the floor of the closet, trying to find something to hit Dean with. Her hand touched an electric iron, but she wasn't quite that mad. Then she came across a cellophane-and-cardboard box that a hairbrush had come in. She smacked Dean on the top of his head with it. Then again.

"Stop hitting me!" Dean said.

The box flew apart after a couple more whacks.

"Then let me up! You're hurting me," she said, although she wasn't really in pain. Just kind of smothered.

"I'm trying to," he said. He was as entangled in clothing as she was.

She was so frustrated she started crying.

"Cheweeeeee!" she screamed, right in Dean's ear. "Chewy, come help me!"

Dean was at last able to stumble to his feet and get out of the closet. He stood there looking chastened. Maybe he was worried that Chewy had heard her calling for help and was dashing up the stairs to pummel him with karate chops and kung fu kicks.

Not that he would. Chewy was the most peaceable person Amy knew.

Thea was sitting on the floor of her living room. She was burning a candle and petting Vervloekt. He was acting nervous. He was a nervous dog anyway, but he seemed more anxious than usual, as if he somehow sensed that changes were coming. She scratched him behind his ears and when he rolled over, she rubbed his tummy. He still looked upset.

Thea and Wim were sitting on a bench in the Public Garden, watching the swan boats and eating lunch. Wim had little esteem for things American, but he did like baseball and he admired Reuben sandwiches. Thea had bought Reubens for both of them at Ken's Deli. It was just after Mr. Q had paid her, and she was feeling wealthy. A dirty, skinny, apprehensive dog was sitting about six feet away from them, watching them eat. Thea plucked a bit of corned beef from her sandwich and held it out to him. The dog whined and shifted his weight from paw to paw, his ears pinned back, his head bowed. He wanted that corned beef, but he was too scared to come get it. Wim said, "Stomme hond. Kom heir, vervloekt. Vervloekt, kom heir!" He said vervloekt so many times that it eventually became the dog's name. "Stomme hond."

"Don't call him stupid," Thea said. "He's just scared." Finally, hunger overcame fear, and the dog gingerly accepted the meat. She gave him more, and he even ate some of the rye bread and sauerkraut. He ended up eating more of Thea's Reuben than she did, which irritated Wim. He considered Reubens far too good for stray dogs.

Vervloekt went home with Thea, over Wim's objections. She put up posters in Back Bay and Beacon Hill with a picture of the dog. She didn't own a camera, so she persuaded Wim to draw a sketch. It was a good likeness, except that there was something odd about the way the dog's paws looked. But no one called; no one wanted Vervloekt to come home. He was hers.

Her apartment felt even emptier than usual, since all of her plants and pillows were already over at Ross's apartment. She'd have to get them back. And she'd have to find a new place to live. She'd already given her landlord notice that she'd be moving out at the end of the month. Maybe she could stay with Amy for a while. Amy's apartment was huge. But then she remembered what Amy had said... no dogs.

It occurred to her that she might need to find another job, too. Maybe work in a hospital again, except she'd hated that, and she still had no Green Card. On Thanksgiving, Mr. Q had offered her another role in one of his films, one that he wanted to call *Behind the Dutch Door*. But she'd never do that again. Now that she had some experience, maybe she could find another waitressing job. Most of the people in the kitchen at ¿Por Que No? were illegal. Maybe that would be true at other restaurants.

Or she could go home. She could stay with her father. That would make him happy. Hugely happy. But what was there for her in Breda?

She thought again about the man in the plaid jacket. He'd paid with a check, and she'd looked at it. Kent de Mint, his name was. No one else in the restaurant had noticed him besides her. Why was Kent de Mint in such a hurry to down his three drinks? Why didn't he speak to anyone? Why did he look so sad? Why did he smile at her? Why did he leave so quickly? Where did Kent de Mint have to go?

"At least I'll be with you, funny looking," she said to Vervloekt. "You probably would have peed on Robin's floor." He peed on Thea's floor about once a week, no matter how many times she took him outside.

She set the dog down and turned on every light in the apartment. She went over to her window. Was that Ross's cat sitting in his window? She couldn't see Ross but she felt—no, she knew he was there, and that he was watching. "*Tot ziens*, Ross," she said. "*Tot ziens als een hotdogwurst.*"

Ross could see a flickering light coming from Thea's apartment. She was burning candles, he could tell that much. Was she alone? When Wim came to the restaurant, had they made plans to be together one last time? Was that why she was being so distant and strange this evening?

He couldn't call her. Her phone had already been disconnected.

Then her lights blazed on. Her apartment was lit up as he'd never seen it before. She was kneeling on her window seat now. Her plants were no longer in the way, but he didn't have Dean's lens. She mouthed something. He couldn't tell what she was saying, but he knew she was talking to him. He guessed that she was saying goodbye. Then she took off her sweater. She whipped if off so fast that her breasts quivered for a second or two afterwards.

WOUNDED MOOSE

(1)

Because of the threat of chicken hawks, Ross didn't want Jeremy going off to the bathroom by himself. Time was running out and they hadn't even checked their luggage. There were rumors, though, that the bus station was rife with men who would swoop down on little travelers, runaways, orphans of the road—chickens, in other words. Ross had no way of knowing if there was any truth to these rumors. No one in the bus station this afternoon looked dangerous. Some looked bored, some looked tired, but none looked menacing. If Thea were here, she could watch their luggage. But there was no Thea. He wished again that he and Jeremy were flying to Colorado. The thought of spending the next forty hours or so on a bus was disheartening.

He'd walked around the block to Thea's building twice this morning and rung the buzzer next to the scrap of paper with her name on it. He remembered standing in this lobby some months before, writing down her name. *Why the hell did I have to do that? How fucked up was that?*

And why the hell did I have to tell Amy. And why the hell did Amy have to tell Thea? After her impromptu striptease last night, there was no doubt that Thea knew about his spying. The only people he'd confided in were Dean and Amy. And Dean wouldn't have told Thea, he knew that much. He'd tried to call Amy, but she didn't answer.

Jeremy became impatient and scornful of his caution and left for the restroom on his own. Ross approached a red-faced woman dressed in what looked like a potato sack and asked her to guard their suitcases. She didn't appear to be waiting for a bus; she seemed to be a resident of the bus station. There was no reason to trust her; she might trade their bags for a bus ticket to Miami or a gallon of pink Catawba. But he had to ask someone.

As he hurried after Jeremy, the bus station seemed to exude a gray seaminess. The P.A. announced that the bus for Chicago and points west, *their* bus, was now loading at Gate 5.

Jeremy was washing his hands by the time Ross came into the restroom. Ross decided he'd better use the facilities himself before boarding. He told Jeremy to wait for him, but Jeremy dried his hands and scooted out.

Ross quickly followed, but he didn't want to appear to be chasing him lest someone—that woman bus driver who was staring at him, for instance —lest someone mistake *him* for a chicken hawk.

He found that Jeremy had relieved the woman in the potato sack who had been watching their luggage. And Jeremy had been joined by Thea.

"I didn't think you were going to come," he told her.

"I wasn't going to," she said. "but I changed my mind."

"You almost missed the bus," he said.

"I had to take Vervloekt to Robin's."

"Robin is working lunch this afternoon."

"I know. It's a good thing her brother was there. I don't think she told her brother that Vervloekt was going to stay with them. He acted confused."

Ross was a little confused himself. "We'd better check our luggage and get to Gate 5."

(2)

Amy woke up to the news on her clock radio. She heard the second half of a news report from California. A bus taking people from a retirement home to gamble in Las Vegas had plunged down an embankment and into a river. Four passengers were dead, a dozen were in the hospital. The driver hadn't been hurt. As a bus driver herself, Amy imagined what he must be going through right now. The announcer didn't say what had caused the bus to plummet into the water, but that might have been explained in the first half of the story.

Amy poked the button that would give her nine more minutes of sleep. *Why nine and not ten?* There would be music on when it woke her up again.

She could decide then if she was going to drive today or call in sick. She'd called in sick twice in the last two weeks.

Gus went on softly snoring. She was glad he'd slept through the news. That bus accident was the kind of thing that he would brood about all day.

A week before, he was spending the night and she had one of her screaming nightmares. She could never remember the dreams that triggered her night terrors—only that a dark, nameless, evil presence was looming over her sleeping body. And she wasn't able to wake up on her own. Someone—Claire, Dean, or in this case Gus—had to rouse her. Gus had shaken her awake, saying, "It's okay, Red, it's all okay," but his tone of voice indicated that he didn't believe that. At least Maud wasn't there when it happened. Whenever Amy screamed in her sleep, Maud howled right along with her.

(3)

The bus had come twenty miles west of Kearny, Nebraska and then refused to go any farther. It was sitting now on the shoulder of Interstate 80. The driver had radioed the Greyhound station back in Kearny and then announced to the passengers that help was on its way; another bus would come and take them on to Cheyenne. That announcement had come quite a while back. A bus should easily have been able to cover twenty miles in that amount of time. Since making the announcement, the bus driver had been getting more and more anxious. Twice he'd opened the door, walked around the bus, and looked back the highway toward Kearny.

They'd been riding on buses for more than a day now. Ross felt like it had been months.

A Nebraska State Police car sped past their stalled bus. Half a dozen police cars had driven past their bus and taken the exit just beyond them. There was a green and white sign with a curved arrow that indicated that this exit led to a place called Patmore. None of the police cars had stopped to offer aid to their driver and his passengers. Ross wondered if some terrible crime had been committed in Patmore. "Where are all the cop cars going?"

"I don't know, buddy," Ross said. "Maybe that's their police station over there. Why don't you go back to sleep?"

"Because I've got a binky," Jeremy said.

The woman sitting next to Ross had also given up trying to sleep for now and turned around in her seat to look at Jeremy. She'd told Ross earlier that she was from Grand Island and was on her way to Cheyenne.

Her daughter and son-in-law owned a couple of laundromats there. She was wearing a sweatshirt that said HUSKERS—GO BIG RED.

She was curious. She asked Jeremy what a binky was, and why it was keeping him awake.

Jeremy took his fingers out of his mouth long enough to answer. "A binky is something you find in your mouth, something that doesn't belong there."

The woman from Grand Island adjusted her hairdo and pretended to go back to sleep. Ross wondered how there could be an island out here in the middle of the prairie. Especially a grand one.

"When are we going to go?" Jeremy asked for the fifth time.

"It won't be long," Thea said. "The driver said another bus was on its way." She patted Jeremy on the knee. Thea had scarcely slept at all since leaving Boston. She'd been staring out the window, though there hadn't been much to see in the way of scenery, and for much of the trip, they had been traveling through darkness. "Once a friend and I were on a bus in Yugoslavia—do you know where Yugoslavia is, Jeremy?—and we were stopped for hours and hours."

"When were you in Yugoslavia?" Ross asked her.

She ignored his question. All the way from Boston to Chicago and then on to Kearny, she'd been carrying on normal conversations with Jeremy. For Ross, there'd been sulky silence. She went on with her story of the Yugoslavian bus ride. "It was the middle of the night. The dead of the night. We were up in the mountains, and we came around a curve, and there were these people standing around on the side of the road by a fire. They were all dressed in white, and they had white masks on. They stopped the bus. We thought they were bandits."

"Were they?"

"No, they were doctors and nurses. They made everyone on the bus roll up their sleeves to prove they had smallpox vaccinations. A few people didn't, and they took them down by the fire and inoculated them right there."

"Oh."

"One woman thought she had gotten her vaccination in her hip, but she wasn't about to take her pants off on the bus, so she went and got another one."

"I wouldn't either. But mine is on my arm."

"Mine, too." Thea rolled up her sleeve and showed him. "There was a smallpox epidemic that year in Yugoslavia. You know what smallpox is, don't you?"

"Uh-huh. People gave it to Indians. It was in their blankets." The story had mostly lost Jeremy's interest when he'd found out that the people in masks weren't bandits.

"I bought a few magazines back in Chicago," Thea said. She opened up her light-blue train case and got them out. "If you want something to look at. Or... do you want some candy?" She shook the box of hopjes Dean had given her. "These are from my country."

"I just want the other bus to come." He was fidgeting in earnest now.

Thea reassured him: "Everything will be fine when we get to Cheyenne." She sounded like someone who knew Cheyenne and its comforts well.

Two more police cars rocked past and took the exit to Patmore.

"I have to go to the bathroom," Jeremy said, "Bad."

"You know the restroom is out of order," Ross said. The toilet had stopped functioning about the same time as the engine had. The drive had taped it closed.

Ross was getting jittery himself and the smell was getting to him. Their seats were too close to the restroom and the back of the bus was beginning to reek. "We can get off the bus and..."

"It's not number one," Jeremy said.

"Well, you can still..."

"No!"

Ross made his way up the aisle and asked the driver about the building just off the exit. "A lot of cops seem to be going there. Is it a police station?"

"How the hell should I know?" The driver had a petulant, bleating way of speaking. "It's a cat house in a cornfield, for all I know."

Ross signaled Jeremy and got the driver to open the door. "If you're not back here when the other bus comes, too bad," the driver said.

The building was farther away than he'd thought. They had to climb a fence and they almost fell into a ditch in the darkness. There was a light dusting of snow and once Ross slipped. He was stiff from sitting, and it was bitterly cold. As they approached the building, they heard sounds like thunder. Or artillery fire. They circled around to the front of the building and saw the sign that had been invisible from the other side: PATMORE LANES. There were ten or twelve police cars in the parking lot. Some of the cars belonged to county cops—cops from Phelps County, Dawson County, Red Willow County. Some belonged to staties.

They walked into the bowling alley and Jeremy scurried off to the restroom. It didn't feel like the kind of place to worry about chicken hawks. While waiting for Jeremy, Ross went up to the counter where shoes could be rented.

"What size?"

"Eleven and a half," Ross said automatically, "but no, wait, I don't need shoes."

"Can't bowl in those," the woman said, looking down at his Hush Puppies.

"No, I'm not bowling, I just .. I was just wondering..."

"Yeah?"

"Why are all the police cars here?" Nothing untoward seemed to be happening at Patmore Lanes, nothing to require a police presence.

"It's league night. They got a league. There some reason why cops shouldn't go bowling?"

Ross shook his head. He couldn't think of any reason why they shouldn't.

By the time they had jumped the ditch and climbed back over the fence, the rescue bus had arrived. All the baggage had been transferred. Thea was standing outside the newly arrived bus, waiting for them. "They almost left without you," she told them.

(4)

"I'm hell when I'm well, and I ain't ever sick," Mojave's mother said.

Dean had dropped the first set to Mojave's mother, 6-0, and they were playing the first game of a second set. It was her serve. She wound up for it like a big-league pitcher. "You're dead meat now," she said.

When Dean had asked Mojave's mother if she'd like to do something with him some time, he hadn't figured on a game of tennis at dawn. This was the first time he'd played tennis since he was in college. Last night, he'd spent an hour looking for his racquet, wondering if Amy had taken it. Finally he found it in the closet under all his clothes. It was surprising that Amy hadn't hit him with it when they'd both been buried in there.

Mojave's mother served and Dean somehow managed to return it, but she slammed it back; the ball hit him in the ear. Maxine, Mojave's mother's Doberman—or Doberperson, as she liked to call her—was sitting by the net like an umpire. The ball rolled off the court and Maxine retrieved it and brought it to Mojave's mother. Fortunately, the dog only retrieved the ball for Mojave's mother; Dean found the dog terrifying and he disliked the idea of handling the ball when it was dripping with dog spit. He glanced over at Maxine; it was hard to tell if she was baring her teeth at him or yawning. He gave her an unfriendly look.

Mojave's mother's next serve came in as a bright yellow blur. The ball was on a low, mean trajectory. It clipped one corner of Dean's court and was gone. It rolled along the back fence, and, before Maxine could swoop it up, it found a hole and went through it.

Dean considered lying about her serve, saying that it was long by an inch or two, but decided not to contest it. That would just prolong the game. Besides, he had a feeling that if he actually managed to win a game, Maxine would chew his face off.

"Excuse me, sir," Dean said to a wino passing nearby. "Could you possibly get that ball for us?"

"Ungrh?" the wino said. "Gaa bleft?" He staggered up to the fence. Was he at the tail end of last night's drunk or just starting in on today's? If he'd just gotten started, it was an auspicious beginning.

"Ylink, grk, fuck. Erghh, shit. Plurp?"

"I said, could you get that ball for us? That one? The yellow ball lying right at your feet? Yes, that's it." Dean pantomimed throwing the ball. "Would you throw it to me?" Dean felt as though he were carrying on a conversation with a box turtle.

The wino made Dean understand that he'd exchange the ball for money. Dean passed a dollar through the fence. The wino threw the ball but it didn't quite clear the fence. He walked away. Dean said to Mojave's mother, "Let's just play with one ball."

"Thirty serving love," she said. She wound up again. "Your ass is grass, and I'm a lawn mower." In fact, Dean's ass was freezing, even if he did have woolies on under his sweat pants. He felt as though they were playing their match out on the Russian steppes. Mojave's mother, though, was wearing a sleeveless white top and a tiny white tennis skirt. She didn't look like anyone's mother in that outfit.

She fired her next serve across the left corner of Dean's court. With a wild backhand, he nicked it. The ball popped up and landed in her fore-court. Mojave's mother was caught unprepared. She may have been thinking about what to say before her next serve.

"If you snooze, you lose," Dean told her.

(5)

After picking them up at the bus station in Grand Junction, Marshall was unable to say much besides "God*damn,* Ross! Goddamn!" Punches in

Ross's arm served as exclamation points. The two brothers had not seen each other for nearly three years. Ross got in a few "Well, hell, Marshalls!" himself.

"Hated to miss your bachelor party," Ross said. "Was it fun?"

"A real blast," Marshall said without enthusiasm. "Would have been a lot better if you'd been there."

Ross asked Marshall, "Was Dad upset that we're getting in late?"

"A little miffed, maybe. You know how Dad feels about people being late."

"I bet he was more than a little miffed. But it's not our fault the bus broke down. And then we missed our connection in Cheyenne. We were stuck there for hours and hours."

"I know that, for Pete's sake. And Dad... he really wasn't all that annoyed."

"That doesn't sound like Dad. How is he, anyway?"

"Dad's still Dad," Marshall said, putting a shrug into his voice. "but he might seem a little more mellow than you remember. I've gotten to know him a lot better since I moved back here. If you can ignore a thing or two about him, you can get along fine with Dad."

Ignore what, his entire persona?

"I'll tell you something," Marshall said. "When I came back from New York, I pretended he wasn't my father at all, that he was someone I wanted to get to know. I'd sit around with him in the evenings, some-times by myself and later with Nikki, and we'd play Scrabble or some-thing—Dad never loses at Scrabble—and if he wanted to say something about himself, I'd just listen. I don't think Dad's ever had anyone who just wanted to listen. Mom doesn't; I think Mom figures she's already heard about everything Dad has to say. And with anyone else, he always expects he'll be getting into arguments, so that's what he's ready for. He's always on the defensive. But I'll tell you what, I found out a lot about him just by sitting back and letting him talk. Like, did you know that, back in the thirties, he went to Cuba? And that he met Louis Armstrong?"

"He met Louis Armstrong in Cuba?"

"No, those were two different things. He interviewed Louis Armstrong for his college newspaper. He got to meet with him back in his dressing room. It was right after Louis's performance, and he was covered with sweat and he was sitting there in his underwear—Louis was, I mean, not Dad. Hey, do you remember what a great shot he was with rocks?"

Ross didn't remember that, but it was easier for him to imagine his father throwing rocks at things than it was to imagine him wandering through Havana or chatting with Satchmo.

"He was a real marksman with rocks. Back when we still lived in Boston, he used to take us for walks—you were probably too young to remember this. A lot of times we'd end up in the alleys. I guess he liked alleys. And Boston must have had a lot of rats in its alleys, because..."

"There aren't that many," Ross said, in Boston's defense.

"I remember there being quite a few. Anyway, Dad could bean a rat at fifty paces."

"What I'd like to know is why he moved us out here to the middle of nowhere."

"Dad and I have talked about that, too. You know, he was there. In Japan."

"He was where?"

"You know he was a corpsman in the Navy, right?"

"Yeah, that's about all I know—he never would talk about the war with me."

"It took a while, but I finally got him to talk about it a little."

"I didn't know he was in Japan. I thought he was in the Mediterranean."

"He was—he was attached to an infantry division in Italy. But he was sent to the Pacific near the end of the war. He was on a medical team that went into Hiroshima right after the bombing. What he saw there... *that's* why he moved us to the middle of nowhere. Although I don't think of it as nowhere. Not anymore."

"Aunt Sophie calls it 'the back of beyond,'" Ross said. "Does Dad still say 'Let's drop it' all the time?"

"What do you mean?"

"You know what I mean. Whenever we used to talk with him and the conversation didn't go the way he liked, he'd say, 'Let's drop it,' and that would be that. End of conversation. I used to hate that."

"I don't remember him saying that all that often," Marshall claimed. "But trust me, Ross, Dad is a lot less uptight than he used to be."

"You say that to me sometimes," Jeremy said to Ross. "You say 'Let's drop it.'"

"I never do."

"Yes, you do. 'Let's drop it, let's drop it,'" Jeremy chanted, mocking two generations at once.

"Let's *do* drop it. Hey Marshall, where's Nikki? I thought she'd come with you to pick us up."

"You'll meet her tonight. She's at the hotel now, working. That Skeets has turned into a real slave driver. I'll be glad when she can quit that job. Jeremy, how much bigger are you going to get? As tall as your dad? You gonna play basketball?"

When Marshall had been in high school, he'd been a star forward on the basketball team even though he was only five foot ten. Everyone loved to watch him out on the court because of the way he hustled, and he was always stealing balls away from players much bigger than he was. His nickname was Hotshot. And fans used to say, "You think Hotshot's something, you just wait till his brother comes along. His brother Ross has at least seven or eight inches on him. He's gonna win us a state championship."

They even had a nickname picked out for him: Bigshot.

The problem was, Ross wasn't any good. It didn't matter that he was closer to the basket than everybody else; he still couldn't make the ball go through the hoop. He missed easy shots, he bounced the ball off his feet when he dribbled, he threw the ball to the wrong players, and at least once he shot a goal for the other team. Not only was he clumsy and a poor shot, he was also slow. The coach used to say, "Jarboe, you ever have to run for your life, you'll be dead." The coach had him come to the gym three times a week at seven to work with him one-on-one, and he would call Ross a klutz and a schlemiel and other names. The coach made Ross take a ball with him everywhere he went—to classes, to the store, even on dates with Winifred. When Ross dislocated his shoulder while skiing during his junior year, he'd been relieved to have an excuse to quit. He didn't even go out for the team his last year. A lot of people in town stopped talking to him then, and the coach, who also taught American history, gave him an F. Only Winifred had taken pity on him.

"I like soccer better," Jeremy said.

"How's work?" Ross asked Marshall.

"Well, pretty slow this time of year—hard to put on a new roof when the old one is covered with snow. But it'll pick up in a few months. And there are some pretty funny guys, some crazy guys on my roofing squad. There's this one guy—Jake, you remember Jake? He was in Skeets' class?"

"I remember seeing him around school. Always dressed like a cowboy, right?"

"Yeah, he did, and he still insists on wearing cowboy boots, even when he's roofing, and those boots have slick soles. He's fallen off twice now. Still wears cowboy boots though."

Thea was moving from window to window in the back seat, trying to take in everything. "God, look at those rocks, the way the sun's hitting them, they look golden. Just look at them! When you live in a city, you start thinking everywhere is like that. Somehow you forget."

"I know," Marshall said. "I used to live in New York City."

"I don't know why anyone would leave a place like this." Thea looked accusingly at Ross.

"If I hadn't left and gone to Boston, I would never have met you," Ross said.

That argument didn't faze her.

"I'm never planning to go east again," Marshall said. "Anyone back there wants to see me, they have to come out here. Nikki and I are going to build here."

"I just can't believe this place," Thea said. "Look at that weird house on the hill over there."

"That's *our* house," Jeremy said.

The house where Ross's parents lived had been designed by an architect from Los Angeles. He and his fiancée, a dental hygienist, had been driving through the Rockies on their way to ski in Telluride, and they'd taken a scenic route. She'd pointed to a gumdrop-shaped hill and said, "Wouldn't it be great to live right on top of that funny little hill?" Without saying anything to his fiancée—he wanted it to be a surprise—the architect designed a home to fit that hilltop. He wasn't able to buy the exact hill his fiancée had pointed at, but there were plenty of funny hills in Colorado, and his agent found a suitable substitute, one called Tuttle Hill. The architect doubted if his intended would be able to tell the difference.

He was never able to test her on this. She started a new job, working for an orthodontist in San Bernardino, and fell hard for him. They moved in together. She never knew that what had been, after all, a pretty whimsical remark, was taking shape as a flying cheeseburger on a hill in western Colorado.

The architect had planned their hilltop house to look like a flying saucer, streamlined and dynamic and futuristic. It didn't, though. It was too fat to pass for a flying saucer; it was shaped more like a cheeseburger. A cheeseburger with everything on it.

The architect lost all enthusiasm for the project after his fiancée left him and moved to San Berdoo; he stopped paying off the mortgage and stopped paying the construction company. The bank eventually foreclosed and the bank manager told the foreman of the construction crew to finish building the house as best he could, and to keep it cheap. Cut off from instructions from California, the foreman fell back on conventional 1950s building techniques. When it was finished, the overall effect that the house gave was that a gigantic flying cheeseburger had wobbled out of the sky and crashed into a split-level ranch house.

When their father was searching for a place safe from blast waves and fallout, he saw the house and made an offer on it. It had been on the market for over two years. The bank was happy to have him take it off their hands.

"I just can't believe it," Thea said again. She'd been saying that a lot since they'd passed through Denver.

"I'm not sure I can believe it either," Ross said, looking up at the house where he had spent most of his childhood. He'd forgotten just how strange that pudgy cheeseburger looked.

They turned up a crooked driveway that wound its way up to Ross and Marshall's parents' house. There was a gate that hadn't been there the last time Ross was back here. Marshall had to get out and enter a code. The gate swung open. "Well, we're home," Marshall said.

(6)

For one horrid moment, Dean thought the older man that Amy was bringing into the restaurant was her subway driver.

It wasn't. This was worse. It was her father. It was Dorky Dan. Dorky Dan, who'd thrown Dean out of his car the day that Nixon had resigned. Dean led them to a table.

"Are you surprised to see us?" Amy asked Dean.

"Not at all," Dean said smoothly, although he was astounded. "I'm surprised you've never eaten here before. This is getting to be the place to be seen, you know." Dean seated them at Table 7, a deuce that looked out on Isabella Street. He gave them menus and took their drink order. Amy had to drive that afternoon, but she ordered a kir anyway. "Perhaps a kir royale? Made with champagne rather than Chablis?" Dean suggested. "You know what Disraeli said: 'Anyone who says they don't like champagne is just a damn liar." *Or was it Gladstone who said that?*

Amy nodded. She loved champagne. They talked her father into a piña colada, something he'd never tried before.

Adriana was working Section 1. She brought their drinks and told them they were on the house. She brought them a basket of tortilla chips and a plate of complimentary appetizers; she said they were called panuchos. After that, Dean helped them order. "I don't like food that's, you know, real spicy hot," Dan said. "It doesn't like me either, you know what

I mean?" Dan ran his fingers nervously through his hair. His hair was not the same shade of red as Amy's and her sister Claire's. Not a rich auburn, but closer to the hair color usually associated with circus clowns.

"That's a common misapprehension about Mexican food, Mr. O'Dell, that it's all very spicy. Mexican food—by that I mean food the way it's actually prepared down in Old Mexico—is made from good, basic, fresh ingredients, and really, much of it is as bland as shredded wheat. You can spice it up as much as you like, of course. That's why we have those cruets of salsa on each table."

Dean suggested the plato combinación as a good place to begin. "Just a hint—if you do taste a little heat when you take your first few bites, just keep digging in—it'll get better."

Amy felt a sense of aptness in being there. Here she was, actually taking her father out to lunch. Not only that, the owner of the restaurant himself had shown them to a table, the best table in the house, she thought, and he'd sent them free drinks and appetizers and helped them order. Not bad, not bad at all, even if the owner was just Dean. It was apt.

She poured some of the red salsa from one of the pitchers on the table into a ramekin and dipped one of the tortilla chips into it. She'd worried about coming here, considering how dreadful her last encounter with Dean had been. *It's not like he's a violent person,* Amy thought. *I didn't handle that situation well. I shouldn't have been badgering him when he was already aggravated. And it wasn't that much of a push. Just a jostle, really. Only a jostle. He caught me off-balance.*

He seems pretty comfortable with the situation now, though. I guess he's accepted facts as facts. And I wanted Daddy to see... to see that Dean could actually be successful with something. Even if he wasn't successful with me.

"You didn't tell me we were coming to *his* restaurant," her father said to her. He didn't look pleased about it.

"Don't be angry, Daddy. Now that I'm not involved with Dean anymore, there's no reason you two can't be friends," she said, though she realized that was unlikely. Highly unlikely. Then she asked her father if he wanted to play pinball in the bar while they were waiting for lunch to arrive.

Dan's bushy red eyebrows shot up. "Pinball?" He shook his head no.

"Why, you afraid I'll beat you?"

"You probably would. I've never played before."

This came as a surprise to Amy. She'd supposed that all men played pinball.

Amy sipped her kir royale. It was delicious. "How's your piña?"

"It's okay. I prefer bourbon and Coke."

It's a good thing I came and got those photos. What if Daddy had come in here and seen my ass plastered all over the place?

"Order up." Cecily put the two lunches Dean had asked for in the pass-through window. He arranged the lettuce on Dorky Dan's plate so that it could accommodate a couple of long yellow chili gueros. He put a few bright red chili serranos in Dan's taco and sprinkled a handful of tiny purple chili piquins on his enchilada. He plopped a habanero Yucateco, a killer pepper that Mama handled with surgical gloves, on top of the rice and topped it all off with a good-sized dollop of Sangre del Diablo hot sauce. When he'd finished, Dorky Dan's plate was a regular fiesta of colors. He took a quick photo of it.

"Here," he said to Adriana. "Do me a favor and take these orders to that deuce in the South 40. Make sure the gentleman gets the plate in my left hand. I'm going home to get a few hours' sleep before the staff meeting. Anyone wants me, you don't know where I am."

(7)

"... and if I hear about anyone else chiseling the hostess or the bus people or the kitchen stiff, I'm going to have him or her taken out and shot at dawn. Clear? Okay, let's move on..."

So far the serving staff meeting had been a success, by Dean's yardstick. No one, so far, had run out crying or cursing. He looked at the notes on his legal pad.

KEYNOTE REMARK: "To serve is to rule." Lao Tzu

AGENDA

- chronic silverware shortage
- sick-leave abuse; e.g., calling in sick, coming in next day with face tanned everywhere except where ski goggles were worn
- ice scoop not to be left in ice machine AGAIN; violators will wake up in the alley with stray cats licking their faces
- no more playing tricks or otherwise hassling Mama
- kitchen stiff has agreed to turn down Mexican music on their radio by two notches
- inappropriate remarks to customers; e.g., "Here's your food" or "This isn't my table"
- inappropriate remarks to Patsy; e.g., "That's not my job"

- why did no one mention the overflowing toilet in Baño de Damas?
- no more failing to tip out hostess, dishwashers, etc.
- no controlled substance use in the basement during hours of operation; go back in the alley
- staffing problems
- lettuce going kaka 'cause crisper's left open

"Next point on the agenda—controlled substances—no need to discuss that. Use 'em if you like, but not inside the restaurant. We don't want to get busted."

"What do you mean, controlled substances?" Robin I asked.

"Like plutonium?" Meredith wanted to know.

"I'm sure you know I don't mean plutonium," Dean said. "Okay, so long as that's clear, we'll move on. Now, you're no doubt aware the wait staff's been dwindling. Thea's on vacation. Robin II's gone. And we have to eighty-six Adriana now. She's starting that cruise ship gig in a couple days. Congrats on that, Adriana."

Adriana stood up and took a bow and threw kisses. "I'll miss everyone!" she said.

"We can't keep taking as many shifts as we have been," Meredith said. Meredith was wearing a blouse that looked two sizes too small. "I mean, the money's nice, but we'll all burn out."

"I'm giving the matter my attention," Dean said, "but I don't want to put an ad in the paper just now. Not with Ross gone."

"Well, then what are you going to do about it?"

"I thought I'd ask around, talk to some people I know in the biz." Dean didn't know that many people in the restaurant business—none, really. "Maybe all of you could do the same. Tell everyone what a great place this is to work."

"If that doesn't help?"

"I still have a few applications from the first set of interviews that look promising," Dean said. "I'll look those over again."

"If you could just hire a couple bus people. It's bullshit that we have to bus our own tables most of the time," Meredith said.

"What happened to Robin II?" Keith asked Dean.

"Oh. Well, there's this guy, Vince, used to be her student, who was harassing her, and..."

"Yeah, we know all about Vince," Keith said. "Robin hardly talked about anything else."

"Well, somehow, he tracked her here. He came in last night, and..."

"Vince was here?" Robin I said. She sounded panicked. "What if he'd gotten us confused? What if he thought *I* was Robin II and not Robin I?"

"I don't think that was a big danger," Dean said. "She was his teacher, remember? He knows what she looks like."

"Oh," Robin I said, "right."

"That Vince asshole comes back here again, I'm gonna talk to that boy by hand," Buzz said. Buzz didn't have to come to this meeting, but there he was, sitting next to Meredith.

"Won't happen," Dean said, "now that Robin has moved on. Anyway, he somehow found her purse and he pocketed her cash, her credit cards, and her driver's license. Since he hadn't been able to harass her for months, I guess he'd been storing up hatefulness all that time. He wrote on the blackboard over the urinals, GUYS, THAT SEXY WAITRESS IN BLUE GIVES GREAT HEAD OUT IN THE ALLEY. $5 A POP!"

"I saw that," Keith said.

"I did, too," Buzz said. "Thing is, almost all the waitresses were wearing blue last night."

"Not me," Robin I said. "I was wearing pink."

"I was wondering why guys were coming up to me and offering me a fiver," Meredith said.

"Yeah, me too. Kept happening," Patsy said. "Wish I hadn't worn that blue blouse."

Meredith stared at Patsy with blatant disbelief. "You could have earned some extra cash, Patsy."

"Shut up, Meredith," Dean told her "So, Robin spotted him and panicked. She grabbed her coat and snatched up her purse and dashed out the door. Vince called the police on the pay phone here. Said he'd been driving behind her and she was weaving all over the road like an addled drunk. Just before she got back to her place, the cops stopped her. Vince had used a screwdriver to gouge a message into her hood: FUCK DA COPS. Luckily, she passed the sobriety test, and they knew after talking to her for a few minutes that she wouldn't have written 'da cops,' but she still got a ticket for not having her license with her."

"How do you know all this?" Meredith asked.

"She called me a couple of hours ago. Woke me up from a nice nap. Said she wouldn't be coming to the meeting and she wouldn't be coming to work tonight. She won't be coming back here at all."

"Do you know where she went?" Keith asked.

"Nope. Well, she said she was moving to Guam, but I don't think she'd tell me or anyone else where's she's really going."

Robin I put up her hand. "Yes, Robin?"

"Can I go back to being Robin?"

"What?"

"Can I just be Robin without the I? I don't like having a number after my name."

"We'll definitely take that under consideration, unless we hire another Robin. Anyway, people, until we can sign on more crew, we'll just have to make do."

"Don't worry," Patsy said confidently. "We'll all pitch in. We'll cope." Patsy had dropped her medieval philosophy course so that she could work more lunches.

Adriana said, "Dean, I should talk to you about that guy at lunch today."

"Which guy is that?"

"You know, the one at Table 7? The one with all the hot peppers. He said he was going to sue the restaurant."

"Oh, that guy. We'll talk about the pepper situation later. Now, on to the lettuce issue."

(8)

"That's where I went to high school," Ross said. "My father's the principal there." Thea looked. The building didn't particularly look like a school. It was squat and nearly windowless. It could have been a paint factory or a secret police headquarters. "Is there anything the matter, Thea?" He'd been asking her that a lot.

She shook her head. It was a half-hearted headshake, though. "Tell me," Thea said, "why does your father talk to me the way he does?"

"What do you mean?" Ross asked her.

"You know what I mean. Whenever I'm around, he talks slowly, and loudly, and he pronounces every syllable perfectly. Is it because he thinks I don't understand English very well?"

"Granddaddy always talks funny," Jeremy said.

"That's true. He does. It was embarrassing when I was in school; I used to hear kids making fun of him. But... you know, it does seem like he's talking slower and enunciating even more carefully these days. It's like he's speaking to dimwitted children."

"Because of me. I'm the dimwit."

"I don't know. I don't think that's the issue. He's been talking like that even when you aren't around. Okay, see that Burger King over there, across from the high school? That used to be the Rocket Ship Drive-In. We used to go over there during lunch break and eat Space Burgers and fries. Anything was better than cafeteria food. We'd pitch pennies in the parking lot in back. And there were these two guys who worked in the kitchen who could spit farther than anyone I've ever seen. They could stand at the back door of the restaurant and spit into a coffee can halfway across the parking lot. If spitting was an Olympic event, those guys could have won a silver and a gold."

"I can spit pretty far," Jeremy claimed. "Want to see?"

"Not out the window, Jer," Ross said. "It'll fly back in your face." They turned onto Uncompahgre Street.

"That strip mall over there, that's where the Mushroom Museum used to be. Marshall and I used to bring mushrooms we'd found in the woods to the museum to see if you could eat them. We got mushroom growing kits from there one Christmas. Oh, and see that little restaurant over there? The Lucky Café? My friend Cap and I used to work there as dishwashers. And that place on the other corner? That's the Pow Wow Steakhouse and the Snakebite Bar. I was the bartender there, at the Snakebite Bar. That's where Marshall's and Nikki's reception is going to be."

They drove through what was now being called "Olde Towne." When Ross had been in high school, the small houses in this part of town were mostly gray and the paint was peeling off, or else they were covered with stucco or siding. Some of the houses were shedding their fish-scale shingles and the fancy gingerbread trim was gone or looked dilapidated.

Nowadays, many of these houses had been refurbished and looked like miniature versions of San Francisco's painted ladies. If they were any cuter, they'd have dimples. There were gas streetlamps on every corner. New shops had popped up: a shop that sold caramel popcorn and fudge, a shop that sold pretty rocks, one that sold Navajo turquoise from New Mexico and Black Hills gold from South Dakota, and one that sold Christmas ornaments all year long. There were bars and bistros and cafés that hadn't been there before. One café had a "for sale" sign on it. Ross thought about what Dean had said—that they should open a restaurant out here.

There were people with cameras wandering through Olde Towne. He couldn't remember ever seeing any tourists when he'd lived here.

Ross turned down Yucca Street. *That's where Winnie used to live. Winifred. Where are you now, winsome Winnie?* A few years ago, his mother had sent him an engagement announcement clipped from the *Daily Search-light*. Winifred was going to get married to some guy from Toronto. Then his mother had sent him another clipping that said that Winifred's mother, an inveterate and grumpy alcoholic, had been run over when she stepped in front of an RV a few days before Winifred was to be married. That was the last he'd heard anything about Winifred.

"Show her where the airplane used to be," Jeremy said.

They drove around the town square in front of the courthouse. "A long time ago, there was a skating rink in the middle of that square," Ross said. "but they tore it out when the Air Force gave the town a Sabre jet from the Korean War. It just sat there on that concrete slab, and after a while, it started falling apart. A kid got hurt playing on it."

"I used to play on it," Jeremy said.

"So did I," Ross said. "Finally, the town asked the Air Force to come and haul it away, but the Air Force said, 'Sabre jet? What Sabre jet?' I don't know whatever became of it. They were talking about putting it in the basement of the courthouse, but I doubt they ever did. Well, there's not much else to show you. What do you want to do?"

"I want to go skiing," Jeremy said.

"I'd like to go skiing while I'm here," Thea said. "Meredith told me that I should give it a try. She said the snow out here is the best in the world."

"I guess we could go sometime while we're out here," Ross said dubiously. His skiing experience had not been a fulfilling one. "There hasn't been that much snow this year, but I guess we could go to Viking Mountain. They have snowmaking equipment. We can't today, though; Nikki's shower is tonight."

"My dad's only been skiing once," Jeremy said. "I've been lots of times in Vermont, with Mojave and his mother. Mojave's mother is a really good skier; she used to be on a ski team. We've gone to Snowbury and Catamount and lots of places."

"First time I went," Ross said, "I dislocated my shoulder."

⁓

Ross, Marshall, and Skeets ditched classes and hitchhiked to Viking Mountain the week that it opened. They rented skiing equipment and signed up for lessons. Because they were self-conscious about being locals who knew nothing about skiing, they pretended to be from Florida, and they spoke in an accent that they believed people in Florida spoke in.

At the foot of Viking Mountain, which until a year before had been a name-

less peak, they got their ski lesson. About ten women from Japan had also signed up for a lesson that day, and the Japanese ladies kept falling down. The instructor was trying to teach them how to carry their skis, how to walk on skis, how to gracefully get on and off the chairlift, and what to do if their skis came off. All through the instructions, the Japanese skiers kept falling down. Even when they were standing stock-still, they fell down. The one in the baby-blue parka fell and the rest of them giggled and took a picture of her splayed out in the snow. She was giving a peace sign. The one in the rose-colored parka fell down and the same thing happened. One of the women, the one in the lavender ski jacket, asked Ross to take a group picture. Afterward, Ross asked her name and she told him it was Akiko. He wanted to keep talking to her, but she fell down.

There was a man getting a private lesson from one of the ski instructors. He was wearing a sign that said BLIND SKIER. "What that mean?" Skeets wanted to know.

"What part don't you understand?" the instructor asked him. "Blind, or skier?"

Skeets had had enough. "I think this eats shit, you all," said Skeets to Ross and Marshall in his faux-Floridian accent. "I think we all can do better on our own." Instead of skiing the bunny slope with the Japanese skiers and the blind skier, they took the Cannonball Creek lift and schussed down a black slope. It was steep and icy and pockmarked with moguls, but Ross skied straight down it, not traversing a bit. Halfway down, Ross fell forward. He fell hard and tumbled a long way down the slope, creating a tiny avalanche and dislocating his shoulder. There had been so much giggling and falling going on that Ross hadn't learned much about turning or stopping.

"At least it got me out of playing basketball," Ross said.

"Let's go to Viking Mountain," Jeremy said.

"I already explained why we can't do that today. Any other suggestions?"

"Let's go to School's Out," Jeremy said.

"Not today," Ross said. He wasn't ready for a trip out there. Not yet. "What do you want to do, Thea?"

"I want to go home."

She said that with such vehemence that he wondered what she meant. *Did she want to go back to his parents' house? Back to Boston? To Breda? To die and go to heaven?*

"I don't feel good," she said. "I've had a headache since yesterday, and it's getting worse."

"It might be the altitude. A lot of people get headaches and nosebleeds when they first come out here."

"I get nosebleeds even back home," Jeremy said.

"I don't want to go to that shower this evening."

"But it's at the house."

"I don't care. I'll just stay in the bedroom or go for a walk. I don't even know Nikki. She won't miss me."

"I want to go to School's Out," Jeremy said again.

"What let's do is, let's go back to my parents' house and have a late lunch. Maybe your headache will go away if you eat something. I'm hungry anyway." Ross turned right on Arroyo Avenue, heading toward the Flying Cheeseburger.

"Over there's where the Ice Palace used to be," Jeremy said. "Tell her about the Ice Palace."

"Oh. Well, back a long time ago, about 1910 or 1912 or something like that, they built an ice palace over where that Kmart is. There used to be a little lake there, years ago. Ice sculptors came all the way from Canada to work on it. The town planned a big winter carnival for when the palace was finished. People were expected to come on the train from Denver, maybe even from farther away. But it turned out to be a warm winter that year, like this year, I guess—what they call an open winter—and when…"

"Ross, I don't want to hear about the Ice Palace," Thea said.

"I do," Jeremy said, though he had heard the story of the Ice Palace many times.

"Okay," Ross said to Thea.

"I'm sorry," Thea said. "I didn't mean to say that. It's just that, this headache…"

"It's okay. I understand," he said, though he didn't.

"Go on with your story," she said.

"No, it's okay."

"Go on, please, Ross."

"Go on, Daddy."

"It melted. The Ice Palace melted. That's about all there is to it."

(9)

Dean came in during that quiet time between lunch and dinner. They weren't theoretically open then, but they never kicked anyone out. The day bartender, Walker, took him aside. "That gentleman at the bar has been sitting there since before lunch."

"So? Is he drunk?"

"I don't know. I don't think he's exactly what you'd call drunk," Walker said. "He's only had two or three old fashioneds. But there's something strange about him."

"Maybe you haven't noticed, Walker, but there's something strange about a lot of the people who come in here."

"He's stranger than most. He keeps asking about these women who..."

"That happens. Some men still think that bartenders know how to find women, and that they..."

"That's not what I mean," Walker said. "He was asking me about a couple specific women, Flora and Esther. You know anything about those two?"

"Never heard of 'em, but..."

"Another thing, he was sweating."

"The way we set the thermostat, he was sweating?" The staff was always complaining about how cold it was in the bar. Dean told them to wear sweaters.

"Don't know about the thermostat," Walker said, "but I do know when a man is sweating. Sweat was pouring off him, but he wouldn't take off his coat—said he was dandy. And another thing..."

"Yes?"

"He said his name was Jack London."

Dean whistled. "Jack London, huh."

"Jack London. Like the man who wrote..."

"I know who Jack London was. Well, you finish closing out for your shift, and I'll talk to him."

The customer in question asked for another old fashioned. Dean made him one. He'd been taking bartending lessons from Walker. "There you go, Mr. London."

"I told you, call me Jack." The man circled the drink with his fingers. He peered at Dean for a long time. "You're not the same bartender, are you?"

He's pretty observant, this Jack, Dean thought. Walker was about twenty-five years older than Dean and more than a foot shorter. Walker wore a red eyepatch. Besides that, he was black.

"Have *you* seen anything of Flora?" the man asked Dean now.

"No, I don't think so. Flora who?"

"Flora my wife. Well, she'll be here."

Jack pulled out a Salem cigarette. Dean lit it for him even though he already had one going. "Another Old Fashioned, if you please," he requested.

He almost toppled off his barstool. He was still sweating, and now he started in with noisy breathing. "Are you okay?" Dean asked him. "Maybe you don't need another drink. You haven't finished the one I just made for you." In fact, he'd only had a few sips.

From the kitchen, Dean heard *trova* music from the Yucatan—lots of acoustic guitars—and knives being sharpened.

"I'm doing just dandy. Better hope you're doing as dandy as I'm doing when you get to be my age."

Dean shrugged. "You should at least take your coat off, the way you're sweating." Jack was wearing a long white duster, the kind of coat one might wear herding cattle in the winter.

"No, I'm dandy. How about Esther? You haven't seen anything of her, have you?"

"I haven't seen Esther either."

"Well, she'll be along."

"And Esther is..."

"My wife."

"I thought Flora was your wife."

"She is. So's Esther. They're both my wives. Both the same, too. Not much good."

Jack started to fall off the stool again; he caught himself only by hooking his elbows on the rim of the bar. He unhooked one elbow, puffed on one of his cigarettes, then took another drink while on the way to the floor. A busboy had been bringing dirty glasses back to the bar, and Jack knocked him over. Jack's drink spilled, and a maraschino cherry rolled across the barroom floor.

Dean had just hired that busboy—now he'd probably quit.

Dean hurried around to the other side of the bar, wishing Thea were there, or anyone who knew something about first aid. "Walker," he yelled, "Dial 911!"

Then Dean noticed that Jack had a revolver tucked into his pants. "Jack," he said, "were you going to rob us, or what?"

"Hell, no, I wasn't. Do I look like a robber?"

Dean had to admit he didn't. At least, he'd never seen a robber wearing a duster and a clip-on tie. With his white hair and flushed face, he looked like what Dean imagined Jack London would have looked like if he'd managed to live to be seventy.

Jack whispered. "That's just to wave around to scare Flora with. Look at it. It's not loaded."

Dean picked up the snub-nosed little pistol. It wasn't loaded. It wasn't even a real gun. "Do you have any idea what might be the matter with you?"

"Course I do. Had open-heart surgery last month in Dallas."

Dean bit his lower lip and chewed on it. This was getting to be a new habit with him, this lip biting. He'd been developing nervous habits at an alarming rate, sometimes two or three new ones a week. "Do you have any pills or anything?"

Cecily came into the bar from the kitchen and Buzz came from downstairs. Buzz had grabbed a ratty blanket from his cot. "He's sweating. Should I cover him anyway?" Buzz had a Boy Scout merit badge in first aid, but he couldn't recall anything useful. Maybe if Jack had been bitten by a snake or cut his hand while whittling...

"I don't know," Dean said.

"I think we should. You cover people with a fever," Cecily said.

"Ambulance on its way," Walker said. "Told them to hurry."

Mama emerged from the kitchen with a knife in one hand and she looked into the bar. She'd been slicing raw meat and her apron was besmeared with blood. She crossed herself and asked, "¿Dónde está Santa Thea?" Jack saw Mama and looked a little frightened.

"I'll get the first-aid kit," Buzz said.

"Great idea," Dean said. "Those Band-Aids should come in handy." He asked Jack, "Is there anyone we can call? Flora, maybe?"

"Don't make me laugh, it hurts too much," Jack said. "You know what Flora would say? She'd say..."

"Don't get yourself all excited, honey bun," Cecily told him. She knelt down beside him and wiped the sweat off his face with a kitchen towel. This was the second red-faced, sweaty customer emergency she'd had to deal with in the last few days. Jack's clothes were pretty well soaked with bourbon and Angostura bitters. With Buzz's help, she got him out of his long coat and covered him with the blanket. That seemed pretty inadequate, but they couldn't think of anything else to do.

"Is there anyone else we can call," Dean asked him.

"Call my brother. He works for the BFD."

Dean said, "Now we're getting somewhere." Not only would they have the police emergency squad to help them but the fire department as well.

"Where does he work? Which station?" Dean asked him.

"Good old Number 5," Jack said.

"Is good old Number 5 the one on Boylston Street?"

Jack didn't know.

"I'm pretty sure it is," Cecily said.

"Call," Dean told Walker. "Tell his brother what's going on."

"What's your brother's name," Walker asked Jack.

"Jack London," Jack told him.

Dean bit his lip again, then said, "I thought *your* name was…"

"There were nine of us brothers, and they called all of us Jack. Wasn't any of our names."

Walker was holding his hand over the receiver. "Man at the station says there's no one there goes by that name," Walker said.

"Ask for Jack," Jack urged him. "Jack London at good old Station Number 5."

Walker talked some more. "Man says someone there knows of a *Phil* London…"

"That's probably him. Talk to him," Dean said.

"But he says this Phil London hasn't been there for five years. Retired. Might be dead, the man thinks."

Dean looked up. There were two policemen in the bar now. One was an attractive Chinese cop; the other looked like he should have retired years ago. They had their guns drawn, and they were pointed at him. "Sir," the woman officer said firmly, "you'll want to put that weapon down and step away from it." Dean suddenly realized he was holding Jack's ersatz pistol.

"No, look, it's not…"

"Put your weapon down NOW, sir. NOW!"

The gun clattered to the floor. "It's not my weapon," Dean told them. "And it's not even a weapon."

The woman cop checked it out. "It's a water pistol. I don't think there's even any water in it," she told her partner.

Now the paramedics were swarming into the place. They broke out oxygen and unlimbered a gurney. Dean admired the speed and efficiency with which they worked and wondered if any of them might want to wait tables in their spare time. He'd read somewhere that EMTs didn't make that much money.

"What's the best way to come out of here with a gurney?"

Dean had never given the matter any thought.

"Through the kitchen and out the alley door. That's where we get all our deliveries," Buzz said. "I'll go prop open the doors for you."

One of the EMTs used a walkie-talkie to tell the ambulance driver to come around to the alley entrance.

Another paramedic was questioning Dean and Walker. "Was he drinking? Did he have anything to eat while he was here?"

Jack pushed the oxygen mask away. "I had three drinks."

"Four," said Walker.

"No, I had three, then I fell off my seat. And I ate... what were those things I ate called?"

"Salbutes," Walker said. "Kind of a fried taco."

"Yeah. That's what I ate. They were good, too." The paramedic was struggling with Jack, trying to get him to breathe through the mask.

"He told me he had open-heart surgery last month in Dallas," Dean said.

"It was in Houston. And it was three months ago," said a gray-haired woman who had come into the bar without anyone noticing.

"Flora?" Dean asked her.

"No," Jack said, "that one's Esther. She's the hoochie-coochie one."

"Well, he was looking for you too, Esther. I don't know why he thought he'd find you here."

"Because he thinks I spend all my afternoons going from bar to bar, looking to meet up with men. And he figures if he just sits in one bar long enough, I'll eventually show up."

"Oh. And Flora?" Dean asked.

"I don't know about Flora," Esther said. "Maybe she did go in for that sort of thing. But they've been divorced for over twenty years. I'm not even entirely sure that Flora is real."

"Never got divorced," Jack said. "Flora's just as much my wife as this one is. In fact, she..."

Jack tried to say something else but the paramedic muzzled him with the oxygen mask. They rolled him out of the bar on the gurney. "The funny thing is," Esther said to Dean, "I really do spend a lot of my afternoons in bars. I have to, to find him. There are about a half dozen around here he goes to, but he adds new ones sometimes, like today. I've tried calling, but for some reason, bartenders tell me he's not there even when he is. This has been happening ever since his surgery."

Dean and Esther walked along side of him. Mama crossed herself again as they wheeled Jack through the kitchen. Rafael asked Cecily if he was dead.

"I don't know if he really thinks I'm interested in chasing men or not," Esther told Dean, "or whether he thinks this is all fun and games. I don't have any idea what he thinks, even after being married to him for fifteen years."

"Fourteen," Jack mumbled from beneath his mask.

"Fifteen," she insisted.

They loaded Jack into the ambulance. Esther got in and sat next to him. "You'd think he'd be ashamed of himself, wouldn't you," Esther asked. "But look at him. Does he look ashamed?" She patted Jack's shoulder nervously.

Dean had to agree; Jack looked, for some reason, pleased, quite pleased with himself. He'd managed to get his wallet out and he pressed a wad of bills on Dean. There was money there to cover his antojitos and his drinks and plenty left over for Walker. No one could say that Jack London didn't know how to tip.

"And this is yours, Jack." Dean handed over the toy pistol butt first. Jack took it and nodded, as if accepting Dean's surrender.

"See you soon," Jack said.

(10)

Laurel liked the sound of wood being split. There was something inherently satisfying about it.

THUNK

She brought a cup of coffee out to the woodpile and gave it to Jay. Jay was out of his neck brace and his casts but was still moving stiffly, like someone pantomiming a clumsy robot. At least he was up and moving. His bones would be brittle from being in casts for a couple of months. She hoped he'd be careful. If he were to break something else, he might never leave.

THUNK. A piece of wood was split into two burnable pieces. Jay flung the pieces onto a pile.

"Jay, my little lumberjack," she said, "I'm making breakfast."

He set the steel wedge into a crack in the top of the next log and gave it a few light taps. He swung the maul and hit the wedge hard. She could see the pain on his face. It was a glancing blow, and the wedge sailed off to one side. He reset the wedge and brought the maul down again, harder.

THUNK. This time the log split perfectly.

"Are you coming with me to Cap's this afternoon?"

THUNK. And then, THUNK.

"I wasn't planning to." Jay was sweating in spite of the cold.

"You didn't go to Marshall's bachelor party," Laurel said. "You didn't even come to his wedding. You're always whining about how bored you are, then when there's something to do, you're all of a sudden not interested."

"I don't know Marshall. Not really."

"I'd like you to come and meet Jeremy."

"And Ross?"

"He'll be there. His new girlfriend is going to bring some hutspot."

"I hate Mexican food."

THUNK

"It's not Mexican. It's Dutch. I told you, Ross's new squeeze is from Holland."

THUNK, THUNK, THUNK, THUNK!

"I'll try to stop by later," Jay said. "I have to see my lawyer this afternoon. What's for breakfast?"

"Poached eggs," Laurel said.

(11)

"Do you remember," Cap said to Ross, "the night we were fired from the Lucky Café?"

Ross said he remembered. Of course he remembered.

"And we stuffed Harvey's car full of snow."

Thea looked quizzical.

Ross told Thea, "See, one night for no reason, Harvey—Harvey was the owner of the Lucky—he told us we were fired. We went outside, feeling sorry for ourselves. It was a pretty crummy gig, but it was all we had. We hung around in the parking lot for a while—it was snowing—and we found out Harvey had left his car unlocked. We started off by just putting a big, fat snowball where he'd sit on it."

"But we decided that wasn't enough," Cap said. "Pretty soon we had the front seat covered with snow, and we thought, 'What the hell, why stop there?'"

"We found a couple of snow shovels and really got to work," Ross said. "Before long, we had the whole passenger compartment packed with snow."

"We hid behind a pickup truck and waited for Harvey to come out. You should have seen the expression on his face."

"But why? Why did you do that?" Thea asked.

"See, like I said, we'd just lost our jobs as dishwashers. Besides, Harvey was a real douchebag."

Cap clarified, "We'd lost our *job* as a dishwasher. We were only getting paid as if we were one person. We'd both go in to work together because that way we'd always have someone to talk to there. Someone to sneak out and get high with."

"We were supporting about twenty people at School's Out on one dishwasher's salary."

"It was a protest," Cap said. "Harvey wanted us to work as hard as two people, which we figured wasn't fair. We figured we only had to work as hard as half a person each."

Cap and Ross had been remembering. They'd spent much of the afternoon remembering. Some of the memories were vivid to Ross; some of them seemed like someone else's memories.

"What about the time you and Poppy and Laurel and I hung all the silverware at School's Out from the trees. Remember that?"

"Course I do," Cap said. "I remember you fell out of a tree."

Thea was baffled. She was laughing, though. It was the best mood she'd been in since Boston. "Why did you do *that*?"

"I lost my balance. I'm not all that agile.

"I know," Thea said, smiling. "I mean, why did you put silverware in the trees?"

"Who knows?" Ross said. "I'm sure at the time we had what we thought was a perfectly good reason."

"It took us all night," Cap said. "When the sun came up, it was a beautiful sight, all those knives and forks and spoons glittering in the sunlight."

"I remember a potato masher, hanging from the highest branch of that tree out front." Ross pointed out the window at a huge cottonwood. "That damn potato masher deserved to be hung from a tree. Every time you tried to get something from the utensil drawer, that masher would jam the drawer shut."

They went on remembering. They remembered:

- the guy who thought he was a lighthouse and made foghorn noises
- the night of a furious winter storm, when the wind blew down the chicken coop, and they had to dash around in the driving snow trying to round up terrified chickens
- the time Andromeda swore she saw a squirrel with a child's face in the woods
- when Stash fell off a cliff when he was tripping on purple double domes (Ross thought) or orange barrels (as Cap remembered) and wasn't hurt at all

- the time a horrified Johnny AWOL thought he saw J. Edgar Hoover at a hardware store in town
- the guy who would stand on his head and say "mom O" any time someone else said "O wow"
- the lunar eclipse, when everyone marched around School's Out banging on pots and pans; the eclipse occurred at the height of an outbreak of Colorado tic fever at Schools out, and at least half the pot-and-pan bangers—Ross included—were marching around dazed and feverish
- Rocco the goat, who committed suicide
- the woman no one knew who arrived one night and sat on the porch of the Earth Cult Lodge, and wept inconsolably for eight hours straight and left at dawn without ever telling anyone why

They were exhausted by memories then, and took a break in the present.

"Your cabin's looking good, Cap," Ross said.

"I've had plenty of time to work on it. It's always had plenty of potential." Cap's cabin had been the camp chaplain's cabin back when School's Out had been the Rocky Mountain Methodist Youth Camp.

"Oh, it's Tara compared to what it used to be."

Thea got up and looked around the living room. "I like this cabin," she said. "It feels so... so *gezellig*."

"What's that mean, Thea?" Cap asked her.

"It's hard to translate exactly. I guess the closest word is cozy. Comfy."

"*Gezellig*," Cap said. "I like that word."

Thea walked around Cap's living room and looked at the black-and-white photos.

- An old photo of the skating rink that had once been in the town square. The women skaters were wearing long skirts and fancy hats.
- A photo of the Ice Palace when it was melting. It looked like it was modeled on one of Mad King Ludwig's fairy-tale castles. The towers were leaning at drunken angles and the palace walls were buckling. It reminded her a little of the wind-battered sandcastle she'd seen on the beach on her last day in Boston.
- A group photo of about twelve people on the front porch of a lodge. It was, she realized, Ross and Laurel's wedding day. She saw a younger Ross standing on the steps with his arm around

Laurel. He was at least a head taller than everyone else in the photo. His hair was longer, his beard shorter, and he was wearing a Mexican shirt. She'd seen that gaudy raspberry shirt with bright yellow pockets hanging in the closet in Ross's old room back in the Cheeseburger. Laurel was holding Jeremy and both of them were looking down at the baby. She was wearing what Thea guessed was a Mexican wedding dress. Next to Ross was his brother Marshall in a suit and tie. Cap was also in the photo, wearing a kaftan and a huge sombrero. Squatting on the steps on the left side of the porch was someone wearing a gorilla suit.

- A portrait of a woman—Poppy, she assumed—standing in a snowstorm. She was wearing a long shearling coat, the kind Meredith wore. Meredith had brought hers back from Afghanistan. Thea remembered seeing a photo of the Beatles wearing coats like that. In this photo, Poppy's eyes were closed, and she was playing the violin. Thea imagined she was playing a sad song. Maybe a sad Beatles song. "Yesterday," maybe.

Cap noticed her looking at that photo. "I took that picture of Poppy on my birthday back in December," he said. "She was playing 'Happy Birthday.'"

Thea looked at the wood carvings scattered around the living room. "Did you carve these animals?"

"Just something to do on those long winter's nights," Cap said.

"I like the moose, and the beaver, but I especially like the bear," Thea said. "I love bears. I've never seen one, though, except at the zoo in London."

"You might see a couple of them if you spend any time up here. There's a three-legged bear we call Tripod and another one we call Mr. Goodbear —we think they're brothers. They come around about once a week and chow down on the garbage. Not this time of year, though; they're still sleeping. Here," he said, handing Thea the bear carving. "This is yours."

"Oh, no, I didn't mean... I couldn't..."

"No, I want you to have it. I can carve another bear. I have plenty of time on my hands lately."

Thea knew that, by *lately*, he meant "since Poppy left." *Why is everyone leaving everyone else? Why can't anyone stay together? Is it something in the water? The air? Are they putting something in the food?*

Ross said to Cap, "I wish you'd been in Boston last year. It would have been great to have you help us when we were remodeling."

"I wouldn't have been happy, being back east," Cap said. "I went there once and I didn't like it." He winked at Thea.

"Cap's a native Coloradan," Ross said. "He thinks that makes him special. That's why he's so smug."

"I'm not smug. Just satisfied," Cap said. "Your hutspot was really good, Thea. It went well with the moose burgers."

Ross said, "Those weren't moose burgers. I saw the package. You bought that hamburger at Matt's store."

"You caught me. Well, what I'm going to do is put a little more weed in the old Doc Grabow and then get dessert. I'm not very good at baking in a wood-fired oven. Poppy could, but I can't. But I've got some Sara Lee from Matt's. Ross, would you toss more wood on the fire?"

He opened the door of the stove and threw in an armload of wood. Orange tongues of flame licked around the logs. He gave the fire a couple of pokes. When Ross had lived at School's Out, the stove in his and Laurel's cabin was an evil deity that took control of his life four or five months a year. The only way to placate it was to feed it wood and more wood. Now, though, it felt good to be stoking a fire again. Thea came and stood beside him. He didn't know if she wanted to be close to him or if she was cold.

"You know, Ross, what you should do is move back here," Cap said from the kitchen.

Ross thought about the café for sale in Olde Towne. "That's what everyone's been telling me: my father, Marshall, now you."

"Your father's a very farseeing person. It took me a while to realize that, but he's pretty brilliant. And Marshall—well, he went east, and now he's back. For good, he says."

"Marshall's not me." Ross could feel the change in his pocket heating up from the heat of the stove. "I've got the restaurant to think of."

"We'd have fun," Cap said. "One thing you gotta say, we had fun here."

Ross agreed. They'd had plenty of fun. Not all of it was fun, but a lot of it was.

Cap went on. "I have a feeling a lot of changes are coming down soon, and not very good changes. Things are going to turn bad out there, I mean, god-awful bad. There's going to be all kinds of weird energy flying around. People—people like us—are going to need a place to sit out all that craziness. People who were here before are going to come back. New people are going to come. It's going to be bustling around here again."

Ross found that somewhat hard to picture. Everything except Cap's cabin and Laurel's cabin was looking ramshackle and neglected. A couple of cabins had even collapsed.

"We *always* thought things were bad out there, and were getting worse."

"We were right," Cap said.

"You sound more and more like my dad."

"Like I said, he's something of a visionary, I think. Things may get ugly out there, but School's Out's going to survive. We'll hang in there. We'll thrive. And this time, it's going to be even more fun."

Cap came from the kitchen with his pipe clenched between his teeth. He brought pound cake with frozen strawberries. And Cool Whip. "It's good to know I'm still welcome," Ross said.

"Always," Cap said, putting his arm around Ross, and then around Thea, holding them. "Both of you, always. Jeremy, too."

(12)

Laurel was walking with her son by the creek. They walked past Johnny AWOL's ancient school bus. He'd driven it to School's Out, lived in it while he was here, and abandoned it when he left to rejoin the Army. Spanning a rivulet that flowed into the creek was a little rainbow-colored bridge that Laurel had made. It was close to the spot where she'd buried Ollie.

"I miss Ollie," Laurel said. "Don't you?"

"Uh-huh," Jeremy said.

"How did you feel when I told you what happened?"

"I don't know. Sad, I guess."

Laurel didn't think he sounded all that sad. Not considering how he and Ollie had wandered the hills around School's Out together during the summers.

Jeremy seemed to have grown distant. *Maybe this is how he's going to be from now on. Maybe he's becoming more like Ross.*

Jeremy had taken off one of his gloves and was digging in his mouth. She asked him what the problem was.

"Just a binky," he said. "Did you know I'm going to work at the restaurant when we get back? I'm going to be a bus person. Every Saturday and Sunday at brunch."

It was hard for Laurel to imagine Jeremy having a job, even a job that Ross had created for him. "What are you going to do with all the money you'll make?"

"I don't know. Buy games. Buy a telescope."

"You can't see any stars from Boston."

"Yes, you can. Dad and I go out on the fire escape or up on the roof and look at them sometimes."

"You can see a lot more out here." Laurel realized with a jolt that she'd missed most of her son's childhood. Three months every summer and Christmas every other year wasn't enough. What if she moved to Boston and opened a studio there? She could see him every day or two. Could she stand living in a city? Or maybe—Jay was a lawyer, he could help her renegotiate the agreement with Ross. Maybe she could have Jeremy come to Colorado and go to school here and spend his summers in Boston. Or at least live half the year here. But Ross would never agree, and if she tried to force the issue, he'd never speak to her again. That was nearly as unthinkable as not seeing Jeremy.

"Jeremy," she said, "do you dream a lot?"

"I don't know. Why?"

"I was just wondering. Tell me one of your dreams."

"I don't remember any." He threw a stick into the creek. If Ollie had been there, he would have looked quizzically at them. Ollie didn't chase sticks. He didn't like cold water. He didn't like water at all.

"Try."

"Well, I had a dream once that my friend Mojave and I were sitting on the floor behind a chair playing The Somme."

"Uh-huh. What's a somme?"

"*The* Somme. It's a war game that Mojave has. And there was paint all over the floor. And a man came into the room, and..."

"What man? Someone you know?"

"No, just a man. And he asked us, 'Who made all this mess. Who got this paint on the floor?' And we said we didn't know."

"What did the man do then?"

"I don't know. Nothing. Went away, I guess."

"Jer, you have pretty uninteresting dreams, don't you?"

"I do not," he said, and smiled at her.

"You do, too. Your dreams are almost as boring as your dad's. But I love you anyway."

• • •

(13)

Thea asked Cap, "Do you play the harpsichord?"

Cap sat on the bench beside her. "I pound away at it sometimes."

There was an old-fashioned book of sheet music open to a song called Roses of Picardy. "Roses are shining in Picardy / In the hush of the silver dew / Roses are flow'ring in Picardy / But there was never a rose like you."

"I saw an ad in the back of a magazine for harpsichord kits once, and I thought it would be fun to build one. Poppy got it for me for Christmas a year ago. Poppy played the violin when she was a kid and so I bought her a violin a few months back. I thought we could play duets, but... but anyway, I'm still trying to learn to play this thing. I took piano lessons when I was a kid, but I don't remember much of what I learned." He shrugged. "It's just something else to keep me busy."

The harpsichord had two keyboards and reverse-color keys—black naturals and white sharps. She asked Cap about that.

"Because, back in Baroque times, the white keys were made of ivory, and the black ones were made of ebony. Ivory was more expensive than wood, and there are fewer sharp notes than natural ones, so... least, that's what I read in the manual that came with the kit. But these keys are all plastic."

Thea hit a couple of chords, an A minor, then a C major. "It's a beautiful instrument. And it has a nice sound, a nice tinkling sound. You must have done a good job."

Cap thanked her, then said, "I like the way that necklace looks on you." When Laurel had come in this afternoon, she'd strolled up to Thea and fastened the necklace around her neck. It was a silver Kokopelli pendant with a flashing blue light for an eye.

She nodded. "That was nice of Laurel."

"So, how do you like it here so far? I've never been to Holland, but I imagine it's a lot different. It's real flat. And there are canals. And you can smoke grass in coffee shops there."

"I guess you can if you want to," Thea said. "Ross tried to tell me what it was like out here. He talks about School's Out a lot. But you can't imagine what a place is like until you go there and see for yourself. I like it here—the mountains, the forest, the creek. It's beautiful. I can see why you and Laurel have stayed."

"I don't know where else I'd go," Cap said.

Thea ran a finger over the gold-leaf script above the center C note on the harpsichord. NON PRO UNA, SED PRO OMNIBUS CANTABO.

"Poppy told me to write that," Cap said. "She took Latin in high school. I think it means that the harpsicord plays for everyone. But really--no one ever hears it but me."

(14)

Laurel and Jeremy were still on their walk. Cap and Thea had gone down to the pig pen; Thea was going to see some pig tricks. Only Lola would be performing; Dotty was suffering from dippity pig syndrome and was in a lot of pain, barely able to walk. Her hind legs were virtually paralyzed. The vet had told Cap that, in a week or so, Dotty would be rejoining Lola in their *pas de deux*. In the meantime, she was too hopped up on piggy goofballs to stir out of her hut.

Ross would have gone with them, but then Jay had come in just as they were having cake. After dessert, Thea and Cap had left without inviting him to come along, and he was stuck in the cabin with Jay. Ross and Jay were both sitting in rocking chairs, rocking chairs that Cap had made.

Even though Jay was a lawyer himself, he'd been in town seeing a lawyer. Jay, it seemed, had a legal problem of an unspecified type. According to Laurel, Jay had had nothing but problems, legal and medical, since the reunion.

They rocked on. Ross's chair wobbled as he rocked. Cap needed to do a little more work on it. Jay was sitting very stiffly in his rocker. Ross tried to think of something to say to him.

He could say, think they'll disbar you for whatever it is you've done?

Or how about: Laurel's a little pile driver in bed, isn't she? Bet you have bruises.

Or even better: You know what Laurel likes best? Put your finger in her butt just at the big moment.

The thing is, Laurel might like that.

Thea didn't.

She'd hated it, in fact. He tried it one night in the bedroom that had once been his and Marshall's. It wasn't easy to talk her into making love in the Cheeseburger; his parents' bedroom was right next door. Then, when he tried out Wim's sexual tip, she let out a loud, piercing screech, like a distressed wolverine. He half expected his father to come crashing into the room, demanding to know what the hell was going on. That was the only time they'd been intimate since leaving Boston.

"That son of a bitch Wim."

"What?" Jay said. He stopped rocking.

Ross realized he'd said that aloud. He blamed Cap's pot. *It's the pot's fault. It makes me say things when I think I'm thinking them. Now Jay thinks I called him a son of a bitch.*

He probably is *an SOB. He looks like one. But I wouldn't have mentioned it to him.*

"I said, that was some good cake. I think I'll have another piece."

"It's just Sara Lee. And Cool Whip tastes like plastic," Jay said, and sneered.

Compared to Wim's, though, Jay's sneer was strictly amateur hour.

(15)

Dean was putting Visine in his eyes when the phone rang. He'd been staring too long at the read-out on the calculator. According to his calculations, after meeting payroll and paying rent, only forty-eight cents would be left in the corporate account for ¿Por Qué No?.

It was Amy calling. "Were you sleeping?"

"No, entertaining," Dean said. "Quiet, girls, quit giggling. I'll come back to bed in just a minute."

Dean could practically hear Amy roll her eyes. "I don't think any woman would get into that rat's nest of a bed," she said.

"There are worse-looking beds," Dean said, thinking of Buzz's cot. "You know, it's funny, but I had an inkling that you'd be calling soon."

"You did, huh. Well, why I'm calling is to warn you: Don't write any big checks."

"How the hell do you know anything about our business finances?"

"I'm talking about *our* account. Our personal account."

"What do you mean, *our* account. We don't have an account."

"Of course we do. We have a joint account, remember?"

"That was for when we were living together. So you could write checks for the rent and the other bills. But you never put any money into that account. That money is clearly..."

"I withdrew half the money, Dean."

"You did what! Aiii-meee, why the hell would you do that? Why? I can't believe you'd do something like that! You hang on. Hang on just a goddamn minute!" Dean went to the kitchen and opened the liquor cabinet. Because of the blizzard, he hadn't been able to get to a liquor store and he'd been rationing himself all day. He poured what he'd been saving for the rest of the night and for tomorrow into a pint glass and lit a cigarette from a gas burner.

Maud was noisily drinking water, her dog tag tinkling against the rim of the metal bowl.

"All right, now listen to me. That money you withdrew, that money is mine, unquestionably mine, no doubt about it. You had no right, no fucking right to take even one penny of..."

"Legally, I've got every right. It was a joint account. I remember going to the State Street Bank with you and opening it. We both signed those forms. I figured I was only entitled to half of it, but I could have drained it completely and still been within my rights."

Dean realized he'd left a flank dangling helplessly. And there wasn't a thing, not one goddamn thing he could do about it. "Legally, yeah, but what about morally? What about morally, huh? You never put one goddamn cent into..."

"I'm not going to argue morals with you, Dean. You're lucky I left you half."

"I still don't believe this. Why are you doing this to me? Could you tell me that, at least? Why?"

"I think you know why. I kept telling Daddy, it's not *that* spicy, because mine was pretty mild, but then I realized you'd doctored Daddy's lunch. His face turned red, and he was clutching at his throat. He drank half a carafe of water to ease the pain, and then..."

"Water doesn't help. It makes it worse. He should have been drinking milk."

"Yeah, that's what the woman in the kitchen, the cookie lady, that's what she told us. She brought him a cup of half & half. Did you know my father has a peptic ulcer? We almost called an ambulance. Daddy was up all night, his tummy hurt so much."

Dean nearly felt a twinge of guilt.

"You're lucky I talked Daddy out of suing the restaurant. That would have cost you a lot more. The only reason I stopped him was, that would hurt Ross, too."

Right now, you could sue us and you'd only get forty-eight cents.

"Still... a few chili peppers... they're going to cost me almost a grand?"

"Actually, there was $1,483.45 in our account, and I withdrew $741.72. Half. I even let you keep the extra penny."

"I wish I could get a job eating hot peppers at those wages." Dean lit another cigarette from the one he was smoking. "I hope you're at least planning to cut Dorky Dan in on your ill-gotten loot. He's the one who ate the peppers."

"I offered to, but he told me to keep it. He doesn't need the money."

"Neither do you. You've got a job. You're just doing this to..."

"I do need it. I quit my job. When it first started snowing, my school bus slid down a hill and skidded right through a stop sign. If there had been a car coming the other way, it would have T-boned my bus. Some of my kids could have been killed. I just can't do it anymore."

"That's not my problem. You call me in the middle of the night like the goddamn Gestapo and you tell me..."

"I don't think the Gestapo called before they came by. Although that's something you need to start doing. I don't want you coming over here again unannounced. Anyway, that's all I have to say to you. I just didn't want you to be overdrawn."

"Oh, yeah, I bet you didn't. Look, Amy..." Dean could hear a Southern whine creeping into his voice. That happened when he was stressed. He took a quick drink. "Look, Amy..." he said again. It sounded better this time. But it was too late. He heard the unmistakable rustle of a phone about to be hung up.

(16)

Ross was trying on his tuxedo when his mother knocked on the door. "You look so handsome in a tux, Ross. I haven't seen you in one since you took Winifred to the prom. It fits pretty well."

"I don't think I've been in one since then."

"I still can't believe you wore that hideous shirt with all the pleats and the pockets when you and Laurel got married. What was it called? It sounded like guacamole."

He told her it was a guayabera. "It's a Mexican wedding shirt. We'd been in Mexico. It was a wedding," Ross said. "These pants are a little short. High water pants, we used to call them."

"They didn't have pants long enough to fit you at the rental place." She straightened his cummerbund. "Where's your bowtie?"

Ross's head shot up as if he'd been given an uppercut so that she could see his bowtie.

His mother said, "When you do that, you look..."

"I know. Like a Pez dispenser."

"I was going to say like a Zippo lighter. You wouldn't consider shaving your beard for the wedding, would you?"

"I've been thinking about shaving it, tell you the truth. It is looking a little raggedy, isn't it? I had Thea trim it for me, but that was over a month ago."

"I think you'd look so much better without it. Fresh faced, younger." She straightened his bowtie. "I heard you and your dad talking in his den last night."

"Yeah, we were talking about Aunt Sophie."

"What about Sophie?"

"He wanted me to assure him that the money she fronted me for the restaurant was a loan. Not a gift. I told him, when she wrote that check, she said that she didn't expect me to pay her back."

"What did he say to that?"

"He said, you know your Aunt Sophie is a little balmy. You should pay her back."

"Did you argue about it?"

"That was the remarkable thing. We didn't. He was being very civil and reasonable. Very... undad-ish. He seems... a little different."

"Yes. Have you and Marshall talked about that?"

"Uh, no. We've talked about Dad, but not about that, really. He just said Dad was mellower these days."

"Your father didn't want me to tell you this, but... the week between Christmas and New Year's, he had a stroke."

Ross found this news shocking. More than shocking. He couldn't remember his father ever being sick. He'd sliced his foot with an ax once, but it hadn't slowed him down. He'd treated the wound himself; compared to some of the wounds his father had seen in the war, a gashed foot was pretty minor.

"Was it a bad stroke?"

"There aren't any good strokes, but... the doctor said it could have been a lot worse. It was strange, though, spending New Year's Eve in the hospital."

"I can't believe he didn't tell me. I can't believe he wouldn't let you tell me."

"You don't know your father very well then. I don't think he would have told Marshall and me if he hadn't needed a ride to the hospital. But you're right, it did change him. Somewhat for the better—he's easier to get along with—but it also changed him for the worse, I think. It's like there's something... something missing, some spark, some..."

Ross tried to think of the phrase. "Elan vital. Life force."

"Yes, life force. He still has it but... some of it's missing, or it's buried inside. So where's your girlfriend?"

"Jeremy's going to miss almost three weeks of school. I got his teachers to give him some assignments and homework to do while we're gone. Thea's been helping him."

"She's very nice," his mother said. "We like her... it's just that..."

"Just that what?"

"She's... a little remote..."

"So am I." Ross thought of how remote his father had been when he was growing up. And his mother too. No wonder he was the way he was.

"It's just that she's kind of hard to get to know. We missed her at Nikki's shower the other evening."

"Yeah, she wasn't feeling very well that night."

"She's coming to the rehearsal? And the rehearsal dinner?"

"I don't know. I hope so."

"Tell me, do you know what size dress Thea wears?"

Ross tried to remember if he'd ever seen her in a dress. A skirt, once or twice. But mostly she wore jeans. "I have no idea."

"I'd guess an eight," Ross's mother said. "Wish I still wore an eight. So, have you seen Laurel yet?"

"Briefly, at Cap's. She and Jeremy took a long walk so... I didn't see much of her."

"It doesn't bother Laurel that you're here with someone else? I mean, you two are still married, aren't you?"

"Well, technically, but... she's with someone else too, mom, some guy from Chicago named Jay."

"We thought we heard Thea scream the other night. What was that about?"

"Nothing. Nothing at all."

Ross's mom nodded. "I see. Well, I'm going to go outside for my cigarette. I'll see you at the rehearsal. Don't mention anything to your dad about our little talk."

Ross sat on the bed and thought. Then he went into the bathroom he and Marshall had once shared. He used a scissors to cut away most of his beard. He found a Schick safety razor in the medicine cabinet. The only other things in the medicine chest were an old styptic pencil and an empty tube of Brylcreem. "A little dab'll do ya." The blade was a little rusty, but it still worked. His chin came into view. *Hello there, chin. It's been a while.* It was a stranger's chin. He had a razor cut on his cheek. He tried to stop the bleeding with the styptic pencil, but it was so old that it crumbled into powder.

. . .

(17)

Dean woke up with the theme song from *Rawhide* running through his head. When he was a child, Dean's mother hadn't allowed him to watch anything remotely violent on TV. She had, however, let him tune in to shows at the beginning to listen to the theme music. He often woke up mentally replaying songs from *Rawhide*, *Maverick*, *Have Gun Will Travel*, and the *Untouchables*, shows that had been gone from the airwaves for years.

Somehow the sound of a ringing phone got tangled up in the melody of the *Rawhide* theme. It didn't seem all that out of place there. He crawled out of bed and answered it.

"Rollin', rollin', rollin'..."

"What the hell you want now?" Dean thought it was Amy, calling back to gloat some more.

"Mr. Burgess?"

"Move 'em on, head 'em up..."

"Is this Mr. Dean Burgess with whom I'm speaking?"

With a last crack of a bullwhip, the music faded from Dean's head. "This is Rick Casey, Mr. Burgess. Rick Casey with Argus Security." He sounded like a kid with an officious voice.

"Yeah? So what?"

"I think we may have a problem, Mr. Burgess."

"Call Ross."

"Would that be Mr. Ross Jarboe?"

"That's right. Call Ross. Tell him about your problem."

"I called him first, actually. No answer."

"That's because he's in Colorado."

"Like I was saying, Mr. Burgess, it appears we have a problem. At oh one hundred one seven..."

"At what?"

"At one seventeen a.m., the security alarm for 95 Isabella Street went off down at Argus. Only for one minute, twenty-three seconds, but that would have given the intruder time to get in and disarm it, if he or she knew what they were doing."

"Why tell me? Call the police."

"I will, Mr. Burgess, if need be. Are you sure you set the alarm properly before you left tonight?"

"We weren't open tonight and we closed early last night because of the blizzard. I think I did when I was there last."

"Hmm. I think I should pick you up so we can check this out."

"Do you know, do you have any idea how much snow there is out there?"

"Fifty-eight centimeters at Boston Logan. Don't worry. Argus vehicles are all 4-WD."

"Listen, before I go down there, I'm going to call the restaurant. We have sort of an amateur night watchman who sleeps there. I'll call you back. Where are you?"

"In my vehicle, sir." *Figures he'd have a phone in his car.* "I'll move to rendezvous with you, Mr. Burgess, at your residence. If your man gives you an all clear, call Argus. Otherwise, my ETA is seven to eight minutes from now."

~

"What did your man inside have to report?"

"Our man inside didn't answer the phone," Dean said.

"Hmm."

"That doesn't mean much, though. I mean, maybe someone's cut his throat, but probably he's playing pinball. He's a very intense pinball player."

The kid from Argus looked like he was about eighteen, only he was completely bald. He reminded Dean of a young Elmer Fudd. "Coffee in the thermos on the dash," the kid said.

They parked—or rather, left the car by a huge snowbank on Isabella Street. The kid put on a leather cap with long earflaps. They approached the restaurant. "Looks like someone may have taken a jimmy to the front door."

"I don't think so," Dean said. "We had a sloppy carpenter. Are we going to go inside?"

"Affirmative. We'll do a quick recon."

"If you think there's someone in there," Dean said, "let's call the police. If you don't, then let's go home. I'm tired and my feet are cold." Dean hadn't had time to put on socks before he pulled on his boots.

The kid had a walkie-talkie. "We're in position," he told the people at Argus Central, "and we're going in." The voice at the other end was too garbled for Dean to make out much, but the kid apparently was used to mangled language; he replied, "Roger that. Over and out."

"Now listen," Dean said. "I think, all kidding aside..."

"You take the flashlight," the kid said, handing him a huge silver Maglite. "Let me have the keys."

They went in.

"I'll get the lights."

"Don't do anything," the kid said in an intimidating whisper. "Just listen."

Dean listened, but he didn't hear anything except ice falling in the ice machine. He hoped the scoop wasn't in there. The only light was the shifting, rainbow light of the jukebox and the eerie glow of Captain Fantastic. *Pretty goddamn spooky,* Dean thought. He accidentally kicked the host stand. The kid put his finger to his lips, shushing him. Dean imagined him saying, "Shh, be vewy, vewy quiet."

There was a long sheepskin coat draped over one of the barstools.

A toilet flushed. The kid grabbed Dean by the elbow and moved him into the dining room. They took position beside Table 12.

Someone came out of the Baño de Damas and Dean shot a dazzling beam of light in that direction. It was Meredith, wearing a blue blouse and striped blue-and-white knee socks and nothing in between. "Freeze!" the kid barked.

The kid definitely had her covered. His legs were flexed, his feet wide apart. He was holding his Ruger semi-auto in front of him with both hands, holding it sideways. Meredith threw her hands up over her head, which hiked her shirttail up.

"Hello, Dean," someone else said. Someone over by the Stag Table.

Holy hell! Trap! Crossfire! The kid whirled around. "Give me some light!"

Dean reluctantly lifted the light off Meredith. It was Buzz. Buzz in his boxers.

"*¿Qué pasa?,* Dean. Sorry you had to come out in the snow and all. I lent Mer my key, but she didn't punch in the code for the alarm."

"I forgot," Meredith said. Dean shifted the beam back to her. The kid's flashlight was as powerful as a searchlight. Meredith stood there blinking. "Is it okay if I put my arms down now?" she asked.

Dean wanted to say no, no you can't put your arms down, you have to stay like that all night.

The kid was shaking his head. He looked more like a young Elmer Fudd than ever, only he was armed with a handgun, not a double-barreled shotgun. Dean could almost hear him saying to Buzz and Meredith, "You wascally wabbits!"

"My dad always told me you shouldn't tilt your gun like that," Buzz said to the kid. "I mean, it looks cool and all, gangsters do it in the movies, but Big Buzz said it makes it harder to aim."

Meredith and Buzz weren't very far away, so Dean didn't think aiming would be a serious problem. It did look pretty cool.

"Ross, is your friend from the police department?" Buzz asked.

"Rick Casey, Argus Security." The kid was slowly putting his weapon back in his shoulder holster.

"In that case, you guys want to do a little toot? As long as you're here?"

"That's a negative. Not while on duty," Rick Casey said. "Actually, not at any time."

Dean said he wanted to go into the bar first to get himself a drink. His hands were trembling. He knew that some people's hands shook because they needed a drink, but he'd never expected to be one himself. "Okay, Buzz," he said, after two belts of Chivas Regal. "Let's do a quick toot."

"I finally decided," Buzz said. "I'm Ian. I made the change a couple of days ago. Do you think that fits?"

"I do," Meredith said. Her smile was as radiant as the glow from the Wurlitzer and Captain Fantastic combined. "He's definitely Ian."

(18)

For the first time since the catastrophic finger-in-the-butt incident, Ross came to the room he used to share with Marshal to see Thea. He'd been sleeping in the guest room with Jeremy, although some nights, Jeremy slept out at School's Out. He knocked and Thea told him he could come in. The lights were out but the moon was shining through the bedroom window. The window was round to simulate a viewport on a flying saucer. Thea was sitting on the bed and putting moisturizer on her feet. She was wearing one of Marshall's old T-shirts. PRATT INSTITUTE ARCHITEC-TURE, it said. She hadn't been sleeping in the nude since they'd arrived in Colorado. She didn't look particularly happy to see him, but she moved over so there was room on the bed for him.

"You know," Ross said, "I feel like we've been drifting further and further apart on this trip."

Thea shrugged. Her whole body shrugged. She didn't want to talk about any drift. "I'm glad we came," she said.

This was news to Ross.

"When we were out at School's Out," she said, "I couldn't help feeling sorry for Cap. He seems so lonely."

"Laurel told me he's pretty shaken by Poppy's leaving," Ross said. "You can't meet women at School's Out, not anymore, and Cap's too stubborn to go anywhere else."

"No, he won't go anywhere else," Thea said. "He's made a stand."

Ross asked Thea if she wanted to make love.

She shrugged again. "I don't care."

He'd come to this room hoping that Thea would want to. She'd been in a good mood—comparatively, anyway—at Cap's cabin. Ross thought that maybe she'd forgiven him. Now, though, she was back to relentless apathy. Ross found apathy contagious. He wasn't sure he wanted to make love to someone who didn't care one way or another.

Besides, there was the noise problem. It seemed as though he and Thea always had to keep it quiet. There was always someone who might wake up: Amy or Jeremy, in Boston, and Ross's parents here. They had to keep the bedsprings from creaking; they had to keep their teeth clenched, or at least Ross did, to keep from growling and groaning too much. And Thea made some pretty weird noises as she climaxed. He wondered if she would get up with him now, in the middle of the night, and go down to the Grandview Hotel. At the Grandview Hotel, they could make as much noise as they pleased. Thea could moan and yip. Ross could bellow like a wounded moose. Like a goddamn wounded moose.

Would she refuse if he were to ask her? She might say, "I don't care" in that same emotionless voice and get up and come with him. Then again, she might not.

Ross dimly heard the phone ring, clear across the house. He jumped off the bed and raced through the Cheeseburger, hoping to get to the kitchen before his father did.

Ross's father had less territory to cover. He was already talking on the phone by the time Ross made it to the kitchen. Ross noticed for the first time that his father had gray in his hair, quite a lot of gray. His father handed him the phone. Ross expected a cuff on the side of the head, or at least a reprimand for having friends who would call so late. Instead he got a sympathetic look and even a pat on the shoulder. It was as if his father were saying, "I'm glad I don't have to deal with a phone call at this hour of the night."

It was Dean. Ross said, "You know it's one a.m. here?"

"That's nothing. It's three a.m. here."

"You woke my father up."

"I know. He told me, and I apologized." Dean actually did sound contrite. "I can't sleep after I do coke. It feels like a bee crawled up my nose and stung me nine times."

"A bee can only sting you once," Ross said, "Then it dies."

"A wasp, then. Or nine bees. Do you want to hear why I was out doing blow in the wee hours of morning?"

Dean told him anyway. And he told him about the luncheon special he'd served Dorky Dan. About Robin II and Vince. About Jack London. About Amy's end run through his bank account. About the snow.

"You closed the restaurant because it snowed?"

"This wasn't an ordinary storm, Ross, it was a killer blizzard."

"Did you shovel in front of the restaurant?" The last time it had snowed hard, back in January, the city had ticketed them for not clearing the sidewalk on Isabella Street in front of ¿Por Qué No?.

"We shoveled."

Usually Buzz shoveled show, but he'd gone to Government Center to make his name change official. Dean sent the entire floor staff out to clear the sidewalk. There was only one snow shovel, so they had to take turns. Those who weren't shoveling threw snowballs at one another. There was a lot of squealing and laughing. Adriana was the best shot; she hit Keith right in the forehead from twelve paces away. When Adriana wasn't looking, Keith dropped a handful of snow down her back. Robin I missed when she fired a snowball at Patsy, but she hit Chris Bean, who was shoveling the sidewalk in front of Copenhagen Cream. Meredith was, surprisingly, the most energetic shoveler. She really attacked the snow, and she did so in high heels. Dean stood at the window by Table 7, looking out, like a dad watching his kids on a snow day. He took a few photographs through the window. And he muttered to himself, over and over, those lines from the Black-bird *poem: "It was evening all afternoon. / It was snowing / And it was going to snow."*

"We didn't have any customers at all. I closed the restaurant about seven. And then it snowed all night, and for most of the morning, so I didn't open today. The whole city's shut down. It's like there's a war on or something. There's not much to eat in my apartment. There're some pickles in the fridge and there's some dried mung beans and a box of those little paper cups for baking muffins in the cabinet. Oh, and some tea bags, but I don't drink tea. There wasn't any booze left either. And my BIC lighter was dead. In a way, it's a good thing I had to go to the restaurant tonight.

If I had to light any more cigarettes from the gas burner, I wouldn't have any eyebrows left."

"And I suppose you brought a couple of bottles home with you, as well as matches."

"I brought *one* bottle home." He didn't mention that it was a half-gallon bottle of Chivas. "I'll replace it when things get back to normal."

"I'm a little worried about you, Dean. You're kind of a mess."

"It's been a difficult time. You would pick a time like this to leave town. You know, I still can't feature Meredith with Ian."

"Who's Ian?"

"Buzz is Ian. He finally decided."

"I didn't know Ian was on his short list."

"I think Meredith liked that name, for some reason. Can you believe she'd trudge through all that snow in the middle of the night to be with him?"

"I can't believe she'd get on that cruddy little cot with him."

"They weren't using the cot. They were using a tablecloth on the floor in the South 40. Oh, and we only have forty-eight cents left in the corporate account."

"Better save that for emergencies," Ross said. "Thing is, last month you figured we had about $140,000 in that account, and we actually had around $14,000."

"Yeah, I'd better get Patsy to check my math. She's a better bookkeeper. So, have things been as dreadful out there as they have been here?"

"I don't know. Thea's been acting weird. I'm pretty sure... no, I'm definitely sure she knows about... you know. "

"Well, I didn't tell her anything. You've seen Laurel?"

"Yeah, we were out at School's Out yesterday and she stopped by for a few minutes and went off with Jeremy. She's looking good. But she's living with someone. Someone named Jay."

"Did she and Thea have a little chat?"

"No. Well, they talked for a few minutes, I guess. Laurel gave her a necklace."

Dean hummed the theme from the movie *Jaws*. "You could be in big trouble. You should never let an old flame talk to a new lover. Never."

It *had* been strange, seeing the two of them together. It was like trick photography, like seeing the Eiffel Tower on the same postcard as the Taj Mahal.

Ross asked Dean why he'd called.

"I'm sick of my own company. Everything's such a mess here; my apartment's a disaster zone. My shirts all stink, and my socks are all mixed up and there are evil bugs living in the kitchen and there's some kind of science fiction mold growing in the sink. I still haven't picked up the clothes that fell down that night I pushed Amy into the closet. There are dust bunnies big as tumbleweeds in my bedroom, and my hemorrhoids have flared up. You know what I hate most about living alone? When you come back home, there are never any surprises. No one's baked muffins or washed the dishes. No one's waiting for you in the nude. No one's made the bed while you were out. I hate unmade beds, they're so depressing, but I never manage to get around to making mine, even when I'm stuck inside all day."

Out in Colorado, Ross yawned. "Sleep on top of the covers. That way you won't have to make it."

"It's too cold in my apartment to do that. And it's too—it's just not..."

"It's not *gezellig*," Ross said.

"It's not what?"

"*Gezellig*. It means cozy. In Dutch."

"Yeah, exactly. Sleeping on top of your covers is the opposite of *gezellig*. You know, whoever said, 'You've made your bed, now you have to lie in it'—whoever said that had it exactly backwards."

30
SLOPPY SECONDS

W<small>HEN</small> R<small>OSS</small> <small>PULLED INTO THE PARKING LOT BEHIND THE</small> L<small>UCKY</small> C<small>AFÉ</small>, <small>ALL HE</small>
could see of Laurel was her jewelry, sparkling away. He parked his father's
Jeep Commando next to the U.S. Grape.

She opened the door for him. "The good old Grape," he said.

"The good old Grape," she repeated. "The Grape's old, all right. The
Grape's practically senile. Plus, it gets about three miles a gallon, and gas
is up to sixty-three cents. Sometimes I spend more on gas than I make at a
fair."

He looked at her pendant, a crystal parrot that kept changing colors.
"Nice things you're doing these days."

"Jay helped me with this one," Laurel said. "He's good with his hands,
for a lawyer. You remember that old clock, the one we bought in Mexico
that never worked right? He fixed that. He fixed the toaster. He fixes all
kinds of things."

"Where are we going?"

"I haven't given it any thought. We can't go to my cabin. We can't go
back to your parents' house, obviously."

"No," Ross said, "we can't."

"So, I don't know. You want to go into the Lucky, get some coffee?"

Ross shook his head. "Harvey might recognize me. He might
remember what Cap and I did to his car. Things could get unpleasant."

"Well, I don't want to just sit in this parking lot," Laurel said. "The
heater isn't working very well."

This was starting to remind Ross of high school, when he'd been with Winifred. *No particular place to go.*

"We could get a room at the Grandview," Laurel said.

Ross had been thinking a few days before about going to the Grandview, and about bellowing like a moose there. Only, according to the original plan, he would have been bellowing with Thea. "We could, I suppose. If you want."

"No. If *you* want."

Ross was starting to get cold. "Well, let's go *some*where."

Laurel started the engine. "Hand me the defroster, would you?"

"What?"

"The defroster. You're sitting on it." The defroster, it turned out, was a pink-and-white dish towel.

"Where did you tell Jay you were going?"

"I told him I was meeting you."

"What did he say about that?"

"He didn't much like it. What did you tell Thea?"

"I didn't tell her anything. I just left right after you called."

Laurel said, "I should have guessed." She pulled out of the parking lot.

Skeets was behind the desk at the Grandview Hotel. He glanced up nervously when Ross and Laurel came in. He shoved his magazine out of sight behind the desk.

Skeets was one year older than Ross and one year younger than Marshall. Neither Marshall nor Ross had considered Skeets a particularly close friend, yet he was always around. Skeets had not been a popular person when they'd all been in high school, partly because of his unusual looks. He had a very angular appearance. Everything on Skeets stuck out. He had a pointy nose and jug ears and an Adam's apple. He had bony elbows and knobby knees. His cowlick could be tamed only by rubbing it with a bar of wet soap. His mother had named him after her favorite rockabilly singer, Skeets Macdonald. His name was not, as popularly rumored, short for Skeezix, despite a certain resemblance to Uncle Wiggily's scrawny, gawky, crow-like nemesis.

Although somewhat odd looking, Skeets had won a certain amount of respect in high school because there was virtually nothing he wouldn't do on a bet, even one involving a paltry sum. Once, surrounded by a cheering crowd of students behind the high school gym, he'd chewed and swallowed the embryo of a white rat that had been pickled in formaldehyde only because someone had bet him two dollars that he wouldn't.

When Ross had started hanging around at School's Out, he'd lost contact with Skeets. Skeets hadn't approved of those people out there. Now Skeets was managing his mother's hotel. Skeets's mother had always had an unhealthy fear that he ran around with women. This was never a very credible threat, but she took it seriously. She would often say to him, "Sweet Jesus didn't kiss no women at night." She'd been pleased when Marshall had whisked away first Annabelle and then Nikki, since those two were the only women who had worked at the Grandview who'd been remotely a danger. Still, she didn't trust Skeets, and she'd taken to dropping by the hotel at odd hours to make sure he was behaving.

"Ross," Skeets said. "You dropping by to say hello, or you want a room?" Skeets laughed a nervous laugh.

"Both," Ross said.

"You want a regular room, or something special?"

"What do you have that's special?"

"I got color TVs. I got waterbeds."

"Waterbeds, huh?"

"Sometimes we get overflow from Viking Mountain. Skiers like waterbeds, things like that. Course, one guest said, when a train went by, there were white caps on her waterbed. Don't know if that's true; never slept on one myself."

"I guess we'll take a regular room with a regular bed."

Skeets cackled again. Another reason he'd not been popular in high school was the awfulness of his laugh.

"You know, I was maybe going to be Marshall's best man. I asked him if he wanted me to be, and he said he'd think about it. Then he heard you were coming..."

Ross apologized.

"You're his brother. Guess it only made sense he'd have you as best man if you were around. Too bad you missed his bachelor's party. We had it in the ballroom here—just Marshall, Jake, Cap, couple of guys from Marshall's b-ball team, and me in that big old room. Kind of depressing."

"Yeah, well, my bus broke down on the way here and I was stuck in Wyoming."

"I heard that girl you had at his wedding was a Dutch girl."

Ross looked over at Laurel. Her face was expressionless.

"Where'd you hear that, Skee?"

"Your mom told her hairdresser. Her hairdresser told my mom."

"Those hairdressers," Ross said, "they'll drag your life right out into the streets."

"That girl you were with, she didn't look very happy. And then she just disappeared."

After Marshall and Nikki had danced their first dance as a married couple, almost everyone in the Snakebite Bar, where'd they'd held the reception, came out on the floor for the next dance, even Ross's mother and father. Although dancing was anathema to Ross, he'd looked for Thea, but didn't see her anywhere. Finally he looked next door, in the Pow Wow Steak House. Thea was over there, sitting in a booth with Cap, drinking coffee and talking. She was wearing the dress his mother had bought her for the wedding. Ross thought about joining them but they seemed to be in the middle of a very intense conversation, and it was time for Ross to give the toast.

"Where's your Dutch girl tonight?"

"Can we just get the key?" Laurel asked him.

"Soon as you sign in," Skeets said

Skeets rotated the register and pushed it in front of Ross. He signed the register MR. AND MS. JARBOE. It came as a small shock when he realized that what he'd written was, in fact, true. He wrote down his Boston address and shoved the book across the desk.

Ross saw a *Hustler Magazine* partly hidden under the blotter on the counter behind the front desk. That's why Skeets had been nervous when they'd come in. He was afraid it was his mother checking up on him, and that she'd caught him fooling around with the women of *Hustler*.

Skeets looked at his sign-in. "Boston, huh? Heard that's where you were. Never been there myself. Heard the people there are real unfriendly."

"Some are. Most people there are about as friendly as people anywhere else."

"Well, I guess there's gotta be something good about every place, or nobody would want to live there."

"I guess," Ross said. "How are things here at the Grandview? Business good?"

Skeets handed Ross a heavy brass key on a worn leather fob. "Business is okay. Nobody hardly skiing this year, not much snow to speak of. Open winter. Last night was the first snow in almost a month. But we had a good summer and lots of people were out here in September to look at the aspen. Anyway... things are okay. In fact, everything would be fine if your brother would quit marrying all the fucking maids."

~

Ross pulled the curtain aside and looked out the window. Despite the hotel's name, it wasn't much of a view: railroad tracks and the back of an auto-parts store.

Laurel threw her backpack on the bed. "There's a bottle of Irish whiskey in there," she said, going into the bathroom. "And instant coffee. You could use hot tap water and make yourself some Irish coffee."

Ross sat down on the bed. He was on vacation from making drinks.

A few minutes later she sat next to him. She was untying her cufflinks. Laura was wearing, as she often did, a man's white dress shirt, size small, with French cuffs. She used little strips of leather as cufflinks.

"So... when you told me Jay was going to see a lawyer... was that about a divorce? Are we getting divorced?"

"No, nothing like that. Jay has a legal problem. Well, maybe both of us do.""

"You have a problem too?"

"Umm... I don't know... I don't really think so, but... "

Ross asked her to tell him about the problem.

"He rented a condo over in Viking Mountain Village from this family who'd gone to Europe. Then he advertised it for sale at a really low price. People came by, took a look, and knew it wouldn't last. Most of them were happy to give him a deposit to hold it for them. Even in cash. He's a lawyer so he could draw up these phony contracts that looked real."

"And you were involved in this how?"

"Sometimes I was there when buyers came in, pretending to be his wife. He thought somehow that made the whole bit look more legit. And Jay threw some money my way. He gave me more money in a week than I usually make in a month. He was only going to do this for one more day, but he scheduled appointments too close together. A couple on their way out talked to three girls on their way in, and they said they'd bought it, and given him a deposit, so when Jay told the girls that the condo was still available if they could come up with a deposit... well, before long the police showed up."

"So you're in trouble?"

"I don't know. I wasn't there when he got busted, and I haven't gotten a visit from the cops. I mean, I helped a little but... it was mostly his show. I don't know what will happen."

"Maybe you should get away from here."

"Yeah, I could run away to Mexico," Laurel said.

Ross said, "Sometimes I feel like doing that."

"We can go together then." Laurel got up and made two cups of instant coffee with hot tap water, and she poured a healthy dollop of Irish whiskey into his. She put half a thimbleful of whiskey into her own.

"So we're still not getting a divorce?"

"I don't see why we should. Unless you want one. Do you?"

"I just thought that you and Jay..."

"No, baby," she said, "I like Jay—most of the time, anyway—and I feel kind of sorry for him. He's one of the unluckiest men I've ever known. But he's picky. He's finicky. I don't do well with finicky men. He has to have his eggs poached just so—not runny, not too hard—and you can't buy frozen orange juice for him, you have to squeeze it, and you have to squeeze it the night before and put it in the fridge so it's cold enough in the morning, and you have to strain out all the pulp—not most of it, all of it. And the stereo has to be at just the right volume, you can't change it, and he put all my books and records in alphabetical order, and even the goddamn blinds all have to be at the same height. It doesn't feel like my cabin anymore. Everything is adjusted to Jay's level of comfort."

"Not to mention... he's something of a criminal," Ross said.

Laurel started unbuttoning her blouse. She made the undoing of each button into an event. "Another thing about Jay, he's not silly. Maybe that comes from being a lawyer, I don't know. These days, you can sleep with just about anyone, but to be silly with someone, really silly, that takes a lot. You have to be totally intimate with someone. You and I—we could get downright silly sometimes, you know? Jay can't hack that. Oh, he tries, but it comes across as ridiculous, not silly."

Ross wondered if he was still silly; if, in fact, he'd ever been all that silly.

Behind the hotel, a whistle screamed as a coal train rumbled by. The bed they were sitting on shook. It felt like an earthquake.

Laurel undid the last button and shed her blouse. She was wearing a bra, black trimmed with white lace. He had seldom seen her in a bra. She hastily reached behind her back, unhooked it, and shrugged it off. The parrot on her left breast seemed to have spread its wings slightly.

Ross poured more Jameson into his lukewarm coffee. He looked at her, but she shook her head.

Laurel took a red scarf out of her backpack and covered the bedside lamp with it. The room was suffused with rosy light. Laurel's jeans disappeared. And then her black panties, which were also trimmed with lace.

He'd definitely never known her to wear matching underwear. "Well, are you just going to lie there?"

"I don't know. What do you want me to do?"

"Oh brother." She reached for his zipper. "You think I'm going to let you come all this way and not make love to me?" She pulled his cock out. "Gilbert!" she squealed happily. "Why hi, Gilbert, remember me?"

That's what she used to call it: Gilbert. He'd never known why.

"No, don't do that," Ross said, but it was too late. She'd already gotten a purple marker out of her backpack and was drawing a face on Gilbert. That was something else she used to do.

Ross rubbed the flesh over his pubic bone. It was sore all right. Laurel was even more energetic than he remembered. Several times she'd said "Faster! Harder," but he'd been going at top speed and as hard as he could. Gilbert's painted face had turned into a purple smear. There were uneven red patches on Laurel's cheeks and chest, a sure sign that she'd had an orgasm.

"We should have gotten the room with the waterbed," Laurel said. Her voice sounded different. It had dropped a notch or two and become softer, dreamier. She was practically humming her words. "I bet we would have made some whitecaps of our own."

"What are you grinning about?" he asked her. Ross hadn't seen her smile like that for a long time.

"I can't help it. I never could keep from grinning after we fucked."

"You didn't always grin. Toward the end there, you..."

"Toward the end, everything went wrong. But right now, my whole body is grinning," Laurel said. "You're grinning, too."

That was true, he was. If he were wearing suspenders, he would have snapped them. If he had a tail, it would be wagging. He put his hand between Laurel's legs and idly ruffled her pubic hair. "Tell me," Ross said, "do you still put pennyroyal on your sheets?"

"What a funny thing to ask. No, because it's hard to come by now. Some women drank pennyroyal tea to give themselves abortions, and one of them overdosed on it and died. Besides, I don't think Jay would like pennyroyal on his sheets very much."

After a while, Ross had another question. "Tell me something else. That time you went to Guanajuato with Heriberto, what really happened? I know it was supposed to be for business, but I always wondered if..."

"Why are you asking me about *that*? That was so long ago."

"I'm just curious."

"You've always been curious about things that don't matter. All the things we could be talking about now, and you want to talk about that?"

"It's just something that I've wondered about for a long time. Come on, tell me."

"You really do wallow in the past, you know that?"

Ross tried to look unhappy. That was something he was good at.

"All right, Jack, I'll tell you what happened. Not because I think it will do you one bit of good, but only so you'll stop acting like a little wah-wah baby."

"I just hope you'll tell me the truth this time."

"Why should I lie now? All right, to begin with, we did go there on business. We sold our jewelry at an outdoor market, went to some jewelry shops and took some orders. And then, that night, when we got to the hotel, Heriberto said, 'Let's save some money and just get one room.'"

"Oh, come on, you must have known that..."

"Sure, I knew he'd put the moves on me. I was naïve back then, but not that naïve. I just didn't think it would be that much of a problem, and I thought I could handle it. He'd come on to me before, but he'd always backed off when I said I wasn't interested. Besides, I'd slept with men before at School's Out, I mean just slept next to them in the same bed, some of them complete strangers, and I'd never had any trouble."

"Yeah, but Heriberto? Mexico isn't School's Out."

"I know, but Heriberto was such a sweetie in a lot of ways. I thought it would be fine."

"Tell me what happened."

"I'm trying to. That night, just what I expected would happen happened. He made a pass at me and didn't get anywhere and so he said *buenas noches y dulces sueños*. But it was a different story in the morning. I woke up with him all over me."

"What—he raped you?"

"Not exactly, no."

"What do you mean, not exactly? Either he did or he didn't."

"I'm not going to go into all the details. I told him I didn't want to do anything, and at first I tried to push him away, sort of, but that got to be too much of an effort, so I just let him do what he wanted to do. I didn't really participate but... but I didn't stop him."

"If he forced you, you should have called the police."

"Yeah, that would have gone over real well. I can just hear what the police would have said."

- 'Now let's get this straight. Did he force you into his room, señorita?'
- 'Well no, I agreed to sleep in the same room with him, but...'
- 'Then, did he make you get into his bed, señorita?'
- 'You couldn't say that, exactly, but he said he wouldn't...'
- 'And did you struggle?'
- 'Well, *un poco*, but I knew it wouldn't do any good, so...'

"They would have snickered."

Ross wondered if she had struggled even a little. "So, what did you do after that?"

"I got dressed and I went for a long walk, and then I came back to the hotel and had a beer. He came in, sat down beside me, and ordered lunch for both of us. I told him what I thought of him, and he looked a little embarrassed, but just a little. He didn't think he'd done anything so awful. He said he could tell that I wanted it, even though I didn't. So after lunch, we went home."

"Why didn't you just leave him there?"

"What was I supposed to do? The Grape was almost out of gas, and I'd spent my last pesos on that beer."

"What I really want to know is, why didn't you tell me about it? Back then, I mean."

"Because you would have gotten bent out of shape and I couldn't have gone on working with Heriberto. I knew things would be okay as long as I stayed out of situations like that, and I was still learning a lot about making jewelry. And anyway, after he'd had me that one time, he was a lot less interested in doing it again. We took a couple trips after that and... *nada*. And why didn't I tell you? Because there are certain things people should keep to themselves. I'm sure you had your own secrets down in Mexico. I heard the rumors. Hey, you're getting upset about this, aren't you? You told me you didn't care."

"I *don't* care. I just can't believe you'd be so dumb. That was dumb as dog shit."

"Don't be such a baby, baby." She squeezed him. "God, jealousy is such a crazy energy. You can store it up for years and years, and when you let it out, it's as powerful as it ever was."

"I told you, I'm not jealous."

"I was jealous," Laurel said, "when I saw you and Thea walk into the wedding together. Not jealous, exactly, but it made me feel funny. A little queasy. You two look good together—she's very pretty—lovely eyes, nice figure, nice dress—and well, I know you've been with women since we split up, but it's different to see you, to actually see you with someone. Soon as I saw you at the wedding, I knew I wanted to sleep with you again. Maybe it was the tux. I've never seen you in one before. And you look good without the beard. I like the look."

She rubbed his smooth chin. She spooned against him. "Do you remember what Jeremy called this? Holding each other like this?"

"Not really," Ross said, though he remembered.

"He called it nudgling. He'd come into our bedroom in the morning and say, 'Can I nudgle with you guys?'"

"I suppose I do remember that. I'm afraid he's gotten too old to want to nudgle much."

"Ross," Laurel said, her voice even more syrupy, "do you ever think about us getting back together?"

"I used to, a lot. For a long time, it was about all I could think about. I think I know what would happen if we did, though. At first it would be magical, like tonight." This made Laurel squeeze him again and nudgle closer to him. "Then things would be just okay, and then, pretty soon, without our even noticing it, we'd get bored with each other. We'd start arguing. You'd start going off and not telling me where you were going. We'd be right back where we were before we split."

"Maybe. We're older now, though. Maybe we've learned a little. You know, sometimes I think there are two diseases, two relationship diseases that people can get. When you have one disease, you're with someone, and you feel claustrophobic. All you can think of is how nice it would be to be on your own, to be independent, to be able to do whatever you want whenever you want. The other disease, you've broken up with someone and you're lonely, and the world feels cold. All you want is to be with someone who understands you, and to feel safe and taken care of. And the nasty thing about these two diseases is, you can't catch one unless you're in the opposite situation."

Ross tried to figure that out.

"There's just one more thing..."

"Oh, stop Ross. Seriously, stop."

"No, just one more thing... Jeremy... Could Jeremy..."

"Don't go there, Ross."

"Jeremy doesn't look anything like me."

"I think he does. He's going to be tall like you. And he doesn't look much like me either."

"But the timing..."

"Listen to me, Ross. You *are* Jeremy's father. That's all there is to it. You are."

"I've thought, a couple of times, about getting a test..."

"Go ahead, if you want. Won't prove anything, no matter how it turns out. You're his dad, and you always will be."

Ross could hear ice falling into an ice machine out in the hall. It reminded him of being in the restaurant late at night.

"I do have one other thing I need to tell you. But I don't want you to say anything to me about it. I just want you to listen."

"Go on."

She created a dramatic pause by sitting up in bed, tucking the sheet under her armpits. More ice fell. "I'm pregnant again."

"I figured that's what you were going to tell me." Ross remembered sitting in the courtyard of Heriberto's house on Christmas Eve when Laurel had last told him she was pregnant. "How long have you known?"

"I've only known for sure for a week or two. But I was pretty sure before that, because I started crying once during a dog food commercial."

"You have television now?"

"Yeah, that's how Jay broke half the bones in his body. He fell off the roof when he was putting up the antenna."

"How did it happen?"

"He slipped in the snow."

"No, I mean..."

"Oh, that. How do you think?"

"I mean, weren't you using anything? Don't you still..."

"I stopped taking the pill because it turns out, it can do scary things to your body. And because, for several years there, I didn't need to do anything, not anything at all. I could have sewn my vagina shut. But then Jay came along and... and diaphragms... you remember, I tried using a diaphragm for a while when we were together—they're so messy and nasty and..."

"Yeah, I remember. I remember that time you didn't turn on the bathroom light and you put Pepsodent in the diaphragm instead of that goo you're supposed to use."

"Yeah. That was an interesting sensation," Laurel said. "See, Jay was supposed to use condoms, but around the time he was laid up, he couldn't get out of bed to get one... and I didn't feel like getting up either... so he said, let's try some of that tantric stuff... you know, go right up to the edge and then stop, and I said okay, we can try, but a couple of times, he got up to that edge, and oops... sailed right over it."

"Sounds to me like you wanted to get pregnant."

"I didn't, though. Not now, not with Jay. Now I have to figure out what to do."

"It's not a big mystery. There *is* something you can do," Ross said.

"I know, I know. But for some reason, I haven't done that yet. I guess because sometimes I think I'd like to be a mommy again."

"Have you told Jay?"

"What? Don't be silly. Of course I have."

"And what does he think?"

She hesitated. "He's not big on the daddy bit. He thinks it would lead to a house in the 'burbs and a station wagon and PTA and an old English sheepdog. The whole Fred MacMurray syndrome. But what Jay thinks isn't a major consideration. He'll be leaving soon anyway, I'm sure. Or he might have to go to jail."

"He really is good at fixing things. He sure fixed you."

"Don't be like that, Ross. You're getting your ego all tangled up in this, and it has nothing to do with you. What I need from you is just for you to be sweet." She let the sheet drop and cupped her breasts. "If these babies get any bigger, I'm going to need a bra size with double letters. And they itch all the time. I think I probably will... will do something about this. I don't know. Maybe next week. I'm going to Santa Fe for a crafts fair, and I have a friend down there. She could probably help me make the arrangements."

"Just don't drink any pennyroyal tea. Hey, what's that smell?"

"It smells like smoke... oh my God, my scarf is smoking!" She jumped up and grabbed her red scarf off the lamp and ran with it to the bathroom. There was the sound of running water. "Damn, there's a big scorch mark in the middle of my scarf. I've had this scarf forever; my dad gave it to me. That idiot Skeets put a 100-watt bulb in a bedside lamp." She hung the dripping scarf on a towel rack and came back to bed.

"It's gonna be all right, babe." He stroked her. After a dozen or so strokes, he said. "There's an expression—sloppy seconds. You ever hear that?"

Laurel nodded. Her hair moved across his chest. "I know what it means. When I was in college, we called it going sharesies."

"At the restaurant, going sharesies, that's what we call it when two people order one dessert."

"Same idea. Did you ever go sharesies or... or have sloppy seconds?"

"Me? No, of course not," Ross asserted, even though there was someone in this very building who could contradict his claim.

~

Marshall met Skeets and Ross at the Greyhound station. He was going to college in this town on a basketball scholarship. They walked down Main Avenue. Not Main Street; in this town it was Main Avenue. Marshall led them down a side street and then along a cross street. There was a stolid three-story brick building with a bright red door. "These are the finest women money can buy," Marshall promised them on the way up to the third floor. Ross hoped so; twenty dollars was half a week's worth of his lifeguarding salary.

An older, severe-looking lady in a faded flowered housedress led them to a sort of waiting room and pointed to a scruffy couch. "I think there's been a change of management since I was here last," Marshall said.

"I hope that's not one of the whores," Skeets whispered.

Ross had only seen the inside of a brothel in movies. He'd been expecting heavy drapes, plush furniture, lamps with tasseled shades, and a player piano. Instead, there were fluorescent lights, gray linoleum floors, and thrift-store furniture. The room did not smell of French perfume but rather of Lysol, cigarette smoke, and strangely, the movie-house smell of popcorn. In one corner of the room there was a Christmas tree. It was June, and all the needles had long since fallen off, but there were still ornaments and glittery tinsel hanging on the branches. Ross tried to imagine the prostitutes drinking eggnog, singing carols, and trimming the tree on Christmas Eve.

The couch they were sitting on was old, and its springs were worn. It was sucking them inside of itself. The room was inordinately hot. From another room came a sound that was like distant machine-gun fire.

The older lady came back with women. Just two women. They needed three. Neither was wearing much in the way of street clothes. That might be why the heat was turned up so high. One was in a baby-blue baby-doll nighty, the other in a lacy bustier and a half slip. The woman in the nighty was about twenty-five and was quite pretty. The other was at least fifteen years older and not so pretty. The one in the nighty said, "You boys shouldn't be here. You're too young. You should be playing basketball or something."

"We do play basketball. Well, two of us do," Marshall said.

She shook her head and sat down in an easy chair on the other side of the waiting room. The chair had a big oily stain on it. She picked up an old copy of

Look and started flipping through it. On the cover, there was a rocket boosting a space capsule into orbit. She lit a cigarette.

The other woman shrugged. It was a classic "money's money and screwing's screwing" sort of shrug. "I'll do 'em." She sounded a little hoarse, like she might be coming down with a cold. She had a big bruise on her left thigh, a purple bruise that was turning green around the edges. Marshall asked her name, and she said it was Ladonna.

One of her. Three of them.

Marshall stood up. "I get to go first, 'cause I'm the oldest." Ladonna led him off.

Skeets had dyed his black hair red a couple of days before to win a bet that he wouldn't. He'd used cheap dye. He was sweating now, and dark red rivulets were running down his face. It looked like he was literally sweating blood. Ross was sweating too, faster than he could wipe it away. They kept sinking deeper into the couch. The woman in the nightie glanced up from her magazine and looked them over. She shook her head. She was glad she didn't have to deal with these sweaty kids. She lit another cigarette from the one she'd been smoking.

Ross found it hard to look away from her. Her nighty was thin and short, and she wasn't wearing anything under it. Once she'd finished her second cigarette, she got up and went into another room and came back with a gold metal bowl full of popcorn. She didn't offer to share. After every few bites, she'd lick her fingers; she must have lavishly buttered her popcorn. Ross found her finger-licking astonishingly erotic. After about ten minutes, Marshall came out, looking self-important. "All right, Ross, you've got sloppy seconds."

"Wait a minute," Skeets complained. "You got to go first because you're the oldest. I'm older than Ross."

"Yeah, but you're not my brother."

"I didn't sleep with Jay today, if that's what you're worried about," Laurel said "We've hardly slept together at all since... since I found out."

"That isn't what I meant. I didn't mean going sloppy seconds, or going sharesies with Jay."

"Don't tell me you're still thinking about Heriberto. I knew I shouldn't have..."

"I meant with myself."

"I'll give you sloppy seconds." She put her tongue in his ear. She remembered that he liked that.

"That's still not what I meant. I mean... this whole thing... our getting together like this... it's like we're trying to go back in time... this whole thing is sloppy seconds. We shouldn't be doing this... I mean, I..."

"I don't care what you meant."

Ross looked under the sheet. "And I don't know if I'm ready."

"Guess I'll just have to have a few words with ol' Gilbert."

Ross's mother came out on the balcony with Thea. Ross's mother seemed to Thea to be more like a frequent houseguest than an actual member of the family. That impression was strengthened by the fact that she often wore her puffy pink down jacket inside the house so that she could duck out quickly for a smoke. Ross's father didn't permit smoking inside the Cheeseburger, and Ross's mom was a heavy, a very heavy smoker. There were two coffee cans on the balcony nearly full of butts, and there was a dusting of ash on the snowbank below.

The balcony was on the side of the house away from the road. A balcony on a spaceship would have looked pretty implausible. She could see the driveway from here, though.

Ross's mother kept her hands in the pocket of her coat as she smoked, so she had to talk around the cigarette. The coat had an elongated hood; her voice and the smoke seemed to be coming from a giant pink fur-lined periscope. "Would you like to come in and play some Scrabble, Thea?"

Thea didn't want to play Scrabble. She'd played with Ross's father and Jeremy a week or so ago. Jeremy had put down the word *moe*. "I believe that's a proper noun, Jeremy," Ross's father carefully said, "and as such, is not allowable." Jeremy said no, he meant *moe* as in "moe the grass." Jeremy had a lot of his words called into question, and he lost every challenge. Ross's father told Thea, "You spell quite well for someone whose native language is not, er, English." But she finished far behind him. He scored two bingos, for *gazebos* and *queenly*, using all seven letters at once and racking up fifty bonus points for each of those words.

"Thanks," Thea said, "but... I just want to stay out here and watch for the deer. Ross told me he used to see deer over there on that ridge all the time."

"I think it's too dark to see any deer now."

Thea shook her head, as if she hadn't realized it was dark.

"I still can't imagine where Ross has gone off to." Ross's mother had been making excuses for Ross all evening, but it was obvious that she didn't know anything... only that someone had called, and that Ross had bolted out right after that. "I think you should come inside. It's cold out here." She flipped her cigarette butt into one of the cans. "Ross can be such an idiot sometimes."

"I won't be out here much longer," Thea said.

Ross's mother said, wistfully, "You know, I'd like to be going back to Boston with you and Ross. I haven't been there in over twenty years. I'd like to see Ross's restaurant and spend more time with Jeremy."

Thea thought about offering Ross's mom her airline ticket. "Why don't you go for a visit?"

The periscope swung from side to side. "I don't know... I might go back there someday. Right now, I have too much to do here."

It didn't seem to Thea that Ross's mom did all that much of anything around here. She'd made a bowl of Chex Mix when they'd played Scrabble, but Thea hadn't seen her do anything else. Ross's dad seemed to be in charge of domestic chores. *But maybe she does things I don't know about. Maybe she does things secretly.*

"Don't stay out here too long—you might get frostbite."

"I won't be long—oh, and thanks again for the wedding dress... I mean for the dress you bought for me to wear to the wedding. Thanks for that. And good night."

Thea looked over at the ridgeline again, where Ross said he'd often seen deer. A low cloud sailed over the pines and appeared to be heading straight for the hilltop where the Cheeseburger sat.

Right this second, where is he? Is he with Laurel? Of course he is. What are they doing? Is he talking to her about me? What is he saying? What is he thinking? Not that it matters. Not that it matters at all.

The wind was picking up and was shredding the clouds. The whole sky seemed to be in motion. In the clear patches of sky, stars burned frantically. The wind seemed to be blowing those burning stars around too. *I'm not going to see any deer tonight. And my nose really might get frostbitten.*

Then, there it was. Down on the driveway that led up to the Cheeseburger, paused by the locked gate, was a canary-yellow taxi. *I'm glad the taxi came before Ross got home. At least I won't have to listen to him try to explain. And I won't have to explain anything to him.*

Thea grabbed her bag from the room where she'd been sleeping. She left the dress Ross's mother had bought for her hanging in the closet next to Ross's raspberry-colored shirt. She headed toward the gate, happily not running into anyone in the house.

She hoped the taxi driver would know the way. She certainly didn't.

~

"What do we do now, buckaroo?"

Ross asked her what she meant.

"Do we stay here or go home? To our respective homes?"

"I don't know. I was almost asleep."

"Well?"

"I suppose we should go. Wouldn't Jay be upset if you stayed out all night?"

"Yes, but I'll stay anyway. I'll stay if you want me to. Decide."

"I don't want to decide. I just want to lie here."

"You know what you're doing? You're rossing. That's what you do at times like these. You just want to lie back and let someone else make decisions."

"You know, I think you've blown this whole bit about me not making decisions way out of proportion. I don't think I have any more trouble making decisions than anyone else does. In fact, I decide lots of things at the restaurant."

"It's easy to decide about things. Making decisions about yourself is a lot harder. And even when you did make a decision, you'd question it forever. If it were up to you, Ross, you would never have left Winifred, you would never have left me, and you would never leave Thea. You'd still be living at your parents' house, you'd still be at School's Out, you'd be in Mexico, and you'd be running your restaurant in Boston, all at the same time."

"You know, just lying here is a decision, it seems to me."

"Maybe, but don't you think it's sort of a half-assed one?"

"All right, I've decided." Ross started to get out of bed.

"Lie down," Laurel told him. She grabbed him by the shoulders and pulled him back. "I'm crazy, you're crazy, we're a couple of goons. We'll stay."

CHANGING PLANES IN ATLANTA

NIKKI AND MARSHALL DROPPED ROSS AND JEREMY OFF AT THE AIRPORT IN Grand Junction. Ross didn't remember anything about the drive there. The flight to Denver was on a loud prop plane not much bigger than a crop duster. It left before dawn, and they flew in darkness over the mountains. Ross didn't remember much about the flight either, except that it was exceptionally uncomfortable. With his long legs, Ross was seldom comfortable when flying, but seating on this flight was especially cramped. When the woman in front of him put her seat back, his knees were practically pressed against his chest. The engines didn't drone like the ones on big jetliners; they sounded more like lawnmower engines. It seemed to Ross that the plane barely cleared the Front Range peaks. No wonder Colorado Airways was known as Colorado Scareways.

Somehow, he stumbled through Stapleton with Jeremy in tow and managed to get to the gate where the flight to Atlanta was departing. Why they should have to go to Atlanta from Denver to get to Boston was beyond him. He decided he needed a new travel agent.

While they were waiting to board, a short delay was announced. Two men in business suits were in line in front of them. One of them said, "If I die and go to hell, I'll have to change planes in Atlanta." Ross had heard that before, only with Chicago in place of Atlanta, but the man had clearly done research, and it was Atlanta, not Chicago, where the connection was made.

The early morning flight from Denver to Atlanta was sparsely populated. After takeoff, Jeremy moved to an empty seat by a window several rows behind their assigned seats. Jeremy was big on sitting by a window. If possible, he would have hung his head out the window of the plane like a dog in a pickup truck.

The sun was up now and lit the Continental Divide behind them. The snow on the peaks turned a rosy gold. In the land below, there appeared to be a sense of purpose at work. Everything was geometrical. Ross saw rectangular fields of tawny gold and perfectly round green circles. There were uncannily straight roads cutting through the fields. It was hard to imagine people driving down a road like that without knowing exactly where they were going and what they would do when they got there.

The sky seen from above the clouds was a different shade of blue than the sky seen from the ground. It was a bluer blue, a dazzling blue. Unwillingly, he thought of Thea's eyes.

Ross had once come across Buzz's *What to Name Baby* book lying next to his disheveled bed in the downstairs office, and Ross had looked up the name Thea. Thea came from the Greek name Theia. Theia, the book said, was the goddess of sight and the shining light in a clear blue sky.

Jeremy came back to his seat just before they landed. Ross asked him what he'd been talking to the stewardess about. "I asked her about those circles you see down on the ground."

Ross had wondered about those himself. "And? What are they?"

"She said they come from giant sprinklers that turn round and round. She said they're used to irritate the crops."

"I see."

They arrived in Atlanta almost half an hour late and Ross and Jeremy had to hurry to make it to their connecting flight. It seemed like every time he was in an airport with Jeremy, running was involved.

~

The flight from Denver was delayed by a thunderstorm over Chicago. He looked out the window and saw the black clouds and the lightning over the skyscrapers. One bolt almost struck the unfinished Sears Tower. It still felt unreal to him that he and Jeremy were leaving Colorado for good. When they finally landed, he picked up Jeremy and ran with him through O'Hare. The flight to Boston left from another terminal. It was an endless run, especially carrying a child as well as their carry-on bags. As they finally approached the gate, a woman said, 'Excuse me, sir, but your little boy's sock came off."

· · ·

"His sock?" Ross said to her, "His sock? Where the hell is his shoe?"

∽

Going from Atlanta to Boston, the plane was packed. Jeremy was chagrined because he didn't have a window. The third seat in their row was empty. That should have been Thea's seat. They remained hopeful until a man in a bottle-green blazer carrying a leather briefcase boarded the plane not long before the doors were closed, and he claimed the seat next to Jeremy, the one by the window. He said he was flying standby, and there had been a no-show. He said he was happy to get a seat, although he didn't look happy. He told them he was an actuarial accountant. *He's the kind of person*, Ross thought, *that you only meet on airplanes.* That was the last thing the man said on the flight. He took out his actuarial tables and his calculator and got down to his accounting. He was pretty blasé about flying. He didn't pay any attention when the stewardess told the passengers about seat belts and emergency exits and how the seat cushions could, in a pinch, be used as flotation devices. Ross didn't think they would make very good ones. *If they did*, Ross reasoned, *people would steal them. But you never see stolen seat cushions at the beach.*

Somewhere over North Carolina, probably, the plane began to shake violently. The captain announced that they had encountered some minor turbulence. The FASTEN SEAT BELTS and NO SMOKING signs came on. A baby began crying. A few seats in front of Ross, one of the oxygen masks disengaged, dropping from the overhead panel like a clumsy cobra uncoiling. Ross heard the stewardess telling the elderly passenger who was directly below the oxygen mask that everything was basically okay, that the cabin was still pressurized, and that the mask had shaken loose, somehow, maybe because of the turbulence. Still, it seemed a bad omen to Ross. On a well-designed plane, things shouldn't simply shake loose, should they?

After a while, their seatmate put his work back in his briefcase. He'd declined a drink earlier and now he shook his head when the stewardess asked if he wanted lunch. Ross had asked for a Virgin Mary but he wasn't having lunch either. He and Marshall and Nikki had stayed up most of the night before drinking and talking. Now, the smell of Jeremy's lunch and the smell of smoke that had wafted in from the smoking section was getting to him. That, and the turbulence. He was thinking about taking the air-sickness bag out of the seat pocket and putting it on his lap.

"Ross," Marshall said, "you look like you're about to pass out." Ross was making his way from the bathroom toward his bed. He was taking short, precise steps as if walking across a skating rink.

"No, no way." Ross believed that it wasn't an actual pass-out if you made it to your own bed first. For a pass-out to count, it had to be in a bar or on the sidewalk or on someone else's floor, not in your own bed. In your own bed, it was just going to sleep drunk. "I just need to lie down." Ross had reached what Dean called "the seventh stage of enlightenment," a sort of alcohol-induced trance. It effectively prevented one from thinking about anything.

While he was lying there, his foot firmly planted on the floor, Marshall and Nikki stumbled around the guest room, throwing his stuff and Jeremy's stuff into their suitcases. They were only marginally less drunk than he was.

Nikki checked the room where Thea had been staying. "The dress she wore to the wedding is in there. And some moisturizing lotion. You want to take those things with you?"

After what felt like a ten-minute sleep, Marshall woke Ross up. He and Jeremy said goodbye to his father; his mother was still asleep. Marshall and Nikki were leaving too, on their way to a skiing honeymoon in Aspen. At the Grand Junction Airport, Marshall helped him get his and Jeremy's bags out of the back of the truck. Ross gave his brother a hug. "See you, Hotshot. Thanks for the ride. You and Nikki have a good time." Ross didn't feel hungover, so much; he still felt drunk. He and Jeremy watched them drive off. Someone had written JUST MARRIED! on the back window of Marshall's red truck. Someone else had drawn a ball and chain. Ross suspected Skeets was the ball-and-chain artist.

The accountant pulled down the shade and went instantly to sleep. This struck Ross as unfair. Jeremy couldn't even look past him at the clouds. *Excuse me sir,* he wanted to say, *but do you really need a window to sleep by? You can have these two seats, one for you and one for your actuarial tables, and I will sit where you are now and my son will sit on my lap, even though he's getting to be too heavy for that, because my son is passionate about seeing the scenery flow past.*

Jeremy was emptying a little paper saltshaker onto his chicken à la king. "How do salt companies stay in business," he asked Ross, "since salt's so cheap and nobody uses much?"

He thought about the last time he'd refilled his saltshaker at home. It was the night he'd first slept with Thea. He'd still not gotten around to refilling his pepper grinder, or even buying any peppercorns.

"Because of people like you. You put salt on your salt."

"No, really."

"Well, the government gives them money to stay in business, because everybody needs salt, and someone has to make it."

"Really? Is that true?"

"Tell you the truth, I don't know, but you should write a letter to Mr. Morton. Ask him how he's gotten along all these years. Ask him who the girl with the umbrella is, while you're at it."

"Why don't you write him now?"

Ross had a piece of airline stationery on the tray table in front of him. The stewardess had brought him half a dozen sheets. He'd written a few sentences on five of them; this was the only one he hadn't torn up and put in the seat pocket in front of him.

"I'm writing your mother." Actually, all he'd written on this sheet so far was this: DEAR LAUREL.

"Why? You just saw her."

"You should really try to spend more time with Jeremy," Laurel said, as Ross was getting out of the Grape. They were back in the parking lot behind the Lucky Café. He noticed that, in the decade or so since its last paint job, the truck had faded from a vivid purple to a drab, dusty color closer to gray than to purple.

It was ten minutes before the time when his father had to leave for work, and Ross had his father's Jeep.

"When you first open a restaurant, it sucks up all your time. It's a black hole. It's unbelievable the number of things you have to do and the hoops you have to jump through. But we're starting to get things under control. I'm planning to switch some shifts with Walker, the day bartender, so I can spend more evenings with Jeremy. And Jeremy will be working Saturday and Sunday brunch, so I'll see him then."

"I don't know about that, either," Laurel said. "Kids shouldn't spend their weekends working."

"He wants to." Ross wondered where this conversation was leading. "Why are you bringing this up now? Did Jeremy say anything about staying here?"

"No," Laurel said, a little sadly. "No, I don't think he's even considered that. He just said he wants to see more of you."

Standing in the parking lot, Ross felt a sudden and fierce gush of love for his son. He wanted to rush back to the Burger and wake him up and tell him that they'd be spending every waking minute together from now on.

"I guess Thea's wondering where the hell you are. Hope you've got a story together. You're going to have to bullshit like a champ when you get home," Laurel said to him. "I'm going to catch hell myself. Not that I really care."

Ross didn't say anything, but he'd woken up in the middle of the night worried about that. Actually, there wasn't much night left when he woke up; the sky was beginning to lighten. He lay there in the semi-dark and tried to imagine what he might tell Thea. Nothing came to him.

"Don't worry," Laurel told him. "It's gonna be all right, babe." She kissed him and patted his crotch. "Goodbye, Ross. Bye, Gilbert."

Ross squeezed his son's knee. Jeremy unnecessarily flipped his hair out of his face. It was a little odd, Ross thought, that hair flipping should be a genetic trait, but Jeremy flipped his hair exactly the way Laurel did.

They hit another patch of turbulence, a rough one, and Ross's stomach bounced. He looked over at the woman across the aisle from him. The plane and everything on it was shaking vigorously, her breasts most of all. What was that called? Sympathetic vibration. It sometimes caused bridges to collapse. She was wearing a gauzy blouse the color of children's aspirins. Probably from India—the blouse, that is, not the woman. She looked up from her book and smiled. Ross interpreted the smile to mean, "Don't worry. Nothing important will shake loose. We'll come through all this."

She leaned into the aisle and asked him, "How did that happen?"

"How did what happen?" It wasn't a question he'd been expecting.

She pointed at his pen. "How did your pen get that way?"

Ross looked at the pen. It was in bad shape. It looked like it had been struck by lightning. "Oh. Well, it was bitten that way. My partner—my business partner—he always bites pens because he's trying to quit smoking. He's back to smoking now, but I think he still bites pens."

"Oh." The woman didn't have any further questions. She went back to her book. She was reading *Future Shock*. Ross had more problems with shocks that came from the past.

The plane flew into yet more turbulence, the worst patch so far. The woman's breasts shook violently. On the pretext of looking out the window on her side of the plane, he watched them vibrate. She clearly wasn't wearing a bra. Clearly. She lifted her book up to cover her chest. He remembered what Dean said: Some women have internal detection devices that let them know when they are being scanned.

What am I doing? Why the hell haven't I learned anything? I've learned nothing. Nada. Why haven't I? He looked away from her.

The plane dropped for a harrowingly long time. Ross looked at Jeremy, who seemed unconcerned. He was drawing a picture of the Ice Palace before it started to melt. The flight leveled off, but the turbulence went on, worse than ever. It knocked Ross's plastic glass off the tray table and ice cubes landed between his legs. His seat belt was fastened and it was hard to get to the ice. The more he tried, the farther toward the back of the seat the ice cubes slithered. The woman across the aisle was giving him an odd look.

He unfastened his seat belt and stood up with as much dignity as he could muster. The ice cubes were, by this time, gone; a couple of wet spots on the seat cushion were all that remained. Ross tried to look as though he'd been planning all along to stand up at this point in the journey. He stretched and walked down the aisle, heading for the rest room in the back of the plane. The stewardess told him to get back to his seat and fasten his seat belt.

～

Amy was waiting for them when they came off the plane. She bent over to kiss Jeremy and stood on tiptoe to kiss Ross on the cheek. "You've shaved. I've never seen all your face before. Looks good."

"For the wedding," Ross said. "What's this?"

"A coming-home present; a bald guy in an orange robe gave it to me." She handed him a copy of the *Bhagavad-Gita* with a gaudy cover.

"Hare, Hare... Krishna, Krishna," Ross said. "I like the perm."

Amy's face was framed in a massive corona of auburn curls.

"Thanks," she said. "I'm still trying to decide if I do. Every time I pass a mirror, I'm startled. And I just read somewhere that the chemicals they use for perms aren't good for your hair, so I'm not sure if I'll do it again. Where's Thea?"

"We don't know," Jeremy said.

"No, we don't," Ross admitted. "She left my parents' house in a taxi a couple of nights ago."

"She left? Where'd she go?"

That was a good question. He assumed she'd already flown back to Boston. He'd given her a key to his apartment. She might be there, but he'd been calling his own phone for the last two days; no answer. She could be in her own apartment; there were still a few days left before her lease was up, but her phone was disconnected. Maybe she was staying with Robin I, along with her dog. Maybe she was living in a tent with Wim. Maybe she was hiding somewhere in the airport and was about to jump out. *"Surprise!"*

"I don't know. I wasn't there when she left. My mother saw her go."

"You could ask the taxi company."

"I don't think they give out that kind of information."

"Oh. I guess taxi drivers are kind of like priests that way, huh?"

"I figured she took the taxi to the airport. I imagine she's back in Boston somewhere. I thought maybe she'd get in touch with you."

"I haven't heard from her, except for this postcard." Amy took the card out of her purse. On one side was a photo of a stretch of four-lane highway with a few cars and trucks on it. INTERSTATE 80, AMERICA'S MAIN STREET. Ross remembered Thea buying postcards during their long layover in the Cheyenne bus station and then mailing them during their tour of the town.

> Hi Amy,
>
> We went by Idaho Springs on Interstate 70 but I didn't get to see anything of it. It was a nice wedding. Ross shaved his beard and he looked good in a tuxedo. I've been looking for a cowgirl hat for you—I thought you'd like that. Ross and Jeremy and I are going to go skiing.
> — Thea

They'd never had a chance to go skiing.

"I wonder why she wrote this thing about Idaho Springs," Ross said.

"Oh, don't you remember? Idaho Springs was my pretend hometown. It sounded better than being from South Boston."

"You and Steve Canyon."

"Who's that?"

"He's a character in a comic strip. He's in the Air Force. He's supposedly from Idaho Springs, too. They have a statue of him there, even though he's not a real person."

They were waiting by the luggage carousel for their bags to arrive. There were an awful lot of people moving through the airport. Ross wondered where they were all going, or coming from. He'd wondered the same thing in Denver and Atlanta. Jeremy's bag was one of the first to come sliding down the ramp. They waited and waited for Ross's.

Everyone he'd seen on their flight had picked up their bags and left, including the woman in the filmy orange blouse and the accountant. Finally, luggage from a flight from Cleveland started arriving. Then Ross saw his luggage tag.

No bag, just his luggage tag, going around and around.

"That's the gaudiest name tag I've ever seen," Amy said. It had red and yellow stars and bright blue flowers.

"I have the plainest black suitcase in the world. I thought if it had a flashy luggage tag…"

"I think your bag was embarrassed to be seen in that thing. It's like an ugly Hawaiian shirt it had to wear. I think it ditched the tag and took off on its own," she said.

Ross reported his suitcase as missing in the Baggage Office. The gloomy agent working there asked if the bag had his name on it. "Well, it used to." The woman made a couple of phone calls. She told him they'd deliver his suitcase to him tomorrow. Probably.

They walked out through the dirty snow to the parking lot. Neither Amy's tall leather riding boots nor Ross's Hush Puppies provided much traction in the icy patches so they walked arm in arm, and Amy held Jeremy's hand. Amy's car had ugly gray chunks of frozen slush in all the wheel wells. She kicked at them. "Sludgesicles, Dean calls these things."

"Dean told me on the phone that it was like another Ice Age here," Ross said.

"We've had two snows since that first big one, and we're supposed to get another one tomorrow. It's been just awful."

They drove up to the short-term parking booths. Jeremy was telling Amy about the Ice Palace. A man in the car in line next to them must have had the stereo in his car cranked up. He was pounding away on the dashboard like a conga drummer. When he stopped drumming and started picking his nose, Ross looked away.

Ross gave Amy money to pay the attendant and she drove through. The Pinto hit a patch of ice and jack-knifed toward the nose-picker's car. She was able to correct in time and drove on.

"It must be miserable," Ross said, "driving a school bus on these icy streets."

"Oh, I guess I didn't tell you—I'm not driving anymore. I'm waitressing."

Ross was afraid to ask where. She told him anyway. "I'm working at a place on the South Shore called Xanadu. It's a Persian restaurant. Iranian, I mean. We have to wear these crazy purple outfits: harem pants and a halter top with gold chains and coins dangling from them."

"What do the waiters wear?"

"Oh, uh, there aren't any—just women. I know, it's a funny outfit, and it's kind of a weird restaurant, but I get good tips. The owner's Iranian. He told me he got out of Iran just in time—things are crazy over there right now, I guess. He's soooo Iranian... he's always saying things like, 'I hate you.'"

"Why does he hate you?" Jeremy asked.

"He doesn't really, Jeremy. I guess that's just something Iranians say when they actually like you. He must like me, because he hired me, and I didn't have any restaurant experience."

They were driving through the Callahan Tunnel. Whenever he went through this tunnel, Ross pictured Godzilla prowling the waters of Boston Harbor above them and stepping on the floor of the harbor above the tunnel. His enormous reptilian foot would come crashing into the tunnel just in front of the car he was in, and a vast cascade of water from the harbor would come pouring in after it.

"Have you heard from Dean lately?" Ross asked her.

Amy's knuckles went white on the steering wheel. "Not really. Did you hear about the chili pepper incident and all?"

"I heard what Dean had to say about it."

"What did you think?"

"I kind of wished I'd been there." Ross had never liked Dorky Dan all that much either.

"It *was* sort of funny, in a horrible sort of way. You know, my father's such a stoic-type person. He never complains because he thinks it makes him look weak. And he doesn't know anything about Mexican food. He ate almost half his lunch before he couldn't go on. He really was in pain. He turned beet red and he was sweating and he kept pawing at his throat. I told Dean he has a peptic ulcer and that we almost took him to the hospital. That wasn't true, though, I just told Dean that to make him feel bad. Tell me, do you think it was wrong, my taking that money out of the joint account?"

"I don't have any opinion."

"That's just a dodge. I'm sure you have an opinion. You just don't want to tell me what it is. Well, if I ever get rich, I'll put $741.72 in an envelope and slide it under Dean's door." They came out of the tunnel.

"Hey, we're in my neighborhood now," Amy said. "Want to stop by my place? Have a glass of wine? It's starting to shape up. I've painted the kitchen orange. It was this toxic green color before. And..."

"Orange? You painted your kitchen orange?"

"Yeah. Well, a shade of orange... it's called papaya. The guy at the Sherwin-Williams store said it was a real up-and-coming color for kitchens. And I've started ripping out the linoleum. Can you believe it—there are oak floors underneath. At least, I think they're oak. They're wood, anyway. I'm going to sand them."

"I just want to get home. It was a long trip. I know, the planes did all the work, we just sat there, but I'm still tired. I'll come down and see your place soon, though. Are those sisters still scowling at you?"

"Stella and Marcella? No. No, I baked them a loaf of banana bread and wrote a nice note and that did the trick. Now they're my best buddies. They've even signed up for Chewy's karate class. They come up every few days and look over what I've done to the apartment, and they always say, 'O, chi bello! Chi bello!' That means..."

"I can guess. It's pretty close to the Spanish."

"They keep hinting, though, that they want me to bake more often. Those ladies do love their banana bread."

"So you haven't seen Dean?"

"Last Saturday, he came by my place without even calling, which pissed me off. He brought cappuccinos and cannoli, but I didn't let him in. He talked to Chewy for a while."

"Why didn't you let him in? Was Gus there for a sleepover?"

"I actually haven't been seeing much of him lately. He was a transition, you know, from the old Amy to the new Amy. The thing about Gus is, he accepted me for what I was, and I needed all kinds of acceptance while I was transitioning. But he's a Virgo and I'm a Pisces, not a good match, and anyway, since I've been working at Xanadu, I've been mostly hanging out with the people there."

"Nice people?"

"Really nice. A little shallow, but nice... fun to hang out with."

"So if Gus wasn't there, why didn't you let Dean in?"

"Because I have nothing, absolutely nothing to say to him. Not at this point, anyway. Besides, there *was* someone there. Just not Gus."

"Someone who spoke Persian?"

"Farsi."

"What?"

"It's called Farsi... the language they speak in Persia. Only Persia's called Iran. Dean left a note for me with Chewy."

"What did it say?"

Amy rooted in her purse without taking her eyes off the road. She plucked out an empty ¿Por Qué No? matchbook. On the inside of the matchbook, Dean had written, in tiny letters, "IF I MUST BE DEVOURED, LET ME BE DEVOURED BY THE JAWS OF A LION, AND NOT GNAWED TO DEATH BY RATS AND VERMIN." SAMUEL SEABURY

"What's this even mean? Lions, and rats, and..."

"I think it means he doesn't approve of my choice of boyfriends. By the way, Dean told Chewy that he was having a thing with one of the waitresses."

"Which one?"

"I don't know. I can never keep them straight."

There was a man walking on Arlington Street across from the Public Garden. He was waving his arms and moving his legs, trying to stay upright. There must have been a sheet of ice coating the sidewalk under the snow. He looked like he was warming up for a dance recital. Ross remembered walking along that stretch of sidewalk one afternoon and hearing an unmistakable voice behind him. He'd turned around and there was Julia Child coming out of the Ritz-Carlton. She wasn't there now, though.

Amy turned onto Commonwealth and into the Back Bay. Things were looking depressingly familiar.

"So, Ross... what went on out there? Why didn't Thea come back with you?"

"The night she left... I got a call from Laurel. And I went to see her."

"You sure like to go looking for trouble." Amy glanced into the back seat to see if Jeremy was paying any attention to their conversation. He didn't appear to be. He seemed to be asleep. "You know, I told Thea about... about what you told me. I told her about your phoning her, and..."

"Figured you did."

Amy double parked in front of Ross's building.

"Are you mad at me? Do you hate me?"

"Not really." Ross felt like he was back on the plane again, flying through choppy air. And he felt the vanguard of a skull-splitting headache coming on. "No, of course I don't hate you."

"I'm sorry now I told her. I didn't know she'd take it so seriously."

"It wasn't just that. It was me. I screwed everything up."

"What did you screw up?" Jeremy asked from the back seat. He'd just woken up. Or else he'd been listening with his eyes closed.

"Everything, as near as I can tell."

"No, you haven't," Jeremy said. He reached up and patted Ross's shoulder. *There's nothing like blanket loyalty,* Ross thought.

"I wish I had a time machine," Ross said. "There are so many things I'd like to go back and do differently, things I'd like to fix."

"I wish I had a time machine too," Jeremy said.

"We all wish we had do-overs sometimes, but you can't change the past," Amy said.

"I'd go to the future," Jeremy said. "That would be a lot more fun."

"She'll get in touch," Amy predicted, "after she's had some time to think."

"She more of less has to. Most of what she owns is in my apartment. Not that she owns that much."

"I want to go to Mojave's," Jeremy said.

"Let's stay home for now, little buddy. Tomorrow you go back to school."

"Tomorrow's Saturday, Ross."

"Oh, right. Anyway, let's take showers and get unpacked. Well, you can get unpacked. My suitcase is probably on its way to Malaysia."

Ross got out of the car and stretched. It felt like he had been sitting down for a week. He looked around. The rows of houses on both sides of Commonwealth Avenue were as stately as ever. The trees were bare. The statue of William Lloyd Garrison was smothered in snow and an icicle was hanging from his nose.

"Call me when you get a chance," Amy said. "I do want you to see my new place."

"I will. Thanks again for picking us up."

"Does it feel good to be home?"

Ross looked around again. "You know, when I'm not in Boston, it feels like I've never really been here. It feels like I've dreamed everything that's ever happened to me here. But when I come back—the minute I come back, it feels like I never left."

3 2

DE HOOGTE

MATT'S STORE WAS BIGGER THAN IT LOOKED FROM THE FRONT. THERE WAS A
back room full of clothing and household goods where it was dark, even
during the day. Matt would wait until customers wandered back there
before he pulled the long string on the overhead light. This afternoon,
though, Matt was already in the back room, taking inventory.

That's where the pay phone was. Thea went back there to use it.

Jeremy answered the phone. He didn't ask where she was or why she'd
gone there. Maybe Ross had told him that it had all been part of some
grand plan.

Ross wasn't home, according to Jeremy. "He said he had some
errands."

"Did he go to the restaurant?"

"I don't know. He said he wasn't going there till tonight."

Thea wasn't sure he could stay away that long.

"Are you by yourself then?" Thea needed to talk to Ross, but she didn't
particularly want to. Not quite yet.

"No, Mojave's here. And Maxine. Valerie's next door."

"How are my plants doing?"

"Okay, I guess. Some of them kinda turned yellow."

"Oh no. Dean must have forgotten to water them. Did he meet you at
the airport?"

"Uh-uh. Amy did."

"How is she? Is her bus-driving job okay?"

"She has a new job. Her boss tells her, 'I hate you.'"

"Oh dear, that doesn't sound like a very good job. I'll have to call her."

She wasn't getting very far with Jeremy. He didn't even sound glad to hear from her. But Ross always said Jeremy hated talking on the phone. "If I give you a message for Ross, will you give it to him?"

"I have to go get a pencil."

That gave Thea a chance to think of what message she wanted Ross to have.

"Look straight up at me," Thea said to Ross.

Thea and Ross were in the downstairs office. In Buzz's boudoir, as Dean called it. She was trimming his beard. She'd never trimmed a man's beard before, but she'd prepped women before they'd gone into labor.

"I don't like working double shifts," Thea said. "I'm not going to see anything today but the inside of this restaurant."

"You're not missing much. It's foggy and nasty out. If you want, though, I could change your schedule so that..."

"Don't do that."

Ross started to nod. She tugged on his beard to keep his head still. "I was going to say, I know what you mean. When I was in high school, and my father was the principal, I was always afraid he'd do something to help me out. I didn't have to worry about it, though. Hey, I don't want it cut too close."

"It's hard to tell where your beard ends and your chest hair begins," she said. "You have such a nice face. I don't know why you want to cover it up."

"I have a weak chin," Ross said.

"No, you don't." She jerked playfully on his beard and leaned over to kiss him.

After the kiss, Ross put his arms around her thighs and pulled her closer. "I like you so much," he told her.

"You know, I don't think I've ever had someone... someone I was involved with... tell me that he likes me. Either tell me you love me or don't say anything at all."

"All right, then, I love you. I love you. You're beautiful and I love you, love you." I sound like Sarah Jefferson, Ross thought.

"Stop talking. I don't want you to tell me you love me because I told you to. And I can't trim your beard with your jaw moving like that. It's just hard for me to figure you out, to figure out how you really feel about me. You know, you told me a few weeks after we first got together that you weren't ready to get too involved, that..."

"I didn't say that. I didn't say that I didn't want to get involved. I said I wanted us to be sure. Since then, I asked you to move in with me, so..."

"You didn't ask me to move in," Thea said. "I asked you if I could."

"Well, I agreed right away, didn't I? There's no sense in you paying all that rent. And I asked you to go to my brother's wedding, didn't I?"

"Umm, I don't know. Seems to me, I invited myself to Colorado too. Don't worry about it. I can't figure out how I feel about you either. Here," she said. She fished her compact out of her purse and opened it. "Take a look. Tell me what you think so far."

Ross shook the whiskers out of the napkin on his lap. Some landed on Buzz's cot. It didn't seem to matter much. "It's a little lopsided, don't you think? Look, it's a little longer over here than over there."

Thea took the mirror from him and looked at herself. Ross often told her that she looked beautiful, but she couldn't see it.

"Are you pouting? You are, aren't you?" Ross asked her. "No, really, you did a good job."

"Tell me something," she said, studying herself in the little mirror. "If I were an animal, what kind of animal do you think I would be?"

Ross hadn't been expecting that question, but without hesitation said, "A duck."

"A duck!" She didn't want him to consider her duck-like.

"When you pout like that, you look something like a duck, yeah. Not an ordinary duck, though, a really pretty duck."

She pulled his head sharply to the right by his beard. Of course, he had no idea that her nickname in lagere school had been Eend—Duck. A nickname she'd hated. She was happy when her family had moved from Breda to Amsterdam when she was nine and she could leave her days as a duck behind.

"I'll try to even it up," she said. She cut off a clump of whiskers. What she felt like doing was lopping off one of his ears. A duck!

~

"Tell him quack," Thea said.

"Quack?" She could picture Jeremy writing that in big letters on the pad by the phone. THEA CALLED AND SAID QUACK. What would Ross make of that when he got home?

"That's right. Quack."

Matt didn't look up while she was quacking into the phone. He was going through tall stacks of overalls like a dealer shuffling cards and would then write the tallies down on his clipboard. According to Cap, a lot of strange calls had gone through Matt's phone over the years. Quacking might seem pretty tame.

"Is that all?" Jeremy asked her. He was sounding a little impatient. Probably he was playing one of his war games with Mojave. Although there was room at the kitchen table or in the middle of the carpet, they always played in an enclosed place behind the easy chair by the window. Maybe it was easier back there to imagine the thunder of the guns and the screams of the wounded.

That was it, she told him. That was all the message there was.

"Well... *goedendag*," Jeremy said.

"You remembered how to say that!"

"Uh-huh. Can I ride your bike until you come back?"

"Sure. You can ride my bike as long as you want. *Goedendag. Ik mis je.*"

She felt a little dizzy.

Cap had been standing a discreet distance away, out in the groceries section. She told him she hadn't been able to talk to Ross but had left a message with Jeremy. "Get more change from Matt. Then you can call him at his restaurant," Cap suggested. "I need to talk to Ross too."

Thea thought about what it would be like if Ross was in the bar now. Lunch rush. Waitresses shouting orders. Dean sitting across the bar from him. "I think I'll wait," she said.

"At least he'll know you're all right," Cap said.

By the steps leading up to the store, they put on their cross-country skis. Thea was using Poppy's boots and skis. She was also wearing Poppy's down jacket and her long underwear. Cap said she wouldn't be needing them in Tallahassee. It was almost noon. When they'd set off from School's Out, the skies had been extraordinarily blue, the air crisp and clear. A "bluebird day," Cap called it; blue skies and fresh snow. Blowing snow glittered in the sunlight.

Now, though, the sky was hazy; the light was brittle and metallic and extraordinarily white, like the light from inside an empty refrigerator.

"There's a trail back to School's Out that goes along the creek. Let's take that instead of the road. It's a lot prettier." They skied across the county highway and she followed Cap to the trail by the creek. Thea didn't feel safe or graceful on skis yet. It was as if her feet had suddenly become six feet long.

Cap got ahead of her on the trail. She was alone among the pines and the snow in a green and white land. She still had trouble adjusting to so much space and so few people. It felt like she was the last person on the planet. It was exhilarating and alarming at the same time.

Cap was waiting for her around a bend of the creek. His head was surrounded by a small white cloud. "Want a toke?" he asked, offering her his pipe.

She shook her head. She didn't have enough breath to inhale. Besides, she'd had a headache off and on for the last few days.

"It's so incredibly quiet here," she said. All she could hear was the creek, bubbling under the ice, and a little bit of wind, and birds singing. It reminded Thea of the record she'd heard at Amy's. "This would be a nice place to live, right here by this creek."

Cap looked around. "You could live by the creek, I suppose. You'd have to put your house up on stilts, because there are floods along here every couple of springs. And you'd have to chop down a few trees."

"I wouldn't want to cut down any trees. The trees are so beautiful, all covered with snow."

"That's their business." By this, Cap didn't mean, this is an affair for trees only. He meant, the trees are doing what they are supposed to be doing, which is to look beautiful.

Then Cap said, "Where we're standing now, this isn't part of School's Out anymore. It used to be, but I've had to sell some land. I sold this last year to a company down in Texas. I hope they don't strip mine it or clear-cut the forest. Now, if I were you, and I wanted to live somewhere around here, I'd fix up that cabin where Andromeda used to live. It's not in bad shape, and it has better views than any other cabin at School's Out."

"I don't have any money to fix up anything," she said, "and I wouldn't know how to even begin to fix something up."

"I could help."

Thea didn't want to tell Cap that she probably wouldn't be here long. He was lonely. He wanted to help fix up a place for her to live. He wanted to cook for her, and play the harpsicord for her. He wanted to carve bears and beavers and give them to her.

"Don't you love the smell? The smell of the pines?" Cap asked.

Thea nodded, although the piney smell reminded her a little of the smell of disinfectant in the hospital where she'd worked in London. All that was missing was the smell of urine.

They skied on a little farther, through a grove of bare, silver-gray aspens. "It's gorgeous here in the fall," Cap said. "The leaves turn gold. They look like gold coins. Gold doubloons, I guess. Or pieces of eight," Cap said, remembering a song about buried treasure from a TV show about the Hardy Boys. "You know, these trees, these aspens, they say they're all part of one organism. It looks like a forest, but it's all one tree.

Aspen groves are the largest living things in the world, they say. I used to think that the people at School's Out were kinda like an aspen grove. We were separate, but we were all connected under the surface. I guess I was wrong."

"I don't know. People still come back for your reunions, don't they?"

Cap shook his head. "It's not the same." Cap pointed with his ski pole. "See where the creek branches up there? The right branch is called Riddle Creek. They call it that because it goes underground in places and then comes back up, and there are a lot of little caves alongside the creek. A few years ago, some people found a case of C.C. in one of those caves."

"What's C.C.?" All she could think of was cubic centimeters.

"Canadian Club. It's a kind of whisky."

"Oh, right. I've had people ask for that at the restaurant. C.C. and Seven."

"Well, the Canadian Club people hid cases of their whisky in elusive places, like Zanzibar and Tasmania and in a glacier in Chile. They put ads in magazines. One said, WE HID A CASE OF C.C. HIGH IN THE ROCK-IES, and had a few vague clues how to get there. Some people from New York found it, after looking for it for a couple of weeks. Was their whole purpose in coming out here, to look for that whisky. They gave Matt a bottle, because he was selling them supplies, and he gave me a drink. It was good whisky, but not *that* good." Cap shook his head, full of marvel at the priorities of New Yorkers.

They had been skiing uphill toward School's Out, but now they came to a place where the trail dipped into a little hollow. Thea stood at the top of the slope and looked down. Cap was already at the bottom. Near the bottom of the hill was an old abandoned school bus. She pictured Amy trying to drive it through the woods. Its tires were flat, its windows broken. Cap had told her that it had belonged to someone named Johnny AWOL, who was hiding out from the Army at School's Out. Once, according to Cap, everyone at School's Out had piled aboard that bus to go to a rock festival back on the East Coast. Halfway to Matt's, it had broken down, and they'd pushed it here. Not long after that, Johnny AWOL turned himself in. And then, a few weeks later, he went AWOL again, and joined some cult. No one had heard anything from him after that, and he'd never come back for his school bus.

It was a steep slope, but there wasn't much she could do but push off and hope she didn't break anything. The aspens and snowy pines whooshed by. She kept speeding up. About three-fourths of the way down, she lost her nerve and took a deliberate tumble. Her right ski came off and slid down the trail on its own, stopping near the old yellow bus. Cap retrieved it and came up the trail to the place where she'd fallen. "Did you hurt yourself?"

"Not really." She remembered Ross telling her how he had dislocated his shoulder the first time he'd gone skiing. "My toes keep coming out of the clips. And these boots are too small for me."

"Poppy had small feet all right." Cap always sounded affectionate when he talked about Poppy, even when he was talking about her feet. "Are you doing okay? You look a little pale. Paler than usual."

Thea felt terrible. Although it was cold, she was sweating under her hat and could feel sweaty hair hanging down on her forehead. Her mouth was full of the taste of dirty pennies. "I have sort of a headache."

"Let's get off this trail and get back on the road."

They skied across a little meadow and regained the road. They set off up Harmony Hill toward School's Out and skied past the tree that had the word TREE painted on it. The paint was old and some of it had flaked off.

"It's not that much farther," Cap said. "You can see the smoke from Laurel's cabin from here."

Before long, they saw Laurel. She was in her truck, heading down the hill toward Matt's. There were chains on the Grape's tires. "Where you off to, Laurel?" Cap asked her.

She told them that she was going to a crafts fair in Santa Fe; she didn't mention that, after the fair, she was going to have an abortion. Probably. But before she left, she needed to pick up a few things at Matt's. And she wanted to make a phone call while she was there.

"Jay still around? I didn't see his car."

"Nope, it's bye bye Blue Jay," Laurel said. "He left a few days ago. But he has to come back for his trial."

Laurel continued along the road, and they kept climbing. They went past an open meadow where there were two freestanding chimneys, past a large rock that looked like a mushroom covered with white icing. They were almost back, but the road was particularly steep and icy there, and Thea was having trouble making her way uphill. "Try to herringbone," Cap suggested.

"I forget how," Thea said. She began to slide backwards, slowly at first, and then she sped up and went off the left side of the road and into a deep trench full of snow, landing in an unnatural position. Her skis and poles and arms and legs were all askew. She struggled to get up, but it was like trying to climb out of a vat of feathers. It got worse, the more she battled the snow, and she was utterly exhausted. Only a helicopter equipped with a winch could get her out, she decided. She stopped struggling for a moment. *I miss being warm. I miss Vervloekt. I miss being at the restaurant. I miss Jeremy. I... God help me, I miss Ross too.*

Thea somehow was able to get her skis unclasped and she tried to wade part of the way out through the hip-deep snow. Cap offered her a hand. His hand was covered in a heavy cowhide mitten that looked like a black oven mitt. He'd brushed the snow off a place on a rock for her to sit down. She tried to catch her breath; the air was sharp and cold. "You okay?"

Thea remembered Meredith talking about the snow in Colorado—the best in the world, she said. Champagne powder, she called it. Thea had champagne powder in her socks and down her collar. There was some between her long underwear—Poppy's long underwear—and her skin. There were little balls of champagne powder hanging from her hair and some wadded in her ears. Her fingers were frozen into stiff fists from gripping her poles. She thought of the way her hands looked in Wim's paintings.

Cap took off his mittens and rubbed her hands in his. His breath was freezing, and there were ice crystals in his bushy, rusty beard.

The tang of metal in Thea's mouth was stronger, and the light had taken on a flickering, grainy quality, as if in an old newsreel. The bottom of her stomach dropped out. She was trembling. She'd felt much like this when she and Wim had been in Greece, and they'd sold her blood for a few drachmas.

Thea and Wim climbed three flights of stairs from the back of a grimy restaurant in a side street off Omonia Square. When they came to the office a nurse—a woman in white, anyway—checked her passport. Then she rubbed Thea's finger with alcohol and stabbed it with a lancet. She took her blood pressure.

After that, they had to wait. Wim wasn't able to give blood; he'd once had hepatitis, he claimed. They were happy, though, to get Thea's blood. Her blood type was O-negative. The nurse told her she was a katholikós doritis. Thea said no, she was agnostic, but the nurse told her that katholikós doritis meant she was a universal donor.

There was a German girl in the waiting room, wearing a long blue cape. She said her father had been in Greece during the war, and he'd told her where to go sightseeing. She said that some of the places he liked had been spoiled, though, since he'd been here. Too many tourists.

There was also an American couple there, two attractive people from California—they looked like surfers—who were with a dog that they had befriended in Corfu and named Buckwheat. People kept asking them if Buckwheat was going to give blood, too.

Then it was Thea's turn to go in. There were three chairs in the inner office that reminded her of dental chairs or barber chairs. The people in the chairs reminded her more of people in an opium den. The nurse sat her down and covered her legs with a large sheet of white paper so that no one could peek up her skirt. This must have simply been standard procedure, because Thea was wearing jeans.

The nurse hit her vein after taking a couple of shots at it, then taped the tube to Thea's forearm and gave her a soft rubber ball. She told Thea to squeeze the ball every few seconds, and then she went away. Thea didn't want to watch her blood filling the plastic bag, but she couldn't help it. It was hard to believe that, just a few seconds before, it had been coursing through her body, and there it was, inside a baggie. Even when she saw a roach crawling up the plastic tubing toward her arm, she couldn't look away.

When there was only about 150 cc's of blood in the bag, she began to feel a little weak, a bit peculiar. The roof of her mouth began to taste like copper. The fluorescent light turned gray and was interwoven with white, wavy lines. The next thing she knew, the nurse—if she was a nurse—was breaking an ammonia ampule under her nose. It made her sneeze. Wim was by her side now, his hand on hers.

The nurse was surprised that she had fainted. Her blood pressure was normal and her red blood cell count fairly high. She asked Thea suspiciously if she had recently sold her blood elsewhere. She denied it; this was her first time.

"Dén tó pistévo," the nurse said. "A miracle." She didn't act impressed, though. She kept muttering in Greek.

Wim stroked Thea's sweaty hair. "We still get paid, don't we?" he asked the nurse.

❧

Thea put her head between her knees. Someone was asking her what was wrong. She was confused. Suddenly she wasn't sure where she was or who was talking to her. Not the Greek nurse. Not Wim. Not Ross. Not Cap. She was sitting on a bench in a sunny park next to an elderly man in a plaid jacket. Kent de Mint. He put his arm around her, which she found immensely comforting. "*De hoogte,*" she said to him.

He smiled. "*Ja, alleen de hoogte,*" he said to her; it's only the altitude. He patted her hand. *"Maak je geen zorgen, Theatje."* Don't worry, dear Thea. She leaned against him.

In a few minutes, she realized she could raise her head from between her legs. She wasn't sitting on a bench in the sunshine, she was once again sitting on a rock by the icy road that led past School's Out. She was worried about the elderly man—Kent de Mint—who had been sitting beside her; he was only wearing that thin plaid jacket. But he had vanished without saying goodbye, as was his habit, and it was now Cap sitting there with his arm around her. A wind had risen and was blowing snow off the trees. The sun was behind a thick cloud cover now.

"De hoogte," she said again.

Cap didn't understand. *Of course*, she thought, *Cap doesn't speak Dutch.*

"You feel... hog-tied?"

She kept trying to think of the words in English. The problem was, there were so many words.

"De hoogte. I think that's all it is. The altitude."

3 3

NIGHT DEPOSIT

Ross didn't recognize the hostess at ¿Por Que No?. She was young. She was so young that she looked unfinished. Her features seemed to be forming right before his eyes.

"Hi there. Can I help you find something?" she asked him politely.

"Find something? Like what?"

"Oh, sorry, that's not what I meant to say. What I meant to say was, 'Good evening, table for one? Oh, and we have a special table for singles— I could seat you there if you want.'"

"No. No, I thought I'd just go into the bar."

"That'll be fine too. Where'd you get that coat, if you don't mind my asking?"

"At an Army-Navy store in Colorado, I think. Why?"

"Just wondering," the hostess chirped. "It looks real cute on you."

"Who are you, anyway?"

"I'm Charlotte. Who are you?"

"I'm Ross."

"Nice to meet... oh, you're Ross. *The* Ross. I should have known. You're so tall. But I thought you had a beard?"

"Is Dean around?"

"I think he's in the bar. Do you want me to show you where that is?"

"No, I think I can find it—I can see it from here."

Ross glanced into the dining room as he walked past. There were two women he'd never seen before waiting tables.

Lizard and Meredith were sitting at the bar and Buzz was behind it. "Hey, Ross, I'm glad you're here. Someone just ordered a couple of mai tais and... what's in a mai tai, anyway?" Buzz acted like Ross had just gone into the kitchen for ice rather than being gone for nearly three weeks.

"I could make them for you," Ross offered, "if you want."

"I'd just as soon you did," Buzz said.

"So Buzz..."

"It's Ian now," Meredith said.

"Yeah, at the last minute, I thought about going with Spencer. I always liked Spencer Tracy, and I loved the Spencer Davis Group, especially Steve Winwood's riffs on the organ in "Gimme Some Lovin'." But Meredith talked me into Ian, so I'm officially Ian now."

"Right," Ross said. "So Ian, did Dean sell you the place and split town?"

"Uh, no, I'm just watching the shop for him. He's training a new waitress. I think they're down in the office."

"He's training someone to wait tables in the office? Are you still sleeping down there, Buzz? I mean Ian?"

Buzz looked over at Meredith. She nodded. "Not anymore. Meredith is letting me crash at her place."

"*Una cerveza mas*, Señor Ross," Lizard said.

"Coming up. Meredith, don't you have some tables?" Meredith was drinking wine and smoking a long cigarette.

"I'm not working tonight. I just came in to spend a little time with Ian. This is the first night I've had off in a week."

"I'd better go deal with the dishes," Ian said. "And I have to peel shrimp."

Dean came up the stairs. He looked surprised to see Ross. Or rather, he looked like a hopeless, rotten actor might look if a director had told him, *Quick, look surprised!* "I'll be damned, there's the big guy now. I was going to have dancing girls for you, but I didn't think you'd be back until tomorrow. I was just telling Lizard, Ross will be back tomorrow, wasn't I, Lizard?" Dean put his arm around Ross and patted him on the back. He smelled like mint and chocolate.

"Yeah, he said, 'I've got to get this place shaped up because Ross's coming back tomorrow,'" Lizard said.

"Guess you got your days mixed up." Ross looked at the woman with the long blonde hair who had come up from the office with Dean. Implausibly, it was the daughter of the critic who had reviewed ¿Por Qué No?, the one who looked like Sarah Jefferson.

"Hello, Ross."

No. No, it wasn't. It *was* Sarah Jefferson.

Ross said hello. She winked at him. There were those arresting jade eyes.

"You remember Ross from... reading stories? To his kid? Years ago?"

"Something like that. How is Jeremy?"

Ross told her Jeremy was just fine.

"Well, Dean tells me I'm ready to take a table, so I'm going to ask Charlotte to seat the next one at Table 11. That's me. We'll have to get caught up sometime, Ross." She glided gracefully toward Section 2. All those years of ballet lessons had paid dividends. Ross and Dean and Lizard all watched her walk away.

"Lost the beard, I see," Dean said. "I guess we're getting too old for facial hair."

"Not me," Lizard said. His huge mustache was dappled with beer foam. "You know what they say—kissing a man without a mustache is like eating a tomato without salt."

"I don't know who says that," Meredith said. "I never put salt on tomatoes."

Dean said, "Well, I decided not to grow my 'stache back. Sometimes I miss Melvin, though."

"Who's Melvin?" Meredith wanted to know.

"Someone I used to be close to," Dean said. He asked Ross: "How was your flight?"

"Flights. There were three of them. The last one was a little rocky at times. Hey, where's my cat?"

"Your cat? Oh. At Robin's."

The plan had been, Ross's neighbor Valerie was to take care of Swizzle and water the plants for the first two weeks that Ross was gone, then Dean was to take over after that because Valerie was going to be out of town herself.

"So why is Swizzle at Robin's?"

"Because I knew I couldn't get over to your place every day, and I couldn't keep her at my place because cats make Maud nervous, and since Robin was watching Thea's dog, I figured she was good with animals, so I took her over there."

"Some of Thea's plants are dying. I don't think God Himself could save the Boston fern."

"Don't berate me, Ross. You don't know what it's been like around here. I watered them once, when I came over to get the cat. And to borrow your masks."

"I was going to ask you about those next."

"Didn't you see them? They're hanging in the dining room. The walls looked so bare after Amy came and got the photographs, I had to do something."

Lizard said, "I never thought those photos were a good idea, though no one asked me. Who wants to look at somebody's butt when they're having tacos? Even a nice butt. Mexican masks are much more appropriate. Although that one mask, that one with the demon coming out of the woman's head, I don't know about that one. I think that one makes your customers uneasy."

"Those butts—those derrières—they were art," Dean insisted. "But you wouldn't know about that, Lizard."

"You know what those photos kind of reminded me of?" Lizard asked. "They reminded me of Wim's paintings. Most of his paintings have a nude woman in some sort of a surreal setting. Like Amy's butt in your photos."

"How the hell do you know anything about Wim's paintings?" Dean asked him.

"I ran into him and his cousin at the Crow Bar last week, and we had some beers and some laughs. Well, it was mostly me laughing—those boys aren't big laughers. But they're not bad guys. After that, we bought some beer and went to their apartment on Marlborough—Thea's old place. We had to sit on the floor because there's no furniture. Wim showed me all his paintings. There's one of Thea sleeping on a broken-down bed with a lion lying next to her. I really liked that one. It felt a little funny, though, seeing Thea naked like that, even though it was just a painting. Hope you don't mind, Ross."

"Wim is living in Thea's place?" He'd looked at her window across the alley last night, but her apartment had been completely dark.

"Yeah, Wim and Hendrik are both staying there. Well, they were. Wim said they'd probably have to leave in a few days because Thea's coming back soon."

"Speaking of Thea, you think she wants to work tonight?" Dean asked. One of the new waitresses came in to get her mai tais.

"It doesn't look to me like you need anyone else on tonight," Ross said. "It seems pretty quiet. And it's snowing out."

"It's *always* snowing. But we've been getting late rushes, snow or no snow."

"Thea won't be coming in tonight. She's still in Colorado."

Dean blinked rapidly twice. This was his newest nervous habit. "I've got her down on the schedule for this week."

The waitress Ross didn't know said to Dean, "Sounds like you might need to put someone else on, huh?"

Dean said he wasn't sure.

"Well, you remember Gretchen, right?" she said to Dean. "She worked at the Denim Den, and then later she came to work at Reynard's with Charlotte and me. She'd make a terrific waitress, I think. She's a real sweet kid."

"I don't think we want to fill that job just yet," Ross said, "even with a real sweet kid like Gretchen."

"Are you the new bartender?" she asked him. She looked aggravated at Ross for blowing the job for Gretchen. "You forgot the garnish on the mai tais."

Ross garnished the drinks with cherries skewered to pineapple slices. "Here you go. Sorry, we're clean out of little paper umbrellas." Actually, they'd never had any. Just lots and lots of swizzle sticks.

"He's not the new anything," Dean said. "That's Ross, come down from the mountains at last."

"Oh, you're Ross. I'm sorry, I'm Jennifer."

Lizard said, "You're sorry you're Jennifer?"

"No, I mean I'm sorry I didn't recognize you, Ross. From what Dean said, I thought you'd be taller, and..."

"You must be hanging out with the Celtics if you don't think Ross is tall," Lizard said.

"... and I thought you had a beard."

"I used to," he said.

When Jennifer was gone, Ross said, "So what happened around here? Where's everyone I used to know?"

"Dean had some personnel problems," Lizard said. "If he'd paid more attention to what Maslow had to say about..."

"What do you know about Maslow?" Dean asked him.

"Who is this Maslow?" Ross asked.

Lizard said, "Albert Maslow. Came up with a theory about what makes people happy. He..."

Meredith corrected him. "*Abraham* Maslow. The hierarchy guy."

Why does everyone know who Maslow is but me? "Oh. At first I thought maybe Dean had hired a new personnel manager. Where'd you hear about this guy, Lizard?"

"I'm taking a night class in management techniques at the Free University."

"Really? Why's that?"

"I might not want to spend all my life doing carpentry. I'm trying to expand my horizons a little. It's an adventure, you might say."

"Listen to this guy," Dean said. "He takes one cruddy adult ed class and he thinks he's on safari."

"Why *did* all the servers quit?"

"We didn't *all* quit," Meredith said. "I'm still here. Robin's still here, she's dancing around the South 40 tonight. Patsy's still here, she's just not on tonight."

"Patsy has been doing doubles for most of the last week," Dean said, "as well as doing the bookkeeping and the ordering, so I finally shoved her out the door and told her to go home and get caught up with her homework. She has a paper on Immanuel Kant due next week."

"Okay, so why did most of them quit?"

"We did have a few personnel disruptions, but... nothing to do with job satisfaction." Dean looked pointedly at Lizard. "I told you about Robin II. After the incident with Vince..."

"Dean likes to call that the Vincident," Lizard said.

"She split right after the Vincident. She didn't even come in to pick up her paycheck. Who knows, maybe she really did go to Guam."

"She should go to Afghanistan. I could fix her up with a job there, at Mom's," Meredith said. "She'd be super safe in Afghanistan."

"Well, at least we only have one Robin now."

"Yeah, but now we have two Jennifers," Meredith said.

"And Adriana, someone came in here for dinner and ended up offering her a job on a cruise ship. She had to tell them yes or no right away, because the ship was set to sail in a few days. She felt bad about leaving with almost no notice, but I told her, just go—I said that job was too cool, she couldn't pass it up."

"They offered me a job, too," Meredith said. "Somehow I managed to pass it up."

"Now Keith, he went back to Maxwell's."

"No. No, I don't believe that. You're making that up. He hated Maxie's."

"Yeah, I know, but what happened was, the manager from Maxwell's came in here one night with a couple of friends, and he asked to sit in Keith's section, and he..."

"The manager? James?"

"I don't know. I guess. He asked about you. Anyway, he came in and he must have been impressed by the way Keith was handling himself, because he offered him the maître d' job at Maxwell's. He'll probably make a lot more money doing that."

Ross had been shaking his head. Now he put his elbows on the bar and his face in his hands.

"When we reopened after the first big snow, Robin and Patsy were both working doubles..."

"And Meredith," Meredith said.

"Right, and Meredith too. I was hostessing and waiting tables, I had Buzz tending bar and doing dishes, Cecily was cooking and cocktail waitressing. The next step would have been to get Mama out on the floor."

"One night I had to go into the kitchen to pick up my own dinner," Lizard said. "Mama yelled at me."

"I didn't want to put another ad in the paper. I just couldn't face a horde of unemployed people by myself. So I went to a couple of the clothing stores where I used to do window work and I recruited some of the clerks when their managers weren't looking. I told them how great the tips were and..."

"That's a bit of an exaggeration," Meredith said.

"... and about the free shift drink, and how it feels like we're all one family here." Dean waited for Meredith to contradict him again, but she didn't. "They jumped at the chance. None of them have any restaurant experience, but they're quick learners. They're clicking in real well."

"They're not bad," Meredith said, "for rookies."

"So that's where they came from," Ross said. "I thought maybe you'd been recruiting at a sorority house at BU."

"One of them is a real looker," Lizard said, "I don't know if it's Jennifer I or II. Which Jennifer was just here?"

"Jennifer I," Meredith said.

"Okay, it's Jennifer II then. Dean, tomorrow night, tell the hostess to seat me in Jennifer II's section."

"I'd steer clear of that Jennifer, if I were you," Dean said. "She's a heart-breaker. She broke a lot of hearts at the Denim Den."

"I don't think a woman like Jennifer II breaks hearts on purpose," Lizard said. "She just goes about her life, and broken hearts are a natural fallout."

"I'm going to the kitchen," Meredith said. "to see if Ian needs any help. Welcome back, Ross."

Lizard said, "She's going to help him wash dishes? On her day off? Man, does she have it bad." His tone was one of sad disbelief.

"That new hostess, what's her name... oh yeah, Charlotte. How old is she?" Ross asked Dean.

"I have an Aunt Charlotte," Lizard said. "My great aunt, really. Nice old broad. I like that name, Charlotte."

"Ask her if she needs a job. Then we can have Charlotte I and II," Ross said.

"I don't have any idea how old our Charlotte is," Dean said. "I forgot to ask for an ID."

"All I can say is, I hope you haven't been letting her serve drinks."

"During happy hour she has, a few times. I'm sure she's older than she looks. She must be at least..."

Ross began banging his head on the copper bar. "She looks like she's fourteen," he said. "Dean, you're going to get our liquor license pulled. I'm afraid to ask, but what else happened while I was gone?"

Dean thought for a moment, "Well, there was this graffito..."

"Graffiti," Ross said.

"No, Dean's right," Lizard said, "for once. Graffiti is the plural. I think he's talking about just one."

Robin breezed into the bar, humming one of the salsa songs she'd heard in the kitchen. "Ross!" She threw herself at him and hugged him. "It's good to see you! We missed you so much!" Robin smelled like mint and chocolate too. It clashed with her usual sandalwood smell in a disconcerting way.

"You did?"

"Uh-huh, we all did. Did you hear? There's no number after my name anymore. I'm just Robin now—isn't that great? Oh, and I need a stinger, a Singapore sling, a rusty nail, and two margs."

Ross started making her drinks. "I was wondering when you were going to come see me." Robin was looking calmer and less befuddled than she had before Ross left.

Robin told him she liked his clean-shaven look. Then she asked, "So where's Thea?"

Thea. His height. His former beard. He was getting tired of those topics. "She hasn't come back yet."

"I have to do something about her dog. Now your cat, she's been a sweetheart."

"I'll come by and get Swizzle tomorrow," Ross said.

""Swizzle isn't the problem. She always uses her litter box, and she's super lovie. But Damn It... I can see why Thea named him Damn It. He barks all the time, for no special reason. And he chewed up my brother's gloves. They were real expensive—made of kangaroo skin. And he..."

"Anyone who has gloves made out of kangaroos deserves to have them chewed up," Lizard said, "in my opinion."

"He's not housebroken real well either," Robin said. "I don't mind cleaning up after him so much, but my brother's real upset at him. Once he even peed on my brother's bed. What should I do about him?"

Ross set her drinks on the bar.

"Do what you have to do," Ross said. "Do what's right."

Robin looked at him squarely. "Will *you* take him?"

Dean paid the cabbie with money from petty cash. Ross wrote it down in the notebook. He wondered how much Dean had spent while he'd been away.

For safety's sake, they always took a cab to their bank near the Prudential Center. Tonight they'd be walking home from the bank to save money. It had stopped snowing for now, but the sky was full of low, sickly yellow clouds, reflecting the lights of the city.

NIGHT DEPOSITS

Dean unlocked the door to the secure area with the key the bank had given them. The drop box creaked as Dean opened it. He dropped in the pouch with the night's receipts. There wasn't a lot in there. There hadn't been much of a late rush. Dean let go of the handle, the box slammed shut, and the pouch dropped into the bowels of the bank. Ross imagined all-night accountants down there, waiting to catch it. Dean made sure the box was empty, and they left the bank and started home.

Dean said, as they walked along, "You know, at one time in my life, I really wanted to be Jewish. Everyone I liked, more or less, was Jewish: Lenny Bruce, Allen Ginsburg, Woody Allen, Abbie Hoffman... all Jewish. If I'd been born a Jew, I figured, I could have been funny and tragic at the same time without any effort, and..."

"You already are," Ross said.

"Thanks," Dean said. "But if I'd been Jewish, I could have been even funnier and so tragic, it would rip your heart out. I could have used a lot of Yiddish slang when I told stories. I love Yiddish slang. I had a girlfriend in college, she was a Jewish woman from Wisconsin, and she taught me. She always called me her *bubelah*. She taught me *shmutz*, and *putz*, *mensch*, *mishugena*—that's my favorite—oh, and *drek*, and *schlemiel*..."

"What's that mean, *schlemiel*?"

"It's like a clumsy person. An unlucky, clumsy person."

"Okay, that makes sense. My basketball coach, when I was in high school—I dunno, maybe he was Jewish—he used to call me a *schlemiel*. And a *klutz*." Ross's coach had also leveled non-Yiddish insults at him, such as candy-ass and chump and teacupper.

"Yeah, well, you are pretty klutzy. And if I were Jewish, I could say *oy vey* all the time. But no, I was born a *shagetz*—but I suppose that's a good thing."

"Why is that?"

"Because I have enough guilt as is."

"That's such a stereotype."

"True, but there's a bit of truth behind every stereotype. A lot of French guys do wear berets. A lot of Chinese people say *lice* instead of *rice*."

"Still, if I were a Jew," Ross said, "I think I'd find you pretty offensive."

"Yeah, but you're not. You're not, are you? Jarboe doesn't sound Jewish."

"My father told me it came from a French name, Charbon. Charbon is someone with dark hair."

"Your hair isn't all that dark. Jeremy's is, though. I guess that..."

"My grandfather on my dad's side was from Kentucky. He said Jarboe was a pretty common name down there."

"Okay, so you're not Jewish, you're from hillbilly stock. Anyway, I wasn't trying to be anti-Semitic. I'm also glad I wasn't born Catholic. Jews, Catholics... they come in first and second in the guilt sweepstakes, or maybe they're tied. And I have enough guilt as is."

"What is it you feel so guilty about?" Ross asked him, though he could think of a few things.

"There's almost nothing I can't work up some guilt about. I feel bad, I can't tell you how truly awful I feel about pushing Amy into the closet. I've never done anything like that, not ever. And I feel a little guilty about tampering with Dorky Dan's lunch. Those were some screamin' hot peppers. He has a peptic ulcer, and after inflaming his ulcer, they probably blew out his lower colon."

"He doesn't."

"He doesn't what?"

"He doesn't have an ulcer. Amy just told you that to make you feel guilty."

"Well, it worked."

Ross slipped on a patch of old ice under new snow. His snow boots were in his suitcase, but his suitcase was still MIA. Dean caught him by the coat sleeve and steadied him. "Is that why you went to see Amy the other day? You were feeling guilty about Dorky Dan?"

"There are tons of reasons to feel guilty where Amy's concerned. But no, that's not why I went to see her. I went to see her because... I guess it was an experiment. An experiment to see just how much I could take," Dean said. "I had to take quite a bit. It was the stuff of nightmares. She told me to go away, but then I ran into her friend Chewy—he lives right below her—and he waved me into his apartment. There I was, sitting in Chewy's apartment, drinking cappuccino and eating a cannoli. He was drinking Morning Thunder tea and he had that big candle going, the one that he and Amy bought somewhere—it's his month to have it, I guess. And we talked about my mouth."

"Your mouth?"

"Yeah, my mouth. He's in dental school—what else were we going to talk about? He asked me what goals I had set for my teeth. It was the first time I'd ever heard him speak in complete sentences. And the whole time we were there, the springs on my girlfriend's bed—my ex-girlfriend's bed—they were just creaking away. There we were, talking about my wisdom teeth, and listening to my ex and his dad. We both pretended not to notice, but it was hard, because after a while, she got to moaning, you know, the way she does, you lived in the room next to us so you know, and they were making that noise that sounds like hands clapping, and then, then she..."

"Dean..."

"How could she do it with someone named Gus? Gus, of all things. Can you imagine her saying 'Gus, that was so good for me. How was it for you, Gus?' That's just disGUSting."

"DisGUSting. You've been saving that up, waiting for the right time, haven't you?"

Dean admitted that he had been.

Ross decided not to tell Dean that Gus was out of the picture, mostly. Dean was doing such a fine job of despising Gus that Ross didn't want to make him start from scratch with someone new.

"Or maybe it wasn't Gus—it might have been that guy from that ridiculous restaurant she's working at now."

"Oh. So you know about that?"

"I know about that. I even went down to Xanadu, to check things out. It's no stately pleasure dome, trust me. It's cheesy as hell. And you should see the silly purple outfits they make the waitresses wear: bare tummies; dangly gold chains. baggy pants. The manager is from Iraq, and I'm pretty sure Amy's screwing him."

"Iran. He's from Iran."

"Whatever. Same difference. I went around back, waiting for someone to come out and have a smoke, and pretty soon the dishwasher came out. His name is Mad Dawg. Good name for a dishwasher, you ask me. Buzz should have considered that."

"It wasn't that guy we interviewed for the dishwashing job, was it? The guy who wouldn't tell us his name? He was pretty much mad."

"No, different guy, but this one looked at least half nuts. He was missing a finger and he had burns on his hands, so I guess he does some cooking too. Anyhow, he said all the waitresses are pissed because Amy gets the best shifts and the best tables. They're sure it's because the owner's banging her. Don't you figure they're right?"

Ross said he didn't know. "She told me she got along with the other waitresses, that they hang out together. She said they were shallow but fun." *Like me. I'm shallow too. But maybe not so much fun.*

"From what Mad Dawg told me, didn't sound like they like her very much. So, speaking of estranged girlfriends, what's the deal with Thea? You even know where she is?"

"This afternoon, when I was out, she called, and she left a message with Jeremy."

"And the message was..."

"Quack."

"Quack? Like a duck? That was the whole message?"

"According to Jeremy, that's all she said."

"That's pretty enigmatic. Got to be some kind of a code, don't you figure? Or maybe quack means something else in Dutch."

"I don't know. After I got back, Laurel called. She said Thea was at School's Out. She's staying with Cap."

"With Cap? The guy who married you and Laurel? Is she..."

"No. No, I'm sure she isn't. Laurel said Thea's sleeping on the fold-out couch. And Cap... Cap took her in because he helps people. That's what he does. And he's lonely. But he wouldn't... he just wouldn't."

"If you say so. But you never know."

"No, I know Cap—I just really don't think he would. Laurel also told me that Jay, that guy who was staying in her cabin, the one who fell off her roof, he split. He kept singing that song about being born a ramblin' man, and a couple of days ago, Laurel told him, please, just ramble on, so he got in his BMW and drove away."

A man, who was coincidentally in a BMW, was spinning his wheels, trying to get out of his parking spot. He wasn't having much luck. Dean and Ross got behind him and pushed him out through a snow bank. He took off without even waving a thank you.

"So... Sarah Jefferson," Ross said.

"Yeah, I feel guilty about her too."

"No reason to. Not anymore. Now that Amy is..."

"Yeah, I know... but that's not what I mean... I'm pretty sure Sarah thinks that... that we're going to be an item."

"I thought maybe that was why you hired her."

"Maybe it was, I don't know, but I do know... right now, I don't want to have a thing with Sarah Jefferson."

"Because of the... the problem with her..."

"I put some Certs and Lavoris in her purse when she wasn't looking. Not for my sake, for the customers."

"That fixed the problem?"

"It helped. Some. But... but that's not the issue. Not the only issue. I just don't want to. I don't even know why. I don't think I want to be with anyone right now; I mean, not for a long-term thing, even though I'm lonely. I was with Amy a long time. I think it's time for me to have a few short, meaningless flings. Of course, Claire gets back from Ghana in a couple of months. Maybe when she gets back we..."

"Don't even think that. Amy would cut off your nuts if you slept with her twin."

"If she can raid my bank account, I can bonk her sister. But I'm not serious. Even though they're identical twins, I was never attracted to Claire, not like I was to Amy. I don't know why, but there it is."

"So, what were you doing down in the office then?"

"With Robin?"

"No, not with Robin, with Sarah."

"Oh. She was filling out her W-4 form."

"Wait. You were down in the office with Robin too? What's that all about?"

"After lunch, I asked her to work another shift. She said she didn't want to. I told her I'd give her a back rub if she did. I told her I'd been trained in the art of massage."

"You gave Robin a back rub? I didn't think you even liked her."

"I'm finally convinced that this is her home planet. Truth to tell, she's been a trouper. And she's got great skin. Soft, supple skin."

"I wondered why you two both smelled like you'd been marinating in Vandermint."

"It was the massage oil. When she left, Amy took the peach and the French vanilla. She left me the almond and the chocolate mint. I'm keeping the chocolate mint down in the desk in the office. If you ever need any."

"You did just rub her back, didn't you?"

"There's no hard and fast line where a person's back ends and a person's front begins. You have to go after tension where you find it. You'd know that if you'd ever taken a massage class."

"She was carrying tension in her boobs?"

"I didn't say that. I..."

"Never mind. I don't care. I'm glad you had fun. I'm glad you like her now, glad you managed to get past the fuzzy toes. Surprised, but glad."

"If Amy ever introduces you to Gus or that Persian guy, try to get close enough to smell them. See if they smell like peaches or vanilla."

"Amy told me you were sleeping with one of the waitresses. Is it Robin? Or one of the Jennifers?"

"No, I'm not, actually. I just told Chewy that to make Amy jealous."

A light snow began falling, and Ross suddenly felt exhausted. So tired he could hardly keep walking. His shoulder ached. He may have pulled a muscle pushing the BMW. If it hadn't been covered with snow, he would have sat down on that bench over there. Once, on a walk between the lunch and dinner shift, he and Thea had sat there together and eaten giant pretzels with mustard on them.

"Do you remember that graffito I was telling you about?" With Dean, it was never safe to assume that a subject had been dropped. "Here's the thing: I've seen the same message before, a couple of times, on the blackboard. Maybe you saw it too. But Buzz—Ian, I should say—cleans off the blackboard every week. So this guy must be a regular. He keeps coming back and writing that message. And after it kept getting erased, the guy gouged it into the inside of the door of the second stall with a knife or a screwdriver or something. He must consider it an important enough message to make sure it's permanently recorded in our men's room."

"What does it say?"

It says, IN THE SUNSET OF EMPIRE, EVEN SMALL MEN CAST GIANT SHADOWS.

There were two dogs on the path that led through the center of the

Commonwealth Avenue mall. The two dogs were barking and biting at the snow and spinning around and rolling in it. They were acting as if they had never seen such a thing as snow before.

"So? What's that got to do with anything? What the hell's that even mean?" Ross's questions came out sounding angry and insulting.

"There's no need to get upset about it. I don't know what it means either, exactly. But I think it's a pretty remarkable line to find written on the door of the second shitter. It's derivative, for sure, of Lin Yutang, but... well, I would say that, historically speaking, it might mean that..."

"I don't want to hear about history tonight. Not your history, or my history, or the history of the goddamned world. I'm through with history for the night."

"'History is a nightmare from which you are trying to wake, huh?'"

"Something like that."

"Someone once said that Napoleon was finished when history got tired of him. And come to think of it, Napoleon was a small man who cast a giant shadow, wasn't he?"

Ross said, "I don't want to hear about Napoleon tonight either. I especially don't want to hear about Napoleon."

"You're being petulant. You don't really have anything against Napoleon. I guess you're being petulant because of Thea, but you should..."

"Mostly I'm just tired. Really tired. I had a long trip yesterday and I had an awful headache, and I didn't sleep at all well last night and... and I guess I'm just tired of everything tonight."

"Stranger! Malarkey!"

There was a woman in a faux fur coat and faux fur bonnet on the stoop of a building they were passing. She'd been sweeping the snow off the steps ineffectively with a fireplace broom. The furs she was wearing looked like they might have come from the same store as Thea's trench coat. "Here, Malarkey! Here, Stranger!" the woman called. "Come on in, boys."

Dean asked Ross: "Do you think she's calling her dogs or talking to us?"

"I don't know."

"Tell you what, I'll be Stranger, you be Malarkey."

"I'd rather be Stranger."

"Fine, have it your way, Stranger. I'm willing to be Malarkey. Let's talk to her."

"I don't want to talk to anyone. I want to go home."

The dogs were still busy quarreling with the snow. They weren't going anywhere.

"It's an opportunity, Ross. Neither of us can afford to pass up opportunities with women these days."

The woman came down the stairs and crossed the street to the mall to get her dogs. In her furs, she looked like a shaggy, genial animal herself. She smiled at Dean. She smiled at Ross. She was friendly.

"Come on, Ross. We don't have anything to lose."

NOTES

- The lines in Chapter 1 are from the poem "Damn Everything but the Circus!" by e.e. cummings (1894-1962).
- The lines from the poem in Chapter 8 are from the poem "Fork" by Charles Simic (1939-).
- The poem referred to in Chapter 22 is "The City of Dreadful Night" by James Thomson (1834-1882).
- The lines from the poem in Chapter 29 are from "Thirteen Ways of Looking at a Blackbird" by Wallace Stevens (1879-1955).